DON QUIXOTE

THE COMPLETE
ADVENTURES

MIGUEL DE CERVANTES

ADAPTED FOR THE CONTEMPORARY READER BY
JAMES HARRIS

ISBN: 9781717746382

CHAPTER 1

INTRODUCING THE CHARACTER AND PURSUITS OF THE FAMOUS GENTLEMAN DON QUIXOTE OF LA MANCHA

Not so long ago, In the village of La Mancha, a place of which I have no desire to mention, there lived one of those gentlemen that keep a lance in the rack, a shield, a lean horse, and a greyhound for running. A pot of beef and a salad on most nights, lentils on Fridays, leftovers on Saturdays, and a pigeon on Sundays, leaving him with three-quarters of his income. The rest of it went on a jacket made of fine cloth, velvet riding trousers and shoes to match for holidays, while on the weekdays his figure filled his home-made clothing. In his house lived a housekeeper over forty, a niece under twenty, and a young boy for the field work, who used to saddle the horse as well as gather the vegetation. He was approaching fifty; he had strong habits, a lean, thin physique, was a very early riser and a great sportsman. You should know, during his leisure time (which was mostly all year round) he dedicated himself to reading books of chivalry with such devotion and desire that he almost entirely neglected the pursuit of any other activity, and even the management of his property; and his eagerness and infatuation went so far, that he sold many acres of land to buy books of chivalry, and brought home as many of them as he could buy. But out of all of them, there were none he liked greater than those written by the famous Feliciano de Silva, because the lucidity of style and complicated word puzzles were pearls in his eyes, particularly when while reading he came across the subject of romance and relationships, where he often found passages like, "The reason for the unreason with which my reason is afflicted weakens my reason so with reason I weep at your beauty;" or again, "My god your divinity divinely align you with the stars, rendering you deserving of the desert your greatness deserves." Over these kind of sentences, the poor gentleman lost his mind, and used to lie awake struggling to understand and find the meaning in them; Aristotle himself couldn't have made out or extracted the meaning, even if he had come to life again purely for that purpose.

He was pedantic about continuity, because whilst reading a book, he became unhappy about the wounds which Don Belianis had taken, because it seemed to him that, as great as the surgeons were, who had cured him, his face and body were left covered with scars. He commended, however, the author's way of ending his book with the promise of a never-ending adventure, and many times he was tempted to pick up his pen and finish it properly, which no doubt he would have done, and made a successful piece of work too, if greater and more absorbing thoughts hadn't prevented him.

He had many arguments with the vicar of his village (an educated man, and a graduate of Siguenza) over who had been the better Knight, Palmerin of England or Amadis of France. Master Nicholas, the village barber, however, used to say that neither of them were as good as the Knight of Apollo, and that if there was any Knight that could compare with him it was Don Galaor, the brother of Amadis of France, because he had a spirit that could rise to any occasion, and was no delicate Knight, or sorrowful like his brother, and in the matter of bravery he wasn't at all behind him. In short, he became so absorbed in his books that he spent his nights from sunset to sunrise, and his days from dawn to dusk, engrossed in them; and with little sleep and extensive reading his brain got so dry that he lost his mind. His imagination grew full of what he used to read about in his books, enchantments, clashes, battles, challenges, wounds, romances, loves, agonies, and all sorts of impossible nonsense; and it possessed his mind to such an extent, that to him, the whole arrangement of his imagination from what he read was true, and that no history in the world had more reality in it. He used to say that Cid Ruy Diaz was a very handsome Knight, but he couldn't be compared to the Knight of the Burning Sword who with one swift-stroke cut in half two fierce and monstrous giants. He thought highly of Bernardo del Carpio because at the battle of Roncesvalles he massacred Roland even though Roland had his armour reinforced, taking advantage of the craftiness Hercules displayed when he strangled Antaeus the son of Terra. He approved highly of the giant Morgante, because, although the giants are usually arrogant and bad-mannered, he was friendly and polite. But above all he admired Reinaldos of Montalban, especially when he saw him leaving his castle and robbing everyone he met, and when he was overseas he stole an image of Mahomet which, as his history says, was made entirely of gold.

In short, with his mind being completely gone, he developed the strangest notion that a madman ever conceived, and that was that he believed it was right and essential, for the support of his own honour and for the service of his country, that he should stray from the ordinary course of life and make himself a Knight, roaming all over the world in full armour and on horseback in search of adventures, and putting into practice everything he had read as being the usual practice of Knights; righting every kind of wrong, and exposing himself to risk and danger from which, he was to secure never-ending recognition and fame. Already the poor man believed he would be crowned by the Emperor of Trebizond; and so, lost by the intense enjoyment he found in these magnificent illusions, he set out immediately to put his scheme into action.

The first thing he did was to clean up some armour that had belonged to his great-grandfather, which had been lying forgotten about in a corner covered with rust and mildew. He rubbed and polished it the best he could, but he observed one great defect in it, the helmet was not complete, it lacked a visor. To this deficiency, however, he applied his ingenuity, because he contrived a kind of half-helmet made of pasteboard which, when fitted to the other half, looked like a whole one. It is true that, in order to see if it was strong and fit for purpose, he took his sword and gave it a couple of slashes, the first of which undid in an instant what had taken him a week to do. The ease of which he had knocked it to pieces unsettled him somewhat, and to guard against that type of danger he went to work again, fixing bars of iron to the inside until he was satisfied with its strength; and then, not caring to try any more experiments with it, he claimed it to be the helmet with the most perfect construction.

He then proceeded to inspect his horse, which, with more marks than the horse of Gonela, that horse of "skin and bones," surpassed in his eyes the horse of Alexander the Great. Four days were spent thinking what name to give him, because (as he said to himself) it was not right that a horse belonging to a Knight so famous, and one with such merits of its own, should be left without some distinctive name, and so, he tried to adapt it to indicate what the horse had been before, and what it now was; because it was only reasonable that, as his master was becoming a new character, he should be given a new name, and that it should be a distinguished and full-sounding one, appropriate for the new calling which was about to follow. And so, after having composed, rejected, added to, made, and remade a number of names out of his memory, he decided to call him: Rocinante, a name, he thought to be proud, deep, and significant to his condition before, and what he now was, the leading, and most legendary horse in the world.

Having decided the name for his horse, he was anxious to make one for himself, and another eight days passed considering this, until at last, he made up his mind to call himself "Don Quixote." Recollecting, however, that the valiant Amadis was not content to call himself Amadis and nothing more, and so, added the name of his Kingdom and country to make it famous, calling himself Amadis of France, he, like a good Knight, decided to extend his name to: Don Quixote of La Mancha, which he considered described accurately his origin and country, and honoured it by taking his surname from it.

So then, his armour being furbished, his helmet repaired, his horse christened, and his name confirmed, he came to the conclusion that nothing else was needed now but to look for a lady to be in love with; because a Knight without love was like a tree without leaves or fruit, or a body without a soul. As he said to himself, "If, for my sins, or by good fortune, I come across a giant nearby, a common occurrence with Knights, and I slaughter him in one strike, or wrestle him to the floor, or, in short, conquer and subdue him, wouldn't it be good to have someone I can send him to as a present, so that he can come in and fall on his knees in front of my sweet lady, and in a humble, obedient voice say, 'I am the giant Caraculiambro, lord of the island of Malindrania, defeated in combat by the never sufficiently commended Knight Don Quixote of La Mancha, who has ordered me to present myself to you, so that you my Queen can do with me what you want with me'?" Oh, how this gentleman enjoyed the delivery of this speech, especially when he had thought of someone to call his Lady!

There was, so the story goes, in a village near to his own a very good-looking farm-girl who at one time he had been in love with, though, so far as it is known, she never knew it or ever thought about it. Her name was Aldonza Lorenzo, and with the image of her in mind, he thought it was fit to grant her the title: Lady of his Thoughts; and after some searching for a name which was not to be out of harmony with her own, and should suggest and indicate that of a

Princess and great lady, he decided to call her Dulcinea del Toboso - a name, in his mind, which was musical, uncommon, and significant, like all those he had already given to himself and the things which belonged to him.

CHAPTER 2

THE FIRST JOURNEY OF THE INGENIOUS DON QUIXOTE

With these things established, he couldn't wait any longer to execute his design, urged on by the thought that the world was losing each day the longer he delayed, as there were many wrongs he intended to right, grievances to amend, injustices to repair, abuses to remove, and duties to discharge. So, without giving anyone notice of his intention, and without anybody seeing him, one morning before the dawn of the day (which was one of the hottest during the month of July) he put on his suit of armour, mounted Rocinante with his patched-up helmet on, clenched his shield, took his lance, and by the back door of his garden charged forward across the land with the highest contentment and satisfaction at seeing with what ease he had made a start toward his grand purpose. But not long after he found himself on the open land, a terrible thought struck him, one which was enough to make him abandon the whole operation before it really begun. It occurred to him that he had not been named a Knight, and that according to the law of chivalry he couldn't draw his weapon against any Knight; and that even if he had been, he still should, as a novice Knight, wear white armour, without any attachments to the shield until due to his expertise he had earned it. These reflections made him waver in his purpose, but his craze being stronger than any form of reasoning, he made up his mind to have himself named a Knight by the first one he came across, following the example of others in the same case, as he had read in the books that encouraged him to do this. As for the white armour, he decided that when the first opportunity presented itself, he would brush his armour until it was whiter than paper; and so, reassuring himself in this manner he continued on his way, taking whichever route his horse chose, because in this he believed to be the essence of adventures.

So, going forward, our new-novice adventurer rode along, talking to himself and saying, "Who knows, in the future, when the genuine history of my famous deeds become known, the sage who writes about them, when he discloses the details of my first adventure in the early morning, will document this? 'Little had the reddish sun spread over the face of the broad spacious earth, the golden threads of its bright hair, little had the birds of colourful feathers adjusted their notes to welcome with sweet and soothing harmony the coming of the rosy Dawn, which was appearing to mortals at the gates and balconies of the Manchegan horizon, when the renowned Knight Don Quixote of La Mancha, mounted his illustrious horse Rocinante and began to navigate the ancient and famous Campo de Montiel;'" which in fact he was actually crossing at the time. "Happy the period, happy the occasion," he continued, "in which my deeds will become known and famous, worthy to be moulded in brass, carved in marble, depicted in pictures, permanently engraved in the history book of life. And so, sage magician, whoever you are, whoever comes to be the chronicler of this wondrous history, do not forget, I ask you, my good Rocinante, the constant companion of my pursuits and adventures." Presently he broke out again, as if he were love-struck, "Princess Dulcinea, lady of this captive heart, a severe wrong has been done to drive me forward with contempt, and with inescapable determination I have been banished from your presence my beauty. Lady, agree to hold in memory this heart, your possession, which in pain longs for your love."

So, he went on stringing together these and other absurdities, all in the style that his books had taught him, imitating their language as well as he could; and all the while he rode so slowly and the sun rose so rapidly and with such intensity that it was enough to melt his brains if he had any left. Nearly all day he travelled without anything remarkable happening to him, because of this he was in despair and became anxious to encounter someone so he could exercise his power.

There are writers who say the first adventure was that of Puerto Lapice; others say it was that of the windmills; but what I have ascertained on this point, and what I have found written in the archives of La Mancha, is that he was on the road all day, and towards the night he and his horse found themselves dead tired and hungry, when, looking all around to see if he could discover any castle or shepherd's home where he could refresh himself and relieve his thirst and hunger, he observed not far in the distance an inn, which was as clear as a star guiding him to the doorways, if not the palaces, of his restoration; and accelerating his pace he reached it just as the night was falling. At the door stood two young women, girls of the district as they call them, on their way to Seville with some transporters who had the chance to stop that night at the inn; and as it happened, to our adventurer, everything he saw seemed to him to be and to happen in the fashion of what he read of, the moment he saw the inn he pictured it to himself as a castle with its four towers and peaks of shining silver, not forgetting the drawbridge and moat and all the other properties usually attributed to castles. Toward this inn, which to him seemed to be a castle, he advanced, and at a short distance from it he stopped to check Rocinante, hoping that some dwarf would appear to discuss the details of the battle, and by sound of a trumpet give notice that a Knight was approaching the castle. But seeing that the dwarf was late, and that Rocinante was in a hurry to reach the stable, he went for the inn door, and observed the girls who were standing there, and who seemed to him to be two lovely ladies in distress lost at the castle gate.

At this moment, it happened that a farmer who was going through the field collecting a group of pigs gave a blast of his horn to bring them together, and immediately it seemed to Don Quixote to be what he was expecting, the signal from some dwarf announcing his arrival; and so with extraordinary satisfaction he rode up to the inn and to the ladies, who, seeing a man of this sort approaching in full armour, lance and shield, ran into the inn, when Don Quixote, guessing their fear by their departure, raising his pasteboard visor, revealed his dry dusty face, and with a polite manner and gentle voice addressed them, "You dear ladies have no need to run in fear of any rudeness, because that does not belong to the law of Knighthood, a service of which I offer to anyone, far less than high-class ladies that your appearance declares you to be." The girls were looking at him and straining their eyes to make out the features which the awkward visor obscured, but when they heard themselves called high-class, something so far out of their line, they could not withhold their laughter, which made Don Quixote infuriated, and say, "Modesty is fair, yet laughter that has no cause is great silliness; this, however, I do not say to upset or anger you, because my desire is nothing other than to serve you."

The incomprehensible language and the unconvincing looks of our Knight only increased the ladies' laughter, and that increased his irritation, and matters might have gone further if at that moment the landlord had not come out, who, being a very fat man, was a quite a peaceful one. He, seeing this grotesque figure covered in armour that did not match any more than his saddle, reins, lance, or shield, was not at all unwilling to join the ladies in their expressions of amusement; but, in truth, standing in amazement of such a complicated arrangement, he thought it best to speak to him fairly, so he said, "Señor Caballero, if you require a room, bath and bed there are none remaining, but there is plenty of everything else here." Don Quixote, noting the respectful manner of the innkeeper (the guard of the fortress in his eyes), replied, "Sir Castellan, for me anything will do, because:

'My armour is my only clothing,
My only rest is the fight.'

The innkeeper thought he called him Castellan because he believed him to be "worthy of Castile," although he was in fact an Andalusian, crafty as a thief and full of tricks. "In that case," he said,

'Your bed is on the hard floor,
Your sleep is to keep watch;'

and if you like, you may dismount and stay for any number of sleepless nights under this roof for up to one year." Whilst saying this, he held the stirrup for Don Quixote, who got down with great difficulty and exertion (because he had not relieved his hunger all day), and then asked the host to take great care of his horse, as he was the best horse that existed in the world. The landlord took a look at the horse but did not find him to be as good as Don Quixote said, not even half as good; and putting him up in the stable, he returned to see what his guest might require. The ladies by this time had made their peace with him, and were now helping him to remove his armour. They had taken off the armour coverings his chest and back, but they did not know or see how to open the protection around his neck, or remove his self-made helmet, because he had tied it with green ribbons, which, as the knots were far too tight, required to be cut. This, however, he would not allow, so all evening he sat with his helmet on, the oddest and strangest figure that can be imagined; and while they were removing his armour, the ladies of such high-class belonging to the castle, he said to them with great inventiveness:

"Never was there a Knight, catered to by the hands of such high-class ladies. As served as he was, Don Quixote of La Mancha; with ladies waiting on him, Princesses of his shield - or Rocinante, because that, ladies, is my horse's name, and Don Quixote of La Mancha is my own; because although I had no intention of declaring my name until the achievement which warrants your service and honour had made me known, the necessity of adapting to the present occasion has given you the knowledge of my name prematurely. A time, however, will come for you ladies to command and for me to obey, and then the power of this Knight will show my desire to serve you."

The girls, who were not used to hearing speech of this type, had nothing to say in reply; they only asked him if he wanted anything to eat. "I would love to eat a bit of something," said Don Quixote, "because I feel it would come at the right time." The day happened to be a Friday, and in the whole inn there was nothing but some pieces of the fish they call in Castile "abadejo," in Andalusia "bacallao," and in some places "curadillo," and in others "troutlet;" so they asked him if he would like to eat troutlet, because there was no other fish to give him. "If enough troutlets," said Don Quixote, "they will be the same thing as a trout; because it is all the same to me; in fact, it may be that these troutlets are like veal, which is better than beef. But whatever it is may it come quickly, because the burden and pressure of my armour cannot be carried without support from the inside." They placed a table for him at the door of the inn, and the host brought him a portion of worse cooked cod, and a piece of bread as black and mouldy as his armour; but it was laughable to see him eating, because having his helmet, he could not with his own hands put anything into his mouth unless someone else did it for him, and this service one of the ladies gave him. But to give him anything to drink was impossible, or would have been if the landlord did not take a large leaf, and putting one end in his mouth poured the wine into him; all of which he accepted with much patience rather than cut the ribbons of his helmet.

While this was going on, a musician entered the inn, who, as he approached, played his flute, and thereby completely convinced Don Quixote that he was in some famous castle, and that they were entertaining him with music, and that the cod was trout, the bread was white, the ladies his, and the landlord the castellan of the castle; and consequently, he believed that his initiative and adventure had served some purpose. But still it distressed him to think he had not been labelled a Knight, because it was plain to him that it was not lawful to engage in any adventure without receiving the official recognition of Knighthood.

CHAPTER 3

THE WAY IN WHICH DON QUIXOTE BECAME A KNIGHT

Agitated by this reflection, he hurried his dinner, and having finished it called the landlord, and locking himself in the stable with him, fell on his knees, saying, "From this spot I will not rise, valiant Knight, until your courtesy grants me the blessing that I seek, one that will contribute to your future praise and benefit the human race." The landlord, seeing his guest at his feet and hearing a speech of this kind, stood staring at him in confusion, not knowing what to do or say, and asking him to rise, which would not work - until he had agreed to grant the blessing demanded of him. "I look for no less, my lord, from your High Magnificence," replied Don Quixote, "and I have to tell you that the blessing I ask for and which your kindness would grant is that you declare me a Knight tomorrow morning, and that tonight I will watch my armour in the chapel of this castle; and tomorrow, as I have said, will see accomplished what I desire, enabling me to lawfully roam through all four quarters of the world seeking adventures on behalf of those in distress, as is the duty of Knights like myself, whose ambition is directed to such deeds."

The landlord, who, as has been mentioned, was something of a joker, and already had some suspicion of his guest's desire, was now quite convinced of it after hearing this speech, and to make a little bit of fun for the Knight he decided to play along. So he told him he was quite right in pursuing this objective, and that a motive like this was very natural for Knights as distinguished as him, and his courageous manner indicated him to be; and that he himself in his younger days had followed the same honourable work, roaming in quest of adventures in various parts of the world, among them the Curing-grounds of Malaga, the District of Seville, the Little Market of Segovia, the Olivera of Valencia, the Rondilla of Granada, the Strand of San Lucar, the Colt of Cordoba, the Taverns of Toledo, and various other places, where he had proved his worth, undoing many wrongs, aiding widows, restoring ruined maids and educating corrupted youths, and, in short, reporting to every tribunal and court of justice in Spain; until at last, he had retired to this castle, where he was living and where he welcomes all Knights of whatever rank or condition they might be in, all for the great love they had so that they might share their substance with him in return for his generosity. He told him, that in this castle there was no chapel where he could watch his armour, as it had been knocked down in order to be rebuilt, but it could be watched from anywhere, and he could watch it that night in the courtyard of the castle, and in the morning, if God desires, the necessary ceremony will be performed to have him declared a Knight. He asked if he had any money with him, to which Don Quixote replied that he had none, as in the histories of Knights he had never read of any of them carrying money. On this point the landlord told him he was mistaken; because, although it's not recorded in the histories, because in the author's opinion there was no need to mention anything so obvious and necessary as money and clean shirts, it was not to be supposed therefore that they did not carry any, and he should regard this as certain and established that all Knights carried well-equipped wallets in case of emergency, and also carried shirts and a little box of ointment to cure any wounds they received. Because on land or desert where they engaged in combat and left wounded, there wasn't always someone there to cure them, unless they had for a friend some sage magician to aid them by seeking some lady or dwarf with a bottle of virtuous water that by tasting one drop of it they were cured of their wounds in an instant and left as if they had not received any damage whatsoever. But in case this did not occur, the Knights made sure their helpers were provided with money and other necessities, such as bandage and ointments for healing purposes; and when a Knight had no helper (which was rarely the case) they themselves carried everything in saddle-bags that were hardly seen on the horse, as if it were something else of more importance, because, unless for a reason like this, carrying saddle-bags was not very favourably regarded among Knights. He therefore advised him (and, as his soon to be godson) never to travel without money and the usual requirements, and he would find the advantage of them when he least expected it.

Don Quixote promised to follow his advice carefully, and it was arranged that he should watch his armour in a large courtyard on one side of the inn; so, collecting it all together, Don Quixote placed it next to the side of a well, and lifting his shield on his arm he held his lance and began with a royal character, to march up and down in front of the armour.

The landlord told all the people staying the inn about the lunacy of his guest, the watching of the armour, and the knighting ceremony he expected. Full of wonder at such a strange form of madness, they gathered to see it from a distance, and observed with what composure he sometimes marched up and down, or sometimes, leaning on his lance, gazed at his armour without taking his eyes off it; and as the night was lit by light from the moon so intense, everything the novice Knight did was clearly seen by all.

Meanwhile one of the guests of the inn became thirsty and required a visit to the well; but seeing the guest approaching Don Quixote spoke in a loud voice, "You, whoever you are, foolish Knight that come to put hands on the armour of the most fearless Knight that ever held the lance, take care what you do; do not touch it unless you hand over your life as the penalty of your rashness." The guest paid no attention to the words, and taking the armour threw it some distance from the well. Seeing this, Don Quixote raised his eyes to heaven, and fixing his thoughts, apparently, upon his lady Dulcinea, exclaimed, "Help me, lady of mine, in this first encounter that presents itself to this man you hold in subjection; do not allow your favour and protection to fail me in this first jeopardy;" and, with these words and others of similar sort, dropping his shield he lifted his lance with both hands and with it struck such a blow to the guest's head that he put him flat on the ground, so stunned that if had he followed it up with a second there would have been no need of a surgeon to cure him. This complete, he picked up his armour and returned to walk up and down with the same serenity as before.

Shortly after this, another, not knowing what had happened (as the other still lay unconscious), came with the same objective of giving water to his donkeys, and was heading to remove the armour, when Don Quixote, without saying a word, once more dropped his shield and lifted his lance, and without actually breaking the second man's head into pieces, made more than three strikes, because he knocked him out in four. Hearing the noise all the people from the inn ran to see what was going on, and among them was the landlord. Seeing this, Don Quixote lifted his shield on his arm, and with his hand on his lance exclaimed, "Lady of Beauty, strength and support of my heart, it is time for the eyes of your greatness to look at me, your captive Knight on the edge of such a mighty adventure." By this he felt so inspired that he would not have hesitated if all the guests in the world had attacked him. The friends of the wounded noticing the dilemma they were in began from a distance to launch stones at Don Quixote, who protected himself as best as he could with his shield, not willing to leave his armour unprotected. The landlord shouted to them to leave him alone, because he had already told them that he was mad, and as a madman he would not be held liable even if he killed them all. Still louder shouted Don Quixote, calling them liars and traitors, and the lord of the castle, who allowed Knights to be treated in this manner, a criminal and a low-class Knight who, had he received his Knighthood, he would summon to account for his treason. "But you," he cried, "dishonourable and dreadful crowd, I create no account; throw, strike, come on, do all you can against me, you will see what the reward of your stupidity and insolence is." This he expressed with so much spirit and boldness that he filled his attackers with terrible fear, and for this reason and the persuasion of the landlord they ceased stoning him, and he allowed them to remove the wounded men, and with the same calmness and composure as before resumed the watch over his armour.

Determined to cut matters short and discuss with him the consequences of Knighthood before any further misfortune could occur; the inn keeper, going up to him, apologised for the rudeness which, without his knowledge, had been directed at him by these low-class people, who, however, had been well punished for their disrespect. As he had already told him, he said, there was no chapel in the castle, and neither was it needed for what remained to be done, because, as he understood the ritual of Knighthood, can be made with a slap on the shoulder, and that could be administered in the middle of a field; and that he had now done all that was necessary by watching the armour, because all requirements were satisfied by a watch of two hours only, while he already done more than four. Don Quixote believed it all, and told him he stood there ready to obey, and to follow through any command with such fury; because, if he were to be attacked again, and knew himself to officially be a Knight, he would not, he thought, leave a man alive in the castle, except those who out of respect he might permit if he was requested.

So, warned and threatened, the castellan took a book in which he used to enter sales and receipts, and, with a young boy holding a candle, and the two ladies already mentioned, he returned to where Don Quixote stood, and asked him kneel down. Then, reading from his book as if he were repeating some sincere prayer, in the middle of his delivery he raised his hand and gave him a strong slap on the neck, and then, with his own lance, another slap on the shoulder, all while mumbling between his teeth as if he was saying his prayers. Having done this, he directed one of the ladies to hold his lance, which she did with great confidence and seriousness, and not much more could be done to prevent a burst of laughter at each stage of the ceremony; but with what they had already seen of the novice Knight's aptitude kept their laughter within. Placing the lance on his shoulder the worthy lady said to him, "May God make your greatness a very fortunate Knight, and grant you success in battle." Don Quixote asked for her name so that he could know from that time forward to who he was in debt for the favour he had received, as he desired to award her a portion of the honour he will acquire. She answered with great humility that she was called La Tolosa, and that she was the daughter of a shoe maker in Toledo who lived in the workshop, and that wherever she would be she would serve and regard him as her lord. Don Quixote said in reply that she would do him a great favour if from then forward she took the "Don" and called herself Dona Tolosa. She promised that she would, and then the other lady approached, and with her followed almost the same conversation as with the lady of the lance. He asked her name, and she said it was La Molinera, and that she was the daughter of a respectable farmer; and likewise Don Quixote requested that she would use the "Don" and call herself Dona Molinera, to make an offer of her further service and favours.

And this, with conciseness and speed, brought to a conclusion these never-till-now-seen ceremonies, Don Quixote was eager to see himself again on horseback charging forward in quest of adventures; and so, mounting Rocinante, saluting his host, and giving thanks for the kindness in knighting him, he spoke in language so extraordinary that it is impossible to convey an idea of it or report it. The landlord, to get him out of the inn, replied with no less eloquence though with shorter words, and without asking him to pay the fee let him go with an expression of good wishes.

CHAPTER 4

WHAT HAPPENED AFTER DON QUIXOTE LEFT THE INN

The day was approaching when Don Quixote left the inn, so happy and so exhilarated at finding himself now labelled a Knight, that his joy was full enough to burst his shirt. However, recalling the advice of his host about the fundamentals he should carry with him, especially referring to money and shirts, he decided to go home and provide himself with these, and a helper, because he thought of acquiring a farm-labourer, a neighbour of his, a poor man with a family, but very well qualified for the position. With this objective, he turned his horse's head towards his village, and Rocinante, remembering the way home, ran so rapidly that he hardly seemed to tread on the earth.

He had not gone far, when out of a bush on his right there seemed to come very quiet cries as if someone was in distress, and the instant he heard them he exclaimed, "Thanks to heaven for the favour it presents me, that so quickly it offers me an opportunity of fulfilling the obligation I have undertaken, and gathering the fruit of my ambition. These cries, no doubt, come from some man or woman in need of help, and requiring my aid and protection;" and twisting suddenly, he turned Rocinante in the direction of the cries. He had gone only a short distance into the woods, when he saw a horse tied to an oak tree, and tied to another, and stripped from the waist upwards, a youth of about fifteen years of age, from who the cries came. These cries had not occurred without cause, because a strong farmer was whipping him with a belt and following up every blow with a telling-off and commands, repeating, "Your mouth shut and your eyes open!" while the youth answered, "I won't do it again, master; I swear to God I won't do it again, and I'll take more care of the sheep next time."

Seeing what was going on, Don Quixote said in an angry voice, "Discourteous Knight, it is disgraceful to attack one who cannot defend himself; mount your horse and take your lance" (because there was a lance leaning against the oak tree which the horse was tied to), "and I will make you aware that you are behaving as a coward." The farmer, seeing in front of him this figure in full armour wielding a lance over his head, thought he was as good as dead, and answered fearfully, "Sir Knight, this youth that I am punishing is my servant, employed by me to watch a herd of sheep that I have, and he is so careless that I lose one every day, and when I punish him for his carelessness and dishonesty he says I do it out of stinginess, to escape paying him the wages I owe him, and I swear to God, and on my soul, he lies."

"Lies in front of me, dishonourable clown!" said Don Quixote. "In the sun that shines on us I have a mind to pierce through you with this lance. Pay him immediately and without another word; if not, by the God that rules us I will make this day an end for you, and annihilate you on the spot; release him instantly."

The farmer lowered his head, and without a word untied his servant, who Don Quixote then asked how much his master owed him.

He replied, nine months at seven coins a month. Don Quixote added it up, found that it came to sixty-three coins, and told the farmer to pay it immediately, if he did not want to die for it.

The trembling farmer replied that he lived honestly by an oath he had sworn (although he had not sworn any) it was not so much; because to be taken into account and deducted there were three pairs of shoes he had given him, and a real for medicine the youth required when he was sick.

"All that may be," said Don Quixote; "but let the shoes and medicine be off set against the whippings you have given him without reason; because if he has damaged the shoes you paid for, you have damaged his body, and if you administered medicine when he was sick, you have damaged him when he was well; so on that balance he owes you nothing."

"The difficulty is, Sir Knight, that I have no money with me; let Andres come home with me, and I will pay him the total."

"Go with him!" said the youth. "No, God forbid! No, señor, not for the world; because he's once alone with me, he would burn me like a Saint Bartholomew."

"He will do nothing of the sort," said Don Quixote; "I only have to command, and he will obey me; and as he has sworn to me under the law of Knighthood which he has received, I let him free, and I guarantee the payment."

"Consider what you are saying, señor," said the youth; "this master of mine is not a Knight, and he has not received a Knighthood; he is Juan Haldudo the Rich, of Quintanar."

"That doesn't matter much," replied Don Quixote; "there can be Haldudos Knights."

"That is true," said Andres; "but this master of mine, is hardly a Knight when he refuses to pay me the wages of my labour?"

"I am not refusing, brother Andres," said the farmer, "be good enough to come with me, and I swear under all the laws of Knighthood there are in the world to pay you what I have agreed and a bonus."

"For the bonus," said Don Quixote; "give it to him in reals, and I will be satisfied; and make sure you do as what you have sworn; if not, I swear to come back, hunt you and punish you; and I will find you. And if you want to know who this command comes from, so you are more firmly bound to obey it, know that I am the fearless Don Quixote of La Mancha, the rectifier of wrongs and injustices; and so, under God's watch, keep in mind what you have promised and sworn as you have already been made aware of the penalties for disobedience."

And with that, he turned Rocinante and was soon fading into the distance. The farmer followed him with his eyes, and when he saw that he had cleared the wood and was no longer in sight, he turned to his boy Andres, and said, "Come here, my son, I want to pay you what I owe you, as that rectifier of wrongs has ordered me to."

"I swear to you," said Andres, "You have been well advised to obey the command of that good Knight – I hope he lives a thousand years because, as he is a brave and fair judge, if you do not pay me, he will come back and do as he said."

"I swear to you too," said the farmer; "but as I have a strong care for you, I want to add to the debt in order to add to the payment;" and grabbing him by the arm, he tied him up again, and gave him such a whipping that he almost passed out.

"Now, Andres," said the farmer, "call the rectifier of wrongs; you will find he won't undo that, and I am not sure that I have finished with you yet, because I have a mind to burn you alive." But he then untied him, and gave him permission to go and look for his judge in order to put the penalty declared into action.

Andres, swearing he would go to look for the courageous Don Quixote of La Mancha and tell him exactly what had happened, and that he would serve his master justice for what he had done; but after that, he left crying, while his master stood laughing.

And so, the valiant Don Quixote believed he had corrected that wrong, and, thoroughly satisfied with what had taken place, as he considered he had made a very good start with his Knighthood, he took the road toward his village in perfect self-contentment, saying in a low voice, "Well may today I call myself fortunate above everyone else on earth, Dulcinea del Toboso, fairest of the fair! Since it has been assigned to my life to be obedient to your will and pleasure, a Knight as renowned as Don Quixote of La Mancha, who, as the whole world knows, yesterday became a Knight, and has today corrected the greatest wrong that injustice ever conceived and cruelty perpetrated: who has today removed the whip from the hand of a ruthless oppressor so shamelessly lashing that gentle child."

He now came to the end of a road splitting in four directions, and immediately he was reminded of those cross-roads where Knights used to stop to consider which road they should take. In imitation of them he paused for a while, and after having deeply considered it, he gave this choice to Rocinante, who followed his first intention, which was to head for his own stable. After he had gone about two miles Don Quixote noticed a large group of people, who appeared to be some traders from Toledo, on their way to buy silk in Murcia. There were six of them coming toward him, with four servants, and three horse keepers on foot. Don Quixote had barely descried them when he perceived that this must be a new adventure; and to help him imitate as much as he could the passages he had read in his books, here seemed to come an adventure made on purpose, which he was determined to attempt. So with a proud manner and resolve he secured himself firmly on his horse, got his lance ready, lifted his shield to his chest, and placing himself in the middle of the road, stood waiting the approach of these Knights, because that's what he now considered them to be; and when they came near enough to see and hear, he exclaimed, "All the world will be on trial, unless all the world confess that in the whole world there is no lady fairer than the Empress of La Mancha, the incomparable Dulcinea del Toboso."

The traders stopped at the sound of this language and the sight of the strange figure that spoke it, and from the figure and language they saw and heard, guessed the madness of their owner; they wanted, however, to understand what was the reason for this confession that was demanded of them, and one of them, who was rather fond of a joke and was very sharp-witted, said to him, "Sir Knight, we do not know who this good lady is that you speak of; show her to us, because, if she if she possesses the beauty as you suggest, with all our hearts and without any pressure we will confess the truth that you require from us."

"If I were to show her to you," replied Don Quixote, "what value would there be in confessing a truth so obvious? The essential point is that without seeing her you must believe, confess, affirm, swear, and defend it; or else you face me in battle, ill-conditioned, arrogant crowd you are; come on, one by one as the law of Knighthood states, or all together as is the custom and disgusting usage of your type, here I stand and wait for you relying on the justice of the cause I uphold."

"Sir Knight," replied the trader, "I ask you to save us from assaulting our consciences with the confession of something we have never seen or heard of, and further to hold a bias toward this lady you speak of over the Empresses and Queens of Alcarria, we hope you will show us a portrait of this lady, and in this way we will be satisfied and relaxed, and you will be content and pleased; actually, I believe we already agree with you that even if her portrait would show her blind in one eye, we would, to satisfy your request, say in her favour everything that you desire."

"Her eyes are perfectly fine, disgusting crowd," said Don Quixote, burning with anger, "nothing of the sort, not one-eyed or humpbacked, but straighter than a new lance: you must pay for the profanity you have said against the beauty of my lady."

And so, he charged with a pointed lance against the one who had said it, with such fury and fierceness that, if luck had not decided that Rocinante should stumble half way and fall down, it would have penetrated the trader. Down went Rocinante, and over went his master, rolling along the ground for some distance; and when he tried to rise he was unable to, being burdened with his lance, shield, helmet, and the weight of his old armour; and all the while he was struggling to get up he kept saying, "Do not run away, cowards! Stay, because not for my fault, but my horse's, am I here."

One of the traders, who could not have had much good nature in him, hearing the poor man speaking in this way, was unable to refrain from giving him an answer; and went up to him, took his lance, and having broken it in pieces, with one of them he began to beat Don Quixote that, in spite of his armour, he flattened him like a pancake. The others shouted not to hit him so hard and to leave him alone, but the traders blood pressure was high, and he did not care to stop until he had vented the rest of his anger, and gathering the remaining pieces of the lance finished with a final strike to the unhappy victim, who all through the storm of blows that struck him never once stopped threatening heaven, and earth, and the lawbreakers, because to him that is what they seemed to be. Finally, the trader was tired, and him and the others continued their journey, taking with them a story to talk about: the poor man who had just been beaten. When Don Quixote found himself alone made another effort to rise; but if he was unable to when he was well, how was he about to after having been beaten and nearly knocked to pieces? And yet he believed himself to be fortunate, as it seemed to him that this was a regular Knight's misfortune, and entirely, he considered it to be the fault of his horse. However, as injured as his body was, to get up was beyond his power.

CHAPTER 5

HOW OUR KNIGHT'S BAD FORTUNE CONTINUED

Finding that he could not move, he thought it was best to resort to his usual solution, which was to think of some passage in his books, and his madness brought to mind a story about Baldwin and the Man of Italy, when Carloto left him wounded on the mountain side, a story known by heart by the children, never forgotten among young men, spoken and even believed by the older generation; and for everyone without a grain of intelligence truer than the miracles of Jesus. This appeared to him to be exactly the case in which he found himself in, so, making a show of severe suffering, he began to roll on the ground and with little breath repeated the very words which the wounded Knight is believed to have spoken:

Where are you, my lady,
I am lost without you.
Although you do not know it,
My love is so true.

And so, he continued with the speech as far as the lines:

Noble man of Italy,
My Uncle – supreme lord!

By chance, when he got to this line a peasant from his village was passing by, a neighbour of his, who was carrying a load of wheat to the mill, and seeing the man on the floor, came to him and asked him who he was and what was wrong with him to make him complain so sadly.

Don Quixote was so persuaded that this was the man of Italy, his uncle, so his only answer was to continue with his speech, in which he told the story of his misfortune exactly as it was written in the book.

The peasant stood in amazement after hearing such nonsense, and releasing his visor, already smashed to pieces by blows, he wiped his face, which was covered with dust, and as soon as he saw his face he recognised him and said, "Señor, who has done this to you?" But in response he continued with his speech.

The peasant removed as well as he could his armour to see if he had any wounds, but he couldn't see any blood or marks. He then lifted him from the ground, and with a little difficulty placed him on his horse, which seemed to him to be the easiest mount for him; and collecting the armour, even the splinters of the lance, he tied them to Rocinante, and leading him by the harness took the road toward the village, very sad to hear what bizarre stuff Don Quixote was talking about.

Don Quixote was also sad because with the blows and bruises he could not sit upright on the horse, and from time to time he made sighs to heaven, which caused the peasant to ask again what troubled him. And it could have only been the devil himself that put the stories into his head, because now, forgetting Baldwin, he thought of himself as the Moor Abindararez, when the mayor of Antequera, Rodrigo de Navarez, took him prisoner and carried him to his castle; so when the peasant asked again how he was and what troubled him, he gave a reply using the same words and phrases that the captive Abindararez gave to Rodrigo de Navarez, just as he had read in the story of "Diana" of Jorge de Montemayor where it was written, applying it to his own case so appropriately that the peasant went along cursing his fate that he had to listen to such nonsense; from which, however, he came to the conclusion that his neighbour was mad, and so he rushed to reach the village to escape the tiring rant of Don Quixote; who, at the end of it, said, "Señor Don Rodrigo de Narvaez, you must know that this fair lady I have mentioned is the lovely Dulcinea del Toboso, for who I have done, am doing, and will do the most famous deeds of chivalry this world has ever seen, are to be seen, and will ever see."

The peasant answered, "Señor – I am a sinner! Can you not see that I am not Don Rodrigo de Narvaez nor the Man of Italy, but Pedro Alonso your neighbour, and that you are not Baldwin or Abindararez?"

"I know who I am," replied Don Quixote, "and I am not only those I have named, but all Twelve Peers of France, as my achievements surpass all they have done individually and collectively."

With this talk and more of the same they reached the village just as the night was beginning, but the peasant waited until it was a little later so the beaten gentleman would not be seen riding in such a miserable state. When it seemed to him to be the proper time he entered the village and went to Don Quixote's house, which he found in a state of confusion: The village vicar and barber who were great friends of Don Quixote were there, and his housekeeper was saying to them in a loud voice, "What do you think has happened to my master? It has been three days now since anyone has seen him, or the horse, or the shield, lance, or armour. I am sure, as true as the day I was born, that these books of chivalry he has, he has read so constantly, have upset his reason; because now I remember hearing him saying to himself that he would become a Knight and go all over the world in quest of adventures. The devil with such books, have ruined the finest understanding there was in all of La Mancha!"

The niece said the same, and, more: "You must know, Master Nicholas" Because that was the name of the barber, "it was often my uncle's way to spend two days and nights reading over these unholy books of adventures, and after he would throw the book and take his sword and start slashing the walls; and when he was tired he would say he had killed four giants; and the sweat that came from him when he was exhausted he said was the blood from the wounds he had received in battle; and then he would drink a large amount of cold water and become calm and quiet, saying that this water was a most precious potion which a sage or a great magician and friend of his, had brought him. But I take all the blame myself for never telling you about my uncle's behaviour, so you could put an end to it before things had gone this far, and burn all these cursed books."

"It is not too late to destroy them," said the vicar, "and I promise that tomorrow will not pass by without a public judgment on them, and they will be directed to the flames in the same way they lead those who read them to behave as my good friend seems to have behaved."

The peasant heard everything, and from it he finally understood what the matter was with his neighbour, so he began to say out loud, "Open the door, for Señor Baldwin and the man of Italy, who have been badly wounded, and to Señor Abindararez, the Moor, who the courageous Rodrigo de Narvaez, brings captive."

Hearing these words, they all rushed outside, and when they recognised their friend, master, and uncle, who had not yet dismounted from the horse because he was unable to, they ran to embrace him.

"Stop!" he said, "I am badly wounded through my horse's fault; carry me to bed, and if possible request a wise man to cure my wounds."

"See!" cried the housekeeper: "did I not tell you exactly what has happened to my master? You have to go to bed at once, and we will arrange to cure you here without seeking the wise man that you ask for. This is a curse, inflicted by those books of chivalry that have lead you to be in this state."

They carried him to bed immediately, and after checking for wounds could not find any, but he said they were bruises from having a severe fall from his horse Rocinante when in combat with ten giants, the biggest and the boldest that could be found on earth.

"So!" said the vicar, "giants are also the cause of this? On the Cross I will burn them tomorrow before the day is over."

They asked Don Quixote many questions, but his only answer was to give him something to eat, and leave him to sleep, because that was what he needed most. And they did, and the vicar questioned the peasant about how he found Don Quixote. He told him, and mentioned the nonsense he had talked about when he was found and on the way home, which only made the vicar more eager to do what he did the next day, which was to call his friend the barber, Master Nicholas, and go with him to Don Quixote's house.

CHAPTER 6

THE IMPORTANT INSPECTION WHICH THE VICAR AND THE BARBER MADE IN THE LIBRARY OF DON QUIXOTE

He was still sleeping; so, the vicar asked the niece for the keys to the room where the books, and the authors of all the mischief were, and willingly she gave them. They all went in, the housekeeper as well, and they found more than a hundred volumes of big books very well bound, and some other small ones. The moment the housekeeper saw them she turned and ran out of the room, and came back immediately with a saucer of holy water, saying, "Here señor, sprinkle this room; don't leave any magician in these books to curse us in revenge for banishing them from the world."

The simplicity of the housekeeper made the vicar laugh, and he asked the barber to give him the books one by one to see what they were about, as there might be some among them that did not deserve to be burnt.

"No," said the niece, "there is no reason to grant mercy to any of them; every one of them have caused mischief." The housekeeper said the same, as they were both eager to slaughter even the innocent books, but the vicar would not agree to it first without reading the titles.

The first that Master Nicholas handed him was "The four books of Amadis of France." "This seems a mysterious thing," said the vicar, "because, as I have heard that this was the first book of chivalry printed in Spain, and from this all the others derive their birth and origin; so. it seems to me that we should unavoidably sentence it to the flames as the founder of such a disgusting genre."

"No," said the barber, "I have heard that this is the best of all the books of this kind, and so, as something so individual as it is, it should be excused."

"True," said the vicar; "and for that reason its life will be saved for the moment. Let us see which is next."

"It is," said the barber, "the 'Sergas de Esplandian,' the lawful son of Amadis of France."

"Then certainly," said the vicar, "the importance of the father must not be considered in the case of the son. Take it, miss housekeeper; open the window and throw it into the garden to lay the foundation for the bonfire we are going to make."

The housekeeper obeyed with great satisfaction, and the worthy "Esplandian" went flying into the garden to await the fire that was in store for it.

"Continue," said the Vicar. "This one is next," said the barber, 'Amadis of Greece,' I believe all of those books on this side are about the Amadis lineage."

"So they belong in the garden," said the vicar; "I think so," said the barber. "And so do I," added the niece.

"In that case," said the housekeeper, "let me take them into the garden to be burnt!"

They were handed to her, and as there were a lot of them, she decided not to take the stairs, and threw them out of the window.

"What is that stack of books there?" said the vicar.

"These," said the barber, "are of 'Don Olivante de Laura.'"

"The author of that book," said the vicar, "was the same that wrote 'The Garden of Flowers,' and surely there is no deciding which of the two books is more truthful, or, to put it better, less lying; all I can say is, send them into the garden to be burnt."

"The next is 'Florismarte of Hircania,'" said the barber.

"Señor Florismarte?" said the vicar; "this must take its place in the garden, in spite of his marvellous birth and visionary adventures, the stiffness and dryness of his style deserve nothing else; take him into the garden."

"With all my heart, señor," said the housekeeper, and she executed the order with great satisfaction.

"This," said the barber, "is Platir, The Knight.'"

"An old book," said the vicar, "but I find no reason for forgiveness; send it to the garden with the rest;" which was done.

Another book was opened, and they saw it was entitled, "The Knight of the Cross."

"Due to the holy name of this book," said the vicar, "its ignorance can be excused; but then, they say, 'behind the cross is the devil; take it to the fire then.'"

Taking down another book, the barber said, "This is 'The Mirror of Chivalry.'" "I know this work," said the vicar; "that is where Señor Reinaldos of Montalvan resided with his friends, who were great thieves, I can only recommend banishment, even if they share in the creation of the famous poet Ludovico Ariosto.

Opening another book, he saw it was "Palmerin de Oliva," and beside it was another called "Palmerin of England," upon seeing these, the vicar said, "The Olive can be made firewood immediately and burned until no ashes remain; and let that Olive of England be kept and preserved.

This book is of importance, for two reasons, first because it is very good, and secondly because it is said to have been written by a wise and witty King of Portugal. All the adventures at the Castle of Miraguarda are excellent and admirable, and the language is polished and clear, written with decency. So then, provided it seems good to you, Master Nicholas, I say let this and 'Amadis of France' be let off the penalty of fire, and for the rest, let them be burnt without any further questions."

"OK," said the barber, "and this that I have here is the famous 'Don Belianis.'"

"Well," said the vicar, "in the meantime, you keep them in your house and do not let anyone read them."

"With all my heart," said the barber; and not caring to continue reading more books of chivalry, he told the housekeeper to take all the big ones and throw them into the garden. This was not said to someone dull or deaf, but to someone who enjoyed burning them more than arsonist; and taking about eight at a time, she threw them out of the window.

Carrying so many at the same time she dropped one at feet of the barber, who picked it up, curious to know what it was, and it said, "History of the Famous Knight, Tirante el Blanco."

"God bless me!" said the vicar, "Tirante el Blanco' here!" "Hand it over" said the barber, "because I reckon inside that book is an immense amount of traeasure, enjoyment and a goldmine of recreation. Inside is Don Kyrieleison of Montalvan, a valiant Knight, and his brother Thomas, and the Knight Fonseca, who the bold Tyrant fought, and the empress in love with Hipolito - in truth, due to his style, it is the best book in the world. " "It deserves to be burnt," said the vicar, "take it home and read it, and you will see that I am right." "OK," said the barber; "but what should we to do with all these little books that are left?"

"These are probably books of poetry not chivalry," said the vicar; and opening one he saw it was the "Diana" of Jorge de Montemayor, and, guessing all the others to would be similar, "these," he said, "do not deserve to be burned like the others, because they cannot do the mischief the books of chivalry have done."

"Ah, señor!" said the niece, "you better order these to be burned as well as the others; because it would be no wonder if, after being cured of his chivalry disorder, my uncle, by reading these, decided to become a shepherd and began walking in the woods and fields singing; or, what would be worse, to turn into a poet, which they say is an incurable and infectious disorder."

"The young girl is right," said the vicar, "it is better to put this stumbling-block and temptation out of our friend's way. Begin, then, with the 'Diana' of Montemayor."

"This next," said the barber, "the 'Diana,' entitled the 'Second Part, by the Salamancan,' and this other book has the same title, and its author is Gil Polo."

"The Salamancan," replied the vicar, "can go along with the others sentenced to be burnt, and let Gil Polo's be preserved as if it came from God himself: but be quick because it is getting late."

"This book," said the barber, opening another, "is the ten books of the 'Fortune of Love,' written by Antonio de Lofraso, a Sardinian poet." "Such an absurd book as this" Said the vicar, "has never been written, and in a way is the best and most unique of that type, anyone who has not read it can be sure he has never read something so delightful. Pass it to me."

He put it aside with extreme satisfaction, and the barber went on, "These next are 'The Shepherd of Iberia,' 'Nymphs of Henares,' and 'The Enlightenment of Jealousy.'" "Then all we have to do," said the vicar, "is hand them to the housekeeper."

"Next is the 'Vicar de Filida.'" "He was no Vicar," said the vicar, "but a highly polished advisor; let it be preserved as a precious jewel."

"This large one here," said the barber, "is called 'The Treasury of various Poems.'" "If there were not so many of them," said the vicar, "they would be appreciated more: this book must be cleansed of certain vulgarities which it contains along with its excellences; let it be preserved because the author is a friend of mine, and out of respect for his other more heroic and grander work."

"This," continued the barber, "is the 'Cancionero' of Lopez de Maldonado." The author of that book, too," said the vicar, "is a great friend of mine, and the verses from his mouth are admired by all that hear them, due to the sweetness of his voice: let it be kept along with those that we have set apart. But what book is that next to it?"

"The 'Galatea' of Miguel de Cervantes," said the barber. "That Cervantes has been a great friend of mine for many years, and to my knowledge he has more experience in converses than in verses. His book contains some distinctive creativity, however it presents us with something but brings nothing to a conclusion: we must wait for the Second Part it promises: perhaps with an amendment it may succeed in winning the full degree of recognition it deserves; and in the meantime, you señor, keep it in your home."

"With pleasure," said the barber; "and here are three more, the 'Araucana' of Don Alonso de Ercilla, the 'Austriada' of Juan Rufo, Justice of Cordova, and the 'Montserrate' of Christobal de Virues, the Valencian poet." "These three books," said the vicar, "are the best that have been written in Castilian in heroic style, and they can be compared with the most famous of Italy; let them be preserved as the richest treasures of poetry that Spain possesses."

The vicar was tired and would not look at any more books, and so he decided that, "with the contents uncertified," all the rest should be burnt; but then the barber held one open, called "The Tears of Angelica." "I would have shed tears myself," said the vicar when he heard the title, "if I ordered that book to be burnt, because its author was one of the most famous poets in the world, not only in Spain, and he was very happy with the translation of some of Ovid's stories."

CHAPTER 7

THE SECOND ADVENTURE OF OUR WORTHY KNIGHT DON QUIXOTE OF LA MANCHA

At this moment Don Quixote began shouting out, "Here, brave Knights! here is the need for you to demonstrate the capability of your weapons!" At hearing this noise and commotion, they proceeded not to continue any longer with the scrutiny of the remaining books, and so it is thought that "The Carolea," "The Lion of Spain," and "The Deeds of the Emperor," written by Don Luis de Avila, went to the fire unseen and unheard; because no doubt they were among those that remained, and perhaps if the vicar had seen them they would not have been destroyed.

When they reached Don Quixote he was already out of bed, and was still shouting and raving, slashing and cutting, as wide awake as if he had never slept.

They circled him and with force got him back into the bed, and when he had calmed down a little bit, looking at the vicar, he said to him, "The truth, Señor Archbishop Turpin, it is a great disgrace for us who call ourselves the Twelve Peers, to carelessly allow the Knights of the Court to gain victory in this competition."

"Be quiet," said the vicar; "The luck may turn, and what is lost today can be won tomorrow; because at present, God is caring for your health, because it seems to me that you are fatigued, if not badly wounded."

"Wounded no," said Don Quixote, "but bruised and battered no doubt, because that bastard Don Roland has beaten me with the trunk of an oak tree, and all out of envy, because he sees that I rival him in his achievements. For the moment bring me something to eat, because that, I feel, is what I require, and after leave it to me to avenge myself."

They did as he asked; they gave him something to eat, and once more he fell asleep, leaving them marvelling at his madness.

That night the housekeeper burned to ashes all the books that were in the garden and in the whole house; along with some that deserved preservation in everlasting archives, but their fate and the laziness of the examiner did not allow it, and so, contained in this act was the proverb 'the innocent suffer for the guilty.'

One of the solutions which the vicar and the barber immediately applied to their friend's illness was to board up and plaster the room where the books were, so that when he got up he would not find them (possibly with the cause being removed the effect might cease), and they would say that a magician had stolen them, the whole room as well. Two days later Don Quixote got up, and the first thing he did was to go and look for his books, and not finding the room where he had left them, he wandered from side to side looking for it. He came to the place where the door used to be, and raised his hands as if to turn the handle, and he rolled and twisted his eyes in every direction without saying a word; but after some time he asked his housekeeper where the was room that held his books.

The housekeeper, who had already been instructed in what to say, said, "What room are you looking for? There is no room or books in this house anymore, because the devil has stolen them."

"It was not the devil," said the niece, "but a magician who arrived on a cloud one night after you left. He entered the room, and what he did in there I do not know, but after a little while he departed, flying through the roof, and left the house full of smoke; and when we went to see what had been done we could not see any books or a room: but we remember very well, the housekeeper and I, that on leaving, the villain said in a loud voice that, for a grudge he owed the owner of the books and the room, he had done the damage; and he said that his name was the Sage Munaton."

"He must have said Friston," said Don Quixote.

"I don't know whether he called himself Friston or Friton," said the housekeeper, "I only know that his name ended with 'ton.'" "It does," said Don Quixote, "He is a sage magician, a great enemy of mine, who has a grudge against me because he knows that in a time I am to engage in combat and conquer, and he will be unable to prevent it; and for this reason he endeavours to do me as much wrong as he can; but I promise him it will be hard for him to oppose or avoid what is ordered by Heaven."

"Who doubts that?" said the niece; "but, uncle, who involves you in these battles? Would it not be better to remain at peace in your own house instead of roaming the world looking for battles?"

"Oh, niece of mine," replied Don Quixote, "how wrong you are in your thinking: I am able to strip off the beards of any man who dares to touch only the tip of a hair of mine."

The two were unwilling to make any further comments, as they could see that his anger was escalating.

In short, he stayed at home for fifteen days very quietly without showing any signs of desire to continue with his former delusions, and during this time he held lively discussions with his housekeeper, niece, the vicar and the barber, on a point that he believed that Knights were what the world was in need of, and that through him there would be a revival of the Knight and his adventures. The vicar sometimes contradicted him, sometimes agreed with him, because if he had not agreed sometimes he would not have been able to calm him down.

Meanwhile Don Quixote work on a farm labourer, a neighbour of his, an honest man (if that title can be given to a man who is poor), with very little wit in his skull. Basically, he talked to him with such persuasion and promises, that the poor clown made up his mind to go with him and serve him as his aide. Don Quixote, among other things, told him he should go with him willingly, because any moment an adventure might occur which might see them win an island in an instant and make him governor of it. Due to these and similar promises Sancho

Panza (as that's what the labourer was called) left his wife and children, and employed himself as the aide to his neighbour.

Don Quixote then aimed to gather some money; and by selling his possessions and making bad deals in every case, he got together a good amount. He provided himself with a new shield, which he begged as a loan from a friend, and, restoring his battered helmet the best he could, he warned his aide Sancho of the day and hour he intends to leave, so that he can equip himself with what he thought was needed. Above all, he instructed him to take saddlebags with him. Sancho said he would, and that he was going to take the very best donkey he had, as he was not inclined to have to go on foot. Over the donkey, Don Quixote hesitated a little, trying to call to mind any Knight taking with him an aide mounted on a horse, but no instance occurred in his memory. Despite that, however, he decided to take him, intending to give him a worthier horse when the chance presented itself, by taking the horse of the first discourteous Knight they encountered. For himself he provided shirts, according to the advice the host had given him; all being done, without giving any notice, Sancho Panza to his wife and children, or Don Quixote to his housekeeper and niece, they left, unseen by anybody from the village one night, and made such a swift departure that by daylight they were safe from discovery, even if a search were made for them.

Sancho rode on his donkey like a King, with his saddlebags and water container, longing to see himself the governor of the island his master had promised. Don Quixote decided to take the same route and road he had taken on his first journey, the Campo de Montiel, which he travelled with less discomfort than the first time, because, as it was early morning and the rays of the sun hit them, the heat did not concern them.

And now said Sancho Panza to his master, "Take care, Señor Knight, not to forget about the island you have promised me, because if it were so big, I would have to be equal to govern it."

Don Quixote replied, "You must know, Sancho Panza my friend, that it was a practice very much in fashion with the Knights in historic times to make their aides governors of the islands or kingdoms they won, and I am determined that there will be no failure on my part in such a generous custom; on the contrary, I mean to improve it, because they sometimes, and perhaps most frequently, waited until their aides were old, and then when they had given enough service and hard days, they gave them a title or other, a count, or at the most nobleman, of some valley or province more or less; but if you live and I live, it may be within six days, that I have won some Kingdom that has others dependent upon it, which will be just the thing to enable you to be crowned King of one of them. You do not need to count this as wonderful, because these things and chances occur often to Knights in ways so unexpected that I might easily give you even more than I promise you."

"In that case," said Sancho Panza, "if I become a King by one of those miracles you speak of, even Juana Gutierrez, my old woman, would come to be the Queen and my children heirs to the throne."

"Well, who doubts it?" said Don Quixote.

"I doubt it," replied Sancho Panza, "because I am convinced that although God can shower kingdoms on the earth, none one of them would suit Mari Gutierrez. Let me tell you, señor, she is not worth two coins; countess will suit her better, and that is only with God's help."

"Leave it to God, Sancho," said Don Quixote, "because he will give her what suits her best; but do not undervalue yourself so much that you become content with anything less than being governor of a province."

"I will not, señor," answered Sancho, "especially as I have a man of such high quality for a master, who knows how to give me all that is suitable for me and all I can bear."

CHAPTER 8

THE GOOD FORTUNE WHICH THE VALIANT DON QUIXOTE HAD IN THE TERRIBLE AND UNDREAMT-OF ADVENTURE OF THE WINDMILLS

While riding they approached thirty to forty windmills, and as soon as Don Quixote saw them he said to his aide, "Fortune has arranged for us more than we could have desired for ourselves, because look there, my friend Sancho, there are thirty or more monstrous giants, which I am going to engage in battle and slaughter, and from that we will begin to make our fortunes; because this is righteous warfare, and it is God's good service to sweep this evil breed from the face of the earth."

"What giants?" said Sancho.

"Those that you see there," answered his master, "with the long arms, and some even have two heads."

"Look," said Sancho; "what we see there are windmills not giants, and what seem to be their arms are the sails that are turned by the wind."

"It is easy to see," replied Don Quixote, "that you are not used to this business of adventures; those are giants; and if you are afraid, then leave, find somewhere to pray while I engage them in fierce and unequal combat."

Once said, he kicked his heel into his horse Rocinante, oblivious to the cries of his aide Sancho, warning him that those were certainly windmills and not giants he was going to attack. He, however, was so positive that they were giants that he did not hear the cries of Sancho, or perceive, near as he was, what they were, but went toward them shouting, "Do not run away, you cowards and disgusting beings, because a single Knight attacks you."

A slight breeze at this moment encouraged the sails to move, seeing this Don Quixote exclaimed, "Although you have more weapons than the giant Briareus, you have me to deal with."

So calling on Dulcinea with all his heart, asking her to support him in such a danger, with the lance lifted and covered by his shield, he charged at the closest windmill as fast as Rocinante could go; but as he drove his lance into the sail the wind rotated it with such force that it shredded the lance to pieces, taking with it the horse and rider, who went flying. Sancho rushed to his assistance as fast as his horse could go, and when he got there he found him unable to move, with such a shock as Rocinante had fallen with him.

"God bless me!" said Sancho, "did I not tell you to be careful with what you were about to do, because they were only windmills? No one could have mistaken that apart from someone who had something wrong in his head."

"Be quiet, Sancho," replied Don Quixote, "the fortunes of war more than any other are liable to frequent fluctuations; and furthermore I think, and it is the truth, that the same sage Friston who took my room and books, has turned these giants into windmills in order to rob me of the glory of vanquishing them, this is the hatred he has toward me; but in the end his evil arts will not profit against my good sword."

"As God wills," said Sancho Panza, and helping him to mount Rocinante again, whose shoulder was half out; they followed the road to Puerto Lapice, because there, said Don Quixote, they would not fail to find adventures in abundance and variety. Don Quixote was very saddened due to the loss of his lance, and saying so to his aide, he added, "I remember reading how a Spanish Knight, Diego Perez de Vargas, having broken his sword in battle, tore from an oak tree a heavy branch, and with it he pounded so many Moors. I mention this because from the first oak tree I see I am going to take a large branch, and with it I am determined to do things that I believe myself very fortunate and worthy to be able to do, and you will be an eyewitness of many things that will not easily be believed by others."

"As God wills," said Sancho, "I believe all that you say; but straighten yourself a little, because you seem to be leaning to one side, which may be because of the fall."

"Exactly," said Don Quixote, "but I make no complaint about the pain, because Knights are not permitted to complain about any wound, even if their bowels were coming out through it."

"If so," said Sancho, "I have nothing to say; but God knows I would rather you complain when something hurts you. Because, I confess I complain no matter how small the ache is; unless this rule about not complaining extends to a Knight's aide as well."

Don Quixote could not help laughing at his aide's simplicity, and he assured him he could complain whenever and however he chose, just as he liked, because, so far, he had never read anything that said the contrary within the laws of Knighthood.

Sancho reminded him it was dinner-time, but Don Quixote was not hungry. With permission Sancho sat as comfortably as he could on his horse, and taking out of the saddlebags what he had stored in them, he jogged along behind his master chewing loudly, deliberately, and from time to time taking a sip from the bottle of water, with a sigh of relief; and while he went on in this way, he never gave any thought to the promises his master had made him, and he did not consider it a hardship but actually as a form of recreation to go in quest of adventures, however dangerous they might be. Finally, they spent the night among some trees, and from one of them Don Quixote took a dry branch to serve as his new a lance, and fixed to the end of it, the head he had removed from the broken one. All night Don Quixote lay awake thinking of his lady Dulcinea, in order to conform to what he had read in his books, about the Knights that used to lie sleepless in the forests and deserts due to the memories of their lovers. Sancho on the other hand it, having his stomach full was asleep all night, and, if his master did not call him in the morning, neither the rays of the sun beating on his face or the notes of birds welcoming the new day would have had the power to wake him. When he got up he reached for the bottle of water, and found it less full than the night before, which bothered him because he was not sure when they would next be able to fill it. Don Quixote did not care to break his fast, for, as it has been said already, he confined himself to his memories for nourishment.

They returned to the road leading to Puerto Lapice, and at three in the afternoon they could see it in the distance. "Here, brother Sancho," said Don Quixote when he saw it, "we will be immersed in what they call adventures; but remember this, even if you see me in the greatest of danger, you must not raise your sword in my defence, unless you perceive that those who attack me are a crowd of dishonourable people; because in that case you may aide me appropriately; but if they are Knights it is not permitted or allowed by the law of Knighthood for you to help me until you have been named a Knight."

"Certainly, señor," replied Sancho, "rest assured I will fully obey in this matter; especially as I am a peaceful man and not accustomed to mixing in conflict: however, in regards to my own defence I will not give much notice to those laws, because human and divine laws allow each man to defend himself against any attacker whatsoever."

"That I agree with," said Don Quixote, "but in this matter of aiding me against Knights you must put a restraint on your natural impulse."

"I will do, I promise you," answered Sancho. While they were talking two monks appeared on the road, mounted on two camels. They wore travelling glasses and carried sunshades; and behind them was a coach being pulled by four or five people on horseback and two helpers on foot. In the coach there was, as afterwards appeared, a lady from Biscay on her way to Seville, where her husband was appointed with a high honour to leave for the Indies. The monks, although going the same way, were not accompanying her; but the moment Don Quixote saw them he said to his aide, "Either I am mistaken, or this is going to be the most famous adventure that has ever been seen, because those we see there must be, doubtlessly, magicians who are trying to kidnap the Princess in that coach, and with all my power I must undo this wrong."

"This will be worse than the windmills," said Sancho. "Look, señor; those are Monks, and the coach clearly belongs to some travellers: I tell you again to be careful you are about to do and don't let the devil mislead you."

"I have told you already, Sancho," replied Don Quixote, "that on the subject of adventures you do not know much. What I say is the truth, as you will shortly see."

So after saying this, he advanced and placed himself in the middle of the road, and as soon as he thought they were near enough to hear him, he shouted, "Devilish and unnatural beings, release instantly the high class Princesses who you attempt to kidnap, or prepare to face an immediate death as the punishment for your evil deeds."

The monks stopped and stood wondering at the appearance of Don Quixote as well as his words, to which they replied, "Señor Knight, we are not

40

devilish or unnatural, but two brothers from the church taking this road, we do not know whether or not there are any captive Princesses in this coach."

"No weak words with me, because I know you, lying fools," said Don Quixote, and without waiting for a reply he made Rocinante run toward them, with his lance raised and with such fury and determination, that, if the friar had not jumped off the camel himself, he would have been knocked to the ground against his will, sore and wounded, if not killed. The second monk, seeing how his friend was treated, kicked his heels into his camel which ran across the land faster than the wind.

When Sancho saw the monk on the ground, he dismounted quickly from his horse, rushed towards him and began to remove his robe. The two aides who were on foot came and asked what he was stripping him for. Sancho answered, that this was lawful as his master Don Quixote had won the battle. The aides, who had no idea of a joke and did not understand all this about battles, seeing that Don Quixote was some distance away talking to the travellers in the coach, attacked Sancho, knocked him down, and leaving hardly a hair in his beard, battered him with kicks and left him breathless and senseless on the ground; and without any more delay helped the monk to mount his camel, who, trembling, terrified, and pale, as soon as he found himself in the saddle, rushed after his companion, who was standing at a distance looking on, watching the result of the attack; then, not caring to wait for the end of what had just begun, they continued on their journey making more crosses than if they were being chased by the devil.

Don Quixote was, as has been said, speaking to the lady in the coach: "Your beauty," he said, "due to my strength the pride of your capturers lie on the ground; and of course you must be craving to know the name of your saviour, I am called Don Quixote of La Mancha, Knight and adventurer, and captive to the unrivalled and beautiful lady Dulcinea del Toboso: and in return for the service you have received from me I ask no more than that you travel to El Toboso, and on my behalf present yourself to my lady and tell her what I have done to set you free."

One of the aides in the coach, a Biscayan, was listening to what Don Quixote was saying, and, perceiving that he would not allow the coach to continue, and was forcing them to travel to El Toboso, attacked him, and snatching his lance spoke him in bad Castilian and worse Biscayan similar to this but omitting the profanities, "Leave immediately, Knight, or as true as God made me, unless you leave this coach, I will kill you as if it were the art of a Biscayan."

Don Quixote understood him quite well, and answered him very quietly, "If you were a Knight, which you are not, I would have already disciplined you for your irrationality and carelessness, miserable creature." To which the Biscayan replied, "I am no gentleman, I swear to God as I am Christian: if you drop the lance and take your sword, soon you will see that this will be as easy as taking water to a cat."

"You will see," replied Don Quixote; and throwing his lance on the ground he drew his sword, lifted his shield, and attacked the Biscayan, determined to take his life.

When the Biscayan saw him coming, although he wanted to dismount his horse, as it was one of those feeble kind which were let out for hire, he had no confidence, and had no choice but to draw his sword; it was lucky for him, however, that he was near the coach, from which he was able to take a cushion to serve as his shield; and they attacked one another as if they had been two mortal enemies. The others struggled to make peace between them, but could not, because the Biscayan declared that if they did not let him finish this battle he would kill his lover and anyone that tried to prevent him. The lady in the coach, amazed and terrified at what she saw, ordered the coachman to move away a little, and was then watching from a distance, during this the Biscayan struck Don Quixote with a huge blow on the shoulder over the top of his shield, which, without armour, would have left him on the ground. Don Quixote, feeling the weight of this blow, shouted loudly, "Lady of my soul, Dulcinea, flower and beauty, come to the aid of your Knight, who, in fulfilling his obligations to your beauty, finds himself in this extreme danger." To say this, to lift his sword, to shelter himself behind his shield, and to attack the Biscayan was the work of a brave man, determined as he was to deliver a single blow. The Biscayan, seeing him act in this way, was convinced of his courage, and decided to follow his example, so he waited for him shielding himself with the cushion, being unable to execute any sort of manoeuvre with his camel, which, was tired and not meant for this type of game, could not make a step.

Don Quixote rushed toward the cautious Biscayan, with his sword lifted and with a firm intention of splitting him in half, while on his side the Biscayan waited for him with his sword ready, and under the protection of his cushion; everyone stood trembling, waiting in suspense for the result of blows to come, and the lady in the coach and the rest of her aides were praying that God would save her aide and all of them from this great danger which they found themselves in. But at this point the author of this history leaves this battle pending, giving as an excuse that he could not find something more written about the achievements of Don Quixote than what has been already mentioned above. It is unbelievable that a history so interesting could have been allowed to fall into obscurity, or that the intelligent people of La Mancha would not have preserved in their archives some documents referring to this famous Knight; and this being the author's belief, he did not worry about finding the conclusion to this story, which, heaven favouring him, he did find and will be relayed in this next chapter.

CHAPTER 9

CONCLUDING THE TERRIFIC BATTLE BETWEEN THE
BISCAYAN AND OUR VALLIANT KNIGHT

In the First Part of we left the valiant Biscayan and the renowned Don Quixote with swords drawn and raised, ready to deliver two furious blows that if they had connected they would have split and left each other open like a pomegranate; and at this critical point the delightful history came to a stop and was cut short without any information from the author where the missing part could be found.

This distressed me a lot, because the pleasure from having read a small portion turned to anger at the thought that a large part was missing from such an interesting story. It seemed to me to be impossible that such a Knight would be without some sage to undertake the task of writing his marvellous achievements; something that almost all Knights who they say, went after adventures; usually had, one or two sages who not only recorded their deeds but described their most unimportant thoughts and stupidities, however secret they might be; and so, such a good Knight could not have been without, what Platir and others like him had in abundance. I could not bring myself to believe that such an amazing story had been left incomplete, so I blamed Time, the devourer and destroyer of all things, that had either concealed or consumed it.

On the other hand, it struck me that among his books there had been such modern ones as "The Enlightenment of Jealousy" and the "Nymphs and Shepherds of Henares," his story must be modern, and that although it might not be written, it might exist in the memory of the people in his village and those nearby. This thought kept me confused and longing to know the truth and the whole life of the famous Spaniard, Don Quixote of La Mancha, the light and reflection of Manchegan chivalry, and the first of our time, and in these evil days, devoted himself to the labour of Knighthood, righting wrongs, comforting widows, and protecting women that used to ride about, on their horses, with their virginity intact, from mountain to mountain and valley to valley - because, if it were not for some brute, or fool with a knife, that forced them, at the end of eighty years, they would have never slept a day under a roof, and went to their graves unmarried. Therefore, I say that in these and other respects our brave Don Quixote is worthy of everlasting and notable praise, and labour and pains spent in searching for the conclusion to this delightful history has not been kept from me; although I know that if Heaven, chance and good fortune had not helped me, the world would have been deprived of this entertainment and pleasure, that for a couple of hours or so each day, will well occupy the man who reads it attentively. The discovery of it occurred in this way:

One day, I was in the Alcana of Toledo, a boy came to sell some pamphlets and old papers to a silk dealer, and, as I like to read even the scraps of paper in the streets, led by this natural tendency of mine I took one of the pamphlets the boy had for sale, and saw that it was in characters which I recognised as Arabic, and as I was unable to read them although I could recognise them, I looked to see if there were any Spanish-speaking Moor, who could read them for me; this was no great difficulty, because even If I searched for an older and better language I would have found him. In short, chance provided me with an interpreter, who when I told him what I wanted and put the book into his hands, opened it in the middle and after reading a little in it began to laugh. I asked him what he was laughing at, and he replied that it was at something the book had written in the margin as a note. I asked him tell me what it said; and he, still laughing said, "In the margin, as I told you, this is written: 'This Dulcinea del Toboso so often mentioned in history, they say, had the best hand out of any woman in all La Mancha for feeding pigs.'"

When I heard Dulcinea del Toboso, I was struck with surprise and amazement, because it occurred to me that these pamphlets contained the history of Don Quixote. I then asked him to read the beginning, and doing so, turning the Arabic into Castilian, he told me it meant, "History of Don Quixote of La Mancha, written by Cide Hamete Benengeli, an Arab historian." It required great restraint to hide the joy I felt when the title of the book reached my ears, and snatching it from the silk dealer, I bought all the papers and pamphlets from the boy for half a coin; and if he had known how eager I was to have them, he would have safely made six coins more. I left immediately with the Moor into the walkway of the local cathedral, and begged him to turn all these pamphlets that related to Don Quixote into the Castilian, without omitting or adding anything to them, offering him whatever payment he required. He was satisfied with two kilos of raisins and two kilos of wheat, and promised to translate them faithfully; but to make the matter easier, and to not let this precious material slip from my hands, I took him to my house, where in little more than a month and a half he translated the whole text just as follows:

In the first pamphlet the battle between Don Quixote and the Biscayan, history describes, their swords raised, and one protected by his shield, the other by his cushion. The Biscayan had an inscription under his feet which said, "Don Sancho de Azpeitia," which must have been his name; and at the feet of Rocinante was another that said, "Don Quixote." Rocinante was marvellously portrayed, so long and thin, so lean, with a huge backbone. Near him was Sancho Panza holding the reins to his donkey, which had an inscription under its feet that said, "Sancho Zancas," and according to the picture, he must have had a big belly, a short body, and long legs, which must be why he was given the names: Panza and Zancas. Some other minor details might be mentioned, but they have little importance and have nothing to do with the history; and no history can be bad as long as it is true.

If there is any objection over its truth, it can only be that its author was an Arab, as lying is very common among those of that nation; and due to that they are enemies of ours, it is possible that there were omissions rather than additions made in the course of the translation. And this is my own opinion;

because, where he could and should give praise to such a worthy Knight, he seems to me to deliberately pass it in silence; which is irresponsible, because it is the duty of historians to be exact, truthful, and free from bias, and neither interest or fear, hatred or love, should make them deviate from the path of truth, whose mother is history, rival of time, storehouse of deeds, witness for the past, example and counsel for the present, and warning for the future. In this book I know all that is desired can be found, and if it is missing anything at all, I say it is the fault of the original author and not the fault of the subject. To be brief, its Second Part, according to the translation, began in this way:

With swords raised high, it seemed as though the two valiant and furious warriors were threatening heaven, earth, and hell, with great resolution and determination. The fiery Biscayan was the first to strike a blow, which was given with such force and fury that had the sword not turned slightly, that single stroke would have sufficiently put an end to the bitter struggle and to all the adventures of our Knight; so although it struck him on the left shoulder, it did not harm him more than to strip that side of his armour, taking with it a part of his helmet and half of his ear, leaving him in serious danger.

Good God! Who could properly describe the rage that filled the heart of our Knight when he saw the way in which he was treated? All that can be said is, it was enough that he raised himself on his horse, and, grasping his sword more firmly with both hands, he attacked the Biscayan with such fury, striking him over the cushion and over the head, that – this good shield proved to be useless – as if a mountain had fallen on him, he began to bleed from his nose, mouth, and ears, staggering as if he was about to fall backwards off his camel, and no doubt he would have done if he had not held on to its neck; at the same time, however, he his feet slipped out of the straps and then his arms released the neck, the camel, ran in fright across the field, and threw its master to the ground. Don Quixote stood and was looking very calmly, and, when he saw him fall, jumped off his horse and with great speed ran to him, and, presenting the point of his sword to his eyes, told him to surrender, or he would cut his head off. The Biscayan was so disoriented that he was unable to say a word, and this would have been the end of him, if the ladies in the coach, who up until now had been watching in great terror, had not ran to where he stood and begged him to grant them the great grace and favour of sparing their aide's life; to which Don Quixote replied with much seriousness and dignity, "In truth, fair ladies, I am content to do what you ask me for; but it must be on one condition and understanding, which is that this Knight promises to go to the village of El Toboso, and on my behalf present himself to the incomparable lady Dulcinea, and tell her that he was defeated in combat by me Don Quixote of La Mancha."

The terrified ladies, without discussing Don Quixote's demand or asking who Dulcinea was, promised that their aide would do what had been commanded.

"Then, on the faith of that promise," said Don Quixote, "I will do no further harm to him, although he deserves far more from me."

CHAPTER 10

THE PLEASANT CONVERSATION BETWEEN DON QUIXOTE AND HIS AIDE SANCHO PANZA

Sancho had finally risen, after the beating he took from the monk's aides, and stood watching the battle of his master, Don Quixote, and praying to God that he will grant him the victory, and that he might win some island to make him governor of, as he had been promised. Seeing, therefore, that the struggle was now over, and that his master was walking back to mount Rocinante, he approached to hold the stirrup for him, and, before he could mount, he went on his knees before him, and taking his hand, kissed it saying, "Would it please you, Señor Don Quixote, to give me the government of the island which has been won in this hard fight, because although it may be very large I feel I have the sufficient force to be able to govern it as much and as well as anyone in the world who has ever governed islands."

To which Don Quixote replied, "You must take notice, brother Sancho, that this adventure and those like it are not adventures of islands, but are the cross-roads, in which nothing is gained except a broken head or half an ear: have patience, because adventures will present themselves from which I will make you, not only a governor, but something more."

Sancho gave him thanks, and again kissing his hand, helped him to mount Rocinante, and mounting his horse himself, proceeded to follow his master, who at a fair pace, without saying anything further to the ladies belonging to the coach, turned into the woods which was nearby. Sancho followed him at his donkey's greatest speed, but Rocinante galloped so fast, that he found himself left behind, he was forced to call to his master to wait for him. Don Quixote slowed down, reining in Rocinante until his tired aide caught up, who on reaching him said, "It seems to me, señor, it would be prudent for us to go and take refuge in some church, because, seeing how beaten the aide was with whom you fought, it would be no surprise if they give information about the affair to the Holy Brotherhood and send them to arrest us, and if they do, before we are released we will be punished for it."

"Peace," said Don Quixote; "where have you ever seen or heard that a Knight has been charged by the court of justice, however many murders he may have committed?"

"I know nothing about murder," answered Sancho, "and niether in my life have had anything to do with one; I only know that the Holy Brotherhood looks after those who fight in the fields."

"Then you do not need to be uneasy, my friend," said Don Quixote, "because I will keep you out of the hands of the Brotherhood. But tell me, as long as you have lived, have you even seen a more valiant Knight than me in the whole world; have you read in history of any who has or had more courage in attack, more spirit in maintaining it, more dexterity in wounding or skill in overthrowing?"

"The truth is," answered Sancho, "that I have never read any history, because I cannot read or write, but what I can confirm is that I have never served a more daring master than you in all the days of my life; now what I ask from you is to patch your wound, because there is a great deal of blood flowing from your ear; and with us I have bandage and ointment in the saddlebags."

"All of that could be easily taken care of," said Don Quixote, "if I had remembered to make the bottle of ointment out of Fierabras, because with that, it could be healed with one single drop

"What bottle and what ointment is that?" said Sancho Panza.

"It is an ointment," answered Don Quixote, "that if possessed, one need not have fear of death, or dying from any wound; and so when I make it and give it to you, if you have nothing to do when we are in some battle and you see they have cut me in half through the middle of the body – which will not happen frequently, carefully place that half of the body which will have fallen to the ground on the other half which remains in the saddle, taking care to fit it evenly and exactly. Then you will give me to drink two drops of the ointment I have mentioned, and you will see me become complete again."

"If that is so," said Panza, "From now, I surrender the government of the promised island, and desire no more in payment for my many and faithful services just give me the name of this supreme liquor, because I am convinced it will be worth more than two coins an ounce anywhere, and I want nothing more than to pass the rest of my life in ease and honour; but it remains to be said if it costs much to make it."

"With less than three coins, twelve pints of it can be made," said Don Quixote.

"Oh god!" said Sancho, "then why do you put off making it and teaching it to me?"

"Peace, friend," answered Don Quixote; "I have greater secrets to teach you and greater favours to ask you for; and so, for the present let us patch the wound, because my ear is in great pain."

Sancho took out some bandage and ointment from the saddlebags; but when Don Quixote saw his helmet shattered, he began to lose his senses, and grabbing his sword and raising his eyes to heaven, he said, "I swear to the Creator of all things that I will not eat bread, or embrace my lady, until I have complete revenge on him who has committed such an offence against me."

Hearing this, Sancho said to him, "You should bear in mind, Señor Don Quixote, that if the Knight has done what you commanded him to do; and has gone to present himself before lady Dulcinea del Toboso, he will have done all that he was asked to do, and does not deserve further punishment unless he commits a new offence."

"You are right and have made a good point," answered Don Quixote; I remember the promise, so I will take no further vengeance on him, but I make and confirm a new promise, to lead the life I have said until at some time I take by force another Knight's helmet."

"Señor," replied Sancho, "you should send all these type of promises to the devil, because they are very cruel and harmful to the conscience; tell me, if in several we find no man with a helmet, what would we do? Are you going to keep this promise even if it causes a lot of inconvenience and discomfort, don't you find more comfort sleeping in a house, rather than a thousand other difficulties which are contained in the stories of the historic Knights, which you now want to revive? Do you not see that there are no men in armour travelling on any of these roads, nothing but traders and transporters, who, not only do not wear helmets, but perhaps never heard of them in their whole lives?"

"You are wrong," said Don Quixote, "because we won't be here for more than two hours before we see more men in armour."

"Enough," said Sancho; "Let it be then, hopefully God will give us success in obtaining an island."

"I have already told you, Sancho," said Don Quixote, "not to give me any pressure for that; because if we do not obtain an island, there is the Kingdom of Denmark, which will fit you just like a ring fits a finger, and being on mainland, you will enjoy yourself better. But let us leave that until the right time comes; see if you have anything for us to eat in those saddlebags, because right now, we must search for a castle where we can stay the night and make the balsam I told you about, because I swear to God, my ear is causing me a lot of pain."

"I have an onion, some cheese and a few pieces of bread," said Sancho, "but this is not fit for a courageous Knight like yourself."

"How little you know," answered Don Quixote; "I want you to know, Sancho, that it is common for Knights to go without eating for a month, and even when they do eat, it is only what they find; and this would have been clear to you if you had read as many histories as I have, because, although they are many of them, among them I have not found a mention of Knights eating, unless by accident or at some luxurious dinner prepared for them, and the rest of the time they went hungry. And although it is obvious that they could not go without eating and performing all the other natural functions, because, in fact, they were men like ourselves, it is obvious too that, wandering like they did for most of their lives through woods and land without a cook, their most usual food consumption would be scraps like those you are offering me now; so friend Sancho, do not worry what food pleases me."

"Forgive me," said Sancho, "because, as I cannot read or write I do not know or comprehend the rules of chivalry: from now on I will stock the saddlebags with all kinds of dry fruit, as you are a Knight; and for myself, as I am not one, I will fill them with chicken and other more substantial things."

"I did not say, Sancho," replied Don Quixote, "that it is imperative for Knight not to eat anything other than the fruits you speak of; only that their usual diet mostly consisted of certain herbs they found in the fields which they knew about and I know too."

"That's a good thing," answered Sancho, "to know those herbs, because I think we will need to put that knowledge into practice someday."

And, taking out what he said he had for them to eat, both of them ate peacefully over general conversation. But anxious to find somewhere to stay for the night, once they finished eating, they mounted their horses, and set off quickly to find somewhere to stay before the night came; but the hope of finding this place started to fade; and instead they found huts belonging to some goat herders, which they decided to stay in. This upset Sancho somewhat as he really wanted to take shelter in a house, but it was his master's pleasure to sleep under the open sky, because he believed that each time this happened to him he had performed an act of ownership that helped to prove his chivalry.

CHAPTER 11

DON QUIXOTE AND THE GOAT HERDERS

He was welcomed by the goat herders, and Sancho, having tied Rocinante and his horse to the nearby tree, walked towards the fragrance that came from some pieces of goat simmering in a pot on the fire; and although he would have liked to try some immediately, if they were ready to be transferred from the pot to the belly, he refrained from doing so as the goat herders removed them from the fire, and laying sheepskin on the ground, quickly making a table on the floor, and with signs of good-will invited them both to share what they had cooked. Around this table on the floor, six of the goat herders seated themselves, then with politeness asked Don Quixote to take a seat in a space they had made for him. Don Quixote seated himself, and Sancho remained standing to serve the cups, which were made of goat horns. Seeing him standing, his master said to him:

"You can see, Sancho, the good that being a Knight contains in itself, and how those who become Knights on the road are to be honoured and esteemed by the world, I want you to seat yourself here by my side and in the company of these worthy people, and that you are one with me, and although I am your master, you may eat from my plate and drink from whatever I drink from; because being a Knight is synonymous with love, which levels all."

"Thank you master," said Sancho, "but I must tell you that as long as I have enough to eat, I can eat it well, or better, by myself, standing rather than seated alongside an emperor. And indeed, if the truth is told, what I eat standing, without formality is much more pleasure for me, even if it were only bread and onions, than those tables where I am forced to chew slowly, drink a little, wipe my mouth every minute, and cannot cough or fart if I want to, or do other things which are the privileges of liberty and solitude. So, señor, for these honours which you offer me as a servant and follower of a Knight, exchange them for other things which may be of more use and advantage to me; because these, although I fully acknowledge them, I abandon them from this moment to the end of the world."

"Despite that," said Don Quixote, "you must seat yourself, because a man who humbles himself, will be exalted by God;" and grabbing him by the arm he forced him to sit down beside him.

The goat herders did not understand this conversation about Knights and aides, and all they did was to eat in silence and stare at their guests, who with great appetite were consuming pieces as big as a fist. The servings of meat finished, they spread on the sheepskin a large heap of roasted acorns, and with them they placed cheese which was harder than if it had been made of mortar. All of this while the cups were continuously refilled. When Don Quixote had satisfied his appetite, he took a handful of the acorns, and contemplating them attentively said out loud:

"A happy day and happy time, which the ancients called golden, not because in that age the gold so sought-after was gained without work, but because they that lived during it did not know the two words "mine" and "yours"! In that blessed age all things were in common; to gather the daily food required no labour only to stretch a hand and gather it from the sturdy oak trees that stood generously inviting him or her with their sweet ripe fruit. The clear streams and running rivers produced water in abundance. The busy bees created their nests in the gaps of the rocks and hollows of the trees, offering without issue the ample produce of their sweet-scented work to every hand. The mighty cork trees, out of courtesy, shed the broad light bark that served to roof the houses, offering protection against fierce weather. Then all was peaceful, all friendship, all harmony; and then the dull crooked men had not dared to pierce the bowels of our first mother (the earth) that without force produced from every portion of her fertile land all that could satisfy, sustain, and delight the children that then possessed her. Then the innocent and fair young shepherdess roamed from valley to valley and hill to hill, with long flowing hair, and no more garments than what was needed modestly to cover what modesty seeks and sought to hide. Neither were their decorations like those we see today, set in purple and silk, twisted in endless fashions, but the beautified leaves of the green land, were where they went bravely. Then there were true thoughts of love, the hearts clothed themselves simply and naturally as the heart perceived these thoughts, and were not artificially awakened by forced and fake speech. Fraud, deceit, or malice had not yet blended with truth and sincerity. Justice held its ground, undisturbed and un-assailed by the efforts of favour and of interest, that now so much impair, pervert, and attack it. Subjective law had not yet established itself in the mind of the judge, because then there was no cause to judge and no one to be judged. Girls modestly, as I have said, wandered alone by choice, and unattended, without fear of insult or sexual assault, and if they decided to be with someone it was their decision. But now we are in this hateful age of ours and no one is safe, not even if a labyrinth like the one in Crete concealed and surrounded her; even there the infection will make its way to them through the cracks or by the intensity of its appeal, and, despite all seclusion, lead them to their downfall. In defence of these, as time has advanced and evil increased, the order of Knights was instituted, to defend women, to protect widows and to assist the orphans and the poor. I belong to this order, brother goat herders, and to you I return thanks for the hospitality and welcome you have offered me and my aide; because although by law all men are obliged to show support to Knights, yet, without knowing this obligation you have welcomed and fed me, it is only right that with all the good-will in my power I should thank you for yours."

This long ranting (which was not necessary) our Knight gave because the acorns reminded him of the golden age; and inspired him to say all this unnecessary information to the goat herders, who listened to him in amazement without saying a word in reply. Sancho likewise was quiet and ate acorns, and made repeated visits to the cork tree, where they were keeping the wine cool.

Don Quixote spoke longer than it took him to finish eating, and at the end one of the goat herders said, "Señor Knight, thank you for appreciating our hospitality and good-will, we will also amuse you by making one of our companions sing: he will be here soon, and he is a very intelligent young man, deep in love, and what is more he can read and write and play his instrument perfectly."

The goat herder had hardly finished speaking, when the notes of a stringed instrument reached their ears; and shortly after, the player came in, a very good-looking young man of about twenty-two. One of his companions asked him if he would like a drink, and he replied that he had already had one, and he who had offered him said:

"In that case, Antonio, can you give us pleasure by singing a little bit for us, so the gentleman, our guest, can see that even in the mountains and woods there are musicians: we have told him about your accomplishments, and we want you to show them and prove what we say is true; so, we ask that you sit down and sing that song about your love, the one which your uncle presented you with an honorary canon for, and was liked so much in the town."

"With all my heart," said the young man, and without waiting for more convincing he seated himself on the trunk of an oak tree, and after quickly tuning his instrument, began to sing to these words.

ANTONIO'S BALLAD

You love me, Olalla;
Well I know it, even though
Love's silent language, your eyes, have never
By their glances told me so.

Because I know my love, you know,
Therefore, for you I claim to dare:
Once it ceases to be a secret,
Love never need to feel despair.

It is true, Olalla, sometimes
Because you have plainly shown
That your spirit can be rock in hardness,
And your heart can be sometimes stone.

Yet with all that, you are shy,
And uncertainty fits between,
Hope is there - at the border
Although sometimes it can't be seen.

I gain faith from those glimpses,

And this faith in you I hold;
Kindness cannot make it stronger,
Coldness cannot make it cold.

If it is true that love is gentle,
Your gentleness I feel
Something giving me a promise
That what we have is real.

If it is found that in devotion
Lies a power to make hearts move,
Every day I'll show you,
And hopefully that will prove.

Many times, you must have noticed
If you care to glance
That the things I do out of love
Cannot be done by chance.

Love's eyes love to look at brightness;
Love loves what is happily dressed;
Sunday to Monday, all I care is
You should see me at my best.

No record I keep of dances,
Or of places you liked to go,
Keeping you awake from midnight
Until the cockerels begin to crow;

And I have said so much I love you
It now creates a row,
It is true, but as I said it,
By the girls I am hated now.

Teresa from the hillside
After my praise of you was sore;
Said, "You think you love an angel;
It's a monkey you adore."

"You are caught by her glittering charms,
And her borrowed braids of hair,
She is a made-up beauty
And true beauty like mine is rare."

'It was a lie, and so I told her,
And her cousin got the word
Gave me his defiance for it;
And what followed you must have heard.

This is no extravagant affection,
I could not ask for more
As they call it - what I offer
Is an honest love, so pure?

Crafty strings can be found,
Threads of the softest silk they could be;
Put your neck in the noose, my dear;
Mine will follow, you will see.

Or else - once and for all I swear it
To the saints of well renown
If I ever leave the mountains,
It will be in a vicar's gown.

Here the young man brought his song to an end, and although Don Quixote asked him to sing more, Sancho was very disinterested, and was more inclined to sleep than listen to songs; so, he said to his master, "It would be better for you to sleep soon where you intend to rest, because these men work all day which does not allow them to spend the whole night singing."

"I understand Sancho," replied Don Quixote; "I see clearly that the wine in you demands compensation in sleep rather than in music."

"All is good, bless God," said Sancho.

"I do not deny it," replied Don Quixote; "but those with my calling are more likely to be watching than sleeping; still it would be good if you could assist me with my ear again, because the pain is returning."

Sancho did as he was asked, but one of the goat herders, seeing the wound, told him not to be worried, as he would apply a remedy which would heal it rapidly; and gathering some leaves of rosemary, as there was a large quantity there, he chewed them and mixed them with a little salt, and applying them to the ear he secured them firmly with a bandage, assuring him that no other treatment would be required, which turned out to be true.

CHAPTER 12

THE STORY OF MARCELA

Just then another young man arrived and said, "Do you know what is going on in the village?"

"How would we know?" replied one of them.

"Well, then, I must tell you," continued the young man, "this morning that famous trainee-shepherd called Chrysostom died, and it is believed that he died of love for that devilish village girl the daughter of Guillermo the Rich."

"You mean Marcela?" said one of them. "Yes, her," answered the goat herder; "and the worst part is, he has instructed in his will that he is to be buried in the fields like a Moor, under a rock where the Cork-tree is, because, as the story goes, that was the place where he first saw her. And he has also left other instructions with the vicar of the village, who will not obey them, because they appear to be irreligious. However, his great friend Ambrosio, another student like him, also dressed as a shepherd, said that everything should be done without any omission according to the directions left by Chrysostom, and now there is a big commotion in the village; I also heard, what Ambrosio and all of his other friends would like to be done, and tomorrow they are going to bury him where I said. I am sure it will be something worth seeing; I won't miss it, even if I cannot return to the village tomorrow."

"We will do the same," answered the goat herders, "I thank you for that," answered Pedro.

Don Quixote asked Pedro to tell him who the dead man and the lady were, to which Pedro replied that all he knew was the dead man was a wealthy gentleman belonging to a village in those mountains, who had been a student in Salamanca for many years, and at the end he returned to his village with the reputation of being very well educated. "Above all, they said, he was highly educated in science of the stars, and he even predicted the exact moment of the cris in advance."

"Eclipse it is called, not cris, the darkening of a star when it is covered," said Don Quixote; but Pedro, not caring about small details, went on with his story, saying, "Also he could foresee when the year was going to bring abundance or scarity."

"Scarcity, you mean," said Don Quixote.

"Scarity or scarcity," answered Pedro, "it is all the same in the end. And I can tell you that his father and friends who listened to his advice became very rich because they did as he said, telling them 'sow barley this year, not wheat; this year you can sow pea seeds and not barley.'"

"That science is called astrology," said Don Quixote.

"I do not know what it is called," replied Pedro, "but I know that he knew all this and more. But, to make an end of the story, not many months passed by after he returned from Salamanca, when one day he appeared dressed as a shepherd having removed the long gown he wore as a scholar; and at the same time his great friend, Ambrosio, who had been his companion in his studies, started dressing as a shepherd as well. I forgot to say that Chrysostom, who is dead, was a great man for writing verses, so skilled he even made carols for Christmas Eve, and plays, which the young men of our village acted, and all said they were excellent. When the villagers saw the two scholars so unexpectedly appearing in shepherd's clothing, they were puzzled, and could not guess what encouraged such an extraordinary change. Around this time the father of Chrysostom died, and he was left heir to a large amount of property as well as land, a great number of cattle and sheep, and a large sum of money. The young man became the owner of all of this, and deserved it all, because he was a very good man, kind-hearted, and a friend of good people. At this point, it became known that he had changed his clothing and had no other objective than to wander around looking for that lady, Marcela, who he had fallen in love with. And I must tell you, because it is important for you to know, who this girl is; perhaps, and even without any perhaps, you will not have heard anything like it in your whole life, even if live more years than sarna."

"Say Sarra," said Don Quixote, unable to endure the goat herder's confusion with words.

"The sarna lives long enough," answered Pedro; "and if, señor, you have to find fault with words at every step, we won't finish this story for another year."

"Pardon me, friend," said Don Quixote; "but, as there is such a difference between sarna and Sarra, I had to tell you; however, you have answered correctly because sarna lives longer than Sarra: so continue your story, and I will not object any more to anything."

"I will continue then," said the goat herder, "that in our village there was a farmer even richer than the father of Chrysostom, who was named Guillermo, who God gave great wealth, and a daughter whose mother died after the birth, the most respected woman there was in this neighbourhood; I can still remember her face which had the sun on one side and the moon on the other; and moreover active, and kind to the poor, and I trust that at the present moment her soul is in bliss with God in the other world. Her husband Guillermo died of grief at the death of such a good wife, leaving his daughter Marcela, a child to be rich, and to take care of an uncle of hers, a priest in our village. The girl grew up with such beauty that it reminded us of her mother's, which was very great, and yet it was thought that the daughter's would exceed it; and so when she reached the age of fourteen to fifteen years nobody attempted to be with her but blessed God that had made her so beautiful, and a great number were in love with her. Her uncle kept her in seclusion, but due to all that, the fame of her great beauty spread so much that her uncle was asked, solicited, and harassed, to give her in marriage not only to those of our town but to those who lived far away, many of them were people of high quality. But he, being a good Christian man, although he desired that she marry soon, seeing her to be old enough, was unwilling to do so without her consent, not that he had anything to gain or profit from it. You should know, Sir, that in these little villages everything is talked about and everything is criticised, and rest assured, as I am, that the priest must be more than good if all speak well of him, especially in villages."

"That is the truth," said Don Quixote; "but go on, because the story is interesting, and you, good Pedro, tell it with much grace."

"In that case I will not delay," said Pedro; "To proceed; you must know that although the uncle spoke to his niece and described to her the qualities of each man who had asked for her hand in marriage, asking her to make a choice according to her own taste, she never gave any other answer than that she had no desire to marry yet, and that being so young she did not think it was the right time for her to accept the responsibility of marriage. And with these reasonable excuses that she made, her uncle stopped encouraging her, and waited until she was older and could make the decision for herself. Because, he said - and was right - parents should not push children in life against their will. But when it was least expected, one day the reserved Marcela made her appearance as a shepherdess; and, in spite of her uncle and all those of the town that strove to dissuade her, she started going to the field with the other shepherd-ladies of the village, and supervising her own herd of sheep. And so, since she appeared in public, and her beauty was seen openly, I could not tell you how many rich young men, gentlemen and peasants, have worn shepherds clothing, roaming the fields attempting to make love to her. One of these, as has been already said, was our deceased friend, of which some say he did not love her, but he adored her. But do not think, because Marcela chose a life of freedom and independence, that she gave herself on any occasion, or even had the appearance of someone who does this; because on the contrary, she possesses great vigilance over her honour, and out of all those who tried to entice her not one of them has boasted, or can truthfully boast, that she has given him any hope however small of obtaining his desire. Because although she does not avoid or shun the society and conversation of the shepherds, and treats them kindly, if any one of them declared his intention to her, even it if were holy like marriage, she then flings him away from her like a catapult. And with this kind of personality she does a lot of harm, because her warmth and her beauty move the hearts of those that associate with her to love her, but her frankness bring them to the point of hopelessness; and so they call her cruel and hard-hearted, and other names which describe the nature of her character; and if you stay here long enough, señor, you will hear in the hills and valleys the sound of the cries of the rejected ones who pursue her. Not far from this spot there are a few dozen trees, and there is not one of them where someone has not carved and written on the bark the name of Marcela, and above some of these inscriptions, a crown has been carved to say Marcela wears a crown which represents all of human beauty. One shepherd is moaning, another is crying; love songs are heard, hopeless poems are written. One man will spend the whole night sat at the bottom of some oak tree or rock, and there, without closing his crying eyes, the sun finds him in the morning confused and lacking sense; and another man without relief from his moans, stretched on the burning sand in the full heat of the summer noon, appeals to heaven, and another one and another, over all of these, the beautiful Marcela triumphs free and careless. And all of us that know her are waiting to see what she will do, and who will be the happy man that will succeed in taming a nature so difficult and gain possession of a beauty so supreme. All I have told you is well-established truth; I am convinced that the cause of Chrysostom's death is the same. And so, I advise you, señor, do not fail to be present tomorrow at his burial, which will be well worth seeing, because Chrysostom had many friends, and the burial will not be very far from here."

I will ensure I attend," said Don Quixote, "and I thank you for the pleasure you have given me by telling me such an interesting a tale."

"Oh," said the goat herder, "I do not even know half of what has happened to the lovers of Marcela, but perhaps tomorrow we might encounter a shepherd on the road who can tell us; and now it would be wise for you to go to sleep under a cover, because the cold night air may hurt your wound, although with the remedy I have applied to you there is no fear of a bad result."

Sancho Panza, who was waiting for the goat herder's long speech to end, begged his master to go to sleep. He did so, and spent the rest of the night thinking of his lady Dulcinea, in imitation of the lovers of Marcela. Sancho Panza settled himself between Rocinante and his donkey, and slept, not like a lover who had been discarded, but like a man who had been thoroughly beaten.

CHAPTER 13

HOW THE STORY OF MARCELA ENDED

The day had hardly begun to show itself through the balconies of the east when five of the six goat herders came to wake Don Quixote and tell him that if he still wanted to go and see the famous burial of Chrysostom he could go with them. Don Quixote got up straight away and ordered Sancho to prepare the horses immediately, which he did. They had not gone a quarter of a mile when at a crossing of two paths they saw coming towards them six sheep herders dressed in black sheepskins. Each of them carried a stick in his hand, and with them were two upper class men on horses in fine-looking clothing, with three servants on foot accompanying them. Courteous greetings were exchanged, and interested in which way they were all going, they soon learned that they were all heading for the scene of the burial, so they continued together.

One of the men on a horse speaking to his companion said, "It seems to me, Señor Vivaldo, that we can consider the delay as time well spent, bearing in mind this remarkable funeral, because it can be nothing else but remarkable judging by the strange things these shepherds have told us, of both the dead shepherd and the murdering shepherdess."

"I think so too," replied Vivaldo, "and I would not only delay one day, but four, for the sake of seeing it."

Don Quixote asked them what they had heard of, about Marcela and Chrysostom. The traveller answered that the same morning they had met these shepherds, and seeing them dressed in mournful clothing had asked them the reason why they were dressed like that; and one of them, described the strange behaviour and beauty of a shepherdess called Marcela, and the loves of all those who wanted her, together with the death of Chrysostom to whose burial they were going. In short, he repeated all that Pedro had said to Don Quixote.

This conversation was dropped, and another commenced by Vivaldo asking Don Quixote what was the reason that led him to go armed in that fashion in a country so peaceful. To which Don Quixote replied, "The pursuit of my calling does not allow or permit me to go in any other way; easy life, enjoyment, and relaxation were invented for soft men, but labour, fighting, and weapons were invented and made for those who the world calls Knights."

The instant they heard this they all considered him mad, and to clarify this and discover what kind of madness he had, Vivaldo proceeded to ask him what being a Knight meant.

"Have you not," replied Don Quixote, "read the archives and histories of England, in which are recorded the famous deeds of King Arthur, who we in our popular Castilian customarily call King Artus. It is an ancient tradition, and commonly believed all over the Kingdom of Great Britain, that this King did not die, but was changed by magic into a raven, and that after the process of time he will return to reign and recover his Kingdom; which is the reason that up until now, no Englishman has ever killed a raven.

In the time of this good King the famous order of chivalry: The Knights of the Round Table was introduced, and the love of Don Lancelot with Queen Guinevere occurred. The go-between and intimate friend was the highly honourable lady Quintanona, who gave us that poem so well-known and widely spread in Spain.

Never never, was there Knight
As helped by the hand of his lady,
Which gave Sir Lancelot his might
And never never she said repay me."

With all the sweet and delicious sequence of his achievements in love and war, handed down from that time, this law of chivalry went on extending and spreading itself over many and various parts of the world; and in it, famous and renowned for their deeds, were the mighty Amadis of France with all his sons and descendants to the fifth generation, and the valiant Felixmarte of Hircania, and the never sufficiently praised Tirante el Blanco, and in our own days almost everyone we talk with knows of the invincible Knight Don Belianis of Greece. This, then, is what it means to be a Knight, and what I have spoken of is the law of his chivalry, which, as I have already said, I, an ex-sinner, have made my profession, and what the Knights I have mentioned declared, I have declared as well, and so I go in seclusion through the land seeking adventures, determined by my soul to raise my weapons in the face of the most dangerous situations that fortune may offer me in aid of the weak and needy."

After hearing these words, the travellers were able to satisfy themselves that Don Quixote was out of his mind and that this form of madness had overpowered him, at which they felt the same astonishment that all felt on first becoming acquainted with it; and Vivaldo, who was a person of great insight and had a lively temperament, in order to entertain himself during the short journey which they said was required to reach the mountain, the scene of the burial, gave Don Quixote ample opportunities to continue with his nonsense. So he said to him, "It seems to me, Señor Knight, that you have chosen one of the most serious professions in the world, and I imagine even the monks are not as serious as you."

"Serious it may be," replied Don Quixote, "but so necessary for the world. Because, if the truth is told, the soldier who executes what his captain orders does no less than the captain himself who gives the order. My meaning, is, that churchmen in peace and quiet pray to Heaven for the welfare of the world, but us soldiers and Knights carry into effect what they pray for, defending it with the might of our weaponry and the edge of our swords, not under shelter but in the open air, a target for the intolerable rays of the sun in summer and the piercing frost of winter. So, we are God's ministers on earth and the method by which his justice is done. And as the business of war and all that relates and belongs to it cannot be conducted without great sweat, work, and exertion, it follows that those who make it their profession have undoubtedly more labour than those who in tranquil peace and quiet are praying to God to help the weak. I do not mean to say, nor does it enter into my thoughts, that the Knight's calling is as good as that of the monk; I would merely conclude from what I endure that it is beyond a doubt a more laborious and a more difficult one, a hungrier and thirstier, challenging, grittier, and meaner one; because there is no reason to doubt that the Knights of the past endured suffering in the course of their lives. And if some of them by their sheer might did rise to be emperors, it cost them in blood and sweat; and if those who attained that rank had not had magicians and sages to help them they would have been completely restricted in their ambition and disappointed in their hopes."

"That is my own opinion," replied the traveller; "but one thing among many others seems to me very wrong in Knights, and that is that when they find themselves about to engage in an immense and hazardous adventure in which there is imminent danger of losing their lives, they never at the moment of engaging in it think of calling on God, as is the duty of every good Christian in danger; instead they call on their ladies with as much devotion as if these were their gods, a thing which seems to me a form of irreverence."

"Sir," answered Don Quixote, "that cannot be on any account omitted, and the Knight would be disgraced if he acted otherwise: because it is usual and customary in Knighthood that the Knight, when engaging in any battle has his lady in mind, he should turn his eyes towards her softly and lovingly, as though with them ask her to favour and protect him in the hazardous duty he is about to undertake, and even though no one can hear him, he is bound to say certain words between his teeth, calling on her with all his heart, and of this we have innumerable instances in the histories. But this does not mean they omit calling on God, because there will be a time and opportunity for doing so while they are engaged in their task."

"Well," answered the traveller, "I still have some doubts, because I have often read how words will arise between two Knights, and one thing leads to another and then their anger has woken, and they turn their horses around and go a long distance up the field, and then without any more words, at top speed they charge, and during this they don't call on God; and what commonly occurs from this encounter is that one falls off of his horse pierced through by his opponent's lance, and as for the other, it is only by holding on to the mane of his horse that he stops himself falling to the ground; but I do not know how the dead had time to call on God in the course of this rapid battle; it would have been better if those words which he said calling on his lady had been devoted to his duty and obligation as a Christian. Moreover, it is my belief that not all Knights have ladies to call on, because not all of them are in love."

"That is impossible," said Don Quixote: "It is impossible that there could be a Knight without a lady, because it is as natural and proper to be in love as it is for the heavens to have stars: most certainly in no history has a Knight been seen without a love, and for the simple reason that without one he would not be considered a legitimate Knight but a bastard, and one who had gained entrance into the fortress of the Knighthood, not by the door, but over the wall like a thief and a robber."

"Nevertheless," said the traveller, "if I remember rightly, I think I have read that Don Galaor, the brother of the valiant Amadis of France, never had a special lady to call on, and yet he was no less esteemed, and was a very famous Knight."

To which Don Quixote replied, "Sir, one hot day does not make summer; furthermore, I know that Knight was in secret very deeply in love; besides that, falling in love with any he liked was a natural tendency which he could not control. But, in short, it is very obvious that he had one woman who he made his lover, to who he called on very frequently and very secretly, because he prided himself on being a discreet Knight."

"Then if it is essential that every Knight should be in love," said the traveller, "It may be inferred that you are too, as you are a Knight; and if you are not as discreet as Don Galaor, I ask you as sincerely as I can, in front of everyone here and myself, to inform us of the name, town, rank, and beauty of your lady, because she will consider herself fortunate if all the world knows that she is loved and served by such a valiant Knight as you appear to be."

Don Quixote gave a deep sigh and said, "I cannot say positively whether my sweet lady would be pleased or not if the world knew that I serve her; I can only say in answer to what has been politely asked of me, that her name is Dulcinea, her town El Toboso, a village in La Mancha, her rank must be at least that of a Princess, since she is my Queen, and her beauty superhuman, since all the impossible and unbelievable attributes of beauty which the poets apply to their ladies are verified in her; her hairs are gold, her eyebrows are rainbows, her eyes are suns, her cheeks are roses, her lips are ruby, her teeth are pearls, her neck is ivory, her heart is marble, her hands are fair, her appearance snow, and what is concealed from sight, I think and imagine, and reflect that I can only worship, not compare."

"We would like to know her lineage, race, and ancestry," said Vivaldo.

To which Don Quixote replied, "She is not ancient Roman, or the Rebellas or Villanovas of Valencia; or Gurreas of Aragon: Mendozas, or Guzmans of Castile; Pallas or Meneses of Portugal; she is from El Toboso of La Mancha, a lineage that although it is modern, comes from a source of gentle blood of which the most illustrious families are to come, and none of you will dispute that with me."

"Although my love is for the Cachopins of Laredo," said the traveller, "I will not compare it to El Toboso of La Mancha, although, to tell the truth, no such surname has ever reached my ears until now."

"What!" said Don Quixote, "how have you never heard?"

The rest of the group were listening with great attention to the conversation, and the goat herders and shepherds started to realise how exceedingly crazy Don Quixote was. Sancho Panza was the only one who thought his master always spoke the truth, knowing who he was and having known him since his birth; but now the only thing he found hard to believe was the story about Dulcinea del Toboso, because he had never heard of this Princess and this name didn't come to his mind, although he lived so close to El Toboso. They all continued to talk while traveling, when they saw a gap between two tall mountains and in-between them, around twenty shepherds, covered in black wool sheepskins, and crowns which, as it appeared afterwards, were made from trees. Six of them were carrying a coffin covered with a variety of flowers and branches, seeing this, one of the goat herders said, "These are the men who carry Chrysostom's body, and the base of that mountain is the place where he ordered them to bury him." They therefore hurried to reach the spot, and managed to arrive in time just as those who were carrying the coffin laid it on the ground, and four of them with shovels were digging the grave by the side of a hard rock. They greeted each other politely, and then Don Quixote and those who were with him turned to examine the coffin, and on it, covered with flowers, they saw a dead body in shepherd's clothing, who had the appearance of a thirty-year-old, which showed them even in death and in life he had handsome features and a gracious presence. Around him in the coffin itself were some books, and several papers, some open, some folded; and those who were looking as well as those who were preparing the grave and all the others who were present noticed a strange silence, until one of those who had carried the body said to another, "Let's make sure Ambrosia, if this is the place Chrysostom spoke about, since you are anxious that what he directed in his will is strictly adhered to."

"This is the place," answered Ambrosia "because many times my poor friend told me the story of his bad fortune. Here it was, he told me, that he saw for the first time that enemy of the human race, and here, too, for the first time he declared to her his love, honourable as it was loyal, and here it was that at last Marcela ended up rejecting him, bringing the tragedy of his poor life to an end; here, in memory of this misfortune, he desired to be buried." Then turning to Don Quixote and the travellers he went on to say, "That body, which you are looking at with compassionate eyes, was the home of a soul which Heaven gave a vast share of its riches. That is the body of Chrysostom, who was unrivalled in wit, unequalled in courtesy, unapproached in gentleness, a phoenix in friendship, generous without limit, serious without arrogance, happy without offensiveness, and, in short, first in all that constitutes goodness and second to none in all that makes up misfortune. He loved deeply, he was hated; he was adored, he was despised; he loved a wild beast, he spoke to marble, he pursued the wind, he cried in the wilderness, he tolerated ingratitude, and for a reward he was made the prey of death in the middle of life, cut short by a shepherdess who he sought to preserve in the memory of men, as these papers which you see fully prove, however he has asked that they be burnt alongside his body"

"Señor Ambrosia while you condemn your friend's body to the earth, you should not transfer his writings with him, because if he ordered that while his heart was bitter, it is not right that you should irrationally obey it. On the contrary, by giving life to those papers, let the cruelty of Marcela live for ever, to serve as a warning to all men to avoid falling into the same danger. I and all of us who have come here know the story of your love-stricken and heart-broken friend, and we know, as well, your friendship, and the cause of his death, and the directions he gave to you; it is a sad story about the cruelty of Marcela, the love of Chrysostom, and the loyalty of your friendship, which demonstrates to those who pursue impulsively the path that insane passion opens to their eyes. Last night we heard about the death of Chrysostom and that he was to be buried here, and out of curiosity and compassion we abandoned our plans and decided to come and see with our eyes the man which when heard of, who had moved our compassion, and in consideration of that compassion and our desire to prove it, we by condolence, beg you, excellent Ambrosia, or at least I on my own account ask you, that instead of burning those papers you allow me to take some of them."

And without waiting for the shepherd's answer, he stretched out his hand and took some of those that were nearest to him; upon seeing this Ambrosio said, "Out of courtesy, señor, for those which you have taken I grant your request, but do not expect me to abstain from burning the rest."

Vivaldo, who was eager to see what the papers contained, opened one of them and saw that its title was "Place of Despair."

Ambrosio said, "That is the last paper the unhappy man wrote; and you can see, señor, what an end his life came to, read it for us to hear, because there will be enough time while his grave is being dug."

"Of course," said Vivaldo; and as all the rest were equally eager they gathered around him, and Vivaldo reading in a loud voice, found that it went as follows.

CHAPTER 14

THE DESPAIR OF CHRYSOSTOM

Cruelty
You inflict, no one to help me.
This Hell, I well know,
My heart has sunken, low.
To ease this burden, I must write,
Although that does not make it right.
I suffer, for all you have done,
So, all the words on this page will not be fun.
Pain in my organs, torn,
No roses, only thorns.
Driven to mad despair,
In my heart you plant a sting in there.

The lion's roar, at night, its late,
The fear of a scary hissing snake.
The sound of a monster without a name,
You could never feel this pain.
The wind as it wrestles with the sea,
This is a part of my history.
The tears,
As the end of my life nears.
My ear hears the choir of Hell,
Confusing my senses, mixed with the fire's smell.
I hope you will hear my soul's complaint,
My words may not display the picture, yet I will try to paint.

In the future echoes of this will be heard
Every line and every word.
To be thrown on the rocks,
My story will leave enduring aftershocks.
Dark valleys and on lonely shores,
When there is sun, suddenly it rains and pours.
Attacked by bees and swarms,
Monsters chasing us in thunderstorms.
Solitude, I feel alone,
With no one else, that is me at home.
No one can match your spite,
All over the world, no one like you, and your type.

The power to kill, you kill me, you do,

Suspicion, whether it is false or true.
Jealousy, made me paranoid.
Long absence creates an empty void.
No hope of happiness, what have I got?
What comes to a man who fears to be forgot?
Death, inevitable, waits in the hall,
But I live, by some strange miracle.
Absence and jealousy, have you heard of me?
Suspicion that becomes a certainty.
Forgotten, left to fan my flame alone,
And while I suffer, the sun is never shown.
I thought we would be a pair,
Now I can't see that in my despair.
But rather than cling, as you get rid of me,
I try to avoid my misery.

Can hope survive in fear?
When we believe so much we make it appear?
Should I shut my eyes to jealousy?
Even if it appears, and inflicts hell in me?
Distrust comes with free access,
Uneven like the earth on an axis.
Suspicions turns to what the worse can be,
And the truth transformed into certainty?
You are cruel in the realm of love,
Jealousy! Chained my hands above.
And bound me with the strongest cord, pain,
All I have is a memory of you, I replay it again and again.

And now I die, since there is no hope,
Of happiness for me in life, so I wrote this note.
Still to my idea of us, I hold on,
Even if I know it's wrong.
The soul which is freest is the most trapped,
As it's Love is expressive and uncapped.
I'll say she is my enemy,
Not a friend of me.
I give this soul and body to the earth,
All I receive, is a crown of bliss for what it's worth.

This injustice has supplied the cause,
Now I've started the process I will stop and pause.
And as I'm wounded can't you see,
This victim of pain, you wouldn't want to be.

My death won't be worth a tear,
In your eyes, you do not care or hear.

And now it is the time, Hell,
To carry the stone like Sisyphus as well.
Lifting the heavy stone,
Forever, and ever, and ever its known.

You will not cry when I am gone,
This is normal for you, and you are wrong.
With death comes life,
But I leave with no children and no wife.

The "Despair of Chrysostom" was met with the admiration of those who listened, although Vivaldo said it did not seem to fit what he had heard of about Marcela, because Chrysostom complained of jealousy, suspicion, and absence, all which opposes the good assigned to the name and fame of Marcela; to which Ambrosio replied as one who knew his friend's most secret thoughts, "Señor, to remove that doubt I should tell you that when the unhappy man wrote this he was far away from Marcela, who he had voluntarily separated himself from, to see if absence would not affect him; but as everything distresses and every fear haunts the rejected lover, so imaginary jealousies and suspicions, dreaded as if they were true, tormented Chrysostom; and therefore the virtue of Marcela remains true, I cannot find any fault except being cruel, and somewhat proud."

"That is true," said Vivaldo; and as he was about to read another paper from those he had saved from the fire, he was stopped by a marvellous vision (as it seemed) that unexpectedly presented itself to their eyes; because on the peak of the rock where they were digging the grave appeared the shepherdess Marcela, so beautiful that her beauty exceeded its reputation. Those who had never seen her until that moment stared at her in wonder and silence, and those who were accustomed to seeing her were not less amazed than those who had never seen her before. But the instant Ambrosio saw her he spoke to her, with anger:

"Do you come, by chance, cruel lady of these mountains, to see if your presence will draw blood flow from the wounds of this poor man of which your cruelty has robbed of life; or is it to celebrate the cruel work of yours, or like another heartless Nero to look down from a height on the ruin of his Rome in flames; or in your arrogance to trample on his corpse? Tell us quickly what you have come for, or what it is you want."

"I have not come, Ambrosia for any of the purposes you have named," replied Marcela, "but to defend myself and to prove how unreasonable everyone who blames for their sorrow and for Chrysostom's death is; and therefore I ask all of you that are here to give me your attention, because I will not take much time or many words to bring the truth to you people of sense. Heaven has made me, so you say, beautiful, and so much that my beauty leads you to love me; and for the love you show me you say, that I am bound to love you. By the natural understanding which God has given me I know that everything beautiful attracts love, but I cannot see how, for being loved, that which is loved for its beauty is bound to love that which loves it; besides, it may be that the lover of that which is beautiful is ugly, and ugliness being repulsive, it would be very absurd to say, "I love you because you are beautiful, you must love me even though I am ugly." But supposing the beauty was equal on both sides, it does not follow that the inclinations must be therefore be alike, because it is not every beauty that excites love, some please the eye without winning the affection; and if every sort of beauty excited love and won the heart, the will would wander vaguely unable to choose someone; because as there is an infinity of beautiful people there must be an infinity of inclinations, and true love, I have heard, is indivisible, and must be voluntary and not forced. If this is so, as I believe it to be, why do you insist I bend my will by force, for no other reason other than you say you love me? Tell me, if Heaven made me ugly, as it has made me beautiful, could I complain to you for not loving me? You must remember that the beauty I possess was not a choice of mine, because, Heaven as a gift, gave it to me without me asking or choosing it; so as the viper, although it kills with it, does not deserve to be blamed for the poison it carries, as it is a gift from nature, neither do I deserve blame for being beautiful; because beauty in a modest woman is like fire or a sharp sword in the distance; one does not burn, the other does not cut, for those who do not go too near. Honour and virtue are the ornaments of the mind, without these the body, although it could be, has no right to be called beautiful; but if modesty is one of the virtues that add grace and charm to the mind and body, why should she who is loved, destroy it to gratify someone who for his pleasure alone strives with all his might and energy to rob her of it? I was born free, and so I can live in freedom I chose the solitude of the fields; in the trees of the mountains I find humanity, the clear waters of the streams are my mirrors, and to the trees and waters I tell my thoughts and charms. I am a fire far away, a sword put aside. Those who I have inspired with love by letting them see me, I have with my words enlightened, and if their desires hang on hope - and I have given none to Chrysostom or to anyone else - it cannot fairly be said that the death of anyone is my fault, because it was his own unreasonableness rather than my cruelty that killed him; and if it is said that his wishes were honourable, and that therefore I was bound to give in to them, I answer that on this very spot where his grave is being made he declared to me his purity of purpose, I told him that mine was to live in everlasting solitude, and that the earth alone would enjoy the fruits of my seclusion and the honour of my beauty; and if, after this open statement, he chose to persist with hope and go against the wind, no wonder he would sink in the depths of his infatuation? If I had encouraged him, I would have done so falsely; if I had gratified him, I would have acted against my own resolution and purpose. He was persistent although he was warned, and he despaired without being hated. Do you now think it is reasonable that his suffering should be blamed on me? Let a man who has been deceived complain, let the man whose encouraged hopes have proved ineffective, let who I entice flatter himself, let who I encourage boast; but don't let him call me cruel when I make no promise, practise no deception, when I have neither enticed or encouraged. So far it has not been Gods will that I love, and to expect me to love because you wish me to, is pointless. Let this general declaration be a notice to any who wish to be with me, and from this moment, let it be understood if anyone dies for me, it is not from jealousy or misery, because she who loves no one can give no cause for jealousy, and truthfulness is not to be confused with disrespect. Whoever calls me a wild beast and a snake, should leave me alone is I am noxious and evil; whoever calls me ungrateful, should provide no service; whoever calls me defiant, should not seek to know me; whoever calls me cruel, should not pursue me; because this wild beast, this snake, this ungrateful, cruel, defiant being has no desire to seek, serve, know, or follow them. If Chrysostom's impatience and violent passion killed him, why should my modest behaviour and cautiousness be blamed? If I preserve my purity in the society of the trees, why should a man who would want me to preserve it when among other men, seek to take it from me? I have, as you know, a wealth of my own, and I do not desire that of others; my taste is for freedom, and I have no appreciation for constraint; I neither love or hate anyone; I do not deceive, date, or play with any. The modest conversation between the shepherd girls and the care of my goats is my recreation; my desires are confined to these mountains, and if they ever wander, it is to contemplate the beauty of heaven, and the steps which the soul travels back to its original home."

With these words, and not waiting to hear a reply, she turned away and disappeared into the thickest part of the woods nearby, leaving all who heard her lost in admiration at her good sense and beauty. Some who were wounded by the irresistible expressions of her bright eyes, were about to go in the same direction to follow her, oblivious to the frank declaration they had just heard; seeing this, and deeming this a perfect opportunity to exercise his chivalry in aid of a distressed lady, Don Quixote, placing his hand on the tip of his sword, exclaimed in a loud and distinct voice:

"Let no one, whatever his rank or condition, dare to follow the beautiful Marcela, or face the pain of incurring my fierce fury. She has shown with a clear and satisfactory argument that little or no fault is to be found with her for the death of Chrysostom, and also how far she is from yielding to the wishes of any of her admirers, for this reason, instead of being followed and persecuted, she should in justice be honoured and esteemed by all the good people of the world, because she shows that she is one of the rare women in it that carries a virtuous resolution."

Whether it was because of the threats of Don Quixote, or because Ambrosio told them to fulfil their duty to their good friend, none of the shepherds moved from the spot until, having finished the grave, they laid his body in it, not without many tears from those who stood by. They closed the grave with a heavy stone which Ambrosio said he had prepared, with an inscription which went as follows:

Beneath the stone before your eyes
The body of a lover lies;
In life he was a very good man,
In death a victim of her plan.
Ungrateful, cruel, shy, and fair,
It was her that drove him to despair,
He loved her more than words can say,
But she didn't love him back for a day.

They then scattered on the grave flowers and branches, and all expressed their condolence to his friend Ambrosio; and Don Quixote said farewell to his hosts and to the travellers, who told him to come with them to Seville, as it was such a convenient place to find adventures, they said they could be found in every street and around every corner. Don Quixote thanked them for their advice, and said that for the present he would not go to Seville until he had cleared these mountains of robbers, as he had a report which said they were full of them. Seeing his good intention, the travellers did not him ask any more, and once more said farewell. They left him and pursued their journey, during which they did not fail to discuss the story of Marcela and Chrysostom as well as the madness of Don Quixote. He, however, had other plans, and decided to go in search of the shepherdess Marcela, and offer her all the service he could give her; but things did not go as he had expected, according to what is told in the course of this history.

CHAPTER 15

AN UNFORTUNATE ADVENTURE WITH HEARTLESS CASTILIANS

It has been said that as soon as Don Quixote left his hosts and those who were present at the burial of Chrysostom, he and Sancho went into the same wood which they had seen the shepherdess Marcela enter, and after having wandered for more than two hours in all directions in search of her without finding her, they came to a stop in an opening covered with gentle grass, beside which ran a pleasant cool stream that invited and compelled them to spend the hours of the noon heat, which by this time was beginning to become quite harsh. Don Quixote and Sancho dismounted, and turning Rocinante and the donkey loose to feed on the grass that was there in abundance, they emptied the saddlebags, and very peacefully and sociably the master and his man made a feast out of what they found in them.

Sancho thought it was not necessary to leash Rocinante, feeling sure, from what he knew of his seriousness and freedom from incontinence, that all the horses in Cordova would not lead him into immodesty. Chance, however, and the devil, who never sleeps, intended that feeding in this valley there would be a group of Galician ponies belonging to Castilians, who usually took their midday rest with their team in places where grass and water flourish. It so happened, then, that Rocinante decided to display himself to the ponies, and abandoning his usual walk and demeanour as he smelt them, he, without asking his master, rushed to make known his wishes to them; they, however, it seemed, preferred their grass to him, and welcomed him with their heels and teeth to such an extent that they broke, and left him without a saddle to cover him; but what must have been worse to him was the Castilians, seeing the violence he had incited in their ponies, came running armed with sticks, and beat him until they brought him battered to the ground.

By this time Don Quixote and Sancho, who had witnessed the beating of Rocinante, came as fast as they could, and Don Quixote said to Sancho:

"As far as I can see, Sancho, these are not Knights but dishonourable men of low birth: I mention it because you can lawfully aid me in taking appropriate vengeance for this insult given to Rocinante."

"What vengeance can we take," answered Sancho, "There are more than twenty of them, and only us two, or, perhaps not more than one and a half?"

"I am the same as one hundred," replied Don Quixote, and without any more words he drew his sword and attacked the Castilians and being excited and impelled by the example of his master, Sancho did the same; and to begin with, Don Quixote delivered a slash to one of them that cut open the leather jacket he wore, along with a large portion of his shoulder. The Castilians, seeing themselves assaulted by only two men while there were so many of them, grabbed their sticks, and attacked with great intensity and energy; in fact, at the first blow brought Sancho to the ground, and Don Quixote as well, all his skill and bravery gaining him nothing, and it so happened that he fell at the feet of Rocinante, who had not yet risen; where it could be seen how furiously sticks can be used in the hands of angry Castilians.

Then, seeing what they had done, the Castilians quickly loaded their horses and continued their journey, leaving the two adventurers an unhappy sight and in an unhappy mood.

Sancho was the first to regain his consciousness, and finding himself near his master he called him in a weak and sad voice, "Señor Don Quixote, ah, Señor Don Quixote!"

"Brother Sancho" answered Don Quixote in the same low tone as Sancho.

"If it is possible," answered Sancho, "please give me some of that healing potion, if you have any there; maybe it will mend broken bones as well as wounds."

"If I only had it, what a fool I am." said Don Quixote; "but I swear to you, Sancho, on the faith of a good Knight, in two days, unless fortune says otherwise, I will have it in my possession, or my hand would have lost its skill."

"But, for how many days do you think we will have good use of our feet?" answered Sancho.

"For myself, I cannot guess how many," said the battered Knight Don Quixote; "but I take the blame for this, because I had no business to raise my sword against men who were not named Knights like myself, and so I believe that in punishment for having disobeyed the laws of chivalry the God of battles has permitted this punishment to be administered to me; so I receive a hint on the matter which I am now about to mention to you, because it is of great importance to the welfare of both of us. It is, when you see crowds of men like this insulting us, you are not to wait until I draw my sword against them, because I will not do so; but you may draw your sword and punish them as much as you like, and if any Knight comes to their aid and defence I will take care to defend you and attack him with all my might; and you have already seen many times what might and power I possess." Reminiscing his victory over the Biscayan.

But Sancho did not fully agree with his master's speech, and said in reply, "Señor, I am a man of peace, humble and quiet, and I can put up with any insult because I have a wife and children to support and bring up; so let it be likewise a hint to you, as it cannot be an order, that on no account I will draw my sword against a clown or a Knight, and that here before God I forgive the insults that I have received, whether they have been, are, or will be given to me by high or low, rich or poor, noble or common."

To which his master said, "I wish I had enough breath to speak easily, and that the pain I feel on my side would decrease so I could explain to you, Sancho, the mistake you are making. Come on, sinner, suppose the wind of fortune, which up until now has been so adverse, should turn in our favour, filling the sails of our desires so that safely and without impediment we drift into the port of one of those islands I have promised you, how would it feel if after winning it I made you the lord of it? You would make it nearly impossible though, not being a Knight or having any desire to be one, or possessing the courage or the will to avenge insults or defend me; because you must know that in newly conquered kingdoms and provinces the minds of the inhabitants are not quiet or welcoming of the new lord, there is no doubt that some of them will make a move to change matters once more, and try, as they say, what chance can do for them; so it is essential that the new possessor has good sense to enable him to govern, and the bravery to attack and defend himself, whatever may happen to him."

"And what has happened to us now," answered Sancho, "I would be pleased to have that good sense and that courage that you speak of, but I swear I am more suited to bandages than arguments. See if you can get up, and let us help Rocinante, he does not deserve it, but he was the main cause of all this beating. I never thought this of Rocinante, because I thought he was as virtuous and as quiet as myself. However, they do say that it takes a long time to know someone, and that there is nothing sure in this life. Who would have thought, after such mighty slashes you gave that unlucky Knight, there was coming for us, such a great number of sticks to beat us?"

"And yet, Sancho," replied Don Quixote, "my own weapons were used against them; and it is clear, they must now feel the pain of this. I know with certainty that all these frustrations are necessary accompaniments as a Knight."

To this Sancho replied, "Señor, as these mishaps are what can occur as a Knight, tell me do they happen very often, or if they have their own fixed times for when they happen; because it seems to me that after two misadventures we will be no good for the third, unless God with his infinite mercy helps us."

"You should know, friend Sancho," answered Don Quixote, "that the life of a Knights is subject to a thousand dangers, and within them contain the immediate possibility for Knights to become Kings and emperors, as experience has shown in the case of many different Knights, whose histories I know well; and I could tell you now, if the pain would let me, of some who simply by their strength have risen to these high peaks I have mentioned; and those men, both before and after, experienced misfortunes and miseries. The brave Amadis of France found himself in the power of his mortal enemy Arcalaus the magician, who, it is positively affirmed, holding him captive, gave him more than two hundred whips with the reins of his horse while tied to one of the pillars of a court; and moreover there is an obscure author with great authority who says that the Knight Phoebus, being caught in a certain pitfall, which opened under his feet in a certain castle, after falling, found himself tied by his hands and feet in a deep pit underground, where they gave him one of those things they call an enema, of sand and snow, that nearly finished him; and if he had not been assisted by a sage, a great friend of his, it would have been much worse for the poor Knight; so I may suffer, because greater sufferings have been given to others, much worse than what we have suffered from. I want you to know, Sancho, that wounds caused by any weapon which happen to be in the hands of enemies inflict no shame, and this is the law of fighting, in other words: if, for instance, the shoemaker strikes another with the last thing in his hand, even if it were a piece of wood, it cannot be said for that reason that he who he struck with it has been beaten. I say this so you can see that because we have been defeated in this fight we have not suffered any shame; because the weapons those men carried, which they pounded us with, were nothing more than sticks, and not one of them, so far as I remember, carried a sword or a dagger."

"They gave me no time to see much," answered Sancho, "I had hardly put my hands on my sword when they beat my shoulders with their sticks in such a way that they took the sight out of my eyes and the strength out of my feet, leaving me now where I lie, and where thinking of whether those strikes were a shame or not gives me no relief from the pain, because they will remain as deeply impressed in my memory as they are on my shoulders."

"I tell you, brother Sancho," said Don Quixote, "that there is no memory which time does not put an end to, and no pain which death does not remove."

"And what greater misfortune can there be," replied Sancho, "than the one that waits for time to put an end to it and death to remove it? If our misfortune were one of those that are cured with a couple of plasters, it would not be so bad; but I am beginning to think that all the plasters in a hospital won't be enough to mend us."

"No more of that talk: take strength out of weakness, Sancho," said Don Quixote, "and let us see how Rocinante is, because it seems to me that most of the misfortune was given to the poor horse."

"There is nothing wonderful in that," replied Sancho, "since he is a Knight too; what I wonder is how my donkey has avoided the whole situation while all of us were beaten."

"Fortune always leaves a door open in adversity in order to bring relief to it," said Don Quixote; "I say so because this donkey may now provide relief to Rocinante, carrying me to some castle where my wounds can be cured. And I will not deem it any dishonour to mount the donkey, because I remember having read how the good old Silenus, the tutor and instructor of the happy god of laughter, when he entered the city of one hundred gates, went very contentedly mounted on a handsome donkey."

"It may be true that he went mounted as you say," answered Sancho, "but there is a great difference between going mounted and going draped like a sack of manure."

To which Don Quixote replied, "Wounds received in battle award honour instead of taking it away; and so, friend Sancho, say no more, but, as I told you before, get up as well as you can and put me on top of your donkey in whatever way you like, and let us go quickly as night will soon come to surprise us."

"And yet I have heard you say," observed Sancho, "that it is very common for Knights to sleep in forests and deserts, and that they believe it to be very good fortune."

"That is," said Don Quixote, "when they cannot help it, or when they are in love; and it is so true that there have been Knights who have remained for two years on rocks, in sunshine and shade and through all the harsh seasons, without their ladies knowing anything about it; anyway, no more of this now, Sancho, let's go quickly before another misfortune happens to the donkey like it did to Rocinante."

"If that were the case, the devil would be responsible," said Sancho; and making many sighs, he raised himself, stopping half-way bent like a bow, without enough power to make himself stand upright, but with all his pain he got up and raised Rocinante.

Sancho then placed Don Quixote on the donkey and tethered Rocinante with a rein, and taking the donkey by the reins, he proceeded more or less in the direction where it seemed to him the main road might be; and, as if chance was conducting their affairs for them, from good to better, he had not gone far when the road came in sight, and on it he saw an inn, which to his annoyance and to the happiness of Don Quixote must be a castle. Sancho insisted that it was an inn, but Don Quixote insisted that it was a castle, and the dispute lasted so long that before the point was settled they had reached it, and into it they entered.

CHAPTER 16

WHAT HAPPENED TO THE INGENIOUS GENTLEMAN IN THE INN WHICH HE THOUGHT WAS A CASTLE

The innkeeper, seeing Don Quixote hanging sideways across the donkey, asked Sancho what was wrong with him. Sancho answered that it was nothing, only that he had fallen from a rock and his ribs were a little bruised. The innkeeper had a wife whose nature was not like those of her profession, because she was by nature very kind-hearted and felt for the suffering of others, so she started to treat Don Quixote for his pain, and made her young daughter, a very pretty girl, help her to take care of their guest. Next to the inn there was a servant, an Asturian girl with a broad face, flat head, and short nose, blind in one eye and not very clear in the other. The elegance of her shape, made up for all her defects. This graceful girl, then, helped the young girl, and the two made a very bad bed for Don Quixote in the attic that showed evident signs of having formerly served for many years as a straw-loft, in which there was also a transporter whose bed was placed a little beyond Don Quixote's, and, although it was made from the contents of his saddlebags, had much advantage over it, as Don Quixote's consisted simply of four hard boards on two not very even slats, a mattress, with such thinness that it might have passed for a quilt, full of small balls which, if there were not seen through the material to be wool, would to the touch have seemed like pebbles in hardness, and two sheets made of leather.

On this horrible bed Don Quixote stretched himself, and the hostess and her daughter soon covered him with plasters from head to toe, while Maritornes (the Asturian girl) held the light for them, and while plastering him, the hostess, observing how full of bruises Don Quixote was in some places, said that this looked more like blows than a fall.

It was not blows, Sancho said, the rock had many points and edges, and each of them have left its mark. "Pray, señora," he added, "please manage to save some energy, as there is someone else to use it on, my body is also rather sore."

"Then you must have fallen too," said the hostess.

"I did not fall," said Sancho, "but from the shock I got when seeing my master fall, my body aches as if I had been hit a thousand times."

"That may be," said the young girl, "because it has happened to me many times in my dreams that I was falling from a tower and never hit the ground, and when I woke from the dream I found myself as weak and shaken as if I had really fallen."

"That is the point, señora," replied Sancho, "I without dreaming at all, but being more awake than I am now, find myself with almost the same amount of bruises as my master."

"How is this gentleman called?" asked Maritornes the Asturian.

"Don Quixote of La Mancha," answered Sancho, "and he is a Knight-adventurer, and one of the best this world has ever seen."

"What is a Knight-adventurer?" said the young girl.

"Are you so new in the world that you do not know?" answered Sancho. "Well, then, I must tell you, sister, that a Knight-adventurer is someone who can be seen bruised one day and an emperor the next, today he could be the most miserable and needy being in the world, and tomorrow he will have two or three kingdoms to give to his aide."

"Then how is it," said the hostess, "that belonging to such good a master as this, you, to judge by your appearance, do not own at least one Kingdom?"

"It is too soon," answered Sancho, "because we have only been searching in quest of adventures for one month, and so far we have not found something that can be called one, because it happens that when one thing is looked for another thing is found; however, if my master Don Quixote gets well from these wounds, and I will not be in any worse condition, I would not change my hopes for the best title in Spain."

Don Quixote was listening very attentively to this conversation, and sitting up in bed as well as he could, and taking the hostess by the hand said to her, "Believe me, fair lady, you may call yourself fortunate for having me in this castle of yours, I have to say so myself, although they say self-praise shames; but my aide will inform you who I am. I only tell you so I can preserve forever inscribed in my memory the service you have given me in order to offer you my gratitude while life allows me to live; and Heaven's love holds me so captivated and subject to its laws, that you lovely ladies here are now the masters of my freedom."

The hostess, her daughter, and Maritornes listened in incomprehension to the words of the Knight; because they understood about as much of them as if he had been speaking in Greek, although they could perceive they were all meant for expressions of good-will and praise; and not being accustomed to this kind of language, they stared at him and wondered to themselves, because he seemed to them a man of a different type from those they were used to, and thanking him for his politeness they left him, while the Asturian gave her attention to Sancho, who needed it no less than his master.

The transporter had made an arrangement with her for pleasure that night, and she had given him her word that when the guests were quiet and the family asleep she would come to find him and gratify his wishes completely. And it is said about this lady that she never made promises of the type without fulfilling them, she held it no disgrace to be employed as a servant in an inn, because, she said, misfortunes and bad-luck had given her that position. The hard, narrow bed of Don Quixote was in the middle of this room, and next to it Sancho made his, which merely consisted of a mat and a blanket that looked as if it was made of canvas rather than wool. Next to these two beds was the transporter's, made up, as already said, out of the contents of his saddlebags, and all the accessories of the two best donkeys he had, although there were twelve of them in total, sleek, plump, and in prime condition, because he was one of the rich transporters from Arevalo, according to the author of this history, who particularly mentions this transporter because he knew him very well, and they even say he was in some degree a relative of his; in addition to this Cide Hamete Benengeli was a historian of great research and accuracy in all things, which is very evident since he would fail to mention something, however insignificant it might be, an example that should be followed by historians who relay actions briefly that we hardly get a taste of them, all the substance of the work being left aside due to carelessness, deviance, or ignorance.

Continuing, then: after having paid a visit to his animals and given them their second feeding, the transporter laid himself on his bed waiting for the reliable Maritornes. Sancho was now covered in plasters and had laid down, and although he tried to sleep the pain of his ribs would not let him, while Don Quixote with the pain of his had his eyes as wide open like an owl.

The inn was silent, and the whole of it was lit by nothing other than a lantern which hung burning in the middle of the gateway. This strange stillness, and the thoughts, always present to Don Quixote's mind, of the incidents described in books that were the cause of his madness, conjured in his imagination the most extraordinary delusion that could ever be conceived, which was that he believed he had reached a famous castle, and that the daughter of the innkeeper was daughter of the lord of the castle, and that she, as he was so handsome, had fallen in love with him, and had promised to come to his bed for a while that night without the knowledge of her parents; and holding all this fantasy that he had constructed as a solid fact, he began to feel uncomfortable and considered the risk which his virtue was about to encounter, and he decided in his heart to commit no disloyalty to his lady Dulcinea del Toboso, even if the Queen Guinevere herself or the lady Quintanona presented themselves to him.

While he was stuck with these notions, the time and the hour, an unlucky one for him - arrived for the Asturian to come, who in her dress, with bare feet and her hair wrapped into a bun, with noiseless and cautious steps entered the room where the three were, in search of the transporter; but barely had she opened the door when Don Quixote noticed her, and sitting up in his bed in spite of his plasters and the pain of his ribs, stretched out his arms to hug his lovely lady. The Asturian, who went in silence with her hands reaching for her lover, encountered the arms of Don Quixote, who grasped her tightly by the wrist, and drawing her towards him, while she remained quiet, made her sit down on the bed. He then felt her dress, and although it was made from cotton it appeared to him to be the finest and softest silk: on her wrists she wore some beads, but to him they had the lustre of precious Orient pearls: her hair, which to some degree resembled a horse's mane, he valued as threads of the brightest gold, and that their brilliance dimmed the sun: her breath, which no doubt smelt of yesterday's stale salad, seemed to him to give a sweet aromatic fragrance from her mouth; and, in short, he drew her portrait in his imagination with the same features and in the same style as that which he had seen in his books of the other

Princesses who, infatuated by love, came to see the deeply wounded Knight; and so great was the poor gentleman's blindness that neither touch, nor smell, or anything else about the lady which would have made anyone but a transporter vomit, were enough to undeceive him; on the contrary, he was persuaded he had the goddess of beauty in his arms, and holding her firmly in his grasp he went on to say in a low, affectionate voice:

"I have found myself, Lovely and glorious lady, in a position to repay such a favour as that which you, by the sight of your great beauty, have granted me; but fortune, which is never exhausted of persecuting the good, has chosen to place me on this bed, where I lie so bruised and broken that although my inclination would gladly comply with yours it is impossible; besides, to this impossibility another yet greater is to be added, which is the faith that I have pledged to the unsurpassed Dulcinea del Toboso, the sole lady of my most secret thoughts; and if this did not stand in the way I would not be such an insensible Knight to miss the happy opportunity which your great goodness has offered me."

Maritornes was sweating, finding herself held so tight by Don Quixote, and not understanding the words he said to her, she struggled without speaking to free herself. The transporter, whose unholy thoughts kept him awake, was aware of the situation the moment she entered the door, and was listening attentively to what Don Quixote said; and jealous that the Asturian had broken her word with him for another, went closer to Don Quixote's bed and stood there to see what would happen after this talk which he could not understand; but when he noticed the lady struggling to get free and Don Quixote determined to hold her, he raised his arm and gave such a terrible punch to the jaw of the passionate Knight that he covered his mouth in blood, and not content with this he stood on his ribs and with his feet tramped all over them. The transporter who was somewhat crazy and not very firm on his feet, and the bed unable to support the additional weight of the transporter, came to the ground, and the mighty crash awoke the innkeeper who at once concluded that there must be some fight over Maritornes', because after calling loudly for her he got no answer. With this suspicion he got up, and lighting a lamp rushed to the room where he had heard the disturbance. The lady, hearing that her master was coming and knowing he had a temper, was frightened, and jumped into the bed of Sancho, who was now sleeping, and she proceeded to tuck herself into a ball.

The innkeeper came in exclaiming, "Where are you?" This disturbed Sancho, and feeling this mass almost on top of him thought he was having a nightmare and began to throw punches all around, some of which landed on Maritornes, who, irritated by the pain, gave back so many in return to Sancho that she fully woke him up. He then, finding himself being beaten by someone he could not recognise in the dark, got himself up as well as he could, and grappled with Maritornes, and between them they began the worse and funniest struggle in the world. The transporter, however, seeing by the light of the innkeepers' lamp what was happening to his lady, left Don Quixote, and ran to bring her the help she needed; and the innkeeper did the same but with a different intention, because his was to punish the lady, as he believed that beyond a doubt she was the cause of the altercation. And so, as it went: the transporter pounded Sancho, Sancho the lady, she pounded Sancho, and the innkeeper pounded her, and all worked so diligently that they did not give themselves a moment's rest; and the best of it was that the innkeeper's lamp went out, and as they were left in the dark they all beat each other unmercifully.

It so happened that there was staying that night in the inn a leader of what they call the Old Holy Brotherhood of Toledo, who, also hearing the extraordinary noise of the conflict, took his stick, and made his way into the dark room shouting: "Stop! in the name of the Holy Brotherhood!"

The first person he noticed was the beaten Don Quixote, who lay stretched senseless on his back on his broken-down bed, and holding him by his beard, continued to cry, "Stop, for the Holy Brotherhood!" but recognising that the man he held did not move, he concluded that he was dead and that those in the room were his murderers, and with this suspicion he raised his voice higher, calling out, "Shut the inn gate; see that no one gets out; they have killed a man here!" This shouting alarmed them all, and each gave up the contest as soon as the voice reached them. The innkeeper ran to his room, the transporter to his pack his saddlebags, the lady to her room; but the unlucky Don Quixote and Sancho alone were unable to move from where they were. The leader let go of Don Quixote's beard, and went out to look for a light to search for and apprehend the offenders; but not finding one, as the innkeeper had purposely extinguished the lantern when retreating to his room, he was compelled to resort to the fireplace, where after much time and trouble he lit another lamp.

CHAPTER 17

THE TROUBLES WHICH THE BRAVE DON QUIXOTE AND HIS GOOD AIDE SANCHO ENDURED IN THE INN

By this time Don Quixote had recovered from his unconsciousness; and in the same tone of voice as the day before when he called for Sancho, after he was beaten with sticks," he began calling him now, "Sancho, are you asleep my friend?"

"How can I sleep!" returned Sancho discontented and bitter, "when it is clear that the devil has found me this evening?"

"You may well believe that," answered Don Quixote, "because, either I am completely mistaken, or this castle is haunted, you must know what I am about to tell you, but you must swear to keep it secret until after my death."

"I swear," answered Sancho.

"I say this," continued Don Quixote, "because I hate taking away anyone's good name."

"I," replied Sancho, "swear to hold my tongue until the end of your days, even if God willed that to be only until tomorrow."

"Would you like to see me dead so soon?" said Don Quixote.

"It is not that," replied Sancho, "but because I hate keeping things inside for too long, and I don't want them to grow rotten inside me from over-keeping."

"Anyway," said Don Quixote, "I have more confidence in your affection and good nature; and so I will tell you that this evening, in this castle, one of the strangest adventures that I could describe happened to me, and to put it briefly you must know that a little while ago the daughter of the lord of this castle came to me. She is the most elegant and beautiful lady that could be found in the world. Oh, what I could tell you about her charms! About her wit! And of other secret matters which, to preserve the faithfulness I owe to my lady Dulcinea del Toboso, I will pass over unnoticed and in silence! I will only tell you that, either fate being envious of such a great blessing placed in my hands by good fortune, or perhaps (and this is more probable) this castle being, as I have already said, haunted, at the time when I was engaged in the sweetest and most passionate conversation with her, there came, without my seeing or knowing where it came from, a hand attached to the arm of some huge giant, that struck my jaw so heavily that I was bathed in blood, and then beat me in such a way that I am now in a worse condition than yesterday when the transporters, on account of Rocinante's misbehaviour, inflicted us with these injuries you already know of; I believe that this was the first indication that there must be some enchanted Moor protecting the treasure of this lady's beauty, and that it is not for me."

"Not for me either," said Sancho, "because more than four hundred Moors beat me as if I was dough being turned into cake and bread. But tell me, señor, what would you call this excellent and rare adventure that has left us as we are now? Although you didn't do as bad as me, having in your arms that incomparable beauty you spoke of; but I, what did I have, except the heaviest blows I think I had in my whole life? Unlucky me! Because I am not a Knight and never expect to be one, and in all these mishaps, I take the greater share."

"Then you have been beaten too?" said Don Quixote.

"Didn't I say so? The worst luck ever!" said Sancho.

"Don't be distressed, friend," said Don Quixote, "because I will now make the precious balm which we will cure ourselves with in the blink of an eye."

By this time the officer had succeeded in lighting the lamp, and came in to see the man that he thought had been killed; and as Sancho caught sight of him at the door, seeing him coming in his shirt, with a cloth on his head, and a lamp in his hand, and a very hostile expression, he said to his master, "Señor, can it be that this is the enchanted Moor coming back to give us more trouble?"

"It cannot be," answered Don Quixote, "because those under enchantment do not let themselves be seen by anyone."

"If they don't let themselves be seen, they let themselves be felt," said Sancho; "if not, let my shoulders tell you about it."

"Mine can speak too," said Don Quixote, "but that is not a sufficient reason for believing that what we see is the enchanted Moor."

The officer came up, and finding them engaged in such a peaceful conversation, stood amazed; although Don Quixote, to be sure, still lay on his back unable to move from a thorough beating. The officer turned to him and said, "you are alive then."

"I would speak more politely if I were you," replied Don Quixote; "is this the way in this country to speak to a Knight, you tit?"

The officer finding himself so disrespectfully treated by such a sorry-looking individual, lost his temper, and raising the lamp full of oil, struck Don Quixote with such a blow on the head with it that he gave him a badly bruised skull; then, all being in darkness, he went out, and Sancho said, "That is certainly the enchanted Moor, Señor, and he keeps the treasure for others, and for us only pain and beatings."

"That is the truth," answered Don Quixote, "there is no point troubling yourself about these matters of enchantment or being angry or aggravated by them, because as they are invisible and imaginary we will find no one to seek revenge on, let us do what we can; rise, Sancho, if you can, and call the commander of this fortress, and get him to give me a little oil, wine, salt, and rosemary to make the healing balm, because I believe I am in great need of it now, because I am losing a lot of blood from the wound that ghost just gave me."

Sancho got up with pain in his bones, and went looking for the innkeeper in the dark, and upon seeing the officer said, "Señor, whoever you are, do us the favour and kindness to give us a little rosemary, oil, salt, and wine, because it is needed to cure one of the best Knights on earth, who lies nearby on one of your beds wounded by the enchanted Moor that is in this inn."

When the officer heard him talk in this way, he took him for a man who had lost his senses, and as the day was now beginning to start, he opened the inn gate, and calling the innkeeper, he told him what this good man wanted. The innkeeper gave him what he required, and Sancho took it to Don Quixote, who, with his hand on his head, was crying in pain from the blow of the lamp, which had done him no more harm than raising a couple of rather large lumps, and what he thought was blood was only the sweat that flowed from him due to his suffering through the night. To be brief, he took the materials, of which he made a compound, mixing them all and boiling them a while until it seemed to him they had come to perfection. He then asked for some container to pour it into, and as there was none in the inn, he decided to put it into a tin oil-bottle or flask which the host gave to him as a free gift; and over the flask he repeated more than eighty prayers and many more to the Virgin Mary, accompanying each word making a cross with his hand as a way of blessing, in front of all who were present, Sancho, the innkeeper, and the officer; because the transporter was now peacefully attending to the comfort of his donkeys.

Once this was accomplished, he felt anxious to treat himself, on the spot, with the virtue of this precious balm, as he considered it, and so he drank nearly a quarter of what could not be put into the flask and remained in the pigskin in which it had been boiled; but barley had he finished drinking when he began to vomit in such a way that nothing was left in his stomach, and with the cramps and spasms of vomiting he broke into a prolific sweat, and because of this he asked them to cover him up and leave him alone. They did so, and he lay sleeping for more than three hours, at the end of this sleep he awoke and felt a great bodily relief and with so much ease from his bruises that he thought himself to be cured, and believed he had discovered the balm of Fierabras; and that with this remedy he can go forward, without any fear, face any kind of destruction, battle, or combat, however dangerous it might be.

Sancho Panza, who also regarded the improvement of his master as miraculous, begged him to give him what was left, which was no small amount. Don Quixote agreed, and Sancho, taking it with both hands, in good faith, swallowed and drained it fully. But the fact is, that the stomach of poor Sancho was even more delicate than his master, and so, before vomiting, he was seized with such cramp and convulsions, and such sweat and faintness, that certainly and truly he believed his last hour had come, and finding himself so tormented he swore at the balm and the man that had given it to him.

Don Quixote seeing him in this state said, "It is my belief, Sancho, that this malice comes to you because you were not made a Knight, I am now persuaded that this liquor cannot be good for those who are not Knights."

"If you knew that," returned Sancho "why did you let me taste it?"

He sweated and perspired with such spasms and convulsions that not only he himself but all present thought his end had come. This pain and suffering lasted about two hours, and at the end of it he was left, not like his master, but so weak and exhausted that he could not stand. Don Quixote, however, who, as has been said, felt himself relieved and well, was eager to leave at once in quest of adventures, as it seemed to him that all the time he stayed there was a fraud to the world and those in it who were in need of his help and protection, and even more now since he had the security and confidence of his balm; and so, urged by this impulse, he prepared Rocinante himself and put the saddlebags on his aide's donkey, who likewise he helped to dress and mount the donkey; after which he mounted his horse and going to a corner of the inn he picked up a stick that stood there, to serve him as a lance. Everyone that were in the inn, more than twenty people, stood watching him; the innkeeper's daughter was likewise observing him, and he too never took his eyes off her.

As soon as they were both mounted, at the gate of the inn, he called the innkeeper and said in a very serious voice, "I respect the many and great favours, Señor commander of this castle, and I remain under the deepest obligation to be grateful to you for them for the rest of my life; if I can repay them in punishing for you any arrogant enemy who may have wronged you, know that my calling is no other than to aid the weak, to avenge those who suffer wrong, and to punish betrayal. Search your memory, and if you find anything of this kind you only need tell me it, and I promise you by the law of Knighthood which I follow, I will secure your satisfaction and compensation."

The innkeeper replied to him with equal calmness, "Sir Knight, I do not want you to avenge for me any wrong, because when any is done to me I can take for myself whatever revenge seems fair to me; the only thing I want is that you pay me the bill that you have run up in the inn last night, for the straw and barley for your two animals, and for the dinner and beds."

"Then this is an inn?" said Don Quixote.

"And a very respectable one," said the innkeeper.

"I have been under an illusion all this time," answered Don Quixote, "because in truth I thought it was a castle, and not a bad one; but since it appears that it is not a castle but an inn, all that can be done now is that you should excuse the payment, because I cannot break the law of Knights, of which I know as a fact (and up to the present I have read nothing to the contrary) that they never paid for housing or anything else in the inn where they might be; because any hospitality that might be offered to them is appropriate by law, and right in return for the insufferable labour they endure in seeking adventures day and night, in summer and in winter, on foot and on horseback, in hunger or thirst, cold or heat, exposed to all the seasons of heaven and all the hardships of earth."

"I have little to do with that," replied the innkeeper; "pay me what you owe me, and let us not talk any more about Knights, because all I care about is receiving my money."

"You are a stupid, worthless innkeeper," said Don Quixote, and digging his heels into Rocinante he rode out of the inn before anyone could stop him, and went some distance without looking to see if his aide was following him.

The innkeeper when he saw him go without paying ran to get the payment from Sancho, who said that as his master would not pay neither would he, because, being an aide to a Knight, he had to follow the same rules as his master with regard to not paying anything for inns. The innkeeper became very angry and threatened if he did not pay he would make him in a way he would not like. To which Sancho answered that by the law of Knights his master follows he would not pay, even if it cost him his life; because the worthy and ancient use of Knights was not going to be violated by him, or would the aides which are yet to come into the world ever complain about him for breaking such laws.

The bad fortune of the unlucky Sancho arranged that among the company of the innkeeper were four woolcutters from Segovia, three needle-workers from Cordova, and two lodgers from Seville, lively men, fond of a joke, and playful, who, almost as if inspired and moved by a common impulse, went up to Sancho and dismounted him from his donkey, while one of them went inside to get a blanket from one of the host's beds; seeing that the ceiling was somewhat lower than what they required for their work, it was decided to go out into the yard, which was restricted by the sky, and there, putting Sancho in the middle of the blanket, they began to throw him as high as they could.

The cries of the poor blanketed man were so loud that they reached the ears of his master, who, stopping to listen attentively, was convinced that a new adventure was coming, until he clearly perceived that it was his aide who emitted them. Turning around he rode up to the inn with a glorious gallop, and finding it shut went round it to see if he could find some way of getting in; but as soon as he came to the wall of the yard, which was not very high, he discovered the game that was being played with his aide. He saw him rising and falling in the air with such grace and agility that, if his rage had allowed him, it is my belief that he would have laughed. He tried to climb from his horse on to the top of the wall, but he was so bruised and battered that he could not do so; and so, from the back of his horse he began to swear and shout at those who were playing with Sancho. It would be impossible to write down accurately what was said: but they, however, did not stop their laughter or their work, and neither did the flying Sancho's cries cease, mingled now with threats, but all with little purpose, or none at all, because this did not stop them until from pure tiredness they came to a stop. They then brought him his donkey, and mounting him on top of it they put his jacket round him; and the compassionate Maritornes, seeing him so exhausted, thought it was appropriate to refresh him with a jug of water, and so it could be cooler she collected it from the well. Sancho took it, and as he was raising it to his mouth he was stopped by the cries of his master exclaiming, "Sancho, my son, do not drink the water, it will kill you; you see here, I have the blessed balm (and he held up the flask), and with drinking two drops of it you will be restored."

At these words Sancho glanced from the corner of his eyes, and in a louder voice replied, "Can it be, you have forgotten that I am not a Knight, or do you want me to vomit whatever I have left from last night? Keep your balm, and let me drink!" and at the same time he stopped talking and began drinking; but at the first sip he perceived it was water and did not care to go on with it, and begged Maritornes to get him some wine, which she did with good will, and paid for it with her own money; because although she was in that line of life, there was some faint and distant resemblance of a Christian about her. When Sancho had done drinking he dug his heels into his donkey, and the gate of the inn being thrown open he left very well pleased at having paid nothing and made his point, although it had been at the expense of his usual pain, his shoulders. However, it is true that the innkeeper seized his saddlebags in payment of what was owed to him, but Sancho left in such a hurry that he did not realise they were missing.

CHAPTER 18

THE CONVERSATION SANCHO HAD WITH HIS MASTER, DON QUIXOTE, AND OTHER ADVENTURES

Sancho reached his master so weak and faint that he could not encourage his donkey to move. When Don Quixote saw the state he was in he said, "I have now come to the conclusion, good Sancho, that this castle or inn is beyond a doubt haunted, because those who have so dreadfully humoured themselves with you, what else can they be but ghosts or beings from another world? And I confirmed this by noticing that when I was next to the wall of the yard witnessing the acts of your sad tragedy, it was out of my power to take action, I could not climb the wall, because they no doubt had placed a spell on me; because I swear to you that if I had been able to climb up or dismount, I would have punished them in such a way that those loudmouth thieves would have remembered it forever, even if I knew that doing it would go against the laws of chivalry, which, as I have often told you, do not allow a Knight to put hands on someone who is not one, expect in the case of urgent and great necessity in defence of his own life or another's."

"I would have punished them myself as well if I could," said Sancho, "whether I were a Knight or not, but I could not; but in my opinion I am convinced that those who amused themselves with me were not ghosts or enchanted men, as you say, but men of flesh and bone like ourselves; and they all had names, because I heard them name each other when they were tossing me in the air, one was called Pedro Martinez, and another Tenorio Hernandez, and the innkeeper, I heard, was called Juan Palomeque; so, señor, you not being able to climb over the wall of the yard or dismount from your horse was due to something else other than enchantment; and what I make out clearly from all of this is, that these adventures we seek will in the end lead us into such disasters that we will not know which is our right foot; and that the best and wisest thing, according to my small wit, would be for us to return home, now that it is harvest-time, and attend to our business, and give up wandering."

"How little you know about chivalry, Sancho," replied Don Quixote; "have peace and have patience; the day will come when you will see with your own eyes what an honourable thing it is to wander in the pursuit of this calling; actually, tell me, what greater pleasure can there be in the world, or what delight can equal a winning a battle, and triumphing over one's enemy? None, beyond all doubt."

"Very likely," answered Sancho, "although I do not know it; all I know is that since we have been Knights, or since you have been one (because I have no right to call myself one of such an honourable calling) we have never won any battle except the one with the Biscayan, and even out of that you left with half an ear and half a helmet; and from then until now it has been all beatings and more beatings, and as I was thrown in the air by people I could not stop, I do not know what the delight, as you call it, of conquering an enemy is like."

"That is what angers me, and what should anger you, Sancho," replied Don Quixote; "but from now on I will endeavour to have some sword made by such craft that no kind of enchantment can have an effect on he who carries it, and it is even possible that fortune may obtain for me that which belonged to Amadis when he was called 'The Knight of the Burning Sword,' which was one of the best swords that any Knight in the world ever possessed, because, besides having the virtue mentioned, it cut like a razor, and there was no armour, however strong and enchanted it might be, that could resist it."

"Knowing my luck," said Sancho, "that even if that happened and you found this sword, it would, like the balm, turn out good for Knights only, and as for the aides, they end up with sorrow."

"Do not fear that, Sancho," said Don Quixote: "Heaven will give you a better deal."

While talking, Don Quixote and his aide were going along, when, on the road they were following, Don Quixote perceived approaching them a large and thick cloud of dust, on seeing this he turned to Sancho and said:

"This is the day, Sancho, which will see the blessing my fortune is reserving for me; this, I say, is the day on which as much as on any will display my might, and on which I will do deeds that will remain written in the book of fame for generations to come. You see that cloud of dust which rises over there? Well, then, that is churned up by a vast army composed of various and countless nations that comes marching."

"According to that there must be two then," said Sancho, "because on the opposite side there is another cloud of dust."

Don Quixote turned to look and found that it was true, and in delight, he concluded that they were two armies about to fight; because at all times and seasons his mind was full of the battles, enchantments, adventures, crazy accomplishments, loves, and defiance that are recorded in the books of chivalry, and everything he said, thought, or did had reference to these things. However, the cloud of dust he had seen was raised by two great herds of sheep coming along the same road in opposite directions, which, because of the dust, did not become visible until they got nearer, but Don Quixote declared so positively that they were armies that Sancho was led to believe it and say, "Well, what should we do, señor?"

"What else?" said Don Quixote: "give aid and assistance to the weak and those who need it; and you must know, Sancho, that this which comes opposite to us is conducted and led by the mighty emperor Alifanfaron, lord of the great island of Trapobana; this other that marches behind me is that of his enemy the King of the Garamantas, Pentapolin the Bare Arm, because he always goes into battle with his right arm bare."

"But why are these lords enemies?"

"They are hostile," replied Don Quixote, "because this Alifanfaron is a furious pagan and is in love with the daughter of Pentapolin, who is a very beautiful and gracious lady, and a Christian, and her father is unwilling to give her to the pagan King unless he first abandons the religion of his false prophet Mahomed, and adopts his."

"I swear," said Sancho, "Pentapolin is quite right, and I will help him as much as I can."

"And that is your duty, Sancho," said Don Quixote; "because to engage in battles of this kind it is not necessary to be a Knight."

"That I can well understand," answered Sancho; "but where shall we put this donkey? Because I believe it is not normal to go into battle on an animal of this kind."

"That is true," said Don Quixote, "and what you should do with him is to leave him and take the chance whether he is lost or not, because when we come out victorious will have so many horses that even Rocinante will run the risk of being changed for another. But for now listen to me and observe, because I want to give you an account of the main Knights who accompany these two armies; so you can see them better, let us go to that hill which rises over there, where we can view both armies."

They did so, and placed themselves on a hill from which the two herds that Don Quixote made armies of might have been plainly seen if the clouds of dust they raised had not obscured them and blinded the sight; nevertheless, seeing in his imagination what he did not see in reality and what did not exist, he began to say in a loud voice:

"That Knight who you see there in yellow armour, whose shield has a lion crowned crouching at the feet of a lady, is the valiant Laurcalco, lord of the Silver Bridge; that one in armour with flowers of gold, whose shield has three crowns, is the feared Micocolembo grand duke of Quirocia; that other with a gigantic frame, on his right, is the ever fearless Brandabarbaran de Boliche, lord of the three Arabias, who for armour wears that snake skin, and has for a shield, according to tradition, one of those from the temple that Samson brought to the ground when he sought revenge on his enemies. But turn your eyes to the other side, and you will see in front of this other army the ever victorious and never vanquished Timonel of Carcajona, prince of New Biscay, who comes in armour and weapons quarter blue, green, white, and yellow, and displays on his shield a cat with the inscription Miau, which is the beginning of his lady's name, who according to reports is the unsurpassed Miaulina, daughter of the duke Alfeniquen of the Algarve; the other, who attacks that powerful charger and has weaponry as white as snow and a blank shield without any engraving, is a novice Knight, a Frenchman, Pierres Papin, lord of the baronies of Utrique; and so he went on naming a number of Knights out of his imagination, and to all he assigned their weaponry, colours, and mottoes, carried away by the illusions of his unheard-of craze; and without a pause, he continued, "People of nations compose this squadron in front; here are those that drink from the sweet waters of the famous Xanthus, those from the Massilian fields, those that sift the pure fine gold of Arabia, the Persians renowned in archery, the Parthians and the Medes that fight like they fly, the Arabs that constantly shift their homes, the Scythians as cruel as they are fair, the Ethiopians with pierced lips, and an infinity of other nations whose features I recognise, although I cannot recall their names. In this other squadron comes those that drink from the crystal streams of the olive-bearing Betis, those that make their faces smooth with the water from the ever rich and golden Tagus, those that rejoice in the fertilising flow of the divine Genil, those that roam the Tartesian fields, those that take their pleasure in the Elysian meadows of Jerez, the rich Manchegans crowned with fields of corn, the wearers of iron, old relics of the Gothic race, those that bathe in the Pisuerga renowned for its gentle current, those that feed their herds in Guadiana, those that shake in the cold of the Pyrenees or the dazzling snow of the Apennine; in a word, practically everywhere."

Good God! what a number of countries and nations he named! giving each their proper attributes with marvellous detail; saturated with what he had read in his lying books! Sancho listened to his words without speaking, and from time to time turned to try and see the Knights and giants his master was describing, and as he could not make out any of them he said to him:

"Señor, I see no sign of any man you talk of, in the whole thing; maybe it's all enchantment, like the ghosts last night."

"How can you say that!" answered Don Quixote; "Do you not hear the sound of the horses, the trumpets, and the drums?"

"I hear nothing but the moaning of sheep," said Sancho; which was true, because by this time the two herds had come closer.

"The fear you are in, Sancho," said Don Quixote, "prevents you from seeing or hearing correctly, because one of the effects of fear is to derange the senses and make things appear different from what they are; if you are in such fear, go to one side and leave me by myself, because I will suffice alone to bring victory to the side which I give my aid to;" and he gave Rocinante the heels, and putting the lance up, galloped down the slope like a thunderbolt. Sancho shouted, "Come back, Señor Don Quixote; I swear to God they are sheep you are charging at! Come back! What madness is this! Look, there is no giant, or Knight, no weapons, or shields." But Don Quixote did not turn back; on the contrary he went on shouting out, "Oh Knights, you who follow and fight under the banner of the valiant emperor Pentapolin of the Bare Arm, follow me; you will see how easily I will give him his revenge over his enemy Alifanfaron of Trapobana."

He then rushed into the middle of the herd of sheep, and began striking them with as much spirit as if he were beating his mortal enemies. The shepherds accompanying the flock shouted at him to stop; seeing it was no use, they began to shower his head with stones as big as a fist. Don Quixote gave no notice to the stones, but, whilst thrusting the lance right and left kept saying:

"Where are you, proud Alifanfaron? Come to me; I am a single Knight who would willingly prove my skill hand to hand, and make you give your life as penalty for the wrong you do to the valiant Pentapolin Garamanta."

Stones continued to hit him and some struck a couple of his ribs. He imagined himself badly wounded, and recollecting his balm he took out his flask, and putting it to his mouth began to pour the contents into his stomach; he succeeded in swallowing what seemed to him enough, then there came another stone striking him on the hand and on the flask with such accuracy that it smashed it to pieces, knocking three or four teeth out of his mouth as well, and sorely damaging two fingers of his hand. The force of the blows was so strong that the poor Knight came down backwards off his horse. The shepherds came, and were sure they had killed him; so in a hurry they gathered their herds, took the dead animals, of which there were more than seven, and left without waiting to ascertain anything further.

All this time Sancho stood on the hill watching the crazy actions of his master, tearing his beard out and swearing from a distance. Seeing him, then, brought to the ground, and that the shepherds had left, he ran to him and found him in a very bad state, but not unconscious; and he said:

"Did I not tell you to come back, Señor Don Quixote; and that what you were going to attack were not armies but sheep?"

"That is how that thief of a sage, my enemy, can alter things," answered Don Quixote; "you must know, Sancho, that it is a very easy matter for those like that to make us believe what they choose; and this evil being who persecutes me, envious of the glory he knew I was going to win in this battle, has turned the squadrons of the enemy into herds of sheep. At any rate, do this, I beg you, Sancho, undeceive yourself, and see that what I say is true; mount your donkey and follow them quietly, and you will see that when they have gone some distance from here they will return to their original shape and, ceasing to be sheep, become men in all respects as I had described them to you. But do not go just yet, because I need your help and assistance; come here, and see how many of my teeth are missing, because I feel as if there is not one left in my mouth."

Sancho came so close that he almost put his eyes into his mouth; and just at that moment the balm started to act on the stomach of Don Quixote, so, at the very instant when Sancho came to examine his mouth, he discharged all of its contents with more force than a gun, fully into the face and and onto the beard of poor Sancho.

"God!" cried Sancho, "what is this that has happened me? Clearly this man is badly wounded, as he vomits blood from the mouth;" but considering the matter a little more closely he perceived by the colour, taste, and smell, that it was not blood but the balm from the flask which he had seen him drink; and he was struck with such disgust that his stomach turned, and he vomited his insides over his master, and both were left in a lovely state. Sancho ran to his donkey to get something from his saddle bags to clean himself with, and to relieve his master; but finding them missing, he nearly lost his senses, and swore loudly, and in his heart determined to leave his master and return home, even though he forfeited the wages of his service and all hopes of the promised island.

Don Quixote rose and putting his left hand to his mouth to keep his teeth from falling out altogether, with the other he took the reins of Rocinante, who had never left is master's side - so loyal and well-behaved – and took himself to where Sancho stood leaning over his donkey with his hand on his cheek, like someone in deep sadness. Seeing him in this mood, looking so sad, Don Quixote said to him:

"Bear in mind, Sancho, that one man is no more than another, unless he does more than the other; all these storms that come to us are signs that fair weather is coming soon, and that things will go well for us, because it is impossible for good or evil to last for ever; and so it follows that as the evil has lasted so long, the good must be now be near; so you must not distress yourself over the misfortunes which happen to me, since you have no share in them."

"How have I not?" replied Sancho; "was he, who they threw in the air yesterday by chance anyone other than my father's son? and the saddlebags that are missing today with all my treasures, did they belong to anyone else than myself?"

"What! Are the saddlebags missing, Sancho?" said Don Quixote.

"Yes, they are missing," answered Sancho.

"In that case we have nothing to eat today," replied Don Quixote.

"That would be so," answered Sancho, "if there are none of the herbs you say you know of in these meadows."

"For all of those," answered Don Quixote, "I would rather have a loaf of bread and a couple of pilchards' heads, than all the herbs described by Dioscorides, even with Doctor Laguna's notes. Nevertheless, Sancho the Good, mount your donkey and come along with me, because God, who provides for all things, will not fail us (especially when we are so active in his service), since he fails neither the birds of the air, or the worms of the earth, or the tadpoles of the water, and is so merciful that he makes his sun rise on the good and on the evil, and sends rain on the fair and on the unfair."

"You would make a better preacher than a Knight," said Sancho.

"Knights knew and should know everything, Sancho," said Don Quixote; "because there were Knights in former times well qualified to deliver a sermon the middle of a battle, as if they had graduated in the University of Paris; so we can see that the lance has never hindered the pen, and the pen never hindered the lance."

"Well, as you say," replied Sancho; "let us leave now and find some place with shelter for the night, and God let it be somewhere where there are no blankets, or ghosts, or enchanted Moors; because if there are, I know the devil controls the whole matter."

"Tell God," said Don Quixote; "that you will go where he wills, because this time we leave our accommodation to his choice; take your hand, and find out how many of my teeth are missing from this right side of my jaw, because it is there I feel the pain."

Sancho put in his fingers into his mouth, and feeling about asked him, "How many teeth did you have on this side?"

"Four," replied Don Quixote, "apart from the back-tooth, all were whole and quite sound."

"Mind what you are saying, señor."

"I say four, if not five," answered Don Quixote, "because never in my life have I lost a tooth or have any fallen out or been destroyed by any decay."

"Well, then," said Sancho, "in this lower side you have no more than two, and in the upper not even a half or any at all, because it is all as smooth as the palm of my hand."

"Just my luck!" said Don Quixote, hearing the sad news his aide gave him; "I would rather they took an arm, if it were not the sword-arm; because I tell you, Sancho, a mouth without teeth is like a mill without a millstone, and a tooth is much more valuable than a diamond; but we who follow the order of chivalry are liable to all this. Mount Sancho, and lead the way, and I will follow you at whatever pace you choose."

Sancho did as he asked him, and proceeded in the direction in which he thought he might find refuge without leaving the main road. As they went along, then, at a slow pace, because the pain in Don Quixote's jaws kept him uneasy and not in good condition for speed, Sancho thought it was best to amuse him by talk of some kind, and among the things he said to him was that which will be told in the following chapter.

CHAPTER 19

THE CLEVER CONVERSATION WHICH SANCHO HAD WITH HIS MASTER

"It seems to me, señor, that all these mishaps that have come to us lately have been without a doubt a punishment for the offence committed by you against the laws of chivalry in not keeping the pledge you made not to eat bread off a tablecloth or embrace the Queen, and all the rest of that you swore to observe until you had taken that helmet of Malandrino's, or whatever the Moor is called, because I do not remember well."

"You are very right, Sancho," said Don Quixote, "but to tell the truth, it had escaped my memory; and you can be sure that the issue of the blanket was my fault, and it happened to you because I was not reminded of these transgressions in time; but I will make up for it, because there are ways of compounding for everything in the laws of chivalry."

"But did I take the oath as well?" said Sancho.

"No, but It makes no difference," said Don Quixote; "You are clear of responsibility; but you are my aide."

"In that case," said Sancho, "please be careful not to forget like you did the oath; because perhaps the ghosts will like to amuse themselves once more with me; or even with you."

While engaged in this and other talk, night fell before they had reached or discovered any place of shelter; and what made it worse was that they were dying of hunger, because with the loss of the saddlebags they had lost their entire supply of food; and to complete the misfortune they encountered yet another adventure. It so happened that the night closed in somewhat darkly, but despite that they pushed on, Sancho feeling sure that as the road was the King's highway they might reasonably expect to find some inn soon. Going along then, in this way, the night dark, Sancho hungry, the master hungrier, they saw coming towards them on the road they were travelling a great number of lights which looked exactly like stars in motion. Sancho was shocked by the sight of them, and Don Quixote did not quite appreciate them either: one stopped his donkey, the other raised his lance, and they stood still, watching anxiously to see what all this would turn out to be, and found that the lights were approaching them, and the nearer they came the greater they seemed. At this spectacle Sancho began to shake like a man dosed with drugs, and Don Quixote's hair stood on end; he, however, plucking up his spirit a little, said:

"This, no doubt, Sancho, will be a most mighty and dangerous adventure, in which it will be necessary for me to put forward all my courage and bravery."

"Unlucky for me!" answered Sancho; "if this adventure happens to be one of ghosts, as I am beginning to think it is, where will I find the ribs to tolerate it?"

"If they are ghosts," said Don Quixote, "I will not permit them to touch a thread of your garments; because if they played tricks with you the time before, it was because I was unable to climb the walls of the yard; but now we are on wide open land where I can exercise my sword however I like."

"And if they enchant and cripple you as they did the last time," said Sancho, "what difference will it make being on the open land or not?"

"Don't worry," replied Don Quixote, "I ask you, Sancho, to keep a good heart, because experience will tell you I am right."

"I will," answered Sancho, and both moved to one side of the road to observe closely what all these moving lights could be; and very soon after they recognised roughly twenty jacketed men, all on horseback, with torches in their hands, this awe-inspiring spectacle completely extinguished the courage of Sancho, who began to chatter with his teeth like someone in the coldest part of Russia; and his teeth chattered even more when they observed distinctly that behind was a coffin covered over with black and followed by six more mounted figures in sorrowful clothing which hung to the very feet of their donkeys. They could clearly tell these were not horses by the slow pace at which they went. And as the men came along they mumbled to themselves in a low sorrowful tone. This strange spectacle at such an hour and in such a solitary place was quite enough to strike terror into Sancho's heart, and it did so, because Sancho's determination had now broken down. It was just the opposite with his master, whose imagination immediately conjured up all of this to him as vividly as one of the adventures of his books.

He took it into his head that the coffin was actually a movable frame, on which some sorely wounded Knight laid on, and to avenge this was a task reserved for him alone; and without any further reasoning he put his lance in a rested position, placed himself firmly in his saddle, and with courageous spirit and attitude took his position in the middle of the road where the men had to pass; and as soon as he saw them coming close he raised his voice and said:

"Halt, Knights, or whoever you are, and give me account of who you are, where you came from, where you are going, what it is you carry on that frame, because, to judge by appearances, either you have done some wrong or some wrong has been done to you, and it is necessary that I know, so I may discipline you for the evil you have done, or so I may seek revenge on your behalf for the injury that has been inflicted on you."

"We are in hurry," answered one of the jacketed men, "and the inn is far away, we cannot stop to give you such an account as you demand."

Don Quixote was mightily provoked by this answer, and grabbing his donkey by the head brace he said, "Halt, and have more manners, and give an account of what I asked you for; or else, I will take your defiance to combat, all of you."

The donkey was shy, and was so frightened at her head brace being seized that she jumped up and flung her rider to the ground over her hips. An attendant who was on foot, seeing the man fall, began to abuse Don Quixote, who now moved to anger, and raising his lance charged at one of the men in mourning and left him badly wounded on the ground, and as he turned around toward the others the agility with which he attacked them was a sight to see, because it seemed as if wings had instantly grown on Rocinante. The mourning men were timid and unarmed, so they quickly made their escape from the fight and ran across the field with their torches. However, being enclosed and wrapped in their attire, they were unable to run away fast enough, and so with entire safety, Don Quixote beat them all and drove them away against their will, because they all thought this was not a man but a devil from hell who had come to carry away the dead body they carried.

Sancho observed in amazement the fearlessness of his lord, and said to himself, "Clearly this master of mine is as brave and courageous as he says he is."

A burning torch lay on the ground near the first man who the donkey had thrown, by the light of this Don Quixote saw him, and coming up to him he presented the point of the lance to his face, telling him to give himself as a prisoner, or else he would kill him; to which the man replied, "I am a prisoner enough as it is; I cannot move, because one of my legs is broken: I ask you, if you are a Christian gentleman, do not kill me, you will be committing serious irreverence, because I am a practising Christian and I hold a certificate to teach in the highest degree."

"Then what the hell brought you here, being a churchman?" said Don Quixote.

"Well, señor?" said the other. "My bad luck."

"Then worse awaits you," said Don Quixote, "if you do not satisfy my request, which I have already asked you."

"You will be satisfied soon," said the churchman; "you must know, then, that although just now I said I was a churchman, I am a graduate, and my name is Alonzo Lopez; I am a native of Alcobendas, I come from the city of Baeza with eleven others, priests, the same men who ran with the torches, and we are going to the city of Segovia accompanying a dead body which is in that coffin, and it is the body of a gentleman who died in Baeza; and now, as I said, we are taking his bones to their burial-place, which is in Segovia, where he was born."

"And who killed him?" asked Don Quixote.

"God, with a nasty fever that took him," answered the graduate.

"In that case," said Don Quixote, "the Lord has relieved me of the task of avenging his death had any other man killed him; but, he who killed him having killed him, there is nothing for us to do but to be silent, and shrug the shoulders; I would do the same if he were to kill me; and I want you to know that I am a Knight of La Mancha, Don Quixote is my name, and it is my business and calling to roam the world righting wrongs and equalising injuries."

"I do not know how you are righting wrongs," said the bachelor, "because from straight you have made me crooked, leaving me with a broken leg that will never be the same again all the days of its life; and the injury you have equalised in my case has been to leave me injured in such a way that I will remain injured forever; and for me it has been a misadventure to meet you who go in search of adventures."

"Things do not all happen in the same way," answered Don Quixote; "it all happened, Sir Alonzo Lopez, due to you, as you did, go at night dress in that clothing, with torches, praying, covered with dark clothing, so naturally you looked like something evil and from the other world; and so I could not avoid doing my duty in attacking you, and I should have attacked you as if I had known, positively that you were the devil from hell, because I certainly believed you to be."

"As my fate has willed it," said the graduate, "I ask you, sir Knight, whose duty has been such an evil one for me, to help me to get up from under this donkey that holds one of my legs caught between the stirrup and the saddle."

"I would have talked until tomorrow," said Don Quixote; "how long were you going to wait before telling me of your distress?"

He called Sancho, who, however, had no mind to come, as he was just then engaged in unloading the saddlebags of one of the donkeys, well stocked with food, which these gentlemen had brought with them. Sancho made a bag out of his coat, and, getting together as much as he could, and as the bag would hold, he loaded his donkey, and then rushed to obey his master's call, and helped him to remove the graduate from under the donkey; then putting him on her back he gave him the torch, and Don Quixote asked him to follow the tracks of his companions, and forgive him for his part in this wrong doing which he could not help.

And Sancho said, "If by any chance these gentlemen want to know who was the hero that served them today, you can tell them that he is the famous Don Quixote of La Mancha, otherwise called the Knight of the Sorrowful Face."

The graduate then left.

I forgot to mention that before he did, he said to Don Quixote, "Remember that you stand excluded for having laid violent hands on a holy thing, juxta illud, si quis, suadente diabolo."

"I do not understand Latin," answered Don Quixote, "but I know I did not lay hands on you; besides, I did not think I was committing an assault on priests or people of the Church, which, like a Catholic and faithful Christian I am, I respect and revere, but on ghosts and threats from the other world."

On hearing this the graduate left, as has been said, without replying; and Don Quixote asked Sancho what had induced him to call him the "Knight of the Sorrowful Face."

"I will tell you," answered Sancho; "it was because I had been looking at you for some time in the light of the torch held by that unfortunate man, and currently you have the saddest face I ever saw: it must be either due to the fatigue of this combat, or the need of some teeth."

"It is not that," replied Don Quixote, "but because the sage whose duty it will be to write the history of my achievements must have thought it was appropriate that I have some distinctive name as all the Knights of the past did;

one being 'Man of the Burning Sword,' another 'Knight of the Unicorn,' another 'Knight of the Ladies,' and another 'Knight of the Phoenix,' another 'The Knight of the Griffin,' and another 'Knight of the Death,' and by these names and titles they were known all around the world; and so I say that the sage must have put it into your mouth and mind just now to call me 'The Knight of the Sorrowful Face,' as I intend to call myself from this day forward; and that this name may fit me better, I mean, when the opportunity offers, to have a very Sad Face painted on my shield."

"There is no occasion, señor, for wasting time or money on making that face," said Sancho; "because all that you need to do is show your own face, to those who look at you, and without anything more, they will call you 'Knight of the Sorrowful Face' and believe me I am telling you the truth, because I assure you, señor, hunger and the loss of your teeth have given you such a sad face that, as I say, the sad picture does not need to be created."

Don Quixote laughed at Sancho's politeness; however, he decided to call himself by that name, and have his shield painted as he said.

Don Quixote wanted to look to see whether the body in the coffin was bones or not, but Sancho would not have it, saying:

"Señor, you have ended this dangerous adventure more safely for yourself than any of those I have seen: perhaps these people, although beaten, may think to themselves that it is a single man that has beaten them, and feeling sore and ashamed of it may decide to come in search of us and give us trouble. The donkey is in good condition, the mountains are near, we have hunger, there is nothing left to do, and, as the saying goes, the dead to the grave and the living to the bread."

And driving his donkey forward he begged his master to follow, who, feeling that Sancho was right, did so without replying; and after proceeding some distance between two hills they found themselves in a wide valley, where they dismounted, and Sancho unloaded his saddle-bags, and laid the contents on the green grass. They then had breakfast, lunch and dinner all at the same time, satisfying their appetites with more than one serving of each. But they suffered from another piece of bad luck, which Sancho said was the worst of all, and that was that they had no wine to drink, not even water to moisten their lips; and as thirst tormented them, Sancho, observed that the meadow where they were was full of green grass, and said what will be told in the following chapter.

CHAPTER 20

THE UNHEARD-OF ADVENTURE WHICH WAS ACHIEVED BY THE VALIANT DON QUIXOTE OF LA MANCHA WITH LESS DANGER THAN ANY OTHER ACHIEVED BY ANY FAMOUS KNIGHT IN THE WORLD

"Señor, this grass has to be proof that there must be a lake nearby to give it moisture, so it would be wise to move a little further, so we can find some place where we can quench this terrible thirst, which beyond a doubt is more distressing than hunger."

The advice seemed good to Don Quixote, and, taking Rocinante by the reins and Sancho taking the donkey by the halter, after he had packed away the remains of the food, they progressed through the meadow feeling their way, because the darkness of the night made it impossible to see anything; but they had not gone far at all when a loud noise of water, as if falling from great rocks, struck their ears. The sound cheered them greatly; but stopping to make out by listening from which direction it came they heard another noise which spoiled the satisfaction the sound of the water gave them, especially for Sancho, who was by nature timid and faint-hearted. They heard a drumming sound, a certain rattling of iron and chains that, together with the furious crashing of the water, would have struck terror into any heart except Don Quixote's. The night was, as has been said, dark, and they had happened to reach a spot among some tall trees, whose leaves encouraged by a gentle breeze made a low tormenting sound; so that, what with the solitude, the place, the darkness, the drumming, the noise of the water, and the rustling of the leaves, everything inspired awe and fear; especially as they perceived that the sounds did not cease, or the wind, or the approach of morning; and to add to this: their ignorance of where they were.

But Don Quixote, supported by his courageous heart, leaped on Rocinante, and placing his shield on his arm, lifted his lance, and said, "Friend Sancho, know that I by Heaven's will have been born in this iron age to revive in it the age of gold, or the golden age as it is called; I am a man for who threats, mighty achievements, and valiant deeds are reserved; I am, I say again, a man who is to revive the Knights of the Round Table, the Twelve Peers of France and the Nine Worthies; and a man who is to consign to oblivion the Tyrants along with the whole group of famous Knights of the past, performing in these in adventures such marvels and feats that will obscure their brightest deeds. You mark my words, faithful and trusted aide, the gloom of this night, it's strange silence, the dull confused murmur of those trees, the awful sound of that water which we came in quest for, that seems as though it were dashing itself down from the high mountains, and that incessant hammering that disturbs our ears; these things all together and each itself are enough to instil fear, terror, and panic into the chest of any man, and much more into those not used to hazards and adventures of this type. Well, then, all this that I put before you is an incentive and stimulant to my spirit, making my heart beat in my chest with eagerness to engage in this adventure, difficult as it indicates to be; therefore tighten Rocinante's straps a little, and God be with you; wait for me here for three days and no more, and if in that time I do not come back, you can return to our village, and then, you will do me a favour and a service, you will go to El Toboso, where you will say to my incomparable lady Dulcinea that her captive Knight has died in attempting things that make him worthy of being called hers."

When Sancho heard his master's words he began to cry in the most pathetic way, saying:

"Señor, I do not know why you want to attempt this terrible adventure; it is night now, no one can see us here, we can easily turn around and take ourselves away from danger, even if we don't drink for another three days; and as there is no one to see us, there is no one to put us down as cowards; besides, I have many times heard the vicar of our village, who you know well, preach that he who seeks danger dies in it; so it is not right to tempt God by trying such an incredible deed from which there can be no escape except by a miracle, and Heaven has performed enough of them for you in saving you from being blanketed as I was, and bringing you out victorious and safe and sound from all those enemies that were with the devil; and if all this does not resonate or soften that hard heart, let this thought and reflection do it, that you will have hardly left this spot when from pure fear I will give my soul to anyone that will take it. I left my home, wife and children to come and serve you, hoping to do better not worse; but as greediness bursts the bag, I have seen my hopes torn apart, because just as I had them at their highest about getting that island you have so often promised me, I see that instead of it you intend to desert me now in a place so far from another human soul: for God's sake, master, do not be so unfair to me, and if you will not give up attempting this deed, at least put it on hold until the morning, because the wisdom I learned when I was a shepherd tells me it cannot be more than three hours until dawn now, because the mouth can be seen in the stars overhead and midnight is in line with the left arm."

"How can you see, Sancho," said Don Quixote, "where it makes that line, or where this mouth you speak of is, when the night is so dark that there is not a star to be seen in the whole sky?"

"That's true," said Sancho, "but fear has sharp vision, and sees things underground, and much more in the sky; besides, there is good reason to believe that this night is in need of day."

"Let it need what it needs," replied Don Quixote, "no one will say of me now, or at any other time that tears or petitions turned me away from doing what was in accordance with knightly duty; and so I beg you, Sancho, to hold your peace, because God, who has put it into my heart to undertake now this terrible adventure, will take care to watch over my safety and comfort your sorrow; what you have to do now is to tighten Rocinante's straps well, and wait here, because I will come back shortly, dead or alive."

Sancho noticing that his master was serious, and how little his tears and petition succeeded with him, was determined to remedy this situation with his inventiveness and persuade him, if he could, to wait until daylight; and so, while tightening the straps of the horse, he quietly and without being noticed, with his donkey's reins tied both of Rocinante's legs, so that when Don Quixote attempted to go he would be unable to as the horse could only move by jumping. Seeing the success of his trick, Sancho Panza said:

"See there, señor! Heaven, moved by my tears and prayers, has ordered it that Rocinante cannot walk; and if you will be stubborn, you will only provoke fortune."

Don Quixote grew desperate, but the more he drove his heels into the horse, the less he moved him; and not having any suspicion about the tying, he was disappointed to resign and wait until day or until Rocinante could move, firmly persuaded that all of this came from something other than Sancho's ingenuity. So, he said to him, "As it is, Sancho, Rocinante cannot move, I am content to wait until dawn comes, even if I cry while it delays its coming."

"There is no need to cry," answered Sancho, "because I will amuse you by telling stories from now until daylight, unless you would like to dismount and lie down to sleep a little on the green grass as Knights do, so you can be fresher when the day comes and the moment arrives for attempting this extraordinary adventure you are looking forward to."

"What are you talking about dismounting or sleeping for?" said Don Quixote. "You think, I am, one of those Knights that take their rest in the presence of danger? Sleep you who are born to sleep, or do as you will, because I will act as I think most consistent with my character."

"Do not be angry, master," replied Sancho, "I did not mean to say that;" and coming close to him he placed one hand on the saddle and the other on the stirrup, not daring to separate from him; as he was so afraid of the drumming noise which still echoed with a regular beat. Don Quixote asked him tell some story to amuse him as he had proposed, to which Sancho replied that he would if his fear of what he heard would let him; "Still," he said, "I will tell a story which, if I can manage to say it, and nobody interferes, is one of the best stories, give me your attention, because here I begin. What was, was; and may the good that is to come, come for everyone, and the evil for him who goes to look for it - you must know that in the beginning, the older generations' stories were not just whatever pleased them; they were proverbs of Cato Zonzorino the Roman, who said 'the evil for him that goes to look for it,' and this fits perfectly to the purpose now, as a ring on a finger, to show that you should keep quiet and not go looking for evil, and that we should go back by some other road, since nobody forces us to follow this path with which so many terrors frighten us."

"Go on with your story, Sancho," said Don Quixote, "and leave the choice of our road to me."

"I say then," continued Sancho, "that in a village of Estremadura there was a shepherd - that is to say, one who tended to sheep - who was called Lope Ruiz, and this Lope Ruiz was in love with a shepherdess called Torralva, and this shepherdess Torralva was the daughter of a rich farmer, and this rich farmer-"

"If that is the way you tell your story, Sancho," said Don Quixote, "repeating twice everything you have to say, you will not be finished in two days; go on with it, and tell it like a reasonable man, or else say nothing."

"Stories are always told in my country in the same way I am telling this," answered Sancho, "and I cannot tell it in any other, neither is it right of you to ask me to make new customs."

"Tell it as you want," replied Don Quixote; "and as fate decides that I cannot help listening to you, go on."

"And so," continued Sancho, as I have said, this shepherd was in love with Torralva the shepherdess, who was a wild curvaceous lady with the look of a man about her, because she had little moustache hairs; I can imagine her now."

"Then you knew her?" said Don Quixote.

"I did not know her," said Sancho, "but he who told me the story said it was so true and certain that when I tell it to another I might safely say and swear I had seen it all myself. And so in course of time, the devil, who never sleeps and puts everything in confusion, contrived that the love the shepherd had for the shepherdess turned into hatred, and the reason, according to some, was a little jealousy she caused, that crossed the line and trespassed on forbidden ground; and so much did the shepherd hate her from that time forward that, in order to escape from her, he determined to leave the country and go where he would never set eyes on her again. Torralva, when she found herself rejected by Lope, was immediately taken with love for him, although she had never loved him before."

"That is the natural way of women," said Don Quixote, "to disrespect the one that loves them, and love the one that hates them: go on, Sancho."

"It came to be," said Sancho, "that the shepherd carried out his intention, and having his sheep in front of him he made his way across the land of Estremadura to reach the Kingdom of Portugal. Torralva, who knew of it, went after him, and on foot and barefoot followed him at a distance, with a walking stick in her hand and a pendant around her neck, in which she carried, it is said, a small mirror, a comb and a little make up for her face; but whatever she carried, I am not going to trouble myself to prove it; all I say is, that the shepherd, they say, went with his flock to cross the river Guadiana, which was at that time full and almost overflowing its banks, and for him there was no ferry or boat or anyone to carry him or his flock to the other side, at which he was quite annoyed, because he noticed that Torralva was approaching and would annoy him a lot with her tears and appeals; however, he went looking and he discovered a fisherman who had a boat so small that it could only hold one person and one sheep; but he spoke to him and agreed with him to carry himself and his three hundred sheep across. The fisherman got into the boat and carried one sheep over; he came back and carried another over; he came back again, and again brought over another - you keep count of the sheep the fisherman is taking across, because if one escapes the memory that will be the end of the story, and it will be impossible to tell another word of it. To proceed, I must tell you the landing place on the other side was muddy and slippery, and the fisherman lost a lot of time coming and going; but still he returned for another sheep, and another, and another."

"OK ok, let us just say he brought them all across," said Don Quixote, "and don't keep coming and going in this way, or the sheep will not have been transported even in a year from now."

"How many have gone across so far?" said Sancho.

"How the hell do I know?" replied Don Quixote.

"There it is," said Sancho, "what did I tell you, that you must keep count; well then, by God, that is the end of the story, it cannot go any further."

"How can that be?" said Don Quixote; "is so essential to the story to know exactly how many sheep that have crossed over, that if there is a mistake in counting, you cannot go on with it?"

"No, señor, not a bit," replied Sancho; "because when I asked you worship to tell me how many sheep have crossed, and you answered that you did not know, at that instant all I had to say left my memory, and, trust, there was much virtue in this story and entertainment."

"So, then," said Don Quixote, "the story has come to an end?"

"As much as my mother has," said Sancho.

"In truth," said Don Quixote, "you have told one of the rarest stories, tales, or histories that anyone in the world could have imagined, and with such a way of telling it and ending it that this will not be heard again in a lifetime; although I expected nothing else from your excellent understanding. But I do not wonder, because perhaps that ceaseless drumming may have confused your head."

"All that may be," replied Sancho, "but I know in regards to my story, all that can be said is that it ends there where the mistake in the count of the sheep begins."

"Let it end there then," said Don Quixote, "and let us see if Rocinante can move now;" and again he dug his heels into him, and again Rocinante jumped and remained where he was.

Just then, whether it was the cold of the morning that was now approaching, or that he had eaten something laxative at dinner, or that it was only natural (as is most likely), Sancho felt a desire to do what no one could do for him; but due to the fear that had penetrated his heart, he could not separate himself from his master as much as the dirt under his nails; to escape doing what he was about to do, however, was also impossible; so what he did was to remove his right hand, which held the back of the saddle, and with it to untie gently and silently the string which held up his trousers, so that on loosening it they immediately fell down around his feet; he then raised his shirt as well as he could. With this accomplished, which he thought was all he needed to do to get out of this situation and embarrassment, another greater difficulty presented itself, because it seemed to him impossible to relieve himself without making some noise, so he grit his teeth and squeezed his shoulders together, holding his breath as much as he could; but in spite of his precautions he was unlucky enough after all of that to make a little noise, far from it.

Don Quixote, hearing it, said, "What noise is that, Sancho?"

"I don't know, señor," he said; "it must be something new, because adventures and misadventures never begin with silence." Once more he tried again, and succeeded so well, that without any further noise or disturbance he found himself relieved of the burden that had given him so much discomfort. But as Don Quixote's sense of smell was as acute as his hearing, and as Sancho was standing so close to him that the fumes rose almost in a straight line, it could not be possible that some would reach his nose, and as soon as they did he relieved himself of the smell by compressing his nose between his fingers, saying, "Sancho, it appears to me that you are in great fear."

"I am," answered Sancho; "but how do you perceive it now more than ever?"

"Because now you smell stronger than ever, and not of perfume," answered Don Quixote.

"Very likely," said Sancho, "but that's not my fault, but yours, for leading me at unusual hours into such unexpected places."

"Then go back, my friend," said Don Quixote, all the time with his fingers on his nose; "because it is my great familiarity with you that has produced this disapproval."

"I bet," replied Sancho, "that you think I have done something I should not do."

"It makes it worse to makes jokes about it, friend Sancho," returned Don Quixote.

With this and other talk of the same sort master and man spent the night, until Sancho, observing that day was coming, very cautiously untied Rocinante. And as soon as Rocinante found himself free, although by nature he was not at all energetic, he seemed to feel lively and began dancing. Don Quixote, then, observing that Rocinante could move, took it as a good sign and a signal that he should attempt the dangerous adventure. By this time day had fully revealed itself and everything could be seen distinctly, and Don Quixote saw that he was among some tall trees, chestnuts, which cast a very deep shade; he perceived likewise that the sound of the strokes did not stop, but could not discover what caused them, and so without any further delay he let Rocinante feel his heels, and once more about to leave Sancho, he told him to wait for him there for three days at the most, as he had said before, and if he had not returned by that time, he could feel sure that it had been God's will that he should end his days during that dangerous adventure. He again repeated the message with which he was to go on his behalf to his lady Dulcinea, and said he was not to be upset about the payment of his services, because before leaving home he had made his will, in which he would find himself fully compensated in the matter of wages in due proportion to the time he had served; but if God returned him safe, sound, unhurt and out of that danger, he could consider the promised island much more than certain. Sancho began to cry again hearing the words of his good master and committed to stay with him until the final outcome of this adventure. From these tears and this honourable firmness of Sancho Panza the author of this history infers that he must have been of good character and at least an old Christian; and the feeling he displayed touched Don Quixote but not enough to make him show any weakness; on the contrary, hiding what he felt as well as he could, he began to move towards where the sound of the water and of the drumming seemed to come from.

Sancho followed him on foot, leading by the halter, as his custom was, his donkey, his constant companion in prosperity or adversity; and advancing some distance through the shady chestnut trees they came to a little meadow at the foot of some high rocks, down which a mighty rush of water threw itself. At the foot of the rocks were some badly constructed houses looking more like ruins, from among which came, they perceived, the sound of the drumming, which still continued without pause. Rocinante was frightened by the noise of the water and the drumming, but leaving him Don Quixote advanced step by step towards the houses, calling with all his heart to his lady, asking for her support to remove any fear, and on the way calling on God, not to forget him. Sancho who never left his side, stretched his neck as far as he could and looked between the legs of Rocinante to see if he could now discover what it was that caused him such fear and apprehension. They went a little closer, when on turning a corner the true cause, beyond the possibility of any mistake, of that fear producing and to them awe-inspiring noise that had kept them all night in such fear and perplexity, appeared plain and obvious; and it was (if, the reader, is not disgusted and disappointed) six hammers designed to clear the impurities of our clothing, which by their alternate strokes made all the noise.

When Don Quixote saw what it was, he was rigid from head to foot. Sancho glanced at him and saw him with his head bent down on his chest in disappointment, and Don Quixote glanced at Sancho and saw him with his cheeks puffed out and his mouth full of laughter, and evidently ready to explode with it, and in spite of his anger he could not help laughing at the sight of him; and when Sancho saw his master begin he let go so heartily that he had to hold his sides with both hands to keep himself from bursting with laughter. Four times he stopped, and many times his laughter started again with the same violence as the first, then Don Quixote grew furious, above all when he heard him say mockingly, "you must know, friend Sancho, that it was Heaven's will that I was born in this iron age to revive in it the golden or age of gold; I am a man reserved for danger, mighty achievements, and courageous deeds;" and he went on repeating the words that Don Quixote had said the first time they heard the drumming.

Don Quixote, then, seeing that Sancho was ridiculing him, was so angered that he lifted up his lance and struck him with two blows that if, instead of catching him on his shoulders, had stuck him on his head, there would have been no wages to pay, unless to his heirs. Sancho seeing that he was getting a bad return for his fun, and fearing his master might carry on further, said to him very humbly, "calm down, sir, I am only joking."

"Well, then, if you are joking I am not," replied Don Quixote. "Look here, lively gentleman, if these, instead of being cleaning hammers, had been some dangerous adventure, do you not think, I have shown the courage required for the achievement? Am I, by chance, being, as I am, a gentleman, obliged to know and distinguish sounds and tell whether they come from cleaning hammers or not; and that, when perhaps, as is the case, I have never in my life seen any of these? But if these six hammers were six giants, and attacked me, one by one or all together, and I did not knock them all out, then you could make whatever jokes you like."

"No more of that, señor," returned Sancho; "I I went a little too far with the joke. But tell me, now that peace has been made between us (and may God bring you out of all the adventures that may come to you as safe and sound as he has brought you out of this one), was it not a thing to laugh at, and is it not a good story, the great fear we were in? At least that I was in; because as I see now that you neither know or understand what fear is."

"I do not deny," said Don Quixote, "that what happened to us may be worth laughing at, but it is not worth making a story about, because not everyone is smart enough to have the right type of thinking around this."

"At any rate," said Sancho, "you knew how to hit the right point with your lance, aiming at my head and hitting my shoulders, thanks to God and my own smartness in dodging it. But let that go, I have heard God say 'he who makes you cry loves you well;' and moreover that it is the way with great lords after any hard words that they give their servant a pair of new trousers; although I do not know what they give after blows, unless maybe Knights after blows give islands, or kingdoms on the mainland."

"That may be on the cards," said Don Quixote, "All you say will come true; overlook the past, because you are smart enough to know that our first movements are not in our own control; and one thing for the future to bear in mind, that you should control and restrain your talkativeness in my company; because in all the books of chivalry that I have ever read, and there are so many, I never discovered any aide who talked so much to his master as you do to me; and in fact I feel it would be a great fault of mine: that you have so little respect for me; that I do not make myself more respected. There was Gandalin, the squire of Amadis of France, and we read of him that he always addressed his lord with his cap in his hand, his head bowed down. And then, there was Gasabal, the aide of Galaor, who was so silent that in order to indicate to us the greatness of his marvellous silence his name is only mentioned once in the whole of that history, as long as it is truthful. From all I have said you will gather, Sancho, that there must be a difference between master and man, between lord and messenger, between Knight and aide: so that from this day forward in our discussions we must observe more respect and be less loose, because in whatever way I may be angered with you it will be bad for the story. The favours and benefits that I have promised you will come in due time, and if they do not your wages at least will not be lost, as I have already told you."

"All that your worship says is very well," said Sancho, "but I would like to know (in case the time of favours do not come, and it might be necessary to fall back on wages) how much did a Knight's aide get in those days, and were they paid by the month, or by the day?"

"I do not believe," replied Don Quixote, "that aides were ever on wages, but were dependent on favours; and if I have now mentioned mine in the sealed will I have left at home, it was with a view to what may happen; because as yet I do not know how chivalry will turn out in these disgraceful times of ours, and I do not wish my soul to suffer in the other world; because you should know, Sancho, that in this there is no condition more hazardous than that of adventurers."

"That is true," said Sancho, "since the mere noise of the hammers of a cleaning mill can disturb and disquiet the heart of such a valiant Knight adventurer as you; you can be sure I will not open my lips from now on to make any fun of you, but only to honour you as my master and natural lord."

"By so doing," replied Don Quixote, "you will live a long life on earth; because after parents, masters are to be respected as though they were parents."

CHAPTER 21

THE GLORIOUS ADVENTURE AND PRIZE OF MAMBRINO'S HELMET, TOGETHER WITH OTHER THINGS THAT HAPPENED TO OUR INVINCIBLE KNIGHT

It began to rain a little, and Sancho wanted to go into the cleaning mills, but Don Quixote had taken a disliking to them due to the jokes made earlier; so, turning to the right they came to another road, different from that which they had taken the night before. Shortly afterwards Don Quixote noticed a man on horseback who wore on his head something that shone like gold, and the moment he saw him he turned to Sancho and said:

"I think, Sancho, there is no other proverb better than this, all sayings being drawn from experience, the mother of all sciences, the one that says, 'where one door shuts, another opens.' I say so because if last night shut the door to the adventure we were looking for, cheating us with the cleaning mills, it now opens another one for a better and more certain adventure, and if I do not plan to enter it, it will be my own fault, and I cannot blame it on my ignorance of the cleaning mills, or the darkness of the night. I say this because, if I am not mistaken, coming towards us is someone who wears on his head the helmet of Mambrino, concerning the oath I took, you remember?"

"Mind what you say sir, and even more what you do," said Sancho, "because I don't want any more cleaning mills to continue hammering and knock our senses out."

"Has the devil got you man?" said Don Quixote; "what has a helmet got to do with cleaning mills?"

"I don't know," replied Sancho, "but, if I may speak as I used to, perhaps I could give some reasons so you would see you were mistaken in what you say."

"How can I be mistaken in what I say, unbelieving traitor?" returned Don Quixote; "tell me, do you not see there, a Knight coming towards us on a small grey horse, who has on his head a helmet of gold?"

"What I see and make out," answered Sancho, "is only a man on a grey donkey like my own, who has something that shines on his head."

"Well, that is the helmet of Mambrino," said Don Quixote; "stand to one side and leave me alone with him; you will see how, without saying a word, to save time, I will bring this adventure to an end and possess for myself the helmet I have longed for."

"I will take care to stand aside," said Sancho; "but, I say once more, that it may be something else like the cleaning mills."

"I have told you, brother, not to mention those cleaning mills to me again," said Don Quixote, "or I promise, and I will not say it again -I will pull the soul out of you."

Sancho was silent in fear believing that his master would carry out the promise.

The fact of the matter in regards the helmet, horse, and Knight that Don Quixote saw, was this: In that neighbourhood there were two villages, one of them so small that it did not have a chemist or barber shop, which the other that was close to it had, so the barber of the larger served the smaller, and in it there was a man who wanted to be shaved, so the barber was travelling for this, carrying with him a brass washbowl; but as luck would have it, as he was on the way it began to rain, and not to spoil his hat, which probably was a new one, he put the basin on his head, and being clean it sparkled in the distance. He rode on a grey donkey, as Sancho said, and this was what made it seem to Don Quixote to be a small grey horse and a Knight and a golden helmet; because everything he saw he made to fall in with his crazy chivalry notions; and when he saw the poor man come closer, without entering into any discussion with him, at Rocinante's top speed he rushed toward him with the lance pointed, fully determined to pierce him right through, and as he reached him, without stopping the fury of his charge, he shouted:

"Defend yourself, miserable being, or yield to me that which is reasonably due."

The barber, who without any expectation or apprehension of it saw this spirit coming toward him, and had no other way of saving himself from the strike of the lance but to let himself fall off his donkey; and no sooner had he touched the ground, he sprang up more quickly than a deer and ran away across the field faster than the wind.

He left the basin on the ground, with which Don Quixote contented himself, saying that the pagan had shown his caution and imitated the beaver, which finding itself chased by the hunters, bites and cuts off with its teeth, by its natural instinct, that which it knows it is pursued for.

He told Sancho to pick up the helmet, and taking it in his hands he said:

"God the basin is a good one, and worth a lot," and handed it to his master, who immediately put it on his head, turning it around, now this way, now that way, in search of the correct fit, and not finding it he said, "Clearly the pagan this famous head-piece was first made for must have had a very large head."

When Sancho heard him call the basin a headpiece he was unable to restrain his laughter but remembering his master's anger he stopped himself in the middle of it.

"What are you laughing at, Sancho?" said Don Quixote.

"I am laughing," he said, "to think of the large head the pagan must have had who owned this helmet, because it looks exactly like a regular barber's basin."

"Do you know what I suspect, Sancho?" said Don Quixote; "that this wonderful helmet must by some strange accident have come into the hands of someone who was unable to recognise or realise its value, and who, not knowing what he did, and seeing it to be of the purest gold, must have melted down one half for the sake of what it might be worth, and of the other made this which is like a barber's basin as you say; but be it as it may, to me who recognises it, its transformation makes no difference, because I will set it right at the first village where there is a metal worker, and in such style that this helmet, the god of helmet makers has created for the god of battles, will not surpass it or even come close to it; and in the meantime I will wear it as well as I can, because something is better than nothing; and it will be enough to protect me from any potential blow from any stone."

"That is," said Sancho, "if it is not shot with a sling as in the battle of the two armies, when they knocked your teeth out and smashed the flask containing that concoction that made me vomit."

"It does not upset me much to have lost it," said Don Quixote, "because you know, Sancho, that I have the recipe in my memory."

"So have I," answered Sancho, "but if ever I make it, or try it again as long as I live, may it be my last hour; I have no intention of putting myself in any need of it, because I intend, with all my five senses, to keep myself from being wounded or from wounding anyone: as to being blanketed again I say nothing, because it is hard to prevent mishaps of that sort, and if they come, there is nothing to do but to squeeze our shoulders together, hold our breath, shut our eyes, and let ourselves go where luck and the blanket may send us."

"You are a bad Christian, Sancho," said Don Quixote after hearing this, "because once an injury has been done to you, you never forget it: but know that it is the part of noble and generous hearts not to attach importance to these things. What injured leg have you got from it, what broken rib, what cracked head, which makes you unable to forget the past? It was not injurious, they did it for fun, and had I not seen it in that light I would have returned and done more damage seeking revenge for you than the Greeks did for the rape of Helen, who, if she were alive now, or if my Dulcinea had lived then, we could depend on it that she would not be as famous for her beauty as she is;"

Sancho said, "Let it pass for fun as it cannot be revenged, but I know what sort of fun it was, and I know it will never be rubbed out of my memory any more than off my shoulders. But putting that aside, will you tell me what are we to do with this little-grey horse that looks like a grey donkey, which that Martino that you overthrew has left deserted here? Because, from the way he ran, he is not likely to ever come back for it; and God the grey horse is a good one."

"I have never been in the habit," said Don Quixote, "of taking the horses of those who I vanquish, neither is it the practice of chivalry to take away their horses and leave them to go on foot, unless the victor has lost his own in combat, in which case it is lawful to take the horse of the vanquished as a thing won in lawful war; therefore, Sancho, leave this horse, or donkey, or whatever you take it to be; because when its owner sees we have left he will come back for it."

"God knows I would like to take it," said Sancho, "or at least to change it for my own, which does not seem to me as good as that one: sure the laws of chivalry are strict, since they cannot be altered to let one donkey be changed for another; I would like to know if I can at least change the accessories."

"On that matter I am not quite sure," answered Don Quixote, "and the matter being doubtful, pending better information, I say you can change them, if you have urgent need of them."

"It is very urgent," answered Sancho, "if they were for me personally I could not want them more;" and so, fortified by this authorisation, he began switching the fittings over, kitting his donkey out to the maximum and making quite another thing of it. This done, they satisfied their hunger with the remains of the rewards from the battle which they raided from the other donkey, and drank from the stream that flowed from the cleaning mills, without looking in that direction, due to the disgust they held for it, for the alarm it had caused them; and, all anger and gloom removed, they mounted and, without taking any determined road (being the right thing for true Knights), they set off, guided by Rocinante's will, which carried along with it that of his master, which found the main road and pursued it without any particular aim.

As they went along, in this way Sancho said to his master, "Señor, would you allow me to speak a little to you? Because since you placed a hard injunction of silence on me several things I should have said have gone rotten, and I have one right now on the tip of my tongue that I don't want to be spoiled."

"Go on, Sancho," said Don Quixote, "and be brief in your speech, because there is no pleasure in one that is long."

"Well then, señor," returned Sancho, "for the past few days I have been considering how little is gained by going in search of these adventures that you seek, when, even if the most dangerous are victoriously achieved, there is no one to see or know of them, and so they must be left untold forever, to the loss of your objective and the credit you deserve; therefore it seems to me it would be better (unless you have better judgment) if we were to go and serve some emperor or other great prince who may have some war going on, in whose service you may prove your worth, your great might, and greater understanding, on observing this the lord in whose service we may be will reward us, each according to his merits; and there you will not be at a loss for someone to put down your achievements in writing to preserve them forever. Of course, my own will not go beyond the limits of an aide, although I make a bold statement to say that, if it is the practice in chivalry to write the achievements of aides, I do not think mine should be left out."

"You are close to being right, Sancho," answered Don Quixote, "but before that point is reached it is necessary for a Knight to roam the world, as he were on trial, seeking adventures, in order that, by achieving some, name and fame may be acquired, so that when he takes himself to the court of some great monarch the Knight will already be known by his deeds, and that the young men, the instant they see him enter the gate of the city, will all follow him and surround him, crying, 'This is the Knight of the Sun' or the Serpent, or any other title under which he may go. 'This,' they will say, 'is the Knight who vanquished in single combat the gigantic Brocabruno of mighty strength; he who rescued the great Mameluke of Persia from the long enchantment under which he had been for almost nine hundred years.' So between one another they will proclaim his achievements; and by the commotion of the boys and the others, the King of that Kingdom will appear at the windows of his royal palace, and as soon as he observes the Knight, recognising him by his design and the engraving on his shield, will of course say, 'Go ahead all of you, the Knights of my court, to welcome the height of chivalry who comes here!' At this command all will go out, and he himself, advancing half-way down the stairs, will embrace him closely, and salute him, kissing him on the cheek, and will then lead him to the Queen's room, where the Knight will find her with the Princess, her daughter, who will be one of the most beautiful and accomplished ladies that could with the greatest pain be discovered anywhere in the known world. Straight-away she will fix her eyes on the Knight and he will fix his on her, and each will seem to the other something more divine than human, and, without knowing how or why they will be taken and entangled in strings of love and distressed in their hearts not to see any way of making their pain and suffering known to each other by words. Then they will lead him, no doubt, to some richly decorated room of the palace, where, having removed his armour, they will bring him a rich scarlet robe to dress himself in, and if he looked noble in his armour he will look even more so in a robe. When night comes he will eat and drink with the King, Queen, and Princess; and all the time he will never take his eyes off her, stealing secret glances, unnoticed by those present, and she will do the same, and with equal cautiousness, being, as I have said, a lady of great discretion. The tables being removed, suddenly through the door of the hall there will enter a hideous and tiny dwarf followed by a charming lady between two giants, who comes with a certain adventure, the work of an ancient sage; and he who resolves it will be regarded as the best Knight in the world.

"The King will then command all those present to attempt it, and none will bring it to an end and conclusion except the new Knight, which only enhances his fame, and by this the Princess will be overjoyed and will esteem herself happy and fortunate for having fixed and placed her thoughts so high. And the best of it is that this King, or Prince, or whatever he is, is engaged in a very bitter war with another as powerful as himself, and the new Knight, after having spent some days at his court, requests to leave him to go and serve him in this war. The King will grant it immediately, and the Knight will politely kiss his hands for the favour he has given him; and that night he will go to speak to his lady the Princess from outside the room where she sleeps, which looks upon a garden, where he has already had many conversations with her, through the messenger, a friend and highly trusted lady of the Princess. He will sigh, she will faint, the lady will get her some water, much distressed because as the morning approaches, and for the honour of her lady she does not want them to be discovered; at last the Princess will wake and will present her white hands through the window to the Knight, who will kiss them a thousand times, covering them with his tears. It will be arranged between them how they are going to inform each other of their good or bad fortune, and the Princess will ask him to make his absence as short as possible, which he will promise to do with many oaths; once more he will kiss her hands, and leave in such heartache that he is almost ready to die. He takes himself to his room, throws himself on his bed, cannot sleep due to the sorrow, rises early the next morning, goes to say goodbye to the King, Queen, and Princess, and, as he leaves, it is said to him that the Princess is reluctant and cannot be visited; the Knight thinks it is from grief over his departure, his heart is pierced, and he is hardly able to maintain hiding his pain. The friend is present, observes everything, goes to tell the Princess, who listens with tears and says that one of her greatest sorrows is not knowing who this Knight is, and whether he is from a kingly lineage or not; the lady assures her that such courtesy, gentleness, and bravery that her Knight possesses could not exist in anyone except someone who was royal and illustrious; her anxiety is relieved, and she tries to be in a good mood otherwise she would excite suspicion from her parents, and at the end of two days she appears in public. Meanwhile the Knight has made his departure; he fights in the war, conquers the King's enemy, wins many cities, triumphs in many battles, returns to the court, sees his lady, and it is agreed that he will ask for her hand in marriage from her parents as the reward for his services; the King is unwilling to give her, as he does not know who he is, however, whether done in secret or any other way, the Princess becomes his bride, and her father then regards it as good fortune; because eventually this Knight is proven to be the son of a valiant King of some Kingdom, I do not know where, because I think it is unlikely to be on the map. The father dies, the Princess inherits, and in few words the Knight becomes King. And this is the point where he presents the rewards to his aide and all who have aided him in rising to such an exalted rank. He marries his aide to a lady of the Princess, who will be, no doubt, the one who was the confidante in their love, and is the daughter of a very great duke."

"That's what I want!" said Sancho. "That's what I'm waiting for; because all of this, word for word, is in store for you under the title of the Knight of the Sorrowful Face."

"You do not need to doubt it, Sancho," replied Don Quixote, "because in the same manner, and by the same steps as I have described here, Knights rise and have risen to be Kings and emperors; all we want now is to find out what King or Christian is at war and has a beautiful daughter; but there will be enough time to think of that, because, as I have told you, fame must be won in other ways before appearing before a King. There is another thing, too, that is missing; because supposing we find a King who is at war and has a beautiful daughter, and that I have won incredible fame throughout the world, I do not know how it can be proven that I am from a royal lineage, or even second cousin to an emperor; because the King will not be willing to give me his daughter in marriage unless he is first thoroughly satisfied on this point, however as much my famous deeds may deserve it; with this deficiency I fear I will lose what my deeds have fairly earned. It is true that I am a gentleman of a known house, estate and property, and entitled to a large salary; and it may be that the sage who will write my history will clear up my ancestry so that I may find myself the fifth or sixth in descent of a

King; because you should know, Sancho, that there are two kinds of lineages in the world; some are traceable and derive their descent from Kings and Princesses, who time has reduced little by little until they end in a point like a pyramid upside down; and others who spring from the common group of men and go forward rising step by step until they become great lords; so the difference is that some were and are no longer are, and the others are now what they were not. And I may be one of those that after investigation my origin may be proven great and famous, with which the King, my father-in-law to be, should be satisfied; and if he is not, the Princess will love me so much that even if she knew me to be the son of a water-carrier, she will take me for her lord and husband despite her father; if not, then I will take her and carry her to wherever I like; because time or death will put an end to the madness of her parents."

"It comes to this, too," said Sancho, "what some naughty people say, 'Never ask as a favour what you can take by force;' although it would be better to say, 'A clear escape is better than good men's prayers.' I say this because if my lord the King, your father-in-law, will not humble himself and give you my lady the Princess, there is nothing you can do but, as you say, take her and transport her. But the trouble is that until harmony is made and you come into the peaceful enjoyment of your Kingdom, the poor aide is hungry as far as rewards go, unless it be that the lady acting as confidante that is to be his wife comes with the Princess, and that with her he repairs his bad luck; because his master, I suppose, can give her to him immediately as a lawful wife."

"Nobody can object to that," said Don Quixote.

"Then since that can be," said Sancho, "there is nothing left but to commit ourselves to God, and let fortune take whatever course it will."

"God guide it according to my wishes and my wants," said Don Quixote, "and he who thinks of himself as mean will be mean."

"In God's name let him be," said Sancho: "I am an old Christian, and to make me a gentleman is enough."

"More than enough for you," said Don Quixote; "and even if you were not, it would make no difference, because I being the King can easily give you nobility without any service rendered by you, because when I make you a nobleman, then you are immediately a gentleman; and they may say what they want, but I will ensure that they will have to call you 'your lordship,' whether they like it or not."

"No doubt; and I will know how to upkeep the tittle," said Sancho.

"You should say Title, not tittle," said his master.

"So be it," answered Sancho. "I say I will know how to behave, because once in my life I was an officer of a brotherhood, and the officer's gown fit so well on me that everyone said I looked as if I was the steward of the same brotherhood. What will it be, then, when I put a duke's robe on my back, or dress myself in gold and pearls like a nobleman? I believe people will come from all over the world to see me."

116

"You will look very well," said Don Quixote, "but you must shave your beard often, because you have it so thick, rough and un-kept, and if you do not shave it every other day at least, they will see what you really are."

"What more will it be," said Sancho, "than having a barber, and keeping him on wages in the house? And even if it is necessary, I will make him go with me like a nobleman's officer."

"How do you know that noblemen have officers?" asked Don Quixote.

"I will tell you," answered Sancho. "Years ago, I spent a month in the capital and there I saw a very small gentleman who they said was a very great man, and a man following him on horseback every turn he took, just as if he was his tail. I asked why this man did not join the other man, instead of always going behind him; he answered that he was his officer, and that it was the custom of noblemen to have such people behind them, and ever since then I knew of it, because I have never forgotten it."

"You are right," said Don Quixote, "and in the same way you may have your barber with you, because customs did not come into use all together, neither were they all invented at once, and you may be the first nobleman to have a barber following him; and, and definitely, shaving someone's beard requires greater trust than saddling someone's horse."

"Let finding a barber be my business," said Sancho; "and yours to strive to become a King and make me a nobleman."

"Let it be," answered Don Quixote, and raising his eyes he saw what will be told in the following chapter.

CHAPTER 22

THE FREEDOM DON QUIXOTE GAVE TO SEVERAL UNFORTUNATE PEOPLE WHO AGAINST THEIR WILL WERE BEING TAKEN WHERE THEY HAD NO WISH TO GO

Benengeli, the Arab and Manchegan author, states in this most serious, and original history that after the discussion between the famous Don Quixote of La Mancha and his aide Sancho Panza which was noted at the end of chapter twenty-one, Don Quixote raised his eyes and saw that going along the road he was following about a dozen men on foot strung together by the neck, like beads on a chain, and all with shackles on their hands. With them there was also two men on horseback and two on foot; those on horseback with guns, those on foot with swords, and as soon as Sancho saw them he said:

"That is a chain of slaves, on the way to a ship by force of the King's orders."

"How by force?" asked Don Quixote; "is it possible that the King uses force against anyone?"

"No, not his direct force, just his orders," answered Sancho, "these people are condemned for their crimes to serve on the King's ship."

"In fact," replied Don Quixote, "however it may be, these people are being taken force, and not by their own will."

"Exactly," said Sancho.

Then if so," said Don Quixote, "here is a case for me to exercise my duty, to stop this force and to help the poor."

"Do you recollect," said Sancho, "The King administers justice himself, not using force or doing wrong to these people, but punishing them for their crimes."

The slaves were now closer, and Don Quixote in very polite language asked those who were leading them to be good enough to tell him the reason or reasons for why they were taking these people in this manner. One of the guards on horseback answered that they were slaves belonging to the King, that they were going to the ship to work, and that was all that was to be said and that he had no business to know.

"Nevertheless," replied Don Quixote, "I would like to know from each of them individually the reason for his misfortune;" to this he added more words to induce them to tell him what he wanted to hear, then the other mounted guard said to him:

"Although we have the register and certificate of the sentence of every one of these poor men, this is no time to take them out or read them; ask them yourself; they can tell you if they choose, and they will, because these men find pleasure in doing and talking about crime."

With this permission, which Don Quixote would have taken even if the they had not granted it, he approached the chain and asked the first what offences he had done which led to this.

He answered that it was for being a lover.

"For that only?" replied Don Quixote; "If for being lovers they send people to the ships I would have been rowing in them a long time ago."

"The love is not the type you are thinking of," said the slave; "mine was that I loved a washerwoman's basket of clean linen so well, and held it so close to me, that if the law had not forced it from me, I would have never let go of it even until now; I was caught in the act, there was no time for torture, the case was settled, then they treated me to a hundred whips on the back, and three years of gurapas, and that was the end of it."

"What are gurapas?" asked Don Quixote.

"Gurapas are galleys, which is the place on a ship where the slaves row the oars," answered the slave, who was a young man of about twenty-four, and said he was a native from Piedrahita.

Don Quixote asked the same question to the second, who gave no reply, as he was so down and depressed; but the first answered for him, and said, "He, sir, goes for being a canary, I mean as a musician and a singer."

"What!" said Don Quixote, "for being musicians and singers are people sent to the ships as well?"

"Yes, sir," answered the slave, "because there is nothing worse than singing while suffering."

"On the contrary, I have heard people say," said Don Quixote, "that a man who sings scares away his suffering."

"Here it is the reverse," said the slave; "because a man who sings cries his whole life."

"I do not understand," said Don Quixote; but one of the guards said to him, "Sir, to sing while suffering means to confess under torture; they tortured this sinner and he confessed to his crime, which was being a cattle-thief, and on his confession they sentenced him to six years on the ships, and two hundred whips that he has already had on the back; and he is always depressed and down because the other thieves that got away mistreat him, ignore, mock, and despise him for confessing and not having the spirit to say no; because, they say, 'no' has less letters in it than 'yes,' and that a criminal is safe when his life or death depends on his own tongue and not on that of a witnesses or evidence; and to my thinking they are not wrong."

"I think so too," answered Don Quixote; then coming to the third he asked him what he had asked the others, and the man answered quickly and casually, "I am going for five years to the ships for wanting ten gold coins."

"I will give you twenty to get you out of that trouble," said Don Quixote.

"That," said the slave, "is like a man having money at sea when he is dying of hunger and has no way of buying what he wants; I say this because if at the right time I had had those twenty gold coins that you now offer me, I would have exercised the notary's pen and stimulated the attorney's wit with them, so that today I would be in the middle of the plaza of Zocodover in Toledo, and not on this road being lead like a greyhound. But God is great; I have patience, and enough of it."

Don Quixote went to the fourth, a man of honourable appearance and white beard down to his chest, who when hearing himself asked the reason of him being there began to cry without answering, but the fifth acted as his tongue and said, "This worthy man is going to the ships for four years, after being publicly exposed."

"That means," said Sancho Panza, "as I take it, to have been exposed to shame in public."

"Exactly," replied the slave, "and the offence which they gave him his punishment for, was being a body-broker; I mean, in short, that this gentleman was a pimp, and additionally for having a touch of the magician about him."

"If that touch had not been thrown in," said Don Quixote, "he would not deserve, for mere pimping, to row in the ships, but actually to command and be an admiral of them; because the office of the pimp is no ordinary one, being the office of people of discretion, one very necessary in a well-ordered state, and only to be exercised by people of good birth; actually, there should be an inspector and overseer of them, as in other offices; in this way many of the evils would be avoided which are caused by this office being in the hands of stupid and ignorant people, such as women more or less silly, and clowns with little experience, who on urgent occasions, and when inventiveness is needed, do not even know not which is their right hand. I would like to go on, and give reasons to show that it is advisable to choose those who are to take this position in such a necessary office in the state, but this is not the place for it; someday I will explain the matter to someone able to see to it and rectify it; all I say now is, that the additional fact of him being a magician has removed the sorrow it gave me to see these white hairs and this respectful appearance in such a painful position on the account of being a pimp; although I well know there are no enchantments in the world that can move or induce the will as some people say, because our will is free, neither is there a herb or charm that can force it. All that some silly women and frauds do is turn men mad with potions and poisons, pretending that they have the power to cause love, because, as I have said, it is impossible to force the will."

"That is true," said the good old man, "and indeed, sir, as far as the charge of magic goes I was not guilty; but being a pimp I cannot deny; but I never thought I was doing any harm, because my only objective was that the world should enjoy itself and live in peace and quiet, without arguments or troubles; but my good intentions were unable to save me from going where I never expect to come back from, with this many years on me and a urinary illness that never gives me a moment's rest;" and again he began to cry like before. Sancho felt such compassion for him that he took out a gold coin and gave it to him as a donation.

Don Quixote went on and asked another what his crime was, and the man answered.

"I am here because I took a joke too far with a couple of cousins of mine, and with a couple of other cousins who were not mine; in short, I carried the joke so far with them all that it ended in such a complicated increase of association that no accountant could make it clear: it was all proven against me, I got no favour, I had no money, they sentenced me to the ships for six years, I accepted my fate, it is the punishment of my fault; I am a young man; hopefully my life lasts longer, and after this all will go right. If you, sir, have anything to help the poor, God will repay it to you in heaven, and us on earth will petition to him and pray for the life and health of you, that it may be as long and as good as your friendly appearance deserves."

This one was dressed as a student, and one of the guards said he was a great speaker and a very sophisticated Latin scholar.

Behind all of these men was a man of about thirty years old, a very likeable man, except that when he looked, his eyes turned in a little one towards the other. He was chained differently from the rest, because he had a chain so long that it was wound all around his body, and two rings on his neck, one attached to the chain, the other hung two irons bars reaching to his waist with two manacles fixed to them in which his hands were secured by a large lock, so that he could neither raise his hands to his mouth or lower his head to his hands. Don Quixote asked why this man had more chains than the others. The guard replied that it was because he had committed more crimes than all the rest put together, and was so daring and such a villain, that although they led him they did not feel sure about him, and feared he would make an escape.

"What crimes did he commit," said Don Quixote, "if they have not deserved a worse punishment than being sent to the ships?"

"He goes for ten years," replied the guard, "which is the same thing as civil death, and all that needs to be said is that this man is the famous Gines de Pasamonte, otherwise called Ginesillo de Parapilla."

"Gently, señor commissioner," said the slave, "let us have no fixed names or surnames; my name is Gines, not Ginesillo, and my family name is Pasamonte, not Parapilla as you say; let each one mind his own business, and he will be doing enough."

"Speak with less disrespect, master thief of extra measure," replied the commissioner, "if you don't want me to make you hold your tongue with your teeth."

"It is easy to see," returned the slave, "that man goes as God wills, but someone will know some day whether I am called Ginesillo de Parapilla or not."

"Don't they call you that? You liar" said the guard.

"They do," returned Gines, "but I will make them stop calling me that, or I will be shaved, where, I can only do it myself. If you, sir, have anything to give us, give it to us now, and I hope God speeds you up, because you are becoming tiring with all this inquisitiveness about the lives of others; if you want to know about mine, let me tell you I am Gines de Pasamonte, whose life is written in books."

"That is true," said the commissioner, "because he has written his grand story, and has left the book in the prison as a deposit for two hundred coins."

"And I will take it out of deposit," said Gines, "although it is there for the two hundred coins at the moment."

"Is it that good?" said Don Quixote.

"So good," replied Gines, " all I will say about it is that it deals with facts, and facts so neat and pleasing that no lies could match them."

"And how is the book entitled?" asked Don Quixote.

"The 'Life of Gines de Pasamonte,'" replied the subject of it.

"And is it finished?" asked Don Quixote.

"How can it be finished," said the other, "when my life is not yet finished? All that is written is from my birth up to the point when they sent me to the ships again."

"Then you have been there before?" said Don Quixote.

"In the service of God and the King I have been there for four years before, and I know by this time what the whip is like," replied Gines; "and it is no big problem for me to go back to it, because there I will have time to finish my book; I still have many things left to say, and on the ships of Spain there is more than enough free time; although I do not need much time for what I have to write, because I know it by heart."

"You seem like a clever man," said Don Quixote.

"And an unfortunate one," replied Gines, "because misfortune always persecutes good wit."

"It persecutes crooks," said the commissioner.

"I told you already to go gently, master commissioner," said Pasamonte; "no one gave you the permission to mistreat us, but to conduct and take us where the King orders you to; if not, by the mouth of this gentleman it may be that someday the stains of this will come out in the cleaning; hold your tongue and behave well and speak better; and now let's continue walking, because we have had quite enough of this entertainment."

The commissioner lifted his sword to strike Pasamonte in return for his threats, but Don Quixote came between them, and begged him not to mistreat him, as it was not too much to allow someone who had his hands tied to have his tongue free; and turning to all of them he said:

"From all you have told me, dear brothers, it is clear that although they have punished you for your faults, the punishments you are about to endure do not give you much pleasure, and that this goes against your will, and that perhaps one lacked courage under torture, one lacked money, the other lacked support, and lastly the perverted judgment of the judge may have been the cause of your failure to obtain the justice you deserved. All which presents itself now to my mind, urging, persuading, and even compelling me to demonstrate in your case the purpose for which Heaven sent me into the world and caused me to make a pledge to the order of chivalry to which I belong, and the promise I made was to give aid to those in need and under the oppression of the strong. But as I know that it is a mark of prudence not to do in a bad way that which may be done in a fair way, I will ask these gentlemen, the guards and commissioner, to be good enough to release you and let you go in peace, as there will be no lack of others to serve the King under more favourable circumstances; because it seems to me unfair to make slaves of those who God and nature has made free. Furthermore, guards," added Don Quixote, "these poor men have done nothing to you; let each one answer for his own sins; there is a God in Heaven who will not forget to punish the wicked or reward the good; and it is not right that honest men should be the instruments of punishment to others. This request I make gently and quietly, that, if you comply with it, I will have reason to thank you; and, if you will not do so voluntarily, this lance and my might will oblige you to comply with it by force."

"Nonsense!" said the commissioner; "a fine piece of humour he has come out with at last! He wants us to let the King's prisoners go, as if we had any authority to release them, or else he will order us to do so! Go away, sir, and good luck to you; put that basin straight that you have on your head, and do not go looking for three feet on a cat."

"'It is you who is the cat, rat, and devil," replied Don Quixote, and acting on behalf of the word he attacked him so suddenly that without giving him time to defend himself he brought him to the ground wounded by the lance; and he was lucky that it was the one that had the gun. The other guards stood amazed at this unexpected event, but recovering their minds, those on horseback took their swords and attacked Don Quixote, who was waiting for them with great calmness; and no doubt it would have gone badly for him if the slaves, seeing the chance of liberating themselves, had not broken the chain on which they were strung. This created such confusion, that the guards, now rushing to detain the slaves who were breaking loose, left Don Quixote free to attack. Sancho, gave a helping hand to release Gines de Pasamonte, who was the first to stand free and unrestricted, and who, attacking the commissioner, took from him his sword and the gun, with which, aiming at one, he, without discharging it, drove every one of the guards off the field, because they made a run for it to escape Pasamonte's gun, along with the shower of stones the now released slaves were raining on them. Sancho was greatly distressed by the affair, because he anticipated that those who had ran would report the matter to the Holy Brotherhood, who would raise the alarm and go forward in quest of the offenders; so he said so this to his master, and asked him to leave immediately, and go into hiding in the mountain that was close by.

"That is all very well," said Don Quixote, "but I know what has to be done now;" and calling together all the slaves, who were now rebelling, and had stripped the commissioner to his skin, he collected them to hear what he had to say, and said to them as follows: "To be grateful for benefits received is customary from the people of good birth, and one of the sins most offensive to God is ingratitude; I say because, you have already seen manifested the proof of the benefit you have received from me; in return for which I desire, and it is my pleasure that, loaded with that chains which I have taken off your necks, you proceed to the city of El Toboso, and there present yourselves to the lady Dulcinea, and say to her that her Knight, Don Quixote, sends them to commit himself to her; and that you relay to her in full detail all of this notable adventure, up to the recovery of your longed-for freedom; and once this has been done you may go wherever you like, and good fortune will await you."

Gines de Pasamonte answered for all, saying, "That which you, sir, our liberator, demand from us, is out of all the impossibilities, the most impossible to comply with, because we cannot go together along the roads, but separately, and each one on his own way, endeavouring to hide ourselves to escape the Holy Brotherhood, which, no doubt, will come in search of us. What you may do, and fairly do, is to change this service and tribute in regards to the lady Dulcinea del Toboso for a certain quantity of prayers which we will say for you, and this is a condition that can be complied with during the day or night, running or resting, in peace or in war; but to imagine that we are now going to return to Egypt, and you want us to go to El Toboso, is to imagine that it is now night, although it is ten in the morning, and to ask this is like asking pears to grow on an orange tree."

"For that" said Don Quixote (now enthused with rage), "Don son of a bitch, Don Ginesillo de Paropillo, or whatever your name is, you will have to go yourself alone, with your tail between your legs and the whole chain on your back."

Pasamonte, who was anything but timid (being by this time thoroughly convinced that Don Quixote was not quite right in his head as he had committed to such a notion as to set them free), finding himself abused in this fashion, winked to his companions, and they began to shower stones on Don Quixote at such a rate that he was unable to protect himself with his shield, and poor Rocinante did not respond to the heels of Don Quixote as if he had been made of brass. Sancho stood behind his donkey, and with him sheltered himself from the hailstorm that showered on them both. More pebbles than I could count struck Don Quixote full on the body with such force that they brought him to the ground; and the instant he fell the student pounced upon him, snatched the basin from his head, and with it struck three or four blows on his shoulders, and many more on the ground knocking it almost to pieces. They then stripped him of a jacket that he wore over his armour, and they would have stripped off his socks if his crying had not prevented them. From Sancho they took his coat, leaving him in his shirt; and dividing among themselves the remaining food won from the battle, they each went their own way, more concerned about keeping clear of the Holy Brotherhood they feared, than about burdening themselves with the chain, or going to present themselves before the lady Dulcinea del Toboso. The donkey and Rocinante, Sancho and Don Quixote, were all that were left; the donkey with a limp neck, shaking his ears from time to time as if he thought the storm of stones that assaulted them was not yet over; Rocinante lying beside his master, because he too had been brought to the ground by a stone; Sancho stripped, and trembling with fear of the Holy Brotherhood; and Don Quixote furious to find himself treated in this way by the very people who he had done so much for.

CHAPTER 23

WHAT HAPPENED TO DON QUIXOTE IN THE SIERRA MORENA, WHICH WAS ONE OF THE RAREST ADVENTURES IN HISTORY

Seeing himself treated in this way, Don Quixote said to his aide, "I have always heard Sancho, that to do good to fools is the same as throwing water into the sea. If I had believed your words, I would have avoided this trouble; but it is done now, I have to be patient and take this as warning for the future."

"You will take warnings as much as I am a Turk," returned Sancho; "but, as you say this trouble could have been avoided if you had believed me, believe me now and greater misfortunes will be avoided; because I tell you chivalry does not stand for much with the Holy Brotherhood, and they don't care for any of the Knights in the world; and I can tell you, I can imagine hearing their arrows flying past my ears."

"You are a coward by nature, Sancho," said Don Quixote, "but you can say I am stubborn, and I never do as you advise, this once I will take your advice, and withdraw out of reach of that fury you fear; but it must be on one condition, that never, in life or in death, will you say to anyone that I retired or withdrew from this danger out of fear, but only in compliance with your request; because if you say otherwise you will lie, and will lie every time you think or say it; because the thought that I am withdrawing or retiring from any danger, above all from this, which does seem to carry a little shadow of fear with it, makes me ready to stand here and await alone, not only against that Holy Brotherhood you speak of and fear, but the brothers of the twelve tribes of Israel, and the Seven Maccabees, and Castor and Pollux, and all the brothers and brotherhoods in the world."

"Señor," replied Sancho, "to retire is not to run in fear, and there is no wisdom in waiting when danger outweighs hope, and it is normal for wise men to preserve themselves today for tomorrow, and not risk all in one day; and let me tell you, although I am a clown and a fool, I have got some notion of what they call safe conduct; so don't regret not taking my advice, but mount Rocinante if you can, and if not I will help you; and follow me, because my intuition tells me we are in need of more legs than hands right now."

Don Quixote mounted without replying, and, with Sancho leading the way on his donkey, they entered the side of the Sierra Morena a system of mountain ranges, which was close by, as it was Sancho's idea to cross it entirely and come out again at El Viso or Almodovar del Campo, and hide for some days among its mountains to escape the search of the Holy Brotherhood if they come looking for them. He was encouraged when he noticed that the stock of supplies carried by the donkey had come out safe after the fight with the slaves, a circumstance that he regarded as a miracle, seeing how the slaves pillaged and ransacked.

That night they reached the very heart of the Sierra Morena, where it seemed prudent to Sancho to spend the night and even some days, at least as many as the supplies he carried would last, and so they settled between two rocks and among some cork trees; but fatal destiny, which, according to the opinion of those who do not possess the light of the true faith, directs, arranges, and settles everything in its own way, directed that Gines de Pasamonte, the famous thief who by the virtue and madness of Don Quixote had been released from the chain, driven by fear of the Holy Brotherhood, which he had good reason to fear, decided to hide in the mountains; and his fate and fear led him to the same spot which Don Quixote and Sancho Panza had been led by theirs, just in time to recognise them and let them fall asleep: and as the evil are always ungrateful, and un-satisfied they are led to wrongdoing, and immediate advantage overcomes all considerations of the future, Gines, who was neither grateful or well-principled, made up his mind to steal Sancho Panza's donkey, not bothering to take Rocinante, as he was no good either to offer or sell. So, while Sancho slept he stole his donkey, and before the day came he was far out of reach.

The sun made its appearance bringing happiness to the earth but sadness to Sancho Panza, because he found that his donkey was missing, and seeing himself without him he began the saddest and most miserable crying in the world, so loud that Don Quixote awoke due to his cries and heard him saying, "Born in my very house, my children's plaything, my wife's joy, the envy of my neighbours, relief of my burdens, and lastly, joint supporter of myself, with the money you earnt me daily I met half of my expenses."

Don Quixote, when he heard the cry and learned the cause, consoled Sancho with the best arguments he could, asking him to be patient, and promising to give him a letter of exchange ordering three out of five donkeys that he had at home to be given to him. Sancho took comfort in this, dried his tears, and returned thanks for the kindness shown to him by Don Quixote, who was rejoiced to the heart on entering the mountains, as they seemed to him to be just the place for the adventures he was in search of. They brought back to his memory the marvellous adventures that had happened to Knights in similar seclusions and wilderness, and he continued reflecting on these things, so absorbed and carried away by them that he had no thought of anything else.

Neither did Sancho have any other care (now that he thought he was travelling in a safe place) than to satisfy his appetite with the remains of what were left of the supplies, and so he marched behind his master loaded with what the donkey used to carry, emptying the sack and packing his stomach, and so long as he could continue doing this, he would not have given anything to encounter another adventure.

While engaged in this manner he raised his eyes and saw that his master had stopped and was trying with the point of his lance to lift some bulky object that lay on the ground. Seeing this, he rushed to join him and help him if it was needed, and reached him just when, with the point of the lance he was raising a bag attached to it, half or rather wholly rotten and torn; but being so heavy Sancho had to help to lift it, and his master directed him to see what the bag contained. Sancho did so with great eagerness, and although the bag was secured with a chain and padlock, from its torn and rotten condition he was able to see its contents, which were four shirts of fine silk, and other articles of linen no less interesting than clean; and in a handkerchief he found a lot of gold coins, and as soon as he saw them he exclaimed:

"Thank God for sending us an adventure that is good for something!"

Searching further he found a little note book luxuriously bound; Don Quixote asked him for it, telling him to take the money and keep it for himself. Sancho kissed his hands for the goodwill, and emptied the bag of its linen, which he put away in his own.

Considering the whole matter, Don Quixote observed: "It seems to me, Sancho - and it is impossible that it can be otherwise - that some traveller must have crossed this sierra and was attacked, and the attackers brought him to this secluded spot to bury him."

"That cannot be," answered Sancho, "because if they had been robbers they would not have left any of this."

"You are right," said Don Quixote, "and I cannot guess or explain what this may mean; but wait; let us see, if in this note book there is anything written by which we may be able to trace or discover what we want to know."

He opened it, and the first thing he found in it, written roughly but in good handwriting, was a poem, and reading it aloud so Sancho could hear it, he found it went as follows:

POEM

A love lacking in intelligence,
To the height of cruelty, it can attain,
Beyond the measure due to my offence,
Now it is my fate to suffer pain.
But if Love is God, I return to those lanes,
He knows all, and that certainty remains,
No God loves cruelty; then who ordains?
Tormented by charms, Chloe, was her name.
Evil with goodness cannot live,
A miracle alone a cure can give,
Against Heaven I cannot charge the blame,
Now it is my time to die in Spain.

"There is nothing to be learned from that rhyme," said Sancho, "apart from that clue contained in it."

"What clue is there?" said Don Quixote.

"I thought you mentioned a clue in it," said Sancho.

"I only said Chloe," replied Don Quixote; "and that no doubt, is the name of the lady the author wrote this poem about; and he must be an acceptable poet, or I must know little of the craft."

"Then you understand rhyming too?"

"Better than you think," replied Don Quixote, "as you will see when you carry a letter written from beginning to end to my lady Dulcinea del Toboso, because you should know, Sancho, that all or most of the Knights in the earlier days were great poets and musicians, because both of these accomplishments, or more properly speaking: gifts, are the unusual property of lovers: it is true that the verses of the Knights have more spirit than simplicity in them."

"Read more," said Sancho, "and maybe you will find something that will enlighten us."

Don Quixote turned the page and said, "This is prose and seems to be a letter."

"A correspondence letter, señor?"

"From the beginning it seems to be a love letter," replied Don Quixote.

"Then read it aloud," said Sancho, "because I am very fond of matters of love."

"With all my heart," said Don Quixote, and reading it aloud as Sancho had requested him to do, he found it went as follows:

Your false promise and my misfortune take me to a place where the news of my death will reach your ears before the words of my complaint. Ungrateful one, you have rejected me for someone wealthier, but not worthier; and if virtue were esteemed wealth, I would neither envy the fortunes of others or cry for the misfortune of my own. Your beauty was high but your actions were low; from your beauty I believed you were an angel; but from your actions I know you are a woman. I wish peace for you who has sent me war, and I hope that the deceit of your husband will be forever hidden from you, so that you do not repent for what you have done, and I do not find my revenge.

When he had finished the letter, Don Quixote said, "There is less to be gathered from this than from the verses, except that he who wrote it is some rejected lover;" and turning over nearly all the pages of the book he found more verses and letters, some of which he could read, while others he could not; but they were all complaints, cries, doubts, wishes and dislikes, favours and rejections, some joyful, some miserable. While Don Quixote examined the book, Sancho examined the bag, not leaving a corner unsearched, or seam that he did not rip, or bit of wool that he did not pick to pieces, in-case anything could escape that was desirable; he had already been thoroughly enthused by the discovery of the coins, which amounted to nearly a hundred; and although he found no more, he held the blanket flight, balm vomiting, transporter's fight, missing saddle bags, stolen coat, and all the hunger, thirst, and exhaustion he had endured in the service of his good master, cheap; as he considered himself more than fully reimbursed for everything with the payment he received as a gift.

The Knight of the Sorrowful Face was still very anxious to find out who the owner of the bag could be, imagining from the poem and letter, from the money in gold, and from the excellence of the shirts, that he must be a lover of distinction who the cruelty of his lady had driven to some desperate action; but as there was no one to be seen in that uninhabited spot, who he could inquire with, he saw nothing else but to continue on their journey, taking whatever road Rocinante chose - where he could make his way firmly persuaded that among this wilderness he would not fail to find some rare adventure.

As he went along then, occupied with these thoughts, and observed on the peak of a mountain that rose before their eyes a man who was jumping from rock to rock with marvellous agility. As far as he could see he was wearing no protection, was bald-headed, had a thick black beard, and bare legs and feet, his thighs were covered by trousers apparently of yellowish-brown velvet but so ragged that they showed his skin in several places.

The Knight of the Sorrowful Face observed and noted all these trivialities, and although he made the attempt, he was unable to follow him, because it was not possible due to the weakness of Rocinante to proceed over such rough ground, he being, slow-paced and sluggish by nature. Don Quixote immediately came to the conclusion that this was the owner of the bag, and decided to search for him, even if he would have to roam a year in those mountains before he found him, and so he directed Sancho to take a short cut over one side of the mountain, while he himself went another way, and perhaps by this they might catch the man who had passed so quickly out of their sight.

"I can't do that," said Sancho, "because when I separate from you, fear immediately takes over me, and attacks me with all sorts of panic; and let what I say now be a notice to you, that from this day I am not going to separate an inch from your presence."

"As you wish," said the Knight of the Sorrowful Face, "and I am very glad that you are willing to rely on my courage, which will never fail you, even though the soul in your body does; so come on now follow me as well as you can, and watch carefully; let us quickly go around this ridge; perhaps we will find this man that we saw, who no doubt is no other than the owner of what we found."

To which Sancho replied, "It would be far better would if we did not look for him, because, if we find him, and he happens to be the owner of the money, it is clear I will have to give it back; it would be better, therefore, that without taking this needless trouble, for me to keep possession of it until in some other less nosy and intrusive way the real owner can be discovered; and perhaps that will be when I would have spent it, and then the King would consider me innocent."

"You are wrong there, Sancho," said Don Quixote, "because now that we have a suspicion who the owner is, and have him close, we are obliged to seek him and make amends; and if we do not try to find him, the strong suspicion we have as to him being the owner would make us guilty if we chose not to; and so, friend Sancho, do not let our search for him give you any nervousness, because if we find him it will relieve mine."

And so, he gave Rocinante the heels, and Sancho followed him on foot, loaded, and after having partly taken the path around the mountain they found lying in a valley, a donkey, half devoured by dogs, saddled and restrained, all further strengthening their suspicion that he who had fled was the owner of the donkey and the bag.

As they stood looking at it they heard a whistle like that of a shepherd watching his flock, and suddenly on their left appeared a large number of goats and behind them on the summit of the mountain the goat herder in charge of them, a man advanced in years. Don Quixote called out to him and begged him to come down to where they stood. He shouted in return, asking what had brought them to that spot, seldom walked on except by the feet of goats, or wolves and other wild beasts that roamed around. Sancho in return asked him come down, and they would explain it all to him.

The goat herder descended, and reaching the place where Don Quixote stood, he said, "I bet you are looking at that donkey that lies dead. It has now been there for the past six months; tell me, have you seen its master anywhere around here?"

"We have seen nobody," answered Don Quixote, "and nothing else except a little bag that we found not far from here."

"I found it too," said the goat herder, "but I would not touch it or go near it, as I feared I would receive some bad luck or be charged with theft, because the devil is crafty, and things can rise up under our feet to make us fall without seeing it coming."

"That's exactly what I say," said Sancho; "I found it too, and I would not go within a stone's throw of it; I left it there, and there it lies just as it was."

"Tell me, good man," said Don Quixote, "do you know who the owner of it is?"

"All I can tell you," said the goat herder, "is that about six months ago, more or less, three men arrived at a shepherd's hut, perhaps, from these men a youth of well-bred appearance and manners, mounted the same donkey which lies dead here, and with the same saddle and bag which you say you found and did not touch. He asked us what part of this mountain was the most rugged; we told him that it was where we are now; because if you go on half a mile further, perhaps you will not be able to find your way out; and I am wondering how you have managed to come here, because there is no road or path that leads to this spot. On hearing our answer, the youth turned around and left for the place we pointed out to him, leaving us all charmed with his good looks, and wondering why he asked this question and the swiftness with which we saw him leave in the direction of the mountain. After that we did not see him anymore, until some days afterwards he crossed the path of one of our goat herders, and without saying a word to him, went up to him and gave him several punches and kicks, and then went to the donkey with our stock and took all the bread and cheese it carried, and having done this went back again into the mountains with extraordinary swiftness. When some of us goat herders heard this we went to look for him for about two days through the most remote part of this mountain, and eventually we found him wedged in the hollow of a large thick cork tree. He came out to meet us with great gentleness, with his clothes now torn and his face disfigured and burned by the sun, that we hardly recognised him, but his clothes, although torn, convinced us, from the recollection we had of them, that he was the person we were looking for. He saluted us courteously, and in a few well-spoken words he told us not to worry about seeing him with this appearance, as it was justification and a self-punishment for his many sins. We asked him to tell us who he was, but we were not able to find out from him: we begged him, when he was in need of food, which he could not do without, to tell us where we could find him, as we would bring it to him with good-will; or if this were not to his taste, at least to come and ask for it and not to take it by force from us. He thanked us for the offer, asked for forgiveness for the assault, and promised in the future to ask for it from God without offering violence to anybody. As for a fixed home, he said he had none apart from whatever chance offered and wherever the night took him; and his words ended in an outburst of crying so strong that while listening to him we must have been stones if we had not joined him, comparing his condition to the first time we saw him; because, as I said, he was a beautiful and gracious youth, and in his courteous and polished language displayed himself to be a good man.

"But in the middle of his conversation he stopped and became silent, keeping his eyes fixed on the ground for some time, during which we stood still waiting anxiously to see what would come from this abstraction; from his behaviour, now staring at the ground with fixed gaze and eyes wide open without moving an eyelid, again closing them, compressing his lips and raising his eyebrows, we perceived that he was going through a fit of madness of some kind; and not long after he showed that what we imagined was the truth, because he got up in a fury from the ground where he had thrown himself, and attacked the first man in front of him with such rage and fierceness that if we had not dragged him off him, he would have beaten or bitten him to death, all the while exclaiming, 'Faithless Fernando, here, here you pay the penalty of the wrong you have done to me; these hands will tear out your heart, you are a man of all injustice, deceit and fraud above all; and to these he added other words of a similar kind about someone called Fernando and accusing him of disloyalty and faithlessness.

"We forced him to release his hold but it was a struggle, and without another word he left us, and rushing off jumped in-between the brambles, to make it impossible for us to follow him; from this event we supposed that the madness comes to him from time to time, and that someone called Fernando must have done him some harm of a serious nature which created the condition he speared to show. All this has been confirmed by those occasions, and others since then, and there has been many of them, on which he has crossed our path, at one time to beg the herders to give him some of the food they carried, another to take it from them by force; because when he is in a fit of madness, even though the he is offered it freely, he will not accept it but snatches it from them and gives them punches; but when he is in a normal condition he begs the herders and God for it, courteously and politely, and when he receives it he gives many thanks with many tears. And to tell you the truth," continued the goat herder, "it was yesterday that we decided, I and four of the lads, two of them our servants, and the other two friends of mine, to go and search for him until we find him, and when we did, to take him, whether by force or with his own consent, to the town of Almodovar, which is eight miles from here, and there strive to cure him (if his condition is curable), or to gather when he is in a normal condition who he is, and if he has relatives that we may give notice of his misfortune. This, is all I can say in answer to what you have asked me; and be sure that the owner of the items you found is the man you saw pass by with such nimbleness."

Because Don Quixote had already described how he had seen the man go jumping along the mountain side, and he was now filled with amazement at what he heard from the goat herder, and more eager than ever to discover who the unhappy madman was; and in his heart he decided, as he had done before, to search for him all over the mountain, not leaving a corner or cave unexamined until he found him. But chance arranged matters better than he expected or hoped for, because at that very moment, in a valley on the mountain that opened where they stood, the youth he wished to find made his appearance, coming along talking to himself in a way that would have been unintelligible even if he were closer, and even worse at a distance. His clothing was what had been described, but as he got closer, Don Quixote noticed the tattered jacket which he wore was amber-tanned, from which he concluded that one who wore such garments could not be of very low rank.

Approaching them, the youth greeted them in a harsh and rough voice but with great courtesy. Don Quixote returned his greeting with equal politeness, and dismounting from Rocinante advanced with grace to embrace him, and held him for some time close in his arms as if he had known him for a long time. The other, who we may call the Ragged One of the Sorry Face, as Don Quixote was the Sorrowful, after submitting to the embrace pushed him back a little and, placing his hands on Don Quixote's shoulders, stood gazing at him as if seeking to see whether he knew him or not, no less amazed, perhaps, at the sight of the face, figure, and armour of Don Quixote than Don Quixote was at the sight of him. To be brief, the first to speak after embracing was the Ragged One, and he said what will be told shortly.

CHAPTER 24

CONTINUING THE ADVENTURE OF THE SIERRA MORENA

Don Quixote listened to the ragged Knight of the mountain, who began by saying:

"Señor, whoever you are, I thank you for the kindness and courtesy you have shown me, and if I were in a condition to repay you with something more than good-will for the pleasant reception you have given me I would do so; but my fate does not provide me with anything to return to you for the kindnesses except my desire to repay it."

"I," replied Don Quixote, "am to be of service to you, so much so that I had decided not to leave these mountains until I had found you, and I sought whether there is any kind of relief to be found for the sorrow from which and with the strangeness of your life you seem to be suffering from; and to search for you with complete diligence. And if your misfortune happened to be irredeemable, it was my purpose to join you in grieving over it, as much as I could; because comfort can be found in misfortune, if there is someone else to share it with. And if my good intentions deserve to be acknowledged with any kind of respect, I ask you, señor, to tell me who you are and the cause that has brought you to live or die in these mountains like a wild animal, dwelling among them in a manner so foreign to your condition as your clothing and appearance deem you to be. And I swear," added Don Quixote, "by the law of Knighthood which I follow, and by my vocation as a Knight, if you gratify me with this, I will serve you with all the intensity my calling demands of me, either in relieving your misfortune if it is possible to relieve, or to join you in your grief as I promised."

The Ragged One, hearing the Knight of the Sorrowful Face talk in this manner, did nothing but stare at him, and stare at him again, and again viewing him from head to foot; and when he had thoroughly examined him, he said to him:

"If you have anything to give me to eat, for God's sake give it me, and after I have eaten I will do all you ask in acknowledgment of the goodwill you have displayed towards me."

Sancho from his saddle-bags, and the goat herder from his pouch, furnished the Ragged One with the means of appeasing his hunger, and what they gave him he ate like a hungry animal, so quickly that he did not pause between mouthfuls, devouring rather than swallowing; and while he ate neither he or they who observed him said a word. As soon as he had done he made signs to them to follow him, which they did, and he led them to a green field which was a little further away around the corner of a rock. On reaching it he laid himself on the grass, and the others did the same, all keeping silence, until the Ragged One, settling himself in his place, said:

"If you wish, that I disclose in a few words the extent of my misfortunes, you must promise not to break the thread of my sad story with any questions or other interruptions, because the instant you do the story will come to an end."

These words of the Ragged One reminded Don Quixote of the story Sancho had told him, when he failed to keep count of the goats that had crossed the river and the story remained unfinished; but returning to the Ragged One, he went on to say:

"I give you this warning because I wish to pass briefly over the story of my misfortunes, because recalling them to memory only serves to add news ones, and the less you question me the sooner I will end the story, although I will not omit anything of importance in order to fully satisfy your curiosity."

Don Quixote gave the promise for himself and the others, and with this assurance he began as follows:

"My name is Cardenio, my birthplace one of the best cities in Andalusia, my family noble, my parents rich, my misfortune so great that my parents must have cried and my family grieved over it without being able with their wealth to resolve it; because the gifts of fortune can do little to relieve opposites sent by Hell. In that same city there was a heaven in which love had placed all the glory I could desire; the beauty of Luscinda, a lady as noble and as rich as I, but with happier fortune. This Luscinda I loved, worshipped, and adored from my earliest years, and she loved me in all the innocence and sincerity of childhood. Our parents were aware of our feelings, and were not upset to know of them, because they saw clearly that as they ripened they must lead at last to a marriage between us, a thing that seemed almost prearranged by the equality of our families and wealth. We grew up, and with our growth the love grew between us, so that the father of Luscinda felt bound for respectability's sake to refuse me admission to his house. Perhaps this intensity intimidated the parents (this love which is celebrated by the poets), but this refusal only added love to love and flame to flame; because although they enforced silence on our tongues they could not impose it on our pens, which can make known the heart's secrets to a loved one more freely than the tongue; because many times the presence of the object of love shakes the firmest will and strikes dumb the boldest tongue. Oh god! how many letters did I write to her, and how many elegant modest replies I received! How many poems and love-songs did I compose in which my heart declared and made known its feelings, described its passionate yearning, delighted in its recollections and lingered with its desires! Growing impatient and feeling my heart suffering with longing to see her, I decided to put into execution and carry out what seemed to me the best mode of winning my desired and deserved reward, to ask her father for her to be my lawful wife, which I did. To this he thanked me for the character I showed to honour him and to regard myself as privileged by the transfer of his treasure; and as he was alive it was his right to make this demand, because if it were not in accordance with his full will and pleasure, Luscinda was not to be taken or given by stealth. I thanked him for his kindness, reflecting that there was reason in what he said, and that my father would agree to it as soon as I would tell him, and with that view I went the very same instant to let him know what my desires were. When I entered the room where he was I found him with an open letter in his hand, which, before I could say a word, he gave to me, saying, 'With this letter you will see, Cardenio, the disposition the Duke Ricardo has to serve you.' This Duke Ricardo, as you, probably know already, is a notable man in Spain who has his seat in the best part Andalusia. I took and read the letter, which was expressed in terms so flattering that even I myself felt it would be wrong if my father did not comply with the request the duke made in it, which was that he would send me immediately to him, as he wished me to become the companion, not servant, of his eldest son, and would place me in a position corresponding to the esteem in which he held me. On reading the letter my voice failed me, and still more when I heard my father say, 'two days from now you will depart, Cardenio, in accordance with the duke's wish, and give thanks to God who is opening a road for you by which you may attain what I know you deserve; and to these words he added others of fatherly advice. The time for my departure arrived; I spoke to Luscinda, I told her all that had occurred, and also to her father, asking him to allow some delay, and to defer granting her hand until I saw what the Duke Ricardo sought from me: he gave me the promise, and she confirmed it with innumerable vows. Finally, I presented myself to the duke, and was welcomed and treated kindly by him, that very soon envy began to do its work, the old servants growing envious of me, and regarding the duke's inclination to show favour to me as an injury to themselves. But the one to who my arrival gave the greatest pleasure was the duke's second son, Fernando, a brave youth, of noble, generous, and passionate disposition, who very soon made me an intimate friend that everyone noticed; because although the elder was attached to me, and showed me kindness, he did not carry his affectionate treatment to the same length as Don Fernando. It so happened, then, that as between friends no secret remains unshared, and as the favour I enjoyed with Don Fernando had grown into friendship, he made all his thoughts known to me, and in particular a love affair which troubled his mind a little. He was deeply in love with a poor girl, a servant of his father's, and she being so beautiful, modest, discreet, and virtuous, no one who knew her was able to decide in which of these respects she was most gifted. The attractions of the poor girl raised the passion of Don Fernando to such a point that, in order to gain his objective and overcome her virtuous resolutions, he determined to give his word to her to that he would become her husband, because to attempt it in any other way was to attempt an impossibility. Bound to him as I was by friendship, I strove by the best arguments and the most forcible examples I could think of to restrain him from this course; but noticing I produced no effect I decided to make the Duke Ricardo, his father, familiar with the issue know; but Don Fernando, being sharp-witted and shrewd, foresaw and apprehended this, knowing that my duty as a good friend made me bound not to keep concealed a thing which opposed the honour of my lord the duke; and so, to mislead and deceive me, he told me he could find no better way of deleting from his mind the beauty that imprisoned him than by going away for some months, and that he asked that I go with him, to my father's house under the pretence, which he would say to the duke, of going to see and buy some fine horses that there were in my city, which produces the best in the world. When I heard him say so, even if his decision had not been so good I considered it as a chance, prompted by my affection, seeing what a favourable opportunity it offered me of returning to see my Luscinda. With this thought and wish I commended his idea and encouraged it, advising him to put it into execution as quickly as possible. But, afterwards, he said to me that he had already enjoyed the poor girl under the title of fiancé and future husband, and was waiting for an opportunity to let me know safely, fearing what his father the duke would do when he came to know of his foolishness. It happened, then, that as with young men love is for the most part nothing more than appetite, which, as its final object is enjoyment, comes to an end after obtaining it, and that which seemed to be love passes quickly, as it cannot pass the limit fixed by nature, which fixes no limit to true love - what I mean is that after Don Fernando had enjoyed this poor girl his passion subsided and his eagerness cooled, and if at first he contrived to be absent in order to cure his love, he was now in reality anxious to go away to avoid keeping his promise.

"The duke gave his permission and ordered me to accompany him; we arrived at my city, and my father welcomed him due to his rank; I saw Luscinda without delay, and, although it had not been dead or weakened, my love gathered fresh life. To my sorrow I told the story of it to Don Fernando, because I thought that in virtue of the great friendship he gave me I was bound to conceal nothing from him. I praised her beauty, her cheerfulness, her wit, so warmly, that my praises excited a desire in him to see a lady with such attractions. To my misfortune I consented to it, showing her to him one night by the light at a window where we used to talk to one another. As she appeared in the window in her dressing-gown, she drove all the beauties he had seen until then out of his memory; speech failed him, his head turned, he was mesmerised and in the end obsessed, as you will see in the course of the story of my misfortune; and to inflame further his passion, which he hid from me and revealed to Heaven alone, it so happened that one day he found a note of hers asking me to arrange the marriage, so delicate, so modest, and so loving, that on reading it he told me that in Luscinda alone were combined all the charms of beauty and understanding that were distributed among all the other women in the world. It is true, and although I knew what good cause Don Fernando had to praise Luscinda, it gave me uneasiness to hear these praises from his mouth, and I began to fear, and with reason to feel distrust of him, because there was no moment when he was not ready to talk about Luscinda, and he would start the subject himself at times mentioning her unexpectedly, a circumstance that aroused in me a certain amount of jealousy; not that I feared any change in the constancy or faith of Luscinda; but still my fate led me to predict what she assured me against. Don Fernando contrived always to read the letters I sent to Luscinda and her answers to me, under the pretence that he enjoyed the wit and sense of us both. It so happened, then, that Luscinda having begged me for a book of chivalry to read, one that she was very fond of, Amadis of France"

As soon as Don Quixote heard a book of chivalry mentioned, he said:

"Had you told me at the beginning of your story that the Lady Luscinda was fond of books of chivalry, no other words would have been needed to make me aware of the superiority of her understanding; so, as far as I am concerned, you do not need to waste any more words describing her beauty, worth, and intelligence; because, on merely hearing what her taste was, I declare her to be a highly beautiful and an intelligent woman; and I wish you had, along with Amadis of France, sent her the worthy Don Rugel of Greece, because I know the Lady Luscinda would have greatly enjoyed Daraida and Garaya, and the shrewd sayings of the shepherd Darinel, and the admirable verses about the countryside, sung and delivered by him with such liveliness, wit, and ease; but a time may come when this omission can be remedied, and to rectify it nothing more is needed than for you to be so good as to come with me to my village, because there I can give you more than three hundred books which are the delight of my soul and the entertainment of my life; although it occurs to me that I have not got one of them now, thanks to the spite of wicked and envious enchanters; but anyway, forgive me for having broken the promise we made not to interrupt your story; because when I hear chivalry or Knights mentioned, I cannot help talking about them as much as the rays of the sun cannot help giving heat; forgive me, please, and proceed."

While Don Quixote was saying this, Cardenio allowed his head to fall on his chest, and seemed to be in deep thought; and although Don Quixote asked him twice to continue his story, he did not look up or say a word in reply; but after some time he raised his head and said, "I cannot get rid of the idea, and no one else in the world will remove it, or make me think otherwise - and only a fool would believe anything else than that complete fool Master Elisabad was with Queen Madasima."

"That is not true," said Don Quixote in anger, turning on him, as his way was; "and it is a very great insult, or rather wickedness. Queen Madasima was a very illustrious lady, and it is not to be supposed that such an exalted Princess would have gone with a fool; and whoever maintains the opposite opinion like a rat, I will let him know about it, on foot or on horseback, armed or unarmed, night or by day."

Cardenio was looking at him steadily, while Don Quixote continued with his mad fit, he had no mood to go on with his story, and neither would Don Quixote have listened to it, after what he had heard about Madasima had disgusted him. Strange to say, he stood up for her as if she were his lady. Cardenio then, being, as I said, now mad, when he heard himself called a liar and other insulting names, not enjoying it, grabbed a stone that he found near him, and with it delivered a blow on Don Quixote's chest that he laid him on his back. Sancho Panza, seeing his master treated in this fashion, attacked the madman with his closed fist; but the Ragged One anticipated it, and gave him a blow that laid him on the floor, and then mounting on him crushed his ribs to his own satisfaction; the goat herder, who came to the rescue, shared the same fate; and after having beaten them all he left and quietly withdrew to his hiding-place in the mountains. Sancho got up, and with the rage he felt at finding himself beaten without deserving it, ran to take vengeance on the goat herder, accusing him of not giving them a warning that this man was at times taken with mad rage, because if they had known it they would have been on their guard to protect themselves. The goat herder replied that he had said so, and that if he had not heard him, that was not his fault. Sancho responded, and the altercation ended in them seizing each other by the beard, and exchanging punches that if Don Quixote had not made peace between them, they would have knocked one another to pieces.

"Leave me alone, Knight of the Sorrowful Face," said Sancho, grappling with the goat herder, "because on this man, who is a clown like myself, and no Knight, I can safely take vengeance against the disrespect he has shown me, fighting with him hand to hand like an honest man."

"That is true," said Don Quixote, "but I know that he is not to blame for what has happened."

With this he pacified them, and again asked the goat herder if it would be possible to find Cardenio, as he felt the greatest anxiety to know the end of his story. The goat herder told him, as he had told him before, that there was no way to know with certainty where his hideout was; but that if he wandered about for some time in that area he could not fail to meet with him, while he was either in or out of his senses.

CHAPTER 25

THE STRANGE THINGS THAT HAPPENED TO THE KNIGHT OF LA MANCHA IN THE SIERRA MORENA

Don Quixote left the goat herder, and once more mounting Rocinante asked Sancho follow him, but having no donkey, he did very unhappily. They proceeded slowly, making their way into the most rugged part of the mountain, Sancho all the while dying to talk with his master, and longing for him to start a conversation, so there would be no breach of the injunction set on him; but unable to keep his silence for long he said to him:

"Señor Don Quixote, give me your blessing and dismissal, because I would like to go home to my wife and children, with them I can talk and converse as much as I like; because to want me to go through these isolations day and night and not speak to you when I feel like talking is burying me alive. If luck would have it that animals spoke, it would not be so bad, because I could talk to Rocinante about whatever came into my head, and put up with my bad-fortune; but it is a hard case, and not to be blessed with patience, to go seeking adventures all one's life and get nothing but kicks, beatings and punches, and with all this to have to sew up my mouth without daring to say what is in my heart, as if I were dumb."

"I understand Sancho," replied Don Quixote; "you are dying to have the order I placed on your tongue removed; consider it removed and say what you like while we are wandering in these mountains."

"So be it," said Sancho; "let me speak now, because God knows what will happen soon; and to take advantage of the permission, I ask, what made you stand up so for Queen Majimasa, or whatever her name is, what did it matter whether that fool was with her or not? Because if you had let that pass, and you were not a judge in the matter - it is my belief the madman would have gone on with his story, and the blow of the stone, and the kicks, and more than half a dozen punches would have been escaped."

"It is my belief, Sancho," answered Don Quixote, "if you knew, as I do, what an honourable and illustrious lady Queen Madasima was, I know you would say I had great patience not to break into pieces the mouth that spoke such profanities, because it is a great violation to say or imagine that a Queen went with a fool. The truth of the story is, Master Elisabad who the madman mentioned was a man of great prudence and sound judgment, and served as governor and physician to the Queen, but to suppose that she was his mistress is nonsense deserving a very severe punishment; and as a proof that Cardenio did not know what he was saying, remember when he said he was out of his mind."

"Exactly," said Sancho; "there is no occasion for taking seriously the words of a madman; because if good luck had not helped you, and he had sent that stone toward your head instead of your chest, you would have been left in a bad state for standing up for this lady! And then, wouldn't Cardenio have gone free as a madman?"

"Against men in their senses or against madmen," said Don Quixote, "every Knight is bound to stand up for the honour of women, whoever they may be, even more for Queens of such high degree and dignity as Queen Madasima, who I have a particular regard for on account of her good-natured qualities; because, besides being extremely beautiful, she was very wise, and very patient during her misfortunes, of which she had many; and the advice of Master Elisabad were a great help and support to her in enduring her difficulties; so the ignorant and ill-disposed vulgar man took this occasion to say and think that she was his mistress; and lied, and I say it once more, those who say this lie two hundred times more, and all who think so."

"I do not say or think so," said Sancho; "let God decide whether they misbehaved or not; I come from the vineyard, I know nothing; I am not fond of prying into other men's lives; he who buys and lies feels it in his wallet; moreover, I was born naked, naked I find myself, I neither lose, or gain; but if they did, what is that to me? Many think, there is something where there is not; but who can put gates on an open field?"

"God bless me," said Don Quixote, "what a set of absurdities you are stringing together! What has what we are talking about got to do with the proverbs you are threading together? For God's sake hold your tongue, Sancho, and from now on don't interfere in what does not concern you; and understand with all your five senses that everything I have done, am doing, or will do, is well founded on reason and in conformity with the rules of chivalry, because I understand them better than all the world that recognise them."

"Señor," replied Sancho, "is it a good rule of chivalry that we go wandering through these mountains without a path or road, looking for a madman, who, when he is found will perhaps like to finish what he began, not his story, but your head and my ribs, and end it by breaking them altogether for us?"

"Peace Sancho," said Don Quixote, "because let me tell you, it is not so much the desire of finding that madman that leads me into these regions than that which I have of performing in them an achievement which will win for me the eternal name and fame throughout the known world."

"And is it very dangerous, this achievement?"

"No," replied the Knight of the Sorrowful Face; "although it may be in the throw of the dice that we will get to aces instead of two sixes; but all will depend on your diligence."

"On my diligence!" said Sancho.

"Yes," said Don Quixote, "because if you return soon from the place where I want to send you, my amendments will be over soon, and my glory will soon begin. But as it is not right to keep you any longer in suspense, waiting to see what comes of my words, I want you to know, Sancho, that the famous Amadis of France was one of the most perfect Knights. I am not wrong to say he stood alone, the first, the only one, the lord of all that were in the world during his time. A seed for Don Belianis, and for all who say they equalled him in any respect, but I swear, they are deceiving themselves! When a painter desires to become famous in his art he endeavours to copy the originals of the rarest painters that he knows; and the same rule holds for all of the most important crafts and callings that serve to decorate a state; there whoever wants to be esteemed as prudent and patient imitates Ulysses, and Homer who presents to us a lively picture of prudence and patience; as Virgil, also, shows us the virtue of a virtuous son and the wisdom of a brave and skilful captain; not representing or describing them as they were, but as they should be, to leave the example of their virtues to future generations. In the same way Amadis was the first of the valiant and devoted Knights, who everyone who fights under the banner of love and chivalry are bound to imitate. This, then, being so, I consider, friend Sancho, that the Knight-who imitates him most closely will come nearest to reaching the perfection of chivalry. Now one of the instances in which this Knight most noticeably showed his prudence, worth, valour, endurance, fortitude, and love, was when he withdrew, rejected by the Lady Oriana, to punish himself, changing his name to Beltenebros, a name definitely significant and appropriate for the life which he had voluntarily adopted. So, as it is easier for me to imitate him in this than in slicing giants apart, cutting off snakes' heads, slaying dragons, directing armies, destroying fleets, and breaking enchantments, and as this place is so well suited for a similar purpose, I must not allow the opportunity to escape which is now so conveniently offered to me."

"What is it in reality," said Sancho, "that you want to do in such an out-of-the-way place like this?"

"Have I not told you," answered Don Quixote, "that I intend to imitate Amadis here, playing the victim of despair, the madman, the maniac, so as at the same time to almost imitate the valiant Don Roland, when at the fountain he had evidence of the fair Angelica having disgraced herself with Medoro and through grief he went mad, and cut down trees, troubled the waters of the clear rivers, killed flocks, burned down huts, destroyed houses, and committed a hundred thousand other outrages worthy of everlasting renown and record? And though I have no intention of imitating Roland, Orlando, or Rotolando (because he went by all of these names), step by step in all the mad things he did, said, and thought, I will make a rough copy to the best of my power of all that seems to me most essential; but perhaps I will content myself with the simple imitation of Amadis, who without giving way to any mischievous madness but merely to tears and sorrow, and gain as much fame as the most famous."

"It seems to me," said Sancho, "that the Knights who behaved in this way had a cause for those irrationalities; but what cause do you have for going mad? What lady has rejected you, or what evidence have you found to prove that the lady Dulcinea del Toboso has been with anyone else?"

"There is the point," replied Don Quixote, "and that is the beauty of this business of mine; there is no thanks for a Knight who goes mad when he has cause; the thing is to turn crazy without any cause, and let my lady know, if I do this when dry, what would I do when moist; furthermore I have cause: the long separation I have endured from my lady Dulcinea del Toboso; as you heard that shepherd Ambrosio say the other day, in absence all troubles are felt and feared; and so, friend Sancho, waste no time in advising me against such a rare, and unheard-of imitation; I am mad, and mad I must be until you return with the answer to a letter that I want to send by you to my lady Dulcinea; and my constancy deserves that my insanity comes to an end; and if it has the opposite effect, I will become sincerely mad, and, being so, I will suffer no more; therefore in whatever way she may answer I will escape from the struggle and affliction in which you will leave me, enjoying in my senses the gift you bring me, or as a madman not feeling the evil you bring me. But tell me, Sancho, have you got Mambrino's helmet safe? Because I saw you pick it up from the ground when that ungrateful fool tried to break it into pieces but could not, which demonstrates the fineness of its build."

To which Sancho answered, "God, Sir Knight of the Sorrowful Face, I cannot endure with patience some of the things that you say; and from them I begin to suspect that all you tell me about chivalry, and winning kingdoms and empires, and giving islands, and granting other rewards which is the custom of Knights, must be all made up of wind, and all pigments or figments, or whatever they are called; because what would anyone think to hear you calling a barber's bowl Mambrino's helmet without ever seeing the mistake all this time, but someone who says and maintains such things must have his brains scrambled? I have the basin in my sack all dented, and I am taking it home to have it mended, to trim my beard in it, if, by God's grace, I am allowed to see my wife and children some day or ever again."

"Look here, Sancho," said Don Quixote, "I swear you have the most limited understanding that any aide in the world has or ever had. Is it possible that all this time you have been going about with me you have never found out that all things belonging to Knights seem to be illusions and nonsense and ravings, and to always be opposites? And not because it really is so, but because there is always a swarm of enchanters in attendance that change and alter everything with us, and turn things into whatever they like, and however they are inclined to aid or destroy us; therefore what seems to a barber's bowl seems to me to be Mambrino's helmet, and to another it will seem to be something else; and what rare foresight in the sage who is on my side to make what is really and truly Mambrino's helmet seem like a bowl to everyone else, because, being held as it is, the whole world would pursue me to rob me of it; but when they see it is only a barber's bowl they do not take the trouble to obtain it; as was clearly shown by him who tried to break it, and left it on the ground without taking it, because, I believe, had he known he would never have left it behind. Keep it safe, my friend, because I have no need of it now; actually, I will have to take off all this armour and remain as naked as the day I was born, if I want to follow Roland rather than Amadis as my punishment."

They reached the foot of a high mountain which stood like an isolated peak among the others that surrounded it. Past its base flowed a gentle stream, all around it nourished a meadow so green and luxuriant that it was a delight to any eyes that look at it, with forest trees in abundance, and shrubs and flowers, which added to the charm of the spot. At this place the Knight of the Sorrowful Face made his choice for the performance of his self-punishment, and exclaimed in a loud voice as though he were out of his senses:

"This is the place, oh heaven, that I select and choose for the misfortune in which you yourselves have given me: this is the spot where the over flowing of my eyes will increase the water of the little stream, and my deep and endless sighs will move unceasingly the leaves of these mountain trees, as proof and mark of the pain my persecuted heart is suffering. Oh God, whoever you are that haunt this spot, hear the complaint of a poor lover who long absence and growing jealousy have driven to this fate among this wilderness to complain about the hard heart of that ungrateful one, the end and limit of all human beauty! Oh, all you, that dwell in this forest, help me to grieve over my hard fate or at least do not tire listening to it! Oh, Dulcinea del Toboso, day of my night, glory of my pain, guide of my path, star of my fortune, may Heaven grant you in full all that you seek, think of the place and condition to which absence from you has brought me, and reply in kindness to that which is due for my faithfulness! Oh, lonely trees, that from this day forward will give me company in my solitude, give me some sign by the gentle movement of your branches that my presence is not distasteful to you! Oh, you, my aide, pleasant companion in my prosperous and adverse fortunes, fix well in your memory what you will see me do here, so that you may relay and report it to the sole cause of all this," and so, he dismounted from Rocinante, and in an instant removed the saddle and harness, and giving him a slap on the bottom, said, "I give you freedom as I am without it myself, oh horse as excellent in actions as you are unfortunate in your life; go wherever you like, because no other can equal you in speed."

Seeing this Sancho said, "Good luck to the man who has saved me the trouble of removing the saddle from the horse! I believe Rocinante would not have gone without a slap on the bottom and something said in his praise; and indeed, Sir Knight of the Sorrowful Face, if my departure and your madness are to work, it will be better to call back and saddle Rocinante again so he may satisfy my need of the donkey, because it will save me time in going and returning: because if I go on foot I don't know when I will get there or when I will return, as I am, in truth, a bad walker."

"I declare, Sancho," returned Don Quixote, "it will be as you wish, because your plan does not seem bad to me, and three days from today you will leave, because I want you to observe in the meantime what I do and say for her, so you are able to tell it."

"But what more do I have to see besides what I have already seen?" said Sancho.

"There is much more to see!" said Don Quixote. "I have now got to tear up my clothes, to scatter my armour, knock my head against these rocks, and more of the same sort of thing, which you must witness."

"For the love of God," said Sancho, "be careful, how you give yourself those knocks on the head, you might come across a rock, and in such a way, the very first may put an end to the whole plan of this self-punishment; and I should think, if indeed knocks on the head seem necessary to you, and this business cannot be done without them, you might be content - as the whole thing is artificial, and fake, and like a joke - you might be content, I say, with giving them to yourself in the water, or against something soft, like cotton; and leave it all to me; because I'll tell her that you knocked your head against a point of rock harder than a diamond."

"I thank you for your good intentions, friend Sancho," answered Don Quixote, "but I want you to know that all these things I am doing are not a joke, but very much serious, because anything else would be an offence to the law of chivalry, which forbids us to tell any lie under the penalty of being removed; and to do one thing instead of another is just the same as lying; so my knocks on the head must be real, solid, and valid, and it will be necessary to leave me a bandage to cover my wounds, since fortune has compelled us to do without the precious balm we have lost."

"It was worse losing the donkey," replied Sancho, "because with him the bandages and all were lost; but I beg you not to remind me again of that cursed liquor, because my soul, not to say my stomach, turns when hearing the very name of it; and I beg you, too, to forget about the next three days you allow me to see the mad things you do, because I take them as already seen, and I will tell wonderful stories to your lady; so write the letter and send me on my way, because I want to return as soon as possible and take you out of this agony where I am leaving you."

"Agony you call it, Sancho?" said Don Quixote, "rather call it hell, or worse if there is anything worse."

"For one who is in hell," said Sancho, "nulla est retentio, as I have heard."

"I do not understand," said Don Quixote.

"Nulla est retentio," answered Sancho, "means that whoever is in hell can never come out of it, which will be the opposite case with you or my trip will be for no reason: let me go to El Toboso and into the presence of your lady Dulcinea, and I will tell her about the irrationalities and madness that you have done and are still doing, so that I will manage to make her softer than a glove although I will find her harder than a cork tree; and with her sweet and honeyed answer I will come back through the air like a witch, and take you out of this agony that seems to be hell but is not, as there is hope of getting out of it; which, as I have said, those in hell cannot, and I believe you will not say anything to the contrary."

"That is true," said the Knight of the Sorrowful Face, "but how will we manage to write the letter?"

"What about the donkies you promised me?" added Sancho.

"All will be included," said Don Quixote; "and as there is no paper, it would be ok write it on the leaves of trees, as the ancients did, or on tablets of wax; although that would be as hard to find now as paper. But it has just occurred to me how it may be conveniently and even more than conveniently written, and that is in the note-book that belonged to Cardenio, and you will take care to have it copied on paper, in good handwriting, at the first village you come to where there is a schoolmaster, or if not, any vicar will copy it; but make sure you do not give it to any notary to copy, because they write in law that even Satan could not make out."

"But what about the signature?" said Sancho.

"The letters of Amadis were never signed," said Don Quixote.

"That is all very well," said Sancho, "but the order needs to be signed, and if it is copied they will say the signature is false."

"The order will go signed in the same book," said Don Quixote, "as for the love letter you can put as a signature, 'Yours till death, the Knight of the Sorrowful Face.' And it will not matter if it is written by someone else, because as well as I recollect Dulcinea can neither read or write, or in the whole course of her life has she seen handwriting or a letter of mine, because my love and hers has always been spiritual, not going beyond a modest look, and even that was so seldom that I can safely swear I have not seen her more than four times in all the twelve years I have been loving her, loving her more than the light of these eyes that the earth will one day devour; and perhaps even out of those four times she has not once noticed that I was looking at her: due to the seclusion in which her father Lorenzo Corchuelo and her mother Aldonza Nogales have brought her up in."

"So!" said Sancho; "Lorenzo Corchuelo's daughter is the lady Dulcinea del Toboso, otherwise called Aldonza Lorenzo?"

"She is," said Don Quixote, "and she is worthy to be lady of the whole universe."

"I know her well," said Sancho, "and let me tell you she can use a crowbar as well as the strongest man in the whole town. She is a brave woman, and fit to be the helper of any Knight that is or is to be, who may make her his lady: what sting she has and what a voice! I can tell you one day she placed herself on the top of the village tower to call some labourers of theirs that were in the plough field of her father's, and although they were about half a mile away they heard her as well as if they were at the base of the tower; and the best of her is that she is not very prudish, because she has plenty of friendliness, and humour with everybody, and has a smile and a joke for everything. So, Sir Knight of the Sorrowful Face, I say you not only can and should do mad things for her sake, but you have a good right to give way to despair and punish yourself; and no one who knows about it will say you did wrong. I wish I were on the road already, simply to see her, because it has been a long time since I saw her, and she must have changed by now, because going out into the fields always, and in the sun and the air spoils women's looks. But I must tell the truth to you, Señor Don Quixote; until now I have been under a great illusion, because I truly believed honestly that the lady Dulcinea must be some Princess you were in love with, or a person great enough to deserve the rich presents you have sent her, such as the Biscayan and the slaves, and many more no doubt, because you must have won many victories in the time when I was not yet your aide as well. But all things considered, what good can it do for the lady Aldonza Lorenzo, I mean the lady Dulcinea del Toboso, to have the conquered people you send or will send coming to her and going down on their knees in front of her? Because maybe when they came she would be shaving her arm pits, or cleaning the floor, and they would be ashamed to see her, and she would laugh, or resent the present."

"I have told you many times, Sancho," said Don Quixote, "that you are a mighty talker, and that with a blunt wit you are always striving at sharpness; but to show you what a fool you are and how rational I am, I want you to listen to a short story. You must know that a certain widow, fair, young, independent, and rich, and above all free and easy, fell in love with a sturdy strapping young man; and his superior came to know of it, and one day said to the worthy widow in brotherly protest, 'I am surprised, señora, and not without good reason, that a woman of such high standing, so fair, and so rich as you are, could have fallen in love with such a low, stupid man, when in this house there are so many masters, graduates, and divinity students from among them you might choose as if they were a bunch of pears, saying I will take this one, I won't take that one; but she replied to him with great frankness, 'My dear sir, you are very much mistaken, and your ideas are very old-fashioned, if you think that I have made a bad choice, a fool as he seems; because all I want his him and he knows as much and more philosophy than Aristotle.' In the same way, Sancho, all I want is Dulcinea del Toboso she is just as good as the most exalted Princess on earth.

You think that the Sylvias, the Dianas, the Galateas, the Filidas, and all the rest of them, that the books, the poems, the barber's shops, the theatres are full of, were really and truly ladies of flesh and blood, and mistresses of those that glorify and have glorified them? Not at all; they only invent them to serve as a subject for their verses, and that they may pass for lovers, or for men valiant enough to be so; and so it suffices me to think and believe that the good Aldonza Lorenzo is fair and virtuous; and as to her pedigree it doesn't matter, because no one will question it for the purpose of delivering any order to her, and I, for my part, consider her the most exalted Princess in the world. Because you should know, Sancho, if you do not know, that only two things alone beyond all others are incentives to love, and these are great beauty and a good name, and these two things are to be found in Dulcinea in the highest degree, because in beauty no one equals her and in good name few come close; and to put the whole thing in a nutshell, I persuade myself that all I say, is as I say, no more or less, and I picture her in my imagination as I want her to be, in beauty and in good condition; does Helen approach her, no, neither does Lucretia come close, or any other of the famous women of the past, Greek or Latin."

"You are entirely right," said Sancho, "and I am a fool. But I do not know how the name fool came into my mouth, because a rope should not be mentioned in the house of a man who has been hung; but now for the letter, and then, I am off."

Don Quixote took out the note-book, and, starting at one side, very deliberately began to write the letter, and when he had finished it he called Sancho, saying he wanted to read it to him, so that he can commit it to memory, in case he loses it on the road; because with evil fortune like his anything could happen. Sancho replied, "write it two or three times in the book and give it to me, and I will carry it very carefully, because to expect me to keep it in my memory is nonsense, because I have such a bad one that I often forget my own name; but anyway repeat it to me, as I would like to hear it, because surely it will be as good as if it were published."

"Listen," said Don Quixote, "this is what it says:

DON QUIXOTE'S LETTER TO DULCINEA DEL TOBOSO

"Supreme and exalted Lady. The pierced by absence, the wounded to the heart's core, sends you, sweetest Dulcinea del Toboso, the health that he himself does not enjoy. If your beauty despises me, if your worth is not for me, if your ridicule is my suffering, although I have been suffering for a long time, I will hardly endure this anxiety, which, besides being oppressive, is extended. My good aide Sancho will relay to you in full, ungrateful one, the condition which I am reduced to due to you: if it is your pleasure to give me relief, I am yours; if not, do whatever pleases you; because by ending my life I will satisfy your cruelty and my desire. "Yours till death, "The Knight of the Sorrowful Face."

"On my father's life," said Sancho, when he heard the letter, "it is the grandest thing I ever heard. How you say everything as you like in it! And how well you fit in 'The Knight of the Sorrowful Face' into the signature. I declare you are indeed the very devil, as there is nothing you don't know."

"Everything is needed for the calling I follow," said Don Quixote.

"Now then," said Sancho, "let you put the order out for a donkey on the other side, and sign it very plainly, so they can recognise it at first sight."

"With all my heart," said Don Quixote, and as he had written it he read it to this effect:

"Dear niece, please pay Sancho Panza, my aide, three of the five donkeys I left at home: three donkeys to be paid and delivered, which on his receipt will be paid. Written in the heart of the Sierra Morena, the twenty-seventh of August of this present year."

"That will do," said Sancho; "now please sign it."

"There is no need to sign it," said Don Quixote, "but merely to put my style on it, which is the same as a signature, and enough for three donkeys, or even three hundred."

"I can trust you," returned Sancho; "let me go and saddle Rocinante, and be ready to give me your blessing, because I am going to leave immediately without seeing the fooleries you are going to do; I will say I saw you do so many that she will not want to hear any more."

"At any rate, Sancho," said Don Quixote, "I would like, and there is reason for it, I say, you to see me naked and performing a dozen insanities, which I can get done in less than half an hour; because having seen them with your own eyes, you can then safely affirm the rest you would add; and I promise you will not even need to tell as many as I will perform."

"For the love of God, master," said Sancho, "do not let me see you naked, because it will upset me, and I will not be able to hold in my tears, and my head already aches with all the tears I shed last night for my donkey, that I am not in the state to start crying again; but if it is you pleasure that I see some insanities, do them in your clothes, short ones; because I myself do not really want to see any, and, as I have said, it will be better to save time so I return sooner, which will be with the news you desire and deserve. And if not, I swear as seriously as I can that I will get a fair answer out of her stomach with kicks and punches; because why should it be that a Knight as famous as you should go mad without a reason? This lady had best not drive me to say it, because by God I will speak and let out everything cheap, even if it doesn't buy: I am pretty good at that! She doesn't know me; believe, if she knew me she would be in awe of me."

"I believe, Sancho," said Don Quixote, "regardless of your appearance you are no sounder in your mind than I am."

"I am not mad," answered Sancho, "but I am spicier; but apart from all this, what have you got to eat until I come back? Will you venture out on the road like Cardenio to force it from the goat herders?"

"Do not be troubled with anxiety," replied Don Quixote, "because even if I do not eat anything but the herbs and the fruits which this meadow and these trees can offer me; the beauty of this business of mine lies in not eating, and in performing other activities."

"Do you know what I am afraid of?" said Sancho, "that I will not be able to find my way back to this spot where I am leaving you, it is such an out-of-the-way place."

"Observe the landmarks well," said Don Quixote, "because I will try not to go far from here, and I will even take care to mount the highest of these rocks to see if I can discover you returning; however, not to miss me and lose myself, the best plan will be to cut some branches around here so it is very clear that this is the place when you return, and as you go cut them at intervals until you have cleared this area; these will serve you, like clues in the labyrinth of Theseus, as marks and signs for finding me on your return."

"I will do so," said Sancho Panza, and having cut a few already, he asked for his master's blessing, and not without many tears on both sides, he mounted Rocinante, which Don Quixote put him in charge of to have as much care as if he was his own. He made his way, cutting at intervals the branches of trees as his master had recommended him to do. He had not gone a hundred metres, however, when he returned and said:

"I must say, señor, you were right, that in order to be able to swear without any weight on my conscience that I had seen you do mad things, it would be better for me to see even if it were only one; although as you are still here I have already seen a great one."

"Did I not tell you so?" said Don Quixote. "Wait, Sancho, and I will do them in no time," and pulling off his trousers in all swiftness he stripped himself to his skin and his shirt, and then, without a pause, he did a couple of somersaults, heels over his head, making such a display that, not to see it a second time, Sancho turned Rocinante around, and felt easy, and satisfied in his mind that he could swear he had left his master in a mad state; and so we will leave him to follow his road until his return, which was a quick one.

CHAPTER 26

DON QUIXOTE PLAYED THE PART OF A LOVER IN THE SIERRA MORENA

Returning to the Knight of the Sorrowful Face when he found himself alone, the history says that when Don Quixote had completed the performance of the somersaults, naked from the waist down and clothed from the waist up, and saw that Sancho had gone off without waiting to see any more crazy acts, he climbed to the top of a high rock, and sat himself himself to consider what he had considered many times before without ever coming to a conclusion on the point: whether it would be better or not to imitate the outrageous madness of Roland, or the depressed madness of Amadis; and conversing with himself he said:

"No wonder Roland was such a good Knight and so valiant as everyone says he was, when, after all, he was enchanted, and nobody could kill him except by thrusting a pin into the bottom of his foot, but he always wore shoes with iron soles? Although crafty plans did not benefit him against Bernardo del Carpio, who knew all about them, and strangled him in his arms at Roncesvalles. But putting the question of his valour aside, what about him losing his mind, because it is certain that he lost it as a consequence of the proof he discovered at the fountain, and the intelligence the shepherd gave him about Angelica having slept more than two siestas with Medoro, a little curly-headed moor, and aide to Agramante. If he was persuaded that this was true, and that his lady had done him wrong, it is no wonder he went mad; but how am I to imitate him in his madness, unless I can imitate him in the cause of it? Because my Dulcinea, I swear, never saw a moor in her life, and I would be doing her wrong if, I believed anything else, and I were to go mad with the same kind of madness as Roland the Furious. On the other hand, I see that Amadis of France, without losing his senses and without doing anything mad, acquired as a lover as much fame as the most famous; because, according to his history, when finding himself rejected by his lady Oriana, who had ordered him not to appear in her presence until she wanted him to, all he did was to retreat to the cliffs with a hermit, and there he did his fair share of crying until Heaven sent him relief in the middle of his great grief and need. And if this is true, as it is said, why should I now bother to strip naked, or do harm to these trees which have done no harm to me, or why should I disturb the clear waters of these streams which give me water to drink whenever I need it? Long live the memory of Amadis and let him be imitated as much is possible by Don Quixote of La Mancha, of whom it will be said, as was said of the him, that if he did not achieve great things, he died in attempting them; and if I am not repulsed or rejected by my Dulcinea, it is enough for me, as I have said, to be absent from her. And so, come to my memory the deeds of Amadis, and show me how I should imitate you. I know already that mainly what he did was to pray and commit himself to God; but what can I do without a rosary, because I have not got one?"

And then it occurred to him how he could make one, and that was by tearing a strip of his shirt, and making eleven knots on it, one bigger than the rest, and this served him as a rosary the whole time he was there, during which he repeated countless prayers. But what distressed him most was not having another hermit there to confess to and receive consolation from; and so he comforted himself with pacing up and down, and writing and carving on the bark of trees a multitude of verses all in harmony with his sadness, and some in praise of Dulcinea; but, when they were found there afterwards, the only ones which were completely legible and could be read were those that follow here:

You on the mountain side that grow,
You, green things, trees, shrubs, and bushes,
Are you aware of the great sorrow?
That this poor chest crushes?
If it disturbs you, and I owe
Some compensation, it may be a
Defence for me to let you know
Don Quixote's tears will flow,
And all for the distant Dulcinea
Del Toboso.

The loyal lover time can show,
Doomed for a lady's love to weaken,
Among these solitudes I go,
A prayer for every kind of pain.
Why Love is like a spiteful foe
Get used to him, he has no idea,
But its full - this he does know
Don Quixote's tears will flow,
And all for the distant Dulcinea
Del Toboso.

Adventure seeking is where I go
To heights, down rocky slopes,
Hills or valleys, high or low,
Mishaps happen in all his ventures:
Still love pushes him to and fro,
And gives him his cruel punishment!
Relentless fate, an endless woe;
Don Quixote's tears will flow,
And all for the distant Dulcinea
Del Toboso.

The addition of "Del Toboso" to Dulcinea's name aroused a lot of laughter among those who found the lines above, because they suspected Don Quixote must have thought that unless he added "del Toboso" when he introduced the name of Dulcinea the verse would be unintelligible; which was indeed the fact, as he himself afterwards admitted. He wrote many more, but, as has been said, these three verses were all that could be perfectly deciphered. In this way, and while sighing and calling on the trees and shrubs of the woods and the streams, to reply, answer, comfort, and hear him, as well as looking for herbs to sustain him, he passed his time until Sancho's return; which had it been delayed three weeks, as it was by three days, the Knight of the Sorrowful Face would have had such an altered expression that the mother that gave birth to him would not have recognised him: and here it will be best to leave him, wrapped up in complaints and verses, to tell how Sancho Panza progressed on his mission.

Sancho, coming out on the main road, went toward El Toboso, and the next day reached the inn where the misfortune of the blanket had happened to him. As soon as he recognised it he felt as if he were flying through the air again, and he could not bring himself to enter it, although it was dinner-time, and he craved to taste something hot as recently he had only had cold food. This craving pushed him closer to the inn, still undecided whether to go in or not, and as he was hesitating two people came out and immediately recognised him, and one said to the other:

"Señor vicar, surely, that man on the horse there is Sancho Panza who, our adventurer's housekeeper told us, went off with her master as his aide?"

"So it is," said the vicar, "and that is our friend Don Quixote's horse;" and the reason why they knew him so well was because this pair of men were the vicar and the barber of his village, the same who had carried out the scrutiny and sentence on the books; and as soon as they recognised Sancho Panza and Rocinante, being anxious to hear about Don Quixote, they approached, and calling him by his name the vicar said, "Friend Sancho Panza, where is your master?"

Sancho recognised them immediately, and determined to keep secret the place and circumstances which he had left his master, he replied that his master was engaged in a matter of great importance which he could not disclose.

"No, no," said the barber, "if you don't tell us where he is, Sancho Panza, we will suspect as we already do, that you have murdered and robbed him, because here you are mounted on his horse; in fact, you must take us to the master of the horse, or else suffer the consequences."

"There is no need to threaten me," said Sancho, "because I am not a man who would rob or murder anyone; my master is engaged doing self-punishment in the mountains;" and then, without stopping, he told them how he had left him, and how he was carrying a letter to the lady Dulcinea del Toboso, the daughter of Lorenzo Corchuelo, who he was head over heels in love with. They were both amazed at what Sancho Panza told them; because although they were aware of Don Quixote's madness and the nature of it, each time they heard more of it they were filled with fresh wonder. They then asked Sancho Panza to show them the letter he was carrying to lady Dulcinea del Toboso. He said it was written in a note-book, and that his master's instructions were that he should have it copied on paper at the first village he came to. The vicar said if he showed it to him, he would make a good copy of it. Sancho put his hand into his inner jacket pocket in search of the note-book but could not find it, and he wouldn't have found it, even if he had been searching until now, because Don Quixote had kept it, and had never given it to him, neither had he thought of asking for it. When Sancho discovered he could not find the book his face went pale, and in a great rush he searched all of his pockets, and seeing it was not to be found, without searching further he seized his beard with both hands and pulled away half of it, and then, as quick as he could and without stopping, gave himself half a dozen punches on his face and nose until they were covered in blood.

Seeing this, the vicar and the barber asked him what had happened to him to provoke such self-abuse.

"What has happened?" replied Sancho, "I have lost from one hand to the other, in a moment, three donkeys, each of them worth a castle."

"How is that?" said the barber.

"I have lost the note-book," said Sancho, "that contained the letter to Dulcinea, and an order signed by my master in which he directed his niece to give me three donkeys out of four or five he had at home;" and then he told them about the loss of his donkey.

The vicar consoled him, telling him that when his master was found he would get him to renew the order, and make a fresh draft on paper, as was usual and customary; because those made in notebooks were never accepted or honoured.

Sancho comforted himself with this, and said if that was the case the loss of Dulcinea's letter did not trouble him too much, because he remembered almost all of it by heart, and it could be written down from him whenever and wherever they liked.

"Repeat it then, Sancho," said the barber, "and we will write it down afterwards."

Sancho Panza stopped to scratch his head to bring back the letter to his memory, and balanced himself now on one foot, now the other, one moment staring at the ground, the next at the sky, and after having half chewed off the end of a finger and kept them in suspense waiting for him to begin, he said, after a long pause, "By God, señor vicar, the devil has stolen from my mind my recollection of the letter; but it said at the beginning, 'Exalted and scrubbing Lady.'"

"It cannot have said 'scrubbing,'" said the barber, "but 'superhuman' or 'sovereign.'"

"That is it," said Sancho; "then, as well as I remember, it continued, 'The wounded, and wanting of sleep, and the pierced, kisses your hands, ungrateful and very unrecognised fair one; and it said something or other about health and sickness that he was sending her; and from that it continued in that manner until it ended with 'Yours until death, the Knight of the Sorrowful Face

Both found it amusing to see what a good memory Sancho had, and they complimented him on it, and begged him to repeat the letter a couple more times, so that they could remember it by heart as well and be able to write it down. Sancho repeated it three times, and as he did, articulated three thousand more absurdities; then he told them more about his master but he never said a word about the blanketing that had happened to him in that inn, into which he refused to re-enter. He also told them, how if he brought him a favourable answer from the lady Dulcinea del Toboso, it was part of a deal after he had become an emperor, or at least a monarch; because it had been agreed between them, and with his personal worth and strength it was an easy accomplishment, that on becoming this his master was to arrange a marriage for him (because he would be a widower by that time) and was to give him as a wife one of the empress's ladies, the heiress of some rich and grand state on the mainland, having nothing to do with islands of any sort, because he did not care much about them. All of this Sancho expressed with so much composure - wiping his nose from time to time -and with little common-sense that his two hearers were again filled with amazement of the force of Don Quixote's madness that it could diminish this poor man's reason. They did not care to take the trouble of correcting his errors, as they considered that since it did not in any way hurt his conscience it would be better to leave it, and they would have more amusement in listening to his irrationalities; and so they asked him to pray to God for his master's health, as it was a very likely and very feasible for him to become an emperor, as he said, or at least an archbishop or some other dignitary of equal rank soon.

To which Sancho answered, "If fortune, should bring these things in such a way that my master wishes, instead of being an emperor, to be an archbishop, I would like to know what archbishops commonly give to their aides?"

"They commonly give them," said the Vicar, a permanent place in the church, or some similar place which brings them a good fixed income, not counting the altar fees, which may be a lot more."

"But for that," said Sancho, "the aide must be unmarried, and must know, at any rate, how to give a sermon, and if that is so, poor me, because I am married already and I don't know the first letter of the A B Cs. What will happen to me if my master decides to be an archbishop and not an emperor, as is usual and customary with Knights?"

"Do not worry, friend Sancho," said the barber, "because we will talk to your master, and advise him, even urging him as a case of conscience, to become an emperor and not an archbishop, because it will be easier for him as he is more valiant than literate."

"So I have thought," said Sancho; "although I can tell you he is ready for anything. What I aim to do for my part is to pray to our Lord to place him where it may be best for him, and where he may be able to grant good things to me."

"You speak like a man of sense," said the vicar, "and you will be acting like a good Christian; but what must be done now is to take the steps to persuade your master out of that useless self-punishment you say he is performing; and we should go into this inn to consider what approach to take, and also to have dinner, as it is now time."

Sancho said that they could go in, but he would wait outside, and that he would tell them afterwards the reason why he was unwilling, and why it did not suit him to enter it; but he begged them to return to him with something to eat, and for it to be hot, and also to bring barley for Rocinante. They left him and went in, and shortly after the barber returned to him with something to eat. After they had between them carefully thought over what they should do to carry out their objective, the vicar came up with an idea very well adapted to humour Don Quixote, and satisfy their purpose; and his notion, which he explained to the barber, was that he himself would assume the disguise of a wandering lady, while the other should try as best he could to pass for an aide, and that they should proceed to where Don Quixote was, and he, pretending to be an upset and worried lady, would ask him for a favour, which as a valiant Knight he could not refuse to grant; and the favour he would ask for was that he would accompany her to wherever she asked, in order to rectify a wrong which an evil Knight had done to her, while at the same time she would ask him not to require her to remove her mask, or ask her any question until he had corrected what the evil Knight had done. And he had no doubt that Don Quixote would comply with any request made under these terms, and that in this way they could remove him and take him to his own village, where they would endeavour to find out if his extraordinary madness accepted any kind of remedy.

CHAPTER 27

HOW THE VICAR AND THE BARBER PROCEEDED WITH THEIR SCHEME; TOGETHER WITH OTHER MATTERS WORTHY OF RECORD IN THIS GREAT HISTORY

The vicar's plan did not seem like a bad one to the barber, actually so good that they decided to execute it immediately. They begged for a coat from the landlady, leaving her with a new garment as a deposit belonging to the vicar, and the barber styled his beard. The landlady asked them what they were doing this for, and the vicar told her in a few words about the madness of Don Quixote and how this disguise was intended to get him away from the mountain where he was. The landlord and landlady immediately came to the conclusion that the madman was their guest, the balm man and master of the blanketed aide, and they told the vicar all that had happened between him and them, not overlooking what Sancho had been silent about. Finally, the landlady dressed the vicar in a style that left nothing to be desired; she put on him a cloth coat with black velvet stripes, and a lace under garment of green velvet set off by binding white satin, which was as well as a coat could be made in the time of King Wamba. The vicar put on his head a little quilted linen cap, and bound his forehead with a strip of black silk, while with another he made a mask with which he concealed his beard and face very well. He then put on his hat, which was broad enough to serve him as an umbrella, and enveloping himself in his new attire seated himself womanly-fashion on his donkey, while the barber mounted his, with a beard down to the waist of mingled red and white, because it was, the tail of a red ox.

They left, and the good Maritornes, who, sinner as she was, promised to pray a rosary of prayers that God would grant them success in such an arduous and Christian undertaking. But hardly had he gone forth from the inn when it struck the vicar that he was doing wrong dressing himself in that fashion, as it was an inappropriate thing for a priest to do, even though much might depend upon it; and saying this to the barber he begged him to exchange dress, as it was more appropriate that he should be the distressed lady, while he himself would play the aide's part, which would be less insulting to his self-respect; otherwise he was committed to have nothing more to do with the matter, and let the devil take Don Quixote. Just at this moment Sancho came, and on seeing the pair in such costume he was unable to restrain his laughter; the barber, however, agreed to do as the vicar wished, and, altering their plan, the vicar went on to instruct him how to play his part and what to say to Don Quixote to induce and compel him to come with them and give up his commitment to that place he had chosen for his worthless self-punishment. The barber told him he could manage it properly without any instruction, and as he did not care to dress himself up until they were nearer to where Don Quixote was, he folded up the garments, and the vicar adjusted his beard, and they continued their journey under the guidance of Sancho Panza, who went along telling them of the encounter with the madman they met in the Sierra, saying nothing, however, about finding the bag and its contents.

The next day they reached the place where Sancho had marked the branches to direct him to where he had left his master, and recognising it he told them that this was the entrance, and that it would be best to dress themselves now, if that was required to free his master; because they had already told him that going in this disguise and dressing in this way was highly important in order to rescue his master from the destructive life he had adopted; and they told him strictly not to tell his master who they were, or that he knew them, and if he asked, as he would, if he had given the letter to Dulcinea, to say that he had, and that, as she did not know how to read, she had answered by word of mouth, saying that she commanded him, on pain of her displeasure, to come and see her immediately; because in this way and with what they intended to say to him they felt sure of bringing him back to a better mode of life and inducing him to take immediate steps to become an emperor or monarch, because he could easily become an archbishop. All this Sancho listened to and fixed well in his memory, and thanked them enthusiastically for intending to recommend his master to be an emperor instead of an archbishop, because he felt sure that when it came to rewards for their aides, emperors could do more than archbishops could. He said, too, that it would be wise for him to go ahead before them to find him, and give him his lady's answer; because that perhaps might be enough to bring him away from the place without putting them through all of this trouble. They approved of what Sancho proposed, and decided to wait for him until he came back after having found his master.

Sancho went ahead into the Sierra, leaving them next to a gentle little stream, and where the rocks and trees gave a cool and grateful shade. It was an August day, and the heat in those parts was intense, and the hour was three in the afternoon, all of which made the spot more inviting and tempted them to wait there for Sancho's return, which they did.

They were relaxing in the shade, when a voice unaccompanied by the notes of any instrument, but sweet and pleasing in its tone, reached their ears, at which they were surprised, as the place did not seem to them a likely place for someone who sang so well; because although it is often said that shepherds with rare voices can be found in the woods and fields, this is closer to a poet's imagination than the truth. And they were more surprised when they perceived that what they heard sung were not the verses of rural shepherds, but songs of the city; and it was proven, because these were the verses that they heard:

What makes my quest of happiness seem vain?
Disdain.
What asks me to abandon hope of ease?
Jealousies.
What holds my heart in anguish and suspense?
Absence.

If that is so, then for my grief
Where do I turn to gain relief?
When hope on every side lies slain
By Absence, Jealousies, Disdain?

What fits my cause of suffering like a glove?
Love.
What will improve my glory's stance?
Chance.
Where is permission to distress me given?
Heaven.
If that is so, but I await
The blow of a resistless fate,
Since, working for my sorrow, these three,
Love, Chance and Heaven, in association I see.

What must I do to find a remedy?
Die.
What is the lure for love when shy and strange?
Change.
What, if all fails, will cure the heart of sadness?
Madness.
If that is so, it is but folly
To seek a cure for melancholy:
Ask where it lies; the answer is left
In Change, in Madness, or in Death.

The hour, the summer season, the solitary place, the voice and skill of the singer, all contributed to the wonder and delight of the two listeners, who remained waiting to hear more; finding however, that the silence continued for some time after, they decided to search for the musician who sang with such a fine voice; but just as they were about to do so they heard the same voice, which once more hit their ears, singing this:

SONNET

Toward heaven, our holy Friendship, did go
Soaring to seek your home beyond the sky,
And take your seat among the saints so high,
It was your will to leave the earth below

Your resemblance, and on it to bestow
Your veil, was at times hypocrisy,
Parading in your shape, deceives the eye,

160

And makes its evil bright as virtues show.

Friendship, return to us, do not cheat,
You wear it now, your former attire should restore,
However, I see, your sincerity is poor.
If you will not unmask your counterfeit,

The song ended with a deep exhale, and again the listeners remained waiting attentively for the singer to resume; but perceiving that the music had now turned to cries and heart-twisting moans they determined to find out who the unhappy man could be whose voice was as rare as his sighs were sad, and they had not proceeded far when on turning the corner of a rock they discovered a man who had the same appearance as Sancho had described to them when he told them the story of Cardenio. He, showing no astonishment when he saw them, stood still with his head resting on his chest like someone in deep thought, without raising his eyes to look at them after the first glance when they suddenly came to him. The vicar, who was aware of his misfortune and recognised him by the description, being a man of good speech, approached him and in a few sensible words asked and urged him to quit this life of misery, or else he would end it there, which would be the greatest of all misfortunes. Cardenio was then in his right mind, free from any attack of that madness which so frequently carried him away, and seeing them dressed in a fashion so unusual among the visitors of this wilderness, could not help showing some surprise, especially when he heard them speak about his case as if it were a well-known matter (because the vicar's words gave him this idea) so he replied to them:

"I see, you sirs, whoever you may be, that Heaven, whose care it is to help the good, and even the evil more often, here, in this remote spot, cut off from human contact, sends me, although I do not deserve it, those who seek to draw me away from this to some better place, showing me by many and forcible arguments how unreasonably I act in leading the life I do; but as they know, that if I escape from this evil I will fall into another greater evil, perhaps people will call me a weak-minded man, or, what is worse, one who lacks reason; it would be no wonder, because I myself can perceive that the effect of the recollection of my misfortunes is so great and works so powerfully to my destruction, that although I try to think otherwise at times I become like a stone, without feeling or consciousness; and I come to feel the truth of it when they tell me and show me proof of the things I have done when the terrible anger overpowers me; and all I can do is moan about my life, and curse my destiny, and try to justify my madness by saying how it was caused, to anyone that cares to hear it; because no reasonable people after learning the cause will be surprised by the effects; and if they cannot help me at least they will not blame me, and the disgust they feel at my wild ways will turn into sympathy for my problems. If it is so, sirs, that you are here with the same objective as the others that have come, before you proceed with your wise arguments, I ask you to hear the story of my innumerable misfortunes, because perhaps when you have heard it you will spare yourselves the trouble you would take in offering consolation to grief that is beyond the reach of it."

As they, both of them, desired nothing more than to hear from his own lips the cause of his suffering, they asked him to tell it, promising not to do anything for his relief or comfort that he did not wish; and then the unhappy gentleman began his sad story in nearly the same words and manner in which he had said it to Don Quixote and the goat herder a few days ago, when, due to Master Elisabad, and Don Quixote's honourable observance of what was due to chivalry, left the story unfinished, as this history has already recorded; but now fortunately the man did not suffer any fit of madness, which allowed him to tell it to the end; and so, coming to the incident about the note which Don Fernando had found in the volume of "Amadis of France," Cardenio said that he remembered it perfectly and that it was in these words:

"Luscinda to Cardenio.

"Every day I discover virtues in you that oblige and compel me to hold you in higher esteem; so if you desire to relieve me of this obligation without cost to my honour, you may easily do so. I have a father who knows you and loves me dearly, who without putting any constraint on my inclination will grant what will be reasonable for you to have, if it is so that you value me as you say and as I believe you do."

By this letter I was induced, as I told you, to demand Luscinda as my wife, and it was through it that Luscinda came to be regarded by Don Fernando as one of the subtlest and prudent women of that time, and it was this letter that suggested to him to ruin me before my plan could be carried into effect. I told Don Fernando that all Lucinda's father was waiting for was for me to ask him for her, which I did not dare to suggest to to my father, fearing that he would not consent to it; not because he did not know perfectly well the rank, goodness, virtue, and beauty of Luscinda, and that she had qualities that would do honour to any family, but because I was aware that he did not wish me to marry so soon, before seeing what the Duke Ricardo would do for me. In short, I told Don Fernando that I did not mention it to my father, because of that difficulty, and it seemed to me that what I desired was never going to happen. To all of this Don Fernando answered that he would speak to my father, and persuade him to speak to Luscinda's father. Traitor, cruel, malicious, treacherous being! When had this poor man failed in his loyalty, who with such frankness showed you the secrets and the joys of his heart? What offence did I commit? What words did I say, or what directions did I give that did not have the continuance of your honour and welfare as their aim? But, poor me, did I continually complain? Yes, and it is that when misfortunes spring from the stars, descending from high and they fall on us with such fury and violence that no power on earth or human device can stop their course. Who could have thought that Don Fernando, a highborn gentleman, intelligent, bound to me by gratitude for my services, one that could win the object of his love wherever he set his affections, could have become so stubborn, as they say, as to rob me of my one lamb that was not even yet in my possession? But putting aside these useless reflections, let us continue the broken thread of my unhappy story.

"To proceed, then: Don Fernando finding my presence an obstacle to the execution of his treacherous and evil plan, decided to send me to his elder brother to ask him for money to pay for six horses which, purposely, and with the sole objective of sending me away so that he could carry out his evil scheme, had bought the horses the very day he offered to speak to my father, and the price he now desired me to pay. Could I have anticipated this treachery? Could I by any chance have suspected it? Not at all; so far from it, I offered with the greatest pleasure to go immediately, I was satisfied by the good bargain he had made. That night I spoke with Luscinda, and told her what had been agreed with Don Fernando, and how I had strong hopes that our fair and reasonable wishes would be realised. She, as unsuspicious as I was of the treachery of Don Fernando, asked me to try to return quickly, as she believed the fulfilment of our desires would be delayed as long as my father put off speaking to hers. I do not know why it was that on saying this to me her eyes filled with tears that prevented her from saying any more although it seemed to me she was striving to say something. I was astonished at this unusual turn, which I never before observed in her. Because we always spoke, whenever good fortune and my ingenuity gave us the chance, with the greatest cheerfulness and happiness, but never mingling tears, sighs, jealousies, doubts, or fears with our words; I praised my good fortune that Heaven had given her to me as my mistress; I glorified her beauty, I celebrated her worth and her understanding; and she paid me back by praising in me what in her love for me she thought worthy of praise; and besides we had a hundred thousand things and activities of our neighbours and acquaintances to talk about, and the extent of my boldness was to take, almost by force, one of her fair white hands and carry it to my lips, as well as the intimacy allowed me to. But the night before the unhappy day of my departure she cried, she moaned, she sighed, and she withdrew leaving me filled with confusion and amazement, overwhelmed at the sight of such strange and distressing signs of grief and sorrow; but not to crush my hopes I attributed it all to the depth of her love for me and the pain that separation gives to those who love deeply. At last I left, sad and depressed, my heart filled with suspicions, but not knowing well what it was I suspected; clearly omens pointing to the sad event and misfortune that was awaiting me.

"I reached the place where I had been sent, gave the letter to Don Fernando's brother, and was kindly welcomed but not promptly dismissed, because he desired me to wait, very much against my will, eight days in some place where the duke his father was not likely to see me, as his brother wrote that the money was to be sent without his knowledge; all of which was part of

163

the scheme of the treacherous Don Fernando, because his brother had no lack of money to enable him to allow me to leave at once.

The command was one that exposed me to the temptation of disobeying it, as it seemed to me impossible to endure life for so many days separated from Luscinda, especially after leaving her in the sorrowful mood I have described to you; nevertheless, as a loyal servant I obeyed, although I felt it would be at the cost of my well-being. But four days later a man came in search of me with a letter which he gave me, and which by the address I noticed to be from Luscinda, and as the writing was hers. I opened it with fear and anxiety, persuaded that it must be something serious that had impelled her to write to me when at a distance, as she rarely did even when I was near. Before reading it I asked the man who it was that had given it to him, and how long he had been on the road; he told me that as he happened to be passing through one of the streets of the city at noon, a very beautiful lady called to him from a window, and with tears in her eyes said to him, 'Brother, if you are, as you seem to be, a Christian, for the love of God I ask you to take this letter without a moment's delay to the place and person named on the address, all which is well known, and by this you will be giving a great service to our Lord; and by doing this you will not be inconvenienced;' he said, 'and with this she threw me a handkerchief out of the window in which were tied up a hundred coins and this gold ring which I bring here together with the letter I have given you. And then without waiting for any answer she left the window, although not before she saw me take the letter and the handkerchief, and I had by signs let her know that I would do as she asked me to; and so, seeing myself so well paid for the trouble I would have in bringing it to you, and knowing by the address that it was to you it was sent (because, señor, I know you very well), and also unable to resist that beautiful lady's tears, I decided to trust no one else, but to come myself and give it to you, and in sixteen hours from the time when it was given to me I have made the journey, which, as you know, is eighteen miles.'

"While the good-natured unrehearsed courier was telling me this, I hung on his words, my legs trembling under me so that I could barely stand. However, I opened the letter and read these words:

"The promise Don Fernando gave you to urge your father to speak to mine, he has fulfilled much more to his own satisfaction than to your advantage. I have to tell you, señor, that he has demanded me for a wife, and my father, led away by what he considers Don Fernando's superiority over you, has favoured him so well, that in two days from today the engagement is to take place with such secrecy and so privately that the only witnesses are to be the Heavens above and a few of the household. Picture to yourself the state I am in; judge if it is urgent for you to come; the issue of the affair will show you whether I love you or not. God please grant this may reach your hand before mine will be forced to link itself with his who keeps so ill the faith that he has pledged to you. "

The words of the letter made me set out at once without waiting any longer for the money; because I now saw clearly that it was not the purchase of horses but of his own pleasure that had made Don Fernando send me to his brother. The enragement I felt against Don Fernando, joined with the fear of losing the prize I had won by so many years of love and devotion, gave me wings; so that almost flying I reached home the same day, by a time which served well for speaking with Luscinda. I arrived unobserved, and left the donkey on which I had come to the house to the worthy man who had brought me the letter, and fortune was for once pleased to be so kind that I found Luscinda. She recognised me immediately, and I her, but not as she should have recognised me, or I her. But who is there in the world that can boast of having fathomed or understood the wavering mind and unstable nature of a woman? The truth: no one. To proceed: as soon as Luscinda saw me she said, 'Cardenio, I am in my bridal dress, and the treacherous Don Fernando and my greedy father are waiting for me in the hall with the others, who will be the witnesses of my death before they witness my marriage. Do not worry, my friend, but plan to be present at this sacrifice, and if it cannot be prevented by my words, I have a dagger concealed which will prevent more deliberate violence, putting an end to my life and giving you proof of the love I have endured and give you.' I replied to her quickly, in fear I would not have time to reply, 'May your words be verified by your deeds, lady; and if you have a dagger to save your honour, I have a sword to defend you or kill myself if fortune is against us.'

"I think she could not have heard all these words, because I perceived that they called her away in a hurry, as the bridegroom was waiting. Now the night of my sorrow set in, the sun of my happiness went down, I felt my eyes bereft of sight, my mind of reason. I could not enter the house, or was I capable of any movement; but reflecting how important it was that I should be present at what might take place on the occasion, I prepared myself as best as I could and went in, because I knew well all the entrances and outlets; and besides, with the confusion of this secret that pervaded the house no one took any notice of me, so, without being seen, I found an opportunity of placing myself in the recess formed by a window of the hall itself, and concealed by the ends and borders of two tapestries, from between which I could, without being seen, see all that took place in the room. Who could describe the agitation of heart I suffered as I stood there - the thoughts that came to me - the reflections that passed through my mind? They were in such a state that cannot be, or would it be well to be told. Suffice it to say that the bridegroom entered the hall in his usual dress, without any ornament of any kind; only the groomsman he had (a cousin of Luscinda's), and the servants of the house were in the hall. Soon afterwards Luscinda came out from a side room, attended by her mother and two of her ladies, clothed and adorned in line with her rank and beauty, and in full event and ceremonial attire. My anxiety and distraction did not allow me to observe or notice particularly what she wore; I could only perceive the colours, which were crimson and white, and the glitter of the gems and jewels on her head dress and apparel, surpassed by the rare beauty of her lovely auburn hair that rivalling with the precious stones and the light of the four torches that stood in the hall shone with a brighter gleam than all. Oh memory, fatal enemy of my peace! Why place in front of me now the incomparable beauty of that adored enemy of mine? Would it not be better, cruel memory, to remind me and recall what she did next, that encourages me by a wrong so evident that I seek, if not vengeance now, at least to free myself of life? Do not be weary, sirs, listening to these deviations; my sorrow is not one of those that can or should be told concisely and briefly, because to me each incident deserves many words."

To this the vicar replied that not only were they not weary of listening to him, but that the details he mentioned interested them deeply, being a kind that should not be omitted and deserve the same attention as the main story.

"To proceed, then," continued Cardenio: "everyone being in the hall, the priest of the town came in and as he took the pair by the hand to perform the necessary ceremony, at the words, 'Will you, Señorita Luscinda, take Señor Don Fernando, here present, for your lawful husband, as the holy Church orders?' I thrust my head and neck out from between the tapestries, and with eager ears and throbbing heart set myself to listen to Luscinda's answer, awaiting, for her reply the sentence of death or the gift of life. Oh, I had dared at that moment to rush forward crying aloud, 'Luscinda, Luscinda! Be careful what you do; remember what you owe me; think that you are mine and cannot be another's; reflect that your declaration "Yes" and the end of my life will come at the same time. O, treacherous Don Fernando! Robber of my glory, death of my life! What do you seek? Remember that you cannot as a Christian attain the object of your wishes, because Luscinda is my bride!' What a fool I am! Now that I am far away, and out of danger, I am saying what I should have done and what I did not do: now that I have allowed my precious treasure to be robbed from me, I despise the robber, on who I might have taken vengeance if I had as much heart for it as I do for moaning about my fate; in short, as I was a coward and a fool, it is little wonder that now I am dying in shame, regretful, and mad.

"The priest stood waiting for the answer of Luscinda, who for a long time withheld it; and just as I thought she was taking out the dagger to save her honour, or struggling for words to make some declaration of the truth on my behalf, I heard her say in a faint and feeble voice, 'I will:' Don Fernando said the same, and giving her the ring they stood linked by a knot that could never be loosened. The bridegroom then approached to embrace his bride; and she, pressing her hand on her heart, fell fainting in her mother's arms. All that remains, is for me to tell you the state I was in when in that consent that I heard I saw all my hopes mocked, the words and promises of Luscinda proved to be false, and the recovery for the prize I had lost in an instant would remain impossible forever. I stood confused, totally abandoned, it seemed, Heaven declared the earth to be my enemy, the air refusing me to breath, the water moisture for my tears; it was only the fire that gathered strength so that my whole frame glowed with rage and jealousy. They were all thrown into confusion by Luscinda's fainting, and as her mother was assisting her to give her air a sealed paper was discovered in her chest which Don Fernando seized at once and began to read by the light of one of the torches. As soon as he had read it he sat himself in a chair, leaning his cheek on his hand in the attitude of one deep in thought, without taking any part in the effort that was being made to recover his bride after she had fainted.

"Seeing all the household in confusion, I wanted to come out regardless whether I were seen or not, and determined, if I were, to do some furious deed that would prove to all the world the righteous anger of my chest in the punishment of the treacherous Don Fernando, and that of the inconsistent fainting lady. But my fate, no doubt reserving me for greater sorrows, if there were such a thing, ordered it that just then I replaced that reason which since has been missing in me; and so, without seeking to take vengeance on my greatest enemies (which might have been easily taken), I decided to take it on myself to inflict the pain they deserved, perhaps with even greater severity than I should have given to them; because sudden pain is over soon, but that which is extended: tortures and is always hurting without ending a life. In a few words, I left the house and reached the man who I had left my donkey with; I made him prepare the saddle for me, mounted without saying goodbye, and rode out of the city, not willing to turn my head and look back to it; and when I found myself alone in the open country, covered by the darkness of the night, and tempted by the stillness to vent my grief without fear of being heard or seen, then I broke the silence and raised my voice cursing Luscinda and Don Fernando, as if this would avenge the wrong they had done to me. I called her cruel, ungrateful, false, thankless, but above all materialistic, since the wealth of my enemy had blinded the eyes of her affection, and turned it away from me and transferred it to someone who fortune had been more generous and liberal to.

And yet, in the middle of this outburst of insulting and scolding, I found excuses for her, saying it was no wonder that a young girl in the seclusion of her parents' house, trained and schooled to obey them always, would have been ready to yield to their wishes when they offered her a husband: a gentleman of such distinction, wealth, and noble birth, that if she had refused to accept him she would have been thought of as out of her senses, or to have placed her affection elsewhere, a suspicion which would be harmful to her name and fame. But then again, I said, if she had declared that I was her husband, they would have seen that in choosing me she had not chosen poorly and that they would excuse her, because before Don Fernando had made his offer, they themselves would not have desired, if their desires had been ruled by reason, a more eligible husband for their daughter than I was; and she, before taking the last fatal step of giving her hand, could have easily said that I had already given her mine, because I would have come forward to support any declaration of hers of this kind. In short, I came to the conclusion that frail love, little reflection, great ambition, and a craving for rank, made her forget the words with which she had deceived me, encouraging and supporting my firm hopes and honourable passion.

"Therefore speaking to myself and agitated, I journeyed onward for the remainder of the night, and by daylight I reached one of the passages in these mountains, among which I wandered for three days more without taking any path or road, until I came to some meadows, and there I asked some herdsmen in what direction the most rugged part of the mountain was. They told me that it was in tat region, and I immediately directed my course there, intending to end my life; but as I was making my way, my donkey dropped dead through fatigue and hunger, or, what I think is more likely, to be done with such a worthless burden as carrying me. I was left on foot, worn out, starving, without anyone to help me or any thought of seeking help: and so I laid on the ground, how long for I do not know, after this I got up and was freed from hunger, and found next to me some goat herders, who no doubt were the people who had relieved my need, because they told me how they had found me, and how I had been acting in a crazy manner that showed clearly I had lost my reason; and since then I am conscious that I am not always in full possession of it, but at times so deranged and crazed that I do a thousand mad things, tearing my clothes, crying aloud in these solitudes, cursing my fate, and calling out the name of her who is my enemy, and only seeking to end my life while crying; and when I recover my senses I find myself so exhausted and weary that I can barely move. Usually I stay in the hollow of a cork tree large enough to shelter this miserable body; the goat herders who roam these mountains, moved by compassion, give me food, leaving it nearby on the rocks, where they think I might pass and find it; and so, even though I may be out of my senses, nature teaches me what is required to sustain me, and makes me crave it and eager to take it. At other times, so they tell me when they find me in an irrational mood, I go out on the road, and although they would gladly give it to me, I snatch food by force from the herders taking it from the village to their huts. This is how I live the worthless life that remains, until it is Heaven's will to bring it to a close, or to reorder my memory so I no longer recollect the beauty and treachery of Luscinda, or the wrong done to me by Don Fernando; because if it will do this without depriving me of life, I will turn my thoughts toward some better channel; if not, I can only pray to heaven to have full mercy on my soul, because in myself I feel no power or strength to release my body from this path which by my own decision I have chosen to take.

"This, sirs, is the miserable story of my misfortune: tell me if it is something that can be told with less emotion than you have seen in me; and do not bother urging or trying to give me what reason suggests likely to serve as my relief, because it will benefit me as much as the medicine prescribed by a wise doctor benefits the sick man who will not take it. I have no wish for health without Luscinda; and since it is her pleasure to be another man's, when she is mine or should be mine, I live in misery when I should have enjoyed happiness. By her inconstancy she strove to make my ruin irrecoverable; I will strive to gratify her wishes by seeking my self-destruction; and it will show generations to come that I was deprived of that which all others in misfortune have in abundance, because to them the impossibility of being consoled is itself a consolation, while to me it is the cause of greater sorrow and sufferings, because I think that even in death there will be no end of them."

Here Cardenio brought to a close his long discourse and story, as full of misfortune as it was of love; but just as the vicar was going to give some words to comfort him, he was stopped by a voice that reached his ear, saying in miserable tones what will be told shortly; because at this point the sagacious historian, Cide Hamete Benengeli, brought this part to a conclusion.

CHAPTER 28

TELLING THE STRANGE AND DELIGHTFUL ADVENTURE THAT HAPPENED TO THE VICAR AND THE BARBER IN THE SAME SIERRA

The times were fortunate when that most daring Knight Don Quixote of La Mancha was sent into the world; because he formed a resolution so honourable, seeking to revive and restore the long-lost and almost obsolete order of Knighthood, we now enjoy in this age of ours, so poor in light entertainment, not only the charm of his ethical history, but also the tales and episodes contained in it which are, no less pleasing, ingenious, and truthful, than the history itself; which, resuming its thread, spun, and woven, states that just as the vicar was going to offer consolation to Cardenio, he was interrupted by a voice that came to his ears saying in miserable tones:

"O God! is it possible I have found a place that may serve as a secret grave for the load of this body that I support unwillingly? If these mountains offer solitude and I am not deceived, how much more grateful will these rocks and trees be, that permit me to complain about my misfortune, than any human being, because there is none on earth to turn to for advice in doubt, comfort in sorrow, or relief in distress!"

All this was distinctly heard by the vicar and those with him, and as it seemed to be coming from nearby, as indeed it was, they got up to look for the speaker, and before they had gone far they discovered behind a rock, sat at the foot of an ash tree, a youth in the clothing of a peasant, whose face they were unable at the moment to see as he was leaning forward, washing his feet in the stream that flowed past. They approached so silently that he did not notice them, being fully occupied washing his feet, which were so white that they looked like two pieces of shining crystal among the other stones of the stream. The whiteness and beauty of these feet struck them with surprise, because they did not seem to have been made to follow the plough as their owner's clothing suggested; and so, finding they had not been noticed, the vicar, who was in front, made a sign to the other two to conceal themselves behind some fragments of rock that were there; which they did, observing closely what the youth was wearing. He had on a loose double-breasted brown jacket clinging tight to his body with a white cloth; he wore brown cloth trousers, and on his head a brown hat; and he had suspenders on, which seemed to be made from a pure white mineral rock.

As soon as he had finished bathing his beautiful feet, he wiped them with a towel he took from under the hat, which when taking it off he raised his face, and those who were watching him had an opportunity of seeing a beauty so exquisite that Cardenio said to the vicar in a whisper:

"This is no human creature but a divine being."

The youth taking of his hat, and shaking his head from side to side shook loose and spread out a mass of hair that the beams of the sun might have envied;

by this they knew what had at first seemed like a peasant boy was actually a lovely woman, actually the most beautiful the eyes of two of them had ever seen, or even Cardenio's if they had not seen and known Luscinda, because afterwards he declared that only the beauty of Luscinda could compare with this. The long auburn strands not only covered her shoulders, but their length and abundance concealed her, so that nothing except the feet of her body was visible. She now used her hands as a comb, and if her feet had seemed like bits of crystal in the water, her hands looked like pieces of snow among her locks; all which increased not only the admiration of the three viewers, but their anxiety to know who she was. With this objective they decided to reveal themselves, and at the sound they made getting up on their feet the lady raised her head, and parting her hair from in front of her eyes with both hands, she looked to see who had made the noise, and the instant she saw them she rose to her feet, and without waiting to put on her shoes or gather her hair, she hastily snatched a bundle of clothes that she had next to her, and, scared and alarmed, attempted to run; but before she had gone a few steps she fell on the ground, her delicate feet being unable to bear the roughness of the ground; seeing this, the three rushed toward her, and the vicar said:

"Stay, señora, whoever you are, because us you see here only wish to be of service to you; you have no need to run, because your feet cannot bear it, and we cannot allow it."

Taken by surprise and confused, she did not reply to these words. They, however, came towards her, and the vicar taking her hand went on to say:

"What your dress would hide, señora, has been made known to us by your hair; a clear proof that there can be no simple cause that has disguised your beauty in a fashion so unworthy of it, and sent it into a place like this where we have had the good fortune to find you, if not to relieve your distress, at least to offer you comfort; because no distress, as long as life lasts, can be so oppressive or reach such a height to make the sufferer refuse to listen to comfort offered with good intention. And so, señora, or señor, or whatever you prefer to be, dismiss the fear that our appearance has caused you and let us know of your good or evil fortunes, because from all of us together, or from each individually, you will receive sympathy for your trouble."

While the vicar was speaking, the disguised lady stood as if she was stunned, looking at them without opening her lips to say a word, just like a villager who has seen something strange that he has never seen before; but after the vicar spoke some further words of the same kind, sighing deeply she broke her silence and said:

"Since the solitude of these mountains has not been able to conceal me, and the escape of my untidy hair will not allow my tongue to tell any lie, it would be pointless for me to make any further façade about which, if you were to believe me, you would believe more out of courtesy than for any other reason. This being so, I thank you, for the offer you have made to me, which places me under the obligation of complying with the request you have made; although I fear the account I will give you of my misfortunes will excite in you as much concern as compassion, because you will be unable to suggest anything to remedy them or any consolation to alleviate them. However, so that my honour is not be left a matter of doubt in your minds, now that you have discovered me to be a woman, and see that I am young, alone, and in this dress, things that taken together or separately would be enough to destroy any good name, I feel bound to tell you what I would willingly keep secret if I could."

All of this she delivered without any hesitation, with so much ease and in such a sweet voice that they were no less charmed by her intelligence than by her beauty, and as they repeated their offers and appeals to her to fulfil her promise, she without further insisting, first modestly covering her feet and gathering her hair, sat herself on a stone with the three placed around her, and, after an effort to hold back some tears that came to her eyes, in a clear and steady voice began her story:

"In Andalusia there is a town from which a duke takes a title which makes him one of those that are called Grandees of Spain. This nobleman has two sons, the elder the heir to his self-respect and apparently to his good qualities; the younger heir to I do not know what, unless it is the treachery of Vellido and the lies of Ganelon. My parents are this lord's servants, modest in origin, but so wealthy that if birth had given them a fortune, they would have had nothing left to desire, and neither would I have had reason to fear trouble like that in which I find myself now; because it may be that my bad fortune came from theirs in not having been nobly born. It is true they are not so low that they have any reason to be ashamed of their condition, but neither are they so high as to remove from my mind the impression that my misfortune comes from their humble birth. They are, in short, peasants, plain homely people, without any stain of disreputable blood, and, as the saying is, old Christians, but so rich that by their wealth and generous way of life they are coming by degrees to be considered noble by birth, and even by position; although the wealth and nobility they thought most of was having me for their daughter; and as they have no other child to make their heir, and are affectionate parents, I was one of the most indulged daughters that any parents ever indulged.

"I was the mirror in which they saw themselves, the remedy of their old age, and the object in which, with submission to Heaven, all their wishes centred, and mine were in accordance with theirs, because I knew their worth; and as I was the love of their hearts, I was also their possession. Through me they engaged or dismissed their servants; through my hands passed the accounts and returns of what was sown and reaped; the oil-mills, the wine-presses, the count of the flocks and herds, the beehives, in summary all that a rich farmer like my father has or can have, I had under my care, and I acted as guardian with diligence on my part and the satisfaction on theirs I cannot describe very well to you. The hours left to me after I had given the necessary orders to the head shepherds, overseers, and other labourers, I spent in such engagements which are not only allowable but necessary for young girls: using the needle, embroidery, cushion making, and to refresh my mind if I was not doing these for a while, I found recreation in reading some holy book or playing the harp, because experience taught me that music soothes a troubled mind and relieves weariness of spirit. This was the life I led in my parents' house and if I have portrayed it thoroughly, it is not with pretention, or to let you know that I am rich, but so you can see how, without any fault of mine, I have fallen from the happy condition I have described, to the misery I am in at present. The truth is, that while I was leading this busy life, in a seclusion that might compare with that of a monastery, and unseen by anyone except the servants of the house (because when I went to Mass it was so early in the morning, and I was so closely joined by my mother and the women of the household, and so thickly veiled and so shy, that my eyes barely saw more ground than I walked on), in spite of all this, the eyes of love, or sloth, more appropriate in this case, discovered me, with the help of the attention of Don Fernando; because that is the name of the younger son of the duke I speak of."

The moment the speaker mentioned the name Don Fernando, Cardenio changed colour and broke into a sweat, with such signs of emotion that the vicar and the barber, who observed it, feared that one of the mad fits which they heard attacked him sometimes was about to come to him; but Cardenio showed no further agitation and remained quiet, observing the peasant girl with fixed attention, because he began to suspect who she was. She, however, without noticing the excitement of Cardenio, continuing her story, went on to say:

"And he had hardly discovered me, when, as he confessed afterwards, was smitten with a violent love for me, as the manner in which it displayed itself clearly showed. But to reduce the long speech of my miseries, I will pass in silence all the tricks used by Don Fernando to declare his passion for me. He bribed the household, he gave and offered gifts and presents to my parents; every day was like a holiday or festivity in our street; at night no one could sleep due to the music; the love letters that used to come to my hand, no one knew how, were innumerable, full of affectionate pledges, containing more promises and oaths than there were letters in them; all which did not soften me, but hardened my heart against him, as if he had been my mortal enemy, and as if everything he did to make me yield were done with the opposite purpose. Not that the high-bred manner of Don Fernando was unpleasant to me, or that I found his insistences tiring; because it gave me a sort of satisfaction to find myself so wanted and esteemed by a gentleman of such distinction, and I was not displeased at being praised in his letters (because however ugly we women can be, it seems to me it always pleases us to hear ourselves being called beautiful) but that my own sense of right was opposed to all of this, as well as the repeated advice of my parents, who now very clearly perceived Don Fernando's purpose, because he cared very little if the whole world knew it. They told me they trusted and confided their honour and good name to my virtue and morality alone, and asked me consider the disparity between Don Fernando and myself, from which I might conclude that his intentions, whatever he might say to the contrary, had as their aim his own pleasure rather than my advantage; and if I desired to oppose his unreasonable attempt, they were ready, they said, to marry me immediately to someone else I preferred, either among the leading people of our own town, or any other in the neighbourhood; because with their wealth and my good name, a match could be found in any part. This offer, and their sound advice strengthened my firmness, and I never gave Don Fernando a word in reply that could encourage in him any hope of success, however remote."

"All this caution of mine, which he must have taken as me being shy, had apparently the effect of increasing his appetite, because that is the name I give to his passion for me; had it been what he declared it to be, you would recognise it now, because there would have been no occasion to tell you about it. Shortly after he discovered that my parents were contemplating marriage for me in order to put an end to his hopes of obtaining possession of me, or at least to secure additional protectors to watch over me, and this intelligence or suspicion made him act as you will now hear. One night, as I was in my room with no other companion than a lady who waited on me, with the doors carefully locked in case my honour would be endangered through any carelessness, I do not know or can conceive how it happened, but, with all this seclusion and these precautions, and in the solitude and silence of the night, I found him standing in front of me, a vision that astounded me so much that it deprived my eyes of sight, and my tongue of speech. I had no power to make a cry for help, neither, did he give me time to, as he immediately approached me, and taking me in his arms (because, as overwhelmed as I was, and powerless, I say, to help myself), he began to make confessions to me that I do not know how could be false or have had the power to be dressed to seem like the truth; and the traitor arranged that his tears should guarantee his words, and his sighs would prove his sincerity.

"I, a poor young girl alone, not used to being among people in cases such as this, began, I do not know how, to think all these lying declarations were true, although without being moved by his sighs and tears to anything more than pure compassion; and so, as the first feeling of confusion passed away, and I began in some degree to recover myself, I said to him with more courage than I thought I could have possessed, 'If, as I am in your arms now, señor, I were in the claws of a fierce lion, and my release could only be obtained by doing or saying something which opposes my honour, it would be no more in my power to do it or say it, than it is now; so then, if you hold my body clasped in your arms, I hold my soul secured by virtuous intentions, very different from yours, as you will see if you attempt to carry them into effect by force. I am a servant, but I am not your servant; your nobility neither has or should have any right to dishonour or degrade my humble birth; and a low-born peasant as I am, I have my self-respect as much as you do, a lord and gentleman: with me your violence will have no purpose, your wealth will have no weight, your words will have no power to deceive me, and neither will your sighs or tears soften me: and if I were to see any of the things I speak of in him who my parents give to me as a husband, his will should be mine, and mine should be his; and my honour being preserved even though my inclinations would willingly yield to him what you, señor, would only obtain by force; and this I say so you know that any other man, other than my lawful husband will never win anything from me.' 'If that,' said this disloyal gentleman, 'is the only hesitation you feel, Dorothea' (because that is the name of this unhappy lady), 'I give you my hand to be yours, and let Heaven, from which nothing is hidden, and this image of Our Lady you have here, be witnesses of this pledge.'"

When Cardenio heard her say she was called Dorothea, he showed fresh anxiety and felt convinced about the truth of his former suspicion, but he was unwilling to interrupt the story, and wanted to hear the end of what he already knew, so he merely said:

"What! Dorothea is your name, señora? I have heard of another woman with the same name who can perhaps match your misfortunes. But continue; and then I will tell you something that will astonish you as much as it will excite your compassion."

Dorothea was struck by Cardenio's words as well as by his strange and miserable attire, and begged him if he knew anything concerning her to say it immediately, because if fortune had left her any blessing it was courage to handle whatever disaster may come to her, as she felt sure that none could reach her capable of increasing in any degree what she had already endured.

"I would not let the occasion pass by, señora," replied Cardenio, "of telling you what I think, if what I suspect is the truth, but so far there has been no opportunity, and it is not of any importance for you to know it."

"Nevertheless," replied Dorothea, "what happened next was Don Fernando, taking an image that stood in the room, placed it as a witness of our engagement, and with the most binding words and extravagant promises promised to become my husband; although before he had ended I asked him to really consider what he was doing, and think of the anger his father would feel seeing him married to a peasant girl and one of his servants; I told him not to let my beauty blind him, because that was not enough to make an excuse for his wrongdoing; and if in the love he offered me he wished to do any kindness for me, it would be to leave my life and let it follow its course at the level my condition required; because marriages so unequal never brought happiness, neither did they last long to grant the enjoyment they began with.

"All of this I have now repeated, I said to him, and much more which I cannot remember; but it had no effect of inducing him to relinquish his purpose; he who has no intention of paying does not trouble himself about difficulties when he is negotiating a bargain. At the same time, I discussed the matter briefly in my own mind, saying to myself, 'I would not be the first who has risen through marriage from low to high, neither will Don Fernando be the first who beauty or, as is more likely, a blind attachment, has led to mate himself below his rank. Then, since I am introducing no new practice, I may as well profit myself with the honour that chance offers me, because even if his inclination for me would not outlast the attainment of his wishes, I would be, after all, his wife before God.

And if I attempt to repel him by scorn, I can see that, being fair means failing, he is in a mood to use force, and I will be left dishonoured and without any method of proving my innocence to those who cannot know how unwillingly I have come to be in this position; because what arguments would persuade my parents that this gentleman entered my room without my consent?'

"All these questions and answers passed through my mind in a moment; but the promises of Don Fernando, the witnesses he appealed to, the tears he gave, and lastly the charm of his character and his high-bred style, which, accompanied by such signs of genuine love, might well have conquered a heart even harder than mine - these were the things that more than all began to influence me and lead me unaware to my ruin. I called my maid, so there could be a witness on earth besides those in Heaven, and again Don Fernando renewed and repeated his promises, invited as witnesses' new saints in addition to the former ones, called on himself a thousand curses if he failed to keep his promise, gave more tears, increased his sighs and pressed me closer in his arms, from which he had never allowed me to escape; and so I was left by my maid, and finished being whole, and he became a traitor and a liar."

"The day following the night of my misfortune did not come so quickly, I imagine, as Don Fernando wished, because when desire has attained its objective, the next greatest pleasure is to flee from the scene. I say this because Don Fernando was in a rush to leave me, and through the skill of my maid, who was the one who let him in, he reached the street before day; but when leaving me he told me, although not with as much sincerity and enthusiasm as when he came, that I should be assured of his faith and of the purity and sincerity of his promises; and to confirm his words he took a ring off his finger and placed it on mine. He then left and I was left, I do not know whether happy or full of sorrow; all I can say is, I was left disturbed and troubled in my mind and almost disoriented by what had happened, and I did not have the spirit, or it did not occur to me, to blame my maid for the betrayal she had been guilty of, by allowing Don Fernando into my room; because in that moment I was unable to make up my mind whether what had happened to me was for good or evil. I told Don Fernando when he was leaving, that now I was his, he can see me on other nights discreetly, until he decided to let the matter become known; but, the following night, he did not come, and for more than a month I did not see him in the street or in church, while I exhausted myself looking for him; although I knew he was in the town, and almost every day he went out hunting, an activity he was very fond of. I remember well how sad and lifeless those days and hours were to me; I remember well how I began to doubt as they went by, and even to lose confidence in the faith of Don Fernando; and I remember, too, how my maid heard the words of me blaming her, and how I was forced to place a restraint on my tears and on the expression of my face, not to give my parents a cause to ask me why I was so miserable, and cause me to invent excuses in reply. But all of this was suddenly brought to an end, because the time came when all of these considerations were disregarded, and there was no further question of honour, when my patience ran out and a secret became known. The reason was, that a few days later it was reported in the town that Don Fernando was to be married in a city nearby to a lady of rare beauty, the daughter of parents in a distinguished position, although not so rich that would entitle her to look for such a brilliant match; it was said, that her name was Luscinda, and that at the engagement some strange things happened."

Cardenio heard the name of Luscinda, but he only shrugged his shoulders, bit his lips, raised his eyebrows, and two streams of tears escaped from his eyes. Dorothea, however, did not interrupt her story, and went on with these words:

"This sad intelligence reached my ears, and, instead of being struck with a chill, I was filled with such rage and fury, my heart burned and I barely restrained myself from rushing out into the streets, crying aloud and broadcasting openly the deceit I was the victim of; but this rage was controlled by a resolution I formed, to be carried out the same night, and that was to wear this clothing, which I got from a servant of my father's, one of the shepherds, who I confided my whole misfortune in, and who I asked to accompany me to the city where I heard my enemy was. Although he argued against for my boldness, and criticised my plan, when he saw me so intent on my purpose, offered to come with me, as he said, to the end of the world. I packed in a linen pillow-case a woman's dress, and some jewels and money to provide for emergencies, and in the silence of the night, without letting my disloyal maid know, I left the house, accompanied by my servant and a lot of anxiety, and on foot went toward the city, as if I had wings given to me by my eagerness to reach it, if not to prevent what I presumed to have already happened, at least to ask Don Fernando to tell me with what conscience he had done it. I reached my destination in two and a half days, and when entering the city, I asked for the house of Luscinda's parents. The first person I asked gave me more in reply than I asked to know; he showed me the house, and told me all that had happened at the engagement, an event of such dishonour in the city that every idle person in the city was talking about it. He said that on the night of Don Fernando's engagement to Luscinda, as soon as she had consented to be his bride by saying 'Yes,' she suddenly fainted, and when the bridegroom approached her to undo the top of her dress to give her air, he found a paper written by her, on which she wrote and declared that she could not be Don Fernando's bride, because she was already Cardenio's, who, according to the man's account, was a gentleman of distinction in the same city; and that if she had accepted Don Fernando, it was only in obedience to her parents. In short, he said, the words on the paper made it clear she was going to kill herself on the completion of the engagement, and gave her reasons for putting an end to herself all of which was confirmed, it was said, by a knife they found somewhere in her clothes. When seeing this, Don Fernando, was confident that Luscinda had fooled, offended, and played with him, and attacked her before she had recovered from her faint, and tried to stab her with the knife that had been found, and would have succeeded if her parents and those who were present had not prevented him. It was said, also, that Don Fernando left immediately, and that Luscinda did not recover from her faint until the next day, when she told her parents how she was really the bride of Cardenio who I have already mentioned. I discovered that Cardenio, according to the report, had been present at the engagement; and when he saw her become engaged, as she opposed his expectation, he left the city in misery, leaving behind, a letter declaring the wrong Luscinda had done to him, and his intention of going somewhere no one would ever see him again. This matter was a great dishonour in the city, and everyone spoke about it; especially when it became known that Luscinda was missing from her father's house and from the city, because she could not be found anywhere, which disturbed her parents, who did not know what to do to recover her. What I found out revived my hopes, and I was pleased not to have found Don Fernando than to find him married, because it seemed to me that the door was not entirely shut yet and gave relief to my case, and I thought that perhaps Heaven had put this obstacle in the way of the second love, to lead him to recognise his obligations to the former one, and reflect that as a Christian he was destined to consider his soul above all human objects. All this passed through my mind, and I attempted to comfort myself without finding it, indulging in faint and distant hopes of treasuring a life that I now despise.

"But while I was in the city, and uncertain what to do, as I could not find Don Fernando, I heard a notice being given by the town announcer offering a great reward to anyone who would find me, and giving the details of my age and the clothing I wore; and I heard it said that the man who came with me had taken me from my father's house; something that cut through my heart, showing how low my good name had fallen, since it was not enough that I would lose it by leaving, but they must add who I left with, someone so much beneath me and so unworthy of my consideration. The instant I heard the notice I left the city with my servant, who now began to show signs wavering in his devotion to me, and the same night, due to the fear of being discovered, we entered the most enveloped part of these mountains. But, as it is commonly said, one evil creates another and the end of one misfortune is often the beginning the next: even greater, and this proved to be my case; because my servant, who until then had been so faithful and trustworthy, when he found we were alone in these woods, encouraged more by his own evil than by my beauty, decided to take advantage of the opportunity which these seclusions seemed to present to him, and with little shame and less fear of God and respect for me, began to make suggestions to me; and when I replied to the boldness of his proposals with severe language, he decided no longer to ask, which was his first strategy, and began to use violence.

"But Heaven, which never fails to watch over and aid good intentions, aided mine, and with my slight strength and with little effort I pushed him off the edge of a cliff, where I left him, dead or alive I do not know; and then, with greater speed than seemed possible in fear and with fatigue, I made my way into the mountains, without any other thought or purpose except hiding myself among them, escaping my father and those who were sent by his order to search for me. Now I no longer know how many months it has been since I came here, where I met a herdsman who employed me as his servant at a place in the heart of this Sierra, and all of this time serving him, striving to hide this hair which has now unexpectedly betrayed me. But all my care was pointless, because my master discovered that I was not a man, and concealed the same desires as my servant; and as fortune does not always provide a remedy in cases of difficulty, and I had no cliff or valley nearby to throw the master and remedy his passion, as I had in the servant's case, I thought it would be less evil to leave him and once again conceal myself in these mountains, than to test my strength again. So, as I say, I went into hiding again to seek a place where I could with tears pray to Heaven to have pity on my misery, and give me help and strength to escape from it, or let me die here, leaving no trace of an unhappy being who, by no fault of her own, has created disgraceful talk at home and in a nearby city."

CHAPTER 29

THE AMUSING METHOD AGREED ON TO RESCUE OUR LOVE-SICK KNIGHT FROM THE SEVERE SELF-PUNISHMENT HE HAD IMPOSED ON HIMSELF

"That, sirs, is the true story of my sadness; judge for yourselves whether the sighs and crying you heard, and the tears that flowed from my eyes, did not have a sufficient cause; and if you consider the nature of my misfortune you will see that consolation is an unlikely remedy, as there is no possible cure for it. All I ask for, something you can easily do: please show me where I can spend the rest of my life without the fear of discovery by those who are looking of me; because although my parents love me dearly which makes me feel sure I will be welcomed back by them, I have a great feeling of shame over the thought that I cannot present myself in front of them as they expect, so I should rather remove myself from their sight forever than look them in the face with the reflection that they consider my stripped of the purity they had a right to expect in me."

With these words she became silent, and the colour that spread over her face clearly displayed the pain and shame she was suffering in her heart. In theirs, the listeners felt just as much pity as they did wonder about her misfortunes; but as the vicar was just about to offer her some consolation and advice Cardenio spoke, saying, "So then, señora, you are Dorothea, the only daughter of the rich Clenardo?" Dorothea was surprised hearing her father's name, and at the depressed appearance of the man who mentioned it, because it has been already said how poorly dressed Cardenio was; so she said to him:

"And who are you, brother, you seem to know my father's name so well? Because so far, if I remember correctly, I have not mentioned it in the whole story of my misfortune."

"I am that unhappy man, señora," replied Cardenio, "who, as you have said, Luscinda declared to be her husband; I am the unfortunate Cardenio, who due to the wrong-doing of he who has brought you to your present condition and has reduced me to the state you see me in, scruffy, dirty and without all human comfort, and what is worse, without reason, because I only possess it when Heaven is pleased for a short space of time to restore it to me. I, Dorothea, am the man who witnessed the wrong done by Don Fernando, and heard the 'yes' spoken by Luscinda which declared herself as his bride: I am the man who did not have the courage to see what happened after she fainted, or to hear what the paper that was found had said, because my heart did not have the fortitude to withstand so many hits of bad-fortune at the same time; and so losing my patience I left the house, and left a letter with my host, who I asked to place it in Luscinda's hands, I took myself to these solitudes, determined to end the life I hated here, as if it were my mortal enemy. But fate would not allow me to, contenting itself instead with stripping me of my reason, perhaps to preserve me for the good fortune I have had in meeting you; because if what you have just told us is true, as I believe it is, it may be that Heaven has in store for both of us a happier ending to our misfortunes than we were seeking; because as Luscinda cannot marry Don Fernando, being mine, as she has declared, and Don Fernando cannot marry her as he is yours, we can reasonably hope that Heaven will restore for us what is ours, as it is still possible and not yet destroyed. And as we have this comfort which has not come from a visionary hope or wild idea, I ask you, señora, to form new resolutions in your mind, as I intend to do in mine, preparing yourself to look forward to happier fortune; because I swear to you, as a gentleman and a Christian not to leave you until I see you in possession of Don Fernando, and if I cannot induce him with my words to recognise his obligation to you, I will exercise my right which my rank as a gentleman gives me, and with a justifiable cause challenge him for the injury he has caused you, not regarding what he has done to me, which I will leave to Heaven to punish, while myself on this earth devote myself to your cause."

Cardenio's words completed the amazement of Dorothea, and not knowing how to thank him for such an offer, she attempted to kiss his feet; but Cardenio would not allow it, and the vicar replied for both, commended the sound reasoning of Cardenio, and finally, begged, advised, and encouraged them to come with him to his village, where they could restore themselves with whatever they needed, and make a plan to discover Don Fernando, or return Dorothea to her parents, or do what seemed most appropriate for them. Cardenio and Dorothea thanked him, and accepted the kind offer he made; and the barber, who had been listening to everything attentively and in silence, offered some kind words as well, and with no less good-will than the vicar who had offered his services in any way that could be useful to them. He also explained to them in a few words the objective that had brought them there, and the strange nature of Don Quixote's madness, and how they were waiting for his aide, who had gone to look for him. Like the recollection of a dream, the disagreement he had with Don Quixote came back to Cardenio's memory, and he described it to the others; but he was unable to say what the argument was about.

At this moment they heard a shout, and recognised it as the voice of Sancho Panza, who, was calling out loud for them as he could not find them where he had left them. They went to meet him, and in answer to their questions about Don Quixote, he told them how he had found him stripped to his shirt, lifeless, yellow, half dead with hunger, and sighing for his lady Dulcinea; and although he had told him that she commanded him to leave that place and come to El Toboso, where she was expecting him, he had said that he was determined not to appear in the presence of her beauty until he had done acts to himself to make him worthy of her favour; and if this went on, Sancho said, he risked not becoming an emperor, or even an archbishop, which was the least he could be; and for this reason they should consider what could be done to get him away from there. The vicar told him not to be worried, because they would make him leave. He then told Cardenio and Dorothea their plan to cure Don Quixote, or at least take him home. Dorothea then said that she could play the distressed lady better than the barber; especially as she had her dress with her, and that they should trust her to act the part in every particular way for carrying out their scheme, because she had read many books of chivalry, and knew exactly the style which afflicted ladies used to beg for help from Knights.

"In that case," said the vicar, "there is nothing else to do except leave immediately, because currently fortune is acting in our favour, since it has unexpectedly begun to open a door for your relief, and smoothed the path for us to complete our objective."

Dorothea then took out of her pillow-case a complete coat of rich texture, and a green veil of fine material, and a necklace and other jewellery out of a little box, and with these in an instant she clothed herself so she looked like a great and rich lady. All this, and more, she said, she had taken from her home in case it was needed, but until then she had no reason to use it. They were all highly delighted with her grace and beauty, and declared Don Fernando to be a man with very little taste as he had rejected such a charm. But the one who admired her most was Sancho Panza, because it seemed to him (which was true) that in his whole life he had never seen such a lovely creature; and he asked the vicar with such interest who this beautiful lady was, and what she was doing here in these mountains.

"This fair lady, brother Sancho," replied the vicar, "is the heiress in direct line to the great Kingdom of Micomicon, who has come to search for your master to beg for his assistance, which is that he rectify a wrong that an evil giant has done to her; and from the fame as a good Knight which your master has acquired far and wide, this Princess has come from there to seek him."

"Lucky seeking and a lucky finding!" said Sancho; "especially if my master has the good fortune to rectify that injury, and right that wrong, and kill that son of a bitch giant that you speak about; and he will kill him he finds him, unless, he happens to be a ghost; because my master has no power at all against ghosts. But one thing I beg of you, señor, which is, to prevent my master favouring to become an archbishop, because that is what I'm afraid of, please recommend him to marry this Princess immediately; because in this way he will be disabled from becoming an archbishop, and will become part of an empire instead, and I will gain my desire; I have been thinking over this matter carefully, and what I found out was, that it will not be good for me if my master became an archbishop, because I would not be good for the Church, because I am married and have a wife and children, for me to obtain the privilege which would enable me to hold a place of profit in the Church, would be endless work; so, señor, it would be better my master marries this lady immediately - and as I do not know her yet, I cannot call her by her name."

"She is called Princess Micomicona," the vicar; said "because as her Kingdom is Micomicon, it is obvious that must be her name."

"There's no doubt of that," replied Sancho, "because I have known many people to take their name and title from the place where they were born and call themselves Pedro of Alcala, Juan of Ubeda, and Diego of Valladolid; and it may be that over there in Micomicon Queens have the same way of taking the name of their Kingdom."

"Indeed," said the vicar; "and as for your master marrying her, I will do everything in my power toward it:" this pleased Sancho as much as the vicar was amazed at his simplicity and what a hold the absurdities of his master had on him, because he had unquestionably persuaded himself that he was going to be an emperor.

By this time Dorothea was on the vicar's donkey, and the barber had fitted the ox-tail beard to his face, and they now told Sancho to lead them to where Don Quixote was, warning him not to mention the vicar or the barber, as his master becoming an emperor entirely depended on him not recognising them. Neither the vicar or Cardenio, however, thought it was wise to go with them; Cardenio even less as he might remind Don Quixote of the argument he had with him, and the vicar as there was no necessity for his presence just yet, so they allowed the others to go on in front of them, while they themselves followed slowly on foot. The vicar did not forget to instruct Dorothea how to act, but she said they can relax their minds, as everything would be done exactly as the books of chivalry required and described.

They had gone about three-quarters of a mile when they discovered Don Quixote amongst some rocks, by this time wearing clothes, but without his armour; and as soon as Dorothea saw him and was told by Sancho that was Don Quixote, she whipped her horse, the well-bearded barber followed her, and on reaching him her aide jumped off his donkey and came forward to assist her, and she dismounting with great ease advanced to kneel in front of the feet of Don Quixote; and although he tried to lift her up, she without rising addressed him in this fashion:

"From this spot I will not rise, valiant and brave Knight, until your goodness and courtesy grant me a favour, which will reflect the honour and renown of your name and render a service to the unhappiest and distressed lady the sun shone upon; and if the strength of your arm corresponds to the reputation of your name, you are sure to aid the helpless being who, led by the value of your renowned name, has come from a far distant land to seek your aid in her misfortune."

"I will not answer a word, beautiful lady," replied Don Quixote, "or listen to anything further, until you rise from the ground."

"I will not rise, señor," answered the afflicted lady, "unless your courtesy grants me the favour I seek."

"I grant it," said Don Quixote, "as long as it is not to the detriment or in opposition to my King, my country, or her who holds the key to my heart and freedom, it may be complied with."

"It will not be to the detriment or in opposition to any of them, my lord," said the afflicted lady; and here Sancho Panza went closer to his master's ear and said to him very softly, "You may very safely grant the favour she asks; it's nothing at all; only to kill a big giant; and she who is asking for it is the exalted Princess Micomicona, Queen of the great Kingdom of Micomicon."

"Whoever she may be," replied Don Quixote, "I will do what is my duty, and what my conscience asks me to, in conformity to what I have declared;" and turning to the lady he said, "Let your great beauty rise, because I grant the aid you ask from me."

"Then what I ask," said the lady, "is that you accompany me immediately, and that you promise not to engage in any other adventure or quest until you have retaliated on my behalf against a traitor who opposes all human and divine law, and has seized my Kingdom."

"I repeat that I grant it," replied Don Quixote; "and so, lady, you may from this day forward put aside the sadness that distresses you, and let your fading hope gain new life and strength, because with the help of God and my strength you will soon see yourself restored to your Kingdom, and sat on the throne of your ancient and mighty realm, despite the criminals who go against it; and now let us get to work, because danger can be found in delay."

The distressed lady attempted with much determination to kiss his hands; but Don Quixote, who as graceful and polite Knight, would not allow it, but made her rise and embraced her with great courtesy and politeness, and ordered Sancho to prepare Rocinante, and to dress him in his armour without a moment's delay. Sancho took down the armour, which was hung on a tree like a trophy, and after preparing Rocinante, equipped his master with his armour, who as soon as he found himself wearing it exclaimed:

"Let us go in the name of God to give aid to this great lady."

The whole time the barber was on his knees trying very hard to hide his laughter and not let his beard fall, because if it had fallen maybe their fine plan would have failed; but now seeing the aid granted, and the eagerness with which Don Quixote was prepared to leave in compliance with it, he got up and took his lady's hand, and they both helped to place her on the donkey. Don Quixote then mounted Rocinante, and the barber sat himself on his donkey, Sancho being left to go on foot, which made him feel the loss of his Donkey again, finding himself in need of him now. But he continued with cheerfulness, as he believed his master was now on the way to becoming an emperor; because he felt no doubt that he would marry this Princess, and be the King of Micomicon at least. The only thing that troubled him was the reflection that this Kingdom was in a land of moors, and that the people they would give him for servants would moorish; but for this he soon found a solution, and he said to himself, "What does it matter to me if my servants are moors? All I have to do is transport them to Spain, where I can sell them and get money for them, and with it live in leisure for the rest of my life. Not unless you go to sleep and haven't got the skill to sell three, six, or ten thousand servants" And so he jogged on, occupied with his thoughts and so relaxed in his mind that he forgot all about the difficulty of travelling on foot.

Cardenio and the vicar were watching all of this from the bushes, not knowing how to join the others; but the vicar, who was very creative, soon thought of a way to achieve their purpose, and with a pair of scissors he had in a case he quickly cut off Cardenio's beard, and put on him a grey jumper of his own and a black coat, leaving himself in his trousers and top. Cardenio's appearance was now so different from what it had been that he would not have recognised himself in a mirror. Having done this, although the others had gone on ahead talking to each other, they easily came out on the high road in front of them, because the branches and awkward places they encountered did not allow those on horses to go as fast as those on foot. They then placed themselves on the level ground at the opening of the Sierra, and as soon as Don Quixote and his companions were exiting it the vicar began to examine him very deliberately, as if he was trying to recognise him, and after having stared at him for some time he rushed towards him with open arms exclaiming, "How fortunate am I, to meet with the reflection of chivalry, my admirable neighbour Don Quixote of La Mancha, the blossom and elite of high breeding, the protection and relief of the distressed, the personification of Knights!" And saying this he held in his arms the knee of Don Quixote's left leg. Don Quixote, amazed by the stranger's words and behaviour, looked at him thoughtfully and finally recognised him, very much surprised to see him there, and made a great effort to dismount. This, however, the vicar would not allow, to which Don Quixote said, "Let me, señor, because it is not right that I am on a horse and someone as respected as you are on foot."

"I will not allow it," said the vicar; "you must remain on horseback, because it is on horseback you achieve the greatest deeds that have been seen in our time; as for me, an unworthy priest, it will be enough for me to mount on the back of one of the donkies of these people who accompany you, if they have no objection."

"I have no objection to that, señor," answered Don Quixote, "and I know it will be the pleasure of my lady the Princess, out of love for me, to order her aide to give up his donkey for you, and he can sit behind you if the donkey can manage it."

"It will, I am sure," said the Princess, "and I am sure, too, that I do not need to order my aide, because he is too polite and considerate to allow a Churchman to go on foot when he could be mounted."

"That he is," said the barber, and immediately descending, he offered his seat to the vicar, who accepted it without petition; but unfortunately as the barber was mounting behind, the donkey, as it happened to be a hired one, which is the same thing as saying poor-conditioned, lifted its back legs and gave a couple of kicks in the air, which would have made Master Nicholas the barber, wish his expedition in search of Don Quixote never happened, had they caught him on the chest or head. But, they took him by surprise and he fell to the ground, without giving any attention to his beard, and so it fell off, and all he could do when he found himself without it was to cover his face quickly with both his hands and shout that his teeth were knocked out. When Don Quixote saw that the bundle of hair had detached, without any teeth or blood, from the face of the fallen aide, he exclaimed:

"By God, this is a great miracle! it has knocked off and plucked away the beard from his face as if it had been shaved off intentionally."

The vicar, realising the danger of discovery that threatened his plan, immediately seized the beard and ran with it to where Master Nicholas lay, still expressing moans, and drawing his head to his chest put it back on him in an instant, mumbling some words which he said was a special prayer for sticking on beards, as they would see; and as soon as he had fixed it, he left him, and the aide appeared well bearded and whole as before, at this Don Quixote was beyond amazed, and begged the vicar to teach him that prayer when he had the opportunity to, as he was convinced its virtue must extend beyond sticking on beards, because it was clear to him that where the beard had been stripped off, the face must have remained torn and cut, and if it was healed, it must be good for more than beards.

"And so it is," said the vicar, and he promised to teach it to him when the first opportunity presented itself. They then agreed that for the present the vicar should mount, and that the three of them should take turns to ride until they reached the inn, which might be about six miles from where they were.

Three being mounted, that is to say, Don Quixote, the Princess, and the vicar, and three on foot, Cardenio, the barber, and Sancho Panza, Don Quixote said to the Princess:

"Let your highness lead where is most pleasing to you;" but before she could answer the vicar said:

"Towards what Kingdom do you wish to direct our course? Is it perhaps towards Micomicon? It must be, or else I do not know much about kingdoms."

She, being ready to follow the plan, understood that she was to answer "Yes," so she said "Yes, señor, we are heading towards that Kingdom."

"In that case," said the vicar, "we must go right through my village, and there we can take the road to Cartagena, where you will be able to embark, if fortune allows it; and if the wind is smooth and the sea is calm and tranquil, in less than nine years you will see the great lake Meona, I mean Meotides, which is a little more than a hundred days' journey from your Kingdom."

"You are mistaken, señor," said she; "because it has not even been two years since I left it, and although the weather was bad, I am here and have found what I hoped for, and that is my lord Don Quixote of La Mancha, whose famous name I heard of as soon as I entered Spain which encouraged me to look for him, to ask for his assistance, and assign the justice of my cause to his superior strength."

"Enough; no more praise," said Don Quixote, "because I despise flattery; and although this might not be, still this language is offensive to my virtuous ears. I will only say, señora, whether I have strength or not, I will be devoted to your service until death; and now, putting this all aside until the right time, I would ask our vicar to tell me what it is was that brought him here, alone, and so lightly dressed."

"I will answer that briefly," replied the vicar; "you should know, Señor Don Quixote, that Master Nicholas (our friend and barber) and I were going to Seville to receive some money that a relative of mine who went to the Indies many years ago had sent me, and not a small amount as it was over sixty thousand pieces of gold, full weight, which is something; and passing by this place yesterday we were attacked by four men on foot, who stripped us of everything even our beards, and so the barber found it necessary to put on a false one, and even this young man here" - pointing to Cardenio - "But the best part is, as the story goes in the neighbourhood that those who attacked us were a number ship slaves who, they say, were set free almost in the very same place by a man of such courage that, in spite of the commissioner and the guards, he released all of them; and no doubt he must have been out of his senses, or he must a lawbreaker just like they are, or some man without a heart or conscience to let the wolf loose among the sheep, the fox among the hens, the fly among the honey. He has deceived justice, and opposed his King and lawful master, because he opposed his righteous commands; he has, I say, robbed the ships of their fleet, disturbed the Holy Brotherhood which for many years has been quiet, and, lastly, has performed an action by which his soul may be lost without any gain to his body." Sancho had told the vicar and the barber about the adventure of the ship slaves, and hence the vicar alluding to it made the most of it to see what would be said or done by Don Quixote; who changed colour during every word, not daring to say it was himself who had been the liberator of those worthy people. "These, then," said the vicar, "were the people who robbed us; and let God with his mercy forgive the man who would not let them receive the punishment they deserved."

CHAPTER 30

THE FAIR DOROTHEA, WITH OTHER AMUSING MATTERS

The vicar had hardly stopped speaking, when Sancho said, "señor, the man who did that deed was my master; and I had told him beforehand and gave a warning to him to mind what he was about to do, and that it was a sin to set them free, as they were all there because they were criminals."

"Idiot!" said Don Quixote, "it is no business or concern of Knights to query whether any people in suffering, in chains, or oppressed that they may meet on the roads go that way and suffer as they do because of their faults or because of their misfortunes. It only concerns them to aid them as people in need of help, having regard for their suffering and not for their offenses. I encountered a string of miserable and unfortunate people, and did for them what my sense of duty demands from me, and whoever objects to it, except the sacred dignity of our vicar here, I say that he knows little about chivalry and lies like a whore, and this I will let him know to the fullest extent with my sword;" and after saying this he sat himself on Rocinante and pressed down his visor on the barber's basin, which according to him was Mambrino's helmet, which he was previously carrying until he could repair the damage done to it by the ship slaves.

Dorothea, who was very smart, by now thoroughly understood Don Quixote's madness, and all except Sancho Panza were playing with him, and not to be out of line with the rest said to him, after observing his irritation, "Sir Knight, remember the aid you have promised me, and that in accordance with it you must not engage in any other adventure, even if you are becoming persuaded to; calm yourself, because if the vicar had known that the slaves had been set free by you he would have closed his mouth, or even bitten his tongue three times before he would have said a word that offered any disrespect toward you."

"That I swear," said the vicar, "and I would have even plucked off my moustache."

"I will relax peace, señora," said Don Quixote, "and I will control the natural anger that had arisen in my chest, and will proceed in peace and quietness until I have fulfilled my promise; but in return for this consideration I ask you to tell me, if you have no objection to do so, what is the nature of your trouble, how many, and what people I am required to take revenge on, on your behalf?"

"That I will do with my whole heart," replied Dorothea, "if it will not be boring for you to hear about miseries and misfortunes."

"It will not be, señora," said Don Quixote; to which Dorothea replied, "Well, if that is so, give me your attention." As soon as she said this, Cardenio and the barber went closer to her side, eager to hear what sort of story the quick-witted Dorothea would invent; and Sancho did the same, because he was as much taken in by her as his master; and she having settled herself comfortably on the saddle, and with the help of coughing to take time to think, began with great liveliness in this fashion.

"First of all, I want you to know, that my name is" and here she stopped for a moment, because she forgot the name the vicar had given her; but he came to her assistance, seeing the difficulty she was having, and said, "It is no wonder, señora, that your highness is confused and embarrassed to tell the story of your misfortune; because such afflictions often have the effect of depriving the sufferers of their memory, so that they do not even remember their own names, as is the case now with you, who has forgotten that she is called Princess Micomicona, lawful heiress to the great Kingdom of Micomicon; and with this help your highness may now recall the rest of the sorrowful story you want to tell us."

"That is the truth," said the lady; "but I think now I will no longer need any prompting, and I will deliver my true story safely, so here it is. My father the King, who was called Tinacrio the Wise, was very educated in what they call magic art, and became aware through his craft that my mother, who was called Queen Jaramilla, was going to die before he was, and that soon after he was going to leave this life, and I was going to be left an orphan without a father or mother. But all of this, he asserted, did not hurt or distress him as much as his knowledge of an extraordinary giant, the lord of a great island close to our Kingdom, Pandafilando the Scowl - because it is stated that, although his eyes are properly placed and straight, he always looks uneven as if he is squinting, and this he does out of malice, to strike fear and terror into those he looks at. He knew, that this giant when becoming aware I was an orphan would invade my Kingdom with a mighty force and strip me of it, not even leaving me a small village to seek shelter; and that I could avoid all of this ruin and misfortune if I were willing to marry him; however, as far as he could see, he never expected that I would consent to marriage so unequal; and he was speaking the truth, because it has never entered my mind to marry that giant, or any other, however great or enormous. My father said, also, that when he was dead, and I saw Pandafilando about to invade my Kingdom, I should not to wait and attempt to defend it myself, because that would be destructive for me, but that I should leave the Kingdom entirely open to him if I wanted to avoid the death and total destruction of my good and loyal servants, because there would be no possibility of defending myself against the giant's devilish power; and that I should immediately with some of my followers head to Spain, where I could obtain relief for my distress when finding a certain Knight whose name and fame by that time would extend over the whole Kingdom, and who would be called, if I remember correctly, Don Azote or Don Gigote."

"He must have said 'Don Quixote,' señora," said Sancho, "otherwise called the Knight of the Sorrowful Face."

"That is it," said Dorothea; "he also said, that he would be a tall lanky man; and that on his right side under the left shoulder, or near it, he would have a grey mole with hairs like bristles."

On hearing this, Don Quixote said to his aide, "Here, Sancho my son, give a hand and help me to strip, because I want to see if I am the Knight that sage King predicted."

"What do you want to strip for?" said Dorothea.

"To see if I have that mole your father spoke of," answered Don Quixote.

"There is no occasion to strip," said Sancho; "because I know you have a mole on the middle of your backbone, which is the mark of a strong man."

"That is enough," said Dorothea, "because with friends we must not look too closely into insignificant matters; and whether it is on the shoulder or on the backbone does not matter much; it is enough if there is a mole, wherever it is, because it is all the same flesh; no doubt my good father was right in every way, and I am lucky to have found Don Quixote; because he is the one my father spoke of, as the features of his face correspond with those assigned to this Knight by that wide fame he acquired not only in Spain but all over the world; because I had barely landed at Osuna when I heard many accounts of his achievements, that immediately my heart told me he was the one I had come looking for."

"But how did you land at Osuna, señora," asked Don Quixote, "when there is no seaport?"

But before Dorothea could reply the vicar anticipated her, saying, "The Princess meant to say that after she had landed at Malaga the first place she heard about you was at Osuna."

"That is what I meant to say," said Dorothea.

"And that would be only natural," said the vicar. "Will your highness please proceed?"

"There is nothing left to add," said Dorothea, "except that finding Don Quixote has been such good fortune, that I already consider and regard myself Queen and mistress of my entire Kingdom, since due to his courtesy and generousness he has granted me the aid of accompanying me wherever I may ask him to go, which will be only to bring him face to face with Pandafilando the Scowl, so he can kill him and restore to me what has been unfairly taken by him: because all of this occurred just as my father Tinacrio the Wise predicted it, who additionally left it declared in writing in Chaldee or Greek characters (because I cannot read them), that if this predicted Knight, after having cut the giant's throat, would be willing to marry me I was to offer myself immediately without objection as his lawful wife, and grant him possession of my Kingdom together with me."

"What are you thinking now, friend Sancho?" said Don Quixote. "Did you hear that? Did I not tell you so? See how we have already got a Kingdom to govern and a Queen to marry!"

"It is so," said Sancho; "and it would be bad fortune for whoever would not marry her after cutting Señor Pandahilado's windpipe!" And after saying this he danced in extreme satisfaction, and then ran to Dorothea's donkey, and fell on his knees in front of her, begging her to give him her hand to kiss in appreciation and acknowledgment of her as his Queen. At this point the spectators had trouble withholding their laughter, seeing the madness of the master and the simplicity of the aide. Dorothea consequently gave her hand, and promised to make him a great lord in her Kingdom, when Heaven would be kind and permit her to recover and enjoy it. For this Sancho returned thanks in words that made them all laugh again.

"This," continued Dorothea, "is my story; the only thing left to tell you is that out of all the attendants I took with me from my Kingdom I have none left except this well-bearded assistant, because all of them drowned in a great storm we encountered when entering the port; and he and I came to land on a couple of planks as if by a miracle; and certainly the whole course of my life is a miracle and a mystery as you may have observed; and if I have not given enough detail in any respect or not as precise as I should be, let it be accounted for by what the vicar said at the beginning of my story, that constant and excessive troubles deprive the sufferers of their memory."

"They will not deprive me of mine, exalted and worthy Princess," said Don Quixote, "however great those which I will endure in your service may be; and here I confirm again the aid I have promised you, and I swear to go with you to the end of the world until I find myself in the presence of your fierce enemy, whose arrogant head I promise to cut off with the edge of this - I will not say good sword, thanks to Gines de Pasamonte who took mine" (this he said in an angry tone, and then continued), "and when it has been cut off and you have been put in peaceful repossession of your realm it will be your own decision on what you would like to do; because as long as my memory is working, my will is imprisoned, and my understanding enchanted by her - I say no more - it is impossible for me to contemplate marriage, even with a Princess."

The last words from his master about not wanting to marry were so distasteful to Sancho that raising his voice he exclaimed with great irritation:

"I swear, Señor Don Quixote, you are not in your right mind; because how can you possibly object to marrying such an exalted Princess as this? Do you think Fortune will offer you another piece of luck as it is offering you now? Is lady Dulcinea fairer? She is not; not even half as fair; and I will even go so far as to say she does not come close to this one here. A poor chance I have of getting that country I am waiting for if you go looking for fine things at the bottom of the sea. God, marry, marry and take this Kingdom that comes to you without any trouble, and when you are King make me governor of a province, and as for the rest let the devil take it all."

Don Quixote, when he heard such profanities spoken against his lady Dulcinea, could not tolerate it, and lifting his lance, without saying anything to Sancho, gave him two blows that brought him to the ground; and had Dorothea not cried out for him to stop he would have no doubt taken his life.

"Do you think," he said to him after a pause, "you drowsy clown, that you have the right to interfere, and that you can always offend and I always forgive? Don't think that, sinful rat, because no doubt you are that, since your tongue goes against the incomparable Dulcinea. Do you not know, fool, tramp, beggar, that if it were not for the power she infuses into my arm I would not have strength to kill a flea? You do not realise, ridiculer with a snake's tongue, I who have gained a Kingdom and cut off this giant's head and made you a governor (because all of this I count as already accomplished), is not the power of Dulcinea, employing me as the instrument of her achievements? She fights and conquers through me, and I live and breathe through her, and owe my life and soul to her. You whore, ungrateful one, you see yourself raised from the dust of the earth to be a great lord, and the return you give for such a great benefit is to speak evil about her who has given it to you!"

Sancho was stunned, hearing all his master said, and rising with some degree of agility he ran to place himself behind Dorothea's horse, and from there he said to his master:

"Tell me, señor; if you decided not to marry this great Princess, it is clear the Kingdom will not be yours; and not being so, how can you make me a lord of something which is not yours? That is what I am complaining about. You should marry this Queen, now that we have her here as if she were sent from heaven, and afterwards you can go back to lady Dulcinea; because there must have been Kings in the world who kept ladies on the side. As for beauty, I have nothing to say about it; and if the truth is told, I like both of them; although I have never seen lady Dulcinea."

"How have you never seen her, irreligious traitor!" Exclaimed Don Quixote; "have you not just brought me a message from her?"

"I mean," said Sancho, "that I did not see her for so long that I could take particular notice of her beauty, or of her charms individually; but taken as a lump I like her."

"Now I forgive you," said Don Quixote; "and forgive me for the injury I done to you; because our first impulses are not always in our control."

"That is true," replied Sancho, "and with me the wish to speak is always the first impulse, and I cannot help saying what I have on the tip of my tongue."

"In that case, Sancho," said Don Quixote, "take care of what you say, because the jug often goes to the well - I say no more to you."

"Well, well," said Sancho, "God is in heaven, and sees all the tricks, and will judge who does the most harm, I not speaking right, or you not doing it."

"That is enough," said Dorothea; "run, Sancho, and kiss your lord's hand and beg his forgiveness, and from now on be more cautious with your praise and abuse; and say nothing mocking lady Dulcinea, of who I know nothing except that I am willing to serve her; and put your trust in God, because you will not fail to obtain some dignity and live like a prince."

Sancho went to Don Quixote hanging his head and begged for his master's hand, which Don Quixote with pride presented to him, giving him his blessing as soon as he had kissed it; he asked him go on ahead with him, as he had questions to ask and matters of great importance to discuss with him. Sancho obeyed, and when the two had gone some distance in front Don Quixote said to him, "Since your return I have had no opportunity or time to ask you many details

192

about your mission and the answer you have brought back, and now that chance has granted us the time and opportunity, do not deny me the happiness you can give me with such good news."

"Ask whatever you like," answered Sancho, "because I will find a way out of anything as I have found a way in; but I ask you, señor, not to be so unforgiving in future."

"Why do you say that, Sancho?" said Don Quixote.

"I say it," he returned, "because those blows just now were likely because of the argument the devil created between us both the other night, rather than what I said against lady Dulcinea, who I have love and reverence for - although there is not much to her – only someone belonging to you."

"Say no more or I will take your life, Sancho," said Don Quixote, "because it is offensive to me; I have already forgiven you for that, and you know the common saying, 'for a fresh sin a fresh punishment.'"

While this was going on they saw coming toward them, on the road they were travelling a man mounted on a donkey, who when he came close seemed to be a gipsy; but Sancho Panza, whose eyes and heart were awakened wherever he saw donkies, as soon as he saw the man knew it was Gines de Pasamonte; and he also recognised the donkey carrying him was his own. Pasamonte, to escape recognition and to sell the donkey had disguised himself as a gipsy, being able to speak the gipsy language, and many more, as well as if they were his mother tongue. Sancho saw him and recognised him, and the instant he did he shouted to him, "Ginesillo, thief, release my treasure, release my life, embarrass yourself, get off my donkey, leave my delight, get off, be gone, thief, and release what is not your own."

It was not necessity for so many words, because after the first one Gines jumped down, and at a racing speed ran away. Sancho rushed to his donkey, and embracing him he said, "How have you been, my blessing, my companion?" While kissing him and hugging him as if he were a human being. The donkey was peaceful, and let himself be kissed and hugged by Sancho without saying a single word. They all came and congratulated him on having found his donkey, Don Quixote especially, who told him that this would not cancel the order for the three donkies, and for this Sancho thanked him.

While the two had been going along talking in this style, the vicar observed that Dorothea had shown great intelligence, in the story and in its conciseness, and the resemblance it had to the books of chivalry. She said that she had amused herself many times reading them; but that she did not know much about the provinces or seaports, and so she said randomly that she had landed at Osuna.

"So I noticed," said the vicar, "and for that reason I quickly had to say what I did, and that set everything right. But is it not strange to see how quickly this unhappy gentleman believes all these fabrications and lies, simply because they are in the same style and manner as the absurdities in his books."

"It seems so," said Cardenio; "and so uncommon, that if someone attempted to invent and create it in fiction, I doubt there would be anyone with enough brain to imagine it."

"But another strange thing about it," said the vicar, "is that, apart from the silly things which this gentleman says in connection with his madness, when other subjects are discussed, he can consider them in a perfectly rational manner, showing that his mind is quite clear and composed; so that, provided chivalry is not mentioned, no one would believe him to be anything other than a man of comprehensive understanding."

While they were having this conversation Don Quixote continued his conversation with Sancho, saying:

"Friend Panza, let us forgive and forget our arguments, and tell me now, dismissing anger and irritation, where, how, and when did you find Dulcinea? What was she doing? What did you say to her? What did she say in reply? How did she look when she was reading my letter? Who copied it out for you? And anything else which would be worth knowing, asking, and learning; neither exaggerating to give me pleasure, or limiting anything to deprive me of it."

"Señor," replied Sancho, "if the truth is told, nobody copied the letter for me, because I carried no letter at all."

"That is true," said Don Quixote, "because the note-book in which I wrote it I found in my possession two days after your departure, which angered me, as I did not know what you would do when you found yourself without the letter; and I thought you would return to take it."

"I would have done," said Sancho, "if I had not remembered by heart when you read it to me, so I repeated it to a vicar, who copied it for me. He said in all the days of his life, although he had read many letters of this type, he had never seen or read one as pretty as that."

"And do you still have it in your memory, Sancho?" said Don Quixote.

"No, señor," replied Sancho, "because as soon as I had repeated it, knowing there was no further use for me to keep it in mind, I slowly started to forget it; and if I can remember any of it, it was about 'Scrubbing, 'I mean to say 'Sovereign Lady,' and the end 'Yours until death, the Knight of the Sorrowful Face;' and between these two places I put into it more than three hundred 'my soul' and 'my life' and 'my eyes.'"

CHAPTER 31

THE CHARMING DISCUSSION BETWEEN DON QUIXOTE AND SANCHO, ALONG WITH OTHER INCIDENTS

"Very good Sancho," said Don Quixote. "Go on; you got there and then? What was that beauty Queen doing? Surely you found her making a necklace of pearls, or sewing some garment with gold thread for me her enslaved Knight."

"No señor," said Sancho, "I found her inspecting two loads of wheat in the garden outside her house."

"Then surely," said Don Quixote, "the grains of wheat turned into pearls when touched by her hands; did you not see my friend? Was it white or brown wheat?"

"Neither, it was red," said Sancho.

"Then I promise you," said Don Quixote, "that, after being touched by her hands, there is no doubt the bread it made was the whitest; but go on; when you gave her my letter, did she kiss it? Did she celebrate, what did she do?"

"When I went to give it to her," replied Sancho, "she was very busy, swaying from side to side with the wheat she was carrying, and she said to me, 'put the letter, on top of the sack, because I cannot read it until I have finished harvesting all of this."

"Discreet lady!" said Don Quixote; "that was in order to read it alone and enjoy it; continue, Sancho; while she was busy harvesting wheat what else did she say to you? What did she ask about me, and what answer did you give? Quickly; tell me everything, and do not leave an atom behind."

"She asked me nothing," said Sancho; "but I told her how I left you punishing yourself in her honour, naked from the waist up, among these mountains like a wild animal, sleeping on the ground, not eating bread off a tablecloth or combing your beard, crying and cursing your fortune."

"Saying I cursed my fortune is wrong," said Don Quixote; "because I am blessed and will be blessed my entire life for having found a love so outstanding: lady Dulcinea del Toboso."

"And she is so outstanding," said Sancho, "that she is at least one hand taller than me."

"What! Sancho," said Don Quixote, "did you measure yourself against her?"

"I measured in this way," said Sancho; "when helping her to put a sack of wheat on the back of a donkey, we came so close together that I could see she was more than a palm taller."

"Well!" said Don Quixote, "is it not the truth that she beautifies this greatness with a thousand million charms of the mind! But one thing you will not deny, Sancho; when you came close to her did you not perceive an Arabian odour, an aromatic fragrance, I do not know what, a delicious, I cannot name it; a perfumed smell, as if you were in the shop of an exquisite glove maker."

"All I can say is," said Sancho, "that I did notice an aroma, something damp; it must have been that she was covered in sweat from her hard work."

"It could not be that," said Don Quixote, "you must have been suffering from a head cold, or must have smelt yourself; because I know well the scent of that rose among the thorns, that lily of the field."

"Maybe," replied Sancho; "quite often the same odour comes from myself as the one which seemed to come from lady Dulcinea; but it is no wonder, because one devil is like another."

"Well then," continued Don Quixote, "after she was done harvesting the wheat and sent it to the mill; what did she do when she read the letter?"

"As for the letter," said Sancho, "she did not read it, because she said she could read or write; instead, she ripped it into small pieces, saying she did not want anyone to read it or her secrets would become known in the village, and what I had told her by word of mouth about the love you have for her, and the extraordinary self-punishment you were doing for her, was enough; and she told me to tell you that she kisses your hands, and that she had a great desire to see you rather than write to you; and therefore she asked and commanded you, to come out of these mountains, finish performing these absurdities, and travel to El Toboso immediately, unless something else of more importance happened, because she had a great desire to see you. She laughed when I told her that you were now called The Knight of the Sorrowful Face; I asked her if that Biscayan the other day had been there; and she told me he had, and that he was an honest man; I asked her about the ship slaves as well, but she said she had not seen any yet."

"So far, all went well," said Don Quixote; "but tell me what charm she gave to you when you said you were going to leave? Because it is an ancient custom with Knights and Princesses to give the aides, ladies, or dwarfs who bring them messages, from Knight to Princess, or Princess to Knight, a rich jewel as a token of appreciation for the good news,' and acknowledgment of the message."

"That is very likely," said Sancho, "and a good custom it was, in my opinion; but that must have been in the past, because now it seems the custom is only to give a piece of bread and cheese; because that was what lady Dulcinea gave me; but it was sheep's-milk cheese."

"She is very generous," said Don Quixote, "and if she did not give you a piece of gold, no doubt it must have been because she did not have one nearby. But you know what amazes me, Sancho? It seems to me that you must have gone and come back through the air, because it took you just over three days to go to El Toboso and return, although it is more than thirty miles from here. This makes me think that the sage magician who is my friend, and watches over my interests (because of course there is and must be one, or else I would not be an official Knight), must have helped you to travel without your knowledge; because some of these sages catch a Knight sleeping in his bed, and without him knowing how or in what way it happened, he wakes up the next day more than a thousand miles away from the place where he went to sleep. And if this did not happen,

Knights would not be able to give aid to one another in danger, as they so often do. Because a Knight, maybe, is fighting in the mountains of Armenia with some dragon, or fierce snake, or another Knight, and gets the worst of the battle, and is at the point of death; but when he least expects it, there appears on a cloud, or chariot of fire, another Knight, a friend of his, who only moments ago had been in England, and who comes to his rescue, and saves him from death; and in the evening he finds himself in his own home drinking and feeling very satisfied; and yet from one place to the other would have been two or three thousand miles. And all of this is done by the craft and skill of the sage enchanters who take care of valiant Knights; so, friend Sancho, I believe that you must have gone from here to El Toboso and returned in such a short time, since, as I have said, some friendly sage must have carried you through the air without you realising it."

"That must have been it," said Sancho, "because Rocinante went like a gipsy's donkey with an unpredictable pace."

"There is the proof!" said Don Quixote, "but putting this aside, what do you think I should do about my lady's command to go and see her? Because although I feel that I must obey her order, I feel that I am also prohibited to by the aid I have granted to the Princess that accompanies us, and the law of chivalry requires me to have respect for my word in preference to my inclination; on one hand the desire to see my lady follows and harasses me, and on the other my sincere promise and the glory I will gain from this adventure urges and calls me; so what I think I should do is to travel as fast as I can to reach quickly the place where this giant is, and on my arrival I will cut off his head, and establish the Princess peacefully back in her realm, and after I will return to see the light that brightens my senses, to who I will give an account of the reasons why I was late and she will be led to approve of my delay, because she will see that it only increases her glory and fame; because all that I have won, am winning, or will win through my strength in this life, comes to me through the power she extends to me, and because I am hers."

"Ah! what a sad condition your brains are in!" said Sancho. "Tell me, señor, are you going to travel all that way for nothing, and let slip and lose such a rich and great opportunity as this, where you would receive a portion of a Kingdom that in truth I have heard is more than twenty thousand miles wide, and contains all the things necessary to support human life, and is bigger than Portugal and Castile put together? For the love of God! You should be embarrassed for what you have said, take my advice, and forgive me, and marry immediately in the first village where there is a vicar; if not, with us is our vicar who will do the business beautifully; remember, I am old enough to give advice, and this advice I am giving comes to serve a purpose; because a sparrow in your hand is better than one in a bush, and a man who has the good in his hand and chooses the opposite, eventually complains that what he wants does not come to him."

"Look, Sancho," said Don Quixote. "If you are advising me to marry, so that immediately after killing the giant I become King, and give you what I have promised, let me tell you I will be able to very easily satisfy your desires without marrying; because before going into battle I will make it a condition that, if I am victorious, even if I do not marry, they will give me a portion of the Kingdom, so I can give it to whoever I choose, and when they give it to me, who else do you think I will pass it on to but you?"

"That sounds fair," said Sancho; "but please take care and choose the coast, so if I don't like the life, I am be able to load a ship off my Moorish servants and deal with them as I have said; I don't mind going to see lady Dulcinea now, but go and kill this giant and let us finish this adventure first; because I feel God is telling us this will be one of great honour and great profit."

"I think you are right, Sancho," said Don Quixote, "and I will take your advice as to accompanying the Princess before going to see Dulcinea; but I advise you not to say anything to any one, or to those who are with us, about what we have considered and discussed, because as Dulcinea is so respectable, she does not wish her thoughts to be known and it is not right that I or anyone else discloses them."

"Well then, if that is so," said Sancho, "why is it that you make all of those who you overpower by your strength go to present themselves to her, is this not the same thing as signing your name that you love her and are her lover? And as those who go must kneel in front of her and say they came from you to submit themselves to her, how can the thoughts of both of you be hidden?"

"O, how silly and simple you are!" said Don Quixote; "Do you not see, Sancho, that improves her acclaim? Because you must know that according to our way of thinking in chivalry, it is an honour for a lady to have many Knights in her service, whose thoughts never go beyond serving her, and who seek no other reward for their great and true devotion than that she is willing to accept them as her Knights."

"It is with that kind of love," said Sancho, "I have heard preachers say we should love God, without being moved by the hope of glory or the fear of punishment; although in my case, I would rather love and serve him for what he could do for me."

"The devil has made you a clown!" said Don Quixote, "what intelligent things you say at times! One would think you have studied."

"In truth, I cannot even read."

Master Nicholas called out to them asking them to wait a while, as they wanted to stop and drink a little from a stream they were near. Don Quixote came to a stop, which gave Sancho a lot of satisfaction, because he was now tired from telling so many lies, and fearing his master catching him, because although he knew that Dulcinea was a peasant girl of El Toboso, he had never seen her in his whole life. Cardenio had now put on the clothes which Dorothea was wearing when they found her, and although they were not very good, they were far better than those he took off. They dismounted together by the side of the stream, and with what the vicar had provided him from the inn they ate, although not very well, as each had a very keen appetite.

While they were eating there happened to be a youth passing by, who stopping to observe the group at the stream, the next moment ran to Don Quixote and holding him around the legs, began to cry, saying, "O, señor, do you not remember me? Look at me; I am Andres the boy you released from the oak-tree where I was tied."

Don Quixote recognising him, took his hand he turned to those present and said: "Now can see how important it is to have Knights to rectify the wrongs and injuries done by tyrannical and evil men in this world, I can tell you that some days ago passing through the woods, I heard cries and complaints as if a person was in pain and distress; I immediately rushed toward the sound, compelled by my duty, and I found this boy tied to an oak tree, who now stands in front of you. I celebrate, because his verification could not allow me to deviate from the truth in any way. He was, as I said, tied to an oak tree, naked from the waist up, and a clown, who afterwards I found to be his master, was whipping him with the reins of his horse. As soon as I saw him I asked him the reason of such a cruel whipping. The clown replied that he was whipping him because he was his servant and it was because of carelessness rather than dishonesty or stupidity; then this boy said, 'Señor, he whips me only because I asked to be paid my wages.' The master gave some speech and explanation, which, although I listened to him, I did not accept. I made the clown untie him, and swear he would take him home, and pay him his wages and more for the pain and suffering he had caused to the boy. Is this not the truth, Andres my son? Did you not notice the authority I commanded him with, and the humility he had when he promised to do everything I had said, specified, and required from him? Tell them; tell these gentlemen what happened, so they can see that it is a great advantage to have Knights in the world."

"All that you have said is true," answered the boy; "but in the end it turned out to be the opposite of what you say."

"How! the opposite?" said Don Quixote; "did the clown not pay you then?"

"Not only did he not pay me," replied the boy, "but as soon as you left the woods and we were alone, he tied me up again to the same oak tree and gave me a fresh whipping, that left me like a Saint Bartholomew; and every lash he gave me he followed up with some remark or insult about making a fool out of you, and I would have laughed at the things he said but I could not because of the pain I was suffering. He left me in such a condition that I have been in hospital until now being taken care of for the injuries that clown inflicted on me ; all of this you are to blame for; because if you had gone your own way and not come where no one called you to, or interfered in other people's affairs, my master would have been content giving me one or two dozen strikes, and would have then untied me and paid me what he owed me; but when you abused him disproportionately, and gave him so many harsh words, his anger was ignited; and as he could not do anything, as soon as he saw you had left, the storm came to me in such a way, that I feel I could never be a man again."

"The damage," said Don Quixote, "can be found in me leaving; because I should not have gone until I had seen you paid; because I should have known well by long experience that there is no clown who will keep his word if he finds it will not suit him to keep it; but remember, Andres, that I swore if he did not pay you I would find him even if he hid himself inside a whale's belly."

"That is true," said Andres; "but it did not help."

"You will see now if it is of use or not," said Don Quixote; and he got up quickly and asked Sancho to prepare Rocinante, who was browsing while they were eating. Dorothea asked him what he was going to do. He replied that he was going to search for this clown and punish him for such evil conduct, and see Andres paid in full. To which she replied that he must remember that in accordance with his promise he could not engage in any other adventure until he had concluded hers; and that as he knew this better than anyone, he should restrain his eagerness until he returned from her Kingdom.

"That is true," said Don Quixote, "and Andres must have patience until my return as you say, señora; and I once more swear and promise not to stop until I have seen him punished and Andres paid."

"I have no faith in those promises," said Andres; "I would rather have something to help me get to Seville than all the revenge in the world; if you have anything to eat that I can take with me, please give it to me, and let God be with you and all Knights; and may their adventures turn out as well for themselves as they have for me."

Sancho took out from his store a piece of bread and another bit of cheese, and giving them to the boy he said, "Here, take this, brother Andres, because all of us have a share in your misfortune."

"Why, what share have you got?"

"This share of bread and cheese I am giving you," answered Sancho; "and God knows whether I will feel the need for it or not; because you should know, friend, that we aides of Knights have to tolerate a great deal of hunger and hard fortune, and even other things which are more easily felt than told."

Andres took the bread and cheese, and seeing that nobody gave him anything else, turned around and took the road. However, before leaving he said, "For the love of God, sir Knight, if you ever meet me again, even if you see someone cutting me to pieces, do not give me any aid or help, just leave me with my misfortune, which will not be as bad as the misfortune that will come from being helped by you. And if not, to all the Knights that have ever been born, God send a curse."

Don Quixote was getting up to punish him, but he ran and left with such pace that no one attempted to follow him. Don Quixote's jaw wide open after hearing Andres' story, and the others had to take great care to restrain their laughter not to make Don Quixote any angrier.

CHAPTER 32

DON QUIXOTE AND THE OTHERS AT THE INN

As the little they had left to eat, now being finished, they prepared to leave, and without any adventure worth mentioning the next day they reached the inn, a place of Sancho Panza's fear; but although he would have rather not entered it, there was no other option. When the landlady, the landlord, their daughter, and Maritornes saw Don Quixote and Sancho coming, they went out to welcome them with signs of sincere happiness, which Don Quixote acknowledged with dignity and seriousness, and asked them to prepare a better bed for him than last time: to which the landlady replied that if he paid better than he did last time she would prepare one suitable for a prince. Don Quixote said he would, so they prepared a tolerable one for him in the same loft as before; and he went to rest immediately, being deeply shaken and in need of sleep.

As soon as the door was shut the landlady went to the barber, and grabbing him by the beard, said:

"You are not going to make a beard out of my tail any longer; give it back, because it is a shame the way that thing of my husband's falls on the floor; I mean the comb that I used to stick in my tail."

But as much as she tugged at it the barber would not let it go until the vicar told him to let her have it, as there was no need for it, and he could now be himself, and tell Don Quixote that he ran to this inn when those ship slaves had robbed him; and if he wonders where is the Princess's aide, they could tell him that she had sent him ahead to give the people of her Kingdom notice that she was coming, and bringing with her the liberator of them all.

The barber was now happy to give the tail to the landlady, and at the same time they returned all the accessories they had borrowed to fool Don Quixote. All the people staying in the inn were astonished by the beauty of Dorothea, and the handsomeness of Cardenio. The vicar asked them prepare whatever food was in the inn, and the landlord, in hope of better payment, served them a fairly good dinner. All this time Don Quixote was asleep, and they thought it best not to wake him, as sleeping now would do him more good than eating.

While at dinner, the company consisting of the landlord, his wife, their daughter, Maritornes, and all the travellers, discussed the strange craze of Don Quixote and the manner in which he had been found; and the landlady told them what had taken place between him and the trader; and then, looking round to see if Sancho was there, when she saw he was not, she told them the whole story of his blanketing, which thoroughly amused them. When the vicar said that it was the books of chivalry which Don Quixote had read that had damaged his brain, the landlord said:

"I cannot understand how that can be, because in my mind there are no better books to read in the world, and I have here two or three of them, with other writings that are the very life, not only of myself but of many others; because when it is time to harvest, the farmers come here on holiday, and there is always one of them who can read and who picks up one of these books, and we gather round him, thirty or more of us, and listen to him with great pleasure that makes our grey hairs grow young again. At least I can say for myself that when I hear about what furious blows the Knights give, I am struck with a craving to do the same, and I would like to hear more about them them all night and day."

"Me as well," said the landlady, "because I never find a quiet moment in my house except when you are listening to someone reading; because then you are so occupied that during that time you forget to complain."

"That is true," said Maritornes; "and, I really love to hear these thing too, because they are very beautiful; especially when they describe a lady or another in the arms of her Knight under the orange trees, and the old lady who is watching out for them them half dead with envy and fear; all of this, I say, is as good as honey."

"And you, what do you think, young lady?" said the vicar turning to the landlord's daughter.

"I don't know, señor," said she; "I listen too, and to tell the truth, although I do not understand it, I like hearing it; but it is not the blows that my father likes that I like, but the sadness from the Knights when they are separated from their ladies; and it is true that sometimes they make me cry with the sympathy I feel for them."

"Then you would comfort them if they cried for you, young lady?" said Dorothea.

"I don't know what I would do," said the girl; "I only know that some of those ladies are so cruel that they call their Knights tigers and lions and a thousand other bad names: and Jesus! I don't know what sort of people they can be, so cold and heartless, that rather than look at the worthy man they leave him to die or go mad. I don't know what is good about such prudery; if it is for honour, why not marry them? That's all they want."

"Quiet, child," said the landlady; "it seems to me you know a lot about these things, and it is not appropriate for girls to know or talk so much."

"As the gentleman asked me, I could not help answering him," said the girl.

"Well then," said the vicar, "bring me these books, señor landlord, because I would like to see them."

"With all my heart," he said, and going into his own room he brought out an old bag secured with a little chain, and after opening it the vicar found it contained three large books and some manuscripts written with very good handwriting. The first he found to be "Don Cirongilio of Thrace," and the second "Don Felixmarte of Hircania," and the other the "History of the Great Captain Gonzalo Hernandez de Cordova, with the Life of Diego Garcia de Paredes."

When the vicar read the two first titles he looked at the barber and said, "We need Don Quixote's niece and housekeeper here."

"No," said the barber, "I can do it, I will carry them to the garden, there is a very good fire there."

"What! you want to burn my books!" said the landlord.

"Only these two," said the vicar, "Don Cirongilio, and Felixmarte."

"Are my books irreligious or something, that makes you want to burn them?" said the landlord.

"Divisive," said the barber."

"OK," said the landlord; "but if you want to burn any of them, make it be the one about the Great Captain and Diego Garcia; because I would rather have a child of mine burnt than either of the other two."

"Brother," said the vicar, "those two books are made of lies, and are full of foolishness and nonsense; but this one about the Great Captain is a true history, and contains the deeds of Gonzalo Hernandez from Cordova, who by his many and great achievements earned the title all over the world of the Great Captain, a famous and illustrious name, and only he deserved it; and Diego Garcia de Paredes was a distinguished Knight from the city of Trujillo in Estremadura, a very suave soldier, and had such physical strength that with one finger he stopped a windmill in full motion; and he kept the whole of an immense army from crossing a bridge he guarded, and achieved so many other deeds that if, instead of the modesty he possessed as a Knight and writing his own history, some free and unbiased writer had recorded them, they would have recorded more than all the deeds of the Hectors, Achilleses, and Rolands."

"Tell that to my father," said the landlord. "That is a thing to be astonished by! Stopping a windmill! You should read what I have read about Felixmarte of Hircania, how with one single slash of the sword he divided five giants in two, right through the middle as if they were pea-pods; and another time he attacked a great and powerful army, which had more than one million six hundred thousand soldiers, all armed from head to toe, and he conquered them all as if they were a herd of sheep.

"And, what do you have to say about the good Cirongilio from Thrace, that was so brave and courageous; as it mentions in the book, where it is said that he was sailing along a river and out of the water came a fiery snake, and as soon as he saw it, he threw himself on it and got behind its scaly shoulders, and squeezed its throat with both hands with such force that the snake, finding it was being strangled, had nothing else to do but to let itself sink to the bottom of the river, taking with it the Knight who would not let go; and when they got down there he found himself among palaces and gardens which were so beautiful that it was an amazing sight to see; and then the snake changed itself into an ancient old man, who told him things which were never heard before. Relax, señor; because if you were to hear this you would go mad with enjoyment!"

Hearing this Dorothea whispered to Cardenio, "Our landlord is close enough to be a second Don Quixote."

"Agreed," said Cardenio, "because, it seems, he accepts everything contained in those books as certain, and that what they say took place exactly as it is written; even the barefooted priests could not persuade him of the opposite."

"But consider this, brother," said the vicar, "there never was any Felixmarte from Hircania in the world, or Cirongilio from Thrace, or any other Knights that the books of chivalry talk about; the whole thing is the fabrication and invention of bored minds, devised by them for the same purpose as you mentioned, passing the time, as your farmers do when they read; because I swear to you in all seriousness there never were any Knights in the world, and no such adventures, this nonsense never happened anywhere."

"Throw that bone to another dog," said the landlord; "as if I do not know how many make five, and where my shoes are; don't think you can feed me that crap, God knows I am no fool. It must be a joke for you to try and persuade me that everything these good books say is all nonsense and lies, do you know they were printed under the license of the Lords from the Royal Council, as if they were people who would allow a lot of lies to be printed, and so many battles and enchantments that they would confuse one's senses."

"I have told you, friend," said the vicar, "that this is done to entertain bored minds; as is the case in well-ordered states, games of chess, cards, and billiards are allowed for the entertainment of those who do not care, are not obliged, or are unable to work, so books of this type are allowed to be printed, on the belief that, the true being evident, there can be nobody so ignorant to take any of these books as true stories; and if I were permitted, and the present company desired it, I would say something about the qualities books of chivalry should possess to be good ones, that would be to the advantage of the reader; but I hope the time will come when I can communicate my ideas to someone who may be able to fix things; and in the meantime, señor landlord, believe what I have said, and take your books, and make up your mind if they are true or not, and with as much good they may have done for you; be careful not end up the same as your guest Don Quixote."

"I have no fear of that," replied the landlord; "I will not be so mad to make myself a Knight; because I can see well enough that things at present are not what they used to be, the days when they say those famous Knights travelled the world."

Sancho had made his appearance in the middle of this conversation, and he was very disturbed by what he heard said about Knights no longer existing in these days, and all the books of chivalry being foolishness and lies; and he decided in his heart to wait and see what would come from this journey of his master's, and if it did not turn out as happily as his master expected, he decided he would leave him and go back to his wife and children and his ordinary work.

The landlord was carrying away the bag and the books, but the vicar said to him, "Wait; I want to see what those papers are that are written in such good handwriting." The landlord took them out handed them to him to read, and he noticed there were about eight sheets of manuscript, with, in large letters at the beginning, the title of "Novel of the Ill-advised Curiosity." The vicar read three or four lines to himself, and said, "I must say the title of this novel does not seem to be a bad one, and I feel quite interested to read it all." To which the landlord replied, "Then it would be good for you to read it then, because I can tell you that some guests who have read it here have been very pleased with it, and have begged me to allow them take it; but I would not let it go, as I intend to return it to the person who forgot the bag, books, and papers here, because maybe he will return someday; and although I know I will miss the books, I will return them; because although I am an innkeeper, I am still a Christian."

"That is very good my friend," said the vicar; "but, if the novel pleases me you must let me copy it."

"With all my heart," replied the host.

While they were talking Cardenio had picked up the novel and begun to read it, and forming the same opinion as the vicar, he begged him to read it so they all could hear.

"I would read it," said the vicar, "but now the time would be better spent sleeping."

"It would help me to rest," said Dorothea, "because whenever I listen to some story it helps me, especially if my spirit is not yet tranquil enough to let me sleep when it should."

"Well then, in that case," said the vicar, "I will read it, perhaps it may contain something pleasant."

Master Nicholas also requested him to read it in a similar manner, and Sancho too; and seeing this, and considering that he would give pleasure to all of them, and receive it himself, the vicar said, "Well then, everyone listen to me, because the novel begins like this."

CHAPTER 33

THE NOVEL OF "THE ILL-ADVISED CURIOSITY"

In Florence, a rich and famous city in Italy in the province called Tuscany, there lived two gentlemen of wealth and quality, Anselmo and Lothario, such great friends that they were called by everyone that knew about them "The Two Brothers." They were unmarried, young, the same age and had the same tastes, which was enough to account for the mutual friendship between them. Anselmo, was somewhat more motivated to seek pleasure in love than Lothario, because for him the pleasure of the chase had more attraction; but sometimes Anselmo would skip his own taste and yield to those of Lothario, and Lothario would surrender his for those of Anselmo, and in this way their preferences kept pace with one another with a harmony so perfect that the best regulated clock could not surpass it.

Anselmo was deep in love with an upper class and beautiful lady from the same city, the daughter of parents so reputable, and so admirable herself, that he decided, with the approval of his friend Lothario, as without him he did nothing, to ask her to marry him, and did so, Lothario conducting the negotiation so much to the satisfaction of his friend that in a short time he was in possession of the object of his desires, and Camilla was happy in having won Anselmo for her husband, that she gave endless thanks to heaven and to Lothario, as this good fortune had come to her through them. The first few days, those of a wedding usually being the days to celebrate, Lothario frequently visited his friend Anselmo's house, striving to honour him and the occasion, and to satisfy him in every way he could; but when the wedding days were over and the number of visits and congratulations had slowed down, he began purposely not to go as much to Anselmo's house, because it seemed to him, as it naturally would to all men with sense, that friends' houses should not be visited after marriage with the same frequency as in their bachelor days: because, although true and genuine friendship cannot and should not be in any way suspicious, a married man's honour is a thing of such delicacy that it can be injured by brothers, much more than friends. Anselmo mentioned the end of Lothario's visits, and complained about it to him, saying that if he had known that marriage was going to stop him from enjoying his friendship as he used to, he would have never married; and that, through the harmony that existed between them while he was a bachelor they had gained such a sweet name "The Two Brothers," he would not allow this title which is so rare and delightful to be lost through a needless anxiety to act cautiously; and so he asked him, to feel free in his house and to come in and go out as he used to, assuring him that his wife Camilla had no other desire than what would satisfy him, and that knowing how sincerely they loved each other she was upset to see such coldness in him.

All of this that Anselmo said to Lothario to persuade him to come to his house as he had been in the habit of doing, Lothario replied with so much prudence, sense, and judgment, that Anselmo was satisfied of his friend's good intentions, and it was agreed that on two days in the week, and on holidays, Lothario would come to eat with him; but although this arrangement was made between them, Lothario decided only to satisfy what he considered to be in agreement with the honour of his friend, whose good name was more important to him than his own. He said, and rightly so, that a married man who heaven had given a beautiful wife should consider carefully what friends he brought into his house and what female friends his wife associated with, because what cannot be done or arranged in the market-place, in church, at public festivals or at stations (opportunities that husbands cannot always deny their wives), may be easily managed in the house of the female friend or relative where the most confidence is placed. Lothario said, as well, that every married man should have a friend who would point out to him any negligence he might be guilty of in his conduct, because it will sometimes happen due to the deep affection the husband has for his wife, that either he does not caution her, or, not to anger her, refrains from telling her to do or not to do certain things, and doing or avoiding them may be a matter of honour or dishonour to him; and errors of this kind he could easily be corrected if warned by a friend. But where can a friend be found like Lothario, so sensible, so loyal, and so true?

Truthfully, I do not know; because Lothario alone was the one, with the utmost care and vigilance he watched over the honour of his friend, and strove to diminish, cut down, and reduce the number of days for going to his house according to their agreement, in case the visits of a young man, wealthy, upper class, and with great attractions he was conscious of possessing, at the house of a woman so beautiful as Camilla, would be regarded with suspicion by the inquisitive and evil eyes of the bored public. Because although his integrity and reputation might restrain defamatory statements, he was still unwilling to risk his own good name or his friend's; and for this reason, on most of the days which they had agreed he devoted his time to some other business which he pretended was unavoidable; so most of the day was used up with complaints on one side and excuses on the other. It happened, however, that on one occasion when the two were walking together outside the city, Anselmo said the following words to Lothario.

"You might think, Lothario my friend, that I am unable to give sufficient thanks for the favours God has given me, making me the son of great parents as mine were, and delivering me with no defects, these are called the gifts of nature as well as those from fortune, and above all for what he has done in giving me you as my friend and Camilla as my wife - two treasures that I value, if not as highly as I should, at least as highly as I am able to. And yet, with all these good things, which all men need to enable them to live happily, I am the most discontented and dissatisfied man in the whole world; because, I do not know for how long now I have been harassed and oppressed by a desire so strange and so unusual, that I blame and criticise myself when I am alone, and strive to supress it and hide it from my own thoughts, but I have no success, as if I were endeavouring deliberately to publish it to the whole world; and as, in short, it must come out, I want to confide it in you for your safe keeping, feeling sure that by this, and by your willingness as a true friend to give me relief, I will soon find myself freed from the distress it causes me, and that your care will give me happiness in the same degree as my own madness has caused me misery."

The words of Anselmo took Lothario by surprise, unable to guess the meaning of such an extensive explanation; and although he strove to imagine what the desire could be that troubled his friend, his guesses were all far from the truth, and to relieve the anxiety which this confusion was causing him, he told him this was unfair to their great friendship, seeking indirect methods of confiding in him his most hidden thoughts, because he should know that he can rely on his advice in diverting them, or his help in carrying them into effect.

"That is the truth," replied Anselmo, "and relying on that I will tell you, friend Lothario, that the thought which harasses me is knowing whether my wife Camilla is as good and as perfect as I think she is; and I cannot be satisfied of the truth on this point except by testing her in such a way that the test can prove her purity and virtue as fire proves what is gold; because I am convinced, my friend, that a woman is virtuous only to the degree she is or is not tempted; and that a woman is strong if she does not yield to the promises, gifts, tears, and insistence of intense lovers; because what thanks does a woman deserve for being good if no one urges her to be bad, and what wonder is it that she is reserved and prudent when there is no opportunity for doing wrong and who knows she has a husband that will take her life the first time he detects her being unfaithful? Therefore I do not believe a woman is virtuous through fear or lack of opportunity in the same degree as a woman who comes out of temptation and a test with a crown of victory; and so, for these reasons and many others that I could give you to justify and support the opinion I have, I am eager that my wife Camilla must pass this test, and be refined and examined by the fire of finding herself pursued by someone worthy to chase her; and if she comes out victorious from this struggle, I will look at my good fortune as unmatched, I will be able to say that the cup of my desire is full, and that the virtuous woman, which the sages say 'are difficult to find' has come to me. And if the result is the opposite of what I expect, knowing that I have been right in my opinion to test her, I will take without any complaint the pain which my experience will naturally cause me. And, as nothing you will say will urge against my wish and keep me from carrying it into effect, it is my desire, friend Lothario, that you should become the instrument for completing this purpose, because I will be able to give you opportunities to test her, and nothing should come from a virtuous, honourable, modest and high-class woman. And among other reasons, I trust this difficult task with you because I know if Camilla is conquered by your pursuit she will not be pushed to extremes, but only far enough to determine her loyalty, and that which is left unfinished from your sense of honour will be left undone; so I will not be betrayed in anything other than her intention. I know this thought will last until death if I do not know for sure, therefore, if you want me to enjoy this thing called life, you will engage in this love struggle, not lazily, but with energy and enthusiasm that the test demands, and with the loyalty our friendship assures me of."

There were the words Anselmo said to Lothario, who listened to them with a lot of attention, apart from what has already been mentioned, he did not open his lips until the other had finished. Then noticing he had no more to say, after observing him for a while, like someone would observe something they have never seen before that excited wonder and amazement, he said to him, "I cannot convince myself, Anselmo my friend, that what you have said to me is not a joke; if I thought that you were speaking seriously I would not have allowed you to go so far; I suspect that either you do not know me, or I do not know you; but no, I know very well who you are Anselmo, and you know that I am Lothario; the misfortune is, it seems to me, that you are not the Anselmo you were, and must have thought that I am not the Lothario I am; because the things that you have said to me are not those of my friend Anselmo who was my friend, and neither should the things you demand from me be asked from the Lothario you know. True friends will prove their friends and make use of them, as a poet once said, usque ad aras; which means that they will not make use of their friendship in things that oppose God's will. If this was an irreligious man's view about friendship, how much more would a Christian's be, who knows that the divine should not be sacrificed for any human friendship? And if a friend would put aside his duty to Heaven to fulfil his duty to his friend, it should not be in matters that are insignificant, but in areas that affect the friend's life and honour. Now tell me, Anselmo, in which of these are you exposed, so I should endanger myself to gratify you, and do something so disgusting? Neither; actually quite the opposite, you are asking me, as far as I understand, to work hard towards robbing you of honour and life, and to rob myself of them at the same time; because if I take away your honour it is clear I take away your life, as a man without honour is worse than dead; and being the instrument, as you want me to be, of so much wrong to you, would I not, also, be left without honour, and consequently without life? Listen to me, Anselmo my friend, do not be impatient to answer me until I have said whatever comes to me about the objective of your desire, because there will be enough time left for you to reply and for me to hear."

"OK," said Anselmo, "say what you like."

Lothario then went on to say, "It seems to me, Anselmo, that you are showing a typical mentality of the Moors, who can never be shown the error of their beliefs by quotations from the Holy Scriptures, or by reasons which depend on the examination of the understanding or are founded upon the articles of faith, but must have examples that are tangible, easy, logical, capable of proof, not welcoming doubt, with mathematical demonstrations that cannot be denied, like, 'If an equal number is taken from another equal number, then the remaining number must be equal:' and if they do not understand this in words, it has to be shown to them with the hands, and put in front of their eyes, and because of this no one can succeed in convincing them about the truth of our holy religion. So I will have to take the same approach with you, because the desire which has been created in your mind is so absurd and distant from everything that has a resemblance of reason, that I feel it would be a waste of time to try reason with your simplicity, because at present I have nothing else I can call it, and I am even tempted to leave you in your irrationality as a punishment for your destructive desire; but the friendship I have with you, which will not allow me to desert you in such obvious danger of destruction, keeps me from dealing with you so harshly. And so you can clearly see this, Anselmo, have you not told me that I must force myself on a modest woman? Entice someone that is virtuous? Make advances to one that is pure-minded? Seduce one that is prudent? Yes, that is what you have told me. If you know you have a wife, modest, virtuous, pure-minded and prudent, what is it that you are seeking? And if you believe that she will overcome all of my attacks, and of course she would - what higher title can you give her than the one she possesses now, or in what way will she be any better than she is now? Either you do not believe her to be what you say, or you do not know what you demand. If you do not believe her to be what you say, why do you seek to prove it instead of treating her as guilty? But if she is as virtuous as you believe, it is an uncalled-for proceeding to test truth itself, because, after the test, it will remain at the same estimation as before. Therefore, it is certain that to attempt things which bring harm rather than an advantage is the product of unreasoning and a reckless mind, especially when they are things which we are not forced or obliged to attempt, and which, when observed from a distance show that it is madness to attempt them.

"Difficulties are attempted either for God or for the world, or for both; those undertaken for God are those which the saints undertake when they attempt to live the lives of angels in human bodies; those undertaken for the world are the type that see men navigate the seas, go through a variety of climates, so many strange countries, to acquire what are called the blessings of fortune; and those undertaken for God and the world together are the type that see brave soldiers, who as soon as they see in the enemy's wall an opening as wide as a cannon ball they, put aside all fear, without hesitating, or regarding the evident danger that threatens them, pushed forward by the desire of defending their faith, their country, and their King, they throw themselves boldly into a thousand opposing deaths that await them. These are the things that men should attempt, because there we find honour and glory in attempting them, however full of difficulty and danger they may be; but that which you say is your wish to attempt and carry out will not gain you the glory of God or the blessings of fortune, or fame among men; because even if it is undertaken as the result is what you would like it to be, you will be no happier, richer, or more honoured than you are at this moment; and if it is the opposite you will be reduced to misery greater than you can imagine. Even if no one is aware about your misfortune; knowing it for yourself will be enough to torture and crush you. And to confirm the truth of what I say, let me repeat a stanza to you by the famous poet Luigi Tansillo at the end of the first part of his 'Tears of Saint Peter,' which says this:

The suffering and the shame, grew greater in Peter's heart as the morning slowly came;
No eyes were there to see him, he knew this, but to himself he felt ashamed,
Exposed to all men's eyes, or separated from view,
Shame can hide which one of these is true;
A victim of shame the sinning soul will be,
Even if, only heaven and earth can see.

So by keeping it secret you will not escape your sorrow, but actually, you will cry continuously, if not tears from the eyes, tears of blood from the heart, like the tears of that simple doctor our poet tells us about, that tried the test of the cup, which the wise Rinaldo, better informed, refused to do; because although this may be a fiction it contains a moral lesson worthy of attention, study and imitation. Furthermore, by what I am about to say to you, you will be about to see the great error you would commit.

"Tell me, Anselmo, if Heaven or good fortune had made you the master and lawful owner of a diamond of the finest quality, with excellence and purity, which all the experts that had seen it being satisfied said in the same way and common consent that in purity, quality, and fineness, it was surely a diamond of the kind, you as well holding the same belief, knowing nothing opposing this, would it be reasonable for you to desire to take that diamond and place on the floor, take a hammer, and hit it as hard as you can to test if it was as hard and as fine as they said it was? And if you did, and if the diamond resisted this silly test, that would add nothing to its value or reputation; and if it were broken, as it might be, do you not think all would be lost? Of course it would, leaving its owner to be regarded as a fool in the opinion of all. Consider, then, Anselmo my friend, that Camilla is a diamond of the finest quality in your estimation and in others, and that it is unreasonable to expose her to the risk of being broken; because if she remains intact she cannot rise to a higher value than she now possesses; and if she breaks and is unable to resist, think about how you will be deprived of her, and you will complain about yourself for being the cause of her ruin and your own. Remember there is no jewel in the world as precious as a faithful and virtuous woman, and that the whole honour of women consists in reputation; and since your wife is of the highest excellence that you know of, why should you seek to call that truth in to question? Remember, my friend, that a woman is an imperfect animal, and that obstacles are not to be placed in her way to make her trip and fall, but that they should be removed, and her path left clear of all obstacles, so that without any hindrance she may walk her path freely to attain the desired perfection, which consists in being virtuous. Zoologists tell us that the ermine is a little animal which has the purest white fur, and that when the hunters want to take it, they use this trick: once they have determined the places which it usually visits and passes, they block the way to them with mud, and as soon as the ermine comes to the mud it stops, and allows itself to be taken rather than go through the mud and spoil its whiteness, which it values more than life and freedom. The virtuous and faithful woman is an ermine, the virtue of modesty is whiter and purer than snow; and he who wishes that she does not lose it, but to keep and preserve it, must implement a strategy which is different from the one used with the ermine; he must not leave in front of her the mud of the gifts and attention of persevering lovers, because perhaps - and even without a perhaps - she may not have sufficient virtue and natural strength in herself to go through and pass these impediments; they must be removed, and the brightness of virtue and the beauty of a good reputation must be highlighted to her. A virtuous woman, is also like a mirror, shining clear like crystal, but likely to be tarnished and dimmed by every breath that touches it. She must be treated as artefacts are; adored, not touched. She must be protected and respected like someone who protects and respects a garden full of roses and flowers, the owner of this allows no one to trespass or pick the flowers; it is enough for others that from afar and through the iron grate they can enjoy its fragrance and its beauty. Finally let me repeat some verses to you, which have come to my mind; I heard them in a modern comedy, and it seems to me they are similar to the point we are discussing.

A prudent old man was giving advice to another man, the father of a young girl, to lock her up, watch over her and keep her in isolation, and among the arguments he used these:

A woman is made of glass;
Who knows what will pass?
But her fragility is the best;
Not also inquisitively to test.

Breaking glass is an easy matter,
It cannot be made whole if you shatter.
And it is madness to expose,
You cannot preserve by giving it blows.

This, everyone knows as true;
And the reason's plain to see.
Ladies like Danae can be;
There are showers of gold too.

"All that I have said to you so far, Anselmo, has reference to what concerns you; and now it is right for me to say something regarding myself; and if this takes some time, forgive me, because the labyrinth which you have entered into and which I need to rescue you from makes it necessary.

212

"You consider me a friend, and yet you would rob me of honour, a thing wholly inconsistent with friendship; and not only is this your aim, but you want me to rob you of it as well. It is clear to see how I will lose honour, because when Camilla sees that I pursued her at your request, she will regard me as a man without honour or good conscience, since I attempt and do something so opposed to friendship. Robbing you of it is clear as well, because when Camilla sees my advances, she will suppose that I have perceived in her something which has encouraged me to show her my dishonourable desire; and if she feels dishonoured, her dishonour touches you as belonging to her; and there arises what commonly takes place, that the husband of the disloyal woman, although he may not be aware of or have given any cause for his wife's failure in her duty, or (being careless or negligent) have had it in his power to prevent his dishonour, nevertheless is stigmatised by a disgusting and disapproving name, and in a manner regarded with eyes of disrespect instead of pity by all who know of his wife's guilt, although they see that he is unfortunate not by his own fault, but by the lust of a vicious wife. But I will tell you why with good reason dishonour attaches to the husband of the immoral wife, although he does not know that she is to blame, or has done anything, or given any incitement to make this happen. Please be patient listening to me, because it will be for your own good.

When God created our first parent in the earthly paradise, the Holy Scripture says that he infused sleep into Adam and while he slept took a rib from his left side, and with this he formed our mother Eve, and when Adam awoke and saw her he said, 'This is flesh of my flesh, and bone of my bone.' And God said 'for this, a man will leave his mother and father, and they will be two in one flesh; and then came the divine ceremony of marriage, which binds these two so that only death alone can loosen them. And this is the force and virtue of this incredible ceremony that it makes two different people become one and the same flesh; and even more than this when the virtuous are married; because although they have two souls they will then have one. And from this it follows that as the flesh of the wife is one and the same with that of her husband the stains that can be thrown on it, or the injuries it can incur affect the husband's flesh, although he, as has been said, may have given no cause for them; because just as the pain of the foot or any member of the body is felt by the whole body, because all is one flesh, the head feels the hurt of the ankle without having caused it, so the husband, being one with her, shares the dishonour of the wife; and as all worldly honour or dishonour is human, and of flesh and blood, the wife's errors of the type that the husband takes a share in, also dishonour him without knowing it. See, then, Anselmo, the danger you are facing when seek to disturb the peace of your virtuous wife; your curiosity would awaken passions that now rest quietly in the chest of your pure wife; reflect - for what is at stake, your win will be very little, and what you stand to lose I will leave undescribed, not having the words to express it. But if all I have said is not enough to turn you away from your disgusting purpose, you must seek some other instrument for your dishonour and misfortune; because I will not consent to be that, even if I lose your friendship, the greatest loss I can conceive."

Having said this, the wise and virtuous Lothario was silent, and Anselmo, troubled in mind and deep in thought was unable for a while to say a word in reply; but finally he said, "I have listened to you Lothario my friend, attentively, as you have seen, to what you have chosen to say to me, and in your arguments, examples, and comparisons I have seen the high intelligence you possess, and the perfection of true friendship you have reached; and likewise I see and confess that if I am not guided by your opinion, but follow my own, I am flying from the good and pursuing the evil. However, this being so, you must remember that I am suffering from that illness which women sometimes suffer from, when the craving takes them to eat clay, plaster, charcoal, and even worse things, so disgusting to look at, and much more to eat; so it will be necessary to have a remedy to cure me; and this can be easily done if you will do it, even if it is was lukewarm and in a make-believe style, to attempt to win Camilla, who will not be so weak in her virtue that she will break on the first attack: with this little attempt I will be satisfied, and you will have done what our friendship binds you to do, not only giving me life, but persuading me not to discard my honour. And this you are bound to do for one reason alone, that, being, as I am, determined to apply this test, it is not for you to permit me to reveal my weakness to another, and so with honour you are striving to keep me from losing mine to someone else; and if your estimation of Camilla is high then it is of little importance if she finds out, because you can plainly tell her the truth about our strategy, and regain your place in her esteem; and as you are only going to try a little, and as it can offer me much satisfaction, how could you refuse not to undertake it; because, as I have said, if you only make a start I will accept the issue as decided."

Lothario seeing the fixed determination of Anselmo, and not knowing what further examples to offer or arguments to give in order to deter him from it, and perceiving that he threatened to confide his destructive scheme to someone else, to avoid a greater evil decided to gratify him and do what he asked, intending to manage this situation to satisfy Anselmo without corrupting the mind of Camilla; so in reply he told him not to communicate his purpose to any other, because he would undertake the task himself, and would begin it as soon as he wanted him to. Anselmo embraced him warmly and affectionately, and thanked him for his offer as if he had done him a favour; and it was agreed between them to start the next day, Anselmo allowing an opportunity and time for Lothario to speak alone with Camilla, and supplying him with money and jewels to offer and present to her. He suggested, as well, that he should play music, and write a poem praising her, and if he was unwilling to take the trouble of composing it, he offered to do it himself. Lothario agreed to all of this with an intention very different from what Anselmo thought, and with this understanding they returned to Anselmo's house, where they found Camilla awaiting her husband anxiously and uneasily, because he was later than usual returning that day. Lothario went to his own house, and Anselmo remained in his, well satisfied, as much as Lothario was troubled in mind; because he could see no satisfactory way out of this ill-advised plan. That night, however, he thought of a plan to deceive Anselmo without any damage to Camilla. The next day he went to eat with his friend, and was welcomed by Camilla, who treated him with great friendliness, knowing the affection her husband felt for him. When dinner was over and the cloth removed, Anselmo told Lothario to stay there with Camilla while he attended to some pressing business, and he would return in an hour and a half. Camilla begged him not to go, and Lothario offered to go with him, but nothing could persuade Anselmo, who on the contrary encouraged Lothario to wait for him there as he had a matter of great importance to discuss with him later. At the same time, he asked Camilla not to leave Lothario alone until he came back. In short, he arranged to create such a good reason, or foolishness, about his absence that no one could have suspected it was deception.

Anselmo left, and Camilla and Lothario were left alone at the table, because the rest of the household had gone out. Lothario saw himself encouraged to undertake his friend's wish, and facing an enemy that could by her beauty alone conquer a group of armed Knights; had a good reason to be hesitant; so what he did was lean his elbow on the arm of the chair, and his cheek on his hand, and, asking Camilla to forgive him for his bad manners, he said he would like to have a nap until Anselmo returned. Camilla in reply said he could rest better in the reception-room than in the chair, and asked him to go and sleep in there; but Lothario declined, and remained asleep on the chair until Anselmo returned, who finding Camilla in her own room, and Lothario asleep, imagined that he had been away for so long he gave them enough time for conversation and even for sleep, and was quite impatient for Lothario to wake up, so that he could go outside with him and question him about his success or failure. Lothario woke up, and both of them left the house, and Anselmo asked what he was anxious to know, and Lothario told him that he had not thought it was advisable to declare himself entirely the first time, and therefore had only praised the charms of Camilla, telling her the city spoke of nothing else but her beauty and intelligence, because this seemed to him an excellent way of beginning to gain her good-will and make her inclined to listen to him with pleasure the next time, therefore gaining an advantage for himself, the methods the devil resorts to when he wants to deceive someone who is on the watch; because he being the angel of darkness transforms himself into an angel of light, and, undercover of this, reveals himself, and executes his purpose even if at the beginning his evil is not discovered. All of this gave great satisfaction to Anselmo, and he said he would give the same opportunity every day, but without leaving the house, because he would find things to do at home so that Camilla should not detect the plan.

Therefore, several days went by, and Lothario, without saying a word to Camilla, reported to Anselmo that he had talked to her and that he had not been able to get from her the slightest indication of consent to anything dishonourable, not even a sign or shadow of hope; on the contrary, he said she would inform her husband of it if he did not stop.

"So far so good," said Anselmo; "Camilla has resisted words; now we must see how she will resist actions. I will give you tomorrow two thousand gold coins to offer her, and as many more you need to buy jewels to lure her, because women are fond of wearing jewels and dressing up, and even more if they are beautiful, however virtuous they may be; and if she resists this temptation, I will be satisfied and will not give you any more trouble."

Lothario replied that now he had begun he would carry out the plan to the end, although he felt he would come out of it tired and defeated. The next day he received two thousand coins, and with them two thousand perplexities, because he did not know what to say to Anselmo; but in the end he made up his mind to tell him that Camilla stood firm against the gifts and promises as she did against the words, and that there was no point continuing, because all the time was spent with no purpose.

But chance, leading things in a different direction, ordered it that Anselmo, having left Lothario and Camilla alone, went into the other room and sat himself to watch and listen through the keyhole to what happened between them, and noticed for more than half an hour Lothario did not say a word to Camilla, and neither would he say a word if he were there for a thousand years; and so he came to the conclusion that what his friend had told him about the replies from Camilla were lies, and to determine if it were so, he came out, and calling Lothario aside asked him what news he had in regards to their plan. Lothario replied that he was not willing to go on with the plan, because she had answered him so angrily and harshly that he had no heart to say anything else to her.

"Ah, Lothario, Lothario," said Anselmo, "how badly you have done in your obligations to me, and the great confidence I had in you! I have just been watching through this keyhole, and I have seen that you have not said a word to Camilla, from this I conclude that on the former occasions you have not spoken to her either, and if this is so, as no doubt it is, why do you deceive me, or why do you seek by deception to deprive me of the means of attaining my desire?"

Anselmo said no more, but he had said enough to cover Lothario with shame and confusion, and he, feeling his honour touched by having been detected in a lie, swore to Anselmo that from that moment he would devote himself to satisfying him without any deception, as he would see if he had the curiosity to watch; although he need not bother to, because the effort he would take to satisfy him would remove all suspicions from his mind. Anselmo believed him, and to give him a better opportunity, he decided to be away from his house for eight days, asking a friend of his who lived in a village not far from the city to invite him to go somewhere with him; and giving a better explanation for his departure to Camilla, he arranged it that the friend would send him an invitation.

Anselmo, what are you doing, what are you plotting, what are you devising? Do you not think you are working against yourself, plotting your own dishonour, devising your own ruin? Your wife Camilla is virtuous, you possess her in peace and quiet, no one attacks your happiness, her thoughts do not wander beyond the walls of your house, you are her heaven on earth, the object of her wishes, the fulfilment of her desires, the ruler where she measures her will, making it conform in all things to yours and Heaven's. If, then, the treasure of her honour, beauty, virtue, and modesty comes to you without work and all the wealth it contains that you can wish for, why would you dig the earth in search of fresh sources, of new unknown treasure, risking the collapse of the current structure, since all rests on the frail legs of her weak nature? Do you not think that when a man seeks impossibilities, that which is possible can be withheld, as was better expressed by a poet who said:

It is up to me to seek for life in death,
Health in disease,
I seek in prison, freedom's breath,
In traitors, loyalty.
Fate, can grant hate,
Or grace or gain to me,
Since what can never be, I want,
Denies me what might be.

The next day Anselmo left the village, leaving instructions with Camilla that during his absence Lothario would come to look after his house and to have dinner with her, and that she was to treat him as well as she would treat herself. Camilla was distressed, as a discreet and right-minded woman would be, at the orders her husband left her, and asked him to remember that it was not appropriate that anyone occupy his seat at the table during his absence, and if he acted like this because he did not feel confident that she would be able to manage his house, let her prove she can, and he would find by experience that she was equal to greater responsibilities. Anselmo replied that he preferred it to be as he said, and that she had only to submit and obey. Camilla said she would do so, but it was against her will.

Anselmo went, and the next day Lothario came to his house, where he was greeted by Camilla with a friendly and modest welcome; but she never allowed Lothario to see her alone, because she was always accompanied by servants, especially by a lady of hers, called Leonela, who she was very attached to (because they had been brought up together from childhood in her father's house), and who she had kept with her after her marriage to Anselmo. The first three days Lothario did not speak to her, although he might have done if the servants were not there; because it was Camilla's orders that Leonela ate with her and never left her side. She, however, having her thoughts fixed on other things more to her taste, and wanting time and opportunity for her own pleasures, did not always obey Camilla's commands, but on one occasion actually left them alone, as if they had ordered her to do so; but the humble manner of

Camilla, the calmness of her expression, and her composure were enough to stop the tongue of Lothario. But the influence which the many virtues of Camilla used in imposing silence on Lothario's tongue proved mischievous for both of them, because if his tongue was silent his thoughts were busy, and he began to think about the perfection of Camilla's goodness and beauty, enough charm to warm with love a marble statue, not to say a heart of flesh. Lothario stared at her when he could have been speaking to her, and thought of how worthy of being loved she was; and this reflection began little by little to assault his allegiance to Anselmo, and a thousand times he thought of leaving the city and going where Anselmo would never see him, and where he would never see Camilla. But already the delight he found in staring at her interrupted his thoughts and held him there. He put a constraint on himself, and struggled to repel and repress the pleasure he found in contemplating Camilla; when alone he blamed himself for his weakness, called himself a bad friend, actually a bad Christian; then he argued the matter and compared himself with Anselmo; always coming to the conclusion that the foolishness and carelessness of Anselmo had been worse than his faithlessness, and that if he could excuse his intentions in front of God, he had no reason to fear any punishment for his offence.

In short, the beauty and goodness of Camilla, combined with the opportunity which the blind husband had placed in his hands, overthrew the loyalty of Lothario; and giving attention to nothing except the object which his inclination led him toward, after Anselmo had been away for three days, during which he had been carrying on a continual struggle with his passion, he began to declare his love to Camilla with so much intensity and warmth of language that she was overwhelmed with amazement, and could only rise from her place and go to her room without answering him. But the hope which always springs up with love, was not weakened in Lothario by this repelling behaviour; on the contrary his passion for Camilla increased, and seeing in him what she had never expected, she did not know what to do; and considering it neither safe or right to give him the chance or opportunity of speaking to her again, she decided to send, as she did that very night, one of her servants with a letter to Anselmo, in which she said the following:

CHAPTER 34

CONTINUING "THE ILL-ADVISED CURIOSITY"

"It can be said that an army looks weak without its general and a castle falls without a leader, and I say that a young married woman looks worse without her husband unless there is a very good reason for it. I find myself unsettled without you, and so weak to endure this separation, that unless you return quickly I will have to go for relief to my parents' house, even if I leave yours without a protector; because the one you left with me, if he deserves that title, has, I think, more regard for his own pleasure than what concerns you: as you possess good judgment I do not need to say anymore to you, and perhaps its best I do not say anymore."

Anselmo received this letter, and from it he gathered that Lothario had begun his task and that Camilla must have replied to him as he would have liked her too; he was extremely happy to see her intelligence, so he replied to her, saying not to leave his house, as he would return very soon. Camilla was amazed by Anselmo's reply, which gave her even greater confusion than before, because she did not want to stay in the house, and was told not go to her parents'; and if she remained her virtue was in danger, and if she left she was opposing her husband's commands.

She knew the worse option for her was to remain, but decided not to run from the presence of Lothario, so she would not create any gossip for her servants; and she now began to regret writing to her husband, fearing he might imagine that Lothario had noticed something in her which had encouraged him to put aside the respect he used to show her; but confident of her morality she put her trust in God and in her own virtuous intentions, with which she hoped to resist in silence all the approaches of Lothario, without saying anything to her husband so she did not involve him in any argument or trouble; and she even began to consider how to excuse Lothario to Anselmo when he would ask her what it was that induced her to write that letter. With these resolutions, more honourable than sensible or effective, she remained in the house the next day listening to Lothario, who continued to apply pressure until Camilla's firmness began to soften, and her virtue struggled to rescue her eyes and keep them from showing signs of compassion which the appeal of Lothario had awakened in her. Lothario observed this, and it excited him more. In short, he felt that while Anselmo's absence offered him time and opportunity he must break into the fortress, and so he attacked her self-esteem - praising her beauty, because there is nothing quicker to reduce and level the castle towers of women's vanity than with a tongue of flattery. In fact, with great attention he destabilised the rock of her purity with various methods that had Camilla been made of brass she would have fallen by now. He cried, he pleaded, he promised, he flattered, he persisted with so much feeling and apparent sincerity, that he overthrew the virtuous Camilla and won the triumph he least expected. Camilla surrendered, Camilla fell;

but what wonder is it that the friendship of Lothario could not stand firm? This is clear proof to us that the passion of love can only be conquered only by running away from it, and that no one should engage in a struggle with an enemy so mighty; because divine strength is needed to overcome this human power. Leonela was the only one that knew of her mistress's weakness, because the two new lovers were unable to conceal it. Lothario did not care to tell Camilla the object Anselmo had in view, or that he had given him the opportunity of reaching that result, because she would have undervalued his love and think that it was made up without intending it and not because he really did love to her.

A few days later Anselmo returned to his house and did not sense what he had lost, that which he so lightly treated and so highly prized. He went immediately to see Lothario, and found him at home; they hugged each other, and Anselmo asked for the report of his life or his death.

"The report I have to give you, Anselmo my friend," said Lothario, "is that you possess a wife that is worthy to be the design and pinnacle of all good wives. The words I gave to her were wasted and went with the wind, my promises were despised, my presents have been refused, my artificial tears were ridiculed. In short, as Camilla is the essence of all beauty, she is also the treasure-house where purity lives, and gentleness and modesty stand with all the virtues that give praise, honour, and happiness to a woman. Take back your money, my friend; here it is, I have had no need to use it, because the virtue of Camilla does not surrender to gifts or promises. Be content, Anselmo, and refrain from seeking further proof; and as you have passed clearly through the sea of those doubts and suspicions that are and may be invited by some women, do not seek to go into the deep ocean of new embarrassments again, or with another captain to test the goodness and strength of the ship Heaven has granted you to journey across the sea of this world; consider yourself now to be in a safe port, lower your anchor, and rest in peace until you are called to pay that debt which no rich man on earth can escape paying."

Anselmo was completely satisfied by the words of Lothario, and believed them fully as if they had been spoken by an oracle; yet he asked him not to abandon the undertaking, out of curiosity and amusement; although now he did not need him to be as serious as before; all he wanted him to do was to write some verses to her, praising her; and if Lothario was unwilling to take the trouble of writing the verses he would compose them himself.

"That will not be necessary," said Lothario, "because the muses are not enemies of mine, actually they visit me now and then during the year.

Therefore, an agreement was made between the friends, the ill-advised one and the treacherous, and Anselmo returning to his house asked Camilla the question she wondered he had not already asked - what it was that caused her to write the letter she had sent to him. Camilla replied that it seemed to her that Lothario looked at her somewhat more freely than when he had been at home; but now she was enlightened and believed it to only be her imagination, because Lothario now avoided seeing her, or being alone with her. Anselmo told her she could relax her suspicion, because he knew that Lothario was in love with a lady in the city who he called Chloris, and that even if he were not, his loyalty and their great friendship gave no room for fear. Camilla, however, had already been informed beforehand by Lothario that this love for Chloris was a lie, and that he had told Anselmo about her so he could secretly discuss Camilla with him, no doubt she would have become jealous; but being alert she received the news without worry.

The next day as the three were at the table Anselmo asked Lothario to recite something that he had composed for his Chloris; because as Camilla did not know her, he could safely say whatever he liked.

"Even if she did know her," returned Lothario, "I would not hide anything, because when a lover praises his lady's beauty, or accuses her of cruelty, he does no damage to her good name; at any rate, all I can say is that yesterday I made a poem about the ungratefulness of Chloris, which goes like this:

POEM:

At midnight, in silence, when the eyes,
To Chloris and to Heaven rise,
Telling the the story of my untold woes,
And then the happier couple sleeps close.

And when the light of day dyes,
The windows from the east with tints of rose,
With undiminished force my sorrow flows
In broken accents and in burning sighs.

And when the sun ascends from his throne,
And pours down his midday beams,
Noon renews my crying and tears.
And again at night I start to moan,
Always in my agony it seems,
To me that neither Heaven or Chloris hears.

The poem pleased Camilla, and even more Anselmo, because he praised it and said the lady was extremely cruel for ignoring such sincerity. To which Camilla said, "Do all poets in love tell the truth?"

"As poets they do not tell the truth," replied Lothario; "but as lovers they are not more defective in expression than they are truthful."

"There is no doubt of that," observed Anselmo, anxious to support and uphold Lothario's ideas with Camilla, who had no idea about his plan and was now deep in love with Lothario; and so she enjoyed anything that was his, and knew that his thoughts and writing were for her, and she was the real Chloris, she asked him to repeat some other poems or verses if he recollected any.

"I do," replied Lothario, "but I do not think they are as good as the first one; but you can judge, it goes like this:

POEM

I know that I am doomed; death is true,
As certain as you are ungrateful I swear,
Dead at your feet you should see me lying there,
My heart regrets its love for you.

If buried in oblivion I should be,
Without life, fame, favour, even there,
It would be found that I can bear,
Engraved in my chest for all to see.

This like some holy relic I do prize,
To save me from the fate my truth entails,
Truth that to my hard heart its vigour owes.
For him there is lowering skies,
Danger on the ocean sails,
No friendly port or a star which shows."

Anselmo praised the second poem too, as he had praised the first; and so he went on adding link after link to the chain which he was binding himself and making his dishonour secure; because when Lothario was doing the most to dishonour him he told him he was honoured; and therefore each step that Camilla descended towards the depths of her belittlement, she climbed, in his opinion, towards the summit of virtue and good fame.

It so happened that finding herself on one occasion alone with her maid, Camilla said to her, "I am ashamed to think, my dear Leonela, how lightly I have valued myself that I did not induce Lothario to purchase by at least some expenditure of his time the full possession of me, that I so quickly surrendered to him using my own free will. I fear that he will think badly of my softness or lightness, not considering the irresistible influence he had on me."

"Do not let that worry you, my lady," said Leonela, "because it does not take away the value of the thing given or make it less precious to give it quickly if it is really valuable and worthy of being prized; actually, that which gives quickly gives twice."

"They also say," said Camilla, "that what costs little is valued less."

"That saying does not apply in your case," replied Leonela, "because love, as I have heard, sometimes flies and sometimes walks; with this one it runs, with some it moves slowly; some it cools, others it burns; some it wounds, others it kills; it begins with its desires, and at the same moment completes and ends it; in the morning it will have attacked a fortress and by the night it will have taken it, because there is no power that can resist it; so what are you worried about, what do you fear, when the same has happened to Lothario, love chose the absence of your husband as the instrument for conquering you? And it was absolutely necessary to complete what love had decided, without allowing enough time for Anselmo to return and by his presence force the work to be left unfinished; because love has no better way for carrying out his projects than opportunity. I know all of this well myself, more by experience than by rumour, and some day, señora, I will enlighten you on the subject, because I am almost your flesh and blood too. Moreover, lady Camilla, you did not surrender yourself or yield so quickly because first you had to see Lothario's whole soul in his eyes, in his sighs, in his words, his promises and his gifts, and by this, his good qualities proved how worthy he was of your love. This, then, being the case, do not let these prudish ideas trouble your imagination, be assured that Lothario honours you as you honour him, and be content and satisfied that as you are caught in the trap of love this is one with worth and value that has taken you, and one that has not only the four S's that they say true lovers should have, but a complete alphabet; listen to me and you will see I am right. He is in my eyes and opinion, Agreeable, Brave, Considerate, Distinguished, Elegant, Fond, Good, Honourable, Illustrious, Jolly, Kind, Loyal, Manly, Noble, Open, Polite, Quick-witted, Rich, Suave, Tender, Unique, Veracious, Wise: 'X'trodinary, Yours; and Zealous for your honour."

Camilla laughed at her maid's alphabet, and noticed her to be more experienced in love affairs than she had previously thought, which she then went on to prove, confessing to Camilla that she had love with a young man of good upbringing in the same city. Camilla was uncomfortable by this, fearing this could endanger her honour, and asked whether her love had gone beyond words, and she with little shame and much brashness said it had; because when she saw her lady make a false step, she thought it was nothing to let her imprudence known. All that Camilla could do was to ask Leonela not to say anything about what she had done, and to be discreet so that it does not reach Anselmo. Leonela said she would, but kept her word in such a way that she confirmed Camilla's apprehension of losing her reputation through her; because abandoning this the bold Leonela, as soon as she noticed that her lady's manner was not what it should be, had the audacity to introduce her lover into the house, confident that even if her lady saw him she would not dare to ask him to leave; because this sin of hers could be used against her by others; and usually these sins make the owners of servants, servants of their servants, and are obliged to hide their carelessness and immoralities; as was the case with Camilla, who although she observed, not once but many times, that Leonela was with her lover in some room of the house, not only did not dare to scold her, but offered her opportunities to conceal him and removed all difficulties, so he would not be seen by her husband. She was unable, however, to prevent him from being seen on one occasion as he left in the morning by Lothario, who, not knowing who he was, thought he was a threat; and as soon as he saw him run away, hiding his face with his cloak and concealing himself carefully and cautiously, considered confronting him, but he rejected this foolish idea, and adopted another, which would have ruined everything if Camilla had not found a remedy. It did not occur to Lothario that this man he had seen leaving at such a strange hour from Anselmo's house could have entered it due to Leonela, and neither did he even remember there was such a person as Leonela; all he thought was that as Camilla had been light and yielding with him, she had been with another; because this is the penalty of the stumbling woman that the sin brings with it, that her honour is distrusted even by the one whose approaches and persuasions she has yielded to; and he believes her to have surrendered more easily to others, and gives implicit credibility to every suspicion that comes into his mind. All Lothario's good sense seemed to have failed him on this occasion; all his prudent proverbs escaped his memory; because without even once reflecting rationally, and without more contemplation, in his impatience and in the blindness of the jealous rage that distressed his heart, and dying to seek revenge on Camilla, who had not done any wrong to him, before Anselmo had woken up he rushed to him and said to him, "You must know, Anselmo, that for several days I have been struggling with myself, striving to withhold from you what it is no longer possible or right that I should conceal from you. Know that Camilla's fortress has surrendered and is ready to submit to my will; and if I have been slow to reveal this fact to you, it was in order to see if it were some light impulse of hers, or if she wanted to try me and ascertain if the love I began to make to her with your permission was made with a serious intention. I thought, as well, that she, if she were what she should be, and what we both believed her to be, would have given you the information of what happen; but seeing that she has not, I believe the promise she has given me is true, that the next time you are absent from the house she will grant me access to the room where your jewels are kept (and it was true that Camilla used to meet him there); but I do not wish you to rush impulsively to take vengeance, because the sin is as yet only committed in intention, and Camilla's mind may change perhaps between this and the appointed time, and her regret may take its place. As until now you have always followed my advice wholly or in part, follow and observe this that I will give you now, so that, without mistakes, and with mature deliberation, you may satisfy yourself as to what may seem the best course; pretend to be absent for two or three days as you have been on other occasions, and arrange to hide yourself in the closet; because the tapestries and other things in there offer a great way to conceal yourself, and then you will see with your own eyes and I with mine what Camilla's purpose may be. And if it is a guilty one, which may be feared rather than expected, with silence, prudence, and discretion you can become the instrument of punishment for the wrong done to you."

Anselmo was amazed, overwhelmed, and astounded by the words of Lothario, which came to him at a time when he least expected to hear them, because now he looked at Camilla as having triumphed over the pretended attacks of Lothario, and was beginning to enjoy the glory of her victory. He remained silent for a considerable time, looking on the ground with a fixed gaze, and finally said, "You have behaved, Lothario, as I expected of your friendship: I will follow your advice in everything; do as you will, and keep this secret as it should be kept in circumstances like this."

Lothario gave him his word, but after leaving him he regretted everything he had said to him, recognising how foolishly he had acted, as he might have got revenge on Camilla in some less cruel and degrading way. He cursed his lack of sense, condemned his reckless impulse, and did not know what to do to undo the damage or find an escape from it. At last he decided to reveal everything to Camilla, and, as there was no lack of opportunity for doing so, he found her alone the same day; but she, as soon as she had the chance of speaking to him, said, "Lothario, I have to tell you I have such sorrow in my heart which fills it so much it is about to burst; and it will be a miracle if it does not; the nerve of Leonela has now reached such a point that every night she conceals a man of hers in the house and stays with him until the morning, risking my reputation; because it is open for anyone to question if they see him leaving my house at these unsuitable hours; but what distresses me is that I cannot punish her, because she knows about us, so this keeps my mouth shut, as I fear she will reveal everything."

As Camilla said this Lothario, he first imagined it was a way to delude him into the idea that the man he had seen leaving was Leonela's lover and not hers; but when he saw how she cried and suffered, and begged him to help her, he became convinced it was the truth, and the conviction completed his confusion and remorse; however, he told Camilla not to worry herself, as he would take action to put a stop to the disrespect of Leonela. At the same time, he told her everything, that driven by the rage of jealousy, he had said to Anselmo, and how he had arranged to hide him in the closet so he could clearly see how little she preserved her loyalty to him; and he asked her to forgive him for this madness, and her advice on how to repair it, and escape safely from the intricate labyrinth in which his imprudence had placed them. Camilla was struck with alarm when hearing what Lothario had said, and with much anger, and good sense, she criticised him and disapproved of his foolish and mischievous plan; but as women have by nature a quicker wit than men, for good or evil, although it usually fails if she attempts to exercise reason deliberately, Camilla immediately thought of a way to repair all that appeared to be irremediable, and told Lothario to arrange that the next day Anselmo should conceal himself in the place he had mentioned, because she hoped from this she could obtain the way to enjoy themselves in the future without any worry; and without revealing her purpose to him entirely she asked him to be careful, and as soon as Anselmo was concealed, to come to her when Leonela calls him, and she said to him to answer as he would have answered had he not known that Anselmo was listening.

Lothario asked her to explain her intention fully, so that he could with more certainty and precaution take care to do what was necessary.

"I tell you," said Camilla, "there is nothing to take care of except to answer what I will ask you;" because she did not wish to explain to him beforehand what she was going to do, fearing he would be unwilling to follow the idea which seemed to her to be a good one, and would try or devise another less practical plan.

Lothario then left, and the next day Anselmo, under the pretence of going to his friend's house, left his home, and then returned to conceal himself, which he was able to do easily, as Camilla and Leonela took care to give him the opportunity; and so he placed himself in hiding, in a state of agitation as he imagined he would see his honour disrespected in front of his eyes, and found himself close to losing the supreme blessing he thought he possessed: his much-loved Camilla. Having made sure Anselmo's was in his hiding-place, Camilla and Leonela entered the room, and the instant they went in Camilla said, with a deep sigh, "Ah! dear Leonela, would it not be better, before I do what I am unwilling to do, you should know and seek to prevent it, that you should take Anselmo's knife that I have asked you to take, and use it to pierce this disgusting heart of mine? But; there is no reason why I should suffer the punishment for another's fault. I will first like to know what it is that the shameless eyes of Lothario saw in me that could have encouraged him to reveal to me an idea so disgusting which he has disclosed regardless of his friendship with my husband, and of my honour. Go to the window, Leonela, and call him, because there is no doubt he is in the street waiting to carry out his evil idea; but mine, however cruel it may be, is honourable, and will be carried out first."

"Ah, señora," said the crafty Leonela, who knew her part, "what is it you want to do with this knife? Can it be that you are going to take your own life, or Lothario's? Because whichever you want to do, it will lead to the loss of your reputation and good name. It is better to avoid this problem and not give this evil man the chance of entering the house and finding us alone; consider, señora, we are weak women and he is a man, and as he comes with such a disgusting purpose, blind and encouraged by passion, perhaps before you can put your plan into execution he may do what will be worse for you than taking your life. I may be punished by my master, Anselmo, for giving the authority for this shameless man to enter the house! And supposing you kill him, señora, as I suspect you intend to do, what will we do with him when he is dead?"

"What?" replied Camilla, "we leave him for Anselmo to bury; because it will be light work for him to hide his own dishonour underground. Call him quickly, because all of this delay in taking vengeance for my wrong seems to me to be an offence against the loyalty I owe to my husband."

Anselmo was listening to all of this, and every word that Camilla spoke made him change his mind; but when he heard that the plan was to kill Lothario his first impulse was to come out and show himself to avoid such a disaster; but in his anxiety to see a resolution so bold and virtuous he restrained himself, intending to come out in time to prevent the action. At this moment Camilla, throwing herself on a bed that was close by, prepared herself, and Leonela began to cry, exclaiming, "Poor me! That I have, dying here the flower of virtue on earth, the crown of true wives, the pattern of modesty!" With more words of similar effect, so that anyone who heard her would have taken her for the most tender-hearted and faithful servant in the world.

Camilla was recovering from her fainting fit and said, "Why do you not go, Leonela, to call the false friend here? Go quickly! Or else the fire of my rage will burn itself out, and the righteous vengeance that I hope for could melt away."

"I am going to call him, señora," said Leonela; "but first you must give me that knife, because I fear while I am gone you will use it and give all those who love you reason to cry for their whole lives."

"Go in peace, dear Leonela, I will not do it," said Camilla, "because impulsive and as foolish as I may be in your mind, in defending my honour, I am not going to do what Lucretia did, who they say killed herself without having done anything wrong, without having first killed the person where the guilt of her misfortune lay. I will die, if I am to die; but it must be after full vengeance on him who has brought me here to cry due to no fault of my own."

Leonela required a lot of encouragement before she would go to call Lothario, but at last she went, and while awaiting her return Camilla continued, as if speaking to herself, "Good God! Would it have not been more prudent to have rejected Lothario, as I have done so many times before, than to allow him, as I am doing now to think of me as disloyal and disgusting, even for this short time while I wait to enlighten him? No doubt it would have been better; but I should not be punished, and the honour of my husband should be blameless, and he should find a clear and easy escape from the path which this immorality has led him. Let the traitor pay with his life for the nerve of his disgusting desires, and let the world know that Camilla not only preserved her allegiance to her husband, but sought vengeance on the man who dared to do him wrong. Still, I think it might be better to disclose this to Anselmo. But then I have called his attention to it in the letter I wrote to him, and, if he did nothing to prevent the trouble I pointed out to him, I suppose it was from the pure goodness of his heart and trustfulness he would not and could not believe that any thought against his honour could live in the chest of such a friend; neither did I believe it myself for many days, neither would I have ever believed it if his disrespect had not gone so far as to make it obvious by presents, promises, and ceaseless tears. This traitor needs to go away! Let the false friend come, approach me and die, give his life. I came pure to the husband that Heaven gave me, and I will leave pure; and at the worst bathed in my own pure blood and in the evil blood of the falsest friend that friendship ever saw in the world;" and as she spoke these words she walked up and down the room holding the knife, with irregular and disordered steps, and gestures that anyone would have thought she had lost her mind, and taken her for a violent criminal instead of a delicate woman.

Anselmo, hidden behind some tapestries where he had concealed himself, observed and was amazed by it all, and already felt that what he had seen and heard was a sufficient answer to even greater suspicions; and now he would have been pleased if the proof offered by Lothario coming was avoided, as he feared there may be some sudden misfortune; but as he was about to reveal himself and come out to embrace and inform his wife, he paused as he saw Leonela returning, leading Lothario. When Camilla saw him, she drew a long line in front of her on the floor with the knife, and said to him, "Lothario, pay attention to what I say to you: if you dare to cross this line you see, or even approach it, the instant I see you attempt to, in the same moment I will pierce my chest with this knife that I hold in my hand; and before you answer me, you must listen, and afterwards you can reply however you like. First, I want you to tell me, Lothario, if you know my husband Anselmo, and how you regard him; and secondly I want to know if you know me too? Answer me, without embarrassment or reflecting deeply what you will say, because these are not riddles."

Lothario was not stupid, the first moment when Camilla directed him to make Anselmo hide himself he understood what she intended to do, and therefore he went along with her idea so willingly and promptly that between them they made the deception look more true than truth; so he answered her: "I did not think, Camilla, that you were calling me to ask questions so far off the objective which I came with; but if you are trying to defer the promised reward, you may defer it even longer, because the desire for happiness gives more distress the nearer the hope of gaining it comes; but in answer to your questions, I know your husband Anselmo, and we have known each other from our earliest years; I do not need to repeat what you also know about our friendship and testify against the wrong that love, the mighty excuse for great errors, makes me inflict on him. I know you and give you the same valuation as he does, because if it were so, I would have, for a less worthy prise acted in opposition to the holy laws of true friendship, now broken and violated by me through that powerful enemy, love."

"If you confess that," returned Camilla, "enemy of all that truly deserve to be loved, how dare you come to me, who you know to be the mirror of him who you seek to do wrong? I now comprehend what has made you give so little notice to what you owe to myself; it must have been some freedom of mine, because I will not call it immodesty, as it did not proceed from any deliberate intention, but from some thoughtlessness which women can be guilty of through carelessness when they think they have no occasion to be unfriendly. But tell me, traitor, when did I with my words or signs give a reply to your prayers that could awaken in you a shadow of hope of attaining your disgusting wishes? When did I not refuse your confessions of love? When did I accept your promises or gifts? As I am convinced that no one can persevere for long in the attempt to win love unsustained by some hope, I am willing to attribute to myself the blame of your assurance, because no doubt some thoughtlessness of mine has encouraged your hopes; and therefore I will punish myself and inflict on myself the penalty your guilt deserves. And so you may see, I have called you here to be a witness of the sacrifice I intend to offer to the injured honour of my husband, wronged by you with all the diligence you were capable of, and by me through a lack of caution in avoiding every occasion, and if I have given any hope, of encouraging and not sanctioning your disgusting desires. Once more, I say the suspicion in my mind that some imprudence of mine has provoked these lawless thoughts in you, is what causes me the most distress and what I desire to punish most, with my own hands, because if any other instrument of punishment were used my error might become more widely known; but before I sacrifice myself, I intend to inflict death, and take with me the one who will fully satisfy my desire for the revenge I hope for; because I will see, the penalty given by inflexible unbending laws on him who has placed me in a such a desperate position."

As she spoke these words, with incredible energy and swiftness she rushed toward Lothario with the knife, so determined to bury it in his chest that he was almost uncertain whether these demonstrations were real or fake, because he was obliged to use his skill and strength to prevent her from striking him; and she acted with such reality and confusion that, to give it a colour of truth, she determined to stain it with her own blood; because observing, or pretending, that she could not wound Lothario, she said, "Fate, it seems, will not grant my desire, but it will not be able to stop me from satisfying it partially;" and making an effort to free the hand with the knife which Lothario held, she released it, and directing the point of the knife to a place where it could not inflict a deep wound, she plunged it into her left side high up close to the shoulder, and then allowed herself to fall to the ground.

Leonela and Lothario stood amazed and astounded at the disaster, and seeing Camilla on the ground bathed in her own blood, they were still uncertain about the true nature of the act. Lothario, terrified and breathless, rushed quickly to pull out the knife; but when he saw how slight the wound was he was relieved of his fears and once more admired the subtlety, coolness, and wit of Camilla; and to support the part he had to play better, he began to say such distressing and unhappy words over her body as if she were dead: and knowing that his friend Anselmo was listening he spoke in such a way as to make a listener feel much more pity for him than for Camilla, even though he assumed she were dead. Leonela took her in her arms and laid her on the bed, asking Lothario to search for someone to treat her wound in secret, and at the same time asking his advice and opinion as to what they should say to Anselmo about his lady's wound if he returned before it was healed. He replied they could say what they liked, because he was not in a state to give advice that would be of any use; all he could tell her was to try and stop the blood, as he was going where he would never be seen again; and with every appearance of deep grief and sorrow he left the house; but when he found himself alone, and where there was nobody to see him, he reflected unceasingly, lost in wonder at the cleverness of Camilla and the consistent acting of Leonela. He reflected how convinced Anselmo would be that he had such a great wife, and he looked forward anxiously to meeting him in order to rejoice together over the lies that most craftily veiled the truth.

Leonela, was trying to stop her lady's blood, which was to support her deception; and washing the wound with a little wine she covered it up with the best of her skill, talking the whole time while patching the wound, although no more needed to be said to assure Anselmo that he had in Camilla a model of purity. To Leonela's words Camilla added her own, calling herself cowardly and lacking spirit, since she was not able to take her own life or her enemy's. She asked her servant's advice whether or not she should inform her beloved husband about all that had happened, but the other told her to say nothing about it, as she would give him the obligation of taking vengeance on Lothario, which he could not do without a great risk to himself; and it was the duty of a true wife not to give her husband incitement to argue, but, on the contrary, to remove it as far as possible from him.

Camilla replied that she believed she was right and that she would follow her advice, but it would be wise to consider how she was going to explain the wound to Anselmo, because he would notice it; to which Leonela answered that she did not know how to tell a lie even as a joke.

"How can I know then, my dear?" said Camilla, "because I would not dare to keep up a lie even if my life depended on it. If we cannot think of an escape from this difficulty, it will be better to tell him the truth than him find out later."

"Do not worry, señora," said Leonela; "between now and tomorrow I will think of what we can say to him, and perhaps the wound being where it is it can be hidden from his sight, and Heaven might be inclined to help with a purpose so good and honourable. Compose yourself señora, and calm your excitement so he does not find you nervous; and leave the rest to mine and God's care, who always support good intentions."

Anselmo had listened with the deepest attention and seen played out the tragedy of the death of his honour, which the performers acted with such amazingly effective acting that it seemed as if they had become the realities of the parts they played. He awaited the night and an opportunity to escape from the house and go to see his good friend Lothario, and let him know of his joy over the precious treasure he had gained having established his wife's purity. Both Camilla and her servant took care to give him time and opportunity to get away, and taking advantage of it he made his escape, and immediately went in search of Lothario, and it would be impossible to describe how he embraced him when he found him, and the things he said to him from the joy of his heart, and the praise he gave to Camilla; all of which Lothario listened to without being able to show any pleasure, because he could not forget how deceived his friend was, and how dishonourably he had wronged him; and although Anselmo could see that Lothario was not happy, he imagined it was only because he had left Camilla wounded and had been the cause of it; and so among other things he told him not to be distressed about Camilla's accident, as the wound was not serious; and that being so, he had no reason to fear, but from now on should be happy and celebrate with him, seeing that by his skilfulness he found himself raised to the greatest height of happiness that he could ever have hope for, and desired to do nothing else than make verses praising Camilla that would preserve her name for the future. Lothario praised his purpose, and promised to assist him in creating such a glorious tribute.

And so Anselmo was left the most deceived man there could be in the whole world. He himself, convinced he had conducted the plan of his glory, led home by the man who had been the destructor of his good name; who Camilla welcomed with an angered face, although her heart smiled. The deception was carried on for some time, until at the end of a few months Fortune turned the wheel and her guilt which had been until then so skilfully concealed was published, and Anselmo paid with his life the penalty of his ill-advised curiosity.

CHAPTER 35

THE HEROIC AND EXTRAORDINARY BATTLE DON QUIXOTE HAD WITH SKINS OF RED WINE, AND BRINGING THE END OF THE NOVEL "THE ILL-ADVISED CURIOSITY" TO A CLOSE

There was little of the novel left to be read, when Sancho Panza burst out with wild excitement from the attic where Don Quixote was, shouting, "Run! quick; and help my master, who is in the middle of the toughest and hardest battle I have ever seen. Oh my God he has given the giant, the enemy of Princess Micomicona, such a slash that he has sliced his head clean off as if it were a turnip."

"What are you talking about brother?" said the vicar, pausing as he was about to read the rest of the novel. "Have you lost your mind, Sancho? How the hell can that be, when the giant is two thousand miles away?"

They heard a loud noise coming from the room, and Don Quixote shouting, "Stand, thief, bandit, villain; now I have got you, your little sword will not help you!" And then it seemed as though he were slashing vigorously at the wall.

"Don't stop to listen," said Sancho, "go in and separate them or help my master: although there is probably no need for that now, no doubt the giant is already dead and is now giving an account to God of his wicked life; because I saw the blood flowing on the ground, and the head cut off, and it is as big as a large melon."

"Let me die," said the landlord, "if Don Quixote or Don Devil has not been slashing some of the skins of red wine that are at the end of his bed, and the spilt wine must be what this man sees as blood;" and after saying this he went into the room and the rest followed him, and there they found Don Quixote in the strangest costume in the world. He was in his shirt, which was not long enough at the front to cover his thighs completely and was even shorter behind; his legs were very long and lean, covered with hair, and anything but clean; on his head he had a little greasy red cap that belonged to the inn-keeper, around his left arm he had rolled the blanket of the bed, which Sancho, for reasons unknown to himself, held a grudge, and in his right hand he held his sword, with which he was slashing in all directions vigorously, emitting exclamations as if he were actually fighting some giant: and the best of all was his eyes were not open, because he was fast asleep, and dreaming that he was having a battle with the giant. Because his imagination was so focused on the adventure he was going to accomplish, that it made him dream he had already reached the Kingdom of Micomicon, and was engaged in combat with his enemy; and believing he was attacking the giant, he had given so many cuts to the wine skins that the whole room was full of wine. On seeing this the landlord was so angered that he attacked Don Quixote, and with his clenched fist began to punch him in such a way, that if Cardenio and the vicar had not dragged him away, he would have brought the war of the giant to an end. But even this did not wake the poor gentleman, until the barber brought a large pot of cold water from the well and threw it with one toss all over his body, and then Don Quixote woke up, but not completely enough to understand what was happening. Dorothea, seeing how short and small his clothing was, would not go in to witness the battle between her champion and her opponent. As for Sancho, he was searching all over the floor for the head of the giant, and not finding it he said, "I see now that it's all enchantment in this place; because the last time, on this very spot where I am now, I got so many thumps without knowing who gave them to me, or being able to see anybody; and now this head is nowhere to be seen, although I saw it cut off with my own eyes and the blood running from the body as if it came from a fountain."

"What blood and fountains are you talking about, enemy of God?" said the landlord. "Don't you see, idiot, that the blood and the fountain are only these wine skins here that have been stabbed and the red wine flowing all over the room? And I wish I saw the man who stabbed them in hell."

"I know nothing about that," said Sancho; "all I know is it will be my bad luck if I do not find this head, because my county will melt away like salt in water;" - because Sancho awake was worse than his master asleep, as his master's promises had confused his mind.

The landlord was angered by the coolness of the aide and the mischievous actions of the master, and swore it will not be like the last time when they left without paying; and that their privileges of chivalry will not work to let them leave without payment, they will have to pay, even for the cost of the plugs that would have to be put in damaged wine-skins. The vicar was holding Don Quixote's hands, who, thinking he had now ended the adventure and was in the presence of the Princess Micomicona, knelt in front of the vicar and said, "High-ranking and beautiful lady, your highness can live from this day onward without fear of any harm from this disgusting being; and I from this day on am released from the promise I gave to you, since by the help of God and by the favour of her who I live and breathe through, I have fulfilled it successfully."

"Did I not say so?" said Sancho. "You see I wasn't drunk; you now see my master has already killed the giant; there's no doubt now; the county is mine!"

Who could have helped laughing at the absurdities of the pair, master and man? And laugh they did, all except the landlord, who was very angered; but finally the barber, Cardenio, and the vicar arranged with no small effort to get Don Quixote on the bed, and he fell asleep with every appearance of exhaustion. They left him to sleep, and went out to the gate of the inn to comfort Sancho Panza for not finding the head of the giant; but they had much more hard work to pacify the landlord, who was furious at the sudden death of his wine-skins; and the landlady said: half telling-off, half crying, "At an evil moment and at an unlucky hour he came into my house, this Knight, I wish I had never seen him, because he has cost me dearly; the last time he left without paying the overnight fee for dinner, bed, straw, and barley, for himself, his aide, horse and donkey, saying he was a Knight adventurer – he said God sent unlucky adventures to him and all the adventurers in the world - and therefore was not bound to pay anything, because the tariff was settled by the laws of Knighthood: and then, all because of him, and for a finishing touch to all of this, he bursts my wine-skins and spills my wine! I wish I saw his own blood on the floor! But I hope he does not deceive himself, because, on the grave of my father and my mother, he will pay me every penny; or my name is not what it is, and I am not my father's daughter." The landlady said all of this and more of a similar nature with great irritation, and her maid Maritornes backed her up, while the daughter was quiet and smiled from time to time. The vicar smoothed matters over by promising to restore all the losses to the best of his ability, not only regarding the wine-skins but also the wine. Dorothea comforted Sancho, promising him, that as soon as it was certain his master had defeated the giant, and she found herself peacefully re-established in her Kingdom, she would give him the best county there was in it. Hearing this Sancho comforted himself, and assured that he had already seen the head of the giant, but that it was not to be seen now because everything that happened was by enchantment, as he himself had endured the last time he was there. Dorothea said she fully believed him, and that he does not need to worry, because all would turn out well and as he wished. Therefore, everyone being appeased, the vicar was anxious to finish reading the novel, as he saw there was only a little more left to be read. Dorothea and the others encouraged him to finish it, and he, as he was willing to please them, and enjoyed reading it himself, continued the story as follows:

The result was, that from the confidence Anselmo felt about Camilla's virtue, he lived happy and free from anxiety, and Camilla purposely looked emotionlessly at Lothario, so Anselmo would suppose her that feelings towards him were the opposite of what they were; and to support this position, Lothario begged to be excused from coming to the house, as the displeasure which Camilla displayed in regard to his presence was clear to be seen. But the deceived Anselmo said he would not allow it, and so in a thousand ways he became the author of his own dishonour, while he believed he was insuring his happiness. Meanwhile the satisfaction with which Leonela saw herself empowered to carry on her romance reached such a height that, regardless of everything else, she followed her passion unrestrained, feeling confident that her lady would cover her, and even show her how to manage it safely. Finally, one night Anselmo heard footsteps in Leonela's room, and when trying to enter to see who it was, he found that the door was held closed against him, which made him more determined to open it; and exerting his strength he forced it open, and entered the room in time to see a man jumping out through the window into the street. He ran quickly to catch him or discover who he was, but he was unable to achieve either purpose, because Leonela threw her arms round him crying, "Calm down, señor; do not worry or follow him; he belongs to me, and in fact he is my husband."

234

Anselmo would not believe it, but blind with rage revealed a knife and threatened to stab Leonela, asking her tell the truth or he would kill her. In her fear, not knowing what she was saying, exclaimed, "Do not kill me, señor, because I can tell you things much more important than any you can imagine."

"Tell me now, or die," said Anselmo.

"It would be impossible for me now," said Leonela, "I am so scared: leave me until tomorrow, and then you will hear from me what will fill you with surprise; but please be assured that the man he who leaped through the window is a young man from this city, who has promised to become my husband."

Anselmo was satisfied with this, and was content to wait until tomorrow, because he never expected to hear anything against Camilla, as he was so satisfied and sure of her virtue; and so he left the room, and left Leonela locked inside, telling her she could not come out until she had told him everything she had to let him know. He went immediately to see Camilla, to tell her, as he did, all that had happened between him and their servant, and the promise she had given him to inform him about matters of serious importance.

There is no need to say whether Camilla was worried or not, because her fear was already great that Leonela would tell Anselmo everything she knew about her faithlessness, she did not have the courage to wait and see if her suspicions were true; and so the same night, as soon as she thought Anselmo was asleep, she packed the most valuable jewels she had and some money, and without being observed by anybody escaped from the house and took herself to Lothario house, to who she told everything that had occurred, begging him to suggest some place for safety or go with her to where they will be safe from Anselmo. Camilla reduced Lothario to such a state of confusion that he was unable to say a word in reply, and less to decide what he should do. Finally, he decided to take her to a nunnery where a sister of his lived; Camilla agreed to this, and with the speed which the circumstances demanded, Lothario took her and left her there, and then he left the city without letting anyone know about his departure.

As soon as daylight came, Anselmo, without realising Camilla was missing from his side, woke eager to learn what Leonela had to tell him, and rushed to the room where he had locked her in. He opened the door and entered, but did not find Leonela; all he found were some sheets knotted out of the window, clear proof that she had let herself down from it and escaped. He returned, anxious, to tell Camilla, but not finding her in bed or anywhere in the house he was lost in confusion. He asked the servants in the house about her, but none of them could give him any explanation. As he was searching for Camilla it happened by chance that he observed her boxes were open, and that a large portion of her jewels were gone; and now he believed the man he had observed jumping through the window was her lover, and that Leonela was not the cause of his misfortune; and, without delaying to dress himself completely, sad in his heart and dejected, went to his friend Lothario to make him aware of his sorrow; but when he failed to find him and the servants reported that he had been absent from his house all night and had taken with him all the money he had, he felt as though he was losing his mind; and to complete everything, when returning to his own house he found it deserted and empty, not one of all his servants, male or female, remaining in it. He did not know what to think, or say, or do, and his reasoning faculty seemed to be leaving him little by little. He reviewed his position, and saw himself in a moment left without a wife, friend, or servants, abandoned, he felt, even by heaven above him, and more than all robbed of his honour, because in Camilla's disappearance he saw his own ruin. After a long reflection he decided to go to his friend's village, where he had been staying when he gave the opportunities of this complication and misfortune. He locked the doors of his house, mounted his horse, and with a broken spirit went on his journey; but he had hardly gone half-way when, harassed by his reflections, he had to dismount and tie his horse to a tree, and he threw himself at the base of it, venting his distress; and he remained there until nightfall, when he observed a man approaching on horseback from the city, who, after greeting him, he asked what was the news in Florence.

The citizen replied, "The strangest things that have been heard for a long time; because it is reported abroad that Lothario, the great friend of the wealthy Anselmo, who lived at San Giovanni, last night took Camilla, the wife of Anselmo, who has also disappeared. All of this has been said by Camilla's servant, who the keeper of the house found last night lowering herself by a sheet from the window of Anselmo's house. I do not know, precisely, what caused this affair to happen; all I know is that the whole city is wondering about it, because no one would have expected something of the sort, when knowing about the great and intimate friendship that existed between them, so great, they say, that they were called 'The Two Brothers.'"

"Is it known at all," said Anselmo, "what road Lothario and Camilla took?"

"Not at all," said the citizen, "although the house keeper has been very active in searching for them."

"God bless you, señor," said Anselmo.

"God be with you," said the citizen and he went his way.

This disastrous intelligence almost robbed Anselmo not only of his senses but of his life. He got up as well as he was able to and got to the house of his friend, who currently did not know about his misfortune, but seeing him approaching, pale, worn out, and haggard, observed that he was suffering with a heavy affliction. Anselmo begged to be allowed to rest there and to be given writing materials. His wish was complied with and he was left alone to rest. Finding himself alone he reflected further over his misfortune that by the signs of death he felt within him he knew his life was coming to a close, and therefore he decided to leave behind a declaration of the cause of his strange end. He began to write, but before he had put down all he wanted to say, his breath failed and he lost his life, a victim of the suffering which his ill-advised curiosity had given him. The master of the house observing that it was now late and that Anselmo did not leave the room, decided to go in and see if he was recovering well, but found him lying on his face, his body partly in the bed, partly on the writing-table, on which he lay with the writing paper open and the pen still in his hand. Having first called him without receiving any answer, his host approached him, and taking him by the hand, found that it was cold, and saw that he was dead. Greatly surprised and distressed he called everyone in the house to witness the sad fate of Anselmo; and then he read the paper, the handwriting he recognised as his, which contained these words:

"A foolish and ill-advised desire has robbed me of life. If the news of my death reaches the ears of Camilla, let her know that I forgive her, because she was not required to perform miracles, and I should have not pressed her to perform them; and since I have been the author of my own dishonour, there is no reason why-"

This is as far as Anselmo had written, and therefore it was plain to see that at this point, before he could finish what he had to say, his life came to an end. The next day his friend sent intelligence of his death to his relatives, who had already determined his misfortune, as well as the nunnery where Camilla was almost at the point of accompanying her husband on that inevitable journey, not due to her husband's death, but because of her lover's departure. Although she knew she was a widow, it is said that she refused to leave the nunnery or die, until, not long afterwards, intelligence reached her that Lothario had been killed in a battle which M. de Lautrec had recently engaged in with the Great Captain Gonzalo Fernandez de Cordova in the Kingdom of Naples. Discovering this Camilla shortly afterwards died, worn out by grief and sadness. This was the end of all three, an end that came from a thoughtless beginning.

"I like this novel," said the vicar; "but I am unsure if it is a true story; and if it has been invented, the author's story is defective, because it is impossible to imagine any husband foolish enough to try such a costly experiment as Anselmo's. If it had been represented as occurring between a man and his mistress it might pass as true; but between a husband and wife there is something of an impossibility about it. In regards to the way in which the story is told, however, I find no fault."

CHAPTER 36

FURTHER INCIDENTS THAT OCCURRED AT THE INN

Just then the landlord, who was standing at the gate of the inn, exclaimed, "Here comes a fine group of guests; if they stop."

"Who are they?" said Cardenio.

"Four men," said the landlord, "riding with lances and shields, and all with black veils, and with them there is a woman dressed in white, whose face is also veiled, and two attendants on foot."

"Are they near?" said the vicar.

"So near," answered the landlord, "that here they come."

Hearing this Dorothea covered her face, and Cardenio went into Don Quixote's room, and they hardly had any time before the whole group, that the host had described, entered the inn, and the four that were on horseback, who were of high appearance, dismounted, and went to take down the woman who rode with them, and one of them taking her in his arms placed her on a chair that was next to the entrance of the room where Cardenio had hidden himself. The whole time neither she or they had removed their veils or spoken a word, only when sitting down on the chair the woman gave a deep sigh and let her arms fall like someone who was ill and weak. The attendants on foot then led the horses away to the stable. Observing this the vicar, curious to know who the people dressed like this and staying silent were, went to where the servants were standing to ask the question, but was replied to with:

"Sorry, sir, I cannot tell you who they are, I only know they seem to be people of distinction, particularly the one took down the lady you saw in his arms; and I say this because the rest of them always show him respect, and nothing is done except what he directs and orders."

"And the lady, who is she?" asked the vicar.

"That I cannot tell you either," said the servant, "because I have not seen her face during the whole journey: I have heard her sigh many times and cry that she seems to be suffering; but we do not know any more than what we have told you, as my friend and I have only been in their company two days, as they met us on the road and begged and persuaded us to accompany them to Andalusia, promising to pay us well."

"And have you heard any of them called by a name?" asked the vicar.

"No," replied the servant; "they all preserve a marvellous silence on the road, not a sound is heard among them except the poor lady's sighs and cries, which make us pity her; and we feel sure that wherever she is going, it is against her will, and as far as I judge from her clothing she is a nun or, what is more likely, about to become one; and perhaps it is because she will be taking the vows against her own free will, which makes her so unhappy as she seems to be."

"That may be so," said the vicar, and leaving them he returned to where Dorothea was, who, hearing the veiled lady sigh, moved by natural compassion went close to her and said, "What are you suffering from, señora? If it is something that women are accustomed to and know how to relieve, I offer you my services with all my heart."

The unhappy lady gave no reply; and although Dorothea repeated her offers more sincerely she still kept her silence, until the gentleman with the veil, who, the servant said, was obeyed by the rest, approached and said to Dorothea, "Do not trouble yourself, señora, making any offers to that woman, because it is her way to give no thanks for anything that is done for her; and do not try to make her answer unless you want to hear some lie from her lips."

"I have never told a lie," was the immediate reply of the lady who had been silent until then; "on the contrary, it is because I am so truthful and so ignorant of lies and deception that I am now in this miserable condition; and this I say you are a witness of, because it is my unstained truth that has made you false and a liar."

Cardenio heard these words clearly and distinctly, being quite close to speaker, because there was only the door of Don Quixote's room between them, and the instant he did, he exclamation loudly, "Good God! What is this I hear? What voice is this which has reached my ears?" Startled by the voice the lady turned her head; and not seeing the speaker she stood up and attempted to enter the room; observing this the gentleman held her back, preventing her from taking a step. In her agitation and sudden movement, the silk which she had covered her face with fell off and revealed a face of incomparable and marvellous beauty, but pale and terrified; because she kept turning her eyes, everywhere she could direct her view, with an eagerness that made her look as if she had lost her mind, and it was so clear that Dorothea could not help but pity her, and everyone else who saw her, although they did not know what caused it. The gentleman held her firmly by the shoulders, and being so fully engaged with holding her back, he was unable to place a hand on his veil which was falling off, and finally it fell off entirely, and Dorothea, raising her eyes saw that the man who held the lady, was her husband, Don Fernando. The instant she recognised him, with a prolonged sorrowful cry which came from the depths of her heart, she fell backwards fainting, and if the barber had not been close by to catch her in his arms, she would have fallen completely to the ground. The vicar immediately rushed to throw water on her face, and as he did, Don Fernando recognised her and stood as if death had taken him; not, however, relaxing his grip on Luscinda, because it was her that was struggling to release herself from his hold, having recognised Cardenio by his voice, as he had recognised her. Cardenio also heard Dorothea's cry as she fell fainting, and imagining that it came from Luscinda burst out of the the room in terror, and the first thing he saw was Don Fernando with Luscinda in his arms. Don Fernando recognised Cardenio immediately; and all three, Luscinda, Cardenio, and Don Fernando, stood silent in amazement barely knowing what had happened to them.

They looked at one another without speaking, Cardenio at Don Fernando, Don Fernando at Dorothea who lay on the ground and Luscinda at

Cardenio. The first to break the silence was Luscinda, saying to Don Fernando: "Leave me, Señor Don Fernando, leave me to cling to the truth, to the support, which neither your insistence, or your threats, or your promises, or your gifts have been able to detach me. See how Heaven, by very strange ways and hidden from our sight, has brought me face to face with my true husband; and you know well that only death alone will be able to erase him from my memory. If this clear affirmation, then, leads you, as you can do nothing else, to turn your love into rage, your affection into resentment, and take my life; because if I give it in the presence of my beloved husband I consider it well donated; because by my death he will be convinced that I kept my faith to him to the last moment of my life."

Meanwhile Dorothea had come to her senses, and had heard Luscinda's words, with which she determined who she was; but seeing that Don Fernando had not yet released her or replied to her, finding her strength as well as she could she knelt at his feet, and with a flood of bright and touching tears said this:

"If, the beams of that sun that you hold eclipsed in your arms did not dazzle and rob your eyes of sight you would have seen by now that she who kneels in front of you is the unhappy and unfortunate Dorothea. I am that poor peasant girl who you in your goodness or for your pleasure raised high enough to call her yours; I am she who in the seclusion of innocence led a contented life until the voice of your insistence, and your true and tender passion, as it seemed, opened the gates of her modesty and surrendered to you the keys of her freedom; a gift received by you but without thanks, as is clear to see by my retreat to the place where you have now found me, and by your appearance under the circumstances in which I see you. Nevertheless, you should know that I have not come here driven by my shame; it is only grief and sorrow seeing myself forgotten by you. It was your will to make me yours, and you followed that will, that now, even if you run away, you can't help being mine. Do you think, the affection I have for you can be compensated for by beauty and noble birth for which you have deserted me. You cannot be Luscinda's because you are mine, and she cannot be yours because she is Cardenio's; and it will be easier, remember, to bend your will to love someone who adores you, than to lead someone to love you who hates you. You took advantage of my simplicity, you took my virtue, you were not ignorant of my position, and you know how I yielded to your will; there is no ground or reason for you to say you were deceived, and if it is so, as it is, and you are a Christian as you are, why do put off making me as happy as you did at first? And if you will not take me for what I am, your true and lawful wife, at least take and accept me as yours, because as long as I am yours I will consider myself happy and fortunate. Do not by abandoning me let my shame become gossip in the streets; do not make my old aged parents miserable; because the loyal services they as faithful servants have given to you do not deserve such a return; and if you think it will dishonour your bloodline to mix it with mine, reflect that there is little or no nobility in the world that has not travelled the same road, and that in illustrious lineages it is not the woman's blood that matters; and moreover, that true nobility consists in virtue, and if you lack that, refusing me the justice you owe me, then even I have a higher claim to nobility than you. To end this, señor, these are my last words to you: whether you will, or will not, I am your wife; witness of your words, which must not and should not be false, if you pride yourself with that which you damage me with; remember the promise which you gave to me, and remember Heaven, which you yourself asked to witness the promise you made; and if all that fails, your own conscience will not fail to raise its silent voice in the middle of all your joy, and assert the truth of what I say and destroy your highest pleasure and enjoyment."

All this and more the injured Dorothea delivered with such heartfelt feeling and such tears that all those present, even those who came with Don Fernando, were bound to join her. Don Fernando listened to her without replying, until, stopping her speech, she gave cries and sighs that only a heart of stone could not be softened by the sight of such great sorrow. Luscinda regarded her with no less compassion for her suffering than admiration for her intelligence and beauty, and would have gone to her to say some words to comfort, but was prevented by Don Fernando's grasp which still held her. He, overwhelmed with confusion and astonishment, after listening to Dorothea for some moments without taking his eyes off her, opened his arms, and, releasing Luscinda, exclaimed:

"You have conquered, Dorothea, you have conquered, because it is impossible to have a heart which could deny the united force of so much truth."

Luscinda in her weakness was at the point of falling to the ground when Don Fernando released her, but Cardenio, who was near, having moved behind Don Fernando to escape recognition, putting his fear aside and regardless of what might happen, ran to support her, and said as he held her in his arms, "If Heaven with its compassion is willing to let you rest at last, lady of my heart, true, constant, and fair, nowhere can you rest more safely than in these arms that now hold you, and held you before when fortune permitted me to call you mine."

Luscinda looked up at Cardenio, at first beginning to recognise him by his voice and then satisfying herself with her eyes that it was him, and hardly knowing what she did, and thoughtless of all modesty, she threw her arms around his neck and pressing her face close to his, said, "Yes, my dear lord, you are the true master of me your love, even if adverse fate would interrupt again, and new danger threatened this life that is bound to yours."

It was a strange sight for Don Fernando and everyone else that stood around, filled with surprise by an incident so unplanned. Dorothea thought that Don Fernando changed colour and looked as if he wanted to take vengeance on Cardenio, because she observed him put his hand on his sword; and the instant the idea struck her, with such quickness she held him round the knees, and kissing them and holding them to prevent him from moving, she said, while her tears continued to flow, "What is it you want to do in this unforeseen event? You have your true wife in front of you: think whether it will be right for you, whether it will be possible for you to undo what Heaven has done, or whether it will be wise for you to seek to keep her as yours in spite of every obstacle, so strong in my truth and constancy, bathing in the tears of love looking at the face of my lawful husband. For God's sake I ask you, and for your own sake I ask you, do not not let this manifestation rouse your anger; but rather let it calm it and allow these two lovers to live in peace and quiet without any interference from you as long as Heaven allows them to; and doing so you will prove the generosity of your grand spirit, and the world will see that your reason was stronger than your passion."

The whole time Dorothea was speaking, Cardenio, although he held Luscinda in his arms, never took his eyes off Don Fernando, determined, if he saw him make any hostile movement, to try and defend himself and resist as best he could any who might attack him, even if it could cost him his life. But now Don Fernando's friends, as well as the vicar and the barber, who had been present the whole time, not forgetting the worthy Sancho Panza, rushed forward and gathered round Don Fernando, asking him to have regard for the tears of Dorothea, and not allow her reasonable hopes to be disappointed, since, as they firmly believed, what she said was the truth; and asked him to observe that through God they had all met in a place where no one would have expected. And the vicar asked him to remember that only death could part Luscinda from Cardenio; and even if some sword were to separate them they would find their death better than being without each other; he asked him to show a generous mind, and allow these two to enjoy the happiness Heaven had granted them. He asked him, also, to turn his eyes toward the beauty of Dorothea and he would see that few if any could equal much less excel her; an in addition to that beauty should be added her modesty and the outstanding love she had for him. But besides all this, he reminded him that if he prided himself on being a gentleman and a Christian, he could not do anything else than to keep his word; and that in doing so he would obey God and meet the approval of all sensible people, who know and recognise it to be the privilege of beauty, even in one of humble beginnings, provided virtue accompany it, to be able to raise itself to the level of any rank, without any disgrace to him who offers it; and furthermore that when the potent influence of passion asserts itself, as long as there is no mixture of sin in it, he cannot be blamed by being influenced by it.

To be brief, they added further arguments that Don Fernando's manly heart, being after all nourished by noble blood, was touched, and yielded to the truth which, even had he wished otherwise, he could not avoid; and he showed his submission, and acceptance of the good advice that had been offered to him, by bending down and embracing Dorothea, saying to her, "Stand, dear lady, it is not right that what I hold in my heart should be kneeling at my feet; and if until now I have not shown gratitude for what is mine, it may have been Heaven's wish in order that, seeing the constancy with which you love me, I would learn to value you as much as you deserve. What I ask from you is that you do not hold against me my misbehaviour and serious wrong-doing; because the same cause and force that drove me to make you mine encouraged me to struggle against being yours; and to prove this, turn and look at the eyes of the now happy Luscinda, and you will see in them an excuse for all my errors: and as she has found and gained the object of her desires, and I have found in you what satisfies all of mine, may she live in peace and contentment as many happy years with her Cardenio, as on my knees I will pray to Heaven to allow me to live with my Dorothea;" and with these words he once more embraced her and pressed his face to hers with so much tenderness that he had to take great restraint to keep his tears from completing the proof of his love and repentance in the sight of all. This was not so for Luscinda, and Cardenio, and almost everyone else, because they had shed so many tears, some in their own happiness, some because of other's, that an onlooker would have thought a serious disaster had happened to them all. Even Sancho was crying; although afterwards he said he only cried because he saw that Dorothea was not the Queen Micomicona as he thought, who he was expecting such great a reward from. Their wonder as well as their crying lasted for some time, and then Cardenio and Luscinda went and fell on their knees in front of Don Fernando, thanking him for the favour he had given them in language so grateful that he did not know how to answer them, and raising them up, hugged them with every sign of affection and courtesy.

He then asked Dorothea how she had managed to come to a place so far from her own home, and she in a few words told all that she had previously told Cardenio. Dorothea described her misfortunes so charmingly that Don Fernando and his companions were so delighted that they wished the story had been longer. When she had finished, Don Fernando described what had happened to him in the city after he had found Luscinda's paper on which she had declared that she was Cardenio's wife, and could never be his. He said he wanted to kill her, and would have done so if he had not been prevented by her parents, and that he left the house full of rage and shame, and decided to avenge himself when a more convenient opportunity occurred. The next day he found out that Luscinda had disappeared from her father's house, and that no one knew where she had gone. Finally, at the end of some months he heard she was in a nunnery and was going to remain there for the rest of her life, if she was not going to share her life with Cardenio; and as soon as he had heard this, taking these three gentlemen as his companions, he arrived at the place where she was, but avoided speaking to her, fearing that if it were known he was there stricter precautions would be taken; and watching for a time when the gatekeeper was busy he left two men to guard the gate, and he and the other entered the nunnery in search of Luscinda, who they found having a conversation with one of the other nuns, and took her without giving her any time to resist; all of this they were able to do in complete safety, as the nunnery was in the country and a considerable distance from the city. He added that when Luscinda found herself in his power she lost all consciousness, and after regaining it she did nothing but cry and sigh without saying a word; and in silence and tears they had reached the inn, which for him was like reaching heaven where all the misfortunes of earth are over and finished.

CHAPTER 37

CONTINUING THE STORY OF THE FAMOUS PRINCESS MICOMICONA, WITH OTHER AMUSING ADVENTURES

Sancho listened to all of this with little sorrow as he saw his hopes of greatness were fading away and vanishing in smoke, and how the Princess Micomicona had turned into Dorothea, and the giant into Don Fernando, while his master was sleeping tranquilly, totally unconscious of everything that had happened. Dorothea was unable to convince herself that her current happiness was not a dream; Cardenio was in a similar state of mind, and Luscinda's thoughts were in the same direction. Don Fernando thanked Heaven for the favour it had shown to him and for rescuing him from the intricate labyrinth in which he had placed himself so near to the destruction of his good name and of his soul; and in short everybody in the inn was full of contentment, satisfaction and happiness over what was once such a complicated and hopeless situation. The vicar as a sensible man had good reflections over the whole matter, and congratulated each of them for their good fortune; but there was one who was in the highest spirit and good humour: the landlady, because of the promise Cardenio and the vicar had given her to pay for all of the losses and damage she had sustained through Don Quixote's madness. Sancho, as has already been said, was the only one who was distressed, unhappy, and depressed; and so with such a miserable face he went to his master, who had just awoken, and said to him:

"Sir Sad Face, you might as well sleep as much as you like, without thinking about killing any giant or restoring the Kingdom to the Princess; because that is over and settled now."

"As I thought it was," replied Don Quixote, "because I have had the most extraordinary and fantastic battle with the giant out of any battle I ever remember having in all the days of my life; and with one swift cut - I made his head fall to the ground, and so much blood came from him that it made streams over the earth like rivers."

"Like red wine, you should say," replied Sancho; "because you should know, if you don't know already, that the dead giant is a sliced wine-skin, and the blood is gallons of red wine that it had in its belly, and the head cut off is the bitch that gave birth to me; and the devil took it all."

"What are you talking about, fool?" said Don Quixote; "have you lost your mind?"

"You get up," said Sancho, "and you will see the nice work you have done, and what we have to pay; and you will see the Queen turned into a normal lady called Dorothea, and other things that will astonish you, if you understand them."

"I will not be surprised by anything of the sort," returned Don Quixote; "because if you remember the last time we were here, I told you that everything that happened here was a matter of enchantment, and it would be no great amazement if it were the same now."

"I could believe that," replied Sancho, "if my blanketing was the same sort of enchantment also; only it wasn't, it was real and genuine; because can see the landlord, who is here today, holding one end of the blanket and throwing me up to the sky very well, and I say on my behalf, that there is no enchantment about it, only a great deal of bruising and bad luck."

"Well, well, God give you a remedy," said Don Quixote; "hand me my clothes and let me go out, because I want to see the transformations and things you speak of."

Sancho got him his clothes; and while he was dressing, the vicar gave Don Fernando and the others present an account of Don Quixote's madness and discussed the strategy they had used to release him from the self-punishment he believed he should give himself because of his lady. He also described to them almost all of the adventures that Sancho had mentioned, at which they were amazed and laughed a lot, thinking it to be, as they all did, the strangest form of madness a crazy intellect could be capable of. But now, the vicar said, that as lady Dorothea's good fortune prevented them from progressing with their purpose, it was necessary to devise some other way of getting him home.

Cardenio proposed they carry out the scheme they had begun, and suggested that Luscinda would act and support Dorothea's part very well.

"No," said Don Fernando, "that cannot be, because I want Dorothea to follow through with this idea of hers; and if the gentleman's village is not very far, I will be happy to help if there is anything I can do for his relief."

"It is no more than two days' journey from here," said the vicar.

"Even if it were more," said Don Fernando, "I would gladly travel further for the sake of doing such good work.

"At this moment Don Quixote came out in full costume, with Mambrino's helmet, completely dented as it was, on his head, his shield on his arm, and leaning on his lance. The strange figure he presented filled Don Fernando and the rest with amazement as they contemplated his slim yellow face (half a mile long), his armour completely mismatched, and the seriousness of his demeanour. They stood silent waiting to see what he would say, and he, fixing his eyes on Dorothea, spoke to her with great seriousness and composure:

"I am informed, fair lady, by my aide here that your greatness has been defeated, since, you have gone from a Queen and lady of high degree as you used to be, into a private lady. If this has been done by the command of the magician King your father, I will offer you the aid you need and are entitled to, I can tell you he knows little of the histories of chivalry; because, if he had read and gone through them as attentively and deliberately as I have, he would have found on every page that Knights of less renown than me have accomplished things which are more difficult: it is no great achievement to kill a giant, however arrogant he may be; because it is not many hours since I myself was fighting one, and I will not talk about it now as they might say I am lying; time, however, which reveals all, will tell the story when we least expect it."

"You were fighting a couple of wine-skins, not a giant," said the landlord; but Don Fernando told him to be quiet and not to interrupt Don Quixote, who continued, "I say in conclusion, high and disinherited lady, that if your father has created this metamorphosis in you for the reason I have mentioned, you should not attach any importance to it; because there is no danger on earth which my sword will not force a way through, and with it, in not too long, I will bring your enemy's head to the ground and place on yours the crown of your Kingdom."

Don Quixote said no more, and waited for the reply of the Princess, who aware of Don Fernando's determination to carry on the deception until Don Quixote had been taken to his home, with great ease of manner and seriousness replied, "whoever told you, brave Knight of the Sorrowful Face, that I had undergone any change or transformation did not tell you the truth, because I am the same as I was yesterday. It is true that certain good fortune, that has given me more than I could have hoped for, has made an alteration in me; but I have not therefore ceased to be what I was before. And so, señor, through your goodness reinstate your previous view of my father, who brought into existence my good opinion of you, and be assured that he was a wise and prudent man, since through his craft he found an easy way to remedy my misfortune; because I believe, señor, that had it not been for you I would never have been granted the good fortune I now possess; and this is perfectly true; as most of these gentlemen who are present can fully testify to. All that remains now, is for us to continue our journey tomorrow, and the rest of the happy result I am looking forward to, I trust to God and courage of your heart."

On hearing this Don Quixote turned to Sancho, and said to him, with an angry manner, "I declare little Sancho, you are the greatest little villain in Spain. What do you say, thief and drifter, did you not just tell me that this Princess had been turned into a lady called Dorothea, and that the head which I cut off the giant was the bitch that gave birth to you, and other nonsense which put me in the greatest confusion I have ever been in my whole life? I promise" (and here he looked up at heaven and clenched his fists) "I am inclined to punish this mischief, in a way that will teach sense to all the future lying aides of Knights in the world."

"Be calm, señor," returned Sancho, "because it may be that I have been mistaken in regards to the change of the lady Princess Micomicona; but the giant's head, or at least the piercing of the wine-skins, and the blood being red wine, I made no mistake, as sure as there is a God; because the wounded skins are there at the end of your bed, and the wine has made a lake of the room; if you do not see now you will see when the eggs come to be fried; I mean when the landlord asks us to pay for all the damage: but, I am very glad that the Queen is as she was, because it concerns me as much as anyone else."

"I will tell you again, Sancho, you are a fool," said Don Quixote.

"That will do," said Don Fernando; "let us say no more about it; and as the Princess proposes to leave tomorrow because it is too late today, so be it, and we will spend the night with pleasant conversation, and tomorrow we will all accompany Señor Don Quixote; because we wish to witness the valiant and unparalleled achievements he is about to perform in the course of this mighty adventure which he has undertaken."

"It is I who will wait and accompany you," said Don Quixote; "and I am much gratified by the favour that has been given to me, and the good opinion you have of me, which I will endeavour to justify even if it will cost me my life, or even more, if it can."

Many compliments and expressions of politeness passed between Don Quixote and Don Fernando; but they were brought to an end by a traveller who at this moment entered the inn, and who seemed from his attire to be a Christian coming from the country of the Moors, because he was dressed in a short coat made of blue cloth with half-sleeves and without a collar; his trousers were also blue cloth, and his hat the same colour, and he wore yellow shoes and had a Moorish short sword attached to a belt across his chest. Behind him, mounted on a donkey, came a woman dressed in Moorish fashion, with her face veiled and a scarf on her head, and wearing a little richly woven cap, and a loose sleeveless coat that covered her from her shoulders to her feet. The man had a well-built frame, aged a little over forty, rather tanned in complexion, with a long moustache and a full beard, and, in short, his appearance was of someone, if he had been well dressed that would have been taken for a person of high quality and good birth. On entering he asked for a room, and when they told him there was none in the inn he seemed distressed, and approaching the lady who by her dress seemed to be a Moor, he helped her down from the saddle in his arms. Luscinda, Dorothea, the landlady, her daughter and Maritornes, attracted by her strange appearance, and to them entirely new costume, gathered round her; and Dorothea, who was always kind, polite, and quick-witted, noticing that both her and the man were annoyed at not finding a room, said to her, "Do not worry, señora, about the discomfort and need of luxuries, because it is common for road-side inns to be full; however, if you will be happy to share our room with us (pointing to Luscinda) perhaps you will have found worse accommodation in the course of your journey."

To this the veiled lady did not reply; all she did was rise from her seat, crossing her hands on her chest, bowing her head and bending her body as a sign that she returned thanks. From her silence they concluded that she must be a Moor and unable to speak their language.

At this moment the man came, and seeing that they all stood round his companion and that she gave no reply to what they said to her, he said, "Ladies, this lady hardly understands my language and can speak nothing but her mother tongue, which is the reason she does not and cannot answer what has been asked of her."

"Nothing has been asked of her," returned Luscinda; "she has only been offered our company for this evening and to share the room we occupy, where she will be made as comfortable as the circumstances allow, with the good-will we are bound to show all strangers that have a need of it, especially if it is for a woman."

"For her gratitude and my own, señora," replied the man, "I kiss your hands, and I respect you highly, as I should, for the favour you have offered, which, on such an occasion and coming from people of your appearance, it is plain to see, is a very great one."

"Tell me, señor," said Dorothea, "is this lady a Christian or a Moor? Because her attire and her silence lead us to imagine that she is what we could wish she was not."

"In her clothing and appearance," he said, "she is a Moor, but at heart she is a thoroughly good Christian, because she has the greatest desire to be one."

"Then she has not been baptised?" returned Luscinda.

"There has been no opportunity for that," replied the man, "since she left Algeria, her native country and home; and up to the present she has not found herself in any imminent danger of death as to make it necessary to baptise her before she has been instructed in all the ceremonies our holy Church commands; but, God willing, she will be baptised with the seriousness appropriate for her which is higher than her attire or mine indicates."

By these words he excited a desire in all who heard him, to know who the Moorish lady and the man were, but no one liked to ask, seeing that it was a better moment for helping them to rest themselves than for questioning them about their lives. Dorothea took the Moorish lady by the hand and leading her to a seat beside herself, requested her to remove her veil. She looked at the man as if to ask him what they were saying and what she should do. He said to her in Arabic that they asked her to take off her veil, and then she removed it and disclosed a face so lovely, that to Dorothea she seemed more beautiful than Luscinda, and to Luscinda more beautiful than Dorothea, and all the observers felt that if any beauty could compare with theirs it was the Moorish lady's, and there were even those who were inclined to give it somewhat the preference. And as it is the privilege and charm of beauty to win the heart and secure good-will, all became eager to show kindness and attention to the lovely Moor.

Don Fernando asked the man what her name was, and he replied that it was Lela Zoraida; but the instant she heard him, she guessed what the Christian had asked, and said hastily, with some disapproval and energy, "No, not Zoraida; Maria, Maria!" leading them to understand that she wanted to be called "Maria" and not "Zoraida." These words, and the touching sincerity with which she spoke, drew more than one tear from some of the listeners, particularly the women, who are by nature soft-hearted and compassionate. Luscinda embraced her affectionately, saying, "Yes, yes, Maria, Maria," to which the Moor replied, "Yes, yes, Maria; Zoraida macange," which means "not Zoraida."

The night was now approaching, and the landlord had taken care to prepare for them the best dinner that was in his power. The hour therefore having arrived they all took their seats at a long table, because there was no round or square table in the inn, and the seat of honour at the end of it, although he was refusing it, they assigned it to Don Quixote, who desired lady Micomicona to place herself by his side, as he was her protector. Luscinda and Zoraida took their places next to her, opposite to them were Don Fernando and Cardenio, and next the other gentlemen, and by the side of the ladies, the vicar and the barber. And so they ate with great enjoyment, which was increased when they observed Don Quixote stopped eating, and, moved by an impulse he begin to say to them all:

"Certainly, gentlemen, if we reflect on it, those who take up Knighthood get to see great and marvellous things. What being is there in this world, who entering the gate of this castle at this moment, and seeing us as we are here, would think or imagine us to be what we are? Who would say that this lady who is beside me was the great Queen that we all know her to be, or that I am that Knight of the Sorrowful Face, known far and wide by word of mouth? Now, there can be no doubt that this art and calling surpasses all those that man has invented, and deserves to be held with more honour compared with others in proportion to the danger it is exposed to. Forget those who assert that letters have supremacy over Knighthood; I will tell them, whoever they may be, that they do not know what they say. Because the reason which they usually assign this to, is that, the work of the mind is greater than that of the body, and that Knighthood only works the body; as if this calling were a porter's trade, for which nothing more is required than good strength; or as if, in what us Knights do, that it did not include acts of energy for the execution of which high intelligence is necessary; or as if the soul of the warrior, when he has an army, or the defence of a city under his care, did not do this as much with his mind as with his body. Actually; see whether by bodily strength alone it is possible to learn or preconceive the intentions of the enemy, his plans, strategies, or obstacles, or to discourage forthcoming damage; because all of this is the work of the mind, and in them the body has no share whatever. Since, therefore, this work has need of the mind, as much as letters, let us see now which of the two minds, the man of letters or the warrior, has most to do; and this will be seen by the goal that each seeks to attain; because the purpose which is worthier is the one which has for its aim a greater objective. The end and goal of letters - I am not speaking of divine letters, the aim of which is to raise and direct the soul to Heaven; because with an end so infinite no other can be compared - I speak of human letters, the end of which is to distribute justice, give to every man that which is his, and see and take care that good laws are observed: an end undoubtedly noble, grand, and deserving of high praise, but not as much as should be given to the Knight's objectives, which have for their end: peace, the greatest gift that men can desire in this life. The first good news the world and mankind received was that which the angels announced, 'Glory to God in the highest, and peace on earth to men of good-will;' and the greeting which the great master of heaven and earth taught his disciples and chosen followers when they entered any house, was to say, 'Peace come to this house;' and many other times he said to them, 'My peace I give to you, my peace I leave you, peace be with you;' a jewel and a precious gift given and left: a jewel without which there can be no happiness either on earth or in heaven. This peace is the true end of war; and war is only another name for arms. This, then, being admitted, that the end of war is peace, and that so far it has the advantage over the goal of letters, let us turn to the work of the body over the man of letters, and those who follow the profession of Knighthood, and see which is greater."

Don Quixote delivered his speech in such a manner and in such correct language, that at this moment he made it impossible for any of his listeners to consider him a madman; on the contrary, as they were mostly gentlemen, who had witnessed arms since their birth, they listened to him with great pleasure as he continued: "Here then, I say is what the student has to undergo; first of all poverty: not that all Knights are poor, but to put the case as strongly as possible: and when I have said that he endures poverty, I think nothing else is needed to be said about his bad fortune, because he who is poor has no share of the good things in life. This poverty he suffers from in various ways, hunger, cold, or nakedness, or all of these together; but all of that might not be as extreme as when he gets something to eat, because it may be at an unreasonable time and from the leftovers of the rich; because the greatest misery of the student is what they themselves call 'going out for soup,' and there is always some neighbour's stove or home for them, which, if it does not warm, at least assists with the cold for them, and lastly, they sleep comfortably at night under a roof. I will not go into other particulars, as for example the need of a shirt, and no abundance of shoes, thin and bare garments, and gorging themselves on food when good luck has treated them to a banquet of some kind. This road that I have described, rough and hard, stumbling here, falling there, getting up again to fall again, eventually leads to the rank they desire. As for the man of letters we have seen many who have travelled far as if luck was on their side; we have seen them, I say, ruling and governing the world from a chair, their hunger turned into satiety, their cold into comfort, their nakedness finely covered, their sleep on a mat turned into luxurious housing, they earned the reward of their virtue; but, contrasted and compared with what the warrior undergoes, all they have undergone falls far short of this, as I am now about to show."

CHAPTER 38

THE CURIOUS SPEECH DON QUIXOTE DELIVERED ABOUT KNIGHTHOOD AND LETTERS

Continuing his speech Don Quixote said: "As we began in the student of letters case, with poverty and its accompaniments, let us see now if the soldier is richer, and we will find that in poverty itself there is no one poorer; because he is dependent on his little pay, which comes late or never, or else on what he can find, seriously risking his life; and sometimes his nakedness will be so great that a ripped jacket is his uniform, and in the depth of winter he has to defend himself against the unpleasant cold of the weather in the open field with nothing better than the breath of his mouth, which I say, coming from an empty place, must come out cold, contrary to the laws of nature. Surely he does not look forward to the approach of night and all of these discomforts that await him, however he can easily sleep on the ground anywhere he likes, and roll himself around on it without any fear that the sheets will slip away from him. Then, after all of this, consider the day and hour for taking his degree in this calling has come; suppose the day of the battle arrives, which requires him to act as a doctor, to heal some bullet-hole, perhaps, that has gone through his temples, or left him with a crippled arm or leg. Or if this does not happen, and the merciful Heaven that watches over him keeps him safe and sound, it could be he continues with the same poverty he had before, and he must go through more travels and more battles, and come out victorious from all of them before he betters himself; but miracles of this kind are not often seen. Because tell me, if you have ever reflected on it, how much do those who have gained from war fall short of the number of those who have died in it? No doubt you will reply that there can be no comparison, that the dead cannot be numbered, while the living who have been rewarded may be summed up with three figures. All of this is reversed in the case of men of letters; because they all find ways of support themselves; so that although the soldier has more to endure, his reward is much less. But against all of this it may be said that it is easier to reward two thousand soldiers, because they may be compensated by giving them positions, which must unavoidably be awarded to men of their profession, while the men of letters can only be compensated out of the property of the master they serve; but this impossibility only strengthens my argument.

"Putting this aside, however, because it is a puzzling question which is difficult to find a solution to, let us return to the superiority of Knighthood over letters, a matter still undecided, as many arguments can be put forward on each side; besides those I have mentioned, letters say that without them arms cannot maintain themselves, because war, too, has its laws and is governed by them, and laws belong to the domain of letters and men of letters. To this arms can answer that without them laws cannot be maintained, because by arms, states are defended, kingdoms preserved, cities protected, roads made safe, seas cleared of pirates; and, in short, if it were not for them, states, kingdoms, monarchies, cities, routes by sea and land would be exposed to the violence and confusion which war brings with it, as long as it lasts and is free to make use of its privileges and powers. And then it is plain that whatever costs most is valued and deserves to be valued most. To attain distinction in letters costs a man time, watching, hunger, nakedness, headaches, indigestions, and other things of the sort, some of which I have already referred to. But for a man to be a good soldier costs him all the student of letters suffers, and in an incomparably higher degree, because at every step he runs the risk of losing his life. Because what fear or poverty can reach or harass the student of letters which can compare with what the soldier feels, who finds himself under attack, and cannot under any circumstances leave or run from the imminent danger that threatens him? All he can do is stand his ground in fear and expectation of the moment when he will fly to the clouds without wings against his will. And if this seems like a little risk, let us see whether it is equalled or surpassed by the encounter of two boats in the middle of the open sea, locked and entangled with one another, when the soldier has no earth to stand on; and yet, although he sees before him, threatening him, as many ministers of death as there are cannons of the enemy pointed at him, not a lance length from his body, and sees as well, that with one wrong step he will visit heaven, but still with a strong heart, encouraged by his honour, he struggles to cross the narrow path to the enemy's ship. And what is more marvellous, as soon as someone has gone down into the depths of the sea he will never rise from it; and if he falls into the sea that waits for him like an enemy, another and another will follow him without a pause between their deaths: courage and bravery the greatest that war can display. It is a happy time when that age does not know the fear of fury of those devilish instruments of war, whose inventor I am persuaded is in hell receiving the reward of his disgraceful creations, by which he made it easy for a disgusting and cowardly man to take the life of a gracious gentleman; that does not know how or where, in the height of passion and enthusiasm that the battle of the brave hearts emanates, some random bullet, discharged perhaps by someone who ran in terror at the flash of gunfire, which in an instant puts an end to the life of someone who deserved to live for ages to come. And so, when I reflect on this, I am almost tempted to say that in my heart I regret adopting this profession of Knighthood in such a detestable age as we live in now; because although no danger can make me fear, it still gives me some uneasiness to think that powder and lead could take away the opportunity of making myself famous and renowned throughout the known earth by the strength of my arm and the edge of my sword. But if Heaven's will is done; if I succeed in my attempt I will be even more honoured, as I have faced greater dangers than the Knights of the past have exposed themselves to."

The others ate while Don Quixote delivered this speech, forgetting to raise any food to his lips, although Sancho told him more than once to eat his dinner, as he would have enough time afterwards to say all he wanted. It created even more pity for him in those who had listened to him to see a man with such rational views on every subject, and apparently good sense so hopelessly lacking in it when he puts his chosen profession into action. The vicar told him he was right in all that he had said in favour of arms, and that he himself, although a man of letters and a graduate, had the same opinion.

They finished their dinner, the table-cloth was removed, and while the hostess, her daughter, and Maritornes were getting Don Quixote of La Mancha's room ready, in which it was arranged that the women were going to sleep by themselves for the night, Don Fernando begged the new guest to tell them the story of his life, because he sensed it would be strange and interesting, judging by the hints he received during the man's arrival in the company of Zoraida. To this the man replied that he would willingly grant his request, only he feared his story would not give them as much pleasure as they hoped for; nevertheless, to act in compliance, he would tell it. The vicar and the others thanked him and added their request for the story of his life, and finding himself so encouraged he said there was no more need to ask, when a command had such weight, and added, "If you will give me your attention you will hear a true story, which perhaps, made-up ones constructed with amazing inventiveness could not compare to." These words made them settle themselves in their places and preserve a deep silence, and seeing them waiting for his words in silence, he began to say the following in a pleasant quiet voice.

CHAPTER 39

THE STORY OF THE CAPTIVE'S LIFE AND ADVENTURES

My family's origins were in a village in the mountains of Leon, and nature had been kinder and more generous to it than fortune; although in the general poverty of those communities even my father passed for being a rich man; and he would have been rich in reality if he had been as clever in preserving his property as he was in spending it. This tendency of his to be liberal had been acquired from his days as a soldier when he was a youth, because the soldier's life is a school in which the saver becomes generous and the generous begins to spend uncontrollably; and if any soldiers are found to be misers, they are labelled monsters of rare occurrence. My father went beyond liberality and bordered on uncontrolled, a temperament which is by no means advantageous to a married man who has children to follow in his name. My father had three children, all sons, and all at an appropriate age to make a choice of profession. Finding, then, that he was unable to resist his inclination, he decided to rid himself of the instrument and cause of his uncontrolled spending and extravagance, to free himself of wealth, without which Alexander himself would have seemed ungenerous; and so calling us three all into a room one day, he said something like the following:

"My sons, to assure you that I love you, no more needs to be known or said than you are my sons; and to encourage a suspicion that I do not love you, no more is needed than the knowledge that I have no self-control as far as the preservation of your inheritance is concerned; therefore, so you can feel sure for the future that I love you like a father, and have no wish to ruin you like a stepfather, I propose to do what I have for some time meditated on, and after mature deliberation decided. You are now at an age to choose your line of life or at least make choice of a profession that will bring you honour and profit when you are older; and what I have decided to do is to divide my property into four parts; three I will give to you, each in the same proportion without making any difference, and the other I will keep to live on and support myself for whatever remainder of life Heaven wishes to grant me. But I ask that each of you, when taking possession of the share that comes to you, follow one of the paths I indicate. In this Spain of ours there is a proverb, which in my mind is very true - as they all are short aphorisms made from long practical experience - and the one I refer to says: 'The church, the sea, or the King's house;' which means in plainer language, whoever wants to flourish and become rich, he should follow the church, or go to sea, adopting commerce as his calling, or go into the King's service in his household, because they say, 'Better to be a King's crumb than a lord's favour.' I say this because it is my will and pleasure that one of you follows the church, another goes into trade, and the third serve the King in the wars, because it is a difficult matter to gain admission to his service in his household, and if war does not bring much wealth it offers great distinction and fame. Eight days from now I will give you your full shares in cash, without withholding from you a penny, as you will see. Now tell me if you are willing to follow my idea and the advice I have given you."

Having called me as the eldest to answer, I, after advising him not to strip himself of his property but to spend it all as he pleased (because we were young men able to gain our own living), consented to comply with his wishes, and said that I would follow the profession of arms and therefore serve God and my King. My second brother having made the same proposal, decided on going to the Indies, to seek and commence trade opportunities. The youngest, and in my opinion the wisest, said he would rather follow the church, or go to complete his studies in Salamanca. As soon as we had come to an understanding, and made the choice of our professions, my father hugged us all, and in the short time he mentioned, he put his plan into effect and delivered all he had promised; and when he had given each of us our share, which as I remember was three thousand gold coins (because an uncle of ours bought the estate and paid for it in total, so it would not be lost from the family), all three of us on the same day left our good father; and at the same time, as it seemed to me inhuman to leave my father with very little to live on in his old age, I persuaded him to take two of my three thousand coins, as the remainder would be enough to provide me with all a soldier needed. My two brothers, moved by my example, gave him each a thousand coins, so that there was four thousand coins left for my father, in addition to his three thousand, the value of the portion that was his he preferred to retain in land instead of selling it. Finally, as I said, we left him, and our uncle who I have mentioned, not without sorrow and tears on both sides, both of them asking us to let them know whenever an opportunity arose how we were doing, whether we were well or ill. We promised to do so, and after our father gave us his blessing, one set out for Salamanca, the other for Seville, and I for Alicante, where I had heard there was a vessel taking cargo of wool to Genoa.

It is now about twenty-two years since I left my father's house, and in all that time, although I have written several letters, I have had no news about him or my brothers; my own adventures during that period I will now say briefly. I embarked at Alicante, reached Genoa after a prosperous voyage, and proceeded from there to Milan, where I provided myself with weapons and a few soldier's accessories; then it was my intention to go and serve in the north west of Italy, but as I was on my way, I heard that the great Duke of Alva was on his way to Flanders. I changed my plans, joined him, served under him in the campaigns he created, was present at the deaths of Egmont and Horn, and was promoted to be a commissioned officer under the famous captain of Guadalajara, Diego de Urbina by name. Sometime after my arrival in Flanders news came that his Holiness Pope Pius had united Venice and Spain against the common enemy, the Turk, who had just then with his fleet taken the famous island of Cyprus, which belonged to the Venetians, a loss disgraceful and disastrous. It was known as a fact that the Most Composed Don John of Austria, brother of our good King Don Philip, was coming as commander-in-chief of the allied forces, and rumours were abroad of the vast warlike preparations which were being made, all of which motivated my heart and filled me with a longing to take part in the campaign which was expected; and although I had a reason to believe, almost certain promises, that on the first opportunity that presented itself I would be promoted to captain, I preferred to leave all of that and take myself, as I did, to Italy; and it was my good fortune that Don John had just arrived at Genoa, and was going on to Naples to join the Venetian fleet, as he afterwards did in Messina. I must say, in short, that I took part in that glorious expedition, promoted by this time to be a captain of infantry, which luckily came from my good fortune rather than my merit; and that day - so fortunate for Christians, because then all the nations on earth were enlightened of the error under which they were imagining the Turks to be invincible on sea - on that day, I say, on which the Ottoman pride and arrogance were broken, among all that were there created a happy day (because the Christians who died that day were happier than those who remained alive and victorious) I alone was miserable; because, instead of some naval crown that I might have expected had it been in Roman times, on the night that followed that famous day I found myself with chains on my feet and shackles on my hands.

It happened like this: El Uchali, the King of Algeria, a daring and successful pirate, having attacked and taken the leading Maltese ship (only three soldiers left alive on it, and they were badly wounded), the main ship of John Andrea, which I and my company were placed on board, came to its relief, and doing as we were bound to do in such a case, I leaped on board the enemy's ship, which, separating itself from the ship which had attacked it, prevented my men from following me, and so I found myself alone among my enemies, who vastly outnumbered me, so I was unable to resist; in short I was taken, covered with wounds; El Uchali, as you know, escaped with his entire group, and I was left a prisoner in his power, the only man among so many filled with joy, and the only captive among so many who were free.

They took me to Istanbul, where the Grand Turk, Selim, made the captain of the ship a general for doing his duty during the battle and took as evidence of his bravery the medal called the standard order of Malta. The following year, which was year seventy-two, I found myself at Navarino rowing in the leading ship with the three lanterns. There I saw and observed how the opportunity of capturing the whole Turkish fleet in harbour was lost; because all the marines and soldiers that belonged to it knew that they were about to be attacked inside the harbour, and due to their great fear, they had their kit and shoes ready to run as soon as they reached the shore without waiting to be attacked. But Heaven decided otherwise, not due to any fault or neglect of the general who commanded on our side, but for the sins of Christians, and because it was God's will and pleasure that we should always have instruments of punishment to correct us. As it was, El Uchali took refuge at Modon, which is an island near Navarino, and arriving forces fortified the mouth of the harbour and waited quietly until Don John retired. On this expedition the ship called the Prize was taken, whose captain was a son of the famous pirate Barbarossa. It was taken by the main ship from Naples called the She-wolf, commanded by that thunderbolt of war, that father of his men, that successful and unconquered captain Don Alvaro de Bazan, Nobleman of Santa Cruz; and I cannot help telling you what took place when the Prize was captured.

The son of Barbarossa was so cruel, and treated his slaves so badly, that, when those who were rowing saw that the She-wolf was approaching them and catching up with them, they all immediately dropped their oars and captured their captain who stood there in front of them shouting at them to row; and passing him forward from bench to bench, from the rear to the front of the ship, they beat him so badly that before he got to the front his soul had already gone to hell; so great, as I said, was the cruelty with which he treated them, and the hatred with which the possessed for him.

We returned to Istanbul, and the following year, seventy-three, it became known that Don John had taken Tunis and the Kingdom from the Turks, and placed Muley Hamet in possession, putting an end to the hopes which Muley Hamida, the cruellest and bravest Moor in the world, entertained of returning to reign there. The Grand Turk took the loss greatly to heart, and with the cunning which all his race possesses, he made peace with the Venetians (who were much more eager for it than he was), and the following year, seventy-four, he attacked the port of Tunis and the fortress which Don John had left half built. While all these events were occurring, I was working hard rowing without any hope of freedom; at least I had no hope of obtaining it by ransom, because I firmly decided not to write to my father telling him about my misfortune. Finally, the port of Tunis was taken, and the fortress collapsed, in front of these places there were seventy-five thousand regular Turkish soldiers, and more than four hundred thousand Moors and Arabs from all parts of Africa and the middle-east, and a vast array of weapons and equipment of war, and so many people that with their hands they might have covered the port of Tunis and the fortress with handfuls of earth. The first to be assailed was the port of Tunis, which until then was considered impregnable, and it fell, not by any fault of its defenders, who did all they could and should have done, but because experimentation proved how easily bases could be made in the desert sand; because water used to be found not far underground, while the Turks found none close by; and so they placed a number of sandbags so high that no one was able to attack or maintain the defence.

It was a common opinion that our men should not have shut themselves in, but should have waited in the open; but those who say so have very little knowledge about such matters; because if in the port of Tunis and in the fortress there were barely seven thousand soldiers, how could such a small number, however determined, go out in the open and hold their ground against the enemy with that many number of soldiers? And how is it possible to help losing a fortress with no additional aid, above all when surrounded by a mass of determined enemies in their own country? But many thought, and I thought so too, that it was a special favour and mercy which Heaven showed to Spain in permitting the destruction of that source and hiding place of trouble, that consumer and sponge of countless money, fruitlessly wasted there for no other purpose than preserving the memory of its capture by the invincible Charles the fifth; as if to make that eternal. The fortress also taken; but the Turks had to take it inch by inch, because the soldiers who defended it fought so bravely and firmly that the number of the enemy killed in twenty-two general assaults exceeded twenty-five thousand. Out of the three hundred that remained alive not one was taken unwounded, clear and obvious proof of their bravery and firmness, and how strongly they had defended themselves and held their position. A small fortress or tower which was in the middle of the water under the command of Don Juan Zanoguera, a Valencian gentleman and a famous soldier, surrendered. They took as a prisoner Don Pedro Puertocarrero, commander of the Goletta, who had done all in his power to defend his fortress, and took the loss of it so much to heart that he died of grief on the way to Istanbul, where they were taking him as a prisoner. They also took the commander of the fortress Gabrio Cerbellon, a Milanese gentleman, a great engineer and a very brave soldier. In these two fortresses many noteworthy people died, among them was Pagano Doria, Knight of the Order of St. John, a man of generous character, as was shown by his extreme liberality to his brother, the famous John Andrea Doria; and what made his death sadder was that he was killed by some Arabs who, when they saw the fortress was now lost, offered to take him disguised as a Moor to Tabarca, a small fortress or base on the coast held by the Genoese who worked in the fisheries. These Arabs cut off his head and took it to the commander of the Turkish fleet, who proved to them the truth of our Castilian proverb, that "although the treason may please, the traitor is hated;" because they say he ordered those who brought him the present to be hanged for not having brought him alive.

Among the Christians who were taken in the fortress one was named Don Pedro de Aguilar, a native of some place, I do not know, in Andalusia, who had been a commissioned officer in the fortress, a soldier of great reputation and rare intelligence, who had in particular a special gift for what they call poetry. I say this because his fate brought him to my ship and to my bench, and made him a slave of the same master; and before we left the port this gentleman composed two poems, one about the port of Tunis and the other about the fortress; actually, I may as well repeat them, because I know them by heart, and I think they will be liked rather than disliked.

The instant the man mentioned the name of Don Pedro de Aguilar, Don Fernando looked at his companions and all three of them smiled; and when he was about to say the poems one of them said, "before you proceed any further I ask you to tell me what happened to Don Pedro de Aguilar that you mentioned."

"All I know is," replied the man, "that after having been in Istanbul for two years he escaped in disguise, accompanied by a Greek spy; but whether he regained his freedom or not I cannot say, although I think he did, because a year afterwards I saw the Greek at Istanbul, although I was unable to ask him what the result of the journey was."

"Well then, you are right," returned the gentleman, "because Don Pedro is my brother, and he is now in our village in good health, rich, married, and with three children."

"Thank God for all the mercy he has shown him," said the man; "because in my mind there is no happiness on earth which compares to recovering lost freedom."

"And what is more," said the gentleman, "I know the poems my brother made."

"Then you repeat them," said the captive, "because you will deliver them better than I can."

"With all my heart," said the gentleman; " the one about the port of Tunis goes like this."

CHAPTER 40

THE STORY OF THE CAPTIVE - CONTINUED

POEM

"Lucky are those, that, from this shell are set free,
In reward of brave deeds purified,
Above this poor globe of ours abide,
Made inheritors of heaven and immortality.

With honourable rage and passion glowing,
Your strength, while strength was yours, in battle used,
And with your own blood and the enemy abused,
The sand can be seen, to the shore keep rowing.

The tired arms; brave hearts that were never down,
Though beaten, yet they earned the victor's crown,
Mourning, yet still triumph was your fall,
Because you won, between the sword and the wall,
In Heaven glory, and on earth renown."

"That was it exactly, according to my recollection," said the captive.

"Well then, the one about the fortress," said the gentleman, "if my memory is right, goes like this:

POEM

"Loyal, toil built on the soil, now a shattered shell,
The walls and towers fell,
Three thousand soldier's souls as well,
The attack they were unable to repel.

Strength and courage, with which they tried,
Unable to resist, persisting shots insist they died,
Tired, a lot fired, far and wide,
Morning came, mourning came, hard men cried."

Everyone liked the poems, and the captive was delighted about the approval they gave him of his companion, and continuing his tale, he went on to say:

"The port of Tunis and the fortress being in their hands, the Turks gave orders to dismantle the port – because the fortress was in such a state that there was nothing left to level - and to do the work quickly and easily they mined it in three places; but they were unable to blow up the part which seemed to be the least strong, that is to say, the old walls, while the new fortifications came to the ground very easily. Finally the fleet returned victorious and triumphant to Istanbul, and a few months later my master died, El Uchali, otherwise Uchali Fartax, which means in Turkish "the dirty renegade;" because he was; and it is common for the Turks to name people from some defect or virtue they possess; the reason being that among them only four surnames belonging to families tracing their descent from the Ottoman house, and the others, as I have said, take their names and surnames either from body blemishes or moral qualities. This "dirty one" rowed as a slave of the Grand Signor's for fourteen years, and when over thirty-four years of age, in resentment for being struck while rowing, became a rebel and renounced his faith in order to be able to revenge himself; however his spirit was so great, that without assigning his advancement to the evil ways by which most of the favourites of the Grand Signor rise to power, he became King of Algeria, and afterwards general-on-sea, which is the third place of trust in the realm. He was born in southern Italy, and a worthy man morally, and he treated his slaves with great humanity. He had three thousand of them, and after his death they were divided, as he directed in his will, between the Grand Signor (who is heir of all who die and shares with the children of the deceased) and his renegades. I came under the Venetian renegade who, when a cabin boy on board a ship, had been taken by Uchali and was loved by him so much that he became one of his most favoured youths. He however became the cruellest renegade I ever saw: his name was Hassan Aga, and he grew very rich and became King of Algeria. I went there with him from Istanbul, rather glad to be closer Spain, not that I intended to write to anyone about my unhappy fortune, but hoping that fortune would be kinder to me in Algeria than in Istanbul, where I had attempted in a thousand ways to escape without ever finding a favourable time or chance; but in Algeria I decided to seek other ways of executing the purpose I held sincerely; because the hope of obtaining my freedom never deserted me; and while plotting, scheming and attempting, the result did not meet my expectations, without losing hope I immediately began to look out for, or conjure up, new hope to support me, however faint or feeble it might be. In this way I lived secluded in a building or prison called a bano by the Turks, in which they confine the Christian captives, as well as those that are the King's or those belonging to private individuals, and slaves of the town who serve the city; but captives of this type recover their freedom with great difficulty, because, as they are public property and have no particular master, there is no one person that can pay for their freedom, even if they were able to. In these banos, as I have said, some private individuals of the town have the habit of bringing their captives, especially when they are to be sold; because there they can keep them in safety and comfort until a buyer arrives. The King's captives as well, that are up for sale, do not go out to work with the rest of the crew, unless when a buyer is delayed; because then, to make use of them, they force them to work and go to retrieve wood, which is no easy work.

I, however, was one of those up for sale, because when it was discovered that I was a captain, although I declared I had little and lacked good fortune, nothing could dissuade them from including me among the gentlemen and those waiting to be sold. They put a chain on me, more as a mark of this than to keep me safe, and so I passed my life in that bano with several other gentlemen and people of high quality marked out as for sale; but although at times, or rather almost always, we suffered from hunger and very little clothing, nothing distressed us as much as hearing and seeing every day the unheard-of cruelties my master inflicted on the Christians. Every day he hanged a man, impaled one, cut off the ears of another; and all with little provocation, or without any entirely, even the Turks acknowledged he did it merely for the sake of doing it, and because he was by nature murderous towards the whole human race. The only one that managed well with him was a Spanish soldier, his name was something de Saavedra, to whom he never gave a strike himself, or ordered a strike to be given, or gave any harsh word, although he had done things that will dwell in the memory of the people there for many years, and all to recover his freedom; and for each and every one of the many things he did we feared he would be killed, and he himself was in fear of it more than once; unfortunately time does not allow, or I would tell you something about what that soldier did, that would interest and astonish you much more than the narration of my own story.

To continue my story however; the courtyard of our prison was overlooked by the windows of the house belonging to a wealthy Moor of high rank; and these, as is usual in Moorish houses, were more like circular holes than windows, and were covered with thick and close lattice-work. It so happened, one day I was in the courtyard of our prison with three other friends. Trying to pass the time, we were seeing how far we could jump with our chains, and being alone, as all the other Christians had gone out to work, I raised my eyes, and from one of these little closed windows I saw a stick appear with a cloth attached to the end of it, and it kept waving to and fro, and moving as if to signal for us to come and take it. We watched it, and one of those who were with me went and stood under the stick to see whether it would be dropped, or what would be done with it, but as he did, the stick was raised and moved from side to side, as if to say "no." My friend came back, and it was lowered again, making the same movements as before. Another of my friends went, and the same happened to him as it did with the first, and then the third went, but he got the same result as the first and second. Seeing this I thought I would try my luck, and as soon as I came under the stick it was dropped and fell in front of my feet. I rushed to untie the cloth, and inside were ten gold coins.

It is needless to say I celebrated this blessing, and my joy was not less than my wonder as I strove to imagine how this good fortune could have come, to me especially. It was evident - the unwillingness to drop the stick for anyone else showed that the favour was intended for me. I took the money, broke the stick, and returned to the terrace, and looking up at the window, I saw a very small and smooth Moorish looking hand shut the window very quickly. From this we thought that it must be some woman living in that house that had done us this favour, and to show that we were grateful for it, we gave bows which was a custom of the Moors, bowing the head, bending the body, and crossing the arms on the chest. Shortly afterwards at the same window a small cross made of sticks was put out and immediately withdrawn. This sign led us to believe that some Christian woman was a captive in the house, and that it was her who had been so good to us; but the colour of the hand and the bracelets we had seen made us dismiss that idea. In all our assumptions we were far wide of the truth; so from that time forward our only occupation was watching the window where the cross had appeared to us, as if it were a guiding star; but at least fifteen days passed without seeing anything, not even the hand, or any other sign and although we attempted with the utmost trouble to ascertain who it was that lived in the house, and whether there were any Christian in it, nobody could ever tell us anything more than a rich Moor of high position lived there, called Hadji Morato, formerly Mayor of La Pata. When we finally thought we were never going to see anything more from that window, suddenly another stick appeared with cloth tied in a larger knot attached to it, and this again, like the first time, was when the bano was empty.

We did the same as the first time, each of the three going forward before I did; but again, the stick was delivered to no one but me. I untied the knot and I found forty Spanish gold coins with a paper written in Arabic, and at the end of the writing there was a large cross drawn on it. I kissed the cross, took the coins and returned to the others, and we all bowed again; but again the hand appeared, and made signs that I should read the paper, and then the window was closed. We were all confused, although filled with joy at what had taken place; and as none of us understood Arabic, we had great curiosity to know what the paper said, and greater difficulty in finding someone to read it. At last I decided to confide in a renegade, a native of Murcia, who became a very great friend of mine, and had promised to carefully guard any secret I entrusted him with; because it is the custom with some renegades, when they return to Christian territory, to carry with them notes from other captives, in whatever form they can, and support these notes by saying things like 'there is a worthy man who has always shown kindness to Christians, and is anxious to escape on the first opportunity that may present itself.' Some carry these testimonials with good intentions, but others use them for evil; because when they go to Christian territory, they produce these notes and say that from these papers the objective they came for can be seen, which is to escape the Turks and stay on Christian soil, but this is solely to divert the attention from their murderous ways. In this way they escape the consequences of the Church before it does them any harm, and then they have the chance to return to cruelty and become what they were before. Others, however, obtain these papers and use them honestly, and remain on Christian soil. This friend of mine, then, was one of the good renegades that I have described; he had notes from all of our companions, which strongly affirmed how trustworthy he was; and if the Moors had found the papers they would have burned him alive.

I knew that he understood Arabic very well, and could not only speak but also write it; but before I disclosed the whole matter to him, I asked him to read the paper for me which I said 'I had found by accident in a hole in my cell.' He opened it and took some time examining it and whispering to himself as he translated it. I asked him if he understood it, and he told me he understood perfectly, and if I wanted him to tell me the meaning word for word, I must give him a pen so he could translate it suitably. I gave him what he required immediately, and he started translating it bit by bit, and when he had done he said:

"Here, written in Spanish is what the Moorish paper contains, and you must keep in mind that when it says 'Lela Marien' it means 'Our Lady the Virgin Mary.'"

I read the paper and it said this:

"When I was a child my father had a slave who taught me to say a Christian prayer in my own language, and told me many things about Lela Marien. The Christian died, and I know that she did not go to the fire, but to Allah, because since then I have seen her twice, and she told me to go to the land of the Christians to see Lela Marien, who had great love for me. I do not know how to go. I have seen many Christians, but none so far have treated me like a gentleman should. I am young and beautiful, and have plenty of money to take with me. See if you can plan how we can go, and if you agree you will be my husband there, and if you do not agree it will not distress me, because Lela Marien will find someone to marry me. I myself have written this: be careful who you allow to read it: trust no Moor, because they are all disloyal. I am very worried about this, because if it were possible I would say do not confide in anyone, because if my father found out he would throw me down a well and cover me with stones. I will attach a string to the stick; tie your answer to it, and if you have no one to write in Arabic for you, give me some signs, because Lela Marien will make me understand you. She, Allah and this cross, which I often kiss and ask for your protection."

You can judge whether we had a good reason for surprise and joy when we read the words on this paper; which were so great, that the renegade asserted that the paper had not been found by chance, but had been in reality addressed to one of us, and he begged us, to trust him and tell him who, because he would risk his life for our freedom; and as saying this he took out from his chest a metal crucifix, and with many tears swore to God, that although he was a sinner, that he was truly and faithfully loyal to us and would keep secret whatever we chose to reveal to him; because he thought and almost foresaw that through the lady who had written the paper, he and all of us would obtain our freedom, and he himself would obtain the objective he desired so much, which

264

was his restoration to the Holy Mother Church, from which through his own sins and ignorance he was now severed like a corrupt limb. The renegade said this with so many tears and such signs of repentance, that with one consent we all agreed to tell him the whole truth, and so we gave him a full account of everything, without hiding anything from him. We pointed out to him the window at which the stick had appeared, and he noted the house, and agreed to discover with care who lived in it. We agreed as well that it would be advisable to answer the Moorish lady's letter, and the renegade without a moment's delay translated the words I said to him, which were exactly what I will tell you, because nothing of importance that took place during this situation has escaped my memory, and never will while my life lasts. This, then, was the answer I gave in response to the Moorish lady:

"The true God will protect you, Lady, and that blessed Marien who is the mother of God, who has put it into your heart to go to the land of the Christians, because she loves you. Ask her if she is pleased to show you how you can execute the command she gives you, because she will, as this is her goodness. On my own part, and on that of all these Christians who are with me, I promise to do all we can for you, until death. Do not fail to write to me and inform me what you plan to do, and I will always answer you; because the great God has given us a Christian captive who can speak and write your language well, as you can see by this paper; without fear, therefore, you can inform us about everything you plan. As to what you say, that if you reach the land of the Christians you will be my wife, I give you my promise on it as a good Christian; and know that the Christians keep their promises better than the Moors. God and Marien his mother watch over you, my Lady."

The paper being written and folded, I waited two days until the bano was empty as before, and immediately went for the usual walk in the courtyard to see if there were any sign of the stick, which did not take long to make its appearance. As soon as I saw it, although I could not distinguish who put it out, I showed the paper as a sign I was going to attach it to the thread, and so, I tied the paper to it; and shortly afterwards our star made its appearance once more with the white flag of peace, and a little bundle was dropped, which I picked up, and found in the cloth, gold and silver coins of all sorts, more than fifty in total, which fifty times more strengthened our joy and doubled our hope of gaining our freedom. That night our renegade returned and said he had discovered that the Moor we had been told of who lived in that house was called Hadji Morato, and that he was enormously rich, that he had only one daughter the heiress of all his wealth, and that it was the general opinion that she was the most beautiful woman in the city, and that several rulers of other cities had come here and had sought her as their wife, but that she had always been unwilling to marry; and he had discovered as well, that she once had a Christian servant who was now dead; all of this agreed with the contents of the paper. We immediately took advice from the renegade as to what course of action could be taken in order to carry off the Moorish lady and bring us all to Christian territory; and in the end it was agreed that for the present we should wait for a second letter from Zoraida (because that was her name, who now desires to be called Maria), because at that moment we thought that she and no one else could find a way out of all these difficulties. When we had decided to wait, the renegade told us not to worry, because he would lose his life to restore our freedom. For four days the bano was filled with people, and the stick delayed its appearance, but at the end of that time, when the bano was, as it sometimes was, empty, it appeared with a cloth so bulky that it promised to be a happy day. The stick and cloth came down to me, and I found another paper and a hundred coins in gold. The renegade was present, and we gave him the paper to read, which was said this:

"I cannot think of a plan, señor, and neither has Lela Marien shown me one, although I have asked her. All that can be done is for me to give you plenty of money in gold from this window. With it pay for yourself and your friends freedom, and one of you go to the land of the Christians, and there buy a boat and come back for the others; and you will find me in my father's garden, which is at the Babazon gate near the seashore, where I will be all summer with my father and my servants. You can carry me away from there at night without any danger. And remember you are going to be my husband, or I will pray to Marien to punish you for lying. I trust you however, and if you cannot trust anyone to go to get the boat, pay for your own freedom and you go, because I know you will return more surely than any other, as you are a gentleman and a Christian. Attempt to make yourself familiar with the garden; and when I see you walking in the courtyard I will know that the bano is empty and I will give you an abundance of money. Allah protect you, señor."

These were the words and contents of the second paper, and on hearing them, each declared himself willing to be the one who was free first, and promised to go and return with the boat; and I made the same offer as well; but to all of this the renegade objected, saying that he would not consent to anyone being set free and that all of us should go together, as experience had taught him how badly those who have been set free keep promises which they made in captivity; because captives frequently had a similar plan, pay the fee for one who was to go to Valencia or Majorca with money to enable him to obtain weaponry and a boat, and return for the others who had paid for him, but then never came back; because recovered freedom and the fear of losing it again delete from the memory all the obligations in the world. And to prove the truth of what he said, he told us briefly what had happened to a certain Christian gentleman, the strangest case that had ever occurred, even there, where astonishing and marvellous things happen every day. In short, he ended by saying that what could and should be done was to give him the money intended for the payment of one of us Christians, so he could buy a boat there in Algeria under the pretence of becoming a merchant and trader at Tetuan and along the coast; and when he became master of the boat, it would be easy for him to find some way of getting us all out of the bano and taking us on board; especially if the Moorish lady gave, as she said, enough money to buy all of our freedom, because once free it would be the easiest thing in the world for us to embark even during the day time; but the greatest difficulty was that the Moors do not allow any renegade to buy or own any boat, unless it is a large boat which is used for trading, because they are afraid that anyone who buys a small boat, especially a Spaniard, only wants it for the purpose of escaping to Christian territory. This however he could get over by arranging with a Moor to share with him in the purchase of the boat, and in the profit of the trading; and under this cover he could become master of the boat. After explaining this he looked at us all as if everything was accomplished. But to me and my companions it seemed a better plan to go to Majorca for the boat, as the Moorish lady suggested, but we did not dare to oppose him, fearing that if we did, he would place us in danger of losing our lives if he were to disclose our dealings with Zoraida. We therefore decided to put ourselves in the hands of God and in the renegade's; and at the same time an answer was given to Zoraida, telling her that we would do all she had recommended, because she had given as good advice as if Lela Marien had sent it. I renewed my promise to be her husband; and therefore the next day that the bano happened to be empty she at different times gave us, using the stick and cloth two thousand gold coins and a paper in which she said that following Friday she was going to her father's garden, but that before she went she would give us more money; and if it were not enough we should let her know, as she would give us as much as we asked for, because her father had so much he would not miss it, and she kept all the keys.

We immediately gave the renegade five hundred coins to buy the boat, and with eight hundred I bought my freedom, giving the money to a Valencian merchant who happened to be in Algeria at the time, and who had me released on his word, promising that on the arrival of the first ship from Valencia he would pay for my freedom; because if he had given the money immediately it would have made the King suspicious. In fact, my master was so difficult to deal with that I did not pay the money all at once. The Thursday before the Friday on which the fair Zoraida was to go to the garden she gave us a thousand more coins, and warned us of her departure, begging me, if I were free, to find her father's garden immediately, and seek an opportunity of going there to see her. I answered in a few words that I would do so, and that she must remember to ask Lela Marien for our assistance, with all the prayers the Christian servant had taught her. This having been done, steps were taken to free my three companions, enabling them to leave the bano, because seeing me free and themselves not, although the money was there, they might make a disturbance about it and the devil would prompt them to do something that might injure Zoraida; because although they acted sufficiently to relieve me from this apprehension, nevertheless I was unwilling to take any risks in the matter; and so I had them freed in the same way as I was, handing over all the money to the merchant so that he could with safety and confidence give security; without, however, confiding our arrangement and secret to him, which might have been dangerous.

CHAPTER 41

THE CAPTIVE CONTINUES HIS ADVENTURES

Within fifteen days the renegade had already purchased an excellent boat with room for more than thirty people; and to make the transaction safe, he thought it was wise, as he did, to take a voyage to a place called Shershel, twenty miles from Algiers, where there is extensive trade in dried figs. He made this voyage two or three times in company of the Moor as already mentioned. To proceed, every time he went there with his boat he anchored in a harbour that was not a shot from the garden where Zoraida was waiting; and there the renegade purposely stationed himself, either going through his prayers, or practising what he was going to perform. And so, he would go to Zoraida's garden and ask for fruit, which her father gave to him, not knowing him; but, as he told me afterwards, he went to speak to Zoraida, to tell her who he was, and that from my orders he was going to take her to the land of the Christians, so that she can feel satisfied and relaxed. Previously he had never been able to do so; because the Moorish women do not allow themselves to be seen by any Moor or Turk, unless their husband or father asked them to: but with Christian captives they grant freedom to talk and communicate, even more than might be considered appropriate. But for me it was better that he had not spoken to her, because perhaps it would have alarmed her to find her affairs talked about by renegades. But God, who ordered it otherwise, gave opportunity for the renegade's well-meant purpose; and he, seeing how safely he could go to Shershel and return, and anchor when, how and where he liked, and that his partner the Moor was happy to go wherever the Renegade pleased, and, now I was free, all we needed was to find some Christians to row. He told me to look out for any I would be willing to take with me, and to prepare them for the next Friday, which he decided as our departure day. I spoke to twelve Spaniards about this, all strong rowers, which were able to easily leave the city; but this was not an easy task, because there were twenty ships out on a cruise and they had taken all the rowers with them; and these would not have been found if their master had not remained at home that summer without going to sea in order to finish making a boat. To these men I said nothing more than the next Friday in the evening they were to come out secretly one by one go to Hadji Morato's garden, waiting there for me until I came. These directions I gave to each one separately, with orders that if they saw any other Christians there, they were not to say anything to them except that I had directed them to wait at that spot.

With this initially settled, another more necessary step had to be taken, which was to let Zoraida know about our plans so she could be prepared, so not to be taken by surprise if we were suddenly to approach her. I decided, therefore, to go to the garden and try to speak to her; and the day before my departure I went there under the pretence of gathering herbs. The first person I met was her father, who spoke to me in a language that is a medium between captives and

Moors, and is neither Morisco or Castilian, or from any other nation, but a mixture of all languages, so we can all understand one another. In this sort of language, he asked me what I wanted in his garden, and who I belonged to. I replied that I was a slave of Arnaut Mami (because I knew that he was a very great friend of his), and that I wanted some herbs to make a salad. He asked me whether I was free or not. While these questions and answers were continuing, Zoraida, who had already noticed me some time before, came out of the house in the garden, and as Moorish women are not bothered about letting themselves be seen by Christians, or, as I have said before, at all shy, she had no hesitation in coming to where her father stood with me; furthermore, her father, seeing her approaching slowly, told to her to come. It would be beyond my power now to describe to you the great beauty, and the brilliant attire of my much-loved Zoraida as she presented herself in front of my eyes. I will content myself with saying that more pearls hung from her neck, her ears, and her hair than she had hairs on her head. On her ankles, were anklets made from the purest gold, set with so many diamonds that she told me afterwards her father valued them at ten thousand coins, and those she had on her wrists were worth much more. The pearls were in excess and very fine, because it is the highest display and beautification of the Moorish women to decorate themselves with rich pearls. Zoraida's father had a reputation of possessing a large number of these, the purest in all Algiers, and also possessing more than two hundred thousand Spanish coins; and she, who is now lady of me only, was lady of all of this. Whether she was adorned with these or not she would have been beautiful, and what she must have been in her prosperity, can be imagined from the beauty remaining after so many hardships; because, as everyone knows, the beauty of some women has its times and seasons, and is increased or diminished by unplanned causes; and naturally the emotions of the mind will intensify or impair it, although indeed more frequently they totally destroy it. In a word she presented to me that day embellished with the highest magnificence, and supremely beautiful; at any rate, she seemed to me the most beautiful thing I had ever seen; and additionally after all I owed to her, I felt as though I had in front of me some heavenly being who had come to earth to bring me relief and happiness.

As she approached her father told her in his own language that I was a captive belonging to his friend Arnaut Mami, and that I had come for salad.

She continued the conversation, and in that mixture of language I have spoken of she asked me if I was a gentleman, and if I had purchased freedom.

I answered that I had, and from the price I deposited it could be seen what value my master has given me, one thousand five hundred coins; to which she replied, "if you had been my father's, I can tell you, I would not have let you free you for twice as much, because you Christians always tell lies about yourselves and make yourselves out to be poor to cheat the Moors."

"That might be, lady," I said; "but I was truthful with my master, as I am and intend to be with everybody in the world."

"And when do you leave?" said Zoraida.

"Next Friday," I said, "because there is a boat here from France which sails and I think I will go on board."

"Would it not be better," said Zoraida, "to wait for the arrival of ships from Spain and go with them and not with the French who are not your friends?"

"No," I said; "if a boat were coming from Spain now, it is true I might go, perhaps, wait for it; however, it is more likely I will depart next Friday, because the longing I feel to return to my country and to those I love is so great that it will not allow me to wait for another opportunity, however more convenient it may be."

"No doubt you are married in your own country," said Zoraida, "and for that reason you are anxious to go and see your wife."

"I am not married," I replied, "but I have given my promise to marry when I arrive there."

"And the lady you have promised this to, is she beautiful?" said Zoraida.

"So beautiful," I said, "that, to describe her respectably and to tell you the truth, she is very much like you."

Her father laughed very enthusiastically and said, "By Allah, Christian, she must be very beautiful if she is like my daughter, who is the most beautiful woman in this whole Kingdom: look at her well and you will see I am telling the truth."

Zoraida's father as the better linguist helped to interpret most of these words and phrases, because although she spoke the bastard language, that, as I have said, is used there, she expressed her meaning more by signs than by words.

While we were still engaged in this conversation, a Moor came running up, exclaiming that four Turks had leapt over the fence or wall of the garden, and were gathering the fruit although it was not yet ripe. The old man was alarmed and Zoraida as well, because the Moors commonly, and, so to speak, instinctively fear the Turks, but particularly the soldiers, who are so disrespectful and domineering to the Moors who are under their power that they treat them worse than if they were their slaves. Her father said to Zoraida, "Daughter, go into the house and shut yourself in while I go and speak to these dogs; and you, Christian, pick your herbs, and go in peace, and I ask Allah to take you safely to your own country."

I bowed, and he went away to look for the Turks, leaving me alone with Zoraida, who acted as if she were about to go as her father had asked her to; but the moment he was obscured by the trees of the garden, turning to me with her eyes full of tears she said, "Tameji, cristiano, tameji?" that is to say, "Are you going, Christian, are you going?"

I answered, "Yes, lady, but not without you, whatever happens let it happen: watch for me, and do not be distressed when you see us; because I promise we will go to the land of the Christians."

This I said in such a way that she understood everything perfectly, and throwing her arm around my neck she began with delicate steps to move towards the house; but as fate decided (and it might have been very unfortunate if Heaven had not ordered it otherwise), just as we were moving in the manner and position I have described, with her arm around my neck, her father, as he returned after having sent away the Turks, saw how we were walking and we noticed that he saw us; but Zoraida, ready and quick-witted, did not remove her arm from my neck, but actually pulled closer to me and placed her head on my chest, bending her knees a little and showing the signs of someone fainting, while I at the same time made it seem as though I were supporting her against my will. Her father came running up to where we were, and seeing his daughter in this state asked what was the matter with her; she, however, giving no answer, he said, "No doubt she has fainted in panic over the entrance of those dogs," and taking her from my chest he drew her to his own, while she breathing, her eyes still wet with tears, said again, "Ameji, cristiano, ameji" - "Go, Christian, go." To this her father replied, "There is no need, daughter, for the Christian to go, because he has done no harm to you, and the Turks have now gone; do not panic, there is nothing to hurt you, because as I say, the Turks have gone back the way they came."

"They terrified her, as you have said, señor," I said to her father; "but since she asks me to go, I have no wish to displease her: peace be with you, and with your permission I will come back to this garden for herbs if necessary, because my master says there is nowhere better for herbs and salad than here."

"Come back for any you need," replied Hadji Morato; "because my daughter does not say this because she is displeased with you or any Christian: she only meant that the Turks should go away, not you; or that you should go and look for your herbs."

After this, I immediately left both of them; and she, looking as though her heart were breaking, went with her father. And so, while pretending to look for herbs I walked around the garden at ease, and studied carefully all the entry points and passages, and the doors of the house and everything that could be taken advantage of to make our task easy.

Having done so I went and gave an account of all that had taken place to the renegade and my companions, and looked forward with impatience to the hour when, all fear aside, I would find myself in possession of the prize which fortune granted me: the lovely Zoraida. The time passed slowly, however the appointed day we awaited arrived; and, all following the arrangement and plan which, after careful consideration and many long discussions, we had decided on, we succeeded as fully as we could have wished; because on the Friday following the day which I spoke to Zoraida in the garden, the renegade anchored his boat at night almost opposite the spot where she was. The Christians who were to row were ready and hiding in different places, all waiting for me, anxious and excited, and eager to row the boat they had in front of their eyes; because they did not know the renegade's plan, but expected that they were going to gain their freedom by a fight and killing the Moors who were on board the boat. As soon as I and my companions made our appearance, all those that were hiding, seeing us, came and joined us. It was now the time when the city gates are shut, and there was no one to be seen anywhere outside. When we were collected together we debated whether it would be better first to go for Zoraida, or to make the Moorish rowers prisoners; but while we were uncertain our renegade came asking us why we were taking so long, as it was now the time, and all the Moors were off guard and most of them asleep. We told him why we hesitated, but he said it was more important first to secure the boat, which could be done with the great ease and without any danger, and then we could go for Zoraida. We all approved of what he said, and so without further delay, guided by him we went to the boat, and he jumping on board first, raised his sword and said in Morisco, "no one move unless you want to lose your life." By this time all the Christians were on board, and the Moors, who were timid, hearing their captain speak in this way, were intimidated, and without any of them raising a sword (and truly they had hardly any) they submitted without saying a word to be bound by the Christians, who quickly secured them, threatening them that if they raised any kind of commotion they would all face the sword. This having been accomplished, and half of our group being left to keep watch over them, the rest of us, again taking the renegade as our guide, rushed towards Hadji Morato's garden, and as good luck had it, when pushing the gate, it opened as easily as if it had not been locked; and so, quite quietly and in silence, we reached the house without being noticed by anyone. The lovely Zoraida was watching out for us at a window, and as soon as she saw that there were people there, she asked in a quiet voice if we were "Nizarani," which meant to ask if we were Christians. I answered that we were, and requested her to come down. As soon as she recognised me she did not delay, and without answering a word she came down immediately, opened the door and presented herself to us all, so beautiful and so richly adorned that I cannot attempt to describe her beauty. The moment I saw her I took her hand and kissed it, and the renegade and my two companions did the same; and the rest, who knew nothing about the circumstances, did what they saw us do, because it only seemed as if we were returning thanks to her, and recognising her as the giver of our freedom. The renegade asked her in Morisco language if her father was in the house. She replied that he was and that he was asleep.

"Then it will be necessary to wake him and take him with us," said the renegade, "and everything with value in this mansion."

"No," she said, "my father should not for any reason be touched, and there is nothing in the house except what I will take, and that will be enough to enrich and satisfy all of you; wait a little and you will see," and so she went in, telling us she would return immediately and asking us stay quiet.

I asked the renegade what had happened between them, and when he told me, I announced that nothing should be done except what was in accordance with the wishes of Zoraida, who now came back with a box so full of gold coins that she could barely carry it. Unfortunately her father woke while this was going on, and hearing a noise in the garden, came to the window, and saw that all those who were there, were Christians, raising an enormously loud shout, he began to call out in Arabic, "Christians, Christians! thieves, thieves!" hearing this we were all placed into the greatest fear and embarrassment; but the renegade seeing the danger we were in and how important it was for him to carry out his purpose before we were heard, went swiftly to where Hadji Morato was, and with him some of our group went; I, however, did not dare to leave Zoraida, who had fallen almost fainting in my arms. To be brief, those who had gone upstairs acted so promptly that in an instant they came down, carrying Hadji Morato with his hands tied and a cloth secured over his mouth, which prevented him from saying a word, warning him at the same time that attempting to speak would cost him his life. When his daughter saw him she covered her eyes, and her father was struck with fear, not knowing how willingly she had placed herself into our hands. But it was now essential for us to move quickly and carefully to the boat, where those who had remained on board were waiting for us in anxiety of some misfortune which had happened to us. It was barely two hours after nightfall when we were all on board the boat, where the cords were removed from the hands of Zoraida's father, and the cloth from his mouth; but the renegade told him again not to say a word, or they would take his life. He, when he saw his daughter there, began to sigh, and even more when he saw that I held her closely and that she lay quiet without resisting or complaining, or showing any reluctance; nevertheless, he remained silent fearing we would put into effect the repeated threats the renegade had given him.

Finding herself now on board, and that we were about to depart, Zoraida, seeing her father there, and the other Moors tied, asked the renegade to ask me to do her the favour of releasing the Moors and letting her father free, because she would rather drown herself in the sea, than see a father that had loved her so dearly be carried away as captive before her eyes due to her. The renegade repeated this to me, and I replied that I was very willing to do so; but he replied that it was not advisable, because if they were left there they would alert the all in the city, and this would lead to the despatch of swift cruisers in pursuit of us, by sea or land, without any possibility of escape; and all we could do was to set them free on the first Christian ground we reached. On this point we all agreed; and Zoraida, who it was explained to, together with the reasons that prevented us from doing immediately what she desired, was satisfied as well; and then in happy silence and with cheerful eagerness each of our rowers took his oar, and thanking God with all our hearts, we began to head to the island of Majorca, the nearest Christian land. However, due to the sea growing a little rough, it was impossible for us to keep a straight direction to Majorca, and we were forced to drift in the direction of Oran, with uneasiness fearing we would be observed from the town of Shershel, which lies on that coast, not more than sixty miles from Algiers. Moreover, we were afraid of meeting on that course one of the ships that usually come with goods from Tetuan; although we felt confident that, if we were to meet a merchant ship, as it is better than a cruiser, we should take the ship with which we could more safely accomplish our voyage. As we pursued our course Zoraida kept her head between my hands so she could not see her father, and I felt that she was praying to Lela Marien to help us.

We might have gone about thirty miles when daylight found us close to land, which seemed to us deserted, and without anyone to see us. For all that, however, by hard rowing we were now a little further out to sea, because it was somewhat calmer, and having gained about two miles we decided to take turns to row, while we ate something, because the boat was well supplied; but the rowers said it was not a time to take any rest; let the food be served to those who were not rowing, and they would not leave their oars for any reason yet. This was done, but now a strong breeze began to blow, which forced us not to row and use the sail to steer for Oran, as it was impossible to go in any other direction. All this was done very promptly, and with the sails we went more than eight miles an hour without any fear, except coming across some ship out on a returning expedition. We gave the Moorish rowers some food, and the renegade comforted them by telling them that they were not held as captives, and we would set them free on the first opportunity.

The same was said to Zoraida's father, who replied, "Anything else, Christian, that I should hope for or think likely from your generosity and good behaviour, but do not think I am so simple as to imagine you will give me my freedom; because you would have never exposed yourselves to the danger of depriving me of it only to restore it to me so generously, especially as you know who I am. Name the sum you require to grant my freedom, I offer you everything you require for myself and for my unhappy daughter there; or for her alone, as she is the greatest and most precious part of my soul."

As he said this he began to cry so intensely that he filled us all with compassion and forced Zoraida to look at him, and when she saw him crying she was so moved that she left me and ran to throw her arms round him, and pressing her face to his, they both gave such an outburst of tears that several of us were forced to do the same.

But when her father saw her in full dress and with all her jewels, he said to her in his own language, "What is this, my daughter? Last night, before this terrible misfortune in which has happened to us, I saw you in your everyday and indoor clothing; and now, without having had much time to dress like this, and without me giving you any joyful occasion for adorning yourself, I see you dressed in the finest it would be in my power to give you when fortune was most kind to us. Answer me this; because it causes me greater anxiety and surprise than even this misfortune itself."

The renegade interpreted to us what the Moor said to his daughter; she, however, gave him no answer. But when he observed in one corner of the boat the box in which she used to keep her jewels, which he well knew he had left in Algiers and had not brought into the garden, he was even more amazed, and asked her how that box came into our hands, and what was inside it. To which the renegade, without waiting for Zoraida to reply, answered, "Do not worry yourself by asking your daughter Zoraida so many questions, señor, because the one answer I will give you will answer them all; you should know that she is a Christian, and she has been the key for our locks and gave us our freedom from captivity. She is here by her own free will, as glad, I imagine, to find herself in this position as one who escapes from darkness into the light, from death to life, and from suffering to glory."

"Daughter, is this true?" cried the Moor.

"It is," replied Zoraida.

"That you are truthfully a Christian," said the old man, "and that you have given your father into the power of his enemies?"

To which Zoraida answered, "A Christian I am, but I have not placed you in this position, because it never was my wish to leave you or do you any harm, only to do good to myself."

"And what good have you done to yourself, daughter?" he said.

"Ask," she said, "Lela Marien, because she can tell you better than I."

The Moor had hardly heard these words when with marvellous speed he ran and threw himself headfirst into the sea, where surely he would have drowned had the long clothing he wore not held him up for a little on the surface of the water. Zoraida cried aloud to us to save him, and we all rushed to help, and grabbing him by his robe we pulled him in half drowned and unconscious, at which Zoraida was in such distress that she cried next to him as severely as if he had died. We turned him face down and he threw up a great quantity of water, and after two hours he came to himself. Meanwhile, the wind had changed and we were being forced to head for the land, so we worked our oars to avoid being driven to the shore; but it was good fortune for us to reach a stream that was on one side of a small cliff, called the "Cava rumia," by the Moors which in our language means "the wicked Christian woman;" because it is believed among them that La Cava, through whom Spain was lost, that buried there on that spot is; "cava" in their language meaning "wicked woman," and "rumia" "Christian;" moreover, they consider it unlucky to anchor the boat there when they are compelled to, and they would never do so otherwise. For us, however, it was not the resting-place of a wicked woman but a sanctuary of safety for our relief. We placed a look-out on shore, and never let the oars out of our hands, and ate from the supplies the renegade had stored on board, asking God and Our Lady with all our hearts to help and protect us, so we could have a happy ending to a beginning so prosperous. At the request of Zoraida orders were given to free her father and the other Moors on the shore, who were still bound, because she could not endure, nor could her sensitive heart bear to see her father restrained and her fellow-countrymen prisoners. We promised her we would do this when we were about to depart, because as it was uninhabited we had no risk to release them there.

Our prayers were successful and must have been heard by Heaven, because after a while the wind changed in our favour, and made the sea calm, inviting us once more to resume our voyage with a good heart. Seeing this we untied the Moors, and one by one put them on the shore, at which they were filled with amazement; but when we came to free Zoraida's father, who had now completely recovered his senses, he said:

"Why is it, you Christians think, that this wicked woman is delighted that you give me freedom? You think it is because of the affection she has for me? No, it is only because of the hindrance my presence offers to the execution of her dishonourable plans. And do not think that it is the belief that yours is better than ours that has led her to change her religion; it is only because she knows that immodesty is more freely practised in your country than in ours." Then turning to Zoraida, while I and another Christian held him by the arms, in case he would do some mad act, he said to her, "Shameful girl, misguided lady, it is in your blindness and madness that you are going into the hands of these dogs, our natural enemies. I regret the hour when I made you! I regret the luxury and indulgence in which I raised you!"

But seeing that he was not likely to stop any time soon I quickly put him on shore, and from there he continued his speech and cries aloud; calling for Mohammed any praying to Allah to destroy us, to confuse us, to make us lost; and so, in consequence when we had started to sail, we could no longer hear what he said but we could see what he did; how he pulled out his beard and tore his hair and lay squirming on the ground. But once he raised his voice to such a pitch that we were able to hear what he said. "Come back, dear daughter, come back; I forgive you; let those men have the money, because it is theirs now, and come back to comfort your poor father, who will lose his life on this barren land if you leave him."

Zoraida heard this, and with sorrow and tears, all she could say in reply was, "God grant that Lela Marien, who has made me become a Christian, give comfort to my father. God knows that I could not do anything other than what I have done, and that these Christians acted in my will; because even if I had not wished to go with them, and remain at home, it would have been impossible for me to stay, as my soul so eagerly urged me to the accomplishment of this purpose, which I feel to be as righteous as to you, my dear father, it seems wicked."

But her father could not hear her and we could not see him when she said this; and so, while I comforted Zoraida, we turned our attention to our voyage, in which a breeze from the right point favoured us and would make sure we found the coast of Spain the next morning at sunrise. But, as good rarely or never comes pure and unmixed, without being attended or followed by some disturbing evil that gives a shock to it, our fortune, or perhaps the curses which the Moor had given his daughter (because whatever kind of father they come from these are always to be feared), brought it about that when we were now in mid-sea, and it was about three in the morning, as we were sailing and had the oars up, because the favouring breeze saved us the trouble of using them, we saw in the moonlight, which shone brilliantly, a square boat sailing close to us, steering in our direction, and so close that we had to steer hard to avoid hitting it. They came to the side of the ship to ask who we were, where we were going, and where we came from, but as they asked this in French our renegade said, "no one answer, no doubt these are French pirates who attack all who pass by."

Acting on this warning no one said a word, and after we had gone a little further, suddenly they fired two gun shots, one of which cut our mast in half which made it and the sail fall into the sea, and the other, at the same moment, broke through the middle of our boat, but without doing any further damage. We, however, finding ourselves sinking began to shout for help and calling for those in the ship to pick us up as we were beginning to go down. They then lowered a small rowing boat, and as many as a dozen Frenchmen, well-armed, got into it and came alongside; and seeing how few there were of us, and that our boat was sinking, they took us in, telling us that this had happened due to our rudeness in not giving them an answer. Our renegade took the box containing Zoraida's wealth and dropped it into the sea without anyone observing what he did. In short we went on board with the Frenchmen, who, after having established all they wanted to know about us, stole from us everything we had, as if they had been our worst enemies, and from Zoraida they even took the anklets she wore around her feet; but the distress they caused her did not distress me as much as the fear I was in, that from robbing her of her rich and precious jewels they might proceed to rob her of the most precious jewel that she valued more than all. However, the desires of those people did not go beyond money, but their greed was insatiable, and on this occasion it was to the extent that they would have taken even the clothes we wore as captives if they had been worth something to them. It was the advice from some of them to throw all of us into the sea wrapped up in a sail; because their purpose was to trade at some of the ports of Spain, and if they brought us alive they would be punished as soon as the robbery was discovered; but the captain (who was the one who had robbed from my treasured Zoraida) said he was satisfied with the prize he had taken, and that there was now no need to go to any Spanish port, his plan now was to pass Gibraltar during night, or as best he could, and go to La Rochelle, from which he had sailed. So they agreed to give us the small rowing boat belonging to their ship as it was all we required for the short voyage that remained for us, and they did this the next day on when the Spanish coast was in sight. When seeing this, the joy we felt made us forget all of our sufferings and miseries as if they had never been endured by us, this is the delight of recovering lost freedom.

It may have been about midday when they placed us in the boat, giving us two barrels of water and some biscuits; and the captain, moved by compassion, as the lovely Zoraida was about to board, gave her forty gold coins, and would not permit his men to take from her the garments which she came with. We got into the boat, giving them thanks for their kindness, and showing our gratefulness rather than offense. They went out to sea, steering toward their destination; we, without looking at any compass except the land in front of us, set ourselves to row with so much energy that by sunset we were so near that we might easily, we thought, arrive before the night came. But as the moon did not show that night, and the sky was clouded, we did not know exactly where we were, but it seemed prudent for us to go ashore, as several of us thought, saying we should head ashore even if it were on rocks and far from any occupancy, because in this way we would be relieved from the apprehensions we naturally felt of the prowling boats of pirates, who leave their shores at night and are on the Spanish coast by day, where they commonly steal and then go home to sleep in their own houses. But out of the conflicting advice it was decided that we should approach gradually, and head where we could, if the sea were calm enough permit us. This was done, and a little before midnight we approached nearer to the base of a huge mountain, not so close to the sea but it left a narrow space on which to land conveniently. We ran our boat onto the sand, and all jumped out and kissed the ground, and with tears of joyful satisfaction gave thanks to God our Lord for all his incomparable goodness given to us on our voyage. We took out of the boat the supplies it contained, and pulled it further on the beach, and then climbed a long way up the mountain, because even there we did not feel safe in our hearts, or sure that we were now on Christian soil.

The morning came, more slowly, I think, than we could have wished; we completed the climb in order to see if from the top any shepherds' huts could be seen, but with much eye strain, no dwelling, or human being, or path or road could be seen. However, we decided to go further, as we thought it could not be long before we must see someone who could tell us where we were. But what distressed me most was to see Zoraida walking with bare foot over that rough ground; because although I carried her on my shoulders once, she was more tired by my tiredness than rested by the rest; and so she would never again allow me to endure the exertion, and continued very patiently and cheerfully, while I led her by the hand. We had gone less than a quarter of a mile when we heard the sound of a little bell, a clear sign that there were herds nearby, and looking carefully to see if any were within view, we observed a young shepherd tranquilly and unsuspiciously trimming a stick with his knife at the base of a cork tree. We called him, and he, raising his head, jumped quickly to his feet, because, as we afterwards discovered, the first he caught sight of was the renegade and Zoraida, and seeing them in Moorish clothing he imagined that all the Moors from Barbary were coming for him; and rushing with marvellous swiftness into the bush in front of him, he began to raise an extraordinary shout, exclaiming, "The Moors - the Moors have landed!" We were in confusion due to these cries, not knowing what to do; but reflecting that the shouts of the shepherd would alert the town and the mounted coast-guard would come immediately to see what was happening, we agreed that the renegade should take off his Turkish garments and put on a captive's jacket or coat which one of our group gave him immediately, although he himself was left in his shirt; and so calling for God's assistance, we followed the same road which we saw the shepherd take, expecting at every moment that the coast-guard would appear. This expectation did not deceive us, because two hours had not passed when, coming out of the woods into the open ground, we observed about fifty men mounted on horses swiftly approaching us. As soon as we saw them we stood still, waiting for them; but as they came close and, instead of the Moors they were searching for, they saw a group of poor Christians, they were surprised, and one of them asked if we were the cause of the shepherd raising the alert. I said "Yes," and as I was about to explain to him what had happened, where we came from and who we were, one of the Christians of our group recognised the horseman who had asked the question, and before I could say anything else he exclaimed:

"Thank God, sirs, for bringing us to such a good place; because, if I am not mistaken, the ground we stand on belongs to Velez Malaga unless, all my years in captivity have made me unable to recollect that you, señor, who ask who we are, are Pedro de Bustamante, my uncle."

The Christian captive had hardly said these words, when the horseman jumped off his horse, and ran to hug the young man, crying:

"Nephew of my soul and life! I recognise you now; and for a long time I have mourned as if you were dead, I, and my sister, your mother, and all your family that are still alive, and who God has been pleased to preserve so that they may enjoy the happiness of seeing you again. We knew for a long time that you were in Algiers, and from the appearance of your garments and those that accompany you, I conclude that you have had a miraculous restoration to freedom."

"It is true," replied the young man, "and soon I will tell you all."

As soon as the horsemen understood that we were Christian captives, they dismounted from their horses, and each man offered his horse to carry us to the city of Velez Malaga, which was a mile and a half away. Some of them went to take the boat to the city, after we had told them where we left it; and Zoraida was placed on the horse of the young man's uncle. The whole town came out to meet us, by this time they had heard of our arrival from one who had gone on in advance. They were not surprized to see liberated captives or captive Moors, because people on that coast were well used to seeing both one and the other; but they were surprised by the beauty of Zoraida, which was now heightened by the exertion of travelling and by the joy of finding herself on Christian soil, and relieved of all fear of being lost; because this had given her face such a bright glow, that unless my affection for her were deceiving me, I would say that there was not a more beautiful creature in the world - at least, that I had ever seen. We went straight to the church to give thanks to God for the mercies we had received, and when Zoraida entered it she said there were faces there like Lela Marien's. We told her they were her images; and as well as he could the renegade explained to her what they meant, and that she could admire them as if each of them were the very same Lela Marien that had spoken to her; and she, having great intelligence and a quick and clear instinct, understood immediately everything he said to her about them. Then they took us away and placed us all in different houses in the town; but the Christian who came with us took the renegade, Zoraida and myself to the house of his parents, who had a fair share of the gifts of fortune, and treated us with as much kindness as they did their own son.

We stayed for six days in Velez, at the end of which the renegade, having informed himself of all that was essential for him to do so, left for the city of Granada to restore himself to the sacred heart of the Church and join the Holy Inquisition. The other released captives left as well, each the way that seemed best to him, and Zoraida and I were left alone, with nothing more than the coins which the courtesy of the Frenchman had given Zoraida, out of which I bought the horse she rides; and, I for the present looking after her like her father and aide and not as her husband, we are now going to find out if my father is living, or if any of my brothers has had better fortune than me; although, as Heaven has made me the companion of Zoraida, I think that no other life could be assigned to me, however happy, that I would rather have. The patience with which she endures the hardships that poverty brings, and the eagerness she shows to become a Christian, are so great that they fill me with admiration, and bind me to serve her for my whole life; although the happiness I feel in seeing myself as hers, and her as mine, is disturbed by not knowing if I will find a place to shelter her in my own country, or whether time and death may have made changes in the fortunes and lives of my father and brothers, that I will find barely anyone who knows me, if they are not alive.

I have no more of my story to tell you, gentlemen; whether it has been an interesting or a curious one let your judgment decide; all I can say is I would have gladly told it to you more briefly; although my fear of tiring you has made me leave out more than one circumstance.

CHAPTER 42

MORE THAT TOOK PLACE AT THE INN, AND SEVERAL OTHER THINGS WORTH KNOWING

After these words the captive was silent, and Don Fernando said to him, "In truth, captain, the manner in which you have told us of this remarkable adventure has been well structured to suit the novelty and strangeness of the situation. The whole story is interesting and uncommon, and contains incidents that fill the hearers with wonder and astonishment; and the pleasure we have found in listening to it has been so great that we would be glad if you began saying it again, even if it took all of tomorrow to tell us the same story." And while he said this Cardenio and the rest of them offered to serve to him in any way that they could, and in words and language so kind and sincere that the captive was very gratified by their good-will. In particular Don Fernando offered, if he would go back with him, to get his brother to become the godfather at the baptism of Zoraida, and he would provide him with the means to make his appearance in his own country with the credit and comfort he was entitled to. For all of this the captive gave thanks very politely, although he would not accept any of their generous offers.

By this time night had come, and as it did, approaching the inn there came a coach attended by some men on horseback, who demanded accommodation; to which the landlady replied that there was not a room in of the whole inn unoccupied.

"Still, despite all of that," said one of the men who had approached on horseback, "a room must be found for the lord Judge here."

Hearing this name, the landlady was surprised, and said, "Señor, the fact is I have no beds; but if the Lord Judge carries one with him, as no doubt he does, let him come in and be welcomed; because my husband and I will give up our room to accommodate him."

"Very good, so be it," said the aide; but in the meantime a man had got out of the coach whose clothing indicated at a glance the office and position he held, because the long robe with ruffled sleeves that he wore showed that he was, as his servant said, a Judge of high rank. He led by the hand a young girl in travel clothing, apparently about sixteen years of age, so beautiful and so graceful, that all were filled with admiration when she made her appearance, and had they not seen Dorothea, Luscinda, and Zoraida, who were there in the inn, they would have thought that a beauty like her would have been hard to find. Don Quixote was present during the entrance of the Judge with the young lady, and as soon as he saw him him said, "You Lord may enter and take your comfort in this castle with confidence; because although the accommodation is poor, there are no rooms so cramped or inconvenient that they cannot make room for arms and letters; above all if arms and letters have beauty as a guide and leader, as letters represented by you Lord have in this fair lady, to who not only should castles throw themselves open and yield themselves, but rocks should split themselves apart and mountains divide and bow themselves to give her a warm reception. Enter, you Lord, I say, into this paradise, because here you will find stars and suns to accompany the heaven you bring with you, here you will find arms in their supreme excellence, and beauty in its highest magnificence."

The Judge was struck with amazement by the language of Don Quixote, whom he scrutinized very carefully, no less astonished by his figure than by his speech; and before he could find the words to answer him he had a fresh surprise, when he saw opposite to him Luscinda, Dorothea, and Zoraida, who, having heard of the new guest and the beauty of the young lady, had come to him and to welcome her; Don Fernando, Cardenio, and the Vicar, however, greeted him in a more comprehensible and polished style. In short, the Judge made his entrance in a state of perplexity, with what he saw and with what he heard, and the ladies of the inn gave the fair lady a pleasant welcome. On the whole he could distinguish that all who were there were people of high quality; but with the figure, face, and manner of Don Quixote he was completely puzzled; and all respect having been exchanged, and the accommodation of the inn looked into, it was settled, as it had been settled before, that all the women would go to the loft that has already been mentioned, and the men would remain outside as if to guard them; the Judge, therefore, was pleased to allow his daughter to go with the ladies, which she did very willingly; and with part of the host's narrow bed and half of what the Judge had brought with him, they made a more comfortable arrangement for the night than they had expected.

The captive, whose heart had leaped within him the instant he saw the Judge, telling him somehow that this was his brother, asked one of the servants who accompanied him what his name was, and whether he knew from what part of the country he came from. The servant replied that he was called the certified Juan Perez de Viedma, and that he had heard that he came from a village in the mountains of Leon. From this statement, and what he himself had seen, he felt convinced that this was his brother who had adopted letters by his father's advice; and excited and delighted, he called Don Fernando, Cardenio and the Vicar aside, and told them what had happened, assuring them that the judge was his brother. The servant had given further information that he was now going to south America being appointed the Judge of the Supreme Court of Mexico; and he had discovered, as well, that the young lady was his daughter, whose mother had died while giving birth to her, and that he was very rich as a consequence of the money left to him with the daughter. He asked their advice about how he should reveal himself to his brother, or to ascertain beforehand whether, when he had made himself known, his brother, seeing him so poor, would be ashamed of him, or would welcome him with a warm heart.

"Leave it to me to find that out," said the vicar; "although señor captive, there is no reason to suppose, that you will not be kindly welcomed, because the worth and wisdom that your brother's manner shows him to possess does not make it likely that he will be insensible, or that he will not know how to assign the accidents of fortune their appropriate value."

"Still," said the captive, "I will not make myself known suddenly, but in an indirect way."

"I have told you already," said the vicar, "that I will manage it in a way to satisfy us all."

By this time dinner was ready, and they all took their seats at the table, except the captive, and the ladies, who had dinner by themselves in their own room.

During dinner the vicar said, "I had a friend of yours, Señor Judge, in Istanbul, where I was a captive for several years, and that same friend was one of the bravest soldiers and captains in the whole Spanish infantry; but he had as much misfortune as he had bravery and courage."

"And what was the captain's name, señor?" asked the Judge.

"He was called Ruy Perez de Viedma," replied the vicar, "and he was born in a village in the mountains of Leon; and he mentioned a circumstance connected with his father and his brothers which, had it not been told to me by such a truthful man as he was, I would have considered it as one of those stories the old women tell each other over the fire in winter; because he said that his father had divided his property among his three sons and had given greater words of advice to them than any of Cato's. But I can say this much, that the choice he made of going to the wars came with great success, that by his brave conduct and courage, and without any help except his own merit, he grew in a few years to be captain of the infantry, and to see himself in the position to be given the command of the soldiers very quickly; but Fortune was against him, because where he expected its favour he lost it, and with it his freedom, on that magnificent day when so many recovered theirs, at the battle of Lepanto. I lost mine at the Port of Tunis, and after a variety of adventures we found ourselves as friends in Istanbul. From there he went to Algiers, where he had one of the most extraordinary adventures to ever occur to anyone in the world."

Here the vicar went on to briefly say his brother's adventure with Zoraida; to which the Judge listened to attentively as if he had never listened to anyone before. The vicar, however, only went as far as to describe how the Frenchmen stole from those who were in the boat, and the poverty and distress in which his friend and the Moor were left, and he said that he had not been able to find out what happened to them after, or whether they had reached Spain, or had been taken to France by the Frenchmen.

The captive, standing a little to one side, was listening to everything the vicar said, and watching every movement of his brother, who, as soon as he noticed the vicar had finished his story, gave a deep sigh and said with his eyes full of tears, "Oh, señor, if you only knew the news you have given me and how it arrives to me, making me show how I feel with these tears that spring from my eyes irrespective of all my worldly wisdom and self-restraint! That brave captain that you speak about is my eldest brother, who, being of a braver and grander mind than my other brother or myself, chose the honourable and worthy calling of arms, which was one of the three careers our father proposed to us, as your friend mentioned in that story he was telling you. I followed the path of letters, in which God and my own exertions have raised me to the position in which you see me. My second brother is in Peru, so wealthy that with what he has sent to my father and to me he has fully repaid the portion he took with him, and has even given my father the means of gratifying his natural generosity, while I too have been enabled to pursue my studies in a more appropriate and creditable manner, which enabled me to attain my present position. My father is still alive, although dying with anxiety to hear about his eldest son, and he prays to God endlessly that death will not close his eyes until he has seen those of his son; but in regards to him what surprises me is, that having so much common sense as he had, he should not have neglected to give any intelligence about himself, either about his trouble and suffering, or his prosperity, because if his father or any of us had known about his condition he would not have needed to wait for that miracle of the stick to obtain his freedom; but what disturbs me now is the uncertainty whether those Frenchmen have restored his freedom, or murdered him to hide the robbery. All this will make me continue my journey, not with the satisfaction in which I began, but with the deepest depression and sadness. Oh dear brother! If I only knew where you are now, I would rush to find you and free you from your suffering, even if it caused me to suffer myself! Oh if I could bring the news to our old father that you are alive, even if you were in the deepest prison in North Africa; because his wealth, my brother's and mine would rescue you! Oh beautiful and generous Zoraida, I would repay you for your goodness to my brother! I would be present at the new birth of your soul, and at your wedding which would give us all so much happiness!"

This and more the Judge said with such deep emotion from the news he had received about his brother that everyone who heard him shared in it, showing their sympathy with his sorrow. The vicar, seeing then, how well he had succeeded in carrying out his purpose and the captive's wishes, had no desire to keep them unhappy any longer, so he rose from the table and going into the room where Zoraida was he took her by the hand, with Luscinda, Dorothea, and the Judge's daughter following her. The captive was waiting to see what the vicar would do. The vicar, returned with them to where the Judge and the other gentlemen were and said, "Let your tears stop flowing, Señor Judge, and the wish of your heart gratified as fully as you could desire, because you have in front of you your admirable brother and your amazing sister-in-law. He, you see here is the Captain Viedma, and this is the fair lady who has been so good to him. The Frenchmen I told you about has brought them to the state of poverty that you see, I hope you will show them the generosity of your kind heart."

The captive ran to embrace his brother, who placed both hands on his chest to have a good look at him, holding him a little, but as soon as he had fully recognised him he clasped him in his arms so closely, shedding so many tears of heartfelt joy, that most of those present could not help but join them. The words the brothers exchanged, the emotion they showed can barely be imagined, I believe, much more than what has been put down in writing. They told each other in a few words about the events of their lives; they showed the true affection of brothers in its strength; then the judge embraced Zoraida, offering her all he possessed; then he made his daughter embrace her, and the Christian and the lovely Moor drew fresh tears from every eye. And there was Don Quixote observing all these strange events attentively without saying a word, and attributing the whole situation to the illusions of Knighthood. Then they agreed that the captive and Zoraida would return with his brother to Seville, and send news to his father about him having been freed and found, to enable him to come and be present at the marriage and baptism of Zoraida, because it was impossible for the Judge to stop his journey, as he was informed that in a month from that time the boat was going to sail from Cadiz to Mexico, and to miss the boat would have been a great inconvenience to him. In short, everybody was well pleased and glad about the captive's good fortune; and as now almost two-thirds of the night had past, they decided to rest for the remainder of it. Don Quixote offered to guard the castle in case they would be attacked by some giant or other evil character, envious of the great treasure of beauty the castle contained. Those who understood him thanked him for this service, and they gave the Judge an account of his bizarre madness, which he was not pleased by. Sancho Panza alone was angered by the lateness of the hour for going to bed; and he out of all was the one that made himself most comfortable, as he stretched himself out on the trimmings which he carried on his donkey, which, as will be told later, cost him dearly.

The ladies, then, having gone to their room, and the others having removed as much discomfort as they could, Don Quixote went out to act as guard of the castle as he had promised. It happened, however, that a little before sunrise a voice so musical and sweet reached the ears of the ladies that it forced them all to listen attentively, but especially Dorothea, who had been awake, next to Dona Clara de Viedma, (as that was the Judge's daughter's name), who lay sleeping. No one could imagine who it was that sang so sweetly, and the voice was unaccompanied by any instrument. At one moment it seemed to them as if the singer were in the courtyard, at another in the stable; and as they were all attentive and wondering, Cardenio came to the door and said, "Listen, whoever is not asleep, and you will hear a donkey herder's voice that charms as it sings."

"We are listening to it already, señor," said Dorothea; after which Cardenio went away; and Dorothea, giving all her attention to it, made out the words of the song to be these:

CHAPTER 43

THE PLEASANT STORY OF A DONKEY HERDER, TOGETHER WITH OTHER STRANGE THINGS THAT HAPPENED IN THE INN

One is on the ocean for retailing,
Another on Love's deep ocean sailing;
And not knowing where the harbour is,
Only seeking a lady to make her his.

One lonely distant star
That is all I have to guide me,
A bright ball, there like a scar,
Lit, by God with a path to provide me.

Drifting since I was born,
Not knowing where it leads me;
Focused on the fuzzy paths, I am torn,
Heedless of anything else that doesn't feed me.

Over-cautious prudery,
Shyness cold and cruel,
What I need might refuse me,
When I need it most for my fuel.

My star, the goal I always have in my eyes,
You above are bright,
I'll know that death is in disguise,
When you hide it from my sight.

    The singer had not yet finished when Dorothea thought that it was not fair to let Clara miss hearing such a sweet voice, so shaking her from side to side, she woke her, saying:
    "Forgive me child, for waking you, but I did it so you can have the pleasure of hearing the best voice you will ever hear, perhaps, in your whole life."
    Clara awoke quite drowsy, and not understanding what Dorothea said, asked her what it was; she repeated what she had said, and Clara became attentive; but she had hardly heard two lines, as the singer continued, when a strange shaking came over her, as if she were suffering from a severe attack of malaria, and throwing her arms round Dorothea she said:
    "Ah, dear lady of my soul and life! Why did you wake me? The greatest kindness fortune could do for me now would be to close my eyes and ears so I never have to hear or see that unhappy musician."

"What are you talking about, child?" said Dorothea. "They say this singer is a Donkey herder!"

"Actually, he is the lord of many places," replied Clara, "and that place in my heart which he holds so firmly will never be taken from him, unless he is willing to surrender it."

Dorothea was amazed at the passionate language from the girl, because it seemed to be far beyond any experience life could offer her at such a young age, so she said to her:

"You speak in such a way that I cannot understand you, Señora Clara; explain yourself more clearly, and tell me what you are saying about hearts and places and this musician whose voice has moved you? But do not tell me anything now; I do not want to lose the pleasure I get from listening to the singer by giving my attention to your words, because I notice he is beginning to sing another song."

"Really, my God," returned Clara; and not to hear him she covered both ears with her hands, at which Dorothea was again surprised; but turning her attention to the song she found that it went like this:

Sweet Hope, please stay,
To push me onward to the goal of my intent,
Please make the way,
Without hindrance or impediment,
Have no fear,
If at each step you find death is near.

No victory,
No joy of triumph will the weak heart know,
Unhappy is he,
If good fortune does not show,
Bad soul and sense,
Becomes a slave to indolence.

If Love is theirs,
If he sold it, we must contest,
What gold compares?
On who has his stamp been pressed?
And all men know,
What cost a little, is rated low.

Love determined,
Does not know the word "impossible,"
And although the path,
Encounters endless obstacles,
There is no despair,

On earth while heaven is there.

At this point the voice stopped and Clara began to cry again, which excited Dorothea's curiosity to know what could be the cause of singing so sweet and weeping so bitter, so she asked her again what it was she was going to say before. Clara, afraid that Luscinda might hear her, put her mouth so close to Dorothea's ear that she could speak without fear of being heard by anyone else, and said:

"This singer, dear señora, is the son of a gentleman of Aragon, lord of two villages, who lives opposite my father's house in Madrid; and although my father had curtains in the windows of his house in winter, and lattice-work in summer, in some way - I do not know how - this gentleman, who was pursuing his studies, saw me, whether in church or somewhere else, I cannot tell, and, in fact, fell in love with me, and decided to let me know it from the windows of his house, with so many signs and tears that I was forced to believe him, and even to love him, without knowing what it was he wanted from me. One of the signs he used to make to me was to link one hand in the other, to show me he wished to marry me; and although I would have been glad if that could be, being alone and motherless I did not know who to open my mind to, and so I left it as it was, showing him no favour, except when my father, and his too, were away from home, to raise the curtain or the lattice a little and let him see me, which made him show such delight that he seemed as if he were going crazy. Meanwhile, when the time for my father's departure arrived, he became aware of it, but not from me, because I had never told him about it. He became sick, of sorrow I believe, and so the day we were going away I did not see him to say goodbye, even if it were only with the eyes. But after my father and I had been on the road for two days, when entering a village, I saw him at the door of an inn dressed as a donkey herder, and so well disguised, that if I did not carry his image engraved on my heart it would have been impossible for me to recognise him. But I knew him, and I was surprised, and glad; he watched me, unsuspected by my father, who he always hides himself from when he crosses my path on the road, or in inns where we stop; and, as I know who he is, and reflect that for his love of me he makes this journey on foot in all this hardship, I am ready to die of sorrow; and where he places his feet there I place my eyes. I do not know what objective he has come with; or how he could have got away from his father, who loves him beyond measure, having no other heir, and because he deserves it, as you will notice when you see him. And moreover, I can tell you, everything he sings is from of his own head; because I have heard them say he is a great intellectual and poet; and what is more, every time I see him or hear him sing I shake all over, and am terrified that my father might recognise him and finally know of our love. I have never said a word to him in my life; but for that I love him so much that I could not live without him. This, dear señora, is all I have to tell you about the musician whose voice has delighted you so much; and from it alone you might easily recognise he is no donkey herder, but a lord of hearts and towns, as I have told you already."

"Say no more, Dona Clara," said Dorothea, at the same time kissing her a thousand times, "say no more, but wait until the day comes; when I trust God will arrange this situation for you so it may have the happy ending such an innocent beginning deserves."

"Ah, señora," said Dona Clara, "what end can be hoped for when his father in such a grand position, and so wealthy, that he would think I was not fit to even be a servant of his son, much less his wife? And as for marrying without the knowledge of my father, I would not do it for the world. I would not ask anything more than that this youth go back and leave me; perhaps without seeing him, and with the long distance we have to travel, the pain I suffer now may become easier; although this remedy I guess will not do me very good. I don't know how the devil has done this, or how this love I have for him got in; I am such a young girl, and he is a young boy; I am not even seventeen yet; because I will be seventeen, next September, my father says."

Dorothea could not help laughing to hear how a child, like Dona Clara spoke. "Let us go to sleep now, señora," said she, because there is little of the night left for us: God will soon send us daylight."

With this they fell asleep, and deep silence set all through the inn. The only people not asleep were the landlady's daughter and her servant Maritornes, who, knowing the weak point of Don Quixote's humour, and that he was outside the inn guarding in armour and on horseback, decided, the pair of them, to play a trick on him, or at least to amuse themselves for a while by listening to his nonsense. As it happened there was no window in the whole inn that looked outwards except a hole in the wall of a straw-loft through which they used to throw out the straw. By this hole the two ladies posted themselves, and observed Don Quixote on his horse, leaning on his lance and from time to time making deep and miserable sighs, that he seemed to pluck up his soul by the roots with each of them; and they could hear him, too, saying in a soft, tender, loving tone, "Oh my lady Dulcinea del Toboso, perfection of all beauty, summit and crown of pleasure, treasure house of grace, depositary of virtue, and finally, image of all that is good, honourable, and charming in this world! What are you doing now? Are you, perhaps, mindful of your enslaved Knight who has of his own free will exposed himself to such great danger, and all to serve you? Give me notification! Perhaps at this moment, you are pacing to and fro in some gallery of your sumptuous palace, or leaning over some balcony, meditating how, whilst preserving your purity and greatness, you may mitigate the tortures I endure for you, the glory you can compensate for my sufferings and rest for my work, the rewards of my services? And you, oh sun, that are no doubt now rushing to surpass bedtimes and rise to see my lady; when you see her I ask you to salute her on my behalf: but have care, when you see her and salute her, that you do not kiss her face; or I will be jealous of you."

Don Quixote had got so far in his pathetic speech when the landlady's daughter began to signal to him, saying, "Señor, come over here, please."

This voice made Don Quixote turn his head to see with the light of the moon, which was in its full splendour, that someone was calling him from the hole in the wall, which seemed to him to be a window, and what is more, with a golden surrounding, as rich castles, such as he believed the inn to be, would have; and it immediately suggested itself to his imagination that, as on the former occasion, the lady, the daughter of the lady of the castle, overcome by love for him, was once more endeavouring to win his heart; and with this idea, not to show himself to be impolite, or ungrateful, he approached the hole mounted on Rocinante, and as he saw the lady, he said:

"I feel sorry for you, beautiful lady, that you have directed your thoughts of love to a place from where it is impossible that a return can be made, which is due to you for your great merit and humble birth, for which you cannot blame this Knight whom love renders incapable of submission to any other than her whom, the first moment his eyes observed her, she became the absolute mistress of his soul. Forgive me, honourable lady, and return to your apartment, and do not, by any further declaration of your passion, oblige me to show myself any more ungrateful; and if, due to the love you have for me, you can find that there is anything else in my power which I can gratify you with, provided it is not love itself, you may demand it from me; because I swear to you I will grant it this instant, even if it you required a lock of Medusa's hair from me, which was all snakes, or even the very beams of the sun trapped and contained in a bottle."

"She wants nothing like that at all, sir Knight," said Maritornes.

"What is it that she wants then, discreet lady?" replied Don Quixote.

"She would like your hand," said Maritornes, "to enable her to express over it the great passion which has brought her to this hole, risking her honour for it; because if the lord her father had heard her, the least he would do is cut off her ear."

"I would like to see him try that," said Don Quixote; "but he better beware, if he does not want to meet the most disastrous end that any father in the world ever met for having placed his hands on the kind-hearted limbs of a love-stricken daughter."

Maritornes felt sure that Don Quixote would present the hand she had asked for, and deciding what to do, she got down from the hole and went into the stable, where she took the leads of Sancho Panza's donkey, and in she quickly returned to the hole, just as Don Quixote had placed himself standing on Rocinante's saddle in order to reach the golden window where he thought the love struck lady was; and giving her his hand, he said, "Lady, take this hand, the tormentor of the evil-doers on the earth; take, I say, this hand which no other hand of a woman has ever touched, not even the one who has complete possession of my entire body. I present it to you, not so you may kiss it, but so you may observe the texture of the ligaments, the close network of the muscles, the extent and capacity of the veins, from which you may infer the strength of the arm that possesses such a hand."

"That we will see now," said Maritornes, and making a knot out of the donkey's leads, she placed it over his wrist and coming down from the hole tied the other end very firmly to the bolt of the door to the loft.

Don Quixote, feeling the roughness of the rope on his wrist, exclaimed, "You seem to be grating rather than caressing my hand; do not treat it so harshly, because it is not to blame for any offence to you, and it is not good to aim your vengeance on such a small part."

But now there was nobody to listen to these words from Don Quixote's, because as soon as Maritornes had tied his hand to the door, her and the other lady ran away, ready to die with laughter, leaving him tied in such a way that it was impossible for him to release himself.

He was, as it has been said, standing on Rocinante, with his arm through the hole and his wrist tied to the bolt of the door was in great fear and dread of being left hanging by the arm if Rocinante moved to one side or the other; so he did not dare to make the any movement, although from the patience and serene nature of Rocinante, he had a good reason to expect that he would stand without budging for a whole century. Finding himself tied then, and that the ladies had left, he began to believe that all of this was done by enchantment, as on the former occasion when in that same castle that enchanted Moor of a trader had beaten him; and he cursed himself and his sense of judgment for deciding to return to the castle again, after the experience of the first time; it being a general rule with Knights that when they have tried an adventure, and have not succeeded, it is a sign that it is not reserved for them but for others, and that they therefore should not try it again. Nevertheless, he pulled his arm to see if he could release himself, but the knot had been made so tight that all his efforts were ineffective. It is true that he pulled it gently in case Rocinante moved, but trying as he did to seat himself in the saddle, there was nothing he could do but stand up upright or pull his hand off. Then he began to wish for the sword of Amadis, as no enchantment had any power against it; then he cursed his bad luck; and the loss the world would sustain by his absence while he remained there enchanted, because he believed he was beyond all doubt; then as usual he started to think of his beloved Dulcinea del Toboso; then he called out for his aide Sancho Panza, who, in a deep sleep and stretched out, was oblivious; then he called for the sages Lirgandeo and Alquife to come to his aid; then he appealed to his good friend Urganda to assist him; and then, at last, the morning found him in such a state of desperation and bewilderment that he was raging like a bull, because he had no hope that the day would bring any relief to his suffering, which he believed would last for ever, inasmuch as he was enchanted; and he was convinced even more of this by seeing that Rocinante never moved, not a little or a lot, and he felt persuaded that he and his horse were going to remain in this state, without eating, drinking or sleeping, until the evil influence of the stars would pass, or until some another sage enchanter would disenchant him.

But he was very wrong in his conclusion, because daylight had hardly begun to appear when there came to the inn four men on horseback, well equipped, with guns across the rear of their saddles. They called out and knocked loudly on the gate of the inn, which was still shut; on seeing this, Don Quixote, even where he was, did not forget to act as guard, and said in a loud and authoritative tone, "Knights, or aides, or whatever you are, you have no right to knock on the gates of this castle; because it is clear to see that those who are within are either asleep, or are not in the habit of throwing open the fortress until the sun's rays are spread over the whole surface of the earth. Withdraw to a distance, and wait until it is broad daylight, and then we will see whether it is appropriate or not to open for you."

"What the hell, what kind of fortress or castle is this," said one of them, "to make us stand here on such a formality? If you are the innkeeper ask them to open for us; we are travellers who only want to feed our horses and continue our journey, as we are in a rush."

"Do you think, gentlemen, that I look like an innkeeper?" said Don Quixote.

"I don't know what you look like," replied the other; "but I know that you are talking nonsense when you call this inn a castle."

"A castle it is," returned Don Quixote, "actually, one of the best in this whole province, and it has within it people who have had the sceptre in the hand and the crown on the head."

"It would be better if it were the other way," said the traveller, "the sceptre on the head and the crown in the hand; but if so, maybe inside there are some thieves, with whom it is a common thing to have those crowns and sceptres you speak of; because in such a small inn as this, and where such silence is kept, I do not believe any people entitled to crowns and sceptres can have taken a room here."

"You know very little of the world," returned Don Quixote, "since you are ignorant of what commonly occurs in Knight-hood."

But the companions of the speaker, getting bored of the dialogue with Don Quixote, continued to knock with great forcefulness, so much so that they woke the host, and not only he, everybody in the inn, and he got up to ask who knocked. It happened at this moment that one of the horses of the four men who were seeking admittance went to smell Rocinante who, sad, dejected, and with floppy ears stood motionless, supporting his poor master; and as he was, after all, flesh, although looked as if he were made of wood, he could not help smelling in return the one who had come to offer him attention. But he had hardly moved at all when Don Quixote lost his balance; and slipping off the saddle, he would have fell to the ground, but was being suspended by his arm, which caused him so much agony that he believed either his wrist would be cut or his arm torn off; and he hung so close the ground that he could just about touch it with his feet, which was worse for him; because, finding how little was needed to enable him to place his feet firmly, he struggled and stretched himself as much as he could to get his toes on the floor; just like those undergoing common torture, when their arms are tied behind their back and they are lifted by them, they then aggravate their own suffering by their violent effort to stretch themselves, deceived by the hope that they can reach the ground.

CHAPTER 44

CONTINUING THE ADVENTURES OF THE INN

Don Quixote's shouting was so loud, that the landlord opening the gate of the inn in a rush, ran to see who was making such a noise, and those who were inside joined him. Maritornes, who had by now been roused by the same outcry, suspecting what it was, ran to the loft and, without anyone seeing her, untied the lead which Don Quixote was suspended by, and down he came to the ground in the sight of the landlord and the travellers, who approaching him asked what made him shout so much. Without saying a word in reply, he took the rope off his wrist, and rising to his feet jumped on Rocinante, raised his shield and his lance, and making a considerable route around the field came back speedily exclaiming:

"Whoever says that I have deserved this enchantment, provided my lady the Princess Micomicona grants me permission to do so, I say he is lying, and challenge him to one on one combat."

The newly arrived travellers were amazed by the words of Don Quixote; but the landlord removed their surprise by telling them who he was, and not to be concerned by him as he had lost his senses. They then asked the landlord if by any chance a young man of about fifteen years of age had come to that inn, one dressed like a donkey herder, and gave a description of an appearance, describing Dona Clara's lover. The landlord replied that there were so many people in the inn he had not noticed the person they were inquiring about; but one of them observing the coach in which the Judge had come, said, "No doubt he is here, because this is the coach he was following: one of us should stay at the gate, and the rest of us go inside to look for him; perhaps one of us should go round the inn, to ensure he does not escape over the wall of the yard." "So be it," said another; and while two of them went in, one remained at the gate and the other patrolled the perimeter of the inn. Observing this, the landlord was unable to guess what they were taking all these precautions for, although he understood they were looking for the young man they had asked about.

Now it was broad daylight; and for that reason, as well as in consequence of the noise Don Quixote had made, everybody was awake and up, but particularly Dona Clara and Dorothea; because although they had been able to sleep that night, the sleep was not very good, one was agitated by having her lover so near her, and the other from curiosity to see him. When Don Quixote saw that none of the four travellers took any notice of him or replied to his challenge, he was furious and ready to die with anger; and if he could have found in the laws of Knighthood that it was lawful for a Knight to undertake or engage in other matters, when he had already given his word and faith not to involve himself in any other until he had finished the one he had pledged himself to, he would have attacked all of them, and would have made them give an answer. But considering that it would not be right, to begin any new endeavour until he had restored Princess Micomicona back to her Kingdom, he was constrained and forced to wait quietly to see what would come of the investigation of those same travellers; one of whom found the youth they were looking for, asleep, without a thought of anyone looking for him, and even less finding him.

The man grabbed him by the arm, saying, "It suits you well, Señor Don Luis, to be in the clothing you wear, and the bed I find you in agrees with the luxury in which your mother raised you."

The youth rubbed his sleepy eyes and stared for a while at the man who held him, but recognising him as one of his father's servants, he was so confused that for some time he could not find a word to say in reply; while the servant went on to say, "There is nothing left now, Señor Don Luis, but to submit quietly and return home, unless it is your wish that my master, your father, should leave for the other world, because nothing else can be the consequence of the grief he has due to your absence."

"But how did my father know that I had taken this road and gone in this clothing?" said Don Luis.

"It was a student to whom you confided your intentions," answered the servant, "that disclosed them to your father, as he was touched with pity when seeing the suffering your father was in while missing you; he then sent four of his servants to look for you, and here we are, all at your service, more pleased than you can imagine that we are able to return so soon and restore you to those eyes that wish to see you again."

"That will be up to me, or as heaven decides," replied Don Luis.

"What else do you or heaven want," said the other, "except to agree to go back? Anything else is impossible."

This conversation between the two was overheard by one of the guests of the inn, and subsequently, he went to report what had happened to Don Fernando, Cardenio, and the others, who by this time had dressed themselves; and told them how the man had addressed the youth as "Don," and how he wanted him to return to his father, which the youth was unwilling to do. With this, and what they already knew about the rare voice that heaven had given him, they all felt very anxious to know more, particularly who he was, and even to help him if anyone attempted to use force against him; so they rushed to where he was, still talking and arguing with his servant.

Dorothea instantly came out of her room, followed by Dona Clara, in shock; and calling Cardenio aside, she told him in a few words the story of the musician and Dona Clara, and he at the same time told her what had happened, how his father's servants had come to search for him; but when telling her Dona Clara over-heard what he said, at which she was so distressed that if Dorothea had not rushed to support her she would have fallen to the ground.

Cardenio then asked Dorothea and Dona Clara to return to their room, as he would endeavour to make the whole situation right, and this they did as he desired. All four who had come in quest of Don Luis had now come into the inn and surrounded him, urging him to return and comfort his father immediately and without any delay. He replied that he could not under any circumstance until he had concluded some business in which his life, honour, and heart were at stake. The servants continued to encourage him, saying that they would not return without him, and that they would take him away whether he liked it or not.

"You will not do that," replied Don Luis, "unless you want to take me dead; although however you take me, I will be without life."

By this time most of those in the inn had been attracted by the dispute, but particularly Cardenio, Don Fernando, his companions, the Judge, the vicar, the barber, and Don Quixote (because now he considered it was not necessary for guarding the castle any longer). Cardenio being already familiar with the young man's story, asked the men who wanted to take him away, what objective they had in seeking to take away this youth against his will.

"Our objective," said one of the four, "is to save the life of his father, who is in danger of losing it through this gentleman's disappearance."

Don Luis exclaimed, "There is no need to make my affairs public here; I am free, and I will return if I want to; and if not, none of you should try to force me."

"Reason will force you," said the man, "and if it has no power over you, it has power over us, to make us do what we came for, and to do what is our duty."

"Let us hear what the whole situation is about," said the Judge; but the man, who knew him as a neighbour of theirs, replied, "Do you not know this gentleman, Señor Judge? He is the son of your neighbour, who has run away from his father's house in a costume so inappropriate to his rank, as you may clearly see."

The judge looked at him more carefully and recognised him, and embracing him said, "What foolishness is this, Señor Don Luis, or what could have been the cause that has induced you to come here in this way, and in this clothing which does not fit your status?"

Tears came to the eyes of the young man, and he was unable to say a word in reply to the Judge, who told the four servants not worry, because everything would be settled reasonably; and then taking Don Luis by the hand, he took him to one side and asked him why he had come there.

But while he was questioning him they heard a loud commotion coming from men at the gate of the inn, the cause of which was that two of the guests who had stayed the night there, seeing that everybody was busy finding out what the four men wanted, had conceived the idea of leaving without paying what they owed; but the landlord, who watched his own affairs more than other people's, caught them trying to go through the gate and demanded his payment, insulting them for their dishonesty with language that drove them to reply with their fists, and so they began to attack on him in such a style that the poor man was forced to shout and call for help. The landlady and her daughter could see no one more free to assist than Don Quixote, and to him the daughter said, "Sir

Knight, with the virtue God has given you, help my poor father, because two evil men are beating him to death."

To which Don Quixote very deliberately and calmly replied, "Fair lady, at present your request is untimely, because I am disallowed from involving myself in any adventure until I have concluded happily the one to which my word has been sworn; but what I can do for you is what I will now say: run and tell your father to fight as well as he can in this battle, and under no circumstance allow himself to be conquered, while I go and seek permission from the Princess Micomicona to enable me to rescue him from his distress; and if she grants it, be assured I will relieve him from it."

"Oh god," exclaimed Maritornes; "before you have got permission my master will be in the other world."

"Let me leave, señora, to obtain the permission I speak of," returned Don Quixote; "and if I get it, it will matter very little if he is in the other world; because even if he was I will give you such a revenge over those who have sent him there that you will be more than satisfied;" and without saying anything else he went and knelt in front Dorothea, requesting in a knightly and high spoken phrase to grant him the permission to assist and rescue the castellan of that castle, who now faced serious danger. The Princess granted it graciously, and he immediately, raising his shield on his arm and holding his sword, rushed to the gate of the inn, where the two guests were still giving the landlord a beating; but as soon as he reached the spot he stopped and stood still. Maritornes and the landlady asked him why he hesitated to help their master and husband.

"I hesitate," said Don Quixote, "because it is not lawful for me to raise my sword against people of an assistant's condition; call my aide Sancho for me; because this defence and vengeance is suited for him."

So as things continued at the inn-gate, where there was a very lively exchange of kicks and punches, giving such sore damage to the landlord. Maritornes, the landlady, and her daughter, were now furious when they saw the timidity of Don Quixote, and the hard treatment their master, husband and father was experiencing. But let us leave him there; because he will surely find someone to help him, and if not, let him suffer from whatever anyone attempts more than his strength allows him to do; and let us go back a bit to see what Don Luis said in reply to the Judge who we left questioning him privately about his reasons for coming to the inn and in such poor dress.

The youth, pressing his hand in a way that showed his heart was troubled with some great sorrow, and releasing a flood of tears, answered:

"Señor, I have nothing else to tell you than from the moment when, through heaven's will and us being close neighbours, I first saw Dona Clara, your daughter and my lady, from that instant I made her the owner of my will, and if yours, my true lord and father, has no objection, then today she will become my wife. Because for her I left my father's house, and for her I wear this disguise, to follow her wherever she goes, as the arrow seeks its mark or the sailor the north star. She does not know any more about my passion than what she may have learned from having sometimes seen from a distance that my eyes were filled with tears. You know already, señor, the wealth and noble birth of my parents, and that I am their sole heir; if this is a sufficient inducement for you to make me completely happy, accept me as your son; because if my father, influenced by other objectives of his own, disapproves of the happiness I have sought for myself, time has more power to alter and change things than human will."

The love-sick youth was silent, while the Judge, after hearing him, was astonished, perplexed, and surprised, by the manner and intelligence with which Don Luis had confessed the secret of his heart, and at the position in which he found himself, not knowing what action to take in a situation so sudden and unexpected. So he answered, that he should relax his mind for now, and arrange with his servants not to take him back that day, so there can be time to consider what was best for everyone involved. Don Luis kissed his hands with force, actually, bathed them with his tears, in a way that would have touched a heart of stone, not to say that of the Judge, who, as a shrewd man, had already perceived how advantageous the marriage would be to his daughter; although, if it were possible, he would have preferred that it should be with the consent of the father of Don Luis, who he knew looked for a title for his son.

By this time the guests had made peace with the landlord, because, by persuasion of Don Quixote's fair words more than by threats, they had paid him what he demanded, and the servants of Don Luis were waiting for the end of the conversation with the Judge and the decision, when the devil, who never sleeps, arranged that the barber, who Don Quixote had taken Mambrino's helmet from, and Sancho had taken the accessories of his donkey in exchange for his own, at this moment entered the inn. As Sancho led his donkey to the stable, the barber observed Sancho Panza engaged in repairing something or other on the saddle bag; and the moment he saw it he recognised it, and went to attack Sancho, exclaiming, "You, sir thief, I have caught you! Hand over my basin and my saddle bag, and all of the accessories which you have robbed me of."

Sancho, finding himself so unexpectedly assaulted, and hearing the abuse thrown at him, held the saddle with one hand, and with the other gave the barber a punch that soaked his teeth in blood. The barber, however, was not ready to relinquish the prize of regaining his saddle bag; on the contrary, he started shouting so loudly that everyone in the inn came running to know what the noise was about. "Here, in the name of the King and justice!" He shouted, "this thief wants to kill me for trying to recover stolen property."

"You lie," said Sancho, "I am no thief; it was in a fair war my master Don Quixote won these items."

Don Quixote was standing nearby at the time, highly pleased to see his aide's bravery, both offensive and defensive, and from that time onward he considered him to be a man of courage, and in his heart decided to make him a Knight when the first opportunity presented itself, feeling sure that the law of chivalry would be rightly granted to him.

During the argument, the barber said among other things, "Gentlemen, this saddle bag is mine as sure as I owe God a death, and I know it as well as if I had given birth to it, and here is my donkey in the stable; try it, and if it does not fit my donkey like a glove, call me a liar; and what is more, the same day I was robbed of these, they robbed me as well of a new brass basin, never used, that would be worth a fair amount."

Don Quixote could not stop himself from answering; and interjecting between the two, and separating them, he placed the saddle bag on the ground, for all to see it, until the truth was established, and said, "You may clearly and plainly see the error under which this man lies when he calls a basin which was, and still is, and always will be the helmet of Mambrino which I won from him in a fair war, making it my legitimate and lawful possession. I do not concern myself with the saddle bag; but on that I must tell you that my aide Sancho asked for my permission to take any possessions attached to the defeated opponent's donkey, and to transfer it to his own; I allowed him to, and he took it; so in regards to the saddle bag, I can give no explanation except the usual one, that such transformations will take place in adventures of chivalry. To confirm all of this, run, Sancho my boy, and bring the helmet which this good man calls a basin."

"Great, master," said Sancho, "if we have no other proof for our case than what you have just said, Mambrino's helmet is just a basin and this is his saddle bag."

"Do as I ask you to fool," said Don Quixote; "not everything in this castle can be enchanted."

Sancho rushed to where the basin was, and brought it back with him, and when Don Quixote saw it, he held it and said:

"As you may see that this man here says that this is a basin and not the helmet I told you about; and I swear under the law of chivalry, that this helmet is the exact same one I took from him, without anything added to or taken away from it."

"There is no doubt of that," said Sancho, "because from the time my master won it until now he has only fought one battle in it, when he let loose those unlucky men in chains; and without this basin-helmet he would not have come away from that adventure very well, as there was plenty of stone-throwing during that affair."

CHAPTER 45

THE DOUBTFUL QUESTION OF MAMBRINO'S HELMET AND THE SADDLE-BAG IS FINALLY SETTLED, WITH OTHER ADVENTURES THAT OCCURRED

"What do you think now, gentlemen," said the barber, "about what these men say, when they want to make out that this is a helmet?"

"And whoever says the opposite," said Don Quixote, "I will let him know that if he is a Knight, he lies, and if he is an aide, that he lies a thousand times."

Our own barber, who was present during this, and understood Don Quixote's madness, decided to back up his delusion and carry on the joke for general amusement; so he said to the other barber:

"Señor barber, or whatever you are, you should know that I am also a barber, and have had a licence to practise for more than twenty years, and I know the barbers equipment, every piece, very well; and I was also a soldier for some time in my youth, and I also know what a helmet is, and other equipment required for soldiers; and I say, in my opinion, that this piece we all see, which this worthy gentleman has in his hands, is no barber's basin, and is as far from being one as white is from black, and true from false; I say, moreover, that this, although it is a helmet, is not a complete helmet."

"Certainly not," said Don Quixote, "half of it is missing."

"Quite true," said the vicar, who perceived the objective of his friend the barber; and Cardenio, Don Fernando and his companions agreed with him; and the Judge, if his thoughts had not been occupied with Don Luis and his daughter, would have helped with the joke; but he was so taken with the serious issue he had on his mind that he paid little or no attention to these unimportant matters.

"God bless me!" exclaimed the barber; "is it really possible that such an honourable bunch of people can say that this is a helmet and not a basin? This is something that would astonish a whole university! If this basin is a helmet, then the saddle-bag must be an embroidered horse cover."

"To me it looks like a saddle-bag," said Don Quixote; "but I have already said that I do not concern myself with that."

"Saddle bag or horse's cover," said the vicar, "it is for Señor Don Quixote to decide; because in these matters of chivalry I bow to his authority."

"Good God, gentlemen," said Don Quixote, "so many strange things have happened to me in this castle on both occasions I have stayed in it, that I will no longer say anything positive in reply to any question related to this place; because it is my belief that everything that happens here is created by enchantment. The first time, an enchanted Moor gave me a lot of trouble, and neither did Sancho do very well here; and last night I was kept hanging by my arm for nearly two hours, without knowing how or why it happened. So now, for me to give an opinion on such a confusing matter, would be a rash decision. In regards to the assertion that this is a basin and not a helmet I have already given an answer; but whether this is a saddle-bag or a horse's cover I cannot give a positive opinion, and will leave it to your better judgment. Perhaps as you are not Knights like myself, the enchantments of this place have nothing to do with you, and your faculties are unrestricted, and you can see things in this castle as they really and truly are, and not as they appear to me."

"There is no doubt," said Don Fernando, "that Señor Don Quixote has spoken very wisely, and that the decision of this matter relies on us; and we may have better ground to stand on, I will take the votes of everyone in secret, and then declare the result clearly and fully."

To those who knew the secret of Don Quixote's madness, all of this gave great amusement; but to those who knew nothing about it, it seemed to be the greatest nonsense in the world, in particular to the four servants of Don Luis, as well as to Don Luis himself, and to three other travellers who had come to the inn by chance, and had the appearance of officers of the Holy Brotherhood, as indeed they were; but the one who above all was completely mystified, was the barber whose basin, there in front of his eyes, had been turned into Mambrino's helmet, and whose saddle-bag was about to become a rich horse's cover. Everyone laughed to see Don Fernando going from one to another collecting the votes, and whispering to them to give him their private opinion whether the treasure over which there had been so much fighting was a saddle-bag or a horse's cover; but after he had taken the votes of those who knew Don Quixote, he said out loud, "The fact is, I am tired of collecting such a large number of opinions, because I find that there no one out of those I ask, who does not tell me that it is absurd to say that this is a saddle-bag and not a horse's cover; so you must accept, because, although you claim it to be a saddle-bag, this is a horse's cover, and you have stated and proved your case very badly."

"God and heaven," said the poor barber, "if you are not all mistaken; may my soul appear in front of God as I see myself, the same way I see a saddle-bag and not a horse's cover; I will say no more; I am not drunk, because I am fasting, except perhaps from sin."

The simple talk of the barber gave as much amusement to all, as the absurdities of Don Quixote, who now said:

"There is nothing left to be done now than for each to take what belongs to him, and who God has given it to."

One of the four servants then said, "Unless this is a deliberate joke, I cannot bring myself to believe that men so intelligent as those present are, or seem to be, can declare and assert that this is not a basin, and that is not a saddle-bag; but as I can see they do assert and declare it, I can only come to the conclusion that there is some mystery in this persistence which is so opposed to the evidence of experience and truth itself; because I swear" - and here he made an oath - "all the people in the world will not make me believe that this is not a barber's basin and that is not a saddle-bag."

On hearing this one of the newly arrived officers of the Holy Brotherhood, who had been listening to the dispute and controversy, unable to restrain his anger and impatience, exclaimed, "It is a saddle-bag I am as sure as my father is my father, and whoever has said or will say anything else must be drunk."

"Liar! - mischievous clown," returned Don Quixote; and lifting his lance, which he had never let out of his hand, he delivered such a blow to his head that, had the officer not dodged it, it would have laid him out flat. The lance was in pieces on the ground, and the rest of the officers, seeing their companion assaulted, raised a shout, calling for help from the Holy Brotherhood. The landlord, who was part of the brotherhood, ran to get his sword, and stood himself on the side of his companions; the servants of Don Luis surrounded him, in case he escaped from them during this confusion; the barber, seeing the commotion, grabbed his saddle-bag and Sancho did the same; Don Quixote raised his sword and charged toward the officers; Don Luis cried out to his servants to leave him alone and go to help Don Quixote, Cardenio and Don Fernando, who were supporting him; the vicar was shouting, the landlady was screaming, her daughter was yelling, Maritornes was crying, Dorothea was shocked, Luscinda scared, and Dona Clara felt faint. The barber punched Sancho, and Sancho punched the barber; Don Luis gave one of his servants, who held him by the arm to keep him from escaping, a punch that covered his chin in blood; the Judge took his part; Don Fernando had knocked one of the officers down and was beating him; the landlord raised his voice again calling for help from the Holy Brotherhood; so now in the whole inn there was nothing but cries, shouts, screams, confusion, terror, shock, misfortune, sword-cuts, punches, beatings, kicks, and bloodshed; and in the middle of this chaos, complication, and general entanglement, Don Quixote had in his head that he had been placed in another adventure; and, in a voice that shook the inn like thunder, he cried out:

"Hold! Everyone cover their swords, all be calm and listen to me as well as you value your lives!"

All paused immediately when hearing this mighty voice, and he went on to say, "Did I not tell you, that this castle was enchanted, and that a team of devils live in it? The proof which you can see with your own eyes is that the discord of Agramante's war has come here, and has been transferred to us. See how they fight, there is a sword, here is a horse, on that side the saddle-bag, on this side the helmet; we are all fighting, and all with opposing purposes. Señor Judge, and you, señor vicar; let one of you represent King Agramante and the other King Sobrino, and make peace among us; because this is such nonsense that so many people of high quality would attack each other for such little causes." The officers, who did not understand Don Quixote's mode of speaking, and found themselves roughly handled by Don Fernando, Cardenio, and their companions, were not appeased; the barber was, however, because his beard and his saddle-bag were not doing too well in the struggle; Sancho like a good servant obeyed any word of his master; while the four servants of Don Luis kept quiet when they saw how little they gained if they did not. The landlord alone insisted that they must punish the insolence of this madman, who continually created a disturbance in the inn; but the commotion was settled for the moment;

the saddle-bag remained a horse's cover until the day of judgment, and the basin a helmet and the inn a castle in Don Quixote's imagination.

Finally, all had been pacified and became friends by the persuasion of the Judge and the vicar, the servants of Don Luis began to urge him again to return with them; and while he was discussing the matter with them, the Judge sought advice from Don Fernando, Cardenio, and the vicar in regards to what he should do with his issue, telling them how it was, and what Don Luis had said to him. After some time, it was agreed that Don Fernando will tell Don Luis's servants who he was, and that it was his desire for Don Luis to accompany him to Andalusia, where he would receive from his brother the welcome his quality entitled him to; because otherwise, it was easy to see from the determination of Don Luis that he would not return to his father at present, even if they tore him to pieces. Discovering the rank of Don Fernando and the resolution of Don Luis, the four servants settled it between themselves that three of them will return to tell his father the situation, and that the other should stay to assist Don Luis, and not leave him until the others came back, or his father's wishes were known. So, with the authority of Agramante and the wisdom of King Sobrino all this complication of disputes was resolved; but the enemy of harmony and hater of peace, feeling himself tricked and made a fool of, and seeing how little he had gained after creating such an elaborate entanglement, decided to try once again by stirring up fresh arguments and disturbances.

So, it happened: the officers had calmed down after learning the rank of those they had been speaking with, and withdrew from the contest, considering that whatever the result might be they were likely to come out of the battle worse off; but one of them, the one who had been punched and kicked by Don Fernando, remembered that among some warrants he carried for the arrest of some troublemakers, he had one for Don Quixote, who the Holy Brotherhood had ordered to be arrested for freeing the ship slaves, which Sancho had, with very good reason, advised against.

Suspecting who it was, then, he wished to satisfy himself as to whether Don Quixote's features corresponded; and taking a paper out of his inner pocket he found what he was in search of, and starting to read it out loud deliberately, because he was not a quick reader, as he said each word he fixed his eyes on Don Quixote, and went on comparing the description in the warrant with his face, and discovered that without any doubt he was the person described in it. As soon as he had satisfied himself, folding up the paper, he held the warrant in his left hand and with his right grabbed Don Quixote by the neck so tightly that he did not allow him to breathe, and shouted, "Help for the Holy Brotherhood! You may see I have the right to detain this criminal, read this warrant which says this highwayman has to be arrested."

The vicar took the warrant and saw that what the officer said was true, and that it agreed with Don Quixote's appearance, who, on his part, when he found himself roughly handled by this man, worked up to the highest pitch of wrath, and all his joints furious with rage, with both hands held the officer by the throat with all of his strength, so that if he had not been helped by his companions he would have given up his life unless Don Quixote released the hold. The landlord, who had to support his brother officers, ran immediately to assist them. When the landlady saw her husband involved in a new argument, she raised her voice, and it was immediately heard by Maritornes and her daughter, calling for heaven and everyone present for help; and Sancho, seeing what was going on, exclaimed, "God, it is quite true what my master says about the enchantments of this castle, because it is impossible to live an hour of peace in it!"

Don Fernando separated the officer and Don Quixote, and to their mutual contentment made them relax the grip by which they held each other; after all of this, however, the officers did not cease to demand for their prisoner and call for help, as it was required for the service of the King and the Holy Brotherhood, who called again for aid and assistance to capture this robber of the highways.

Don Quixote smiled when he heard these words, and said very calmly, "Listen to me, lower, weak-born man; you call it highway robbery to grant freedom to those in slavery, to release the captives, to assist the unhappy, to raise the fallen, to relieve the needy? Dishonourable beings, your vile intellects deserve heaven to inform you that virtue lies in Knighthood, and to show you the sin and ignorance in which you live, when you refuse to respect the shadow, or the presence, of any Knight! Come on; group, not of officers, but of thieves; with the licence of the Holy Brotherhood; tell me who is the fool is, who signed a warrant of arrest against such a Knight as I? Who was the idiot that did not know that Knights are independent of all jurisdictions, that their law is their sword, their license their skill, and their orders their will? Who, I say again, was the clown that does not know that there are no positions of nobility that offer the same privileges or exemptions as a Knight acquires on the day he becomes a Knight, and devotes himself to the demanding profession of chivalry? What Knight ever paid tax, duty fees, Queen's money, King's royalties, tolls on the roads or for the ferry? What tailor ever took payment from a Knight for making his clothes? What Spaniard that hosted him in his castle ever made him pay for his room? What King did not have him at his table? What lady was not in love with him and did not give herself fully to his will and pleasure? And, lastly, what Knight has there been, is there, or will there ever be in the world, not brave enough to give, single-handed, four hundred beatings to four hundred officers of the Holy Brotherhood if they get in his way?"

CHAPTER 46

CONCLUDING THE ADVENTURE OF THE HOLY BROTHERHOOD; AND THE GREAT FIERCENESS OF OUR WORTHY KNIGHT - DON QUIXOTE

While Don Quixote was talking in this tone, the vicar was trying to persuade the officers that he was out of his senses, as they could observe by his words and actions, and that they should not pursue the matter any further, because even if they arrested him and took him away, they would have to release him as a madman; to which the holder of the warrant replied that it was not for him to inquire into Don Quixote's madness, but only to execute his superior's commands, and that once he had been arrested they could let him go three hundred times if they liked.

"Regardless of that," said the vicar, "you must not take him away this time, and neither will he, in my opinion, let himself be taken away."

In short, the vicar used this type of argument, and Don Quixote did such mad things, that the officers would have been madder than he was, if they had not noticed his lack of sense, and so they thought it would be best to be calm, and even to act as peacemakers between the barber and Sancho Panza, who still continued their disagreement with much anger. In the end, they as officers of justice, settled the question by mediation in such a manner that both sides were, if not perfectly contented, at least to some extent satisfied; because they gave a saddle-bag to the barber; and for Mambrino's helmet, the vicar, without Don Quixote knowing it, paid eight gold coins for the basin, and the barber gave a full receipt and agreement not to demand anymore, forever, amen. With these two disputes, which were the most unimportant, settled, all that remained remained was for the servants of Don Luis to consent that three of them should return while one was left to accompany him wherever Don Fernando desired to take him; and good luck and better fortune, having already begun to solve difficulties and remove obstructions in favour of the lovers and warriors of the inn, were pleased to persevere and bring everything to a happy ending; because the servants agreed to do as Don Luis wished; which gave Dona Clara such happiness that no one could have looked at her face without seeing the joy of her heart. Zoraida, although she did not fully comprehend all that she saw, was happy without knowing why, as she watched and studied the various appearances of everyone, but particularly her future husband's, who her eyes followed and she stuck to with her soul. The gift and compensation which the vicar gave the barber had not escaped the landlord's notice, and he demanded Don Quixote's payment, together with an amount for the damage to his wine-skins, and the loss of his wine, swearing that Rocinante and Sancho's donkey will not leave the inn until he had been paid everything. The vicar settled the bill amicably, and Don Fernando paid; although the Judge had also offered to pay the fee; and all became so peaceful and quiet that the inn no longer reminded anyone of the discord of Agramante's war, as Don Quixote had said, but peace and tranquillity: all agreed, and it was the universal opinion that their thanks were due to the great zeal and eloquence of the vicar, and to the generosity of Don Fernando.

Now he was clear of all arguments, his aide's as well as his own, Don Quixote considered that it would be sensible to continue the journey he had begun, and bring to a close the great adventure which he had been chosen for; and with this determination he went and knelt in front of Dorothea, who, however, would not allow him to say any word until he had risen; so to obey her, he got up, and said, "It is a common proverb, fair lady, that 'diligence is the mother of good fortune,' and experience has often shown in important matters that the sincerity of the negotiator brings the doubtful circumstance to a successful end; but in nothing does this truth show itself more plainly than in war, where speed and action anticipate the strategies of the enemy, and win the victory before the foe has time to defend himself. All this I say, exalted and esteemed lady, because it seems to me that for us to stay in this castle is useless, and may be harmful to us in a way that we will find out some day; because who knows, your enemy the giant may have discovered through secret and diligent spies that I am going to destroy him, and if the opportunity is given to him he may decide to protect himself in some impenetrable castle or stronghold, against which all my efforts and the strength of my arm may not do much. Therefore, lady, let us, as I say, foresee his schemes by our activity, and let us leave immediately in search of better fortune; because you are only kept from enjoying it as fully as you desire, by delaying my encounter with your enemy."

Don Quixote said no more, calmly awaiting the reply of the beautiful Princess, who, with commanding dignity and in a style modified to match Don Quixote's, replied to him with these words, "I thank you, sir Knight, for the eagerness you, like a good Knight, display to me in aid of my trouble; and heaven grant that your wishes and mine may be realised, so that you may see that there are women in this world capable of gratitude; in regards to my departure, let it be immediately, because I have no will other than yours; organise me entirely in accordance with your pleasure; because I who have entrusted you with my defence, and placed in your hands the recovery of my Kingdom, must not think about offering opposition to that which your wisdom may order."

"in God's name then," said Don Quixote; "because, when a lady humbles herself to me, I will not lose the opportunity of raising her and placing her on the throne of her ancestors. Let us leave now, because the common saying that in delay there is danger, encourages my eagerness to take the road; and as neither heaven has created, or hell has seen, any that can deter or intimidate me, saddle Rocinante Sancho, and get your donkey ready and the Queen's, and let us leave the castellan and these gentlemen, and go this very moment."

Sancho, who was standing nearby the whole time, said, shaking his head, "Ah! master, master, there is more danger in the village."

"What danger can there be in any village, or in all the cities of the world, you fool, that can hurt my reputation?" said Don Quixote.

"If you are angry," replied Sancho, "I will be quiet and leave unsaid what I am bound to say, and what a good servant should tell his master."

"Say what you like," returned Don Quixote, "provided your words are not meant to invoke fears; because you, if you fear, are behaving like yourself; but I like myself, am not fearing."

"It is nothing like that," said Sancho, "but I consider it to be sure and certain that this lady, who calls herself Queen of the great Kingdom of Micomicon, is no more a Queen than if my mother were; because, if she was what she says, she would not go talking to anyone that is here every instant and behind every door."

Dorothea turned red by Sancho's words, because the truth was that her husband Don Fernando had now and then, when the others were not looking, taken from her lips some of the reward his love had earned, and Sancho had seen this and considered that this freedom was more like a lover than a Queen of a great Kingdom; she, however, being unable or not caring to answer him, allowed him to proceed, and he continued, "This I say, señor, because, if after we have travelled roads and highways, and passed bad nights and worse days, someone who is now enjoying himself in this inn is going to receive the fruit of our labour, there is no need for me to be in a hurry to saddle Rocinante, or put the pad on the donkey; because it will be better for us to stay quiet, and go to dinner."

The anger of Don Quixote when he heard the daring words of his aide was so great, that in a voice inarticulate with rage, with a stammering tongue, and eyes that flashed living fire, he exclaimed, "Mischievous clown, ill-mannered, insolent, and ignorant, ill-spoken, foul-mouthed, fool! Did you dare to say these words in my presence and in the presence of these distinguished people? Do you dare to harbour such disgusting and shameless thoughts in your bewildered mind? Leave my presence, idiot, storehouse of lies, hoarder of shame, inventor of dishonour, enemy of the respect due to royals! Go, do not show yourself any more in front of me or face the pain of my fury;" and saying this he raised his eyebrows, puffed out his cheeks, looked around him, and stamped on the ground violently with his right foot, showing in every way the rage that was contained in his heart; and with these words and furious gestures Sancho was so scared and terrified that he would have been glad if the earth had opened that instant and swallowed him, and his only thought was to turn around and make an escape from the angry presence of his master.

But the quick-witted Dorothea, who by this time understood Don Quixote's madness well, said, to calm his anger, "Do not be irritated by the absurdities of you good aide, Sir Knight of the sorrowful face, because perhaps he did not say them without a cause, and from his good sense and Christian conscience it is not likely that he would intently make false statements against anyone. We may therefore believe, without any hesitation, that since, as you say, sir Knight, everything in this castle happens by enchantment, I say, Sancho may possibly have seen, through this enchantment, what he says he saw although it dishonours my modesty."

"I swear to almighty God," exclaimed Don Quixote, "you have hit the nail on the head; and that some vile illusion must have come to this sinner Sancho, that made him see what it would have been impossible to see without any enchantment; because I know well enough, from the poor man's goodness and harmlessness, that he is incapable of making false statements against anybody."

"That is true," said Don Fernando, "and for this reason, Señor Don Quixote, you should forgive him, and consider, as you did in the beginning, that illusions of this type have taken away his senses."

Don Quixote said he was ready to forgive him, and the vicar called for Sancho, who came in very respectfully, and falling on his knees begged for forgiveness from his master, who gave him his blessing and said, "Now, Sancho my son, you will be convinced about the truth of what I have told you many times, that everything in this castle is done by enchantment."

"So it is, I believe," said Sancho, "except the affair of the blanket, which happened in reality by ordinary people."

"I do not believe so," said Don Quixote, "because if it had been, I would have avenged you that instant, or even now; but I could not, neither now or then, and neither have I seen anyone who I can seek revenge on."

They were all eager to know what the issue of the blanket was, and the landlord gave them a short account of Sancho's flights, at which they laughed a lot, and at which Sancho would have been upset by if his master had not assured him it was all enchantment. And with all his simplicity he persuaded himself that the plain and simple truth, without any deception, was that he had not been blanketed by people of flesh and blood, but by visionary and imaginary ghosts, as his master believed and protested.

Two days had passed in the inn; and as it seemed to them time to leave, they devised a plan so that, without giving Dorothea and Don Fernando the trouble of going back with Don Quixote to his village under pretence of restoring Queen Micomicona, the vicar and the barber could take him with them as they proposed, and the vicar would be able to deal with his madness at home; and to assist with the fulfilment of their plan, they arranged with the owner of a cart who happened to be passing that way, to take him in the following way. They constructed a kind of cage with wooden bars, large enough to hold Don Quixote comfortably; and then Don Fernando and his companions, the servants of Don Luis, and the officers of the Brotherhood, together with the landlord, by the directions and advice of the vicar, covered their faces and disguised themselves, some in one way, some in another, to appear to Don Quixote to be quite different from the people he had seen in the castle. This done, in profound silence they entered the room where he was asleep (taking his rest after the past arguments), and progressing to where he was sleeping tranquilly, not dreaming of anything of the sort happening, they held him firmly and tied his hands and feet quickly, so that, when he awoke startled, he was unable to move, and could only stare and wonder about the strange figures he saw in front of him; at which he immediately had an idea, which his crazy mind invariably conjured up, and took it into his head that all these shapes were ghosts of the enchanted castle, and that he himself was unquestionably enchanted as he could not move or help himself; precisely what the vicar, the concoctor of the scheme expected would happen. Out of everyone there, Sancho was the only one who had his senses and was in his own proper character, and he, although he was very close to sharing his master's illness, did not fail to notice who all these disguised figures were; but he did not dare to open his lips until he saw what came from this attack and capture of his master; and neither did Don Quixote say a word while waiting to see what would happen next. They proceeded to bring in the cage, and then shut him inside and nailed the bars so firmly that they could not be burst open.

They then placed the cage on their shoulders, and as they left the room an awful voice – of the barber, not the one who argued about the saddle bag, the other one was heard to say, "Knight of the Sorrowful Face, do not let this captivity bother you, this has to be done, the quick accomplishment of the adventure in which your great heart has engaged you; the powerful Manchegan lion and the white Tobosan bird will be linked together in marriage. And from this marvellous union will come the light of the world, brave children that will rival their courageous father. And you, noble and obedient aide that ever lifted the sword, by his side, beard on his face, nose to smell with, do not be discouraged or distressed to see the amazing Knight taken away; because soon, if it pleases the creator of the universe, you will see yourself promoted to such a height that you will not recognise yourself, and the promises which your good master has made will not prove to be false; and I assure you, that your wages will be paid, as you will see in due course. Follow the footsteps of the courageous enchanted Knight, because it is beneficial that you go to the destination assigned to you both; and as it is not permitted for me to say any more, I hope God goes with you;" and as he brought the prophecy to an end he raised his voice in a high pitch, and then lowered it to such a soft tone, that even those who knew it was all a joke, were almost persuaded to take what they heard seriously.

Don Quixote was comforted by the prophecy he heard, because he comprehended its meaning perfectly, and perceived he was promised to be united in holy and lawful matrimony with his much loved Dulcinea del Toboso, and from her sacred womb will come his children, his sons, who will be the eternal glory of La Mancha; and being thoroughly and firmly persuaded of this, he raised his voice, and with a deep sigh exclaimed, "You, whoever you are, who has told me so much good, I request that on my part you ask the sage enchanter who takes control of my interest, that he does not leave me to die in this captivity in which they are now taking me away, I hope to see fulfilled these promises so joyful and incomparable; let this happen, and I will travel in glory with the pain of my prison, find comfort in these chains which bind me, and regard this bed where I lay, not as a hard battle-field, but as a soft and happy couch; and console Sancho Panza, my aide, I rely on his goodness and decency that he will not desert me during my good or evil fortune; because if, by his bad luck or mine, it does not happen to be in my power to give him the island I have promised, or anything equivalent, at least his wages will not be lost; because in my will, which is already made, I have declared the amount to be paid to him, measured, not only by his great service, but by what I am able to give him."

Sancho bowed his head very respectfully and kissed both his hands, because, being tied together, he could not kiss one; and then the 'ghosts' lifted the cage from their shoulders and placed it on the cart.

CHAPTER 47

THE STRANGE MANNER IN WHICH DON QUIXOTE OF LA MANCHA WAS TAKEN AWAY ENCHANTED, ALONG WITH OTHER REMARKABLE INCIDENTS

When Don Quixote saw himself caged and lifted on to the cart in this way, he said, "Many of the serious histories of Knights I have read; but I have never read, seen, or heard any of them being carried off enchanted in this manner, or at the slow pace of these lazy sluggish animals; because they always take them away through the air with spectacular swiftness, enclosed in a dark cloud, or on a chariot of fire; but to take me like this on an ox-cart! God, it confuses me! But perhaps the chivalry and enchantments of our time take a different course from that of the past; and it may be, as well, that as I am a new Knight in the world, and the first to revive the already forgotten calling of Knight-adventurers, they may have invented new kinds of enchantments and other modes of transporting the enchanted. What do you think about this matter, Sancho my son?"

"I don't know what to think," answered Sancho, "not having read as much books about Knights as you; but all I dare to say and swear that these ghosts that are around us are not quite catholic."

"Catholic!" said Don Quixote. "My God! how can they be Catholic when they are all devils that have assumed shapes to come and do this, and put me into this condition? And if you want to prove it, touch them, and feel them, and you will find they have bodies of air, and no consistency except in appearance."

"God, master," returned Sancho, "I have touched them already; and that devil, that one over there, has firm flesh, which is very different from what I have heard the devils are made of, because by all descriptions they smell of brimstone and other bad smells; but this one smells of amber half a mile away." Sancho was speaking about Don Fernando, who, like a gentleman of his rank, was likely to be wearing perfume as Sancho said.

"Do not wonder about that, Sancho my friend," said Don Quixote; "because let me tell you devils are crafty; and even if they have an odour, they themselves have no smell, because they are spirits; or, if they have any smell, they do not smell sweet, but of something foul; and the reason is that as they carry hell with them wherever they go, and cannot get any peace from whatever torments them, and as a sweet smell is a thing that gives pleasure and enjoyment, it is impossible that they can smell sweet; if then, this devil you speak of seems to smell like amber, either you are deceiving yourself, or he wants to deceive you by making you think he is not a devil."

This was the conversation between master and man; and Don Fernando and Cardenio, who were anxious about Sancho making a complete discovery of their plan, which he had already uncovered slightly, decided to hurry their departure, and calling the landlord aside, they told him to prepare Rocinante and put the saddle on Sancho's donkey, which he did with much enthusiasm. In the meantime, the vicar had made an arrangement with the officers that they accompany them as far as his village, and he would pay them so much a day. Cardenio hung the shield on one side of Rocinante's saddle and the basin on the other, and commanded Sancho to mount his donkey and take Rocinante's reigns, and at each side of the cart he placed two officers with their guns; but before the cart left, the landlady, her daughter and Maritornes came out to give Don Quixote a farewell, pretending to cry with misery at his misfortune; and to them Don Quixote said:

"Do not cry good ladies, because all these mishaps are common in the life of those who follow the profession I chose; and if these things did not happen to me I could not regard myself as a famous Knight; because these things never happen to Knights with little reputation and fame, because nobody in the world thinks about them; but when it comes to courageous Knights they do, because they are envied for their virtue and bravery by many princes and other Knights. Nevertheless, virtue is in itself so mighty, that, in spite of all the magic in the world, it will be victorious in every test, and shine light on the earth as the sun does. Forgive me, ladies, if, through carelessness, I have in any way offended you; because I have never done so intentionally or knowingly to anyone; and please pray to God that he releases me from this captivity which some wicked enchanter has consigned me to; and if I find myself released because of this, the favours that you have given me in this castle will be held in my memory, for me to acknowledge, recognise, and repay as they deserve to be."

While this was happening between the ladies of the castle and Don Quixote, the vicar and the barber said farewell to Don Fernando and his companions, to the captive, his brother, and the ladies, who were all happy, and in particular to Dorothea and Luscinda. They all hugged one another, and promised to let each other know how things went with them, and Don Fernando told the vicar where to write to him, to tell him about how it went with Don Quixote, assuring him that there was nothing that could give him more pleasure to hear, and that he as well, on his part, would write to him about everything he thought he would like to know, about his marriage, Zoraida's baptism, Don Luis's affair, and Luscinda's return to her home. The vicar promised to follow his request carefully, and they hugged again, and renewed their promises.

The landlord approached the vicar and handed him some papers, saying he had discovered them in the lining of the bag in which the novel of "The Ill-advised Curiosity" had been found, and that he could take them with him as their owner had never returned; and, as he could not read, he did not want them himself. The vicar thanked him, and opening them he saw at the beginning of the text the words, "Novel of Rinconete and Cortadillo," which made him perceive that it was a novel, and as "The Ill-advised Curiosity" had been good he concluded this would good as well, as they were both probably by the same author; so he kept it, intending to read it when he had an opportunity. He then mounted and his friend the barber did the same, both masked, so they were not recognised by Don Quixote, and they started to follow the rear of the cart. The order was like this: first was the cart with the owner leading it; at each side of it marched the officers of the Brotherhood, with their guns; then followed Sancho Panza on his donkey, leading Rocinante by the reins; and behind everyone was the vicar and the barber on their donkeys, with their faces covered, in a serious manner, measuring their pace to match the slow steps of the ox. Don Quixote was seated in the cage, with his hands tied and his feet stretched out, leaning against the bars as silent and as patient as if he were a stone statue and not a man of flesh. Slowly and silently they travelled two miles, until they reached a valley which the transporter thought was a convenient place for resting and feeding his ox, and so he said this to the vicar, but the barber had the opinion that they should go on a little further, as at the other side of a hill which appeared close by he knew there was a valley that had more grass and much better than the one where they proposed to stop; and his advice was taken and they continued their journey.

Just then the vicar, looking back, saw coming behind them six or seven mounted men, well equipped, who soon overtook them, because they were travelling, not at the slow deliberate pace of the ox, but like men who rode canons, and in a rush to take their rest as soon as possible at the inn which was in sight not far away. The quick travellers came close to the slow ones, and polite greetings were exchanged; and one of the new comers, who was, in fact, from Toledo and the master of the others who accompanied him, observing the order of everyone, the cart, the officers, Sancho, Rocinante, the vicar and the barber, and above all Don Quixote caged and confined, could not help asking what the meaning was of carrying a man in that way; although, from the badges of the officers, he already concluded that he must be some robber or other troublemaker whose punishment fell within the jurisdiction of the Holy Brotherhood. One of the officers replied, "Let the gentleman tell you himself the meaning of going in this way, señor, because we do not know."

Don Quixote overheard the conversation and said, "Gentlemen, are you familiar with matters of Knights and chivalry? Because if you are I will tell you my misfortunes; if not, there is no point in me taking the trouble to tell you them;" but here the vicar and the barber, seeing that the travellers were engaged in conversation with Don Quixote, came forward, in order to answer in such a way that would save their strategy from being discovered.

The man from Toledo, replying to Don Quixote, said, "Truthfully, brother, I know more about the books of chivalry than I do about Villalpando's elements of logic; so if that satisfies the requirement, you can safely tell me what you like."

"In God's name, then, señor," replied Don Quixote; "if that is so, you should know that I am held enchanted in this cage by the envy and fraud of wicked enchanters; because virtue is more mistreated by the wicked than loved by the good. I am a Knight, and not one of those whose names Fame has never thought of immortalising in the record books, but one of those who, in defiance of envy itself, and all the magicians that Persia, India, or Ethiopia ever produced, will place their names in the temple of immortality, to serve as examples and patterns for ages to come, where Knights can see the footsteps in which they must tread if they want to attain the pinnacle and peak of honour in Knighthood."

"What Señor Don Quixote of La Mancha says," said the vicar, "is the very truth; because he goes enchanted in this cart, not from any fault or sins of his, but because of the malice of those to whom virtue is repulsive and valour detestable. This, señor, is the Knight of the Sorrowful Face, if you have ever heard this name, whose courageous achievements and mighty deeds will be written on lasting brass and imperishable marble, despite all the efforts of envy to obscure them and malice to hide them."

When the man from Toledo heard the prisoner and the man who was free to talk in such a manner he was astonished; and all his followers were in the same state of amazement.

At this point Sancho Panza, who had come closer to hear the conversation, said, in order to make everything clear, "Well, sirs, you may like or dislike what I am going to say, but the fact of the matter is, my master, Don Quixote, is as enchanted as my mother. He has his full senses, he eats and he drinks, and he has his demands like other men and the same as he had yesterday, before they caged him. And if that's the case, why do they want me to believe that he is enchanted? Because I have heard many say that enchanted people do not eat, sleep, or talk; and my master, if you don't stop him, will talk more than thirty lawyers." Then turning to the vicar he exclaimed, "Ah, señor vicar, señor vicar! do you think I don't know you? Do you think I don't guess and see the purpose of these new enchantments? Well then, I can tell you I know you, and just because your face is covered, and I can tell you I see you, however you hide your tricks. After all, where envy reigns virtue cannot live, and where there is meanness there can be no freedom. If it had not been for you, my master would be married to Princess Micomicona right now, and I would be a ruler; as no less was expected from the goodness of my master, the Knight of the Sorrowful Face, for the greatness of my services. But now I see how true it is what they say around here, that the wheel of fortune turns faster than the wheel of the mill, and that those who were up yesterday are down today. I am sorry for my wife and children, because when they might fairly and reasonably expect to see their father return to them as a governor of some island or Kingdom, they will see him come back as a horse-boy. I have said all this, señor vicar, only to urge to come to your conscience your mistreatment of my master; and be careful that God does not call you to give an account in another life for making him a prisoner in this way, and charge you for all the relief any good deeds that my lord Don Quixote leaves unfinished while he is caged.

"Be quiet!" exclaimed the barber; "are you the same as your master, Sancho? God, I am beginning to think that you will have to keep him company in the cage, and be enchanted like him for having caught some of his absurdity. It was an evil hour when you let yourself be taken by his promises, and that island you hope for so much found its way into your head."

"I am not taken by anything," returned Sancho, "neither am I someone to be influenced, even if it was by the King himself. Although I am poor, I am an old Christian, and I owe nothing to anybody, and if I hope for an island, other people hope for worse. Each of us is the son of his own actions; and being a man my actions might make me the pope, or alternatively governor of an island, especially as my master may win so many that he will not know who to give them to. Mind how you talk, barber; because shaving is not everything. I say this because we all know one another, and it will not work to speak falsely to me; and in regards to the enchantment of my master, God knows the truth; leave it as it is; it only makes it worse to stir it."

The barber did not care to answer Sancho because by encouraging Sancho to speak he might disclose what the vicar and he himself were trying hard to conceal; and under the same apprehension the vicar asked if he could ride a little in front with the man from Toledo, so that he could tell him the mystery of this man in the cage, and other things that would amuse him. The man from Toledo agreed, and going on ahead with his servants, listened with attention to the account of the character, life, madness, and ways of Don Quixote, given to him by the vicar, who described to him briefly the beginning and origin of his insanity, and told him the whole story of his adventures up to him being placed in the cage, together with the plan they had of taking him home to try if by any method they could discover a cure for his condition. The man from Toledo and his servants were surprised again when they heard Don Quixote's strange story, and when it was finished he said, "To tell the truth, señor vicar, I consider what they call books of chivalry to be damaging to the State; and although, led by idle and bad taste, I have read the beginnings of almost all that have been printed, but I could never manage to read any of them from beginning to end; because it seems to me they are all more or less the same thing; and one has nothing more in it than another; this no more than that. And in my opinion this sort of writing and composition is the same type as the stories they call the Milesian, nonsensical tales that aim solely at giving amusement and not instruction, exactly the opposite of the moral stories which amuse and instruct at the same time. And although it may be the main objective of these books to amuse, I do not know how they can succeed, when they are so full of shocking nonsense. Because any enjoyment the mind feels must come from the beauty and harmony which it perceives or contemplates in things that the eye or the imagination sees; and nothing that has any ugliness or imbalance can give any pleasure. What beauty, then, or what proportion of the parts in the whole, or the whole in the parts, can there be in a book or story where a sixteen-year-old boy cuts down a giant as tall as a tower and splits him into two halves as if he were an almond cake? And when they want to give us a picture of a battle, after having told us that there are a million soldiers on the side of the enemy, the hero of the book is opposed to them, and we have inevitably to believe, whether we like it or not, that this Knight wins the victory by the sole might of his arm. And then, what should we say about the stupidity with which a born Queen or empress will give herself to the arms of some unknown wandering Knight? What mind, that is not totally barbaric and uncultured, can find pleasure in reading about how a great tower full of Knights sails away across the sea like a ship in the wind, and will be between the Alps tonight and tomorrow morning in the land of the Indies? And if, in answer to this, I am told that the authors of these types of books write them as fiction, and therefore are not bound to regard workings of truth, I would reply that fiction is better the more it looks like truth, and gives more pleasure the more probability and possibility there is in it. Fictional stories should be attached to the understanding of the reader, and be constructed in such a way that, reconciling impossibilities, smoothing over difficulties, keeping the mind alert, they may surprise, interest, amuse, and entertain, so that wonder and pleasure may keep pace with one another; all which an author will fail to create who avoids authenticity and truth to nature, in this lies the perfection of writing. I have never yet seen any book of chivalry that puts together a connected plot complete in all its parts, so that the middle agrees with the beginning, and the end with the beginning and middle; on the contrary, they construct them with so many parts that it seems as though they want to produce an illusion or monster rather than a well-proportioned figure. And besides all this, they are insensitive in their style, incredible in their achievements, immoral in their love, rude in their speech, tedious in their battles, silly in their arguments, absurd in their travels, and, in short, lacking in everything like intelligent art; for this reason, they deserve to be banned from the Christian nation as a worthless breed."

The vicar listened to him attentively and felt that he was a man of sound understanding, and that there was good logic to what he said; so he told him that, having the same opinion himself, and disliking books of chivalry, he had burned all of Don Quixote's; and gave him an account of the scrutiny he gave them, and of those he had condemned to the flames and those he had spared, with which the man from Toledo was quite amused, adding that although he had said so much in disapproval of these books, he still found one good thing in them, and that was the opportunity they presented to a gifted intellect for revealing itself; because they presented a wide and spacious field over which the pen might move freely, describing shipwrecks, storms, wars, battles, portraying a courageous captain with all the qualifications necessary to make one, showing him educated in foreseeing the deceit of the enemy, fluent in speech to encourage or restrain his soldiers, suitable to give advice, rapid in decision making, brave and patiently waiting during an attack; now seeing some sad tragic incident, now some joyful and unexpected event; here a beautiful lady, virtuous, wise, and modest; there a Christian Knight, brave and gentle; here a lawless, vicious loudmouth; there a polite prince, loyal and gracious; going forward with the devotion and faithfulness of servants, the greatness and generosity of lords. "Or again," he said, "the author may show himself to be an astronomer, or a skilled cosmographer, or musician, or one who understands the matters of the state, and sometimes he will have the chance to be a magician if he likes. He can possess the craftiness of Ulysses, the religiousness of Aeneas, the bravery of

Achilles, the misfortune of Hector, the treachery of Sinon, the friendship of Euryalus, the generosity of Alexander, the boldness of Caesar, the forgiveness and truth of Trajan, the faithfulness of Zopyrus, the wisdom of Cato, and in short all the faculties that serve to make a distinguished man perfect, uniting them in one individual, but distributing them among many; and if this is done with charm, style and clever invention, aiming at the truth as much as possible, he will surely weave a web of vivid and varied threads that, when finished, will display such perfection and beauty that it will reach the worthiest objective any writing can seek, which, as I said before, is to give instruction and pleasure combined; because the unrestricted range of these books enables the author to show his power: heroic, poetic, tragic, or comic, and all the moods that the sweet and captivating arts of poetry and oratory are capable of; because the epic can be written in prose just as well as in verse."

CHAPTER 48

THE MAN FROM TELEDO PURSUES THE SUBJECT OF BOOKS OF CHIVALRY, WITH OTHER MATTERS WORTHY OF HIS INTELLIGENCE

"It is as you say, señor," said the vicar; "and for that reason those who have up until now written books of this kind deserve full criticism for writing without paying any attention to good taste or the rules of art, by which they should guide themselves and become as famous in prose as the two princes of Greek and Latin poetry are in verse."

"I myself," said the Toledoan, "was once tempted to write a book of chivalry in which all the points I have mentioned were observed; and if I must speak the truth I have more than a hundred pages written; and showed them to people who liked this kind of reading, to educated and intelligent men as well as ignorant people who cared for nothing but the pleasure of listening to nonsense, and from all of them I obtained gratifying approval; but I continued no further with it, because it seemed to me to be an occupation inconsistent with my profession, and also because I perceived that there are more fools in the world than the wise; and, although it is better to be praised by the wise few than applauded by the many fools, I have no inclination to offer myself to the stupid judgment of the silly public, who would be the majority of the readers of this type of book.

"But what made me hold my writing hand the most and even abandon the idea of finishing it was an argument I put to myself taken from the plays that are acted these days, which was this: if those that are now in fashion, those that are pure invention, which are, all or most of them, illogical and things that make no sense, and yet the public listens to them with pleasure, and regards them as perfection when they are so far from it; and if the authors who write them, and the actors who act them, say that this is what they must produce, because the public wants this and will have nothing else; and that those who work out a plot according to the laws of art will only find half a dozen intelligent people to understand them, while all the rest remain blind to the excellence of their composition; and that for themselves it is better to get bread from the majority than praise from a few; then my book will go the same way, after I have burnt off my eyebrows trying to follow the principles I have spoken about, and I will be 'the tailor to the small corner.' And although I have sometimes endeavoured to convince actors that they are mistaken in this notion they have adopted, and that they would attract more people, and get more credit, by producing plays in accordance with the rules of art, than by absurd ones, they are so thoroughly devoted to their own opinion that no argument or evidence can turn them away from it.

"One day I remember saying to one of these stubborn men, 'Tell me, do you not remember that a few years ago, there were three tragedies acted in Spain, written by a famous poet of these kingdoms, which filled everyone who heard them with wonder, enjoyment, and interest, the ignorant as well as the wise, the masses as well as the higher few, and brought in more money to the performers, these three alone, than thirty of the best that have been produced since?'

"'No doubt,' replied the actor in question, 'you mean the "Isabella," the "Phyllis," and the "Alexandra."'

"'Those are the ones, exactly,' I said; 'see if they did not follow the principles of art, and if, by following them, they failed to show their superiority and please the whole world; so that the fault does not lie with the public that insists on nonsense, but with those who don't know how to produce anything else. "The Ingratitude Revenged" was not nonsense, neither was there any in "The Numantia," or any to be found in "The Merchant Lover," or in "The Friendly Fair Foe," neither in some others that have been written by other gifted poets, which led to their fame and recognition, and to the profit of those that acted them out;' I added some further remarks to these, with which, I think, I left him rather astonished, but not satisfied enough or convinced that I could correct his error."

"You have touched on an important subject, señor," said the vicar, "that has awakened an old hate I have against the plays in fashion presently, quite as strong as that which I have toward the books of chivalry; because while the drama, according to Tully, should be the mirror of human life, the model of manners, and the image of truth, those which are presented these days are mirrors of nonsense, models of madness, and images of filthiness. Because what greater nonsense can there be in connection with what we are now discussing than for an infant to appear in loose clothes in the first scene of the first act, and in the second a grown-up bearded man? Or what greater absurdity can there be than putting in front of us an old man as a pirate, a young man as a coward, a servant using fine language, a little boy giving sage advice, a King playing a porter, a Princess who is a kitchen-maid? And what more should I say in regards to their attention to the time in which the action they represent may or can take place, than that I have seen a play where the first act began in Europe, the second in Asia, the third finished in Africa, and no doubt, had it been four acts, the fourth would have ended in America, and so it would have taken place in in all four quarters of the globe. And if the truth of life is the main thing the drama should keep in view, how is it possible for any average understanding to be satisfied when the action is supposed to pass in the time of King Pepin or Charlemagne, and the principal person represented in it is the Emperor Heraclius who entered Jerusalem with the cross and won the Holy Tomb, when there are innumerable years between one and the other? Or, if the play is based on fiction and historical facts are introduced, or bits of what occurred to different people and at different times mixed up with it, all, without any resemblance of probability, but with obvious errors that from every point of view are inexcusable? And the worst of it is, there are ignorant people who say that this is perfection, and that anything beyond this is pretentious refinement. And then if we turn to sacred dramas -

what miracles they invent in them! What fictional, ill-devised incidents, attributing to one saint the miracles of another! And even in irreligious plays they venture to introduce miracles without any reason or objective except that they think some miracle, or transformation as they call it, will do well to astonish stupid people and draw them to the play. All of this leans toward altering the truth and the corruption of history, actually, to the deprecation of intellectuals in Spain; and foreigners who carefully observe the dramas look at us as vicious and ignorant, when they see the absurdity and nonsense of the plays we produce. And it is not a sufficient excuse to say that the main objective well-ordered governments have in view when they permit plays to be performed in public is to entertain the people with some harmless amusement; and as this may be attained by any sort of play, good or bad, there is no need to lay down laws, or bind those who write or act them to make them as they should be made, since, as I say, the objective they seek may be secured by any sort of play. To this I would reply that the same objective would be, beyond all comparison, better attained by good plays than by those that are not; because after listening to an artistic and properly constructed play, the hearer will leave invigorated by the jokes, instructed by the serious parts, full of admiration by the incidents, his mind sharpened by the arguments, warned by the tricks, wiser due to the examples, irritated against vice, and in love with virtue; because in all these ways a good play will stimulate the mind of the hearer even if he is ignorant or dull; and the greatest impossibility is that a play containing all of these qualities will not entertain, satisfy, and please much more than one lacking in them, like the greater number of those which are commonly acted presently. The poets who write them are not to be blamed for this; because some among them are perfectly well aware of their faults, and know what they should do; but as plays have become a saleable commodity, they say, and with truth, that the actors will not buy them unless they are made in this way; and so the poet tries to adapt himself to the requirements of the actor who is to pay him for his work. And this truth may be seen by the countless plays that most prolific intellectuals of these kingdoms have written, with so much brilliancy, so much grace and happiness, such polished versification, such choice of language, such profound reflections, and in a word, so rich in eloquence and elevation of style, that he has filled the world with his fame; and yet, in consequence of his desire to suit the taste of the actors, not all of them, as some of them have, come as near to perfection as they should do. Others write plays with such thoughtlessness that, after they have been acted, the actors have to run and escape, afraid of being punished, as they have been before, for having acted something offensive to some King or other, or insulting to some noble family. All of these evils, and many more that I have not mentioned, would be removed if there were some intelligent and sensible person in the capital to examine the plays before they were acted, not only those produced in the capital itself, but all that were intended to be acted in Spain; without whose approval, seal, and signature, no local court would allow any play to be acted. In that case actors would take care when sending their plays to the capital, and could act them in safety, and those who write them would be more careful and take more consideration with their work, fixed in respect of having to submit it to the strict examination of one who understood the matter; and therefore good plays would be produced and the objectives they strive for would be happily attained; satisfying the amusement of the people, crediting the intellectuals of Spain, taking care of interest and safety of the actors, and saving the trouble of inflicting punishment on them. And if the same or some other person were authorised to examine the newly written books of chivalry, no doubt some would appear with all the perfection you have described, enriching our language with the gracious and precious treasure of eloquence, and forcing the old books into obscurity before the light of the new ones that would come out for the harmless entertainment, not only for the lazy but for the very busiest; because the bow cannot always be bent, neither can weak human nature exist without some legal amusement."

The man from Toledo and the vicar had proceeded this far with their conversation, when the barber joined them, and said to the vicar, "This is the spot, señor vicar, that I said was good for fresh grass and for the ox, while we rest."

"It seems so," returned the vicar, and he told the Toledoan what he proposed to do, who also made up his mind to stop with them, attracted by valley in front of their eyes; and to enjoy it as well as the conversation with the vicar, who he had begun to really like and respect, and also to learn more about the madness of Don Quixote. He desired some of his servants to go on to the inn, which was not far distant, and to get something to eat for everyone, as he intended to rest for the afternoon where he was; to which one of his servants replied that the donkey for carrying supplies carried enough to make it unnecessary to get anything from the inn except barley.

While this was going on, Sancho, noticing he could speak to his master without having the vicar and the barber, which he had his suspicions about, present all the time, approached the cage in which Don Quixote was placed, and said, "Señor, to relieve my conscience I want to tell you the state of your enchantment, and that these two here, with their faces covered, are the vicar of our village and the barber; and I suspect they have this plan of taking you away like this, out of pure envy because you surpasses them in doing famous deeds; and if this is the truth it follows that you are not enchanted, but have been deceived and made a fool of. And to prove this I want to ask you one thing; and if you answer me as I believe you will answer, you will be able to notice the trick, and you will see that you are not enchanted but have been confused."

"Ask what you like, Sancho my son," returned Don Quixote, "because I will satisfy you and answer your request. In regards to what you say, that these who accompany us are the vicar and the barber, our neighbours and acquaintances, it is very possible that they may seem to be the same people; but do not believe it; what you should believe and think is that, if they look like them, as you say, it must be that those who have enchanted me have taken this shape and likeness; because it is easy for enchanters to take any form they please, and they may have taken the form of our friends in order to make you think as you do, and lead you into a labyrinth of thinking from which you will find no escape; and they may have done it to make me uncertain in my mind, and unable to estimate where this evil comes from; because if on one hand you tell me that the barber and vicar of our village are here accompanying us, and on the other I find myself shut in a cage, and know in my heart that no power on earth that was not supernatural would have been able to shut me in it, what else do you think I would believe, other than my enchantment has to be something that transcends all that I have ever read in the histories that deal with Knights? So you may let your mind rest and forget the idea that they are what you say, because they are as much as I am a Turk. But you wanted to ask me something, so go on, and I will answer you, even if you asked questions from now until tomorrow morning."

"God be good to me!" said Sancho, lifting up his voice; "is it possible that you have such a thick skull and so short of brains that you cannot see that what I say is the simple truth, and that malice has more to do with your imprisonment than misfortune and enchantment? But as it is so, I will prove to you that you are not enchanted. Now tell me, so God can release you from this affliction, and so you can find yourself when you least expect it in the arms lady Dulcinea"

"Don't try your trickery on me," said Don Quixote, "and ask what you want to know; I have already told you I will answer with all possible precision."

"That is what I want," said Sancho; "without adding or leaving out anything, but telling the whole truth as one expects it to be told, and as it is told, by all Knights, which you are"

"I will tell no lies," said Don Quixote; "finish your question; because truthfully you are tiring me with all of these requirements and precautions, Sancho."

"Well, I rely on the goodness and truth of my master," said Sancho; "and so, because it has an impact on what we are talking about, I would ask, speaking sincerely, whether since your worship has been shut, as you think, enchanted in this cage, you have felt any desire or inclination to go anywhere, as the saying goes?"

"I do not understand what you mean by 'going anywhere,'" said Don Quixote; "explain yourself clearly, Sancho, if you want me to answer the point."

"Is it really possible," said Sancho, "that you do not understand what 'going anywhere' means? The schoolboys knew it from the time they were babies. You must know that I mean have you had any desire to do what cannot be avoided?"

"Ah! now I understand you, Sancho," said Don Quixote; "yes, quite often, and even this minute; get me out of this cage."

CHAPTER 49

THE CLEVER CONVERSATION SANCHO PANZA HAD WITH HIS MASTER DON QUIXOTE

"Aha, I have caught you," said Sancho; "this is what in my heart and soul I wanted to know. Come on, Señor, can you deny what is commonly said about this, when a person is not acting the same, not knowing what the problem is, he does not eat, or drink, or sleep, or give a proper answer to any question; one would think he was enchanted? From this it is understood that those who do not eat, drink, or sleep, or do any of the natural acts I am speaking of are enchanted; but not those that have the desire you have, and drink when drink is given to them, and eat when there is anything to eat, and answer every question that is asked."

"What you say is very true, Sancho," replied Don Quixote; "but I have already told you there are many sorts of enchantments, and it may be that in the course of time they have been changed one for another, and that now it may be the way with enchanted people to do all that I do, although they did not do so before; so it is pointless to argue or make conclusions against a difference of time. I know and feel that I am enchanted, and that is enough to relieve my conscience; because it would weigh heavily on it if I thought that I was not enchanted, and that in a faint-hearted and cowardly way I allowed myself to be put in this cage, cheating thousands of people out of the assistance I could offer to those in distress, who at this very moment may be in desperate need of my aid and protection."

"For all of that," replied Sancho, "I say that, for your greater and fuller satisfaction, it would be good if you were to try to get out of this prison (and I promise to do all in my power to help, and even to take you out of it), and see if you could mount your good Rocinante once again, who seems to be enchanted too, he is so sad and depressed; and then we can look for adventures again; and if we have no luck there will be enough time to go back to the cage; in which, on the word of a good and loyal aide, I promise to shut myself in along with you, if you are so unfortunate, or I am so stupid, not to be able to carry out my plan."

"I am content to do as you say, brother Sancho," said Don Quixote, "and when you see an opportunity for achieving my release I will obey you completely; but you will see, Sancho, how mistaken you are in your idea of my misfortune."

The Knight and the aide kept up their conversation until they reached the place where the vicar, the Toledoan, and the barber, who had already dismounted, were waiting for them. The carter immediately released the ox and left it to roam around the pleasing green area, the freshness seemed to invite, not enchanted people like Don Quixote, but wide-awake, sensible people like his aide, who begged the vicar to allow his master to leave the cage for a little while; because if they did not let him out, the prison might not be as clean as such a gentleman as his master required. The vicar understood him, and said he would gladly comply with his request, only he feared his master, finding himself free, would run away where nobody could ever find him again.

"I assure you he will not run away," said Sancho.

"And I do too," said the Toledoan, "especially if he gives me his word as a Knight not to leave us without our consent."

Don Quixote, who was listening to all of this, said, "I give my word; and one who is enchanted as I am cannot do as he likes; because he who had enchanted him could prevent him moving from one place forever, and if he attempted to escape would bring him flying back." - And that being so, they might as well release him, particularly as it would be an advantage to all; because, if they did not let him out, he would be unable to avoid offending their nostrils unless they kept their distance.

The Toledoan took his hands, which were tied together, and with his word and promise they released him, and he was happy beyond measure to find himself out of the cage. The first thing he did was to stretch himself all over, and then he went to where Rocinante was standing and giving him a couple of slaps on the leg said, "I still trust in God, elite reflection of horses, that we will soon see ourselves, both of us, as we wish to be, you with your master on your back, and I mounted on top of you, following the calling which God sent me into the world for." And accompanied by Sancho, he went to a quiet spot, from which he came back very relieved and more eager than ever to put his aide's plan into execution.

The Toledoan stared at him, wondering about the extraordinary nature of his madness, and that in all his remarks and replies he could show such excellent sense, but when the subject of chivalry was spoken about he lost his mind. And so, moved by compassion, he said to him, as they all sat on the green grass awaiting the arrival of the supplies:

"Is it possible, sir, that reading books of chivalry could have had such an effect on you as to upset your reason so you believe you are enchanted, which is as far from the truth as lies are? How can there be any human understanding that can persuade itself that there ever was an infinity of romances in the world, or all of those famous Knights, all those emperors, all those horses, and ladies, and snakes, and monsters, and giants, and marvellous adventures, and enchantments of every kind, and battles, and extraordinary encounters, wonderful costumes, love-sick Princesses, aides becoming governors, dwarfs, love letters, and, in a word, all that nonsense the books of chivalry contain? For myself, I can only say that when I read them, as long as I do not stop to think that they are all lies and foolishness, they give me a certain amount of pleasure; but when I come to consider what they are, I throw the very best of them against the wall, and would throw it into the fire if there were one nearby, as the punishment they deserve just like the cheaters and deceivers out of the range of ordinary toleration, and like the teachers that lead the ignorant public to believe and accept as truth all the foolishness they contain. And their audacity is so great, they even dare to confuse the minds of gentlemen who were born with intelligence, which is clear to see by the way they have disturbed you, when they have brought you to such a condition that you have to be shut in a cage and carried on an ox-cart as one would carry a lion or a tiger from place to place to make money by showing it. Señor Don Quixote, have some compassion for yourself, return to common sense, and make use of the great share of it that heaven has been pleased to give you, using your gifts of mind in some other reading may serve to benefit your conscience and add to your honour. And if, still carried away by your natural inclination, you desire to read books of achievement and of chivalry, read the Book of Judges in the Holy Scriptures, because there you will find grand reality, and deeds which are as true as they are heroic. Lusitania had a Viriatus, Rome a Caesar, Carthage a Hannibal, Greece an Alexander, Castile a Count Fernan Gonzalez, Valencia a Cid, Andalusia a Gonzalo Fernandez, Estremadura a Diego Garcia de Paredes, Jerez a Garci Perez de Vargas, Toledo a Garcilaso, Seville a Don Manuel de Leon, to read about their valiant deeds will entertain and instruct the grandest minds and fill them with delight and wonder. This, Señor Don Quixote, will be reading worthy of your understanding; from which you will come away educated in history, in love with virtue, strengthened in goodness, improved in manners, brave without foolishness, prudent without cowardice; and all in the honour of God, your own advantage and the glory of La Mancha, where, I am informed, you were born."

Don Quixote listened with the greatest attention to the Toledoan's words, and when he found he had finished, after considering them for some time, he replied to him:

"It appears to me, sir, that you intend to persuade me that there never were any Knights in the world, and that all the books of chivalry are false, lying, mischievous and useless to the State, and that I have done wrong in reading them, and worse in believing them, and still worse in imitating them, when I undertook to follow the calling of Knighthood; because you deny that there ever were Amadises of France or Greece, or any other of the Knights which appear many times across the books."

"Precisely as say," said the Toledoan; to which Don Quixote returned, "You also went on to say that books of this kind had done much harm to me, as far as they had upset my senses, and shut me in a cage, and that it would be better for me to reform and change my studies, and read other truer books which would offer more pleasure and instruction."

"Exactly," said the Toledoan.

"Well then," returned Don Quixote, "in my mind it is you who are the one that is out of his senses and enchanted, as you have expressed such profanities against a thing so universally acknowledged and accepted as true that whoever denies it, as you do, deserves the same punishment which you say you inflict on the books that irritate you when you read them. Because to try to persuade anybody that Amadis, and all the other Knights which the books are filled with, never existed, would be like trying to persuade him that the sun does not give light, ice does not give cold, or the earth does not give nourishment. What mind in the world can persuade another that the story of the Princess

Floripes and Guy of Burgundy is not true, or the story of Fierabras and the bridge of Mantible, which happened during the time of Charlemagne? On all that is good, it is as true as it is daylight now; and if it is a lie, it must also be a lie that there was a Hector, or Achilles, or Trojan war, or Twelve Peers of France, or King Arthur of England, who still lives transformed into a raven, and is never-endingly looked for in his Kingdom. You might as well try to make out that the history of Guarino Mezquino, or the quest of the Holy Grail is false, or that the loves of Tristram and the Queen Yseult are mythical, as well the love of Guinevere and Lancelot, when there are people who can almost remember having seen the lady Quintanona, who was the best servant in Great Britain. And this is so true, that I recollect a grandmother of mine on my father's side, whenever she saw any lady in respectable clothing, used to say to me, 'Grandson, that one is like lady Quintanona,' from which I conclude that she must have known her, or at least had managed to see some portrait of her. And who can deny that the story of Pierre and lady Magalona is true, when even to this day it can be seen in the King's armoury the pin which the valiant Pierres guided the wooden horse he rode through the air with? And alongside the pin is Babieca's saddle, and at Roncesvalles there is Roland's horn, as large as a tree; from which we may infer that there were Twelve Peers, and a Pierre, and a Cid, and other Knights like them, the sort people commonly called adventurers. Or perhaps I will be told, as well, that there was no such Knight as the valiant Lusitanian Juan de Merlo, who went to Burgundy and in the city of Arras fought with the famous lord of Charny, Mosen Pierre was his name, and afterwards in the city of Basle with Mosen Enrique de Remesten, coming out of both encounters covered with fame and honour; or adventures and challenges achieved and delivered, also in Burgundy, by the valiant Spaniards Pedro Barba and Gutierre Quixada (from this family I come in the direct male line), when they defeated the sons of the Governor of San Polo. I will be told, as well, that Don Fernando de Guevara did not go in search of adventures in Germany, where he engaged in combat with Micer George, a Knight from the house belonging to the Duke of Austria. I will be told that the battles of Suero de Quinones, and Mosen Luis de Falces against the Castilian Knight, Don Gonzalo de Guzman, were fake; as well as many other achievements of Christian Knights from here and foreign realms, which are so authentic and true, that, I repeat, he who denies them must be totally lacking in reason and sense."

The Toledoan was amazed to hear the combination of truth and fiction Don Quixote had said, and to see how well acquainted he was with everything relating or belonging to the achievements of Knighthood; he said in reply:

"I cannot deny, Señor Don Quixote, that there is some truth in what you say, especially in regards to the Spanish Knights; and I am willing to grant as well that the Twelve Peers of France existed, but I am not prepared to believe that they did all the things that the Archbishop Turpin says they did. Because the truth of the matter is they were Knights chosen by the Kings of France, and called 'Peers' because they were all equal in worth, rank and ability (at least if they were not they should have been), and it was a kind of religious order like those in Santiago and Calatrava in the present day, in which it is assumed that those who follow it are courageous Knights of distinction and good upbringing; and just as we say now a Knight of St. John, or of Alcantara, they used to say then a Knight of the Twelve Peers, because twelve equals were chosen for that military order. That there was a Cid, as well as a Bernardo del Carpio, there can be no doubt; but that they did the deeds people say they did, I am very doubtful of. That other matter of the pin of Count Pierre that you speak of, and say is near Babieca's saddle in the Armoury, I confess; because I am either so stupid or so short-sighted, that, although I have seen the saddle, I have never been able to see the pin, in spite of it being as big as you say it is."

"It is all there, without any doubt," said Don Quixote; "and they say it is enclosed in a covering of cowskin to keep it from rusting."

"That may be," replied the Toledoan; "but, I do not remember seeing it. However, assuming it is there, that is no reason why I am bound to believe the stories of all those Amadises and the number of Knights they tell us about, neither is it reasonable that a man like you, so worthy, and with so many good qualities, and gifted with such a good understanding, should allow yourself to be persuaded that such wild crazy things as those that are written in those absurd books of chivalry are really true."

CHAPTER 50

THE SHREWD ARGUMENT BETWEEN DON QUIXOTE AND THE TOLEDOAN, TOGETHER WITH OTHER INCIDENTS

"That must be a joke!" returned Don Quixote. "Books that have been printed with the King's licence, and with the approval of those to whom they have been submitted, and read with universal delight, and commended by great and small, rich and poor, educated and ignorant, smart and simple, in a word by people of every type, of whatever rank or condition they are - that these are lies! And above all when they have such an appearance of truth to them; because they tell us the father, mother, country, age, place, and the achievements, step by step, and day by day, performed by a Knight or Knights! Be quiet, sir; do not speak such profanity; trust me I am advising you now to act as a sensible man should; read them, and you will see the pleasure you will gain from them. Because, tell me, can there be anything more delightful than to see, as it were, here displayed in front of us a huge lake with a swarm of snakes, serpents and lizards, and ferocious and terrible creatures of all types swimming in it, while from the middle of the lake there comes a sad voice saying: 'Knight, whoever you are who observes this lake of terror, if you want to win the prize that lies hidden beneath these waves, prove the courage of your strong heart and throw yourself into the middle of its dark burning waters, or else you are not worthy to see the mighty wonders contained in the seven castles of the seven fairies that lie beneath this dark area;' and then the Knight, when the awful voice has ceased, without stopping to consider, without pausing to reflect about the danger to which he is exposing himself, without even relieving himself of the weight of his massive armour, handing himself to God and to his lady, jumps into the middle of the boiling lake, and when he does not look for it, or knows what his fate will be, finds himself among extravagant fields, which the Elysian fields cannot be compared with.

"The sky seems more transparent there, and the sun shines with a unique brilliancy, and a delightful orchard of green leafy trees presents itself to the eyes and charms the sight with its luxuriance, while the ear is soothed by the sweet melody of the countless happy birds that fly among the interlacing branches. Here he sees a stream with clear waters, like liquid crystal, ripple over fine sand and white pebbles that look like pure gold and the clearest pearls. There he notices a cleverly formed fountain of multi-coloured quartz and polished marble; nearby in country fashion are little mussel-shells and spiral white and yellow mansions for the snail positioned in thoughtful order, mingled with fragments of glittering crystal and emeralds, make up a work of high quality, where art, imitating nature, seems to have outdone it.

"Suddenly there is a strong castle or gorgeous palace with walls of gold, towers of diamond and gates of gemstone; in short, its structure is so marvellous that although the materials from which it is built are nothing less than diamonds, rubies, pearls, gold, and emeralds, the workmanship is even more rare. And after having seen all this, what can be more charming than to see how a crowd of ladies comes out from the gate of the castle in fine and gorgeous clothing, that if I were to portray it as the histories describe it to us, I would not be able to do so; and then how the lady who seems to be the first among them all takes the hand of the bold Knight who jumped into the boiling lake, and without saying a word to him leads him into the rich palace, and strips him as naked as when he was born, and washes him in lukewarm water, and massages him all over with sweet-smelling oils, and clothes him in a shirt of the softest silk, all scented and perfumed, while another lady comes and throws over his shoulders a robe which is said to be worth at least a city, and even more? How charming is it, then, when they tell us how, after all of this, they lead him to another room where he finds the table set in such style that he is filled with amazement and wonder; to see how they pour water for his hands distilled from amber and sweet-scented flowers; how they seat him on an ivory chair; to see how the ladies serve him in profound silence; how they bring him a variety of food so temptingly prepared that the appetite does not know what to select; to hear the music that echoes while he is at the table, by whom or where it is produced he does not know. And then when the meal is over and the tables removed, the Knight rests in the chair, plucking the food from his teeth perhaps as usual, and a lady, much lovelier than any of the others, enters unexpectedly through the door, and herself by his side, begins to tell him what the castle is, and how she is held enchanted there, and other things that amaze the Knight and astonish the readers who are following his history.

"But I will not amplify this any further, as it may be gathered from it that whatever part of whatever history of a Knight one reads, it will fill the reader, whoever he is, with delight and wonder; and take my advice, sir, and, as I said before, read these books and you will see how they will remove any sadness you may feel and raise your spirit if it is depressed. Because I can say that since I have been a Knight I have become courageous, polite, generous, considerate, fearless, gentle, patient, and have learned to tolerate hardships, imprisonment, and enchantments; and although it is only such a short time since I have seen myself shut in a cage like a madman, I hope by the might of my arm, if heaven assists me and fortune does not go against me, to see myself King of some Kingdom where I may be able to show the gratitude and generosity that lives in my heart; because, señor, a poor man is unable to show the virtue of generosity to anyone, although he may possess it in the highest degree; and gratitude that rises from mood only is a dead thing, just as faith without action is dead. For this reason, I will be glad for fortune to offer me an opportunity of making myself an emperor, so I can show my heart in doing good to my friends, particularly to poor Sancho Panza, my aide, who is the best companion in the world; and I would gladly give him a county as I have promised him for so long, the only thing is, I am afraid he does not have the capacity to govern his realm."

Sancho partly heard the last words of his master, and said to him, "Try hard, Señor Don Quixote, to give me that county you have often promised me, because I promise you there will be no lack of capacity in me to govern it; and even if there is, I have heard there are men in the world who go to lords and pay so much a year to take charge of the government, while the lord relaxes and enjoys the revenue they pay him, without bothering himself with anything else. That's what I'll do, forget the whole business, and enjoy my rent, and let things go their own way."

"That, brother Sancho," said the Toledoan, "would be as good as far as the enjoyment of the revenue goes; but the lord still must attend to the administration of justice, and here capacity and sound judgment come in, and above all a firm determination to find out the truth; because if this is lacking in the beginning and the middle, the end will always go wrong; however, God commonly aids the honest intentions of the simple as he frustrates the evil designs of the crafty."

"I don't understand the philosophy," returned Sancho Panza; "all I know is I would like the county as soon as I know how to govern it; because I have as much soul as another, and as much body as anyone, and I will be as much a King of my realm as any other of his; and being so I will do as I like, and doing as I like I will please myself, and pleasing myself I will be content, and when one is content he has nothing more to desire, and when one has nothing more to desire there is a good end; so let the county come, and God be with you, and let us see one another, as one blind man said to the other."

"That is not a bad philosophy, Sancho," said the Toledoan; "but there is a lot to be said on the matter of governance."

To which Don Quixote returned, "I do not know what more there is to be said; I only guide myself by the example set for me by the great Amadis of France, when he made his aide the governor of the Insula Firme; and so, without any doubts of conscience, I can make a Sancho Panza a governor, because he is one of the best aides any Knight ever had."

The Toledoan was astonished by the methodical nonsense (if nonsense is capable of method) that Don Quixote expressed, at the way in which he had described the adventure of the Knight of the lake, at the impression that the deliberate lies of the books he read had given him, and lastly he marvelled at the simplicity of Sancho, who desired so eagerly to obtain the county his master had promised him.

By this time the Toledoan's servants had returned with the Donkey with the supplies, and making a carpet out of the green grass of the meadow to act as a table, they sat themselves in the shade of some trees and made their meal there. As they were eating they suddenly heard a loud noise and the sound of a bell that seemed to come from among some bushes that were nearby, and the same instant they observed a beautiful goat, spotted all over white and brown, jump out of the bush with a goat herder after it, shouting at it and saying the usual things to make it stop or turn around. The run-away goat, scared and frightened, ran towards the group as if seeking their protection and then stood still, and the goat herder came and held it by the horns and began to talk to it as if it possessed reason and understanding: "Ah runner, Spotty; how are you limping all the time? What wolves have frightened you, my daughter? Won't you tell me what is the matter, my beauty? What else can it be except that you are a female, and cannot keep quiet? There is a curse on you and those of the same kind! Come back, come back, my darling; and if you will not be happy, at least you will be safe among your companions; because if you who are the one to lead them, run away, what will happen to them?"

The goat herders talk amused those who heard it, but especially the Toledoan, who said to him, "As you live, brother, take it easy, and do not be in such a hurry to drive this goat back to the group; because, being a female, as you say, she will follow her natural instinct regardless of all you can do to prevent it. Take this bread and drink some soup, and that will soothe your irritation, and in the meantime the goat will rest herself," and then, he handed him the thigh of a cold rabbit on a fork.

The goat herder accepted it with thanks, and drank and calmed himself, and then said, "I am sorry if you take me for a foolish man for having spoken so seriously as I did to this animal; but the truth is there is a certain mystery in the words I used. I may appear to be foolish, but not so foolish that I do not know how to behave to men and to animals."

"That I can believe," said the vicar, "because I know by experience that the woods breed educated men, and shepherds' huts harbour philosophers."

"Always, señor," returned the goat herder, "they shelter men of experience; and so you may see the truth of this and grasp it, although I may seem to put myself forward without being asked, I will, if it will not tire you, gentlemen, and you will give me your attention for a little while, tell you a true story which will confirm this gentleman's word (as he pointed to the vicar) as well as my own."

To this Don Quixote replied, "Seeing that this story has a certain feeling of chivalry about it, I, brother, will listen to you gladly, and so will all these gentlemen, from the high intelligence they possess and their love of curious stories that interest, charm, and entertain the mind, as I feel quite sure yours will do. So begin, friend, because we are all prepared to listen."

"I decline," said Sancho, "and will leave with this pastry and go to the stream over there, where intend to satisfy myself for three days; because I have heard my lord, Don Quixote, say that a Knight's aide should eat until he can hold no more, whenever he has the chance to, because it often happens that by accident they find themselves in a wood so thick that they cannot find a way out for six days; and if the man is not well filled or his saddlebags well stored, there he may stay, as he does very often, turned into a dried corpse."

"You are right, Sancho," said Don Quixote; "go where you like and eat all you can, because I have had enough, and only want to give my mind its refreshment, as I will by listening to this good man's story."

"This is what we should all do," said the Toledoan; and then asked the goat herder to begin the story.

The goat herder gave the goat which he held by the horns a couple of slaps on the back, saying, "Lie down here, Spotty, because we have enough time to return to our group later." The goat seemed to understand him, because as her master seated himself, she stretched herself quietly beside him and looked up in his face to show him she was focussed on what he was going to say, and then in these words he began his story.

CHAPTER 51

WHAT THE GOAT HERDER TOLD THOSE WHO WERE CARRYING DON QUIXOTE

Three miles from this valley there is a village which, although it is small, is one of the richest in this neighbourhood, and in it lived a farmer, a very worthy man, and so respected that, although to be so is the natural consequence of being rich, he was even more respected for his virtue than for the wealth he had acquired. But what made him even more fortunate, as he said himself, was having a daughter of such exceeding beauty, rare intelligence, gracefulness, and virtue, that everyone who knew her and observed her admired the extraordinary gifts with which heaven and nature had given her. As a child she was beautiful, she continued to grow in beauty, and at the age of sixteen she was absolutely lovely. The fame of her beauty began to spread through all the villages around - but why do I only say the villages around, when in fact, it spread to distant cities, and even made its way into the halls of royalty and reached the ears of people of every class, who came from all sides of the globe to see her as if to see something rare, or some sacred image?

Her father watched over her and she watched over herself; because there are no locks, or guards, or bolts that can protect a young girl better than her own modesty. The wealth of the father and the beauty of the daughter led many neighbours as well as strangers to seek her as a wife; but he, as one should be, who had to decide who to give such a rich jewel to, was confused and unable to make up his mind to which of her countless admirers he should assign her to. I was one among the many who felt a desire so natural, and, as her father knew who I was, and I was from the same town, of pure blood, at the peak of life, and very rich in possessions, I had great hope of success. There was another from the same place with similar qualifications who also sought her, and this made her father's choice hang in the balance, because he felt that with either of us his daughter would be well presented; so to escape from this state of confusion he decided to refer the matter to Leandra (because that is the name of the rich lady who has reduced me to misery), reflecting that as we were both equal it would be best to leave it to his dear daughter to choose according to her preference - something that should be practised by all fathers who wish to settle their children in life. I do not mean that they should leave them to make a choice of what is disgraceful and bad, but that they should place before them what is good and then allow them to make a well informed choice. I do not know who Leandra chose; I only know her father told us about the young age of his daughter and vague words that showed him to be unassured but did not dismiss us. My rival is called Anselmo and I am Eugenio – so you may know the names of the people that appear in this tragedy, the end of which is still in suspense, although it is plain to see it is disastrous.

Around this time in our town there appeared one Vicente de la Roca, the son of a poor peasant of the same town, this Vicente having returned from service as a soldier in Italy and other parts. A captain who had been taken from our village when he was a boy of about twelve years, and now twelve years later the young man came back in a soldier's uniform, clothed in a thousand colours, and covered in glass jewels and fine steel chains. Today he would appear in one suit, tomorrow in another; bright and flashy, but with little substance. The peasants, who are naturally malicious, and when they have nothing to do can be spiteful, spoke about this, and took note of his fine jewellery, piece by piece, and discovered that he had three suits of different colours; but he made so many arrangements and combinations out of them, that if they had not counted them, anyone would have sworn that he had displayed more than ten suits. Do not think that I am telling you about the clothes for no reason, because they have a great deal to do with the story. He used to seat himself on a bench under a large tree in our area, and there he would astonish us with the stories he told us about his adventures. There was no country on the face of the globe he had not seen, no battle he had not been engaged in; he had killed more Moors than there are in Morocco and Tunisia combined, and fought more single combats, according to his own account, than Garcilaso, Diego Garcia de Paredes and a thousand others he named, and out of all he had been victorious without losing a drop of blood. On the other hand, he showed marks of wounds, which, although they could not be made out, he said were gunshot wounds. Lastly, with outrageous rudeness he used to say "you" to everyone and even those who knew him, and declared that being a soldier he was as good as the King himself. And to add to these boastful ways he was a good musician, and played the guitar with such skill that some said he made it speak; but his accomplishments did not end there, because he was a good poet too, and for anything that happened in the town he made a song.

This soldier, then, that I have described, this Vicente de la Roca, this soldier, heroic, musician, poet, was often seen and watched by Leandra from a window of her house which faced the street. The glitter of his attire captivated her, his songs charmed her (because he gave away twenty copies of every one he made), and she heard the stories of his adventures which he told about himself; and in short, as the devil no doubt had arranged it, she fell in love with him before the thought of making love to her had suggested itself to him; and as in love-affairs none are more easily concluded than those which have an inclination of the lady, Leandra and Vicente came to an understanding without any difficulty; and before any of her numerous admirers had any suspicion of her plan, she had already executed it, having left the house of her dearly beloved father (as she no longer had a mother) and disappeared from the village with the soldier, who came out more triumphantly from this adventure than out of any of the large number he claimed. All the village and all who heard of it were amazed by the affair; I was horrified, Anselmo shocked, her father full of grief, her relatives angry, the authorities all in agitation, the officers of the Brotherhood in uproar. They searched the roads, they explored the woods, and at the end of three days they found Leandra in a mountain cave, stripped to her underwear and robbed of all the money and precious jewels she had taken from her home with her.

334

They brought her back to her unhappy father, and questioned her about her misfortune, and she confessed without any pressure that Vicente de la Roca had deceived her, and with the promise of marrying her had induced her to leave her father's house, as he declared to take her to the richest and most delightful city in the whole world, which was Naples; and that she, naive and deluded, had believed him, and robbed her father, and handed over to him everything she disappeared with that night; and that he had taken her to a rugged mountain and shut her inside where they had found her. She said, that the soldier, without robbing her of her honour, had taken from her everything she had, and left, leaving her in the cave, something that surprised everybody. It was not easy for us to believe in the young man's continence, but she assured it with such seriousness that it helped to comfort her distressed father, who thought nothing about what had been taken, because the jewel that once lost can never be recovered, had been left with his daughter. The same day that Leandra made her appearance her father removed her from our sight and shut her in a nunnery in a town nearby, with the hope that time will wear away some of the disgrace she had incurred. Leandra's youth provided an excuse for her fault, not to those who did not care whether she was good or bad; but to those who knew her of intelligence, leading them not to attribute her misbehaviour to ignorance or shamelessness but to the natural disposition of women, which is quite often erratic and not well regulated.

With Leandra gone from sight, Anselmo's eyes became blind, or at least found nothing to look at that gave them any pleasure, and mine were in darkness without any light to direct them to anything enjoyable while Leandra was away. Our sadness grew greater, our patience was running out; we blamed the soldier's clothing and criticised the carelessness of Leandra's father. Finally, Anselmo and I agreed to leave the village and come to this valley; he has a flock of sheep and I have a large herd of goats, we spend our time among the trees, expressing our sorrow, both of us at times praising her, and other times criticising her, and sometimes we give heaven our complaints alone. Following our example, many more of Leandra's lovers have come to these mountains and adopted our way of life, and there are so many that one would think the place had been turned into the promised land, so full of shepherds and sheep; there is not a place in it where the name of the Leandra is not heard of. One criticises her and calls her impulsive, indecisive, and arrogant, then another calls her frail and silly; one forgives and excuses her, another despises and insults her; one speaks of her beauty, another attacks her character, and in short, all abuse her, and all adore her, and this general infatuation has reached a point that there are some who complain about her disrespect without ever having exchanged a word with her, and even some that complain and grieve with an intense fever of jealousy, which she never directly caused to anyone, because, as I have already said, her misconduct was never known before her passion. There is no place among the rocks, no land, no shade under the trees that is not occupied by some shepherd telling his problem to the breeze; wherever there is an echo it repeats the name of Leandra; the mountains say "Leandra,"- "Leandra" the streams say, and Leandra keeps us all confused, hoping without hope and fearing without knowing what we fear. Out of everyone the one that shows the least and also the most sense is my rival Anselmo, because having so many other things to complain about, he only complains of the separation, while playing his guitar, which he plays well, and he sings his complaints in verses that show his creativity. I follow another, easier, and in my opinion wiser course, and that is to criticise the foolishness of women, their inconstancy, their deceitfulness, their broken promises, and in short the lack of consideration they show in fixing their love and passion. This, was the reason for the words and expressions I used with this goat when I came just now; because as she is a female I have a dislike for her, although she is the best in my whole herd. This is the story I promised to tell you, and if it has taken me a long time to say it, I will not be slow to serve you; my hut is close by, and I have fresh milk and cheese there, as well as a variety of fruit, no less pleasing to the eye than to taste.

CHAPTER 52

THE ARGUMENT THAT DON QUIXOTE HAD WITH THE GOAT HERDER, TOGETHER WITH THE RARE ADVENTURE ABOUT REMOSE, WHICH WITH A LOT OF SWEAT HE BROUGHT TO A HAPPY CONCLUSION

Everyone totally enjoyed the goat herder's story, especially the Toledoan, because he praised the style it had been told in, as it was unlike the usual clownish goat herder's style and was more polished like it came from the city; and he observed that the vicar was quite right when he said educated men can be found in the mountains. They all offered their service to Eugenio but the one who offered the most was Don Quixote, who said to him, "Most certainly, brother goat herder, if I found myself in a position to attempt any adventure, I would, this very moment, go on your behalf, and would rescue Leandra from that nunnery (where she is no doubt being kept against her will), regardless of the nunnery and anyone who would try to prevent me, and I would place her in your hands to deal with her according to your will and pleasure, observing, however, the laws of chivalry which uphold no violence of any kind toward any lady. I trust in God our Lord that the power of one evil enchanter may not be so great that the power of another cannot overturn this situation I find myself in, and then I promise you my support and assistance, as I am bound to do by my profession, which is none other than to give aid to the weak and needy."

The goat herder observed him, and noticing Don Quixote's poor appearance and looks, was filled with wonder, and asked the barber, who the man next to him was, "Señor, who is this man of such a figure and talks in this manner?" "Who else could it be," said the barber, "but the famous Don Quixote of La Mancha, the corrector of injustice, the righter of wrongs, the protector of ladies, the terror of giants, and the winner of battles?"

"That," said the goat herder, "sounds like what someone reads in the books of Knights, who did all that you say this man does; although it is my belief that either you are joking, or this gentleman has empty space in his head."

"You dirty criminal," said Don Quixote, "it is you who is empty and a fool. I am fuller than the whore that gave birth to you;" and going from words to actions, he picked up a loaf of bread that was near him and threw in the goat herder's face, with such force that he flattened his nose; but the goat herder, who did not understand jokes, and found himself roughly handled, giving no respect to the carpet, tablecloth, or diner, attacked Don Quixote, and grabbing him by the throat with both hands would have choked him to death, if Sancho Panza had not instantly come to the rescue, and holding him by the shoulders threw him on the table cloth, smashing plates, breaking glasses, and upsetting and scattering everything on it. Don Quixote, finding himself free, went to get on top of the goat herder, who, with his face now covered with blood, and being kicked by Sancho, was on his hands and knees searching for one of the table-knives to take revenge with. The Toledoan and the vicar, however, prevented him, but the barber arranged it that the goat herder got Don Quixote under him, and he gave such a shower of punches that the poor Knight's face streamed with blood as freely as his own. The Toledoan and the vicar were bursting with laughter, the officers were jumping with amusement, and all encouraged them, as they do dogs that are attacking one another in a fight.

Sancho was frantic, because he could not free himself from the grasp of one of the Toledoan's servants, who kept him from going to assist his master.

At last, while they were all, with the exception of the two who were busy punching each other, in excitement and joy, they heard a trumpet sound a note so loud that it made them all look in the direction where it seemed to come from. But the one most excited by hearing it was Don Quixote, who although against his will was under the goat herder, and looking more than beaten, said to him, "Devil (because it is impossible that you are not one, because you had the strength to overcome mine), I ask you to agree to a truce because in one hour from the note of that trumpet that we hear, seems to me to be the start of a new adventure." The goat herder, who was by this time tired of punching and being punched, released his grip, and Don Quixote rising to his feet and turning his eyes to where the sound had been heard, suddenly saw coming down the slope of a hill several men covered in white like Knights representing atonement.

The fact was that the clouds had withheld their moisture from the earth, and in all the villages of the area they were organising marches, preparing for the day of the ascension, repenting for sins and asking God to open the hands of his mercy and send the rain; and because of this the people in one of the villages were on their way to a holy retreat which was on one side of the valley. When Don Quixote saw the strange clothing of those on their way to repent for their sins, without reflecting how often he had seen this before, took it into his head that this was some sort of adventure, and that it was his responsibility as a Knight to engage in it; and his notion was further confirmed, by the idea that an image they had with them covered in black was some distinguished lady that these villains and disrespectful thieves were taking away by force. As soon as this occurred to him he ran with full speed to Rocinante who was eating grass, and taking the reins and the shield hanging from the saddle, he mounted him instantly, and calling Sancho for his sword he raised his shield on his arm, and in a loud voice exclaimed to those who stood nearby, "Now, honourable friends, you will see how important it is that there are Knights in the world upholding the law of chivalry; now, I say, you will see, by the freedom of that admirable lady who is captive there, whether Knights deserve to be treated with respect," and so, he kicked his heels into Rocinante - and at a full speed (because in the whole of this genuine history we never read of Rocinante running slowly) he went to encounter those covered in white, although the vicar, the Toledoan, and the barber ran to stop him. But it was not in their power to do so, and he did not even stop for Sancho shouting, "Where are you going, Señor Don Quixote? What devil has possessed you to go against our Catholic faith? Stop! Can you not see that is a parade of people repenting, and the lady they are carrying on that stand there is the blessed image of the immaculate Virgin? Take care what you are doing, señor, because this time it can be safely said that you don't know what you are doing." Sancho's words had no effect, because his master was so fixed on approaching the figures covered in white and releasing the lady in black that he did not hear a word; and even if he had heard, he would not have turned back even if the King had ordered him to. He approached the marchers and slowed Rocinante, who was already anxious enough to relax the speed a little, and in a rough, excited voice he exclaimed, "You who hide your faces, perhaps because you are not good people, pay attention and listen to what I am about to say to you."

The first to stop were those carrying the image, and one of the four priests who were chanting the prayers, struck by the strange figure of Don Quixote, the leanness of Rocinante, and the other ludicrous peculiarities he observed, said in reply to him, "Brother, if you have anything to say to us say it quickly, because these people are going to repent, and we cannot stop, and neither is it reasonable that we stop to hear anything, unless it is short enough to be said in two words."

"I will say it in one," replied Don Quixote, "and it is this; that you release that lady whose tears and sad face clearly show that you are taking her against her will, and that you have committed some shameful crime against her; and I, who was born in the world to rectify wrongs like this, will not permit you to go another step until you have restored the freedom she desires and deserves."

All that heard these words concluded that he must be a madman, and began to laugh out loud, and their laughter acted as ignition for Don Quixote's fury, because raising his sword and without another word he rushed toward them. One of those who saw it, rushed to meet him, holding a big forked stick that he had for propping himself up when resting, Don Quixote attacked him and severed it into two pieces; but with the portion that remained in his hand he gave such a blow to Don Quixote's shoulder (which the shied could not protect against) that he made him fall to the ground in such a sad state.

Sancho Panza, who was coming as fast as he could, puffing and blowing, seeing him fall, shouted to his attacker not to hit him again, because he was a poor enchanted Knight, who had never harmed anyone in all the days of his life; but what stopped the man was not Sancho's shouting, but seeing that Don Quixote did not move his hands or feet; and so, believing he had killed him, he quickly tucked his shirt under his belt and ran across the field like a deer.

By this time all of Don Quixote's companions had come to where he lay; but those covered in white seeing them coming, along with officers of the Holy Brotherhood with their crossbows, feared trouble, and gathering around the image, raised their hoods, and held their horse whips, as the priests did their candles, and awaited the attack, determined to defend themselves and even to become offensive against their attackers if they could. Fortune, however, arranged the matter better than they expected, because all Sancho did was to throw himself onto his master's body, leaning over him and giving the saddest and laughable cry that was ever heard, because he believed he was dead. The vicar was known to another vicar who walked in the march, and their recognition of one another removed the anxiety of both groups; the first then told the other in a few words who Don Quixote was, and he and the whole bunch of atoners went to see if the poor gentleman was dead, and heard Sancho Panza saying, with tears in his eyes, "Oh Knight of chivalry, that blow with a stick has ended the course of your well-spent life! Oh pride of your race, honour and glory of all La Mancha, actually, of all the world, which without you will be full of evil people, no longer in fear of punishment for their crimes! Oh you, generous man even more than Alexander, since in only eight months of service you have taken me to the most beautiful places the sea surrounds! Humble with the proud, proud with the humble, facing dangers, enduring the outrage, loving without reason, imitator of the good, tormentor of the evil, enemy of the mean, in short, Knight, of all that can be said!"

Hearing the cries and moans of Sancho, Don Quixote regained his senses, and the first thing he said was, "The man who lives separated from you, sweetest Dulcinea, has greater misfortune to endure than this. Aid me, friend Sancho, to mount the enchanted cart, because I am not in a condition to take the saddle of Rocinante, as this shoulder has been knocked to pieces."

"That I will do with all my heart, señor," said Sancho; "and let us return to our village with these gentlemen, who seek the good for you, and there we will prepare for another adventure, which may turn out more profitable for us."

"You are right, Sancho," returned Don Quixote; "It will be wise to let the harmful influence of the stars which now conquers to pass."

The Toledoan, the vicar, and the barber told him he would act very wisely in doing as he said; and so, highly amused at Sancho Panza's simplicity, they placed Don Quixote in the cart as before. The marchers reformed themselves and continued on their journey; at this point the goat herder decided to leave the group; and the officers of the Brotherhood declined to go any further, and the vicar paid them what was due; the Toledoan begged the vicar to let him know how Don Quixote did, whether he was cured of his madness or still suffered from it, and then asked to leave to continue his journey; in short, they all separated and went their own way, leaving the vicar, the barber, Don Quixote, Sancho Panza, and the carter alone. The carter took his ox and made Don Quixote comfortable on a bed of hay, and at his usual careful pace took the road the vicar directed him to, and at the end of six days they reached Don Quixote's village, and entered it at about mid-day, which so happened to be a Sunday, and the people were all in the town square, through which Don Quixote's cart passed.

They all rushed to see what was in the cart, and when they recognised their townsman they were filled with amazement, and a boy ran off to tell the news to his housekeeper and his niece that their master and uncle had come back very skinny, yellow and stretched on a bed of hay in an ox-cart. It was pathetic to hear the crying of the two good ladies, and how they cursed the books of chivalry; which was repeated again when they saw Don Quixote coming through the gate.

With the news of Don Quixote's arrival Sancho Panza's wife came running, because by this time she knew that her husband had gone away with him as his aide, and on seeing Sancho, the first thing she asked him was if he was well. Sancho replied that he was, better than his master was.

"Thanks to God," said she, "for being so good to me; but now tell me, my friend, what have you have you earned from this? What pretty dress have you brought back for me? What shoes have you brought for your children?"

"I bring nothing of the sort, wife," said Sancho; "although I bring other things of more value."

"I am very glad to hear that," returned his wife; "show me these things of more value, my friend; because I want to see them to cheer my heart that has been so sad the whole time you have been away."

"I will show them to you at home, wife," said Sancho; "be content for the present; because if it pleases God we will go again on our travels in search of adventures, you will soon see me a governor of an island, and not one of those everyday ones, but the very best that can be governed."

"I hope heaven grants it, husband," said she, "because certainly, we need it. But tell me, what is this about islands, because I don't understand?"

"Honey is not for a donkey's mouth," replied Sancho; "all in good time and you will see, wife - actually, you will be surprised to hear yourself called 'my lady' by all your servants."

"What are you talking about, Sancho, my lady, islands, and servants?" returned Teresa Panza - which was the name of Sancho's wife, because in La Mancha it is customary for wives to take their husbands' surnames.

"Don't be in such a hurry to know all this, Teresa," said Sancho; "it is enough that I am telling you the truth, so be quiet. But I can tell you this much by the way, that there is nothing in the world more delightful than to be a person of reverence, aide of a Knight, and a seeker of adventures. To be sure most of the adventures we find do not end as nicely as I could wish, out of a hundred will be ok, ninety-nine will turn out badly. I know by experience, because in one of them I came out blanketed, and in others beaten. Still, apart from all that, it is a fine thing to be looking out for what might happen, crossing mountains, searching woods, climbing rocks, visiting castles, staying at inns, all for free."

While this conversation passed between Sancho Panza and his wife, Don Quixote's housekeeper and niece took him inside and undressed him and laid him in his old bed. He watched them suspiciously, and could not make out where he was. The vicar asked his niece to be very careful to make her uncle comfortable and to watch over him in case he tried to make an escape, telling her what they had done to bring him home. Hearing this, the pair raised their voices again and renewed their anger toward the books of chivalry, and asked heaven to throw the authors of such lies and nonsense into a bottomless well. They were, in short, kept in anxiety and fear that their uncle and master would escape the moment he felt better – and this is exactly what happened.

But the author of this history, although he has devoted much research to the discovery of the deeds achieved by Don Quixote during his third time leaving, has been unable to obtain any information derived from authentic documents in regards to them; but tradition has preserved in the memory of La Mancha the fact that Don Quixote, the third time he left his home, took himself to Saragossa, where he was present at some famous battles which happened in that city, and that his adventures there were worthy of his spirit and high intelligence. In regards to his death he was unable to discover any information, and neither would he have ascertained it or known it, if good fortune had not produced an old physician for him who had in his possession a heavy box, which, according to him, had been discovered among the crumbling foundations of an ancient nunnery that was being rebuilt; in the box was found writing in ancient lettering, but in Castilian, containing many of his achievements, and discussing the beauty of Dulcinea, the form of Rocinante, the faithfulness of Sancho Panza, and the burial of Don Quixote along with assorted inscriptions and tributes to his life and character; but all that could be read and deciphered were those which the trustworthy author of this supreme history presents. And the author asks from those who read it nothing in return for the work which it has taken him in examining and searching the Manchegan archives in order to bring it to light, except that they give him the same credit that people of sense give to the books of chivalry that permeate the world and are so popular; because with this he will consider himself paid and fully satisfied, and will be encouraged to seek out and produce other histories, if not as truthful, at least equal in invention and no less entertaining. The first words written found in the heavy box were these:

THE ACADEMICS OF ARGAMASILLA, A VILLAGE IN
LA MANCHA, ON THE LIFE AND DEATH OF DON QUIXOTE OF LA MANCHA

ON THE TOMB OF DON QUIXOTE:

The brave man that gave La Mancha more
Richness; after him no one else was seen
Without his wit, a happier town could not have been
Now he passed through Gods door;

The Knight renowned as far as any shore,
And all the lands that lie between;
The Knight of sorrowful thin and lean
History filled with his days before;

One who surpassed the Amadises, all,
Not one have the French accounted,

Supported by his love and light:
Who made the Belianises look small,
And sought his renown on Rocinante mounted;
Here, underneath this cold stone, is our Knight.

PANIAGUADO, ACADEMIC OF ARGAMASILLA: DULCINEA DEL TOBOSO

POEM

She, whose full features may be here described,
Big-chested, with a character of disdain,
Is Dulcinea, who Don Quixote loved in vain
The great Don Quixote of La Mancha sighed.

For her, his Queen Toboso, from side to side
He crossed the high mountains, on a campaign
Of Spain, and Montiel's famous plain:
Although Rocinante was a weary ride.

Evil planet, cruel destiny,
Pursued them both, for the Manchegan dame,
And the unconquered star of chivalry.
No youth or beauty saved her from the claim
Of death; he paid love's bitter penalty,
And left in marble to preserve his name.

CAPRICHOSO, ACADEMIC OF ARGAMASILLA, IN PRAISE OF ROCINANTE, HORSE OF
DON QUIXOTE OF LA MANCHA

POEM

On that proud throne with a diamond sheen,
Which the feet of Don Quixote degrade,
The mad Manchegan has been seen,
On Rocinante, in all his bravery displayed.

There he hung his arms and forceful blade,
With which, achieving deeds until now not seen,
He eliminates, cuts, chops; but art has made,
A novel style for the twelve pears, and a new scene.

If Amadis is the proud boast of France,
If through his children has his fame, In Greece,
Then through all the regions of the earth is spread

Great Don Quixote's name, which is by no chance.
Today promotes La Mancha over these,
Above Greece or France, La Mancha holds her head.

His glory does not end here, because his good horse,
Exceeds Brillador and Bayard far by force;
With all the horses compared with Rocinante,
The reputation they have won is scanty.

BURLADOR, ACADEMIC OF ARGAMASILLA, ON SANCHO PANZA

POEM

The admirable Sancho Panza here you see;
A great soul once was in that body so small,
There never was an aide on this earthly ball
So plain and simple, or of cleverness so free.

Within an inch of being Governor was he,
And would have been but he took a fall,
Because of these awful times, mean and illiberal,
That cannot even let a donkey be.

Because mounted on an ass (excuse the word),
By Rocinante's side this gentle aide,
Was there for his master to attend.
Delusive hopes that entice the common herd
With promises of ease, the heart is made,
In shadows, dreams, and smoke you will always end.

CACHIDIABLO, ACADEMIC OF ARGAMASILLA, ON THE TOMB OF DON QUIXOTE

The Knight lies here below,
A bad adventure, bruised and sore,
Who Rocinante was for,
In his wanderings to and fro.

By the side of the Knight is laid,
Unresponsive man, Sancho too,
Never an aide more true,
Not even in the aristocrats' trade.

TIQITOC, ACADEMIC OF ARGAMASILLA, ON THE TOMB OF DULCINEA DEL TOBOSO

Here Dulcinea lies.
Desirable and robust:
Now she is ashes and dust:
The end of all flesh that dies.
A lady of high degree,
With fame, and a proud name,
The great Don Quixote's flame,
And the pride of her village was she.

These were all the verses that could be deciphered; the rest, the writing being worm-eaten, were handed over to one of the Academics to determine their meaning by conjecture. We have been informed that at the cost of many sleepless nights and much work he has succeeded, and that he intends to publish them and relay Don Quixote's third venture.

END OF PART 1

PART 2

DEDICATION

TO THE GOVENOR OF LEMOS

These past days, when sending you my plays, that were published before appearing on the stage, I said, if I remember well, that Don Quixote was putting on his boots to go and offer service to you. Now I can say that "with his boots, he is on his way." When he reaches the destination I think I will have given some service to you, as I am continually encouraged to send him to many parts of the world, to stop the disgust which would be caused by another imitating, and sending a second Don Quixote through the whole world. And the one who has shown the greatest desire for him has been the great Emperor of China, who wrote me a letter in Chinese a month ago and sent it by a special courier. He asked me, or to be truthful, he begged me to send him Don Quixote, because he intended to create a college where the Spanish language would be taught, and it was his wish that the book to be read should be the History of Don Quixote. He also added that I should go and be the director of this college. I asked the transporter if His Majesty had offered a sum to assist me with my travel expenses. He answered, "No, not even in thought."

"Then, brother," I replied, "you can return to China, immediately or at whatever pace you are obliged to go, as I am not fit for such long travel and, apart from being ill, I have very little money, and while there are Emperors and Emperors, Monarchs and Monarchs all over the globe, I have in Naples the great Governor of Lemos, who, without such a grand title, offering colleges and directorships, sustains me, protects me and does for me more favours than I can wish for."

Therefore, I authorised his departure and wish you well on yours. I offering you "The work of Persiles and Sigismunda," a book I will finish within four months, God willing, and which will be either the worst or the best that has been composed in our language, I mean out of those intended for entertainment; at which I apologise for possibly saying it could be the worst, because, in the opinion of friends, it is certain to attain the peak of possible quality. May you return in the perfect health that is wished for you; Persiles will be ready to kiss your hand and I your feet, being as I am, your humblest servant.

From Madrid, the last day of October of the year one thousand six hundred and fifteen.

PREFACE

God bless me, gentle (or it may be common) reader, how eagerly you must be looking forward to this preface, expecting to find revenge, scolding, and abuse against the author of the second Don Quixote - I mean the one who was, they say, produced at Tordesillas and born in Tarragona! Well then, the truth is, I am not going to give you that satisfaction; because, although damage stirs up anger even in a humble man's heart, in mine it must offer an exception. You would like me to call him an ass, a fool, and disrespectful, but I do not have this intention; let his offence be his punishment, let him eat his bread, and that is the end of it. What I cannot help taking personally is that he blames me for being old and one-handed, as if it had been in my power to keep time from passing, or as if the loss of my hand had happened in some pub, and not on the finest occasion the past or present has seen, or the future can hope to see. If my wounds have no beauty in the eye of the beholder, they are, at least, honourable to those who know where they were received; because the soldier gains a greater advantage dead in battle than running away alive; and I feel so strongly about this, that if it were my time to perform an impossibility for me, I would rather share in that mighty action, than be free from wounds right now without having been present. Those injuries the soldier shows on his face and chest are stars that direct others to the heaven of honour and ambition of deserved praise; and moreover it is to be noted that it is not grey hairs that makes one write, but, with the understanding, and that commonly improves with years. I take it offensively as well, that he calls me envious, and explains it to me, as if I were ignorant of what envy is; because really and truly, out of the two kinds that there are, I only know the one which is holy, honourable, and ethical; and if that is so, as it is, I am not likely to attack a priest, above all if, in addition, he holds the rank of the Holy Office. And if he said it on behalf of who I think he did, he is completely mistaken; because I worship the genius of that person, and admire his nonstop and tireless work. After all, I am grateful to this gentleman, the author, for saying that my novels are more entertaining than usual, and that they are very good; because they could not be that unless if there was a little bit of everything in them.

I suspect that you will say I am taking a very humble approach, and keeping myself too much within the boundary of my control, from a feeling that additional suffering should not be inflicted on a sufferer, and that what this gentleman has to endure must be very great, as he does not dare to come out into the open field and broad daylight, but hides his name and disguises his country as if he had been guilty of some crime. If by chance you find out who he is, tell him from me that I do not hold resentment; because I know what the temptations of the devil are, and that one of the greatest is putting into a man's head that he can write and print a book by which will give him as much fame as money, and as much money as fame; and to prove it I ask you, in your own lively, pleasant way, to tell him this story:

There was a madman in Seville who performed one of the funniest irrationalities and impulses that any madman in the world ever did. It was this: he made a tube of reed sharp at one end, and catching a dog in the street, or wherever it might be, with his foot he held one of its legs, and with his hand lifted up the other, and as best he could place the tube where, by blowing, he made the dog as round as a ball; then holding it in this position, he gave it a couple of slaps on the belly, and let it go, saying to the spectators (and there were always plenty of them): "Do you think, that it is an easy thing to blow up a dog?" - Do you think, that it is an easy thing to write a book?

And if this story does not suit him, you may tell him this one, which is similar to the madman and the dog:

In Cordova there was another madman, who carried a very heavy piece of marble slab or a stone on his head, and when he came across any vicious dog he used to get close to him and let the weight fall right on top of him; and then the dog in a rage, barking loudly, would run through the streets without stopping. It so happened, however, that one of the dogs he dropped his load on was a cap-maker's dog, which was very much loved by his owner. The stone came down hitting it on the head, the dog made a loud howl, the master saw everything and was furious, and picking up a large stick rushed toward the madman and did not leave a solid bone in his body, and with every hit he gave him he said, "You are the dog - you thief! My lurcher! Don't you see, you fool, that my dog is a lurcher?" and repeating the word "lurcher" again and again, he sent the madman away beaten to jelly. The madman took the lesson to heart, and vanished, and for more than a month no one saw him in public; but after that he came out again with his old trick and a heavier load than ever. He came to where there was a dog, and examining it very carefully without letting the stone fall, he said: "This is a lurcher!" In short, all the dogs he came across, if they were mastiffs or terriers, he said were lurchers; and he dropped no more stones. Maybe it will be the same with this author; that he will not dare to drop the weight of his mind in books, which, being bad, are harder than stones. Tell him, too, that I do not care about the threat he holds against me of depriving me of my profit due to his book; because, to borrow from the famous interlude of "The Perendenga," I say to him, "Long life to my lord and let Christ be with us all." Long life to the great Governor of Lemos, whose Christian charity and well-known generosity support me against the strokes of my bad fortune; and long life to the supreme compassion of Don Bernardo of Sandoval and Rojas from Toledo; and I do not care if there were no printing-presses in the world, or if they print more books against me than there are letters in the verses of the drama 'Mingo Revulgo!' These two princes, do not request any praise from me, and out of their own goodness, have decided to show me kindness and protect me, and from this I consider myself happier and richer than if Fortune had raised me to the greatest of heights. A poor man may retain honour, but the vicious cannot; poverty can cast a cloud over graciousness, but cannot hide it altogether; and as virtue sheds a certain light, even though it be through the passages and cracks of poverty, it wins the respect of grand and honourable spirits, and as a consequence their protection. You do not need to say any more to him, and I will say no more to you, except to tell you to keep in mind that this Second Part of "Don Quixote" which I offer to you is cut by the same craftsman and from the same cloth as the First, and that in it I present to you Don Quixote continued, and the remaining story until dead and buried, so that no one can dare to bring forward any further evidence of his life, because that which is produced here is sufficient; and it is safe to say that a trustworthy person has given an account of all the insanities of his, without having to go into the matter again; because an abundance, even of good things, prevents them from being valued; and scarcity, even in the case of what is bad, has a certain value. I was forgetting to tell you that you may also expect the "Persiles," which I am now finishing, and also the Second Part of "Galatea."

CHAPTER 1

THE INTERVIEW THE VICAR AND THE BARBER HAD WITH DON QUIXOTE ABOUT HIS ILLNESS

Cide Hamete Benengeli, in the Second Part of this history, and third excursion of Don Quixote, says that the vicar and the barber went a whole month without seeing him, to avoid bringing back to his memory what had happened. They did not, however, forget to visit his niece and housekeeper, and encourage them to be careful, treat him with attention, and give him comforting things to eat, those which were good for the heart and the brain, from where, it was clear to see, all of his misfortune came. The niece and housekeeper replied that they did so, and would continue to do so with all possible care and diligence, because they had started to notice that their master was now and then beginning to show signs of being in his right mind. This gave great satisfaction to the vicar and the barber, because they concluded they had taken the right course of action when taking him away as enchanted on the ox-cart, as has been described in the First Part of this great as well as accurate history, in the last chapter of it. So they decided to visited and test the improvement in his condition, although they thought that it was almost impossible there could be any; and they agreed not to discuss any point connected with Knighthood so they did not run the risk of reopening wounds which were still healing.

Therefore, they came to see him, and found him sitting in bed in a green waistcoat and a red cap, so thin and dried up that he looked as if he had been turned into a mummy. They were very well welcomed by him; they asked him about his health, and he talked to them about himself very naturally and in very well-chosen language. In the course of their conversation they started to discuss what they call State-craft and systems of government, correcting this abuse and condemning that, reforming one practice and eliminating another, each of the three acting like a new legislator, and they completely remodelled the State, that they seemed to have placed it into an oven and then taken out something quite different from what they had put in; and on all the subjects they dealt with, Don Quixote spoke with such good sense that the pair of examiners were fully convinced that he had recovered and had his full senses back.

The niece and housekeeper were present during the conversation and could not find enough words to express their thanks to God for seeing their master so clear in his mind; the vicar, however, changing his original plan, which was to avoid talking about matters of chivalry, decided to test Don Quixote's recovery thoroughly, and see whether it were genuine or not; and so, from one subject to another, he came at last to talk about the news that had come from the capital, and, among other things, he said it was considered true that a Turk was coming with a powerful fleet, and that no one knew what his purpose was, or when the great storm would arrive; and that all the Christians were in anxiety over this, which almost every year calls us to fight, and that the King had made preparations for the security of the coasts of Naples, Sicily and the island of Malta.

To this Don Quixote replied, "His Majesty has acted like a wise warrior in providing for the safety of his realms in time, so that the enemy may not find him unprepared; but if my advice were taken I would recommend to him to adopt an action which at present, no doubt, the King is very far from thinking of."

The moment the vicar heard this he said to himself, "God keep you in his hand, poor Don Quixote, because it seems to me you are advancing from the height of your madness into the profound depth of your simplicity."

But the barber, who had the same suspicion as the vicar, asked Don Quixote what would be his advice in regards to the actions that he said should be taken; because it might prove to be one that would have to be added to the list of the many disrespectful suggestions that people were in the habit of offering to princes.

"Mine, master shaver," said Don Quixote, "will not be disrespectful, actually, quite the opposite, very respectful."

"I don't mean that," said the barber, "but experience has shown that all or most of the methods which are proposed to the King are either impossible, absurd, or harmful to the King and the Kingdom."

"Mine, however," replied Don Quixote, "is not impossible or absurd, but the easiest, the most reasonable, the quickest and most efficient that could be suggested to anyone's mind."

"You take a long time to say it, Señor Don Quixote," said the vicar.

"I don't choose to say it here, now," said Don Quixote, "and have it reach the ears of the lords of the council tomorrow morning, and someone else receive the thanks and rewards of my trouble."

"I swear," said the barber, "I give you my word here and as God as my witness, that I will not repeat what you say, to King, bishop or man - an oath I learned from a story from the vicar, who, in the introduction, told the King about the thief who had robbed him of a hundred gold coins and his donkey."

"I am not familiar with this story," said Don Quixote; "but I know the oath is a good one, because I know the barber is an honest man."

"Even if he were not," said the vicar, "I will confirm on his behalf that in this matter he will be as silent as a dummy, or else in consequence suffer the pain of any penalty you propose."

"And who will be the security for you, señor Vicar?" said Don Quixote.

"My profession," replied the vicar, "which is to keep secrets."

"Very well!" said Don Quixote, "what more does the King have to do but to command, by public announcement, all the Knights that are scattered all over Spain to come together on a fixed day in the capital, because even if no more than half a dozen come, there may be one among them who will be sufficient enough to destroy the entire power of the Turk. Give me your attention and listen to me. Is it any new thing for a single Knight to demolish an army of two hundred thousand men, as if they all had only one throat or were made of glass?

Actually, tell me, how many histories are there filled with these miracles? If only the famous Don Belianis were alive now, or any one of the innumerable children of Amadis of France! If any these were alive today, and were to come face to face with the Turk, I swear, the Turk would not have a chance. But God will protect his people, and will provide some one, who, if not as courageous as the Knights of the past, at least will not be inferior to them in spirit; God knows what I mean, and I say no more."

"Oh God!" exclaimed the niece, "let me die if my master does not want to turn into a Knight again;" to which Don Quixote replied, "A Knight I will die, and let the Turk come when he likes, and with as much force as he can, once more I say, God knows what I mean." But here the barber said, "I ask you all to allow me to tell a short story of something that happened in Seville, which is so appropriate right now that I would really like to tell it." Don Quixote gave him permission, and the rest prepared to listen, and he began like this:

"In the madhouse at Seville there was a man who had been placed there by his relations for being out of his mind. He was a graduate of Osuna in law; but even if he had been from Salamanca, the opinion of most people was that he would have been mad anyway. This graduate, after some years of confinement, took it into his head that he was sane and in his full senses, and under this impression wrote to the Archbishop, asking him seriously, and in very fine language, to have him released from the misery in which he was living; because by God he had now recovered his lost reason, although his relations, in order to enjoy his property, kept him there, and, despite the truth, would make him out to be mad until he dies. The Archbishop, encouraged by repeated sensible, well-written letters, directed one of his ministers to make an inquiry with the madhouse in regards to the truth of the man's statements, and to have an interview with the madman himself, and, if it appeared that he was in his senses, to take him out and restore his freedom. The minister did so, and the governor assured him that the man was still mad, and that although he often spoke like a highly intelligent person, he would in the end break out into nonsense that counterbalanced all the sensible things he had said before, which could be easily tested by talking to him. The minister decided to try the experiment, and obtaining access to the madman and speaking with him for an hour or more, found that, during the whole the time he never said a word that was incoherent or absurd, but, on the contrary, he spoke so rationally that the minister was compelled to believe he was sane. Among other things, he said the governor was against him, not to lose the fee his relations paid for reporting him to still be mad; and that the worst enemy he had in his misfortune was his large property. In short, he spoke in such a way that he threw suspicion on the governor, and made his relations appear to be acquisitive and heartless, and himself to be so rational that the minister decided to take him away so the Archbishop could see him, and ascertain for himself the truth of the matter. Going forward with this view, the worthy minister asked the governor to give him the clothes in which the man of law had entered the house. The governor asked him to be careful in regards to what he doing, as the man of law was without a doubt still mad; but all his cautions and warnings had no effect to discourage the minister from taking him away. The governor, seeing that it was an order from the Archbishop, obeyed, and they dressed the man in his own clothes, which were new and decent. As soon as he saw himself clothed like someone in his senses, and separated from the appearance of a madman, he asked the minister to allow him to go and say goodbye to the madmen in the house. The minister said he would go with him to see what madmen there were; so they went upstairs. Approaching a cage in which there was a furious madman, although at that moment he was calm and quiet, the man of law said to him, 'Brother, do you have any requests for me, because I am going home, as God has been pleased, in his infinite goodness and compassion to restore my reason. I am now cured and in my senses, because with God's power nothing is impossible. Have strong hope and trust in him, because as he has restored me to my original condition, likewise he will restore yours if you trust in him too. I will take care to send you some good things to eat; and be sure you eat them; because I am convinced, as someone who has gone through it, that all this madness comes from having the stomach empty and the brains full of wind. Have courage! Have courage! because hopelessness in misfortune breaks down health and brings us to death faster.'

Another madman in a cage opposite the furious one was listening; and getting up from an old mat on which he lay completely naked, he asked in a loud voice who it was that was leaving cured and with his senses. The man of law answered, 'It is I, brother, who am going; I now have no need to stay here any longer, and because of this I return infinite thanks to Heaven that has had such great mercy on me.'

"'Mind what you are saying; don't let the devil deceive you,' replied the madman. 'Be quiet, stay where you are, and you will save yourself the trouble of coming back.'"

"'I know I am cured,' returned the man of law, 'and will not have to return again.'"

"'You, cured?' said the madman; 'well, we will see; God be with you; but I swear to you, that for this crime, which Seville is committing today by releasing you from this house, and treating you as if you were in your senses, I will have to inflict such a punishment that will be remembered for ages and ages, amen. Do you not know, miserable little man, that I can do it, being Jupiter the Thunder Cloud, who holds in my hands the fiery bolts which I am able to threaten the world with? So I will punish this town, but in another way, and that is by not raining on it, or on any part of its district or territory, for three whole years, to be started from the day and moment when this threat is given. You free, you cured, you in your senses! And I am mad? I am disordered? I am stuck here! I will not rain and instead think of hanging myself.

"Those present stood listening to the words and exclamations of the madman; but our man of law, turning to the minister and holding him by the hands, said to him, 'Do not worry, señor; attach no importance to what this madman has said; because if he is Jupiter and will not send the rain he promised, I, who am Neptune, the father and god of the water, will rain, as often as I like and as often as needed.'

"The governor and the bystanders laughed, and from their laughter the minister was half ashamed, and he replied, 'because of that, Señor Neptune, it is not wise to anger Señor Jupiter; stay where you are, and some other day, when there is a better opportunity and more time, we will come back for you.' So they stripped the man of law, and he was left where he was; and that's the end of the story."

"So that's the story, master barber," said Don Quixote, "which is apparently appropriate that you could not help telling it? Master shaver, master shaver! How blind is a man who cannot see through a sieve? Is it possible that you do not know that comparisons of intelligence with intelligence, courage with courage, beauty with beauty, birth with birth, are always repulsive and unwelcome? I, master barber, am not Neptune, the god of the waters, and neither do I try to make anyone take me for an intelligent man, because I am not one. My only endeavour is to convince the world of the mistake it makes in not reviving the happy time when the laws of chivalry were around. But our degenerate present does not deserve to enjoy such a blessing as the past enjoyed when Knights defended the kingdoms, protected ladies, comforted orphans and children, punished the proud, and recompensed the humble. With the men of these days, mostly, it is the attire, fabrics, and rich stuff they wear, that rustle as they walk, not the chains of their armour; no man these days sleeps in the open field exposed to the weather of heaven, and with full equipment from head to foot; no one now takes a nap, as they call it, without climbing down from his horse, and leaning on his lance, as the Knights used to do; no one now, goes through the woods, penetrates the mountains, and then treads on the lonely shore of the sea - mostly a wild and stormy one - and then finding himself a little boat without oars or sail of any kind, in the fearlessness of his heart places himself into it and commits himself to the furious swirls of the deep sea, that one moment lift him up to heaven and the next plunge him into the depths; and finds himself, when he least expects it, three thousand miles or more away from the place where he embarked; and leaping ashore in a distant and unknown land, has adventures that deserve to be written, not on paper, but inscribed on brass. But now laziness triumphs over energy, inactivity over effort, vice over virtue, arrogance over courage, and theory over practice in chivalry, which flourished and shone brightly only in the golden ages and Knights of the past. Because tell me, who was more virtuous and more brave than the famous Amadis of France? Who more modest than Palmerin of England? Who more gracious and easy than Tirante el Blanco? Who politer than Lisuarte of Greece? Who more daring than Don Belianis? Who more fearless than Perion of France? Who more ready to face danger than Felixmarte of Iran? Who sincerer than Esplandian? Who more impetuous than Don Cirongilio of Greece? Who bolder than Rodamonte? Who more prudent than Sombrino? Who more courageous than Reinaldos? Who more invincible than Roland? And who more gracious and civil than Ruggiero, from whom the dukes of Ferrara of the present have descended, according to Turpin and his 'genealogy.' All these men, and many more that I could name, señor vicar, were Knights, the light and glory of chivalry. These, or Knights like these, I would have to carry out my plan, and the King would find himself well served and would save great expense, and the Turk would be left pulling out his beard. And so I will stay where I am, as the vicar does not want to take me away; and if Jupiter, as the barber has told us, will not send rain, here am I, and I will rain when I please. I say this so that Master Basin may know that I understand him."

"Indeed, Señor Don Quixote," said the barber, "I did not mean it in that way, my intention was good, and you should not be angered."

"In regards to whether I should be angry or not," returned Don Quixote, "I am the best judge of that."

"I have hardly said a word; and I would gladly be relieved of a doubt, arising from what Don Quixote has said, that worries and works my conscience." Said the vicar.

"Señor vicar I offer you more than that," returned Don Quixote, "so please declare your doubt, because it is not pleasant to have a doubt on your conscience."

"Well then, with that permission," said the vicar, "my doubt is that, after all I can do, I cannot persuade myself that all of the Knights you, Señor Don Quixote, have mentioned, were really and truly people of flesh and blood, that ever lived in the world; but actually, I suspect it is all fiction, stories, false, and dreams told by men who are awake, or rather still half asleep."

"That is another mistake," replied Don Quixote, "which many have fallen into who do not believe that there were such Knights in the world, and I have often, with numerous people and on numerous occasions, tried to expose this almost universal error to the light of truth. Sometimes I have not been successful in my purpose, sometimes I have, placing it on the shoulders of the truth; it is so clear that I can almost say I have seen Amadis of France with my own eyes, who was a man of great stature, fair complexion, with a handsome although black beard, with a facial expression between gentle and harsh, careful with words, slow to be angered, and quick to calm from any anger; and as I have depicted Amadis, I could also, I think, portray and describe all the Knights that are in the histories of the whole world; because by the perception I have that they were what their histories describe them as, and by the deeds they did and the dispositions they displayed, it is possible, with the aid of sound philosophy, to deduce their features, complexion, and stature."

"How big, in your opinion, would the giant Morgante have been, Señor Don Quixote?" asked the barber.

"With regard to giants," replied Don Quixote, "opinions differ as to whether there ever were any or not in the world; but the Holy Scripture, which cannot deviate from the truth, tells us that there were, when it gives us the history of that giant, Goliath, who was nine and a half feet in height, which is a huge size. Likewise, in the island of Sicily, leg-bones and arm-bones have been found so large that their size makes it clear that their owners were giants, and as tall as great towers; geometry puts this fact beyond a doubt. But, despite all that, I cannot speak with certainty in regards to the size of Morgante, although I suspect he cannot have been very tall; and I form this opinion because I find in the history in which his deeds are particularly mentioned, that he frequently slept under a roof and as he found houses to contain him, it is clear that his size could not have been excessive."

"That is true," said the vicar, and while he was enjoying hearing such nonsense, he asked him what was his opinion of the features of Reinaldos from Montalban was, and Don Roland and the rest of the Twelve Peers of France, because they were all Knights.

"Reinaldos," replied Don Quixote, "I would say, was broad-faced, had a reddish complexion, with mischievous and somewhat prominent eyes, excessively thorough and sensitive. In regards to Roland, or Rotolando, or Orlando (because he has gone by all of these names), the opinion I hold is, that he had average height, was broad-shouldered, rather bent-legged, tanned-complexioned, red-bearded, with a hairy body and severe expression, a man of few words, but very polite and well-mannered when he did speak."

"With that description," said the vicar, "it is no wonder that Lady Angelica rejected him and left him for the joyful liveliness, and grace of that full-bearded little Moor to whom she surrendered herself; falling in love with the gentle softness of Medoro rather than the roughness of Roland."

"That Angelica, señor vicar," returned Don Quixote, "was an unstable lady, erratic and somewhat unrestrained, and she left the world as full of her impulses as the fame of her beauty. She treated a thousand gentlemen with disrespect, men of courage and wisdom, and went with a smooth-faced little twig, without fortune or fame, except a reputation for gratitude which he showed for the affection his friend had for him. The great poet who always sang about her beauty, the famous Ariosto, completely stopped singing about her after her disgraceful surrender, and finally dropped her when he said:

Some other poet of skilful writing may sing about her; and this was no doubt a kind of prophecy, because poets have also been called psychics; and the truth of this was made clear; because since then a famous Andalusian poet has cried and sung in tears over her, and another famous and rare poet, a Castilian, has sung about her beauty."

"Tell me, Señor Don Quixote," said the barber, "among all those who praised her, has there ever been a poet who wrote a mockery of this Lady Angelica?"

"I believe," replied Don Quixote, "that if Sacripante or Roland had been poets they would have ridiculed the lady; because this is the natural way with poets who have been rejected, whether fabricated or not, they select these ladies of their thoughts, to avenge themselves in mockeries and publishing false statements; but up until now I have not heard any defamatory verses against Lady Angelica, who turned the world upside down."

"Strange," said the vicar; but at this moment they heard the housekeeper and the niece, who had previously withdrawn from the conversation, shouting in the courtyard, and because of the noise they all ran outside.

CHAPTER 2

THE NOTABLE ARGUMENT WHICH SANCHO PANZA HAD WITH DON QUIXOTE'S HOUSEKEEPER AND NIECE, ALONG WITH OTHER AMUSING MATTERS

History states that the shouting Don Quixote, the vicar, and the barber heard came from the niece and the housekeeper screaming at Sancho, who was striving to force his way in to see Don Quixote while they held the door against him, "What does the tramp want in this house? Go away! Because it is you, and no one else, that deludes my master, and leads him astray, and takes him roaming around the country."

To which Sancho replied, "The devil's housekeeper! It is I who am deluded, and led astray, and taken roaming around the country, and not your master! He has taken me all over the world, you are completely mistaken. He enticed me away from my home with a trick, promising me an island, which I am still waiting for."

"I hope the evil islands choke you, disgraceful Sancho," said the niece; "What are islands? Something to eat, greedy sloth that you are?"

"It is not something to eat," replied Sancho, "but something to govern and rule, and better than four cities or four terms as a judge in the courts."

"Who cares what you say," said the housekeeper, "you don't enter this house, you bag of mischief and sack of dishonesty; go govern your own house, and stop searching for islands."

The vicar and the barber listened to the three of them with great amusement; but Don Quixote, was unsettled because Sancho might divulge a whole heap of mischievous stupidities, and touch on points that might not be suitable for him to say, so he called for him and made the other two let him come in. Sancho entered, and the vicar and the barber decided to leave Don Quixote, whose recovery they now considered unlikely after they saw how stuck to these crazy ideas he was, and how saturated he was with his nonsense of chivalry; so the vicar said to the barber, "You will see, when we are not thinking about it, these gentlemen will be go again on another adventure."

"I have no doubt about it," returned the barber; "I understand the madness of the Knight but cannot understand the simplicity of the aide, who has such a firm belief about the island, that I suppose exposing him to the truth would still not get it out of his head."

"God help them," said the vicar; "let us watch carefully to see what comes from all these absurdities of the Knight and aide, because it seems as if they had both been made from the same material, and the madness of the master without the simplicity of the man would not be worth much."

"That is true," said the barber, "I would like to know what the pair are talking about right now."

"I promise you," said the vicar, "the niece or the housekeeper will tell us soon, because they are not the type to forget to listen."

Meanwhile Don Quixote shut himself in his room with Sancho, and when they were alone he said to him, "It saddens me greatly Sancho, that you have said, and say, that I led you astray when we left together, we took the road together, we wandered abroad together; we have had the same fortune and the same luck; if they blanketed you once, they beat me a hundred times, and that is the only advantage I have over you."

"That was only reasonable," replied Sancho, "because, by what you say, misfortune belongs more to Knights more than their aides."

"You are mistaken, Sancho," said Don Quixote, "according to the maxim quando caput dolet, etc."

"I don't understand any language but my own," said Sancho.

"I mean to say," said Don Quixote, "that when the head suffers the members of the body suffer also; and so, being your lord and master, I am your head, and you are a part of me as you are my servant; and therefore any evil that affects or will affect me should give you pain, and what affects you will give pain to me."

"That should be so," said Sancho; "but when I was blanketed as a member, your head was on the other side of the wall, looking at me while I was flying through the air, and I did not feel any pain; so if the members are obliged to feel the suffering of the head, the head should be obliged to feel the member's suffering."

"Are you trying to say, Sancho," said Don Quixote, "that I did not feel anything when they were blanketing you? If you do, you should not say so or think so, because I felt more pain then in spirit than you did in your body. But let us put that aside for the moment, because we will have enough opportunities to consider and settle the point; tell me, Sancho my friend, what do they say about me in the village here? What do the common people think of me? The ladies? The gentlemen? What do they say about my courage; my achievements; my courtesy? How do they treat the task I have undertaken in reviving and restoring to the world the now forgotten laws of chivalry? In short, Sancho, I want you to tell me everything that has come to your ears on this subject; and you have to tell me, without adding anything to the good or taking away anything from the bad; because it is the duty of loyal servants to tell the truth to their lords just as it is, not adding flattery to it or any excessive admiration to obscure it. And I want you to know, Sancho, that if the pure truth, undisguised by flattery, was given to princes, now would be different, and an earlier date would have been considered the iron age more than ours. You can profit from this advice Sancho, and report to me clearly and authentically the truth of what you know about what I have asked from you."

"I will do with all my heart, master," replied Sancho, "provided you will not be angry in anyway by what I say, as you wish me to say it in its naked form, without adding any clothes to it, than how it came to my knowledge."

"I will not be angry at all," returned Don Quixote; "you can speak freely, Sancho, and without going around the subject."

"Well then," he said, "first of all, I have to tell you that the common people consider you a great madman, and me a fool. The hidalgos say that you have made up the 'Don,' and called yourself a Knight, with a couple of acres of land, and barely a shirt on your back. The caballeros say they do not want to oppose the hidalgos, and say the hidalgo's aides polish their own shoes and wear better clothing than us."

"That," said Don Quixote, "does not apply to me, because I am always well dressed; and if I am ragged, I am ragged from the wear and tear of combat not from time."

"In regards to your bravery, politeness, accomplishments, and tasks, there is a variety of opinions. Some say, 'mad but amusing;' others, 'heroic but unlucky;' others, 'polite but interfering,' and then they go into so much detail about us that they don't leave a whole bone in either you or myself unexamined."

"Remember, Sancho," said Don Quixote, "that wherever virtue exists in a prominent degree it is persecuted. Very few or perhaps none of the famous men that have lived escaped being defamed by malice. Julius Caesar, the boldest, wisest, and bravest of captains, was charged with being ambitious, and not particularly clean in his dress, or pure in his morals. Alexander, whose actions gained him the title of Great, they said was an alcoholic. Hercules, the man of much work, they said was lustful. Don Galaor, the brother of Amadis of France, they said was argumentative, and his brother they said was sad. So, Sancho, amongst all the insults against good men, I will let mine pass, since there are no more than you have said."

"No more?"

"Is there more, then?" asked Don Quixote.

"We have only skimmed the surface," said Sancho; "like icing on fancy cakes and bread; but if you want to know all insults they say against you, I will bring you someone who can tell you all of them without missing any; because last night the son of Bartholomew Carrasco, who has been studying at Salamanca, came home after completing his bachelor's degree, and when I went to welcome him, he told me that your history is already published in books, with the title: 'THE INGENIOUS GENTLEMAN DON QUIXOTE OF LA MANCHA'; and he says they mention me in it using my own name: Sancho Panza, and lady Dulcinea del Toboso as well, and various things that happened to us when we were alone; so I wonder how the historian who wrote them could have known them."

"I promise you, Sancho," said Don Quixote, "the author of our history must be some sage enchanter; because whatever they choose to write about can never be hidden."

"What!" said Sancho, "a sage and an enchanter! Samson Carrasco (that I spoke of) says the author of the history is called Cid Hamete Benengeli."

"That is a Moorish name," said Don Quixote.

"That may be so," replied Sancho.

"You must have mistaken his surname 'Cide' - which means in 'Lord' in Arabic" said Don Quixote.

360

"Very likely," replied Sancho, "but if you wish to speak to Samson Carrasco I will go and get him."

"That would be a great pleasure for me, my friend," said Don Quixote, "because what you have told me has amazed me, and I will not eat anything until I have heard all about it."

"Then I am off to get him," said Sancho; and leaving his master he went in search of Samson Carrasco, who he returned with not too long later, and, all three together, had a very amusing discussion.

CHAPTER 3

THE AMUSING CONVERSATION BETWEEN DON QUIXOTE, SANCHO PANZA, AND SAMSON CARRASCO

Don Quixote remained in very deep thought, waiting for Samson Carrasco, who was going to tell him how he had been placed into a book as Sancho said; and he could not persuade himself that any such book could exist, because the blood of the enemies he had battled was not even dry on the blade of his sword, and now they claimed his great achievements were published in print. Because of that, he believed some sage, either a friend or an enemy, might have, with the aid of magic, given them to the press; if it were a friend, this was to magnify and exalt his deeds above the most famous that were ever achieved by any other Knight; if this was done by an enemy, this was to degrade them below the worst ever recorded of any low ranking aide, although as he said to himself, the achievements of aides were never recorded. If, however, it was a fact that this book was in existence, it must be, being the story of a Knight, grand, impressive and true. He comforted himself with this somewhat, although it made him uncomfortable to think that the author was a Moor, judging by the title of "Cide;" and that no truth ever came from Moors, as they are all deceivers, cheaters, and traitors. He was afraid his love affairs may have been written about in some inappropriate manner that might dishonour the purity of his lady Dulcinea del Toboso; and this writing may not include the faithfulness and respect he always had towards her, rejecting Queens, empresses, and all types of ladies who threw themselves at him, and keeping under control the recklessness of his natural impulses. Absorbed and wrapped up in these thoughts and other considerations, he was found by Sancho and Carrasco, whom Don Quixote welcomed with great courtesy.

The graduate, although he was called Samson, had no great bodily size, but he was a very good joker; he had a yellow complexion, and was very sharp-witted, roughly about twenty-four years old, with a round face, a flat nose, and a large mouth, all the indications of a mischievous character with a love of fun and jokes; and he gave a sample of this as soon as he saw Don Quixote, by falling on his knees in front of him and saying, "Let me kiss your hand, Señor Don Quixote of La Mancha, because, this is a habit of St. Peter that I follow, and you are one of the most famous Knights that there has ever been, and ever will be, all over the world. God bless Cide Hamete Benengeli, who has written the history of your great deeds, and God bless the connoisseur who took the time to translate if from Arabic into our Castilian vulgar tongue for the universal entertainment of the people!"

Don Quixote made him rise, and said, "So, then it is true that there is a book about me, and that it was a Moor and a sage who wrote it?"

"It is so true, señor," said Samson, "that I believe there are more than twelve thousand copies of this book in print to date. They can be found in

Portugal, Barcelona, and Valencia, where they have been printed, and I also heard it is being printed in Antwerp, and I am sure there will be no country or language in which it will not be translated into."

"One of the things," said Don Quixote, "I notice that gives pleasure to a virtuous and distinguished man is to find himself in print during his lifetime, spoken about by people, and having a good name; I say a good name, because if it is the opposite, then not even death can be compared to that."

"A good name and fame," said Samson, "you alone tower over any other Knight; because the Moor in his own language, and the Christian in his, have taken care to make us aware of your bravery, your courage in encountering danger, your fortitude in adversity, your patience through misfortune, as well as all the wounds taken for the greater good, along with the purity and continence of the amicable love of you and Dona Dulcinea del Toboso"

"I never heard Dulcinea called Dona," said Sancho; "nothing more than the lady Dulcinea del Toboso; so this already proves the history is wrong."

"That is not an objection of any importance," replied Carrasco.

"Certainly not," said Don Quixote; "but tell me, señor, what deeds of mine are written in this history?"

"In regards to that," replied the Samson, "opinions differ, as tastes do; some swear over the windmills that you believed were giants; others mention the cleaning mills; another gives the description of two armies that afterwards had the appearance of two herds of sheep; another mentions the dead body on its way to be buried at Segovia; a third says the liberation of the slaves is the best of all, and a fourth says that nothing is better than the battle with the brave Biscayan."

"Tell me, señor Carrasco," said Sancho, "is the adventure with the horses mentioned, when our good Rocinante went off looking for something to eat?"

"The sage has left nothing in the ink-bottle," replied Samson; "he has written down everything, even the holes that Sancho made in the blanket."

"I cut no holes in the blanket," returned Sancho; "coming back down from the air I did, and more of them than I liked."

"There is no human history in the world, I suppose," said Don Quixote, "that does not have its ups without downs, but more than others in the books of chivalry, because they can never be entirely made of prosperous adventures."

"True, and in regards to that," replied Samson, "there are some who have read the history and say they would have been glad if the author had left out some of the numerous beatings that were inflicted on Señor Don Quixote during in his various encounters."

"That's where the truth of the history comes in," said Sancho.

"These they could have fairly passed over in silence," said Don Quixote; "because there is no need to record events which do not change or affect the truth of the history, especially if they tend to disrespect the hero of it. Aeneas was not as serious and so religious as Virgil represented him to be, and neither was Ulysses as wise as Homer describes him."

"That is true," said Samson; "but it is one thing to write as a poet, another to write as a historian; the poet may describe or sing things, not as they were, but as they should have been; but the historian has to write them down, not as they should have been, but as they were, without adding anything to the truth or taking away anything from it."

"Well then," said Sancho, "if this Moor is telling the truth, then there is no doubt among my master's beatings mine are to be found as well; because for every beating to my masters shoulders my whole body received worse; but I have no right to complain about that, because, as my master says, the members must share the pain of the head."

"You are a sly dog, Sancho," said Don Quixote; "you have no lack of memory when you choose to remember."

"If I tried to forget the blows they gave me," said Sancho, "my bruises would not let me, because they are still fresh on my ribs."

"Quiet, Sancho," said Don Quixote, "and don't interrupt the man, who I ask to continue and tell all that is said about me in this book."

"And about me," said Sancho, "because they say, as well, that I am one of the principal persons in it."

"People, not persons, friend Sancho," said Samson.

"What! Another word-smith!" said Sancho; "if I am always corrected, I will never make a complete sentence in a lifetime."

"God shortens mine when I make corrections Sancho," returned Samson, "you are the second person in the history, and there are even some who would rather hear you talk than the cleverest in the whole book; although there are some, also, who say you showed yourself as naive in believing there was any possibility to become a governor of that island Señor Don Quixote offered you."

"There is still sun shining on that," said Don Quixote; "and when Sancho is more advanced in life, with the experience that years bring, he will be fitter and better qualified for being a governor than he is at present."

"God, master," said Sancho, "if the island that I cannot govern is due to my age, I'll will not be able to govern it even with the years of the ancient; the true difficulty is that the island keeps its distance somewhere, I do not know where; and not because there is a lack of brain to govern it."

"Leave it to God, Sancho," said Don Quixote, "because all will be and perhaps even better than you think; no leaf on the tree moves without God's will."

"That is true," said Samson; "and if it is God's will, there will be no lack of islands, not only one, for Sancho to govern."

"I have seen governors," said Sancho, "that are not worth being compared to the sole of my shoe; and they are called 'lord' and served food on silver plates."

"Those are not governors of islands," said Samson, "They govern easier things: those that govern islands must at least know grammar."

"I could manage grammar well enough," said Sancho; "but in regards to the sea I have no education or preference for it, because I don't know what it is; so I will leave this matter of government in God's hands, to send me wherever I can be of best service to Him, I tell you, señor Samson Carrasco, it has pleased me greatly that the author of this history has spoken of me in such a way that gives me no offence; because, I promise you, if he had said anything about me that did not resemble an old Christian, which I am, the deaf would have heard about it."

"That would be a miracle," said Samson.

"Miracles or no miracles," said Sancho, "everyone should be careful how they speak or write about people, and not put down randomly the first thing that comes into their head."

"One of the faults they find with this history," said Samson, "is that its author inserted in it a novel called 'The Ill-advised Curiosity;' not that it is bad, but it is out of place and has nothing to do with the history of Señor Don Quixote."

"I bet the son of a dog has mixed the cabbages and the baskets," said Sancho.

"Then, I say," said Don Quixote, "the author of my history was no sage, but some ignorant bigmouth, who, in a disorganised way, decided to write it however it came to him, just as Orbaneja, the painter of Ubeda, used to do, who, when they asked him what he was painting, answered, 'whatever comes to my mind.' Once he painted a rooster in that style, and it looked so different, that he had to write next to it, 'This is a rooster; and so I believe my history will require commentary to clarify it."

"Do not worry about that," returned Samson, "because it is clear that there is nothing confusing in it; the children turn the pages, the young people read it, the grown men understand it, the elderly praise it; in a word, it is so well read, and known by heart by all types of people, that the moment they see any thin horse they say, 'There goes Rocinante.' And those that read it most are the young Knights, because there is no lord's hall where there is not a 'Don Quixote' to be found; one picks it up if another puts it down; this one grabs it, and another begs for it. In short, the history is the most enjoyable and least harmful entertainment there has been up to the present, because in the whole of it there is not to be found even the resemblance of an immodest word, or a thought that is anything other than Catholic."

"To write in any other way," said Don Quixote, "would not be the truth, but lies, and historians who choose lies should be burned, like those who make counterfeit money; and I do not know what could have led the author to novels and irrelevant stories, when he had so much to write about in mine; no doubt he must have used the proverb 'with straw or with hay,' which generally means use hay, which is for nourishing the animals, not straw which is used for their bed, and by merely writing my thoughts, my upsets, my tears, my grand purpose and my work, he might have made a book so large, possibly larger than all the work from La Mancha combined. In fact, the conclusion I arrive at, señor Carrasco, is that to write history, or books of any kind, there is need for great judgment and understanding. To give expression to humour, and to write with grace, is the gift of great geniuses. The cleverest character in comedy is the clown, because someone who makes people take him for a fool, is no one. History is a sacred thing, because it should be true, and where the truth is, there is God; but despite this, there are some who write books and broadcast lies to the world."

"There is no book that is so bad that it does not contain something good in it," said Samson.

"No doubt about that," replied Don Quixote; "but it often happens that those who have acquired and attained a well-deserved reputation by their writing, lose it entirely, or damage it in some degree, when they give these bad books to the press."

"The reason for that," said Samson, "is, that as printed works are examined during leisure, their faults are easily seen; and the greater the fame of the writer, the more closely are they scrutinised. Men famous for their genius, great poets, well-known historians, are always, or most commonly envied by those who take pleasure in criticising the writing of others, without having produced any of their own."

"There is no mystery in that," said Don Quixote; "because there are many psychics who are no good for the church, but excellent in detecting the defects of those who preach."

"All that is true, Señor Don Quixote," said Carrasco; "but I wish these fault-finders were more lenient and less pedantic, and did not pay so much attention to the spots that the bright sun does not cover; because sometimes even the wisest person makes errors, they should remember how long he has been awake to shed the light of his work with as little shade as possible; and perhaps it may be that what they find fault with may be moles, that sometimes enhance the beauty of the face that has them; and so I say, this is a risk that the person who prints a book exposes himself to, because out of all the impossibilities the greatest is to write a book that will satisfy and please all who read it."

"The book about me must have pleased many," said Don Quixote.

"Quite true," said Samson; "but the number of fools is infinite, and they are as many of them as those who have enjoyed the book; some criticised the author's memory, as he forgot to say who the thief was who stole Sancho's donkey; because it was not stated, but only to be inferred from what is written, that he was stolen, and a little later Sancho is mounted on the same donkey, without any reappearance of it. They say, as well, that he forgot to mention what Sancho did with those hundred coins that he found in the bag in the Sierra Morena, as he never alludes to them again, and there are many who would love to know what he did with them, or what he spent them on, because this is one of the most serious omissions in the book."

"Señor Samson, I am not in the mood to give accounts or explanations," said Sancho; "because a stomach pain has come over me, and unless I remedy it soon with medicine I will sitting on the throne. I have some at home, and my lady waiting for me; after dinner I will come back and answer every question you choose to ask, and those about the loss of the donkey and spending of the coins;" and without another word or waiting for a reply he left.

Don Quixote begged Samson to stay and to repent for any sins with him. Samson accepted the invitation and remained, a couple of pigeons were cooked, and at dinner they talked about chivalry, Carrasco went along with his host's eccentricity, the dinner came to a close, they had their afternoon sleep, Sancho returned, and their conversation was resumed.

CHAPTER 4

SANCHO PANZA GIVES A SATISFACTORY REPLY TO THE DOUBTS AND QUESTIONS OF SAMSON CARRASCO, TOGETHER WITH OTHER MATTERS WORTH KNOWING AND TELLING

Sancho came back to Don Quixote's house, and returning to the subject, he said, "in regards to what Señor Samson said, that he would like to know by who, or how, or when my donkey was stolen, I say in reply that the same night we went into the Sierra Morena, running from the Holy Brotherhood after that unlucky adventure with the ship slaves, and the other of the body going to Segovia, my master and I concealed ourselves in a bush, and there, my master leaning on his lance, and I sat on my donkey, exhausted and weary we fell asleep as if it had been on a feather mattress; and I, in particular slept so well, that, whoever he was, was able to come and pick me up with four sticks, and remove me from the saddle and took my donkey away from under me without me feeling it."

"That is an easy matter," said Don Quixote, "and it is no new occurrence, because the same thing happened to Sacripante at the siege of Albracca; the famous thief, Brunello, took his horse from between his legs."

"The morning came," continued Sancho, "and the moment I woke the sticks gave way and I fell to the ground; I looked for the donkey, but could not see him; the tears poured from my eyes and I gave such a cry that, if the author of our history has not put it in, he should know he has left out the loudest sobbing possible. Some days later, I do not know how many, travelling with the Princess Micomicona, I saw my donkey, and mounted him. Dressed as a gipsy, was Gines de Pasamonte, the great rogue and rascal that my master and I freed from the chain."

"That is not where the mistake is," replied Samson; "it is, that before the ass turned up, the author says Sancho was mounted on it."

"I don't know what to say about that," said Sancho, "unless that the historian made a mistake, or perhaps it might be a printing error."

"No doubt it must be that," said Samson; "but what happened to the coins? Did they vanish?"

To which Sancho answered, "I spent them on my wife and children, and my own good, and those coins made my wife have more patience with me while I was wandering the roads and highways in service of my master, Don Quixote; because if after all this time I had come back to the house without any money and without the donkey, it would have been bad news for me; and if anyone wants to know anything else about me, here I am, ready to answer even the King if he had questions; and it is no one else's business if I took or did not take it, whether I spent or did not spend; because the beatings I have received on these journeys had to be paid for in money, even if they were valued at no more than four coins each, so another hundred coins would not pay me for half of them.

Everyone should mind their own business and not try to make white black, and black white; because each of us is just as God created, and often worse."

"I will make sure," said Carrasco, "to let the author of the history know, that if he prints it again, he should not forget what Sancho has said."

"Is there anything else that needs to be corrected in the history, señor Carrasco?" asked Don Quixote.

"No doubt there is," he replied; "but probably nothing that will have the same importance as those I have mentioned."

"Does the author promise there will be a second part at all?" said Don Quixote.

"He does indeed promise," replied Samson; "but he said he has not found it yet, and does not know who has got it; and we cannot say whether it will appear or not; and so, on that note, as some say that no second part has ever been as good as the first, and others say that enough has been already written about Don Quixote, it is thought there will be no second part; although some, who are cheerful rather than sad, say, 'Let us have more stories, let Don Quixote charge forward and Sancho speak, and no matter what will happen, we will be satisfied with that.'"

"And what does the author intend to do?" said Don Quixote.

"Well," replied Samson; "as soon as he has found the history which he is now searching for with extraordinary diligence, he will immediately give it to the press, motivated by the profit he may gain rather than any thought of praise."

Sancho observed, "The author looks for money and profit, does he? It will be a miracle if he succeeds, because it will be done in a hurry, like the tailor on Easter Eve; whose works are done in a hurry and never finished as perfectly as they should be. This master Moor, or whatever he is, should pay attention to what he is doing, and I and my master will give him as many stories his hand requires, all types of adventures and accidents, which would not only make up a second part, but a hundred. The good man believes, no doubt, that we are fast asleep in the straw here, but let him hold up our feet and see the callouses, these feet have been extremely busy. All I say is, that if my master would take my advice, we would be travelling again by now, repairing outrage and righting wrong, which is the custom of good Knights."

Sancho had hardly finished his words when they heard Rocinante neighing, which Don Quixote considered a good signal, and he decided to leave for more adventures in three or four days. Announcing his intention to Samson, he asked for his advice in regards to where he should commence his journey, and Samson replied that in his opinion he should go to the Kingdom of Aragon, and the city of Saragossa, where they could be sure to find fighting at the festival of St. George, where he could win fame above all the Knights of Aragon, which by winning it would place him above all the Knights in the world. Samson applauded this very admirable and courageous purpose, but warned him to proceed with great caution in encountering danger, because his life did not belong to him, but to all those who had a need for him to protect and aid them in their misfortune.

"That is true, and that's why he must go, Señor Samson," said Sancho; "my master will attack a hundred armed men as a greedy boy would a half dozen cakes. I have heard it said, there is a time to attack and a time to retreat (and I think by my master himself, if I remember correctly) that the middle ground of bravery lies between the extremes of cowardice and impulsiveness; and if that is so, I don't want him to leave without having a good reason, or to attack when the odds are not in his favour. But, above all things, I warn my master that if he is to take me with him it must be on the condition that he does all the fighting, and that I am not to be asked to do anything except what concerns keeping him clean and comfortable; for that purpose, I will serve him gladly; but to expect me to use a sword, even against mischievous fools wearing hoods and brandishing knives, is pointless. I am not a fighting man, Señor Samson, but I am the best and most loyal aide that ever served a Knight; and if my master Don Quixote, in consideration of my many faithful services, is pleased to give me some island out of the many he says we may stumble upon during our travels, I will take it as a great favour; and if he does not give it to me, I was born like everyone else, and a man must not live in dependence on anyone except God; and what is more, my bread will taste good, and perhaps even better, without a government than if I were a governor; and how do I know that in these governments the devil hasn't prepared a trip for me, to make me lose my balance and fall and knock my teeth out? I was born as Sancho, and I intend to die as Sancho. But despite all of that, if heaven were to make me a fair offer of an island or something like that, without much trouble and without much risk, I am not such a fool to refuse it; because they say, 'when they offer you a cow that cannot give birth, run; but 'when good luck comes to you, take it.'"

"Brother Sancho," said Carrasco, "you have spoken like a professor; but, despite all that, put your trust in God and in Señor Don Quixote, because he will give you a Kingdom, not a mere island."

"It is all the same, more or less," replied Sancho; "although I can tell you Señor Carrasco that my master would not place the Kingdom he would give me into a sack with holes in it; because I have felt my own pulse and I find myself alive enough to rule Kingdoms and govern islands; and I have told my master this already."

"Take care, Sancho," said Samson; "titles change manners, and perhaps when you find yourself a governor you won't remember your own mother."

"That may be true for those that are born in the street," said Sancho, "but not for those who have the fat of an old Christian, as I have. Actually, look at my character, does it appear likely to show ingratitude to anyone?"

"Let God grant it," said Don Quixote; "we will see when the government comes; and I believe that will be soon."

He then asked Samson, if he were a poet, to do him the favour of composing some verses for him conveying the farewell he wanted to say to his lady Dulcinea del Toboso, and to place a letter of her name at the beginning of each line, so that, at the end of the verses, "Dulcinea del Toboso" could be read by putting together the first letters. Samson replied that although he was not one of the most famous poets in Spain, which he said there were only three and a half, he would not fail to compose the required verses; although he knew the task would be difficult, as there were seventeen letters in the name; so, if he made four sections of four lines each, there would be one letter extra, and if he made them each with five lines, what they would require three extra letters ; nevertheless he would try as well as he could, so that the name "Dulcinea del Toboso" would be split into four line stanzas.

"It must be done, by some method or other," said Don Quixote, "because unless the name is clear to see, no woman would believe the verses were made for her."

They agreed on this, and that the departure should take place in three days. Don Quixote asked Samson to keep it a secret, especially from the vicar and the barber, and from his niece and the housekeeper, or else they might try to prevent the execution of his admirable and courageous purpose. Carrasco promised to keep the secret, and then left, asking Don Quixote to inform him of his good or bad fortune whenever he had an opportunity to do so; and therefore they said farewell to each other, and Sancho went away to make the necessary preparations for their expedition.

CHAPTER 5

THE SHREWD AND AMUSING CONVERSATION BETWEEN SANCHO PANZA AND HIS WIFE TERESA PANZA, AND OTHER MATTERS WORTHY OF BEING RECORDED

The translator of this history, when he comes to write this fifth chapter, says that he considers it legendary, because in it Sancho Panza speaks in a style which is unlike what might have been expected from his limited intelligence, and says things so subtle that he does not think it could be possible that he conceived them; however, desirous of doing what his task required him to do, he was unwilling to leave it untranslated, and therefore he went on to say:

Sancho came home in such a cheerful and joyful spirit that his wife noticed his happiness from a distance, so much that it made her ask him, "What have you got, Sancho, that makes you so glad?"

To which he replied, "Wife, if it were God's will, I would be very glad not to be so pleased as I show myself to be."

"I don't understand you, husband," she said, "and I don't know what you mean by saying you would be glad, if it were God's will, not to be pleased; because, unless I am a fool, I don't know how someone can find pleasure in not having it."

"Listen you, Teresa," replied Sancho, "I am glad because I have made up my mind to go back to serve my master Don Quixote, who intends to go out a third time to seek for adventures; and I am going with him again, and the hope I have that I may find another hundred coins like those we have spent cheers me up; although it makes me sad to have to leave you and the children; and if God would be pleased to let me have my daily bread, while I am at home, without taking me out on the roads and highways, and he could do it easily if he wills it - it is clear my happiness would be more solid and longer lasting, because now the happiness I have is mingled with sorrow for leaving you; so I am right in saying I would be glad, if it were God's will, for me not to be glad."

"Look here, Sancho," said Teresa; "ever since you joined that so called Knight you talk in such an indirect way that you cannot be understood."

"It is enough that God understands me, wife," replied Sancho; "because he understands all things; that will do; but remember, wife, you must take care of the donkey for the next three days, so he may be fit to carry a load; double his portions of food, fit the saddle and harness, because it is not a wedding we are going to, but around the world, fighting giants, dragons and monsters, and to hear hissing, roaring and howling; and all of this would be lavender, if we did not have to deal with enchanted Moors."

"I know well enough, husband," said Teresa, "that aides don't get to eat their bread for nothing, and so I will always pray to our Lord to free you quickly from all that hard fortune."

"I can tell you, wife," said Sancho, "if I did not expect to see myself as a governor of an island soon, I would drop dead on the spot."

"Actually, then, husband," said Teresa; "let the devil take all the governments in the world; you came out of your mother's womb without a government, you have lived until now without a government, and when it is God's will that you go, you are carried to your grave without a government. How many are there in the world who live without a government, and continue to live well. The best sauce in the world is hunger, and as the poor are never without that, they always eat well. But remember, Sancho, if with good luck you do find yourself with some government, don't forget me and your children. Remember that Sanchico is now fifteen, and it is time he should go to school, his uncle wants to have him trained for the Church. Consider, as well, that your daughter Mari-Sancha will be upset if we do not marry her; because I have a suspicion that she is as eager to have a husband as you are to be a governor; and, after all, a daughter looks better in a bad marriage than as a whore."

"I swear," replied Sancho, "if God grants me any government, I intend, wife, to find such a high match for Mari-Sancha that there will be no one approaching her without calling her 'my lady.'"

"No, Sancho," returned Teresa; "marry her to someone equal to her, that is the safest plan; because if you take her out of her old shoes and put her into high-heels, out of her grey coat into silk gowns, out of plain fashion and called 'my lady,' the girl won't know where she is, and she will make a thousand mistakes."

"You fool," said Sancho; "she only needs to practise it for two or three years; and then dignity and politeness will fit her like a glove; and if not, then what? Let her be 'my lady,' and never mind what happens."

"Keep your character, Sancho," replied Teresa; "don't try to raise yourself higher, and remember the proverb that says, 'wipe the nose of your neighbour's son, and take him into your house.' Would it be so great to marry Maria to some great lord or grand gentleman, who, when he decided, would abuse her and call her low-bred, a foolish man's daughter and good for nothing. I have not been bringing up my daughter all this time for that, I can tell you, husband. You bring home the money, and leave marrying her to me; there is Lope Tocho, Juan Tocho's son, a short, strong young man that we know, and I can see he does not take his eyes off the girl; and with him, one of our own sort, she will be well married, and we will always have her in front of our eyes, and be one family, parents and children, grandchildren and in-laws, and the peace and blessing of God will be with us; so don't go marrying her in those courts and grand palaces where they won't know what to think of her, or she what to think of herself."

"Idiot of a wife," said Sancho, "what do you mean by trying, without a valid reason, to keep me from marrying my daughter to someone who will give me grandchildren that will be called 'Lord'? Look, Teresa, I have always heard my elders say that he who does not know how to take advantage of luck when it comes to him, has no right to complain if it leaves him; and now that it is knocking at our door, it is not wise to shut it out; let us go with the favouring breeze that blows toward us."

It is this sort of talk, and what Sancho says after, that made the translator say he considered this chapter fictional.

"Don't you see, you animal," continued Sancho, "that it would be good for me to gain some profitable government that will lift us out of this place, and marry Mari-Sancha to whoever I like; and you yourself will find yourself called 'Dona Teresa Panza,' and sitting in church on a fine carpet and cushions, above all the ladies of the town? No, stay as you are, growing neither greater or worse, like a wooden figure - say no more about it, because Sanchica will be a high lady, and that's that."

"Are you sure about everything you say, husband?" replied Teresa. "Because I am afraid this rank for my daughter will ruin her. You do as you like, make her a Princess if you want, but I can tell you it will not be with my will and consent. I was always a lover of equality, and I don't like to see people give themselves a rank without any right for it. They called me Teresa at my baptism, a plain, simple name, without any additions or tags like Dona. Cascajo was my father's name, and as I am your wife, I am called Teresa Panza, although I should be called Teresa Cascajo; but 'Kings go where laws live,' and I am content with this name without having the 'Dona' put on top of it to make it so heavy that I cannot carry it; and I don't want to make people talk about me when they see me dressed like a lord or governor's wife; because they will say, 'See what the whore gives herself? Only yesterday she was going to mass with a simple coat, and today she goes in a gown with her broaches, as if we didn't know her!' If God keeps my seven senses, or five, or whatever number I have, I am not going to bring myself to do such a thing; you go, husband, and be a government or an island man, and boast as much as you like; because I swear on the soul of my mother, neither my daughter or I are going to move a step from our village; a respectable woman should have a broken leg and stay at home; and to be busy working is a virtuous lady's holiday; go on your adventures along with Don Quixote, and leave us with our misfortune, because God will repair them for us according to what we deserve. I don't know, who fixed the 'Don' to him, something neither his father or grandfather ever had."

"I swear you have a devil of some sort in your body!" said Sancho. "God help you, what a lot of things that you have strung together, one after the other, without a head or tail! What have Cascajo, and the broaches and the proverbs got to do with what I say? Look here, fool (because I may call you that, when you don't understand my words, and run away from good fortune), if I had said that my daughter had to jump from a tower, or go roaming the world, as the holy grail wanted to, you would be right not to give in to my will; but if in an instant, in less than the blink of an eye, I put the 'Dona' and 'my lady' on her, and take her out of poverty, and place her in the shade, and on a couch, with more velvet cushions than all the Almohades of Morocco ever had in their whole family, why won't you consent and respect my wishes?"

"You know why, husband?" replied Teresa; "because of the proverb that says 'who covers you, discovers you.' People barely look at the poor man; but they fix their eyes on the rich; and if the rich man used to be a poor man, this brings hate, gossip, and in the streets here they move in a swarm as thick as bees."

"Look here, Teresa," said Sancho, "and listen to what I am going to say to you now; maybe you never heard it in your whole life; and I am not giving my own ideas, because what I am about to say are the opinions of a revered preacher, who preached in this town last Easter, and said, if I remember correctly, that all things that our eyes now see, bring themselves to us, and remain and fix themselves in our memory much better and more forcibly than the past."

These observations which Sancho makes here go along with the other ones which makes the translator say he regards this chapter as dubious, as they are beyond Sancho's capacity.

"When it arises," he continued, "that we see any person well dressed in rich garments and followed by servants, it seems to lead and impel us inevitably to respect him, although our memory might at the same moment remind us of some poor condition which we have seen him in, but whether it may have been poverty or low birth, that becomes a thing of the past, and has no existence; while the only thing that has any existence is what we see in front of us; and if this person has been fortunate and raised from his original low condition to his present height of prosperity, well bred, generous, courteous to all, without seeking to compete with those whose nobility has preceded his, believe it, Teresa, no one will remember what he was, and everyone will respect what he is, except of course the envious, who no one is safe from."

"I do not understand you, husband," replied Teresa; "do what you like, and don't hurt my head with any more campaigning and speechmaking; and if you have revolved to do what you say"

"Resolved, you should say, woman," said Sancho, "not revolved."

"Don't argue with me, husband," said Teresa; "I speak as God wants me to; and as you are so obsessed with having a government, take your son Sancho with you, and teach him from now how to hold a government; because sons should inherit and learn the trades of their fathers."

"As soon as I have the government," said Sancho, "I will request him by letter, and I will send you money, which you will have no lack of, because there is never any lack of people to lend it to governors when they have not got it; and you are to dress him to hide what he is and make him look as what he going to be."

"You send the money," said Teresa, "and then I will dress him for you as fine as you like."

"Then we agree that our daughter is to be a lady," said Sancho.

"The day that I see her a lady," replied Teresa, "will be the same day as if I was burying her; but once again I say do what you like, because us women are born for this burden of being obedient to our husbands, even if they are dogs;" and she began to cry, as if she already saw Sanchica dead and buried.

Sancho comforted her by saying that although he must make her a lady, he would delay it as long as possible. Their conversation came to an end, and Sancho went back to see Don Quixote, to make arrangements for their departure.

CHAPTER 6

WHAT TOOK PLACE BETWEEN DON QUIXOTE, HIS NIECE AND HOUSEKEEPER; ONE OF THE MOST IMPORTANT CHAPTERS IN THE WHOLE HISTORY

While Sancho Panza and his wife, Teresa Cascajo, held the above irrelevant conversation, Don Quixote's niece and housekeeper were not wasting time, because they began to perceive that their uncle and master intended to discreetly leave for the third time, and once again return to his, for them, madness of chivalry. They tried by all the means in their power to divert him from such a tragic plan; but it was like preaching in the desert and hammering cold iron. Nevertheless, among many other arguments made to him, the housekeeper said to him, "In truth, master, if you do not stay still and stay quiet at home, and forget about roaming mountains and valleys like a troubled spirit, looking for what they say are called adventures, but what I call misfortunes, I will have to make a complaint to God and the King with a loud request to send some remedy."

To which Don Quixote replied, "I do not know what answer God will give to your complaints, housekeeper, and neither what his Majesty will say; I only know that if I were the King I would decline to answer the countless silly petitions they receive every day; because one of the greatest among the many troubles Kings have is being obliged to listen to and answer them all, and therefore I doubt that any affairs of mine would worry him."

The housekeeper said, "Tell us, señor, are there no Knights at his Majesty's court?"

"There are," replied Don Quixote, "and plenty of them; and it is right there should be, to set off the dignity of the prince, and for the greater glory of the King's majesty."

"Then can you not," said she, "be one of those that, without moving much, serve their King and lord in his court?"

"Remember, my friend," said Don Quixote, "all Knights cannot be in the court, and not all court's men can be Knights, and neither do they need to be. There must be all types in the world; and although we may all be Knights, there is a great difference between one and another; because the court's men, without leaving their rooms, or threshold of the court, roam the world by looking at a map, without it costing them a penny, and without suffering the heat or cold, hunger or thirst; but we, the true Knights, measure the whole earth with our own feet, exposed to the sun, to the cold, to the air, to the mood of heaven, day and night, on foot and on horseback; we do not only know our enemies in pictures, but in their own real shapes; and with all the risk and on all occasions we attack them, without any regard to any childish points or rules of single combat, whether one has or does not have a shorter lance or sword, whether one carries any devices with him, whether or not the sun is obscured, these things you know nothing about, but I do. And you must know, that a true Knight, although he may see ten giants, that not only touch the clouds with their heads but pierce through them, and that climb tall towers with their legs, and whose arms are like the masts of large ships, and each eye like a great wind-mill, and glowing brighter than a furnace, cannot be discouraged by them at all. Actually, he must attack them with courage and a fearless heart, and, if possible, conquer and destroy them, even though they have armour like the shells of certain fish, that are harder than diamonds, and instead of swords they use blades of steel, or clubs dotted with spikes also made of steel, which I have seen more than once. I say this, housekeeper, so you can see the difference between the one sort of Knight and the other; and it would better if there were no prince who did not place a higher value on this second, or more appropriately speaking first kind of Knight; because, as we read in their histories, there have been some among them who have been the salvation, not merely of one Kingdom, but of many."

"Ah, señor," exclaimed the niece, "remember that all this you are saying about Knights is story and fiction; and their histories, if they were not burned, would each deserve, to have some kind of mark placed on them to make it known that they are the corrupters of good manners."

"God that angers me," said Don Quixote, "if you were not my niece, the daughter of my own sister, I would inflict a serious punishment on you for the profanity you have just spoken. Can it really be that a young girl that hardly knows how to write dares to show her tongue and criticise the histories of Knights? What would Señor Amadis say if he heard such a thing? He, however, would forgive you no doubt, because he was the most humble-minded and polite Knight of his time, and furthermore a great protector of ladies; but some other Knights might have heard you, and it would not have gone well for you in that case; because they are not all polite or mannerly; some are poor-conditioned mischiefs; not everyone that calls himself a gentleman, is in all respects; some are gold, others bronze, and all may look like gentlemen, but not all can stand the truth. There are men of low rank who strain themselves to look like gentlemen, and high gentlemen who, one would think were dying look like men of low rank; the former raise themselves by their ambition or by their virtues, the latter debase themselves by their lack of spirit or by their vices; and experience and discernment is needed to distinguish these two kinds of gentlemen, so much alike by name but so different in conduct."

"God bless me!" said the niece, "you know so much, uncle - enough, if it must be, get a podium and go preach in the streets – but it is delusional to try to make yourself out to be vigorous when you are old, strong when you are sick, able to put straight what is crooked when you yourself are bent, and, above all, a Knight when you are not one; because although some men might be, poor men are not!"

"There is a great deal of truth in what you say, niece," returned Don Quixote, "and I could tell you somewhat about birth that would astonish you; but, not to mix up things which are human and divine, I refrain. Look you, my dears, all the lineages in the world can be reduced to four categories, which are these:

those that had humble beginnings, and went on spreading and extending themselves until they surpassed greatness; those that had great beginnings and maintained them, and still maintain and uphold the greatness of their origin; those that had a great beginning but have reduced their original greatness until it has come to nothing, like the point of a pyramid, which, relatively to its base or foundation, is nothing; and then there are those - and it is these that are the most numerous - that have had neither an distinguished beginning or a remarkable mid-life, and so end without a name, like an ordinary working-class line. And out of these, the first that had a humble origin and rose to the greatness, the Ottoman house may serve as an example, which from a humble and lowly shepherd, its founder, has reached the height at which we now see it. For examples of the second sort of lineage, that began with greatness and maintained it without adding to it, there are many princes who have inherited dignity, and maintain their inheritance, without increasing or diminishing it, keeping peacefully within the limits of their states. Those that began great and ended with nothing, there are thousands of examples, all the Pharaohs Egypt, the Caesars of Rome, and the whole herd (if I may apply such a word to them) of countless princes, monarchs, lords, Assyrians, Persians, Greeks, and barbarians, all these lineages have ended in a point and come to nothing, they themselves as well as their founders, because it would be impossible now to find one of their descendants, and, even if we find one, it would be in some low and humble condition. For the working-class lineages I have nothing to say, except that they merely serve to swell the number of those that live, without any distinction to entitle them to any fame or praise beyond this. From all that I have said you should gather, that there is great confusion among lineages, and that only those that are seen to be great and illustrious show themselves to be so by the virtue, wealth, and generosity of their possessors. I have said virtue, wealth, and generosity, because a great man who is vicious will be a great example of vice, and a rich man who is not generous will be merely a miserly beggar; because the possessor of wealth is not made happy by possessing it, but by spending it, and not by spending as he wishes, but by knowing how to spend it well. The poor gentleman has no way of showing that he is a gentleman without virtue, by being pleasant, well-bred, polite, well-mannered, and kind, not proud, arrogant, or critical, but above all by being charitable; because by giving two coins with a cheerful heart to the poor, he will show himself to be as generous as a rich man, and no one that perceives him to be gifted with the virtues I have named, will fail to recognise and consider him as someone with good blood; and it would be strange if it were not so; but praise has never been the reward of virtue, and those who are virtuous cannot fail to receive commendation. There are two roads, by which men can reach wealth and honours; one is being a man of words, the other is through arms. My composition leans more toward arms than letters, and, judging by my inclination for arms, I was born under the influence of the planet Mars. I am, therefore, constrained to follow that road, and by it I must travel regardless of what the whole world might tell me, and you will be wasting your time to urge me to resist what heaven wants, fate orders, reason requires, and, above all, my own preference favours; because knowing as I do the countless work that accompanies Knights, I know, too, the infinite blessings that are attained by it; I know that the path of virtue is very narrow, and the road of vice is broad and spacious; I know their ends and goals are different, because the broad and easy road of vice ends in death, and the narrow and hard road of virtue leads to life, and not transitory life, but that which has no end; I know, as our great Castilian poet says:

Through rugged paths like these they go
They attain the height of immortality,
Unreached by those that are lost below."

"God!" exclaimed the niece, "you are a poet, too! You know everything, and can do everything; I bet, if you chose to be a mason, you could make a house as easily as a bird cage."

"I can tell you, niece," replied Don Quixote, "if these chivalrous thoughts did not occupy all my faculties, there would be nothing that I could not do."

At this moment they heard a knocking on the door, and when they asked who was there, Sancho Panza answered "it is me." Straight away the housekeeper knew who it was, and ran to hide herself so she did not see him; as she was so disgusted by him. The niece let him in, and his master Don Quixote welcomed him with open arms, and the pair shut themselves in his room, where they had another conversation not inferior to the previous one.

CHAPTER 7

WHAT HAPPENED BETWEEN DON QUIXOTE AND HIS AIDE, TOGETHER WITH OTHER NOTABLE INCIDENTS

The instant the housekeeper saw Sancho Panza shut himself in the room with her master, she guessed what they were talking about; and suspecting that the result of the consultation would be to go on a third adventure, she grabbed her coat, and in deep anxiety and distress, ran to find Samson Carrasco, as she thought that, being a well-spoken man, and a new friend of her master's, he might be able to persuade him to give up such a crazy notion. She found him pacing the patio of his house, sweaty and flustered, and kneeled in front of him as soon as she saw him.

Carrasco, seeing how distressed she was, said to her, "What has happened, mistress housekeeper? Are you heart-broken."

"No, Señor Samson," said she, "my master is breaking out, clearly breaking out."

"Where is he breaking out, señora?" asked Samson; "has any part of his body burst?"

"He is only breaking out through the door of his madness," she replied; "I mean, dear señor Samson, that he is going to break out again (and this will be the third time) to go all over the world on what he calls adventures, although I cannot figure out why he calls them that. The first time he returned to us laying across the back of a donkey, and beaten all over; and the second time he came in an ox-cart, shut inside a cage, in which he persuaded himself he was enchanted, and the poor creature was in such a state that the mother that gave birth to him would not have recognised him; lean, yellow, with his eyes sunk deep into his skull; to bring him back to his senses, little by little, cost me more than six hundred eggs, I am unable to lie about this, God knows, the world knows, and my hens do as well."

"That I can well believe," replied Samson, "because they are so good and so fat, and so well-bred. In short then, mistress housekeeper, that is all, and there is nothing else, except this fear of what Don Quixote may do?"

"Nothing else, señor," she said.

"Well then," returned Samson, "don't be worried, go home in peace; get something hot ready for me for breakfast, and while you are on the way say the prayer of Santa Apollonia, that is if you know it; because I will come shortly and you will see miracles."

"God," cried the housekeeper, "you want me to say the prayer of Santa Apollonia? That would do if my master had a toothache; but this problem is in the brain."

"I know what I am saying, mistress housekeeper; go, and do not argue with me, because you know I am a graduate of Salamanca, and no one can be more of a graduate than that," replied Carrasco; and with this the housekeeper left, and the graduate went to look for the vicar, to arrange with him what will be told when the time is appropriate.

While Don Quixote and Sancho were shut in the room together, they had a discussion which the history records with great precision and reliable accuracy. Sancho said to his master, "Señor, I have educed my wife to let me go with you wherever you choose to take me."

"Induced, you mean, Sancho," said Don Quixote; "not educed."

"Once or twice, as well as I remember," replied Sancho, "I have asked you not to correct my words, if you understand what I mean by them; and if you don't understand them say, 'Sancho', I don't understand you; and if I don't make my meaning clear, then you may correct me, because I am so facile"

"I don't understand you, Sancho," said Don Quixote; "because I do not know what 'I am so facile' means."

"'So focile' means I am very much like that," replied Sancho.

"I understand you less now," said Don Quixote.

"Well, if you can't understand me," said Sancho, "I don't know how to put it; I know no more, God help me."

"Oh, now I get it," said Don Quixote; "you want to say you are so docile, compliant, and gentle that you will take what I say and accept what I teach you."

"I bet," said Sancho, "from the beginning you understood me, and knew what I meant, but you wanted me to speak more so you could hear me make another couple of mistakes."

"Maybe so," replied Don Quixote; "but to come to the point, what does Teresa say?"

"Teresa says," replied Sancho, "that I should be careful with you, and 'let papers speak and jaws be still,' because 'he who is bound does not dispute,' since one 'take' is better than 'two', and I say a woman's advice is a great thing, and he who won't take it is a fool."

"I say so as well," said Don Quixote; "continue, Sancho my friend; go on; you speak pearls today."

"The fact is," continued Sancho, "that, as you know better than I do, we are all liable to death, and today we might be, and tomorrow we are not, and the lamb is born as soon as the sheep dies, and nobody can promise himself more hours of life in this world than God is pleased to give him; death is deafening, and when it comes to knock at the door of our life, it is always urgent, and no prayers, or struggle, or sceptre, or clothing, can stop it."

"All of that is very true," said Don Quixote; "but I cannot make out what you are trying to say."

"What I am trying to say," said Sancho, "is that you pay me some fixed wages, to be paid monthly while I am at your service; because I do not care to hope for rewards which either come late, or never at all. In short, I would like to know what I am going to get, a lot or a little; because the hen will lay on one egg, and many little things make a lot, and so long as I gain something there is nothing lost. If it be the case (which I do not believe or expect) that you were to give me that island you have promised me, I would be willing to have the revenue of such an island valued and deducted from my wages in promotion."

"Sancho, my friend," replied Don Quixote, "sometimes proportion may be as good as promotion."

"I see," said Sancho; "I will bet I should have said proportion, and not promotion; but clearly you understood me."

"And so well understood," returned Don Quixote, "that I have seen into the depths of your thoughts, and know the mark you are shooting at with the countless pokes of your proverbs. Look here, Sancho, I would fix your wages if I had ever found any instance in the histories of the Knights to show or indicate, in the slightest degree, what their aides used to get monthly or yearly; but I have read all or the best part of the histories, and I cannot remember reading of any Knight having assigned fixed wages to his aide; I only know that they all served for rewards, and that when they least expected it, if good luck came to their masters, they found themselves compensated with an island or something equivalent to it, or at the least they were left with the title of a lord. If with these hopes and additional enticements, you Sancho, will return to my service, that would be fine; but to suppose that I am going to disturb the ancient usage of Knighthood, is all nonsense. And so, my Sancho, go back to your house and explain my intentions to Teresa, and if she likes, and you agree to be paid with reward, great; if not, we remain friends; because if the pigeon-house does not lack food, it will not lack pigeons; and bear in mind, my son, that good hope is better than bad holdings, and a good grievance better than bad compensation. I speak in this way, Sancho, to show you that I can shower proverbs just as well as you; and in short, I mean to say, and I do say, that if you do not like to come based on reward with me, and run the same chance that I run, I hope God makes a saint out of you; because I will find plenty of aides more obedient and conscientious, and not so thick-headed or talkative as you are."

When Sancho heard his master's firm resolute language, a cloud came over the sky and the wings of his heart drooped, because he did not want his master to go without him for all the wealth of the world; and as he stood there speechless, Samson Carrasco came in with the housekeeper and niece, who were anxious to hear what arguments he would use to deter their master from going to seek adventures. Samson came forward, and embracing him as he had done before, said with a loud voice, "Bloom of Knighthood! Shining light of arms! Honour and mirror of the Spanish nation! May God Almighty in his infinite power grant that any person or persons, who aim to impede or hinder you in your third adventure, find no way out of the labyrinth of their schemes, or ever accomplish what they desire most!" And then, turning to the housekeeper, he said, "Mistress housekeeper you might as well stop saying the prayer of Santa Apollonia, because I know it is the positive determination of God that Señor Don Quixote will proceed to put into execution his new and grand plan; and a heavy burden would weigh on my conscience if I urged and persuaded this Knight not to keep the strength of his arms and the virtue of his courageous spirit restricted and kept in check, because by his inactivity he is defrauding the world of the restoration of wrongs, the protection of orphans, the honour of virgins, the aid of widows, and the support of wives, and other matters of this kind relating, belonging, appropriately and particularly to the order of Knighthood. Go, then, my lord Don Quixote, beautiful and brave, leave today rather than tomorrow; and if anything is required for the execution of your purpose, here am I ready in person, and have a wallet to satisfy any need you may have; and if it were necessary to attend with you as your aide, I would regard it as the happiest good fortune."

Don Quixote, turning to Sancho, said, "Did I not tell you, Sancho, there would be plenty of aides for me? Look who offers to become one now; no other than the illustrious graduate Samson Carrasco, the perpetual joy and delight of the courts in the Salamancan schools, strong in body, discreet, patient through the heat or cold, hunger or thirst, with all the qualifications necessary to make a Knight's aide! But heaven forbid that, to gratify my own inclination, I shake or shatter this pillar of letters and vessel of the sciences, and cut down this towering tree of the fair and liberal arts. Let Samson remain in his own country, and, bringing honour to it, bring honour at the same time to the grey heads of his respected parents; because I will be content with any aide that comes to me, as Sancho does not want to accompany me."

"I do," said Sancho, deeply moved and with tears in his eyes; "that should not be said about me, master of mine," he continued, "the bread we have eaten and the journeys shared. I am not ungrateful, the world knows, but particularly my own town, where the Panzas from whom I am descended came from; and, what is more, I know and have learned, through your many good words and deeds, you have a desire to show me favour; and if I have been asking more or less about my wages, it was only to please my wife, who, when she presses a point, no hammer can drive a nail in more than her who drives me to do what she wants; but, after all, a man must be a man, and a woman a woman; and as I am a man, which I cannot deny, I will be one in my own house too, regardless of whoever dislikes it; and so there's nothing more to do than to follow our own will in such a way that it cannot be provoked, so we should leave immediately, to save Señor Samson's soul from suffering, as he says his conscience obliges him to persuade you to travel the world a third time; so I offer again to serve you faithfully and loyally, as well and better than all the aides that served Knights in past or present."

Samson was filled with amazement when he heard Sancho's expression and style of talk, because although he had read the first part of this history he never thought that it could be as amusing as it was described; but now, hearing Sancho talk of a "will that could not be provoked," instead of "will that could not be revoked," he believed all he had read about him, and now regarded him as one of the greatest fools of modern times; and he said to himself that these two, master and man, are the greatest lunatics the world had never seen.

Don Quixote and Sancho hugged one another, and with the advice and approval of the great Carrasco, who was now their oracle, it was arranged that their departure should take place in three days, by which time they could have all that was required for the journey ready, and obtain a closed helmet, which Don Quixote said he should take. Samson offered to give him one, as he knew a friend of his had one and would give it to him, although it was covered with rust and mildew.

The housekeeper and niece tore out their hair, clawed their faces, and in the style of those in mourning, they cried over the departure of their master and uncle, as if it had been his death. Samson's intention in persuading him to once again venture out was to do what the history relates further on; which was the advice of the vicar and barber, with whom he had previously discussed the subject. Finally, then, during those three days, Don Quixote and Sancho provided themselves with what they considered necessary, and Sancho having pacified his wife, and Don Quixote his niece and housekeeper, at night, unseen by anyone except Samson, who thought it was wise to accompany them half a mile out of the village, they left, going in the direction of El Toboso, Don Quixote on Rocinante and Sancho on his old donkey, his saddlebags full of food, and his wallet with money that Don Quixote gave him for emergencies. Samson hugged him, and asked him to let him know about his good or bad fortune, so that he could celebrate the former or comfort him over the latter, which is the law of friendship. Don Quixote promised him he would do so, and Samson returned to the village, and the other two took the road toward the great city of El Toboso.

CHAPTER 8

WHAT HAPPENED TO DON QUIXOTE ON HIS WAY TO SEE HIS LADY DULCINEA DEL TOBOSO

"Allah the all-powerful has blessed us!" says Hamete Benengeli on beginning this eighth chapter; "bless Allah!" he repeats three times; and he says this because he has now got Don Quixote and Sancho to travel again on more adventures, and that the readers of this delightful history are now able to read about the achievements and humour which Don Quixote and his aide are now about to begin; and he urges them to forget the former adventures of the ingenious gentleman and to fix their eyes on those that are about to come, which now begin on the road to El Toboso, he goes on to say:

Don Quixote and Sancho were left alone, and the moment Samson left them, Rocinante began to neigh, and the donkey began to sigh, which, by both the Knight and aide, was accepted as a good sign; although, if the truth is to be told, the sighs of the donkey were louder than the neighing of the horse, from which Sancho inferred that his good fortune was greater than that of his master, building, perhaps, on some official astrology that he may have known, although the history says nothing about it; all that can be said is, that whenever he fell, he was heard to say that he wished he had not come, because by falling there was nothing to be gained but a damaged shoe or a broken rib; and, as he was a fool at times, this was quite common.

Don Quixote said, "Sancho, my friend, night is approaching as we go, and it will be too dark to allow us to reach El Toboso by the morning; because I aim to arrive there before I engage in another adventure, and there I will obtain the blessing and generous permission of the incomparable Dulcinea, with which permission I expect and feel assured that I will conclude and bring to a happy ending every dangerous adventure; because nothing in life makes Knights more courageous than finding themselves favoured by their ladies."

"So I they say," replied Sancho; "but I think it will be difficult for you to speak with her or see her, and receive her blessing; unless, she throws it over the wall of the garden where I saw her the last time, when I took the letter to her which mentioned the self-punishment and mad things you were doing in the heart of the Sierra Morena."

"You thought that was a garden wall, Sancho," said Don Quixote, "where you saw that insufficiently praised grace and beauty? It must have been the gallery, corridor, or doorway of some rich and royal palace."

"It might have been that," returned Sancho, "but to me it looked like a wall, unless I have a really bad memory."

"Either way, we are going there, Sancho," said Don Quixote; "because, for me to see her, it is the same to me whether it be over a wall, at a window, through the crack in a door, or the grate of a garden; because any beam of the sun of her beauty that reaches my eyes will give light to my reason and strength to my heart, so that I will be unmatched and unequalled in wisdom and courage."

"Well, to tell the truth, señor," said Sancho, "when I saw that sun of a lady Dulcinea del Toboso, it was not bright enough to send out beams at all; she appeared to be sifting the wheat I told you about, and the thick dust she raised from doing that covered her face like a cloud and dimmed it."

"What! Are you still persisting, Sancho," said Don Quixote, "saying, thinking, believing, and maintaining that my lady Dulcinea was sifting wheat, that being an occupation and task entirely in opposition to what is and should be the employment of Princesses, who are obligated and reserved for other occupations and pursuits that show their rank a gunshot away? You have forgotten, dear Sancho, the lines of a famous poet where he paints for us how, in their crystal homes, four Princesses rose from their seats and placed themselves in a luxuriant meadow to embroider tissues which the ingenious poet describes to us, and how they worked with and merged gold, silk and pearls; so it must have been something like this that she was doing when you saw my lady, only that some evil enchanter seems to go against everything of mine that gives me pleasure, and turns everything into shapes unlike their own; and so I fear that in the history of my achievements which they say is now in print, if its author was some sage who is an enemy of mine, he will have put one thing instead of another, mingling a thousand lies with one truth, and amusing himself by telling stories which have nothing to do with the sequence of the true history. It is envy, the root of numerous evils that harm the virtues! All the vices, Sancho, bring some kind of pleasure with them; but envy brings nothing but irritation, anger, and rage."

"I agree," replied Sancho; "and I suspect in that history which Samson Carrasco told us about, he saw, my honour dragged in the dirt, knocked about, up and down, sweeping the streets, as they say. And yet, speaking as an honest man, I never spoke badly about any enchanter, and I am not so rich that I should be envied; but, I am quite sly, and can have a dangerous tongue, a bit of a rogue in me; but all of this is covered by my great coat of simplicity, always natural; and if I had no other merit to be envied except as I believe, as I always do, firmly and truly in God, that I am a mortal enemy of the Moors, the historians should have mercy on me and treat me well in their writing. But let them say what they like; I was born naked, and if I find myself naked, I neither lose or gain; actually, while I see myself put into a book and passed on from hand to hand over the world, I don't care at all, let them say what they like about me."

"That, Sancho," returned Don Quixote, "reminds me of what happened to a famous poet of our time, who, having written a humorous poem about all the upper class ladies, did not insert the name of a certain lady of whom it was questionable whether she was one or not. Seeing she was not in the list, she asked him what he had seen in her that made him not include her with the others, telling him he should add to his poem and put her in the new part, or else watch out for consequences. The poet did as she asked him to, and left her without a scrap of reputation, and she was satisfied by getting fame even if it was shame. And it is the same when they talk about that shepherd who set fire to the famous temple of Diana, one of the seven wonders of the world, and burned it with the sole objective of making his name known for decades to come; and, although it was forbidden to name him, or mention his name or put it in writing, so the objective of his ambition could be stopped, nevertheless it became known that he was called: Erostratus. And something similar is what happened in the case of the great emperor Charles the 5th and another gentleman in Rome. The emperor was anxious to see the famous temple of Rotunda, called in ancient times the temple 'of all the gods,' but these days, there it is called by a better terminology, temple 'of all the saints,' which is the best preserved building out of all of those pagan constructions in Rome, and the one which best sustains the reputation of the immense work and magnificence of its founders. It is in the form of a half orange, has enormous dimensions, and well lit, although no light penetrates it except that which is admitted through a window, a skylight, at the top; and it was from this that the emperor examined the building. A Roman gentleman stood by his side and explained to him the skilful construction and ingenuity of the vast fabric and its wonderful architecture, and when they had left the skylight he said to the emperor, 'A thousand times, your Majesty, the impulse came to me to hold you in my arms and jump from the skylight, to leave behind my name in the world, a name that would last for ever.' 'I am thankful that you did not carry such an evil thought into effect,' said the emperor, 'and I will not give you an opportunity in future of testing your loyalty again; and I now forbid you to speak to me or to be where ever I am again; and he followed up these words by having him arrested. The meaning is, Sancho, that the desire of acquiring fame is a very powerful motive. What do you think it was that flung Horatius in his full armour down from the bridge into the depths of the river Tiber? What burned the hand and arm of Mutius? What impelled Curtius to plunge into the deep sea that opened in the middle of Rome? What, against all the signs which came to him, made Julius Caesar cross the river Rubicon? And with more modern examples, what destroyed the ships, and left the courageous Spaniards stranded while they were under the command of the great Cortes? All of these and a variety of other great adventures are, were and will be, the work of fame that mortals desire as a reward and a share of the immortality their famous deeds deserve; although we Catholic Christians and Knights care more about the future glory that is everlasting in the regions of heaven than the vanity of fame that can be acquired in this present transitory life; a fame that, however long it may last, must after all end with the world itself, which has its own appointed end. So with that, dear Sancho, we must not go beyond the limits which the Christian religion we recognise has assigned to us. We have to kill the pride in giants, envy by generosity and honour of heart, anger by calmness of attitude and composure, gluttony and sloth by eating little and increasing the length of the intervals in-between, lust by the loyalty we preserve to who we have made the mistresses of our thoughts, laziness by navigating the world in all directions seeking opportunities of making ourselves, besides Christians, famous

Knights. This, Sancho, is the way in which we reach those extremes of praise that fame carries with it."

"All that you have said so far," said Sancho, "I have understood quite well; but I would be glad if you would dissolve a doubt for me, which has just come to my mind."

"Resolve, you mean, Sancho," said Don Quixote; "say it, and in God's name, I will answer as well as I can."

"Tell me, señor," Sancho went on to say, "all of those courageous Knights that you say are now dead - where are they now?"

"The atheists," replied Don Quixote, "are, no doubt, in hell; the Christians, if they were good Christians, are either in limbo or in heaven."

"Very good," said Sancho; "but now I want to know - the tombs where the bodies of those great lords are they lined with silver, winding-sheets, locks of hair, legs and eyes preserved in wax? Or what are they covered with?"

To which Don Quixote replied: "The tombs of the atheists were generally extravagant temples; the ashes of Julius Caesar's body were placed on the top of a large stone pyramid, which they now call in Rome Saint Peter's needle. The emperor Hadrian had for a tomb a castle as large as a good-sized village, which they called the Moles Adriani, and is now the castle of St. Angelo in Rome. The Queen Artemisia buried her husband Mausolus in a tomb which was considered one of the seven wonders of the world; but none of these tombs, or tombs of many of the atheists, were lined with winding-sheets or any of those decorations that would show them to be saints."

"That's the point I'm coming to," said Sancho; "and now tell me, which is greater work, to bring a dead man to life or to kill a giant?"

"The answer is easy," replied Don Quixote; "it is greater work to bring a dead man to life."

"Now I have got you," said Sancho; "in that case the fame of those who bring the dead to life, who give sight to the blind, cure cripples, restore health to the sick, and in front of their tombs have lamps burning, and whose chapels are filled with sincere people on their knees adoring their remains have better fame in this life and in the other than that which all the atheist emperors and Knights that have ever been in the world have left or may leave behind them?"

"That I agree with," said Don Quixote.

"Then this fame, these favours, these privileges, or whatever you call it," said Sancho, "belong to the bodies and remains of the saints who, with the approval and permission of our holy mother the Church, have lamps, candles, winding-sheets, pictures, eyes and legs, which increase devotion and add to their own Christian reputation. Kings carry the bodies or remains of saints on their shoulders, and kiss bits of their bones, and enrich and decorate their favourite altars with them."

"What would you like me to infer from all you have said, Sancho?" asked Don Quixote.

"My meaning is," said Sancho, "we should become saints, and we will obtain much quicker the fame we are striving for; because you know, señor, yesterday or the day before yesterday, they idolised and adored two little barefoot friars, and it is now considered the greatest good luck to kiss or touch the iron chains which their bodies were secured and tortured with, and so it is said, that those that God preserve are held with greater admiration than the sword of Roland in the armoury of our lord the King. So, señor, it is better to be a humble little friar, regardless of rank, than a courageous Knight; when a couple of dozen lashings which atone for sins are worth more than two thousand lance-thrusts, whether they are given to giants, monsters, or dragons."

"All that is true," returned Don Quixote, "but we cannot all be friars, and there are many ways which God uses to take his own; chivalry is a religion, and there are sainted Knights in heaven."

"Yes," said Sancho, "but I have heard it said that there are more friars in heaven than Knights."

"That," said Don Quixote, "is because there are more in religious orders than Knights."

"There are many Knights," said Sancho.

"Many," replied Don Quixote, "only a few who deserve to be called Knights."

They discussed these matters and others of the same kind as the night passed into the following day, without anything else worth mentioning.

Don Quixote was quite unhappy; but finally, as the day was approaching, they caught sight of the great city of El Toboso, which lifted Don Quixote's spirit and made Sancho's fall, because he did not know where Dulcinea's house was, and in his entire life he had never seen her, any more than his master; so they were both anxious, one to see her, the other as he had not seen her. In the end, Don Quixote decided to enter the city as sunrise approached, and so, they waited among some oak trees that were near El Toboso; and when the moment they had agreed on arrived, they entered the city, where something happened to them that we be relayed in the next chapter.

CHAPTER 9

WHAT HAPPENED IN EL TOBOSO?

It was midnight - more or less - when Don Quixote and Sancho left the woods and entered El Toboso. The town was in deep silence, because all the inhabitants were asleep, and stretched on their backs, as the saying goes. The night was dark, which made Sancho glad, as it offered an excuse for his disorientation. Nothing could be heard except the barking of dogs, which deafened the ears of Don Quixote and troubled the heart of Sancho. Now and then a donkey snorted, pigs grunted, cats meowed, and various other noises occurred which seemed louder in the silence of the night; all of which the captivated Knight took to be a sign of evil; nevertheless, he said to Sancho, "Sancho, my son, lead us to the palace of Dulcinea, perhaps we will find her awake."

"What palace can I lead us to," said Sancho, "when what I saw her in was only a little house?"

"Most likely she had gone into some small apartment of her palace," said Don Quixote, "to socialise with some other ladies, as great ladies and Princesses are accustomed to do."

"Señor," said Sancho, "if you believe, in spite of me telling you otherwise, that the house is a palace, do you think this is this the right time to find the door open, and will it be right for us to knock until they hear us and open the door; making a disturbance and confusion throughout the whole household? Do you think we are going to a house of whores, like men who go and knock at any hour, however late it may be?"

"Let us first find the palace," replied Don Quixote, "and then I will decide Sancho, what is best to do; but look, Sancho, because either I see badly, or that dark mass other there appears to be Dulcinea's palace."

"Then you lead the way," said Sancho, "perhaps you are right; however even if I could see it with my eyes and touch it with my hands, I would believe it as much as I believe it is daylight now."

Don Quixote took the lead, and having gone two hundred yards he arrived at the mass that produced the shade, and found it was a great tower, and then he perceived that the building was no palace, but the main church in the town, and he said, "This is a church we have discovered, Sancho."

"So I see," said Sancho, "and God willing we do not find our graves here; it is not a good sign to find ourselves wandering in a graveyard at this time of night; I am telling you that the house of this lady will be found in an alley way somewhere."

"You are a blockhead!" said Don Quixote; "where have you ever heard that castles and royal palaces are built in alleyways?"

"Señor," replied Sancho, "every city has a way of its own; perhaps here in El Toboso it is the way to build palaces and grand buildings in alleys; so I ask you to let me search among these streets or alleys, and perhaps, in some corner or other, I may find this palace - and I wish I saw the dogs eating it for leading us astray."

"Speak respectfully about what belongs to my lady, Sancho," said Don Quixote; "let us go in peace, and not give up."

"Forgive me," said Sancho, "but how am I meant to be patient when you want me, after only seeing it once to find the house of your lady, and find it in darkness, when you can't find it, someone who must have seen it a thousand times?"

"You are trying to lead me into desperation, Sancho," said Don Quixote. "Look here, pagan, have I not told you a thousand times that I have never seen the incomparable Dulcinea or entered her palace, and that I am in love purely by hearing about her and the great reputation she has for beauty and discretion?"

"Now I hear it," returned Sancho; "and I can tell you that if you have not seen her, neither have I."

"That cannot be," said Don Quixote, "because you said, on bringing back the answer to the letter I sent you with, that you saw her sifting wheat."

"Forget that, señor," said Sancho; "I must tell you that I saw her and the answer I brought back to you was by what I hear too, because I cannot tell who lady Dulcinea is than more than I can touch the sky."

"Sancho, Sancho," said Don Quixote, "there are times for joking and times when joking is out of place; if I tell you that I have neither seen or spoken to the lady of my heart, it is not a reason for you to joke and say you have not spoken to her or seen her, when that is not the case, as you well know."

While the two were engaged in this conversation, they perceived someone with a pair of donkeys approaching the spot where they stood, and from the noise the plough made, as it dragged along the ground, they guessed it was a labourer who had got up before sunrise to do his work, which proved to be the case.

He came along singing a known song called: Roncesvalles pursuit.

"May I die, Sancho," said Don Quixote, when he heard him, "will any good come to us tonight! Do you not hear what that clown is singing?"

"I do," said Sancho, "but what has Roncesvalles pursuit got to do with anything? He might as well be singing the song of Calainos."

By this time the labourer had come closer, and Don Quixote asked him, "Can you tell me friend, where is the palace of the incomparable Princess Dona Dulcinea del Toboso?"

"Señor," replied the labourer, "I am a stranger, and I have only been in this town for a few days, doing farm work for a rich man. In the house opposite the vicar of the village he lives with his assistant, and both or either of them will be able to tell you about this lady Princess, because they have a list of all the people in El Toboso; although it is my belief there is no Princess living here;

however there are many ladies of high quality, and in their own houses each of them may be a Princess."

"Well, then, who I am inquiring about will be one of these, my friend," said Don Quixote.

"That may be," replied the labourer; "God be with you, because here comes the daylight;" and without waiting for any more of his questions, he whipped his donkies and departed.

Sancho, seeing his master sad and somewhat dissatisfied, said to him, "Señor, daylight will be here soon, and it will not be wise to let the sun find us in the street; it will be better for us to leave the city and to hide in some forest in the neighbourhood, and I will come back in the daytime, and I won't leave any place or corner of the whole village unsearched, for the house, castle, or palace of lady Dulcinea, and it will be bad luck if I don't find it; but as soon as I have found it, I will speak to her, and tell her where you are waiting for her and arrange some plan for you to see her without any damage to her honour and reputation."

"Sancho," said Don Quixote, "you have delivered a thousand sentences condensed into a few words; I thank you for the advice you have given, and fully accept it. Let us look for some place where I can hide, while you return, as you say, to seek and speak with my lady."

Sancho was so anxious to get his master out of the town, in-case he discovered the lie about the reply he had brought to him in the Sierra Morena on behalf of Dulcinea; so he rushed their departure, and about two miles out of the village they found a forest where Don Quixote hid himself, while Sancho returned to the city to speak to Dulcinea, upon which many things happened to him which demand fresh attention and a new chapter.

CHAPTER 10

THE CRAFTY METHOD SANCHO ADOPTED TO ENCHANT LADY DULCINEA, AND OTHER INCIDENTS AS LUDICROUS AS THEY ARE TRUE

When the author of this great history comes to relay what is put forward in this chapter he says he would have preferred to leave it out, fearing it would not be believed, because here Don Quixote's madness reaches the pinnacle of the greatest insanity that can ever be conceived, and even goes beyond the greatest. But after all, although still under the same fear and apprehension, he has recorded it without adding to the story or leaving out any part of the truth, and entirely disregarding the accusations of lying that might be brought against him; and he was right to, because the truth will not break, and always rises above lies like oil above water; and so, going on with his story, he says that as soon as Don Quixote had hid himself in the forest near El Toboso, he asked Sancho to return to the city, and not to come back without having first spoken on his behalf to his lady, and begged her to allow herself to be seen by her loyal Knight, and consent to offer her blessings to him, so he may hope for a happy conclusion to all of his encounters and difficult undertakings. Sancho accepted to execute the task according to the instructions, and to bring back an answer as good as the one he brought back before.

"Go, my son," said Don Quixote, "and do not be stunned when you find yourself exposed to the light of that sun of beauty you are going to seek. You will be the happiest aide in the whole world! Keep in mind, and do not let it escape your memory, how she welcomes you; if she changes colour while you are giving her my message; if she is agitated and disturbed when hearing my name; if she cannot rest on her cushion, if you find her happily seated in the sumptuous room appropriate to her rank; and if she is standing, observe if she poises herself on one foot, and then on the other; if she repeats the reply she gives to you two or three times; if she goes from gentleness to seriousness, from seriousness to sensitivity; if she raises her hand to smooth her hair even though it is not tangled. In short, my son, observe all of her actions and motions, because if you are to report them to me as they were, I will understand what she hides in the recesses of her heart in regards to my love; because you should know, Sancho, if you do not know, that with lovers the outward actions and motions they make when there is conversation of their loves are the faithful messengers that carry the news of what is going on in the depths of their hearts. Go, my friend, I hope you find better fortune than I have, and it brings you a happier future than that which I have in this bleak solitude."

"I will go and return quickly," said Sancho; "cheer up that little heart of yours master, because at the moment you seem to have one no bigger than a hazel nut; remember what they say, that a strong heart breaks bad luck, and where there are arrows there are no targets; and they say, the rabbit jumps up where it is not looked for. I say this because, if we could not find Dulcinea's palaces or castles tonight, now that it is daylight I think I will find them when I least expect it, and once found, leave it to me to manage her."

"With certainty, Sancho," said Don Quixote, "you always use the proverbs happily, whatever we deal with; may God give me better luck in regards to what I am anxious about."

Sancho turned around and gave his donkey a kick, and Don Quixote remained behind, seated on his horse, resting in his stirrups and leaning on the end of his lance, filled with sad and troubled thoughts; and there we will leave him, and accompany Sancho, who went off no less troubled than he left his master; so much so, that as soon as he had got out of the woods, and looking around saw that Don Quixote was not within sight, he dismounted from his donkey, and seating himself at the foot of a tree began to talk to himself, saying, "Now, brother Sancho, where are you going. Are you going to look for some donkey that has been lost? Not at all. Then what are you going to look for? I am going to look for a Princess, that's all; and in her for the sun of beauty and the whole heaven at once. And where do you expect to find all this, Sancho? Where? In the great city of El Toboso? And for who are you going to look for her? For the famous Knight Don Quixote of La Mancha, who corrects wrongs, gives food to those who are thirsty and drink to the hungry. That's all very well, but do you know where her house is, Sancho? My master says it will be some royal palace or grand castle. And have you ever seen her by any chance? Neither I or my master have ever seen her. And does it strike you that it would be fair and right if the people of El Toboso, finding out that you were here with the intention of going to interfere with their Princesses and trouble their ladies, were to come and punch your ribs, and leave you without a whole bone in your body? They would have a very good reason, if they did not see that I am under orders, and that 'you are a messenger, my friend, no blame belongs to you.' Don't trust that, Sancho, because the Manchegan people are as hot-tempered as they are honest, and won't put up with mischief from anybody. I swear to God, if they find out, it will be worse for you, I promise. Go, you rascal! Why should I go looking for three feet on a cat, to please another man; and what is more, looking for Dulcinea would be like looking for the graduate in Salamanca? The devil, the devil and nobody else, has mixed me up in this business!"

This was the speech Sancho held with himself, and the conclusion he could come to was to say to himself again, "Well, there's a remedy for everything except death, which is inescapable for all, whether we like it or not, when life is finished. I have seen by a thousand signs that this master of mine is a madman who should be confined, and, I am as well, because I am a greater fool than he is when I follow him and serve him, if there's any truth in the proverb that says, 'Tell me what company you keep, and I will tell you what you are,' or in another, 'Not with who you are bred, but with who you are fed.' Well then, if he is mad, as he is, and with a madness that mostly takes one thing for another, and white for black, and black for white, as was seen when he said the windmills were giants, and the monks' donkies to be camels, flocks of sheep to be armies of enemies, and much more of the same tune, it will not be very hard to make him believe that some country girl, the first I come across here, is lady Dulcinea; and if he does not believe it, I will swear it is true; and if he swears it is not, I will swear again; and if he persists I will persist further. Maybe, by persisting in this way, I may finally stop him sending me with messages of this type, or maybe he will think, as I suspect he will, that one of those evil enchanters, who he says have spite against him, has changed her form for the sake of doing harm and injury to him."

With this reflection Sancho calmed his mind, considering the matter as good as settled, and stayed there until the afternoon to make Don Quixote think he had been gone long enough to go to El Toboso and return; and things progressed so quickly and luckily for him that as soon as he got up to mount his donkey, he saw, coming from El Toboso towards the spot where he stood, three peasant girls on three horses which looked more like donkeys.

To be brief, the instant Sancho saw the peasant girls, he returned immediately to seek his master, and found him weeping and giving a thousand passionate cries. When Don Quixote saw him he exclaimed, "What is the news, Sancho, my friend? Should I mark this day as good or bad?"

"You," replied Sancho, "had better mark it with something meaningful, like the inscriptions on the walls of class rooms."

"Then you bring good news," said Don Quixote.

"So good," replied Sancho, "that you only need to mount Rocinante and go out into the open field to see lady Dulcinea del Toboso, who, with two other lady friends of hers, is coming to see you."

"Holy God! what are you saying, Sancho, my friend?" exclaimed Don Quixote. "Do not be deceiving me, or seeking to create a false joy to cheer my real sadness."

"What would I get by deceiving you," returned Sancho, "especially when the truth of what I say would be revealed to quickly? Come on, señor, get up, and you will see the Princess coming. She and her ladies are all one glow of gold, all bunches of pearls, all diamonds, all rubies; with their hair loose on their shoulders like so many sunbeams playing with the wind; and moreover, they come mounted on three hoses, the finest ever seen."

"Horses, you mean, Sancho," said Don Quixote.

"There is not much difference between hoses and horses," said Sancho; "but no matter what they are coming on, they are there, the finest ladies you could wish for, especially Princess Dulcinea, who overwhelms my senses."

"Let us go, Sancho my son," said Don Quixote, "and in reward for this, as unexpected as it is good, I offer you the best of what I win in the next adventure I have; or if that does not satisfy you, I promise you the ponies I will have this year from my three horses that you know are ready for breeding in our village."

"I'll take the ponies," said Sancho; "because it is not quite certain if what you win in the next adventure will be any good."

By now, they had exited the woods, and saw the three village girls nearby. Don Quixote looked all along the road to El Toboso, and as he could see nobody except the three peasant girls, he was completely puzzled, and asked Sancho if it was outside the city where he had left them.

"Outside the city?" returned Sancho. "Are your eyes in the back of your head, you can't see that they are those coming along there, shining like the very sun at noon?"

"I see nothing, Sancho," said Don Quixote, "but three country girls on three donkeys."

"What the devil!" said Sancho, "Can it be that you see and take three hoses or whatever they are called, as white snow, for donkeys? God, I could tear my beard out if that was the case!"

"Well, I can only say, Sancho, my friend," said Don Quixote, "that it is clear that they are donkies - as clear as I am Don Quixote, and you are Sancho Panza."

"Quiet, señor," said Sancho, "don't talk that way, open your eyes, and pay your respects to the lady of your thoughts, who is getting closer;" and after saying he went to meet the three village girls, and dismounting from the donkey, caught hold of one of the donkies of the three country girls by the reigns, and dropping on both knees, he said, "Queen and Princess of beauty, may it please your greatness to receive into your favour and good-will your captive Knight who stands here turned into marble stone, and quite dazed and numb, finding himself in the presence of your high magnificence. I am Sancho Panza, his aide, and he is the wandering Knight Don Quixote of La Mancha, otherwise called 'The Knight of the Sorrowful Face.'"

Don Quixote had by this time placed himself on his knees beside Sancho, and, with his eyes staring out of his head and a puzzled gaze, was regarding the so called Queen and lady that Sancho made her out to be; and as he could see nothing in her except a village girl, and not a very good looking one, because she was spotty-faced and snub-nosed, he was confused and bewildered, and did not open his lips. The country girls, at the same time, were speechless to see these two men, so different in appearance, on their knees, preventing their companion from continuing her journey. She, however, who had been stopped, breaking the silence, said angrily, "Get out of the way and let us pass, we are in a hurry."

To which Sancho returned, "Oh, Princess and universal lady of El Toboso, is your generous heart not softened by seeing the pillar of Knighthood on his knees in your presence?"

On hearing this, one of the others exclaimed, "Woah! See how the men these days come to play games with the village girls, as if we could not see what they are trying to do. Go your own way, and let us go ours, and it will be better for you."

"Get up, Sancho," said Don Quixote; "I see that fortune, 'with evil intent,' has taken possession of all the roads by which any comfort may reach 'this poor soul' that I carry in my body. And you, highest perfection of excellence that can be desired, utmost upper limit of grace in human shape, sole relief of this afflicted heart that adores you, although the destructive enchanter that persecutes me has brought clouds and cataracts to my eyes, and to them, and them only, transformed your exemplar beauty and changed your features into those of a poor peasant girl, and he at the same time has changed mine into those of some monster to render me detestable to your sight, do not refuse to look at me with tenderness and love; seeing that I on my knees regard your transformed beauty with the humility which my soul adores you with."

"My great grandfather!" cried the girl, "I do not care for your love-making! Get out of the way and let us pass, and we will thank you."

Sancho stood aside and let her go, feeling happy to have got himself out of the trouble he was in. The instant the village girl who had played the part of Dulcinea found herself free, poking her "donkey" with a spike she had on the end of a stick, she left with full speed across the field. The donkey, however, feeling the point more acutely than usual, began to jump, and flung lady Dulcinea to the ground; seeing this, Don Quixote ran to pick her up, and Sancho went to adjust the saddle-bag, which had also slipped under the donkey's belly. The saddle-bag being secured, as Don Quixote was about to lift up his enchanted mistress in his arms and put her back on her donkey, the lady, getting up from the ground, saved him the trouble, because, stepping back a little, she took a short run, and putting both hands on the ass of the donkey she jumped and landed on the saddle more lightly than an eagle, and sat like a man, which made Sancho say, "Rogue! Our lady is lighter than a bird, and could teach the cleverest Mexican how to mount; she cleared the back of the saddle in one jump, and without spurs she is making the donkey go like a zebra; and her ladies are all behind her, because they all fly like the wind;" which was the truth, because as soon as they saw Dulcinea mounted, they rushed after her, and sped away without looking back, for more than half a mile.

Don Quixote followed them with his eyes, and when they were no longer in sight, he turned to Sancho and said, "Now, Sancho? Can you see how I am hated by enchanters! And see to what extent the malice and spite they have for me goes, when they seek to deprive me of the happiness it would give me to see my lady in her proper form. The fact is I was born to be an example of misfortune, and the target and mark at which the arrows of adversity are aimed and directed. Note as well, Sancho, that these traitors were not content with changing and transforming my Dulcinea, but they transformed and changed her into a shape as ugly as a mere village girl; and at the same time they robbed her of that which is an unusual property of ladies of high class, that is to say, the sweet fragrance that comes from always being among perfumes and flowers. Because I must tell you, Sancho, that when I approached to put Dulcinea on her horse (as you say it was, although to me it appeared to be a donkey), she gave me a whiff of raw garlic that made my head spin, and poisoned my heart."

"Scum of the earth!" cried Sancho, "miserable, spiteful enchanters! I hope to see you all strung up like sardines! You know a lot, can do a lot, and will do a lot more. It should have been enough for you, you crooks, to have changed the pearls of lady Dulcinea's eyes into tree bark, and her hair of purest gold into the bristles of an ox's tail, and in short, all her features from beauty to ugliness, without altering her smell; because by that you hoped we would not find what was hidden underneath that ugly coating; although, to tell the truth, I never perceived her ugliness, but only her beauty, which was raised to the highest of perfection by a mole she had on her right lip, like a moustache, with seven or eight red hairs like threads of gold as long as a foot."

"From the correspondence which exists to date," said Don Quixote, "Dulcinea has another mole on the thigh on the same side on which she has the one on her face; but hairs the length that you have mentioned are very long for moles."

"Well, all I can say is it was plain to see," replied Sancho.

"I believe it, my friend," returned Don Quixote; "because nature gave nothing to Dulcinea that was not perfect and well-finished; and so, if she had a hundred moles like the one you have described, on her they would not be moles, but moons and shining stars. But tell me, Sancho, that which seemed to me to be a saddle you were fixing, was it a flat-saddle or a side-saddle?"

"It was neither," replied Sancho, "it was quite a unique saddle, with embroidery worth half a Kingdom."

"And I could not see this either, Sancho?" said Don Quixote; "again I say, and will say a thousand times, I am the most unfortunate of men."

Sancho, had enough to do to hide his laughter, when hearing the simplicity of the master he had so nicely fooled. Finally, after a lot more conversation between them, they remounted, and followed the road to Saragossa, which they expected to reach in time to take part in a grand festival which is held every year in that famous city; but before they got there, things happened to them, so many, so important, and so strange, that they deserve to be recorded and read, as will be seen later.

CHAPTER 11

THE STRANGE ADVENTURE WHICH THE COURAGEOUS DON QUIXOTE HAD WITH THE CART OF "THE CORTES OF DEATH"

Dejected beyond measure Don Quixote pursued his journey, going over in his mind the cruel trick the enchanters had played on him, changing his lady Dulcinea into the disgusting shape of a village girl, and was not able to think of any way of restoring her to her original form; and these reflections absorbed him so much, that without being aware of it he let go of Rocinante's reins, and Rocinante, noticing the freedom that was granted to him, stopped at every step to eat the fresh grass with which the field was covered.

Sancho recalled him from his daydream. "Depression, señor," he said, "was made, not for animals, but for men; but if men give in to it too much they turn into animals; control yourself; be yourself again; hold Rocinante's reins; cheer up, arouse yourself and show that gracious spirit that Knights should have. What the devil is this? What weakness is this? Are we here or in France? The devil can take all the Dulcineas in the world; because the well-being of a single Knight carries more consequence than all the enchantments and transformations on earth."

"Quiet, Sancho," said Don Quixote in a weak and faint voice, "quiet and say no more profanities against that enchanted lady; because I am to blame for her misfortune; her disaster has come from the hatred the wicked have for me."

"I can imagine it is sad if you cannot see her beauty," returned Sancho.

"You may well say that, Sancho," replied Don Quixote, "as you saw her in the full perfection of her beauty; because the enchantment does not go so far as to pervert your vision or hide her loveliness from you; against me however and against my eyes the strength of their venom is directed. Nevertheless, there is one thing which has occurred to me, and that is that you described her beauty incorrectly to me, because, as I recall, you said that her eyes were pearls; but eyes that are like pearls are the eyes of a fish rather than a lady, and I am persuaded that Dulcinea's must be green emeralds, full and soft, with two rainbows for eyebrows; take away those pearls from her eyes and transfer them to her teeth; because beyond a doubt, Sancho, you have mistaken one for the other, the eyes for the teeth."

"Very likely," said Sancho; "because her beauty disoriented me as much as her ugliness did to you; but let us leave it all to God, who alone knows what is going to happen in this evil world of ours, where there is hardly a thing to be found without some mixture of evilness, dishonesty, and mischievousness. But one thing, señor, troubles me more than all the rest, and that is thinking what will be done when you conquer some giant, or some other Knight, and order him to go and present himself to the beauty of lady Dulcinea. Where is this poor giant, or this poor vanquished Knight going to find her? I think I can see them wandering all over El Toboso, looking like fools, and asking for lady Dulcinea; and even if they meet her in the middle of the street they won't know it is her any more than they would my father."

"Perhaps, Sancho," returned Don Quixote, "the enchantment does not go so far as to deprive conquered giants and Knights the power of recognising Dulcinea; we will try this experiment with one or two of the first I vanquish and send to her, whether they see her or not, by commanding them to return and give me an account of what happened in respect to this."

"I say, I think what you have proposed is excellent," said Sancho; "and that by this plan we will find out what we want to know; and if it is true that she is hidden only from you, the misfortune will be more yours than hers; but as long as lady Dulcinea is well and happy, we on our part will make the most of it, and get on as well as we can, seeking our adventures, and leaving time to take its course; because time is the best physician for these and greater ailments."

Don Quixote was about to reply to Sancho Panza, but he was prevented by a cart crossing the road full of the most diverse and strange people and figures that could be imagined. He who led the donkeys and acted as the carter was a hideous demon; the cart was open to the sky, without a roof, and the first figure that presented itself to Don Quixote's eyes was that of Death itself with a human face; next to it was an angel with large painted wings, and at one side an emperor, with a crown, with an appearance of gold on his head. At the feet of Death was the god called Cupid, without his bandage, but with his bow and arrows; there was also a Knight in full armour, except that he had no visor or helmet, but only a hat and hair with curls of various colours; and along with these were others with a variety of costumes and faces. All this, unexpectedly encountered, took Don Quixote by surprise, and struck terror into the heart of Sancho; but the next instant Don Quixote was glad, believing that some new dangerous adventure was presenting itself to him, and under this impression, and with a spirit prepared to face any danger, he planted himself in front of the cart, and in a loud and menacing tone, exclaimed, "Carter, or coachman, or devil, or whatever you are, tell me immediately who you are, where you are going, and who these people are that you carry in your wagon."

To which the devil, stopping the cart, answered quietly, "Señor, we are actors of Angulo el Malo's company; we have been acting out the play 'The Cortes of Death' this morning, in a village behind that hill, and we have to act it again this afternoon which you can see from our attire; and to save the trouble of undressing and dressing again, we travel in the costumes in which we perform. That boy there appears as Death, that other as an angel, that woman, the manager's wife, plays the Queen, this one the soldier, that one the emperor, and I play the devil; and I am one of the principal characters in the play, because in this company I take the leading parts. If you want to know anything else about us, ask me and I will answer, because as I am the devil I am up for anything."

"On the word of a Knight," replied Don Quixote, "when I saw this cart I thought some great adventure was presenting itself to me; but illusions are to be avoided. Continue, good people; keep your festival, and remember, if you demand that I render you any service, I will do it gladly and willingly, because from a child I was always fond of the plays, and in my youth a keen lover of the actor's art."

While they were talking, fate arranged that one of the group in a costume with a great number of bells, joined them, and this merry-man approaching Don Quixote, began waving his stick and banging the ground with a great jingling of the bells, which annoyingly startled Rocinante that, in spite of Don Quixote's efforts to hold him, he ran across the field with greater speed than the bones of his anatomy ever indicated possible.

Sancho, who thought his master was in danger of being thrown, jumped off his donkey, and ran to help him; but by the time he reached him he was already on the ground, and beside him was Rocinante, who had fallen with his master, the usual end of Rocinante's high-spiritedness. But the moment Sancho jumped off his donkey to go and help Don Quixote, the dancing devil with the bells jumped on the donkey, and beating him with the bells, the fright of the noise more than by the pain of the blows, made him fly across the fields towards the village where they were heading to. Sancho witnessed his donkey run and his master's fall, and did not know which of the two cases he should attend to first; but in the end, like a good aide and good servant, he let his love for his master prevail over his affection for his donkey; although every time he saw the bells rise in the air and come down on his Donkey he felt the pain and terror of death, and he would have rather had the blows fall on his own eyes than on a hair of his donkey's tail. In this trouble and perplexity, he came to where Don Quixote lay in a far sorrier state than he liked, and having helped him to mount Rocinante, he said to him, "Señor, the devil has taken my donkey."

"What devil?" asked Don Quixote.

"The one with the bells," said Sancho.

"Then I will recover him," said Don Quixote, "even if he is shut with him in the deepest and darkest dungeons of hell. Follow me, Sancho, because the cart goes slowly, and with their donkeys I will compensate for the loss of yours."

"Do not worry about it, señor," said Sancho; "keep cool, because as I now see, the devil has let my donkey go and is coming back;" and so it turned out, because the devil ran on foot to the town, and the donkey came back to his master.

"Despite that," said Don Quixote, "it will be best to discuss the discourtesy of that devil with some of those in the cart, even if he were the emperor himself."

"Don't do it," returned Sancho; "take my advice and do not interfere with actors, because they are a favoured class; I myself have known an actor taken away for two murders, and yet left the trial without a punishment; remember, as they are happy people who give pleasure, everyone favours and protects them, above all when they belong to royal companies."

"Despite that," said Don Quixote, "the devil must not go off boasting about this, even if the whole human race favours him."

Don Quixote chased the cart, which was now very near to the town, shouting out as he went, "Hold! Stop! you merry, jolly crew! I want to teach you how to treat donkeys and animals that serve the aides of Knights."

The shouts of Don Quixote were so loud, that those in the cart heard and understood them, and, guessing by the words what the speaker's intention was, Death in an instant jumped out of the cart, and the emperor, the devil carter and the angel did too, and neither did the Queen or the god Cupid stay behind; and all armed themselves with stones and formed a line, prepared to welcome Don Quixote with their pebbles. Don Quixote, when he saw them raise such an array of weapons, ready for a mighty shower of stones, checked Rocinante and began to consider in what way he could attack them with the least danger to himself. As he halted Sancho came, and seeing him willing to attack this well-ordered team, said to him, "It would be the height of madness to attempt such a thing; remember, señor, there is no better defensive armour in the world, except to hide oneself under a brass shield; and besides, one should remember that it is impulsiveness, and not bravery, for a single man to attack an army that has Death in it, and where emperors fight in person, with good and bad angels to help them; and if this reflection will not make you keep quiet, perhaps it will help to know for certain that among all these, although they look like Kings, princes, and emperors, there is not a single Knight."

"You have discovered a good point, Sancho," said Don Quixote, "which may and should turn me away from the resolution I had already formed. I cannot and must not raise a sword, as I have many times told you before, against anyone who is not a Knight; it is up to you, Sancho, to take vengeance for the wrong done to your donkey; and I will help you from here with shouting and helpful advice."

"There is no reason to take vengeance on anyone, señor," replied Sancho; "because it is not the part of good Christians to revenge wrongs; and besides, I will arrange it with my donkey to leave his grievance and live in peace as long as heaven grants me life."

"Well," said Don Quixote, "if that is your decision, good Sancho, sensible Sancho, Christian Sancho, honest Sancho, let us leave these actors alone and turn to the pursuit of better and worthier adventures; because, from what I see on this road, we cannot fail to find plenty of marvellous ones on it."

Don Quixote turned his horse around, and Sancho ran to take possession of his donkey, Death and his team returned to their cart and pursued their journey, and therefore the dreaded adventure of the cart of Death ended happily, thanks to the advice Sancho gave to his master; who had, the following day, a fresh adventure, of greater interest than the last, with an infatuated Knight.

CHAPTER 12

THE STRANGE ADVENTURE DON QUIXOTE HAD WITH THE BOLD KNIGHT OF MIRRORS

The following night after the encounter with Death, Don Quixote and his aide passed under some tall shady trees, and Don Quixote by Sancho's persuasion ate a little from the store carried by the donkey, and over their dinner Sancho said to his master, "Señor, what a fool I would have been if I had chosen for my reward the winnings of the first adventure you achieved, instead of the ponies. After all, 'a sparrow in the hand is worth two in the bush.'"

"At the same time, Sancho," replied Don Quixote, "if you had let me attack them as I wanted, at the very least the emperor's gold crown and Cupid's painted wings would have been yours, because I would have taken them by force and placed them into your hands."

"The sceptres and crowns of those play-actor emperors," said Sancho, "were never pure gold, only brass foil or tin."

"That is true," said Don Quixote, "because it would not be right that the accessories of the drama should be real, instead of being mere fictions and resemblances, like the drama itself; which, Sancho − toward us and as a necessary consequence, towards those who represent and produce it − places in front of us a mirror in which we may vividly see displayed what goes on in human life; and there is nothing else similar that shows us more faithfully what we are and should be than the plays and the actors. Tell me, have you not seen a play acted in which Kings, Emperors, Knights, ladies, and other people were introduced? One plays the villain, another the fool, this one the merchant, that one the soldier, one the sharp-witted man, another the foolish lover; and when the play is over, and they have removed the costumes they wore in it, all the actors become equal."

"Yes, I have seen that," said Sancho.

"Well then," said Don Quixote, "the same thing happens in the comedy and life of this world, where some play emperors, others popes, and, in short, all the characters that can be brought into a play; but when it is over, that is to say when life ends, death strips them of all the garments that distinguish one from the other, and all are equal in the grave."

"A fine comparison!" said Sancho; "although not so new that I have not heard it many times before, as well as the other one about the game of chess; how, so long as the game lasts, each piece has its own particular place and value on the board, but when the game is over they all go back in the same box."

"You are growing less foolish and more sharp each day, Sancho," said Don Quixote.

"Yes," said Sancho; "it must be that some of your insightfulness sticks to me; a land that is barren and dry, will yield good fruit if you fertilise it and cultivate it; what I mean is that your conversations have been the fertiliser that has fallen on the barren soil of my dry mind, and the time I have been in your service has been the cultivation; and with the help of this I hope to produce good fruit in abundance that will not fall away or slide from the paths of the good refinement that you have made in my dry understanding."

Don Quixote laughed at Sancho's phrasing, and perceived that what he said about his improvement was true, because now and then he spoke in a way that surprised him; although always, or mostly, when Sancho intended to speak like this and attempted polite language, he ended up falling from the summit of his simplicity into the abyss of his ignorance; and where he showed this most was when he included proverbs, no matter whether or not they had anything to do with the subject he was speaking about, as has been seen already and will be noticed in the course of this history.

They passed the night having conversation of this kind, but Sancho felt a desire to let down the curtains of his eyes, as he used to say when he wanted to go to sleep; and stripping the donkey he left him to roam and eat as much grass as he liked. He did not remove Rocinante's saddle however, as his master's orders were, that so long as they were in the field and not sleeping under a roof Rocinante was not to be stripped - the ancient rule established and observed by Knights was being able to take the harness off and hang it on the saddle, but to not remove the saddle from the horse – ever! Sancho acted accordingly, and gave him the same freedom he had given the donkey.

Between him and Rocinante there was a friendship so unequalled and so strong, that the author of this genuine history devoted some special chapters to it, which, in order to preserve the appropriateness and dignity due to a history so heroic, he did not insert them; although at times he forgets this and describes how eagerly the two animals would scratch one another when they were together and how, when they were tired or full, Rocinante would lay his neck across the donkey's, and the pair would stand gazing thoughtfully on the ground, for three days, or at least as long as they were left alone, or hunger did not drive them to go and look for food. I may add that they say the author left it on record that he compared their friendship to that of Nisus and Euryalus, and Pylades and Orestes; and if that is so, it may be perceived, to the admiration of mankind, how firm the friendship must have been between these two peaceful animals, shaming men, who preserve friendships with one another so badly. This was why it was said:

A friend, no longer a friend;
The leaves turn to knives.

And someone else has said;
Friend to a bug.

No one can disagree with the author when he compared the friendship of these animals to that of men; because men have received many lessons from animals, and learned many important things, as, for example, gratitude from the dog, watchfulness from the crane, foresight from the ant, modesty from the elephant, and loyalty from the horse.

Sancho finally fell asleep at the base of a cork tree, while Don Quixote dozed at the base of a sturdy oak; but a short time passed when a noise he heard behind him woke him up, and rising to his feet in a startled manner, he listened and looked in the direction the noise came from, and perceived two men on horseback, one of whom, letting himself drop from the saddle, said to the other, "Dismount, my friend, and take the reins off the horses, because as far as I can see, this place has enough grass for them, and has the solitude and silence my love-sick thoughts require." As he said this he laid himself on the ground the armour in which he was in rattled, which indicated to Don Quixote that he must be a Knight; and going over to Sancho, who was asleep, he shook his arm and with great difficulty brought him back to his senses, and said in a low voice to him, "Brother Sancho, we have got an adventure."

"God please make it a good one," said Sancho; "and where may this adventure be?"

"Where, Sancho?" replied Don Quixote; "turn your eyes and look, and you will see over there a Knight, who, it strikes me, is not happy, because I saw him throw himself off his horse and onto the ground with a certain misery, and his armour rattled as he fell."

"Well," said Sancho, "how do make that out to be an adventure?"

"I did not say," returned Don Quixote, "that it is a complete adventure, but that it is the beginning of one, because it is in this way adventures begin. But listen, because it seems like he is tuning a guitar, and from the way he is spitting and clearing his chest he must be getting ready to sing something."

"I believe you are right," said Sancho, "and no doubt he is some love sick Knight."

"There is no Knight that is not," said Don Quixote; "but let us listen to him, because, if he sings, with that thread we can extract the ball of his thoughts; because out of the heart the mouth speaks."

Sancho was about to reply to his master, but the Knight's voice, which was neither very bad or very good, stopped him, and listening attentively the pair heard him sing this:

POEM

Your pleasure, my lady, you unfold,
Declare the terms, and I obey,
My will to yours, obediently I mould,
And from your laws, my feet will never stray.

Without you I die, in silent grief I prey,
Then count me now as dead and cold,

Could I tell my grief in some new way?
Then let the tale of my Love be told.

The harmony of opposites, below above,
You the soft wax and me a hard diamond,
Hard or soft, I offer you my chest,
But still, obedient to the laws of love,
Yours for eternity I am,
To the grave I forsake the rest.

With an "Ahhhh!" that seemed to be drawn from depths of his heart, the Knight of the Grove brought this poem to an end, and shortly afterwards exclaimed in a depressed voice, "fairest and most ungrateful woman on earth! Can it be, most serene Casildea de Vandalia, that you will allow this captive Knight to waste away and perish in ceaseless wandering and tiring labour? Is it not enough that I have compelled all the Knights of Navarre, all the Leonese, all the Tartesians, all the Castilians, and finally all the Knights of La Mancha, to confess that you are the most beautiful in the world?"

"Not so," said Don Quixote, "because I am from La Mancha, and I have never confessed anything of the sort, and neither could I, or should I confess something against my lady's beauty; you see how this Knight is crazed, Sancho? But let us listen, perhaps he will tell us more about himself."

"That he will," returned Sancho, "because he seems in a mood to grieve for at least a month."

But this was not the case, because the Knight of the Grove, hearing the voices near him, instead of continuing his weeping, stood up and exclaimed in a distinct but polite tone, "Who goes there? What are you? Do you belong to the happy or the miserable?"

"The miserable," answered Don Quixote.

"Then come to me," said the Knight of the Grove, "and be assured you are coming to me: misery and sorrow itself."

Don Quixote, finding himself answered in such a soft and courteous manner, went over to him, and so did Sancho.

The sad Knight took Don Quixote by the arm, saying, "Sit down here, sir Knight; because, as you are one, and one who practises the order of Knighthood, which is apparent as I have found you in this place, filled with solitude and night which are the natural sofa and proper retreat of Knights, I will keep you company." To which Don answered, "A Knight I am of the profession you mention, and although sorrows, misfortunes, and disasters have made my heart their home, the compassion I feel for the misfortunes of others has not been removed from it. From what you have just now sung I gather that yours come from love, I mean from the love you have for that ungrateful lady you named in your song."

In the meantime, they had seated themselves together on the hard ground peacefully, just as if, as soon as it was sunrise, they were not going to break each other's heads.

"Are you, sir Knight, by any chance, in love?" the Knight of the Grove asked Don Quixote.

"I am," replied Don Quixote; "although the pain arising from well given affection should be esteemed rather than considered misfortune."

"That is true," returned the Knight of the Grove, "if scorn did not unsettle our reason and understanding, because if it is excessive it looks like revenge."

"I was never scorned by my lady," said Don Quixote.

"Certainly not," said Sancho, who stood close by, "because my lady is like a lamb, and softer than butter."

"Is this your aide?" asked the Knight of the Grove.

"He is," said Don Quixote.

"I never yet saw an aide," said the Knight of the Grove, "who spoke when his master was speaking; at least, there is mine, who is as big as his father, and it cannot be proven that he has ever opened his mouth while I am speaking."

"I am favoured" said Sancho, "I have spoken, and am fit to speak, in your presence."

The aide of the Knight of the Grove took Sancho by the arm, saying to him, "Let us go where we can talk as much as we like, and leave these gentlemen our masters to fight it out over the story of their loves; and, I am sure, when sun rises will find them continuing without coming to an end."

"My pleasure," said Sancho; "and I will tell you who I am, and you may see whether I am known among the number of the most talkative aides."

The two aides withdrew to one side, and between them a conversation passed as humorous as that which passed between their masters was serious.

CHAPTER 13

CONTINUING THE ADVENTURE OF THE KNIGHT OF THE GROVE, TOGETHER WITH THE SENSIBLE, ORIGINAL, AND PEACEFUL CONVERSATION BETWEEN THE TWO AIDES

The Knights and the aides were now two groups, two telling the story of their lives, the others the story of their loves; but the history describes first of all the conversation between the aides, and afterwards continues with the masters; and it says that, withdrawing a little from the others, the aide of the Knight of the Grove said to Sancho, "It is a hard life that we lead and live, señor, we aides of Knights; eating our bread covered with the sweat of our faces, which is one of the curses God gave us."

"It can be said, as well," added Sancho, "that we eat while our bodies are cold; because who gets more cold than the miserable aides of Knights? Actually, it would not be so bad if we had something to eat, because worries are lighter if there's bread; but sometimes we go a day or two without eating, except whatever the wind brings."

"All of that," said the Aide of the Knight of the Grove, "may be endured and put up with when we have hopes of a reward; because, unless the Knight he serves is excessively unlucky, after a few adventures the aide will at least find himself rewarded with the government of some fine island or great county."

"I," said Sancho, "have already told my master that I will be content with the government of some island, and he is so noble and generous that he has promised me it so many times."

"I," said the aide of the Knight of the Grove, "will be satisfied with an office for my services, and my master has already assigned me one."

"Your master," said Sancho, "no doubt is a Knight from the Church, and can bestow rewards of that sort on his good aide; but mine is only a normal man; although I remember some clever, but, to my mind, manipulative people, attempted to persuade him to become an archbishop. He, however, would not be anything but an emperor; but I worried the whole time that he might decide to go into the Church, and not find myself fit to hold the office in it; because I can tell you, although I seem a man, I am no better than an animal for the Church."

"Well, then, you are wrong there," The aide to the Knight of the Grove said; "because governing islands is not always satisfactory; some are awkward, some are poor, some are boring, and, in short, the best bring with it a heavy burden of care and trouble which can be unfamiliar to a man who carries this on his shoulders. It would be far better for us who have adopted this service to go back to our own houses, and there engage ourselves in pleasant occupations - in hunting or fishing, for instance; because what aide in the world is there so poor, not to have a horse and a couple of greyhounds and a fishing rod to amuse himself with in his own village?"

"I am not in need of any of those things," said Sancho; "I do not have a horse, but I have a donkey that is worth two of my master's horse. In regards to greyhounds, I have no lack, because there are enough of them to spare in my town; and, moreover, there is more pleasure in sport when it is at other people's expense."

"In truth, sir aide," said the aide to the Knight of the Grove, "I have made my mind up and determined to quit following the drunken impulses of these Knights, and go back to my village, and bring up my children; because I have three, like three Oriental pearls."

"I have two," said Sancho, "so graceful they could be presented to the Pope himself, especially a girl who I am raising to be a Lady, God willing, although her mother does not want her to be."

"And how old is this girl that is being raised to be a lady?" he asked.

"Fifteen, more or less," answered Sancho; "but she is as tall as a lance, and as fresh as an April morning, and as strong as a gatekeeper."

"Those gifts suit her not only to be a lady but a lady of the forest."

To which Sancho answered, somewhat moodily, "She's no whore, neither was her mother, and neither will either of them be, God willing, while I live; speak more civilly; for someone associated with Knights, who are the embodiment of politeness, your words don't seem to me to be very kind."

"Little do you know about compliments, sir aide," he returned. "Don't you know that when a horseman delivers a good lance thrust at the bull in the arena, or when anyone does anything very well, the people say, 'Whore! How well he does it!' And what seems to be abuse in expression is high in praise?

"Hmm," replied Sancho, "in this way, and by the same reasoning, you might call me and my children and my wife all the whores in the world, because all they do and say is that which in the highest degree deserves the same praise; and to see them again I pray to God to free me from sin, or, to free me from this dangerous calling into which I have fallen a third time, enticed by a wallet with a hundred coins that I found one day in the heart of the Sierra Morena; the devil is always putting a bag full coins in front of my eyes, here, there, everywhere, until I believe I am putting my hand on it everywhere I go, and hugging it, and carrying it home with me, and making investments, gaining interest, and living like a prince; and so long as I think like this I endure all the hardships with this simpleton of a master of mine, who, I well know, is more of a madman than a Knight."

"This is why they say that 'greed bursts the bag,'" the aide of the Knight of the Grove said; "but if you want to talk about madness, there is no one greater in the world than my master."

"Is he in love?" asked Sancho.

"He is," said the aide of the Knight of the Grove, "with Casildea de Vandalia, the rawest and best produced lady the whole world could yield; but that rawness is not only the foot she limps on, because she has greater rumbling in her bowels, as will be seen I assure you – shortly."

"There's no road so smooth that does not have some hole or hindrance," said Sancho; "in other houses they cook beans, but in mine it's potted stew; madness will have followers; but if there is any truth in the common saying, that to have companions in trouble gives some relief, I may take consolation from you, inasmuch as you serve a master as crazy as my own."

"Crazy but courageous," replied the aide to the Knight of the Grove, "and more mischievous than crazy or courageous."

"Mine is not like that," said Sancho; "I mean he has nothing of a rogue in him; on the contrary, he has the soul of a Christian; he has no thought of doing harm to anyone, only good to all, neither has he any malice whatsoever in him; a child might persuade him that it is night at noon; and because of this simplicity I love him at the core of my heart, and I can't bring myself to leave him, or let him do foolish things."

"Despite that, brother and señor," the aide to the Knight of the Grove said, "if the blind lead the blind, both are in danger of falling into the pit. It is better for us to depart and go back to our own homes; because those who seek adventures don't always find good ones."

Sancho kept spitting from time to time, and his spit seemed somewhat long and dry, and observing this, the compassionate aide to the Knight of the Grove said, "It seems to me that with all this talk of ours our tongues are sticking to the roofs of our mouths; but I have a pretty good loosener hanging from the saddle of my horse," and getting up he came back the next minute with a large bottle of wine and a pastry two foot long; and this is no exaggeration, because it was made from a rabbit so big that Sancho, as he handled it, mistook it to be made from a goat,, and looking at it he said, "Do you always carry this with you, señor?"

"Why, what are you thinking about?" said the other; "do you take me as a weak aide? I carry more on my horse than a general takes with him when he goes to war."

Sancho ate without being encouraged, and taking large mouthfuls he said, "you are a proper faithful aide, one of a kind, magnificent and grand, as this banquet shows; not like me, an unlucky beggar, I have nothing more in my saddle-bags than a scrap of cheese, so hard that one might attack a giant with it, and, to keep it company, a few dozen carrots and walnuts; thanks to the strictness of my master, and the idea he has and the rule he follows, that Knights must not live or sustain themselves on anything except dried fruits and the herbs of the field."

"Brother," the aide to the Knight of the Grove said, "my stomach is not made for grass, or wild pears, or roots of the woods; let our masters do what they like, with their notions of chivalry and laws, and eat what that entails; I carry my basket and this bottle hanging on the saddle with me despite what they say; and it is an object of worship for me, I love it so much, that there is hardly a moment I am not kissing and embracing it over and over again;" and he thrust it into Sancho's hands, who raising it upward pointed it to his mouth, gazed at the stars for a quarter of an hour; and when he had done drinking let his head fall to one side, and giving a deep sigh, exclaimed, "Ah, whore, how catholic is this?"

"There, you see," the other said, hearing Sancho's exclamation, "how you have called this wine whore as a way of praise."

"Well," said Sancho, "I own it, and I grant it is no dishonour to call anyone whore when it is to be understood as praise. But tell me, señor, as you love this, is this the city's real wine?"

"Rare wine-taster!" he replied; "it comes from nowhere else, and it has quite a few years' age as well."

"Let me think," said Sancho; "I will know the place it came from somehow. What would you say, sir aide, to me having such a great natural instinct in judging wines that you have only to let me smell one and I can positively tell its country, its kind, its flavour, the changes it will undergo, and everything that relates to it? It is no wonder, because I have had in my family, on my father's side, the two best wine-tasters that have been known in La Mancha for many long years, and to prove it I'll tell you now something that happened them. They were given some wine in a flask, to try, asking their opinion in regards to the condition, quality, goodness or badness of the wine. One of them tried it with the tip of his tongue, the other did no more than bring it to his nose. The first said the wine had a flavour of iron, the second said it had a stronger flavour of leather. The owner said the flask was clean, and that nothing had been added to the wine from which it could have got a flavour of either iron or leather. Nevertheless, these two great wine-tasters held to what they had said. Time went by, the wine was sold, and when they came to clean the flask, they found in it a small key attached to a strap of leather; so of course someone who comes from the same line has the right to give his opinion in similar cases."

"Therefore, I say," the other replied, "let us forget going in search of adventures, and as we have bread let us not go looking for cake, but return to our homes, and God will find us there if is his will."

"Until my master reaches Saragossa," said Sancho, "I'll remain in his service; after that we will see."

The two aides talked so much and drank so much that sleep had to stop their tongues and moderate their thirst, because to quench it was impossible; and so the pair of them fell asleep clinging to the now nearly empty bottle and with half-chewed bits of food in their mouths; and there we will leave them for the present, to relate what occurred between the Knight of the Grove and the Knight of the Sorrowful Face.

CHAPTER 14

CONTINUING THE ADVENTURE OF THE KNIGHT OF THE GROVE

Among the things discussed between Don Quixote and the Knight of the Grove, the history tells us the Knight of the Grove said to Don Quixote, "Sir Knight, you should know that my destiny, or, more appropriately speaking, my choice led me to fall in love with the incomparable Casildea de Vandalia. I call her incomparable because no one can compare, whether it be in physique or in the supremacy of her rank and beauty. This same Casildea, then, that I speak of, enticed my honourable passion and gentle aspirations by compelling me, in the same manner Hercules was impelled by a woman, to engage in many dangers of various sorts, at the end of each promising me that, at the end of the next, the objective of my hope would be attained; but my work has been increasing task by task until I am unable to recount them, and I do not know when the last one will come, which will be the beginning of the accomplishment of my virtuous desire. On one occasion she asked me to go and challenge the famous giant of Seville, Giralda, who is as mighty and strong as if made of brass, and although she never moves from one spot, she is the most restless and changeable woman in the world. I came, I saw, I conquered, and then I heard nothing for more than a week.

Another time I was ordered to lift ancient stones, an endeavour more appropriate for porters than Knights. Again, she asked me to throw myself into the cave of Cabra - an unparalleled and awful danger - and bring her an account of all that is concealed inside. I stopped Giralda, I lifted the stones, I threw myself into the cave and brought to light the secrets of its abyss; but my hopes are as dead as dead can be, and her scorn and her commands are as lively as ever. To be brief, last of all she commanded me to go through all the provinces of Spain and compel all the wandering Knights to confess that she surpasses all women alive in beauty, and that I am the most courageous and the most deeply infatuated Knight on earth; in support of this claim I have already travelled over most of Spain, and have vanquished several Knights who have dared to contradict me; but what I most pride myself on, is having vanquished in single combat the famous Knight Don Quixote of La Mancha, and made him confess that my Casildea is more beautiful than his Dulcinea; and with this one victory I hold myself to have conquered all the Knights of the world; because this Don Quixote that I speak of has vanquished them all, and as I have vanquished him, his glory, his fame, and his honour have passed and are transferred to me; because:

Those vanquished of great renown,
Greater glory goes to the victor's crown.

Therefore, the innumerable achievements of Don Quixote are now added to my account and have become mine."

Don Quixote was amazed when he heard the Knight of the Grove, and was on the verge of telling him he lied, and had the word 'liar' directly on the tip of his tongue; but he restrained himself as well as he could, in order to force him to confess the lie with his own lips; so he said to him quietly, "In regards to what you say, sir Knight, about having vanquished most of the Knights in Spain, or even of the whole world, I have nothing to say; but that you have vanquished Don Quixote of La Mancha I consider very doubtful; it may have been some other Knight that resembled him, although there are few like him."

"How! Not vanquished?" said the Knight of the Grove; "God knows I fought Don Quixote and overcame him and made him yield. He is a man of tall stature, lean features, long, lanky limbs, with hair turning grey, a curved nose more like a hook, and a large black drooping moustache; he fights under the name of 'The Sorrowful Face,' and his aide is a peasant called Sancho Panza; he rules the reins of a famous horse called Rocinante; and lastly, the mistress of his will is called Dulcinea del Toboso, previously known as Aldonza Lorenzo, just like I call mine Casildea de Vandalia because her name is Casilda and she is from Andalusia. If all this is not enough to assert the truth of what I say, this is my sword, and it will compel any disbelief to give credibility to it."

"Calm yourself down, sir Knight," said Don Quixote, "and listen very carefully to what I am about to say to you. This Don Quixote you speak of is the greatest friend I have in the world; so great that I regard us as one person; and from the precise and clear description you have given I would be compelled to believe he was the one you vanquished. On the other hand, I see with my eyes and feel with my hands that it is impossible it could have been the same man; unless, as he has many enemies who are enchanters, and one in particular who is always persecuting him, one of these may have taken his shape in order to allow himself to be vanquished, to defraud him of the fame that his glorious achievements as a Knight have earned and acquired for him throughout the known world. And in confirmation of this, I must tell you also, it has only been ten hours since these enchanters transformed the shape of Dulcinea del Toboso into a foul and mean village girl, and in the same way they must have transformed Don Quixote; and if all of this does not serve to convince you of the truth of what I say, here is Don Quixote himself, who will prove it by battle, on foot or on horseback or in any way you like."

And he stood up and placed his hand on his sword, waiting to see what the Knight of the Grove would do, who in an equally calm voice said in reply, "Guarantees don't distress me; I who succeeded in vanquishing you once when transformed, Sir Don Quixote, may fairly hope to subdue you in your own proper shape; but as it is not appropriate for Knights to battle in the dark, like robbers and bullies, let us wait until daylight, so the sun may observe our deeds; and the conditions of our combat will enable us to perform at our best, providing the victor with the best conditions to do all that he can."

"I am more than satisfied with these conditions and terms," replied Don Quixote; and so they took themselves to where their aides lay, and found them snoring, and in the same posture as when they fell asleep. They woke them up, and asked them get the horses ready, as at sunrise they were to engage in bloody and arduous single combat. Upon hearing this Sancho was horrified and shocked, and in fear for the safety of his master because the aide to the Knight of the Grove had described the deeds of his master; but without a word the two aides went in search of the horses; because by this time the horses and the donkey had smelt one another, and were all together.

On the way, the aide said to Sancho, "You must know, brother, that it is the custom with the fighting men of Andalusia, that godfathers don no stand idle with their arms folded while their godsons fight; I say this to remind you that while our masters are fighting, we, too, have to fight, and knock each other to pieces."

"That custom, sir aide," replied Sancho, "may be true among those bullies and fighting men you talk about, but certainly not among the aides of Knights; at least, I have never heard my master speak about any custom like this, and he knows all the laws of Knighthood by heart; but granting it is true and there is a law that requires aides to fight while their masters are fighting, I will not obey it and pay the penalty that may be placed on peacefully minded aides like myself; because I am sure it cannot be more than two pounds of wax, and I would rather pay that, because I know it will cost me less than the expense of mending my head, which I consider already broken and split; there's another thing that makes it impossible for me to fight, I have no sword, and have never carried one in my life."

"I know a good remedy for that," said the other aide; "I have two bags of linen here, both the same size; you take one, and I take the other, and we will fight with blows of the bag."

"If that's the way, so be it," said Sancho, "because that sort of battle will knock the dust out of us instead of hurting us."

"That will not do," said the other, "because we must put something heavy into the bags, to keep the wind from blowing them away, half a dozen pebbles, all of the same weight; and in this way we will be able to bash each other to pieces."

"Great God!" said Sancho, "see what he is putting into the bags, so our heads may be broken and our bones beaten to jelly! Even if they were only filled with silk, I can tell you, señor, I am not going to fight; let our masters fight, that is their job, and let us drink and live; because time will eventually ease us of our lives, without us looking to beat each other so that they may be finished before the appropriate time comes."

"Still," returned the other aide, "we must fight, even if it is only for half an hour."

"Not at all," said Sancho; "I am not going to be so uncivil or so ungrateful to have any argument, even if it is small, with someone I have drunk and eaten with; besides, who could bring himself to fight, without any anger or aggravation?"

415

"I can fix that," said the other aide, "and in this way: before we begin the battle, I will come to you fairly, and give you three or four buffets, and then knock you to my feet and arouse your anger, even if it were sleeping sounder than a dormouse."

"To match that plan," said Sancho, "I have another; I will take a stick, and before you come near enough to waken my anger I will send yours to sleep with whacks, so much so, that it won't wake unless it were in the other world, where it is known that I am not a man to let my face be handled by anyone; let each look out for arrows, although the safer way would be to let everyone's anger sleep, because nobody knows the heart of anyone, and a man may come for wool and go back cut up; God gave his blessing to peace and his curse to arguments; if a hunted cat, surrounded, turns into a lion, God knows what I, who am a man, may turn into; and so I warn you, sir, that all the harm and mischief that may come from our disagreement will not be solely on my account."

"Very good," the other aide replied; "God will send daylight soon and we will begin."

And now happy birds of all types began to sing in the trees, and with their varied notes welcome and greeted the fresh morning that was beginning to show its beauty at the gates and balconies of the east, shaking in its hair a profusion of liquid pearls; in which sweet moisture bathed, the plants, too, seemed to shed and shower a pearly spray, the willows distilled sweet leaves, the fountains laughed, the streams spoke, the woods celebrated, and the meadows displayed themselves in all their magnificence. But hardly had the light of day made it possible to see and distinguish things, when the first object that presented itself to the eyes of Sancho Panza was the aide of the Grove's nose, which was so big that it almost overshadowed his whole body. It is, in fact, stated, that it was of such enormous size, hooked in the middle, covered with warts, and of a mulberry colour like an egg-plant; it hung down two fingers' length below his mouth, and the size, the colour, the warts, and the bend in it, made his face so revolting, that Sancho, as he looked at him, began to shake his hands and feet like a child with seizures, and he swore in his heart he would rather have two hundred buffets, than be provoked to fight that monster. Don Quixote examined his adversary, and found that he already had his helmet on and visor lowered, so he could not see his face; he observed, however, that he was a strongly built man, but not very tall in stature. Over his armour he wore a coat which seemed to be made from the finest gold cloth, all embroidered with glittering mirrors like little moons, which gave him an extremely gracious and impressive appearance; above his helmet was a large quantity of curls, green, yellow, and white, and his lance, which was leaning against a tree, was very long and wide, and had a steel point bigger than a hand.

Don Quixote saw all, and took note, and from what he observed he concluded that the Knight must be a man of great strength, but despite that he had no fear, unlike Sancho Panza; and with a composed and confident manner, he said to the Knight of Mirrors, "If, sir Knight, your great eagerness to fight has not displaced your courtesy, I ask you to raise your visor a little, in order for me to see if the intention of your face corresponds to that of your equipment."

"Whether you come out victorious or vanquished from this, sir Knight," replied the Knight of Mirrors, "you will have more than enough time and leisure to see me; and if I do not comply with your request now, it is because it seems to me I would be doing serious wrong to the fair Casildea de Vandalia in wasting time while I stop to raise my visor before compelling you to confess what you are already aware I maintain."

"Well then," said Don Quixote, "while we are mounting you can at least tell me if I am the Don Quixote who you said you vanquished."

"To that I answer you," said the Knight the Mirrors, "that you are just like the Knight I vanquished, as one egg is like another, but as you say enchanters persecute you, I will not say positively whether you are the same person or not."

"That," said Don Quixote, "is enough to convince me that you are under some deception; however, to relieve you of it entirely, let us be brought our horses, and in less time than it would take you to raise your visor, if God, my lady, and my strength assist me, I will see your face, and you will see that I am not the vanquished Don Quixote you believe me to be."

With this, cutting short the discussion, they mounted, and Don Quixote turned Rocinante around in order to get the appropriate distance to charge at his adversary, and the Knight of the Mirrors did the same; but Don Quixote had not moved twenty feet when he heard himself being called by the other, and, each having gone half-way, the Knight of the Mirrors said to him, "Remember, sir Knight, that the terms of our combat are, that the vanquished, as I said before, will be at the victor's disposal."

"I am already aware of it," said Don Quixote; "provided what is commanded and imposed on the vanquished are things that do not disobey the laws of chivalry."

"That is understood," replied the Knight of the Mirrors.

At this moment the extraordinary nose of the aide presented itself to Don Quixote's view, and he was no less amazed than Sancho at the sight; so much so that he considered him a rare type of monster, or a new species of human. Sancho, seeing his master withdrawing to run his course, did not like to be left alone with the nosy man, fearing that with one flap of that nose, on his own, the battle would be over for him and he would be left stretched on the ground, either by the blow or with fright; so he ran after his master, holding on to Rocinante's stirrup, and when it seemed time for him to turn around, he said, "I beg you master, señor, before you turn to charge, help me up into this cork tree, from which I will be able to witness the courageous encounter you are going to have with this Knight, which will be better than observing from the ground."

"It seems to me Sancho," said Don Quixote, "that you would climb a giraffe in order to see the bulls without danger."

"To tell the truth," returned Sancho, "the monstrous nose of that aide has filled me with fear and terror, and I dare not to stay near him."

"It is," said Don Quixote, "such a nose, that if I were not who I am, would terrify me as well; so I will help you up."

While Don Quixote waited for Sancho to climb into the cork tree the Knight of the Mirrors took as much ground as he considered necessary, and, supposing Don Quixote to have done the same, without waiting for any sound of a trumpet or other signal to direct them, he turned his horse, which was no more agile or better-looking than Rocinante, and at his top speed, which was a slow trot, he proceeded to charge at his enemy; seeing him, however, engaged in placing Sancho in the cork tree, he halted, which his horse was very grateful for, as he was already tiring. Don Quixote, perceiving that his enemy was about to attack him, drove his heels vigorously into Rocinante's lean sides and made him move in such style that the history tells us that on this occasion it appeared to be something like running, because on all others it was more like a simple trot; and with this unparalleled fury he attacked the Knight of the Mirrors who stood digging his heels into his horse as hard as he could, without being able to make him move a finger's length from the spot where he had come to a standstill. At this lucky moment and crisis, Don Quixote attacked his adversary, in trouble with his horse, and struggling with his lance, which he either could not manage, or had no time to lift. Don Quixote, however, paid no attention to these difficulties, and in perfect safety and without any risk at all, he hit the Knight of the Mirrors with such force that he brought him to the ground, and from such a heavy fall he lay with the appearance of being dead, not moving a hand or foot. The instant Sancho saw him fall he jumped down from the cork tree, and rushed to where his master was, who, dismounting from Rocinante, went and stood over the Knight of the Mirrors, and undoing his helmet to see if he were dead, and to give him air if he happened to be alive, who can say what he saw, without filling anyone who hears it with astonishment, wonder, and amazement? He saw, the history says, the very face, the very look, the very appearance, and the very image of Samson Carrasco! As soon as he saw it he called out in a loud voice, "Run here, Sancho, and see what you are to see but not to believe; quick, my son, and learn what magic can do, and what wizards and enchanters are capable of."

Sancho came, and when he saw the face of Carrasco, he fell to his knees – making a cross gesture across his chest a thousand times. During this time the Knight showed no signs of life, and Sancho said to Don Quixote, "It is my opinion, señor, that you should take and thrust your sword into the mouth of this one who looks like Samson Carrasco; perhaps this will kill one of those evil enchanters, your enemies."

"Your advice is not bad at all," said Don Quixote, "because in the case of enemies - fewer the better;" and as he was raising his sword to carry into effect Sancho's advice and suggestion, the other aide came, now without the nose which had made him so hideous, and cried out in a loud voice, "Careful what you are about to do, Señor Don Quixote; that is your friend, Samson Carrasco, and I am his aide."

"And the nose?" said Sancho, seeing him without the hideous feature he had before; to which he replied, "I have it here in my pocket," and putting his hand into his right pocket, he pulled out a fake nose made of varnished pasteboard; and Sancho, examining him more and more closely, exclaimed in a voice of amazement, "Holy Mary be good to me! Is that Tom Cecial, my neighbour and gossiper?"

"You can be assured I am!" returned the now un-nosed aide; "Tom Cecial I am, gossiper and friend of Sancho Panza; and I will tell you the methods, tricks and lies which have brought us here; but in the meantime, I beg and ask for your master not to touch, mistreat, wound, or kill the Knight of the Mirrors because, beyond all dispute, it is the thoughtless and foolish Samson Carrasco, our fellow townsman."

At this moment the Knight of the Mirrors was coming round, and Don Quixote perceiving it, held the point of his sword over his face, and said to him, "You are a dead man, Knight, unless you confess that the incomparable Dulcinea del Toboso exceeds your Casildea de Vandalia in beauty; and in addition to this you must promise, if you survive this encounter, to go to the city of El Toboso and present yourself to her on my behalf, so she can deal with you according to her will; and if she sets you free, you are to return to me (because the trail of my mighty deeds will serve as a guide to lead you to where I may be), and tell me what happened between you and her, and these orders, in accordance with what we specified before our combat, do not disobey the laws of chivalry."

"I confess," said the fallen Knight, "that the dirty tattered shoe of the lady Dulcinea del Toboso is better than the clean shoes of Casildea; and I promise to go and return from her presence to yours, and to give you a full and particular account of all you demand from me."

"You must also confess and believe," added Don Quixote, "that the Knight you vanquished was not and could not be Don Quixote of La Mancha, but someone else in his likeness, just as I confess and believe that you, though you seem to be Samson Carrasco, are not, but some other person resembling him, whom my enemies have put here in front of me, in his shape, in order for me to restrain and moderate the intensity of my wrath, and be gentle when celebrating my victory."

"I confess, and believe everything to be as you say," said the crippled Knight; "let me rise, I beg you; if, indeed, the shock of my fall will allow me to, because it has left me in a bad state."

Don Quixote helped him to rise, with the assistance of his aide Tom Cecial; who Sancho never took his eyes off, and to whom he questioned. The replies gave clear proof that he really and truly was the Tom Cecial; but the impression made on Sancho's mind by what his master said about the enchanters having changed the face of the Knight of the Mirrors into that of Samson Carrasco, would not permit him to believe what he saw with his eyes. Both the master and the man remained under the delusion; and, in a bad state, and out of luck, the Knight of the Mirrors and his aide left Don Quixote and Sancho, with the intention to look for some village where he could plaster and strap his ribs. Don Quixote and Sancho resumed their journey to Saragossa, and at this point the history leaves them in order that it may tell who the Knight of the Mirrors and his long-nosed aide were.

CHAPTER 15

WHO THE KNIGHT OF THE MIRRORS AND HIS AIDE WERE

Don Quixote left satisfied, delighted, and triumphant in the highest degree after having won a victory over such a courageous Knight as he believed him to be, and from him he expected he would learn whether the enchantment of his lady still continued; as the vanquished Knight was bound, under the penalty of ceasing to be one, to return and render to him an account of what took place between him and her. But while Don Quixote had this in mind, the Knight of Mirrors had other thoughts, because he had no intention of anything other than finding some village where he could plaster himself, as has been already said. The history goes on to say then, that when Samson Carrasco recommended Don Quixote to resume his Knighthood which he had put aside, it was a consequence of having had discussions about it with the vicar and the barber on how to induce Don Quixote to stay at home in peace and quiet without worrying himself with his unwarranted adventures; and the conclusion of the consultation was decided by the unanimous vote of all, and on the special advice of Carrasco, that Don Quixote should be allowed to go, as it seemed impossible to restrain him, and that Samson would go to meet him as a Knight, and battle with him, because there would be no difficulty of vanquishing him; and that it should be agreed and settled that the vanquished was to do as the victor ordered. Then, Don Quixote being vanquished, Samson was to command him to return to his village and his house, and not leave it for two years, or until he received further orders from him; all which it was clear Don Quixote would wholeheartedly obey, rather than violate or fail to follow the laws of chivalry; and during the period of his seclusion perhaps he might forget his madness, or there might be an opportunity of discovering some remedy for his madness. Carrasco undertook the task, and Tom Cecial, a gossiper and neighbour of Sancho Panza's, a lively fellow, offered himself to be his aide. Carrasco armed himself in the manner described, and Tom Cecial, not to be detected fitted on over his own natural nose the false one that has been mentioned; and so they followed the same route Don Quixote took, and were almost close enough behind to be present at the adventure of the cart of Death and finally encountered them in the grove, where all that the intelligent reader has been reading about took place; and had it not been for the extraordinary madness of Don Quixote, and his conviction that Samson was not Samson, señor graduate would have been incapacitated forever, finding nests where he thought to find birds.

Tom Cecial, seeing how badly they had succeeded, and what a poor ending their expedition had come to, said to the graduate, "Sure enough, Señor Samson Carrasco, we are served right; it is easy enough to plan something, but it is often a difficult thing to bring it to a happy conclusion. Don Quixote a madman, and we sane; he goes off laughing, safe, and sound, and you are left beaten and sorry! I would like to know now who is madder, he who is because he cannot help it, or he who is due to his own choice?"

To which Samson replied, "The difference between the two sorts of madmen are, one who is because he cannot help it, will always be one, while he who is due to his choice can stop being one whenever he likes."

"In that case," said Tom Cecial, "I was a madman due to my own choice when I volunteered to become your aide, now I'll stop being one and go home."

"That's your choice," returned Samson, "but to suppose that I am going home until I have given Don Quixote a beating is absurd; and it is not my wish that he may recover his senses, which induces me to hunt him out now, but a wish due to the pain I am in, and my ribs won't let me entertain more charitable thoughts."

While talking, the pair travelled until they reached a town where it was their good luck to find a doctor, with whose help the unfortunate Samson was cured. Tom Cecial left him and went home, while Samson stayed behind meditating on vengeance; and the history will return to him again at the appropriate time, so it does not omit to relay Don Quixote's happiness.

CHAPTER 16

WHAT HAPPENED TO DON QUIXOTE WITH A DISCREET GENTLEMAN OF LA MANCHA

Don Quixote pursued his journey with in highest spirit, satisfaction, and self-complacency already described, believing himself to be the most courageous Knight in the world because of his victory. All the adventures that could come to him from that time forward he regarded as already finished in his favour; he no longer cared about enchantments and enchanters; he thought no more about the countless beatings that had been administered to him in the course of his Knighthood, or the shower of stones that had knocked out half his teeth, or the ingratitude of the ship slaves; in short, he said to himself that if he could discover any way, method, or technique to disenchant his lady Dulcinea, he would not envy the highest fortune that the most fortunate Knight ever reached or could reach.

He was going along entirely absorbed in these thoughts, when Sancho said to him, "Isn't it odd, señor, that I have still have in my mind that monstrous enormous nose of the gossiper, Tom Cecial?"

"Do you believe, Sancho," said Don Quixote, "that the Knight of the Mirrors was Carrasco, and his aide was Tom Cecial the gossiper?"

"I don't know what to say to that," replied Sancho; "all I know is that the answers he gave to me about my own house, wife and children, nobody else but himself could have given me; and the face, once the nose was off, was the very face of Tom Cecial, as I have seen it many times in my town and next door to my own house; and the sound of the voice was exactly the same."

"Let's consider the matter, Sancho," said Don Quixote. "By what process of thinking can it be asserted that Samson Carrasco would come as a Knight, with weapons acting offensively and defensively, to fight with me? Have I ever been by any chance his enemy? Have I ever given him any reason to hold a grudge against me? Am I his rival, or is he a real Knight, that would make him envy the fame I have acquired?"

"Well, what can we say, señor," returned Sancho, "about that Knight, whoever he is, being so like Carrasco, and his aide so like the gossiper, Tom Cecial? And if that is enchantment, as you say, was there no one else the world for them to take the likeness of?"

"It is all," said Don Quixote, "a scheme and plot of the evil magicians that persecute me, who, foreseeing that I was to be victorious in the conflict, arranged that the vanquished Knight should display the face of my friend Samson, so that the friendship I have with him would halt the edge of my sword, and calm the wrath of my heart; so that he who sought to take my life by fraud could save his own. And to prove it, you already know, Sancho, by experience which cannot lie or deceive, how easy it is for enchanters to change one face into another, turning beauty into ugliness, and ugliness into beauty; because it has only been two days

423

since you saw with your own eyes the beauty and elegance of the incomparable Dulcinea in all its perfection and natural harmony, while I saw her in the repulsive and disgraceful form of a rough country girl, with cataracts in her eyes and a foul smell in her mouth; and when the perverse enchanter decided to produce such a disgusting transformation, it is no wonder if he did the same for Samson Carrasco and the gossiper in order to snatch the glory of the victory from my grasp. For all that, however, I comfort myself, because, after all, in whatever shape he may have been, I was victorious over my enemy."

"God knows the truth of it all," said Sancho; and knowing as he did that the transformation of Dulcinea had been a trick, his illusions were not satisfactory to him; and he did not like to reply to you in-case he said something that might disclose his trickery.

As they were engaged in this conversation they were overtaken by a man who was following the same road behind them, mounted on a very handsome flea-bitten horse, dressed in fine green cloth, with velvet patches, and a hat made from the same velvet. The trimmings of the horse were in a mulberry colour and green. He carried a Moorish sword hanging from a broad green and gold belt; the boots were the same make as the belt; the spurs were lacquered green, and so brightly polished that, matching as they did the rest of his apparel, they looked better than if they had been pure gold.

When the traveller came up to them he gestured to them with courteously, and digging his heels into his horse was passing them without stopping, but Don Quixote called out to him, "Courteous sir, if you are taking the same road as us, and have no occasion for speed, it would be a pleasure if we were to join company."

"In truth," replied the man on the horse, "I would not pass you so quickly but I fear that your horse might become restless in the company of my horse."

"You may safely stop your horse, señor," said Sancho in reply to this, "because our horse is the most virtuous and well-behaved horse in the world; he never does anything wrong on occasions such as this, and the only time he misbehaved, my master and I suffered for it in excessive proportion for it; I say again you may stop if you like; because if she was offered to him on a plate the horse would not obsess for her."

The traveller pulled the reins, amazed at the trim and features of Don Quixote, who rode without his helmet, which Sancho carried like luggage in front of the donkey's saddle; and if the man in green examined Don Quixote closely, Don Quixote examined the man in green even closer, who struck him as being a man of intelligence. In appearance - he was about fifty years old, but with very few grey hairs, and an expression between serious and happy; and his clothing and trimmings made him appear to be a man of good condition. What he thought about Don Quixote of La Mancha was that he had never seen a man of that sort and shape; he marvelled at the length of his hair, his long stature, the awkwardness and yellowness of his face, his armour, his facial expression and his seriousness - a figure and picture that had not been seen in those regions before.

Don Quixote saw very plainly the attention with which the traveller was regarding him, and read the curiosity in his astonishment; and as courteous as he was and ready to please everybody, before the other could ask him any question, he said, "I would not be surprised if the appearance I present to you being so strange and out of the ordinary filled you with wonder; but you will cease to wonder when I tell you, as I do, that I am one of those Knights who, as people say, go seeking adventures. I have left my home, have mortgaged my estate, have given up my comfort, and committed myself to Fortune, to take me wherever it pleases. My desire was to bring to life again Knighthood, now dead, and for some time previously, stumbling here, falling there, coming down completely, then raising myself up again, I have carried out a great amount of my plan, comforting widows, protecting ladies, and giving aid to wives, orphans, and children, the proper and natural duty of Knights; and, therefore, because of my many courageous and Christian achievements, I have been found worthy to find my name in print across almost all of the nations of the earth. Thirty thousand volumes of my history have been printed, and it is on the-road to be printed thirty thousand, a thousand times, if heaven does not put a stop to it. In short, to sum up everything in a few words, I tell you I am Don Quixote of La Mancha, otherwise called 'The Knight of the Sorrowful Face;' because although self-praise is degrading, I must unavoidably blow my own trumpet sometimes, that is to say, when there is no one else to do it for me. So that sir, neither this horse, or this lance, or this shield, or this aide, or all these weapons put together, or the yellowness of my face, or my thin leanness, will continue to astonish you, now that you know who I am and what profession I follow."

With these words Don Quixote became quiet, the man in green seemed to be speechless; but after a long pause he replied, "You were right when you saw the curiosity in my amazement sir Knight; but you have not succeeded in removing the astonishment I feel by seeing you; because although you say, señor, that knowing who you are should remove it, it has not done so; on the contrary, now that I know, I am left even more amazed and astonished than before. What! Is it possible that there are Knights in the world these days, and history of real chivalry printed? I cannot believe that there can be anyone on earth these days who aid widows, or protects ladies, or defends wives, or comfort orphans; and I would not have believed it had I not seen it in you with my own eyes. Blessed is heaven! Because with this history of your noble and genuine chivalrous deeds, which you say has been printed, the countless stories of fictitious Knights with which the world is filled, much to the damage of morality and the discredit of good histories, will have been driven into oblivion."

"There is a good deal to be said about that," said Don Quixote, "in regards to whether the histories of the Knights are fiction or not."

"Why, is there anyone who doubts that those histories are false?" said the man in green.

"I doubt it," said Don Quixote, "but never mind that for now; if our journey lasts long enough, I trust in God, and will show you that you are wrong if you agree with the stream of those who regard it as a matter of certainty that they are not true."

From this last observation of Don Quixote's, the traveller began to have a suspicion that he was a madman, and was waiting for him to confirm it by something further; but before they could turn to any new subject Don Quixote begged him to tell him who he was, since he himself had given an account of his position and life. To this, the man in green replied "I, Sir Knight of the Sorrowful Face, am a gentleman by birth, native of the village where, God willing, we are going to eat today; I am more than fairly well off, and my name is Don Diego de Miranda. I pass my life with my wife, children, and friends; my pursuits are hunting and fishing, but I possess neither hawks or greyhounds, nothing but a tame partridge or a bold ferret or two; I have around six dozen books, some in our mother tongue, some in Latin, some of them history, others religious; those about chivalry have not yet crossed the threshold of my door; I turn the pages of the irreligious more than the religious, as long as they are books of honest entertainment that charm with their style and attract and interest me with the distinctiveness they display, although there are very few of these in Spain. Sometimes I dine with my neighbours and friends, and often invite them over; my entertaining of guests is neat and well served. I have no taste for gossip, and neither do I allow gossiping in my presence; I do not interfere into my neighbours' private lives, and I do not have eyes for what others do. I attend mass every day; I share my money with the poor, making no display of it, in-case hypocrisy and pride, two enemies that subtly take possession of the most watchful heart, may find an entrance into mine. I strive to make peace between those whom I know to be in disagreement; I am the devoted servant of Our Lady, and my trust is forever in the infinite mercy of God our Lord."

Sancho listened with the greatest attention to the account of the gentleman's life and occupation; and thinking it to be a good and holy life, and that he who led it could work miracles, he threw himself off the donkey, and running in haste took his right stirrup and kissed his foot again and again with a sincere heart and almost with tears.

Seeing this the gentleman asked him, "What are you doing, brother? What are these kisses for?"

"Let me kiss," said Sancho, "because I think you are the first saint in the saddle I have ever seen in all the days of my life."

"I am no saint," replied the gentleman, "but a great sinner; but you are, brother, because you must be a good fellow, as your simplicity displays."

Sancho went back to his donkey, after having extracted a laugh from his master, and excited fresh amazement in Don Diego.

Don Quixote then asked him how many children he had, and observed that one of the things which the ancient philosophers did who were without the true knowledge of God was to place the highest good in the gifts of nature, in those of fortune, in having many good friends and many good children.

"I, Señor Don Quixote," answered the gentleman, "have one son, without whom, perhaps, I should count myself happier than I am, not because he is a bad son, but because he is not as good as I could wish for. He is eighteen years of age; he has been at Salamanca studying Latin and Greek for six years, and when I wanted him to the study the other sciences I found him so wrapped up in poetry (if that can be called a science) that there is no getting him interested in law, which I wished him to study, or to study divinity, the Queen of them all. I would like him to be an honour to his family, as we live in times where our Kings generously reward learning that is virtuous and worthy; because learning without virtue is a pearl on a dunghill. He spends the whole day in discussing whether Homer expressed himself correctly or not in some line, whether Martial was indecent or not in some epigram, whether some lines of Virgil are to be understood in this way or another; in short, all his talk is about the work of these poets, and those of Horace, Perseus, Juvenal, and Tibullus; because out of the modern poets in our own language he knows little; but with all his apparent indifference to Spanish poetry, his thoughts are now absorbed in making some lines, which I suspect are for some poetical contest."

To all this Don Quixote said in reply, "Children, señor, are portions of their parents' bowels, and therefore, if they are good or bad, are to be loved as we love the souls that give us life; it is for the parents to guide them from infancy in the ways of virtue, modesty, and worthy Christian conduct, so that when grown up they may be the continuation of their parents' in their old age, and the glory of their future; and to force them to study this or that science I do not think is wise, although it may be no harm to persuade them; and when there is no need to study for the sake of money, and it is the student's good fortune that heaven has given them parents who will provide them with it, it would be my advice to them to let him or her pursue whatever science they may be most inclined to; and although poetry is less useful than pleasurable, it is not one of those that bring discredit to the possessor. Poetry, gentle sir, is, as I take it, like a tender young lady of supreme beauty, to dress and beautify several other ladies, who are all the rest of the sciences; and she must offer herself to help them, and all derive their shine from her. But this lady will not be controlled, or dragged through the streets, or be exposed in market-places, or in the closets of palaces. She is the product of an Alchemy of such virtue that he who is able to practise it, will turn her into pure gold of incalculable worth. He that possesses her must keep her within boundaries, not permitting her to break out in vulgar sarcasm or soulless sonnets. She must on no occasion be offered for sale, unless, indeed, it is in heroic poems, moving tragedies, or lively and ingenious comedies. She must not be touched by fools, or by the ignorant vulgar people, incapable of comprehending or appreciating her hidden treasures. And do not think, señor, that I apply the term vulgar here merely to commoners and the lower class; because everyone who is ignorant, whether a lord or prince, may and should be included among the vulgar. He, then, who can embrace and cultivate poetry under the conditions I have named, will become famous, and his name honoured throughout all the civilised nations on earth. And in regards to what you say, señor, of your son having no great regard for Spanish poetry, I am inclined to think that he is not quite right there. The great poet Homer did not write in Latin, because he was a Greek, neither did Virgil write in Greek, because he was Latin; in short, all the ancient poets wrote in the language they drank their mother's milk from, and never went in search of foreign ones to express their beautiful conceptions; and that being so, the usage should in fairness extend to all nations, and the German poets should not be undervalued because they write in their own language, neither the Castilian, or even the Biscayan, for writing in theirs. But your son, señor, I suspect, is not prejudiced against Spanish poetry, but against those poets who are mere Spanish verse writers, without any knowledge of other languages or sciences to adorn and give life and vigour to their natural inspiration; and yet even in this he may be wrong; because, according to a true belief, a poet is born one; that is to say, the poet by nature comes as a poet from his mother's womb; and following the skill that heaven has granted him, without the aid of study or art, he produces things that show how true the man who said, 'there is God inside,' was. At the same time, I say that the poet by nature who calls in art to his aid will be a far better poet, and will surpass him who tries to be one relying on his knowledge of art alone. The reason is, that art does not surpass nature, but only brings it to perfection; and therefore, nature combined with art, and art with nature, will produce a perfect poet. To bring my argument to a close, I would say then, gentle sir, let your son go on as his star leads him, because being so studious as he seems to be, and having already successfully surmounted the first step of the sciences, which is that of the languages, with their help he will by his own exertions reach the summit of polite literature, which suits an independent gentleman, and adorns, honours, and distinguishes him, as much as the headdress does the bishop, or the gown does for the educated counsellor. If your son writes sarcasm reflecting on the honour of others, correct him, and tear it up; but if he composes discourses in which he reprimands vice in general, in the style of Horace, and with elegance like his, commend him; because it is legitimate for a poet to write against envy and whip the envious in his verse, and the other vices too, provided he does not single out individuals; there are, however, poets who, for the sake of saying something spiteful, would run the risk of being banished to the coast of Pontus. If the poet is pure in his morals, he will be pure in his verses too; the pen is the tongue of the mind, and as the thought arises there, so will be the things that it writes down. And when Kings and Princes observe this marvellous science of poetry in wise, virtuous, and thoughtful subjects, they honour, value, exalt them, and even crown them with the leaves of that tree which the thunderbolt does not strike, as if to show that those whose heads are honoured and adorned with such a crown are not to be attacked by anyone."

He was filled with astonishment at Don Quixote's argument, so much that he began to abandon his notion about him being crazy. But in the middle of the conversation, it being not very much to his liking, Sancho had wandered from the road to beg for a little milk from some shepherds, who were milking their sheep; and just as the gentleman, highly pleased, were about to renew the conversation, Don Quixote, raising his head, perceived a cart covered with royal flags coming along the road they were travelling; and convinced that this must be some new adventure, he called aloud to Sancho to come and bring him his helmet. Sancho, hearing himself being called, left the shepherds, and, prodding the donkey vigorously, came to his master, who was about to have a terrific and frantic adventure.

CHAPTER 17

THE FURTHEST AND HIGHEST POINT WHICH THE COURAGE OF DON QUIXOTE REACHED OR COULD REACH; TOGETHER WITH THE HAPPILY ACHIEVED ADVENTURE OF THE LIONS

The history says that when Don Quixote called for Sancho to bring him his helmet, Sancho was buying some cakes the shepherds had agreed to sell to him, and being disturbed by the situation his master was in did not know what to do with them or what to carry them in; so, not to lose them, because he had already paid for them, he thought it best to place them into his master's helmet, and acting on this bright idea he went to see what his master had called him for. And as Sancho approached, Don Quixote exclaimed to him:

"Give me that helmet, my friend, because either I know little about adventures, or what I observe ahead is one that will, and does, call me to arm myself."

The man dressed in green, on hearing this, looked in all directions, but could see nothing, except a cart coming towards them with two or three small flags, which led him to conclude it must be carrying treasure belonging to the King, and he said this to Don Quixote. He, however, would not believe him, being always persuaded and convinced that all that happened to him must be an adventure; so he replied to the gentleman, "He who is prepared has his battle half won; nothing is lost by preparing myself, because I know by experience that I have enemies, visible and invisible, and I do not know when, or where, or at what moment, or in what shapes they will attack me;" and turning to Sancho he called for his helmet; and Sancho, as he had no time to take out the cakes, had to give it to him just as it was. Don Quixote took it, and without knowing what was in it, thrust it down in a rush on his head; but as the cakes were pressed and squeezed they began to run all over his face and beard, which startled him so much that he cried out to Sancho:

"Sancho, what is this? I think my head is softening, or my brains are melting, or I am sweating from head to toe! If I am sweating it is not from fear. I am convinced beyond a doubt that the adventure which is about to happen is a terrible one. Give me something to wipe myself with, if you have it, because this sweat is blinding me."

Sancho stayed quiet, and gave him a cloth, and gave thanks to God at the same time that his master had not found out why this had happened. Don Quixote then wiped himself, and took off his helmet to see what it was that made his head feel so cool, and seeing that there was all white mash inside his helmet he put his nose inside, and as soon as he had smelt it he exclaimed:

"On the life of my lady Dulcinea del Toboso, you have put cakes in here, you treacherous, disrespectful, ill-mannered aide!"

To which, with great composure and pretended innocence, Sancho replied, "If there are cakes in there let me have them, your worship, and I'll eat them; but let the devil eat them, because it must have been him who put them there. I would not dare to dirty your helmet! You have guessed the offender finely! Sir, by the light God gives me, it seems I must have enchanters too, that persecute me as a creature and limb of yourself, and they must have put that nastiness in there in order to provoke your patience into anger, and make you attack my ribs as I am sure you want to do. Well, this time, indeed, they have missed their mark, because I trust in my master's good sense to see that I have got no cakes or milk, or anything of the sort; and that if I had it I would put it in my stomach and not in the helmet."

"Maybe so," said Don Quixote.

All this the gentleman was observing with astonishment, especially when, after having wiped his head, face, beard, and helmet clean, Don Quixote put it on again, and settling himself firmly in his saddle, placing his sword in the scabbard, and grasping his lance, he cried, "Now, come whoever you are, here am I, ready to battle with Satan himself in person!"

By this time the cart with the flags had come closer, unattended by anyone except the carter on a donkey, and a man sitting in front. Don Quixote planted himself in front of it and said, "Where are you going, brothers? What cart is this? What have you got in it? What flags are those?"

To this the carter replied, "The cart is mine; inside is a pair of wild caged lions, which the governor of Oran is sending to the court as a present to his Majesty; and the flags are our lord the King's, to show that what is here is his property."

"And are the lions large?" asked Don Quixote.

"So large," replied the man who sat at the door of the cart, "that none as large or larger have ever crossed from Africa into Spain; I am the keeper, and I have brought over others, but never any like these. They are male and female; the male is in the first cage and the female in the one behind, they are both hungry, because they have not eaten today, so please move aside, because we must take them quickly to the place where we can feed them."

Smiling slightly, Don Quixote exclaimed, "Lion-puppies to me! Puppies of lions, and at such a time! God! Those gentlemen who send them here will see if I am a man to be frightened by lions. Get down my good fellow, and as you are the keeper open the cages, and let the beasts loose, and in the middle of this road I will let them know who Don Quixote of La Mancha is, in spite of the enchanters who send them to me."

"Very well," said the gentleman to himself at this."

Our Knight has shown what sort he is; the cakes, no doubt, have softened his skull and let his brains leak from his head."

At this moment Sancho came to him, saying, "Señor, for God's sake do something to keep my master, Don Quixote, from attacking these lions; because if he does they'll tear us all to pieces."

"Is your master so mad," asked the gentleman, "that you believe and are afraid he will attack such fierce animals?"

"He is not mad," said Sancho, "but he is daring."

"I will prevent it," said the gentleman; and going over to Don Quixote, who was insisting that the keepers open the cages, said to him, "Sir Knight, Knights should attempt adventures which encourage the hope of a successful issue, not those which entirely oppose it; because bravery that reaches recklessness is an act of madness rather than courage; furthermore, these lions have not come to attack you; they are passing by as presents to his Majesty, and it will not be right to stop them or delay their journey."

"Gentle sir," replied Don Quixote, "you go and mind your tame partridge and your bold ferret, and leave everyone to manage their own business; this is mine, and I know whether these lions come to me or not;" and then turning to the keeper he exclaimed, "With all that's good, sir rascal, if you don't open the cages right now, I'll pin you to the cart with this lance."

The carter, seeing the determination of this spirit in armour, said to him, "Please señor, first let me untie the donkeys and place myself in safety along with them before the lions are released; because if they kill them, I will be ruined for life, because all I possess is this cart and donkeys."

"Man of little faith," replied Don Quixote, "get down and untie them; you will soon see that you are exerting yourself for nothing, and that you might have spared yourself the trouble."

The carter got down and with all speed untied the donkeys, and the keeper shouted out at the top of his voice, "I call all here to witness that against my will and under compulsion I open the cages and let the lions loose, and that I warn this gentleman that he will be accountable for all the harm and mischief which these animals might do. You, gentlemen, place yourselves in safety before I open the cages, because I know they will not harm me."

Once more the gentleman strove to persuade Don Quixote not to do such a mad thing, as it was tempting God to engage in such a piece of madness. To this, Don Quixote replied that he knew what he was about to do. The gentleman in return asked him to reflect, because he knew he was under a delusion.

"Well, señor," answered Don Quixote, "if you do not like to be a spectator of this tragedy, as in your opinion it will be, take yourself and your flea-bitten horse, and place yourself in safety."

Hearing this, Sancho with tears in his eyes asked him to give up an adventure which could be compared to the one of the windmills, and the awful one of the cleaning mills, and, in fact, all the adventures he had attempted in the whole course of his life. "Look, señor," said Sancho, "there's no enchantment here, nothing of the sort, because between the bars and chinks of the cage I have seen the paw of a real lion, and judging by the size of that paw, I recon the lion must be bigger than a mountain."

"Fear," replied Don Quixote, "will make him look bigger than he really is. Run away, Sancho, and leave me; and if I die here you know what to do; you will console Dulcinea - I say no more." To these he added some further words that removed all hope of him giving up his insane project. The man in green would have offered resistance, but he found himself inadequate to fight, and did not think it was prudent to get into a conflict with a madman, which Don Quixote now showed himself to be in every respect.

Don Quixote proceeded to renew his commands to the keeper and repeating his threats, warned the gentleman to take his horse, Sancho his donkey, and the carter his donkies as well, all striving to get away from the cart as far as they could before the lions were loose. Sancho was already crying over his master's death, because this time he firmly believed it was coming for him; and he began to regret being at service to him again; but with all his tears and crying he did not forget to spank his donkey to put a good space between himself and the cart. The keeper, seeing that the everyone were now some distance away, once more asked and warned him as before; but he replied that already heard him, and that he should not bother to trouble himself with any further warnings, as they would be ineffective, and asked him to hurry up.

During the delay that occurred while the keeper was opening the first cage, Don Quixote was considering whether it would be well to battle on foot, instead of on horseback, and finally decided to fight on foot, fearing that Rocinante might be frightened by the sight of the lions; he therefore jumped off his horse, threw his lance aside, placed his shield on his arm, and raising his sword, advanced slowly with spectacular fearlessness and firm courage, to place himself in front of the cart, calling with all his heart to God and to his lady Dulcinea.

It is to be noted, that on coming to this part of the adventure, the author of this genuine history breaks out into exclamations. "Indomitable Don Quixote! Bravery past worshiping! The mirror, where all the heroes of the world can see themselves! Second modern Don Manuel of Leon, once the glory and honour of Spanish Knighthood! In what words can I describe this dreaded adventure, with what language can I make it credible to ages to come, what tributes have not been given to you already! On foot, alone, fearless, high-souled, with a simple sword, but no sharp blade, a shield, but not one of bright polished steel, there you stood, awaiting the two fiercest lions that Africa ever bred! Your deeds should be your praise, valiant Manchegan, and here I leave them awaiting the words to glorify them!"

Here the author's outburst came to an end, and he proceeded to continue the thread of his story, saying that the keeper, seeing that Don Quixote had taken his position, and that it was impossible for him to avoid letting out the male without incurring the hostility of the fiery and daring Knight, threw open the doors of the first cage, containing, as has been said, the lion, which was now seen to be of enormous size, with a grey and hideous mien. The first thing he did was to turn around in the cage in which he lay, and protrude his claws, and stretch himself thoroughly; he then opened his mouth, and yawned very leisurely, and with nearly two hands' length of tongue that he had released, he licked the dust out of his eyes and washed his face; having done this, he put his head out of the cage and looked around with eyes like glowing coals, a spectacle and demeanour to strike terror into terror itself. Don Quixote merely observed him steadily, anticipating for him to jump from the cart and come closer to him, when he hoped to cut him into pieces.

The noble lion, more courteous than arrogant, not troubling himself about silly bravado, after having looked around, as has been said, turned and presented his rear-end to Don Quixote, and very calmly and tranquilly lay down again in the cage. Seeing this, Don Quixote ordered the keeper to take a stick and provoke him to make him come out.

"That I won't do," said the keeper; "because if I anger him, the first person he will tear into pieces will be myself. Be satisfied, sir Knight, with what you have done, and do not seek to tempt fortune a second time. The lion has the door open; he is free to come out or not to come out; but as he has not come out so far, he will not come out today. Your great courage has been fully displayed already; no brave man is required more than to challenge his enemy and wait for him on the field; if his adversary does not come, he will be the disgrace, and the one who waits for him takes the crown of victory."

"Very true," said Don Quixote; "close the door, my friend, and let me have, what you have seen me do, in the form of a certificate; stating that you opened the cage for the lion, that I waited for him, that he did not come out, that I still waited for him, and that he still did not come out, and lay down again. I am not bound to do more; enchantments be gone, and God uphold the right, the truth, and true chivalry! Close the door as I asked you, while I make signals to those who have left us, so they can know the outcome of this adventure."

The keeper obeyed, and Don Quixote, placing on the point of his lance the cloth he used to wipe his face with after the downpour of cake, and by waving it, proceeded to call the others, who still continued to flee, looking back at every step. Sancho, however, happening to observe the signal of the white cloth, exclaimed, "God kill me, if my master has not overcome the wild beasts, because he is calling us."

They all stopped, and observed that it was Don Quixote who was making signals, and shaking off their fears to some extent, they approached slowly until they were near enough to hear distinctly Don Quixote's voice calling them. After some time, they returned to the cart, and as they came, Don Quixote said to the carter, "Put your donkeys to use once more, brother, and continue your journey; and you, Sancho, give him two gold coins for himself and the keeper, to compensate for the delay they have incurred due to me."

"That I will do with all my heart," said Sancho; "but what has happened to the lions? Are they dead or alive?"

The keeper, then, in full detail, and bit by bit, described the end of the contest, praising to the best of his power and ability the courage of Don Quixote, who by being seen made the lion tremble in fear, and not dare to come out of the cage, although he had held the door open for a long time; and saying how he protested to the Knight that it was tempting God to provoke the lion in order to force him out, which he wished to have done, but very reluctantly, and against his will, had allowed the door to be closed.

"What do you think of this, Sancho?" said Don Quixote. "Is there any enchantment that can triumph over true bravery? The enchanters may be able to rob me of good fortune, but they cannot rob me of fortitude and bravery."

Sancho paid the coins, the carter put the donkeys to work, the keeper kissed Don Quixote's hands for the coins given to him, and promised to give an account of the heroic deeds to the King himself, as soon as he saw him.

"Then," said Don Quixote, "if his Majesty should happen to ask who performed them, you must say THE KNIGHT OF THE LIONS; because it is my desire that the name I have up until now: The Knight of the Sorrowful Face be from this time forward, changed, altered, transformed, and turned into The Knight of the Lions; and I can do this this because I follow the ancient practise of Knights, who changed their names when they liked or when it suited their purpose."

The cart went on its way, and Don Quixote, Sancho, and the man of green went their own. All this time, Don Diego de Miranda had not said a word, being entirely captivated with observing and noting all that Don Quixote did and said, and the opinion he formed about him was, that he was a man of brains gone mad, and a madman on the edge of rationality. The first part of his history had not yet reached him, because, if he had read it, the amazement with which his words and deeds filled him would have vanished, as he would have then understood the nature of his madness; but knowing nothing about it, he took him to be rational one moment, and crazy the next, because what he said was sensible, elegant, and well expressed, and what he did, absurd, impulsive, and foolish; and he said to himself, "What could be madder than putting on a helmet full of cakes, and then persuading oneself that enchanters are softening one's skull; or what could be greater recklessness and foolishness than wanting to fight lions against all advice?"

Don Quixote roused him from these reflections and this monologue by saying, "No doubt, Señor Don Diego de Miranda, you have me placed in your mind as a fool and a madman, because you believe my deeds do not demonstrate anything else. But despite that, you should notice that I am neither so mad or so foolish as I must have seemed to you. A brave Knight uses his lance skilfully against a fierce bull under the watch of his King, in the middle of a spacious arena; a Knight presents himself in glittering armour, running up the slopes in front of the ladies in some festive tournament, and all those Knights that entertain, and, if we may say so, honour the courts of their princes with warlike exercises, or what resemble them; but what is more impressive than all these is a Knight-who wanders the deserts, solitudes, cross-roads, forests, and mountains, in search of dangerous adventures, determined to bring them to a happy and successful conclusion, all to win glorious and lasting fame. A greater advantage, I maintain, the Knight gains from bringing aid to some widow in some lonely wasteland, than the court Knight conversing with some city girl. All Knights have their own special parts to play; let the court Knight devote himself to the ladies, let him add lustre to his King's court with his costumes, let him entertain poor gentlemen with the luxurious food on his table, let him arrange tournaments, and prove himself to be noble, generous, and magnificent, and above all a good Christian, and doing so he will fulfil the duties that are especially his; but let the Knight explore the corners of the earth and penetrate the most intricate labyrinths, at each step let him attempt impossibilities, on barren hills let him endure the burning rays of the midsummer sun, and the bitter rage of the winter wind and frost; let no lions daunt him, no monsters terrify him, no dragons make him run; because to seek these, to attack those, and to vanquish all, are in truth his main duties. I, then, as it is my calling to be a member of Knighthood, cannot avoid attempting all that to me seems to come within the sphere of my calling; therefore it was my duty to attack those lions, although I knew it was the height of foolishness; because I know what courage is, that it is a virtue that occupies a place between two vicious extremes, cowardice and recklessness; but it is less evil for a man who is brave to rise until he reaches the point of rashness, than to sink until he reaches the point of cowardice; because, as it is easier for the uncontrolled than for the miser to become generous, it is easier for a rash man to be truly brave than for a coward to rise to true fearlessness; and believe me, Señor Don Diego, in attempting adventures it is better to lose by rashness than to lose by cowardice; because to hear it said, 'such a Knight is rash and daring,' sounds better than 'such a Knight is timid and cowardly.'"

"I confess, Señor Don Quixote," said Don Diego, "everything you have said and done has proved to be correct by the test of reason itself; and I believe, if the laws and orders of Knighthood should be lost, they might be found in you as their depository and house; but let's leave quickly, and reach my village, where you can rest after your recent exertion; because if the body has not been used, certainly the spirit has, and this sometimes tends to produce bodily fatigue."

"I take the invitation as a great favour and honour, Señor Don Diego," replied Don Quixote; and going forward at a better pace than before, at about two in the afternoon they reached the village and house of Don Diego, or, as Don Quixote called him, "The Knight of the Green Hat."

CHAPTER 18

WHAT HAPPENED TO DON QUIXOTE IN THE CASTLE OR HOUSE OF THE KNIGHT OF THE GREEN HAT, TOGETHER WITH OTHER MATTERS OUT OF THE ORDINARY

Don Quixote found Don Diego de Miranda's house built in a village style; in the patio was the store-room, and at the entrance the cellar, with plenty of wine-jars around, which, coming from El Toboso, brought back to his memory his enchanted and transformed Dulcinea; and with a sigh, and not thinking of what he was saying, or in whose presence he was, he exclaimed:

"Oh you my treasure, enchanted in sorrow!
Once sweet and welcoming when 'it was heaven's will."

"Oh Tobosan jars, how you bring back to my memory the sweet object of my bitter thoughts!"

The student poet, Don Diego's son, who had come out with his mother to welcome him, heard this exclamation, and both the mother and son were filled with amazement at the extraordinary figure presented to them; he, however, dismounting from Rocinante, advanced with great politeness to ask permission to kiss the lady's hand, while Don Diego said, "Señora, please welcome with your kindness Señor Don Quixote of La Mancha, who you see in front of you, a Knight, and the bravest and wisest in the world."

The lady, whose name was Dona Cristina, welcomed him with every sign of good-will and great courtesy, and Don Quixote placed himself at her service with an abundance of well-chosen and polished phrases. Almost the same courtesies were exchanged between him and the student, who listening to Don Quixote, took him to be a sensible, clear-headed person.

Here the author describes minutely everything belonging to Don Diego's house, giving us a picture the whole contents of a rich gentleman-farmer's house; but the translator of the history thought it best to pass over these and other details of the same sort in silence, as they are not in harmony with the main purpose of the story, the main point of which is truth rather than boring additives.

They led Don Quixote into a room, and Sancho removed his armour, leaving him in loose trousers and a leather jacket, all stained with the rust of his armour; his shirt was relaxed, without starch, his socks white-coloured, and his shoes polished. He carried his good sword, which hung from a belt made of wolf's skin.

With five or six buckets of water (in regards to the number of buckets there is some dispute), he washed his head and face, and the water remained white-coloured, thanks to Sancho's greediness and purchase of those cakes that turned his master white. In this manner, and with an easy, energetic, and gracious style, Don Quixote passed into another room, where the student was waiting to entertain him while the table was being laid; because on the arrival of such a distinguished guest, Dona Cristina was anxious to show that she knew how and was able to give a welcoming to distinguished guests that came to her house.

While Don Quixote was taking off his armour, Don Lorenzo (which is the name of Don Diego's son) took the opportunity to say to his father, "What are we to think about this gentleman you have brought home to us, sir? Because his name, his appearance, and you describing him as a Knight have completely puzzled mother and I."

"I don't know what to say, my son," replied. Don Diego; "all I can tell you is that I have seen him perform the acts of the greatest madman in the world, and heard him make observations so sensible that they undo all that he does; you talk to him and feel the pulse of his wit, and as you are sharp, form the most reasonable conclusion you can in regards to his wisdom or madness; although, to tell the truth, I am more inclined to consider him to be mad than sane."

With this Don Lorenzo went away to entertain Don Quixote as has been said, and in the course of the conversation that passed between them Don Quixote said to Don Lorenzo, "Your father, Señor Don Diego de Miranda, has told me about the rare abilities and intellect you possess, and, above all, that you are a great poet."

"A poet, I may be," replied Don Lorenzo, "but a great one, not at all. It is true that I am somewhat into poetry and reading the work of good poets, but not so much to justify the title of 'great' which my father gives me."

"I do not dislike that modesty," said Don Quixote; "because there is no poet who is not conceited and does not think he is the best poet in the world."

"There is no rule without an exception," said Don Lorenzo; "there may be some who are poets and yet do not think they are."

"Very few," said Don Quixote; "but tell me, what verses do you have now which your father tells me keep you somewhat restless and absorbed? If they are a form of commentary, I know something about commentary, and I would like to hear them; and if they are for a poetical tournament, arrange to win the second prize; because the first always wins by favour or personal standing, the second by simple justice; and so the third becomes the second, and the first, winning in this way, will be the third, in the same way as degrees are awarded at the universities; but, despite that, the title of first is a great distinction."

"So far," said Don Lorenzo to himself, "I do not take you to be a madman; but let us continue." So he said to him, "You have apparently attended the schools; what sciences have you studied?"

"Knighthood," said Don Quixote, "which is as good as poetry, and even a finger or two above it."

"I do not know what science that is," said Don Lorenzo, "and until now I have never even heard of it."

"It is a science," said Don Quixote, "that encompasses in itself all or most of the sciences in the world, because he who practices it must be the jury, and must know the rules of justice, allocate it in a reasonable manner, to give to each one what belongs to him and is due to him. He must be a theologian, to be able to give clear and distinctive advice derived from the Christian faith he practices, wherever it may be asked of him. He must be a physician and herbalist, so when travelling the lands he knows the herbs that have the property of healing wounds, because a Knight must not go looking for someone to cure him at every step. He must be an astronomer, to know by the stars how many hours of the night have passed, and what part of the world he is in. He must know mathematics, because there is always some occasion which requires it and will present itself to him; and, additionally he must be adorned with all the virtues, fundamental and theological, down to the minor details, he must, I say, be able to swim as well as Nicholas or Nicolao the Fish could, as the story goes; he must know how to shoe a horse, and repair his saddle and reins; and, to return to higher matters, he must be faithful to God and to his lady; he must be pure in thought, well-mannered in words, generous in work, fearless in deeds, patient in suffering, compassionate towards the needy, and, lastly, an upholder of the truth although its defence could cost him his life. With all these qualities, great and small, a true Knight is made; judge then, Señor Don Lorenzo, whether it is a shameful science which the Knight who studies and practices it has to learn, and whether it does not compare with the finest which are taught in schools."

"If that is so," replied Don Lorenzo, "this science, I say, surpasses all the others."

"Why do you say: if that is so?" said Don Quixote.

"What I mean to say," said Don Lorenzo, "is, that I doubt whether there are now, or ever were, any Knights, especially adorned with such virtues."

"Many times," replied Don Quixote, "have I said what I will say now once again, that the majority of the world have the opinion that there never were any Knights in it; and as it is my opinion that, unless heaven by some miracle brings home the truth to them that there were and are, all the trouble I take to explain will be useless (as experience has often proven to me), I will not stop now to enlighten you about the error you share with the crowd. All I will do is pray to heaven to free you from it, and show you how beneficial and necessary Knights were in days of the past, and how useful they would be in these days if only they were in fashion; but now, due to the sins of the people, sloth and indolence, gluttony and luxury are triumphant."

"Our guest has lost it," said Don Lorenzo to himself at this point; "but, despite that, he is a glorious madman, and I would be a total fool to doubt it."

Here, being summoned to dinner, they brought their conversation to a close. Don Diego asked his son what he had been able to make out in regards to their guest's madness or sanity. To which he replied, "All the doctors in the world will not make sense out of his madness; he is a madman full of flashes of sanity, and full of articulate intervals."

They sat themselves for dinner, and the meal was in the style which Don Diego said on the road he was in the habit of giving to his guests, neat, generous, and tasty; but what pleased Don Quixote most was the marvellous silence that reigned throughout the house, because it was like a Catholic monastery.

When the cloth had been removed, grace had been said and their hands washed, Don Quixote seriously pushed Don Lorenzo to repeat to him his verses for the poetical tournament, to which he replied, "Not to be like those poets who, when they are asked to recite their verses, refuse, and when they are not asked for them vomit them up, I will repeat my lines, which I do not expect any prize for, having composed it merely as an exercise for ingenuity."

"A perceptive friend of mine," said Don Quixote, "had the opinion that no one should waste time speaking verses; and the reason he gave was that the speaking can never be as good as the text, and that often or most frequently it wanders away from the meaning and purpose it aimed at; and besides, that the laws of the oratory were too strict, as they did not allow questioning, or 'he said,' or 'I say,' or turning verbs into nouns, or altering the construction, not to speak of other restrictions and limitations that hold back writers, as you no doubt already know."

"Definitely, Señor Don Quixote," said Don Lorenzo, "I wish I could catch you tripping in your speech, but I cannot, because you slip through my fingers like water."

"I don't understand what you say, or mean by slip," said Don Quixote.

"I will explain myself another time," said Don Lorenzo; "but for now the verses go like this:

Could 'was' become an 'is' for me,
Then would I ask no more than this;
Or could, for me, the time that is,
Become the time that is to be!

Lady Fortune once upon a day,
Was generous and kind;
But all things change; she changed her mind,
And what she gave she took away.

Lady Fortune, for long I've asked you to;
Restore the gifts of history,
Because, trust me, I would ask no more from you,
Could 'was' become an 'is' for me.

No other prize I seek to gain,
No triumph, glory, or success,
Only the long-lost happiness,
Yet the current memory is pain.

One taste, I think, of missing bliss,

The heart-consuming fire might stay;
And, so let it come without delay,
Then would I ask no more than this.

I ask what cannot be, sadly!
That time should ever be, and then,
Come back to us, and be again,
No power on earth can bring it gladly;

The times we miss,
And uselessly, therefore pray,
That what has left us may,
Become for us, the time that is.

Perplexed, uncertain, to remain,
Hope and fear, is death, not life;
Better, sure, to end the strife,
And dying, seek release from pain.

And yet, even if it were the best for me.
This thought to the side I fling,
And to the present I fondly cling,
And dread the time that is to be."

When Don Lorenzo had finished reciting his verses, Don Quixote stood up, and in a loud voice, almost a shout, exclaimed as he gripped Don Lorenzo's right hand in his, "Great God, noble youth, you are the best poet on earth, and deserve to be crowned with laurel, not by Cyprus, but by the Academies of Athens, if they still flourished, and by those that flourish now, in Paris, Rome and Salamanca. Heaven grant that the judges who rob you of the first prize are pierced with arrows, and the Muses never pass the thresholds of their doors. Repeat for me some of your longer verses, señor, as you are so good, because I want to thoroughly feel the pulse of your rare genius."

Is there any need to say that Don Lorenzo enjoyed hearing himself praised by Don Quixote, although he looked at him as a madman? The power of flattery, what a far reaching art you are, and how wide are the boundaries of your jurisdiction! Don Lorenzo gave further proof of his genius, because he complied with Don Quixote's request, and repeated to him this poem on the story of Pyramus and Thisbe.

POEM

The lovely maid, now holds the wall,
Heart-pierced by her young Pyramus, by a lie;

And Love spreads its wings to fly,
A crack to see so great and small.

The silence speaks, no voice at all,
Can pass so slow; but love will try
Without its power, it can die;
But real love will find a way whatever will fall.

Impatient delay, with reckless pace,
The careless lady wins the fatal spot where she,
Sinks, not into her lover's arms but death's embrace.

The strange story, of how the lovers unite,
One sword, one death, one memory,
Kills, and brings back to life.

"Greatest God," said Don Quixote when he had heard Don Lorenzo's poem, "out of a bunch of irritable poets I have found one excellent one, which, señor, the art of this poem proves to me that you are!"

For four days Don Quixote was magnificently entertained in Don Diego's house, at the end of which he requested permission to leave, telling him he thanked him for the kindness and hospitality he had received in his house, but that, as it did not fit Knights to give themselves to idleness and luxury for too long, he was anxious to fulfil the duties of his calling in seeking adventures, of which he was informed there was an abundance in that neighbourhood, where he hoped to use his time until the day came for the tournaments at Saragossa, because that was his proper destination; and that, first of all, he intended to enter the cave of Montesinos, of which so many marvellous things were reported all throughout the country, and at the same time to investigate and explore the origin and true source of the seven lakes commonly called the lakes of Ruidera.

Don Diego and his son praised his admirable resolution, and asked him to take for himself all he wanted from their house, as they would most gladly be of service to him; which, indeed, his personal worth and his honourable profession made mandatory for them.

Finally, the day of his departure came, which was as welcome to Don Quixote as it was sad and sorrowful to Sancho Panza, who was very well satisfied with the abundance of Don Diego's house, and objected to return to the starvation of the woods and wilderness and the barely filled saddle bags; these, however, he filled and packed with what he considered necessary.

When leaving, Don Quixote said to Don Lorenzo, "I do not know whether I have told you already, but if I have I will tell you again, that if you wish to spare yourself the fatigue and work to reach the inaccessible summit of the temple of fame, you have nothing to do but to turn away from the narrow path of poetry and take the narrower one of Knighthood, wide enough, however, to make you an emperor in the blink of an eye."

With this speech Don Quixote gave full evidence of his madness, but even better in what he added when he said, "God knows, I would gladly take Don Lorenzo with me to teach him how to comfort the humble, trample the proud under your foot, and the virtues that are part of the profession I belong to; but since his age does not allow it, or his praiseworthy pursuit permit it, I will simply content myself with impressing on you that you will not become famous as a poet if you are guided by the opinion of others rather than by your own; because no fathers or mothers ever think their own children are unattractive, and this sort of deception succeeds even more strongly in the case of the child's intellect."

Both father and son were amazed again at the strange jumble of words Don Quixote spoke, at one moment sense, at another nonsense, and at persistence he displayed in going through thick and thin in search of his unlucky adventures. There was a renewal of offers of service and courtesies, and then, with the gracious permission of the lady of the castle, they left, Don Quixote on Rocinante, and Sancho on the donkey.

CHAPTER 19

THE ADVENTURE OF THE LOVE SICK SHEPHERD, TOGETHER WITH OTHER TRULY HUMUROUS INCIDENTS

Don Quixote had not gone far beyond Don Diego's village, when he came across a couple of either priests or students, and a couple of peasants, mounted on four animals of the donkey type. One of the students carried, wrapped up in a coarse green linen travel bag, what seemed to be a little linen and a couple of pairs of ribbed socks; the other carried nothing but a pair of new fencing-swords. The peasants carried various articles that showed they were on their way from some large town where they had bought them, and were taking them home to their village; and both students and peasants were struck with the same amazement that everybody felt when seeing Don Quixote for the first time, and were dying to know who this man, so different from ordinary men, could be. Don Quixote greeted them, and after ascertaining that they were heading in the same direction as him, offered to accompany them, and asked them to slow their pace, as their young donkeys travelled faster than his horse; and then, to gratify them, he told them in a few words who he was and the calling and profession he followed, which was that of Knighthood, seeking adventures in all parts of the world. He informed them that his own name was Don Quixote of La Mancha, and that he was called, by surname, the Knight of the Lions.

All this was like hearing Greek or gibberish to the peasants, but not to the students, who very soon perceived the crack in Don Quixote's head; despite that, however, they regarded him with admiration and respect, and one of them said to him, "If you, sir Knight, have no fixed direction, as it is the way with those who seek adventures not to have any, please come with us; you will see one of the finest and richest weddings that up to this day has ever been celebrated in La Mancha."

Don Quixote asked him if it was some prince's, as he spoke of it in this way. "Not at all," said the student; "it is the wedding of a farmer and a farmer's daughter, he the richest in this country, and she is the fairest lady ever seen. The display is to consist of something rare and out of the ordinary, because it will be celebrated in a meadow adjoining the town of the bride, who is called: Quiteria the fair, and the bridegroom is called Camacho the rich. She is eighteen, and he is twenty-two, and they are fairly matched, although some say, who know all the lineages in the world by heart, that the family of lady Quiteria is better than Camacho's; but no one minds that these days, because wealth can patch many great flaws. At any rate, Camacho is generous, and it is his wish to use the whole meadow and cover it, so that the sun will have hard work trying to reach the grass that shields the soil. He has provided dancers as well, not only sword but also bell-dancers, because in his own town there are those who jingle bells to perfection; in regards to shoe-dancers - perhaps, because for them he has engaged a host. But none of these things, or many others I have omitted to mention, will do more to make this a memorable wedding than the part which I suspect the despairing Basilio will play in it. This Basilio is a youth of the same village as Quiteria, and he lived in the house next door to her parents, out of this circumstance Love took advantage to reproduce in the world the long-forgotten loves of Pyramus and Thisbe; because Basilio loved Quiteria from his earliest years, and she responded to his passion with proof of affection, so the love of the two children, Basilio and Quiteria, were the talk and the amusement of the town. As they grew up, the father of Quiteria made up his mind to refuse Basilio freedom of access to the house, and to relieve himself of constant doubts and suspicions, he arranged a match for his daughter with the rich Camacho, as he did not approve of marrying her to Basilio, who had not so large a share of the gifts of fortune as of nature; because if the truth is told fairly, he is the most agile youth we know, a mighty thrower of the spear, a first-rate wrestler, and a great ball-player; he runs like a deer, and leaps better than a goat, bowls over the nine-pins as if by magic, sings like a bird, plays the guitar making it speak, and, above all, handles a sword as well as the best man."

"For that excellence alone," said Don Quixote "the youth deserves to marry, not merely lady Quiteria, but Queen Guinevere herself, if she were alive now, despite Lancelot and all who would try to prevent it."

"Say that to my wife," said Sancho, who had listened in silence until now, "because she won't listen to anything but each one marrying their equal, holding the proverb 'each to their own.' What I would like is that this good Basilio (because I am beginning to like him already) should marry this lady Quiteria; with blessings and good luck— and the opposite for people who would prevent those who love one another from marrying."

"If all those who love one another were to marry," said Don Quixote, "it would deprive parents of the right to choose, and marry their children to the proper person and at the proper time; and if it was left to daughters to choose husbands as they pleased, one would choose her father's servant, and another, someone she has seen passing in the street appearing to be gracious and confident, although he may be a drunken bully; because love and attraction easily blind the eyes of judgment, so much is required in choosing one's future; and the matrimonial choice is very liable to error, and it needs great caution and the special favour of heaven to make it a good one. He who has to make a long journey, will, if he is wise, look out for some trust worthy and pleasant companion to accompany him before he goes. Why, then, should someone not do the same when making the whole journey of life down to the final end of death, especially when the companion has to be his companion in bed, at dinner time, and everywhere, as the wife is to her husband? The companionship of one's wife is no article of merchandise, that, after it has been bought, may be returned, or bartered, or changed; because it is an inseparable commitment that lasts as long as life lasts; it is a noose that, once you put it around your neck, turns into a knot, which, if the sword of Death does not cut it, there is no untying. I could say a great deal more on this subject, if I were not prevented by the anxiety I feel to know if señor lawyer has anything else to say about the story of Basilio."

To this the student, graduate, or, as Don Quixote called him, lawyer, replied, "I have nothing further to say, but that from the moment Basilio heard that lady Quiteria was to be married to Camacho the rich, he has never been seen to smile, or heard to say rational word, and he always goes about moody and dejected, talking to himself in a way that shows plainly he is out of his senses. He eats little and sleeps little, and all he eats is fruit, and when he sleeps, if he sleeps at all, it is in the field on the hard earth like an animal. Sometimes he gazes at the sky, at other times he fixes his eyes on the earth in such a preoccupied way that he might be taken for a clothed statue, with its drapery moved by the wind. In short, he shows such signs of a heart crushed by suffering, that all who know him believe that when tomorrow lady Quiteria says 'yes,' it will be his death sentence."

"God will guide it better," said Sancho, "because nobody knows what will happen; there are a good few hours between now and tomorrow, and at any one of them, or any moment, the house may fall; I have seen the rain coming down and the sun shining all at the same time; many people have gone to bed in good health and cannot get up the next day. And tell me, is there anyone who can boast of having driven a nail into the wheel of fortune? Not at all; and between a woman's 'yes' and 'no' I wouldn't undertake to put the point of a pin, because there would not be room for it; if you tell me Quiteria loves Basilio with her heart and soul, then I'll give him a bag of good luck; because love, I have heard, looks through spectacles that make copper seem like gold, poverty like wealth, and dirty eyes like pearls."

"What are you getting at, Sancho? For God's sake!" said Don Quixote; "when you start stringing proverbs and sayings together, no one can understand you except Judas himself. Tell me, you animal, what do you know about nails or wheels, or anything else?"

"Oh, if you don't understand me," replied Sancho, "it is no wonder my words are taken for nonsense; but no worries; I understand myself, and I know I have not declared anything very foolish in what I have said; only you, señor, are always compaigning about everything I say, actually, everything I do."

"Complaining, not compaining," said Don Quixote, "you deviant of honest language, God deal with you!"

"Don't find fault with me, sir," returned Sancho, "because you know I have not been bred at court or trained at Salamanca, to know whether I am adding or dropping a letter or so in my words. Why! God bless me, it's not fair to force a simple-man to speak like a Toledoan."

"That is true," said the student, "because those who have been bred on the farms cannot talk like those who are almost all day in the cathedral square, and yet they are all Toledoans. Pure, correct, elegant and lucid language will be found in men of courtly breeding and discrimination, although they may have been born in Majalahonda; I say discrimination, because there are many who are not, and discrimination is the grammar of good language, if it is accompanied by practice. I, sirs, have studied at Salamanca, and I rather pride myself on expressing my meaning in clear, plain, and intelligible language."

"If you did not pride yourself more on your dexterity with those swords you carry than your dexterity of tongue," said the other student, "you would have been head of the class, where you are now a tail."

"Look here, Corchuelo," returned the student, "you have the most mistaken idea in the world about skill with a sword, if you think it useless."

"It is no idea, but an established truth," replied Corchuelo; "and if you wish me to prove it to you by experiment, you have swords there, and it is a good opportunity; I have a steady hand and a strong arm, and these joined with my resolution, which is not small, will make you confess that I am not mistaken. Dismount and put into practice your positions, circles angles and science, because I hope to make you see starting now with my rude raw swordsmanship, in which, next to God, I place my trust that no man is yet to be born who will make me turn my back, and that there is no one in the world I will not compel to face the ground."

"Whether you turn your back or not, I do not concern myself," replied the master of fencing; "although it might be that your grave would be dug on the ground where you plant your feet; I mean that you will be stretched dead there for despising skill with the sword."

"We will soon see," replied Corchuelo, and getting off his donkey briskly, he drew out furiously one of the swords he carried with him.

"It must not be that way," said Don Quixote at this point; "I will be the director of this fencing match, and judge of this often disputed question;" and dismounting from Rocinante and grasping his lance, he planted himself in the middle of the road, just as the student, with an easy, graceful manner and step, advanced towards Corchuelo, who came toward him, with fire in his eyes, as the saying goes. The other two, the peasants, without dismounting from their donkeys, served as spectators of the tragedy. The cuts, thrusts, down strokes and back strokes that Corchuelo delivered were past counting, and came thicker than hail. He attacked like an angry lion, but he was met by a tap on the mouth from the tip of the student's sword that checked him in the middle of his furious onset, and made him kiss it as if it were a holy monument, although not as devoutly as holy monuments are and should be kissed. The end of it was that the student returned against every one of his thrusts a slice which cut the buttons of the short shirt he wore, tore the seams into strips, like the tails of a cuttlefish, knocked off his hat twice, and so completely tired him out, that in vexation, anger, and rage, he took the sword and threw it away with such force, that one of the peasants that were there, who was a notary, and who went to retrieve it, made an affidavit afterwards that he sent it nearly three-miles away, a testimony that will serve, and has served, to show and establish with all certainty that strength is overcome by skill.

Corchuelo sat down tired, and Sancho approaching him said, "Señor graduate, if you take my advice, you will never challenge anyone to fence again, only to wrestle and throw the spear, because you have the youth and strength for that; but for these fencers as they call them, I have heard it said they can put the point of a sword through the eye of a needle."

"I am satisfied with having dismounted my donkey," said Corchuelo, "and with having had the truth I was so ignorant of proven to me by experience;" and getting up he hugged the student, and they were better friends than ever; and not caring to wait for the notary who had gone for the sword, as they saw he would be a long time, they continue so they could reach the village of Quiteria (to which they all belonged) in good time.

During the remainder of the journey the student discussed with them the excellence of the sword, with such conclusive arguments, and such statistics and mathematical proofs, that all were convinced about the value of the science, and Corchuelo was cured of his dogmatism.

It began to get dark; but before they reached the town it seemed to all of them as if there was a heaven full of countless glittering stars in front of it, and they also heard the pleasant mingled notes of a variety of instruments: flutes, drums, pipes and tambourines, and as they came closer they perceived that the trees that had been placed at the entrance of the town were filled with lights unaffected by the wind, because the breeze at the time was so gentle that it did not have the power to disturb the leaves. The musicians were the life of the wedding, wandering through the pleasant grounds in separate bands, some dancing, others singing, others playing the various instruments already mentioned. In short, it seemed as though laughter and cheerfulness were running and jumping all over the meadow.

Several other people were busy in erecting raised benches from which people could conveniently see the plays and dances that were to be performed the next day on the spot dedicated to the celebration of the marriage of Camacho the rich and the death of Basilio. Don Quixote would not enter the village, although the peasant as well as the student encouraged him to; he excused himself, however, on the grounds, amply sufficient in his opinion, that it was a custom of Knights to sleep in the fields and woods in preference to towns, even if it were under golden ceilings; and so he turned away from the road a little, very much against Sancho's will, as the good housing he had enjoyed in the castle or house of Don Diego came back to his mind.

CHAPTER 20

AN ACCOUNT IS GIVEN OF THE WEDDING OF CAMACHO THE RICH, TOGETHER WITH THE INCIDENT OF BASILIO THE POOR

Barely had the night given the bright sun time to dry the liquid pearls of her golden hair with the heat of his mighty rays, when Don Quixote, shaking off the laziness from his limbs, sprang to his feet and called for his aide Sancho, who was still snoring. Seeing this Don Quixote woke him and said: "Happy you, above all the inhabitants on the face of the earth, that, without envying or being envied, sleep with a tranquil mind, and that neither enchanters persecute or enchantments attempt to frighten you. Sleep, I say, and will say a hundred times, without any jealous thoughts of your mistress to make you keep incessant watch, or any cares as to how you are to pay the debts you owe, or find tomorrow's food for yourself and your needy little family to interfere with your rest. Ambition does not break your rest, or does this world's empty display disturb you, because the utmost reach of your anxiety is to provide for your donkey, as you have laid the support of yourself on my shoulders, the weight and burden that nature and custom have imposed on masters. The servant sleeps and the master stays awake thinking how he will feed him, elevate him, and reward him. The distress of seeing the sky turn and withhold its needed moisture from the earth, is not felt by the servant but by the master, who in times of scarcity and famine must support him who has served him in times of adequacy and abundance."

Sancho made no reply because he was asleep, and neither would he have woken up if Don Quixote had not brought him to his senses with the end of his lance. He awoke at last, drowsy and lazy, and rolling his eyes in every direction, and then said: "There comes, if I am not mistaken, from beyond the gates of that town over there a smell more like fried rashers than thyme; a wedding that begins with smells like that, I say, will be abundant and generous."

"Gluttonous man," said Don Quixote; "come, let us go and witness this, and see what the rejected Basilio does."

"Let him do whatever he likes," returned Sancho; "if he were not poor, he would marry Quiteria. Believe señor, it's my opinion the poor man should be content with what he can get, and not go looking for food in the bottom of the sea. I will bet my arm that Camacho could bury Basilio in gold coins; and if so, as it no doubt is, what a fool Quiteria would be to refuse the fine dresses and jewels Camacho must have given her and will give her, and take Basilio's spear-throwing and sword-play. They won't give a pint of wine at the tavern for a good throw of the spear or a neat thrust of the sword. Talents and accomplishments that can't be turned into money, let the unintelligent have them; but when such gifts come to one that has cash, I wish my condition of life was as great as theirs is. On a good foundation you can construct a good building, and the best foundation in the world is money."

"For God's sake, Sancho," said Don Quixote, "stop that rant; it is my belief, if you were allowed to continue you would have no time left for eating or sleeping; because you would spend it all talking."

"If your memory serves you well," replied Sancho, "you would remember the articles of our agreement before we left our village this last time; one of them was that I was able to say all that I wanted to, as long as it was not against my neighbour or your authority; and so far, it seems to me, I have not broken the article."

"I remember no such article, Sancho," said Don Quixote; "and even if it were so, I ask that you to hold your tongue and come along; because the instruments we heard last night are already beginning to invigorate the fields again, and no doubt the marriage will take place in the cool morning, and not in the heat of the afternoon."

Sancho did as his master asked him to, and putting the saddle on Rocinante and the saddle-bag on the donkey, they both mounted and at a leisurely pace entered the town. The first thing that presented itself to Sancho was a whole ox hanging from an elm tree, and in the fire which it was to be roasted there was a burning mountain of sticks, and six stew pots that were placed around the blaze which had not been made in the ordinary mould of standard pots, because they were twice as large, each fit to hold the contents of a slaughter-house; they swallowed whole sheep and hid them away without showing any more sign of them as if they were pigeons. There were countless rabbits skinned and ready, and plucked chickens that hung on the trees ready for their burial in the pots, numberless wild birds and animals of various sorts suspended from the branches so the air can keep them cool. Sancho counted more than sixty wine skins of over six gallons each, and all filled, as it proved afterwards, with gorgeous wines. There were, also, piles of the whitest bread, like the heaps of corn one sees on the threshing-floors. There was a wall made of cheeses arranged like brick-work, and two giant pots full of olive oil, bigger than those found in a dyer's shop, served for cooking croquettes, which when fried were taken out with two large shovels, and plunged into another pot of honey that was close by. There were over fifty cooks and cook's-maids, all clean, sharp, and happy. In the spacious belly of the ox were a dozen soft little pigs, which, sewn up in there, served to give it tenderness and flavour. The spices of different kinds did not seem to have been bought by the kilo but by pound, and all were open to view in a huge rack. In short, all the preparations made for the wedding were in countryside style, but abundant enough to feed an army.

Sancho observed all, contemplated all, and everything won his heart. The first to captivate and take it were the pots, out of which he would have very gladly helped himself to a moderate plate full; then the wine skins secured his affection; and lastly, the produce of the frying-pans, if, indeed, such imposing pots may be called frying-pans; and unable to control himself or watch any longer, he approached one of the busy cooks and politely but hungrily begged permission to soak a piece of bread in one of the pots; to which the cook answered, "Brother, this is not a day on which hunger is to have any influence, thanks to the rich Camacho; look around for a dish and help yourself."

"I don't see one," said Sancho.

"Wait a minute," said the cook; "how shy you are!" and seizing a bucket and plunging it into one of the pots, he filled it with three hens and a couple of geese, and said to Sancho, "Here friend, take the edge off your appetite with these skimmings until dinner-time comes."

"I have nothing to put them in," said Sancho.

"Well then," said the cook, "take a spoon; because Camacho's wealth and happiness furnishes everything."

While Sancho managed this, Don Quixote was watching the entrance, at one end of the walkway, where there stood around twelve peasants, all in holiday and festive attire, mounted on twelve beautiful horses with rich handsome harnesses and a number of little bells attached to their coats, who, organised in formation gave shouts and cries of "Long live Camacho and Quiteria! He as rich as she is fair; and she the fairest on the earth!"

Hearing this, Don Quixote said to himself, "It is easy to see these men have never seen my lady Dulcinea del Toboso; because if they had they would be more moderate in their praise of this Quiteria of theirs."

Shortly after this, several groups of dancers of various sorts began to enter at different points, and among them a group of sword-dancers composed of twenty-four men of gracious and high-spirited appearance, dressed in the finest and whitest of linen, and with handkerchiefs embroidered in various colours with pure silk; and one of those on the horses asked an active youth who led them if any of the dancers had been wounded. "As yet, thank God, no one has been wounded," he said, "we are all safe and sound;" and he immediately began to execute complicated movements with the rest of his company, with so many turns and such great dexterity, that although Don Quixote was well used to seeing dances of the same kind, he thought he had never seen any as good as this. He also admired another group that came in composed of fair young ladies, none of whom seemed to be under fourteen or over eighteen years of age, all dressed in green, with their hair partly braided, partly flowing loose, but all of such bright gold to compete with the sunbeams, and over them they wore crowns of Jasmin, roses, amaranth, and honeysuckle. Leading them was a respected old man and an ancient woman, both brisker and more active, however, than might have been expected from their age. The notes of a bagpipe accompanied them, and with modesty exhibited in their faces and in their eyes, and lightness in their feet, they looked like the best dancers in the world.

Following these came an artistic dance – the type that they call "speaking dances." It was composed of eight fairies in two lines, with the god of Love Cupid leading one and another called 'Interest' leading the other line, the former furnished with wings, bow and arrows, the latter in a rich dress of gold and silk in various colours. The ladies that followed Cupid had their names written in large white letters on their backs. "Poetry" was the name of the first,

"Wit" the second, "Birth" the third, and "Courage" the fourth. Those that followed "Interest' were distinguished in the same way; the badge of the first announced "Kindness," the second "Generosity," the third "Treasure," and the fourth "Peaceful Possession." In front of them all was a wooden castle carried by four wild men, all covered in ivy and hemp stained green. On the front of the castle and on each of the four sides of its frame it had the inscription "Castle of Caution." Four skilful drum and flute players accompanied them, and as the dance had begun, Cupid, raised his eyes and pulled back his bow and aimed at a lady who stood between the towers of the castle, and addressed her as follows:

I am the mighty God whose sway,
Is potent over the land and sea.
The heavens above do not have a say,
And the depths below acknowledge me.

I do not fear, I have my will,
Whatever my urge or desire be;
For me there's no impossible,
I order, bind, forbid, set free.

Having concluded this poem, he sent an arrow flying toward the top of the castle, and went back to his place. Interest then came forward and as the drums and flutes ceased, he said:

But mightier than Love am I,
Where do you think Love begun?
Through me no lineage is more high,
Or older, underneath the sun.

To use me wisely, few know how,
To act without me, fewer still,
Because I am Interest, and I vow
For evermore to do your will.

Interest withdrew, and Poetry came forward, and fixing her eyes on the lady of the castle, she said:

Without pride and conceit,
Fair Lady, charming Poetry,
Her soul, an offering at your feet,
Poems to encourage knowing me.

If you respect and will not scorn,
Your fortune, watched by envious eyes,

On wings of poetry will be bourne,
And exalted to the skies.

Poetry withdrew, and coming from the side of Interest Kindness came forward, and said:

To give, while avoiding each extreme,
The tight fisted, the over-free,
Therein consists, wise men deem,
The virtue Liberality.
But you, fair lady, to enrich,
Myself - I'll prove,
A vice not totally shameful, which
May find its excuse in love.

In the same manner all the characters of the two bands came forward and retired, and each danced, and delivered its verses, some of them graceful, some burlesque, but Don Quixote's memory (although he had an excellent one) only retained those that have just been quoted. All then mingled together, forming chains and breaking off again with graceful, unconstrained cheerfulness; and whenever Love passed in front of the castle he shot his arrows up at it, while Interest fired golden pellets against it. Finally, after they had danced for a while, Interest revealed a large purse, made from the skin of a large brown cat which appeared to be full of money, and threw it at the castle, and with the force of the blow the boards fell apart, leaving the lady exposed and unprotected. Interest and the characters of his band advanced, and throwing a large chain of gold over her neck pretended to take her and lead her away as a captive, on seeing this, Love and his supporters advanced as though they would release her, the whole action being accompanied by the drums and in the form of a dance. The wild men made peace between them, and with great dexterity readjusted and fixed the boards of the castle, and the lady once more shielded herself inside; and with this the dance came to an end, to the great enjoyment of the beholders.

Don Quixote asked one of the ladies who it was that had composed and arranged it. She replied that it was a beneficiary of the town who had a nice taste in devising this sort of thing. "I will bet," said Don Quixote, "that the same beneficiary is a greater friend of Camacho than Basilio, and that he is better at sarcasm than religious service; he has introduced the accomplishments of Basilio and the riches of Camacho very neatly into the dance."

Sancho Panza, who was listening to all this, exclaimed, "The King is my bread; I stick to Camacho."

"It is easy to see you are a clown, Sancho," said Don Quixote, "and one that cries 'Long live the conqueror."

"I don't know of what type I am," returned Sancho, "but I know very well I'll never get such generous amounts of food from Basilio's pots as what I have taken from Camacho's;" and he showed him the bucketful of geese and hens, and taking one, began to eat with great enthusiasm and appetite, saying, "A walnut for the accomplishments of Basilio! As much as you have as much you are worth, and as much as you are worth as much you have. As a grandmother of mine used to say, there are only two families in the world, the Haves and the Have nots; and she stuck to the Haves; and to this day, Señor Don Quixote, people would rather be around the 'Haves,' and 'Know;' an ass covered with gold looks better than a horse with a saddle. So I say again that I stick to Camacho, whose pots offer abundant geese, hens and rabbits; but Basilio's, if he has any, would only provide scraps."

"Have you finished with this rant, Sancho?" said Don Quixote. "Of course I have finished it," replied Sancho, "because I see you take offence from it; but if it was not like that, I would have enough to say for three days."

"God grant that I see you dumb before I die, Sancho," said Don Quixote.

"At the rate we are going," said Sancho, "I'll be chewing soil before you die; and then, maybe, I'll be so dumb that I'll not say a word until the end of the world, or, at least, until the day of judgment."

"Even if that happened, Sancho," said Don Quixote, "your silence will never come make up for all you have said, are saying, and will say in your whole life; moreover, it naturally stands to reason, that my death will come before yours; so I never expect to see you dumb, not even when you are drinking or sleeping, and that is the most I can say."

"In good faith, señor," replied Sancho, "there's no trusting the fleshless one, I mean Death, who devours the lamb as well as the sheep, and, as I have heard our vicar say, treads through the grand towers of Kings and the modest huts of the poor. That lady is more mighty than dainty, she is in no way fussy, she devours all and is ready for all, and fills herself with all sorts of people, ages, and ranks. She is no reaper that sleeps all day; at all times she is reaping and cutting down, the dry grass as well as the green; she never seems to chew, but swallows all that is in front of her, because she has a canine appetite that is never satisfied; and although she has no belly, she shows she has a thirst to drink the lives of all that live, as one would drink a jug of cold water."

"Say no more, Sancho," said Don Quixote; "don't try to better it, and risk a fall; because in truth what you have said about death in your countryside phrasing is what a good preacher might have said. I tell you, Sancho, if you had discretion equal to your mother's, you might run a church, and go around the world preaching fine sermons."

"He who preaches well lives well," said Sancho, "and I know no more theology than that."

"And you need no more," said Don Quixote, "I cannot conceive or make out how it is, that the fear of God being the beginning of wisdom, you, who are more afraid of a lizard than of him, know so much."

"Make judgments on your adventures, señor," returned Sancho, "and don't set yourself up to be the judge of other men's fears or bravery, because I am as good a fearer of God as my neighbours; but leave me to eat this delicious food, because all the rest is only talk that we shall be called to account for in the other world;" and so saying, he began a fresh attack on the bucket, with such an appetite that he aroused Don Quixote's, who no doubt would have helped him had he not been prevented by what must be told next.

CHAPTER 21

CAMACHO'S WEDDING IS CONTINUED, WITH OTHER DELIGHTFUL INCIDENTS

While Don Quixote and Sancho were engaged in the discussion of the last chapter, they heard loud shouts and a great noise, which were made by the men on the horses as they went at full charge, shouting, to welcome the bride and bridegroom, who were approaching with musical instruments and ceremony of all sorts around them, which were accompanied by the priest and the relatives of both, and all of the most distinguished people of the surrounding villages.

When Sancho saw the bride, he exclaimed, "wow, she is not dressed like a country girl, but like some fine court lady; as well as I can make out, the dress she wears is rich coral with green velvet; and then the white trimming – I swear it must be satin! Look at her hands - rings on them! May I never have luck if they are not gold rings, and real gold, and set with pearls as white as a milk, and every one of them worth an eye of one's head! Heavens, what hair she has! if it's not a wig, I never saw longer or fairer hair in all the days of my life. See how bravely she carries herself - and her shape! Wouldn't you say she was like a walking palm tree loaded with dates? Because the charms she has hanging from her hair and neck look just like them. I swear in my heart she is a brave lady, and fit 'to pass through the finest countries.'"

Don Quixote laughed at Sancho's discourteous tributes and thought that, apart from his lady Dulcinea del Toboso, he had never seen a more beautiful woman. The fair Quiteria appeared somewhat pale, which was, no doubt, because of the bad night brides always have dressing themselves for their wedding on the night before the day. They advanced towards a theatre that stood on one side of the meadow decked with carpets, where they were to highlight their attendance, and from which they were to observe the dances and plays; but at the moment of their arrival at the spot they heard a loud outcry behind them, and a voice exclaiming, "Wait a little, you, as inconsiderate as you are hasty!" At these words all turned round, and perceived that the speaker was a man dressing in what seemed to be a loose black coat garnished with crimson patches like flames. He was crowned (as was presently seen) with a crown of dark leaves, and in his hand he held a long stick. As he approached he was recognised by everyone as Basilio, and all waited anxiously to see what would come from his words, in fear of some upheaval in consequence of his appearance at such a moment. Finally, he came, fatigued and breathless, and placing himself in front of the bridal pair, drove his stick, which had a steel spike at the end, into the ground, and, with a pale face and eyes fixed on Quiteria, he addressed her in a rough and unsteady voice:

"Well do you know, ungrateful Quiteria, that according to the holy law we acknowledge, as long as you live you cannot take a husband; or are you ignorant either that, with my own exertions and in my hope that time would improve my fortunes, I have never failed to observe the respect due to your honour; but you, throwing behind you all that you owe to my true love, would surrender what is mine to another whose wealth serves to bring him not only good fortune but supreme happiness; and now to complete it (not that I think he deserves it, but inasmuch as heaven grants it to him), I will, with my own hands, eliminate the obstacle that may interfere with it, and remove myself from between you. Long live Camacho the rich! May he live many happy years with the ungrateful Quiteria! And let the poor Basilio die, Basilio whose poverty clipped the wings of his happiness, and brought him to the grave!"

And so saying, he went to pick up the stick he had driven into the ground, and leaving one half of it fixed there, removed what appeared to be a cover that concealed a long blade; and, he swiftly and deliberately threw himself on it, and in an instant the bloody point and half the steel blade appeared through his back, the unhappy man falling to the earth bathed in his blood, and pierced by his own weapon.

His friends immediately ran to his aid, filled with grief at his misery and sad fate, and Don Quixote, dismounting from Rocinante, rushed to support him, and took him in his arms, and found he had not yet ceased to breathe. They were about to draw out the blade, but the priest who was standing nearby objected, and said that the moment of it being withdrawn would be the same as his death. Basilio, however, reviving slightly, said in a weak voice, as though in pain, "If you consent, cruel Quiteria, to give me your hand as my bride in this last fatal moment, I might still hope that my rashness would be excused, by the bliss attained of you taking me as yours."

Hearing this the priest asked him think of the welfare of his soul rather than the cravings of the body, and in all sincerity seek God's forgiveness for his sins and for his rash undertaking; to which Basilio replied that he was determined not to unless Quiteria first gave him her hand in marriage, because that happiness would compose his mind and give him courage to repent to God.

Don Quixote hearing the wounded man's appeal, exclaimed aloud that what Basilio asked was fair and reasonable, and moreover a request that might be easily complied with; and that it would be as much to Señor Camacho's honour to receive the lady Quiteria as the widow of the brave Basilio as if he received her directly from her father.

"In this case," he said, "it will be only to say 'yes,' and no consequences can follow the word, because the honeymoon of this wedding must be the grave."

Camacho was listening to all this, perplexed and bewildered and not knowing what to say or do; but as the request of Basilio and his friends were so urgent, pleading to allow Quiteria to give him her hand, so that his soul, leaving this life in despair, would not be lost, that they moved, actually, forced him, to say that if Quiteria were willing to give it he was satisfied, as it was only putting off the fulfilment of his wishes for a moment. Immediately all attacked Quiteria and encouraged her, some with prayers, and others with tears, and others with persuasive arguments, to give her hand to poor Basilio; but she, harder than marble and more unmoved than any statue, seemed unable or unwilling to say a word, neither would she have given any reply had the priest not asked her to decide quickly what she intended to do, as Basilio now had his soul at his teeth, and there was no time for hesitation.

The fair Quiteria, to all, appeared to be distressed, grieved, and regretful, and moved by what happened she advanced without a word to where Basilio lay, his eyes already turned in his head, his breathing short and painful, murmuring the name of Quiteria between his lips, and apparently about to die like an atheist and not like a Christian. Quiteria approached him, and kneeling, demanded his hand by signs without speaking. Basilio opened his eyes and staring at her, said, "O Quiteria, why have you turned compassionate at a moment when your compassion will serve as a dagger to rob me of life, because I now do not have the strength left either to bear the happiness you give me in accepting me as yours, or to suppress the pain that is rapidly drawing the shadow of death over my eyes? What I ask from you, fatal star, is that the hand you demand from me and would give to me, is not given out of kindness or to deceive me, but that you confess and declare that without any constraint on your will you give it to me to be your lawful husband; because this is not a moment that you should approach me with lies, as one who has already been dealt with so badly by you."

While uttering these words he showed such weakness that the bystanders expected each return of faintness would take his life with it. Then Quiteria, overcome with modesty and shame, holding in her right hand the hand of Basilio, said, "No force would bend my will; as freely, therefore, as it is possible for me to do so, I give you the hand of a lawful wife, and take yours if you give it to me with your own free will, untroubled and unaffected by the tragedy my hasty act has brought you."

"Yes, I give it," said Basilio, "not agitated or distracted, but with unclouded reason that heaven is pleased to grant me, therefore I do give myself to be your husband."

"And I give myself to be your wife," said Quiteria, "whether you live many years, or they carry you from my arms to the grave."

"For one so badly wounded," observed Sancho at this point, "this young man has a great deal to say; they should make him stop, and attend to his soul; because I think he has it more in his tongue than at his teeth."

Basilio and Quiteria having therefore joined hands, the priest, deeply moved and with tears in his eyes, pronounced the blessing on them, and asked heaven to grant an easy opening for the soul of the newly wedded man, who, the instant he received the blessing, sprang smoothly to his feet and with unparalleled boldness pulled out the blade that had penetrated his body.

All the bystanders were astonished, and some, more simple than inquisitive, began shouting, "A miracle, a miracle!" But Basilio replied, "No miracle, no miracle; only a trick, a trick!" The priest, confused and amazed, rushed to examine the wound with both hands, and found that the blade had passed, not through Basilio's flesh and ribs, but through a hollow iron tube full of blood, which he had skilfully fixed in place, the blood, as was afterwards ascertained, had been prepared in a way not to congeal. In short, the priest and Camacho and most of those present saw they were tricked and made fools of. The bride showed no signs of unhappiness by the deception; on the contrary, hearing them say that the marriage, being fraudulent, would not be valid, she said that she confirmed it again, which made them all conclude that the affair had been planned by agreement and understanding between the pair. Camacho and his supporters were so humiliated that they proceeded to revenge themselves by violence, and a great number of them drawing their swords attacked Basilio, who was protected by as many more swords that were in an instant unsheathed, while Don Quixote taking the lead of his horse, with his lance over his arm and well covered with his shield, told all to make way for him. Sancho, who never found any pleasure or enjoyment in such things, retreated to the wine-jars from which he had taken his mouth-watering share, considering that, as a holy place, that spot would be respected.

"Hold, everyone, hold!" cried Don Quixote in a loud voice; "we have no right to take vengeance for wrongs that love may do to us: remember love and war are the same thing, and as in war it is allowable and common to make use of tricks and strategy to overcome the enemy, so in the contests and rivalries of love the tricks and plans employed to attain the desired end are justifiable, provided they are not to the discredit or dishonour of the loved. Quiteria belonged to Basilio and Basilio to Quiteria by the fair approval of heaven. Camacho is rich, and can purchase his pleasure when, where, and as it pleases him. Basilio has this lady, and no one, however powerful he may be, can take her from him; these two whom God has joined man cannot separate; and he who attempts it must first pass the point of this lance;" and once said, he wielded it so firmly and dexterously that he overwhelmed all who did not know him.

Such a deep impression had the rejection of Quiteria made on Camacho's mind that it banished her immediately from his thoughts; and so the advice of the priest, who was a wise and kindly inclined man, overcame him, and by his words Camacho and his followers were pacified and tranquillised, and to prove it they covered their swords again, protesting against the malleability of Quiteria rather than the craftiness of Basilio; Camacho maintaining that, if Quiteria as a lady had such love for Basilio, she would have loved him also as a married woman, and that he should thank heaven for having taken her more than for having given her.

Camacho and his followers, therefore, being consoled and pacified, those on Basilio's side were appeased; and the rich Camacho, to show that he felt no resentment for the trick, and did not care about it, desired the festival to go on just as if he were married in reality. Neither Basilio, however, or his bride, or their followers would take any part in it, and they withdrew to Basilio's village; because the poor, if they are people of virtue and good sense, have those who follow, honour, and uphold them, just as the rich have those who flatter and dance for them. With them they took Don Quixote, regarding him as a man of high worth and bravery. Sancho alone had a cloud on his soul, because he found himself expelled from Camacho's fine feast and festival, which lasted until the night; and therefore dragged away, he reluctantly followed his master, who accompanied Basilio's group, and left behind him the great pots of food; although in his heart he took them with him, and his mind conjured up visions of the now nearly finished portions that he carried in the bucket, which reminded him of the glory and abundance of the good he was losing. And so, angry and unhappy although not hungry, without dismounting from his donkey he followed the footsteps of Rocinante.

CHAPTER 22

THE GRAND ADVENTURE OF THE CAVE OF MONTESINOS IN THE HEART OF LA MANCHA, WHICH THE BRAVE DON QUIXOTE BROUGHT TO A HAPPY ENDING

Great attention was shown to Don Quixote by the newly married couple, who felt themselves under an obligation to him for coming forward in defence of their cause; and they praised his wisdom to the same level as his courage, rating him as high as El Cid in arms, and Cicero in eloquence. Worthy Sancho enjoyed himself for three days at the expense of the pair, from whom they learned that the fake wound was not a scheme arranged with the fair Quiteria, but a trick of Basilio's, who calculated the result they had seen; he confessed, it is true, that he had disclosed his idea to some of his friends, so that at the proper time they could aid him with his purpose and insure the success of the deception.

"That," said Don Quixote, "which aims at a virtuous ending is not and should not be called deception;" and the marriage of lovers he maintained to be an excellent ending, reminding them, however, that love has no greater enemy than hunger and constant want; because love is all joy, satisfaction, and happiness, especially when the lover is in the possession of the object of his love, and poverty and want are the declared enemies of them both;" which he said to urge Señor Basilio to abandon the practice of those accomplishments he was skilled in, because although they brought him fame, they brought him no money, and to apply himself to the acquisition of wealth by legitimate industry, which will never fail those who are prudent and persevering. "The poor man who is a man of honour (if indeed a poor man can be called one) has a jewel when he has a good wife, and if she is taken from him, his honour is taken from him and butchered. The good woman who is a woman of honour, and whose husband is poor, deserves to be crowned with the glory and crowns of victory and triumph. Beauty by itself attracts the desires of all who observe it, and the royal eagles and soaring birds in flight view it as an elegant lure; but if beauty is accompanied by need and poverty, then the ravens and the other birds of prey attack it, and she who stands firm against such attacks deserves to be called the crown of her husband."

"Remember, prudent Basilio," added Don Quixote, "it was the opinion of a certain sage, I do not know whom, that there was no more than one good woman in the whole world for each man; and his advice was that each should think and believe that this one good woman was his own, and in this way he would live a happy life. I myself am not married, neither, so far, has it ever entered my thoughts to be so; nevertheless, I would risk giving advice to anyone who might ask for it, in regards to the method he should use to seek a wife he would be content to marry. The first thing I would recommend to him, would be to look for a good name rather than wealth, because a good woman does not win a good name merely by being good, but by letting it be seen that she is, and open looseness and freedom do much more damage to a woman's honour than secret immorality. If you take a good woman into your house it will be an easy matter to keep her good, and even to make her better; but if you take a bad one you will find it hard work to restore her, because it is no very easy matter to go from one extreme to the other. I do not say it is impossible, but I look at it as difficult."

Sancho, listening to all this, said to himself, "This master of mine, when I say anything that has weight and substance, says I could be a preacher, and go around the world giving fine sermons; but I say that, when he begins stringing proverbs together and giving advice not only could he be a preacher, but worth two of them, and go around the world preaching as much as he likes. The Devil takes you as a Knight, what a lot of things you know! I used to think in my heart that the only thing he knew was what belonged to chivalry; but there is nothing he doesn't have a finger on."

Sancho mumbled this somewhat aloud, and his master overheard him, and asked, "What are you muttering there, Sancho?"

"I'm not saying anything or muttering anything," said Sancho; "I was only saying to myself that I wish I had heard what you have just said now before I married; perhaps I'd say now, 'The ox that is loose licks himself well.'"

"Is your Teresa so bad then, Sancho?"

"She is not very bad," replied Sancho; "but she is not very good; at least she is not as good as I could wish."

"You do wrong, Sancho," said Don Quixote, "to speak badly of your wife; because after all she is the mother of your children."

"We are equal," returned Sancho; "because she speaks badly of me whenever she takes it into her head, especially when she is jealous; and even Satan himself could not put up with her then."

They remained for three days with the newly married couple, by whom they were entertained and treated like Kings. Don Quixote begged the fencing student to find him a guide to show him the way to the cave of Montesinos, as he had a great desire to enter it and see with his own eyes if the wonderful tales that were told about it all over the country were true. The student said he would get him a cousin of his own, a famous scholar, and one very much in to reading books of chivalry, who would have great pleasure in taking him to the mouth of the cave, and would show him the lakes of Ruidera, which were likewise famous all over La Mancha, and even all over Spain; and he assured him he would find him entertaining, because he was a youth who could write books good enough to be printed and dedicated to princes. The cousin finally arrived, leading a donkey, with a saddle covered with a multi-coloured cloth; Sancho saddled Rocinante, got his donkey ready, and stocked his saddle-bags, along with those belonging to the cousin; and so, calling on God's greatness and saying farewell to all, they left, taking the road toward the famous cave of Montesinos.

On the way Don Quixote asked the cousin what the type and character of his pursuits, job, and studies were, to which he replied that he was by profession a humanist, and that his pursuits and studies were making books for the press, all of great usefulness and no less entertainment to the nation. One was called "The Book of Outfits," in which he described seven hundred outfits, with their colours and symbols, from which gentlemen of the court might pick and choose any they liked for festivals and celebrations, without asking anyone, or confusing their brains to dress suitably for their purpose; "because," he said, "I give the jealous, the rejected, the forgotten, the absent, what will suit them, and fit them without fail. I have another book, as well, which I will call 'Transformation,' one of rare and original invention, for imitating Ovid in satire style. In it I show what the Tower of Seville and the Angel of Magdalena were, what the sewer in Cordova was, what the bulls of Castile and León were, the Sierra Morena, the streets and fountains in Madrid, not forgetting the insects which attack the tomatoes, and it contains all their parables, metaphors, and changes, so that they are amusing, interesting, and instructive, all at once. Another book I have which I call 'The Supplement to Polydore Vergil,' which discusses the invention of things, and is a work of great scholarship and research, because I establish and reveal elegantly some things of great importance which Polydore omitted to mention. He forgot to tell us who was the first man in the world that had a cold in his head, and who was the first to invent a cure for the French disease, but I accurately describe these, and quote more than twenty-five authors to prove it, so you can tell I have worked for a good purpose and that the book will be of service to the whole world."

Sancho, who had been very attentive to the cousin's words, said to him, "Tell me, señor - and God give you luck in printing your books - can you tell me (because of course you know, as you know everything) who was the first man that scratched his head? Because I think it must have been our father Adam."

"Must have been," replied the cousin; "because there is no doubt that Adam had a head of hair; and being the first man in the world he would have scratched himself sometimes."

"I think so too," said Sancho; "but now tell me, who was the first acrobat in the world?"

"Really, brother," answered the cousin, "I could not at this moment say positively without investigating it; I will look it up when I go back to where I have my books, and will satisfy your question the next time we meet, because this will not be the last time."

"Look here, señor," said Sancho, "don't trouble yourself about it, because I have just figured it out. The first acrobat in the world, you must know, was Lucifer, when they threw or dropped him out of heaven; because he went somersaulting into the bottomless pit."

"You are right my friend," said the cousin; and Don Quixote said, "Sancho, that question and answer are not your own; you have heard them from someone else."

"I come in peace, señor," said Sancho; "in good faith, if I start asking questions and answering, I'll go on from now until tomorrow morning. Actually! To ask foolish things and answer with nonsense I do not need to go looking for help from my neighbours."

"You have said more than you are aware of, Sancho," said Don Quixote; "Because there are some who weary themselves out in learning and proving things that, after they are known and proven, are not worth anything to the understanding or memory."

In this and other pleasant conversation the day went by, and that night they put up at a small tent from where it was no more than two miles to the cave of Montesinos. The cousin told Don Quixote, adding, that if he was sure he wanted to enter it, it would be necessary for him to provide himself with ropes, so that he could be tied and lowered into its depths. Don Quixote said that even if it reached to the bottomless pit he wanted to see where it went to; so they bought about two hundred meters of rope, and next day at two in the afternoon they arrived at the cave, the mouth of which was spacious and wide, but full of thorns, wild-fig bushes and prickly shrubs, so thick and tangled that they completely covered and closed the entrance.

On coming within sight of it the cousin, Sancho, and Don Quixote dismounted, and the first two immediately tied Don Quixote very firmly with the ropes, and as they were binding and wrapping him Sancho said to him, "Careful what you are about to do master of mine; don't go burying yourself alive, or putting yourself where you'll be like a bottle put to cool in a well; it's no business of yours to become the explorer of this cave, which must be worse than a Moorish dungeon."

"Tie me and be quiet," said Don Quixote, "because an exploration like this, friend Sancho, was reserved for me;" and the guide said, "I beg you, Señor Don Quixote, to observe carefully and examine with a hundred eyes everything that is within there; perhaps there may be some things for me to put into my book of 'Transformations.'"

"I have the drum and know how to beat it well enough," said Sancho Panza.

When he had said this and finished the tying (which was not only over the armour but over the jacket) Don Quixote observed, "It was careless of us not to have provided ourselves with a small bell to be tied on the rope close to me, the sound of which would show that I was still descending and alive; but as that is out of the question now, in God's hand it will be to guide me;" and so he fell on his knees and in a low voice gave a prayer to heaven, asking God to aid him and grant him success in this dangerous and untried adventure, and then exclaimed aloud, "O mistress of my actions and movements, illustrious and incomparable Dulcinea del Toboso, if the prayers and appeals of this unfortunate lover can reach your ears, by your unparalleled beauty I ask you to listen to them, because they ask you not to refuse me your favour and protection now that I stand in such need of them. I am about to sink, to plunge myself into the abyss that is here in front of me, only to let the world know that while you do this favour for me there is no impossibility I will not attempt and accomplish."

With these words he approached the cavern, and perceived that it was impossible to let himself down or create an entrance except by sheer force or by cutting a passage; so drawing his sword he began to demolish and cut away the brambles at the mouth of the cave, and by the noise of this a vast swarm of crows flew out of it so thick and so fast that they knocked Don Quixote down; and if he had been as much of a believer in divination as he was a Catholic Christian he would have taken it as a bad omen and declined to bury himself in such a place. He got up, however, and as there no more crows came, or bats that flew out at the same time with the crows, he lowered himself into the depths of the dreaded cave; and as he entered it Sancho sent his blessings, making a thousand crosses over his chest and saying, "God guide you, bloom and cream of Knighthood. There you go, you dare-devil of the earth, heart of steel, arm of brass; once more, God guide you and send you back safe, sound, and unhurt to the light this world you are leaving to bury yourself in the darkness;" and the cousin gave almost the same prayers.

Don Quixote kept calling to them to give him more rope, and they gave it little by little, and by the time the calls, which came out of the cave as out of a pipe, ceased to be heard they had let down the two hundred meters of rope. They were inclined to pull Don Quixote up again, as they could give him no more; however, they waited about half an hour, at the end of this time they began to gather in the rope again with great ease and without feeling any weight, which made them think Don Quixote was remaining below; and persuaded that it was so, Sancho cried excessively, and pulled in great haste in order to settle the question. When, however, they had come to, as it seemed, rather more than eighty meters they felt a weight, at which they were greatly delighted; and at last, at ten meters more, they saw Don Quixote distinctly, and Sancho called out to him, saying, "Welcome back, señor, because we had begun to think you were going to stop thay to start a family." But Don Quixote did not say a word, and drawing him out entirely they noticed he had his eyes shut and every appearance of being fast asleep.

They laid him on the ground and untied him, but still he did not wake up; however, they rolled him back and forwards and shook and pulled him about, so that after some time he came to himself, stretching himself just as if he were waking up from a deep and sound sleep, and looking about he said, "God forgive you, friends; you have taken me away from the sweetest and most delightful existence and spectacle that any human being ever enjoyed or witnessed. Now I know that all the pleasures of this life pass away like a shadow and a dream, or fade like a flower in the field!"

The cousin and Sancho Panza listened with deep attention to the words of Don Quixote, who spoke them as though he was in immense pain. They begged him to explain himself, and tell them what he had seen in that hell down there.

"Hell you call it?" said Don Quixote; "do not call it by such a name as that, because it does not deserve it, as you will soon see."

He then begged them to give him something to eat, as he was very hungry. They spread the cousin's cloth on the grass, and put the supplies from the saddle-bags down, and all three sitting down lovingly and sociably, had lunch and a supper all in one; and when the cloth was removed, Don Quixote of La Mancha said, "No one rise, and listen to me, my sons, both of you."

CHAPTER 23

THE WONDERFUL THINGS THE INCOMPARABLE DON QUIXOTE SAID HE SAW IN THE PROFOUND CAVE OF MONTESINOS, THE IMPOSSIBILITY AND MAGNITUDE OF WHICH SEEMED TO BE FICTIONAL

It was about four in the afternoon when the sun, veiled in clouds, with subdued light and tempered beams, enabled Don Quixote to say, without trouble or inconvenience, what he had seen in the cave of Montesinos to his two distinguished listeners, and he began as follows:

"About twelve or fourteen times a man's height down in this pit, on the right-hand side, there is a recess or space, large enough to contain a cart with its donkeys. A little light reaches it through some cracks or crevices, communicating with it and opening it to the surface of the earth. This recess or space I perceived when I was getting tired and disgusted at finding myself hanging suspended by the rope, travelling downwards into that dark region without any certainty or knowledge of where I was going, so I decided to enter it and rest myself for a while. I called out, telling you not to release any more rope until I asked you to, but you must not have heard me. I then gathered in the rope you were sending me, and making a coil out of it I sat myself on it, reflecting and considering what I should do to lower myself to the bottom, having no one to hold me up; and as I was deep in thought and confusion, suddenly and without provocation a profound sleep came over me, and when I least expected it, I do not know how, I awoke and found myself in the middle of the most beautiful, charming meadow that nature could create or the most lively human imagination could conceive. I opened my eyes, I rubbed them, and found I was not asleep but thoroughly awake. Nevertheless, I felt my head and chest to satisfy myself whether it was myself who was there or some empty deceptive ghost; but touching, feeling and the thoughts that passed through my mind, all convinced me that I was the same then and there that I am this moment. Next presenting itself to my sight was a royal palace or castle, with walls that seemed built of clear transparent crystal; and through two great doors that opened wide, I saw coming out and advancing towards me a revered old man, dressed in a long gown of mulberry-coloured twill that dragged on the ground. On his shoulders and chest, he had a green satin hood, and covering his head a black Milanese hat, and his snow-white beard fell below his waist. He carried no weapons, nothing but a rosary of beads bigger than hazelnuts, each tenth bead being a bit bigger like an ostrich egg; his manner, his step, his dignity and imposing presence had me mesmerised and in admiration. He approached me, and the first thing he did was to hug me closely, and then he said to me, 'For a long time now, O courageous Knight Don Quixote of La Mancha, we who are enchanted here in these solitudes have been hoping to see you, so that you may make known to the world what is shut and concealed in this deep cave, called the cave of Montesinos, which you have entered, an achievement reserved only for your invincible heart and astonishing courage alone to attempt. Come with me, illustrious sir, and I will show you the marvels hidden within this transparent castle, of which I am the commander and everlasting warden; because I am Montesinos himself, from whom the cave takes its name.'

"The instant he told me he was Montesinos, I asked him if the story they told in the world above was true, that he had taken out the heart of his great friend Durandarte from his chest with a little dagger, and carried it to the lady Belerma, as his friend at the point of death had commanded him to do. He said in reply that they spoke the truth in every respect except in regards to the dagger, because it was not a dagger, neither wat it little, but a shimmering sword sharper than an axe."

"That sword must have been made by Ramon de Hoces the Sevillian," said Sancho.

"I do not know," said Don Quixote; "it could not have been by that maker, however, because Ramon de Hoces was a man of the past, and the matter of Roncesvalles, where this mishap occurred, was a long time ago; but the question is of no great importance, nor does it affect or make any alteration to the truth or substance of the story."

"That is true," said the cousin; "continue, Señor Don Quixote, because I am listening to you with the greatest pleasure in the world."

"And with no less pleasure do I tell the story," said Don Quixote; "and so, to proceed - the respected Montesinos led me into the palace of crystal, where, in a lower room, strangely cool and entirely of alabaster rock, was an intricately formed marble tomb, on which I observed, stretched out at full length, a Knight, not of bronze, or marble, or jasper, as are seen on other tombs, but of actual flesh and bone. His right hand (which seemed to me somewhat hairy and bony, a sign of great strength in its owner) lay on the side of his heart; but before I could put any question to Montesinos, he, seeing me gazing at the tomb in amazement, said to me, 'This is my friend Durandarte, the flower and mirror of the true lovers and valiant Knights of his time. He is held enchanted here, as I myself and many others are, by that French enchanter Merlin, who, they say, is the devil's son; but my belief is, he is not the devil's son, but that he knows, as the saying is, a bit more than the devil. How or why he enchanted us, no one knows, but time will tell, and I suspect that time is not far away. What I find incredible is, that I know it to be as sure as I know it is now day, that Durandarte ended his life in my arms, and that, after his death, I took out his heart with my own hands; and it must have weighed more than two pounds, because, according to naturalists, he who has a large heart is more largely endowed with courage than he who has a small one. Then, as this is the case, and as the Knight really did die, how comes he now moans and sighs from time to time, as if he were still alive?'

"As he said this, the heartless Durandarte cried out in a loud voice:

O cousin Montesinos!
It was my last request of you,

When my soul had left the body,
And that when my death was true,

With your sword or dagger,
Cut the heart out from my chest,
And take it to Belerma,
This was my last request."

On hearing this, the esteemed Montesinos fell on his knees in front of the unhappy Knight, and with tearful eyes exclaimed, 'Long since, Señor Durandarte, my beloved friend, long since have I done what you asked me to do on that sad day when I lost you; I took out your heart as well as I could, not leaving an atom of it in your chest, I wiped it with a lace handkerchief, and I took the road with it, having first laid you in the earth with enough tears to wash and cleanse my hands of the blood that covered them after they wandered within your body; O cousin of my soul, at the first village I came to after leaving Roncesvalles, I sprinkled a little salt on your heart to keep it sweet, and bring it, if not fresh, at least preserved, into the presence of the lady Belerma, whom, together with you, myself, Guadiana your aide, the elder Ruidera and her seven daughters and two nieces, and many more of your friends and acquaintances, the sage Merlin has been keeping you enchanted here for many years; and although more than five hundred years have gone by, not one of us has died; however Ruidera and her daughters and nieces are missing, because of the tears they have shed, Merlin, out of the compassion he seems to have felt for them, changed them into lakes, which to this day in the world of the living, and in the province of La Mancha, are called the Lakes of Ruidera. The seven daughters belong to the Kings of Spain and the two nieces to the Knights of a very holy order called the Order of St. John. Guadiana your aide, likewise grieving over your fate, was changed into a river in his own name, but when he came to the surface and observed the sun of heaven, his pain was so great when finding he was leaving you, that he plunged into the depths of the earth; however, as he cannot help following his natural course, he from time to time rises to the surface and shows himself to the sun and the world. The lakes as mentioned send him their waters, and with these, and others that come to him, he makes a grand and imposing entrance into Portugal; but despite that, wherever he goes, he shows his depression and sadness, and takes no pride in breeding fish, only rough and tasteless ones, very different than those from the golden river Tagus. All this I tell you now, O friend of mine, I have told you many times before, and as you never answer, I fear that either you do not believe me, or do not hear me, and because of this God knows my grief. I now have news to give you, which, if does not serve to alleviate your suffering, will not in any way increase it. Know that you have here in front of you (open your eyes and you will see) that great Knight of whom the sage Merlin has foretold such great things; Don Quixote of La Mancha, who has again, and with a better purpose than in past times, revived in these days:

Knighthood, which has long since been forgotten, and by whose intervention and aid we may be disenchanted; because great deeds are reserved for great men.'

"'And if that may not be,' said the heartless Durandarte in a low and feeble voice, 'if that may not be, then, my friend, I say "patience;"' and turning over on his side, he relapsed into his former silence without speaking another word.

"And then we heard a great outcry, accompanied by deep sighs and bitter crying. I looked around, and through the crystal wall I saw passing through another room a march of two lines of fair ladies all mourning, and with white turbans of Turkish fashion on their heads. Behind, at the rear of these, there came a older lady, because from her dignity she appeared to be so, also covered in black, with a white veil so long and ample that it swept the ground. Her turban was twice as large as the largest of any of the others; her eyebrows met, her nose was rather flat, her mouth was large but with reddish lips, and her teeth, which she allowed a glimpse of at times, seemed to be rather separated or crooked, although as white as peeled almonds. She carried in her hands a fine cloth, and in it, as well as I could make out, a heart that had been preserved, which was so dehydrated and dried.

Montesinos told me that all those forming the march were the attendants of Durandarte and Belerma, who were enchanted there with their master and mistress, and that the last, she who carried the heart in the cloth, was the lady Belerma, who, with her ladies, four days in the week went marching and singing, or rather crying, chanting over the body and the miserable heart of his friend; and that if she appeared to me somewhat unattractive or not as beautiful as fame reported her to be, it was because of the bad nights and worse days that she passed in that enchantment, as I could see by the great dark circles under her eyes, and her sickly complexion; 'her yellowness, and the rings round her eyes,' he said, 'are not caused by the monthly weakness expected with women, because it had been many months and even years since she had any, but the grief her own heart suffers because of that which she holds in her hand continuously, and which recalls and brings back to her memory the sad fate of her lost lover; were it not for this, barely would the great Dulcinea del Toboso, so celebrated in all these parts, and even in the world, come close to her for beauty, grace, and elegance.'

"'Hold it there!' I said, 'tell your story as you should do, Señor Don Montesinos, because you know very well that all comparisons are detestable, and there is no occasion to compare one person with another; the incomparable Dulcinea del Toboso is what she is, and the lady Dona Belerma is what she is and has been, and that's enough.' To which he answered, 'Forgive me, Señor Don Quixote; I admit I was wrong and spoke incorrectly in saying that the lady Dulcinea could barely come close to the lady Belerma; because it was enough for me to have known, I do not know how, that you are her Knight, to make me bite my tongue before I compared her to anything except heaven itself.' After this apology which the great Montesinos made, my heart recovered itself from the shock I had received in hearing my lady compared with Belerma."

"Still I wonder," said Sancho, "did you not attack the old fellow and bruise every bone of him with kicks, and pluck his beard until you didn't leave a hair in it."

"No, Sancho, my friend," said Don Quixote, "it would not have been right for me to do that, because we are all bound to pay respect to the aged, even though they are not Knights, but especially to those who are, and have been enchanted."

"I cannot understand, Señor Don Quixote," remarked the cousin, "how it is that you, in such a short space of time as you have been below there, could have seen so many things, and said and answered so much."

"How long has it been since I went down?" asked Don Quixote.

"A little more than an hour," replied Sancho.

"That cannot be," returned Don Quixote, "because the night overtook me while I was there, and the day came, and it was night again and day again three times; so that, by my estimate, I have been in those remote regions three days without your awareness."

"My master must be right," replied Sancho; "because as everything that has happened to him is by enchantment, maybe what seems to us an hour would seem three days and nights there."

"Precisely," said Don Quixote.

"And did you eat anything during that time, señor?" asked the cousin.

"I never touched a crumb," answered Don Quixote, "nor did I feel hunger, or even think of it."

"And do the enchanted eat?" said the cousin.

"They neither eat," said Don Quixote; "or are they subject to great excrements, though it is thought that their nails, beards, and hair still grow."

"And do the enchanted sleep señor?" asked Sancho.

"Certainly not," replied Don Quixote; "at least, during those three days I was with them not one of them even closed an eye, and neither did I."

"The proverb, 'Tell me what company you keep and I'll tell you what you are,' sums up the point here," said Sancho; "you keep company with enchanted people that are always fasting and watching; no wonder, then, that you neither eat or sleep while you are with them? But forgive me, señor, if I say that out of all this you have now told us, let God take me - I was just about to say the devil - if I believe a single particle."

"What!" said the cousin, "has Señor Don Quixote been lying then? Even if he wished to he has not had enough time to imagine and put together such a heap of lies."

"I don't believe my master lies," said Sancho.

"If not, what do you believe?" asked Don Quixote.

"I believe," replied Sancho, "that this Merlin, or those enchanters who enchanted all the people you say you saw and spoke with down there, stuffed your imagination with all this you have been telling us, and all that is still to come."

"All that might be, Sancho," replied Don Quixote; "but it is not so, because everything that I have told you I saw with my own eyes, and touched with my own hands. But what will you say when I tell you now, how, among the countless other marvellous things Montesinos showed me (of which at leisure and at the appropriate time I will give you an account of in the course of our journey, because it would not be in place here), he showed me three country girls who went skipping and jumping like goats over the pleasant fields there, and the instant I saw them I recognised one to be the incomparable Dulcinea del Toboso, and the other two were those same country girls that were with her and that we spoke to on the road from El Toboso! I asked Montesinos if he knew them, and he told me he did not, but he thought they must be some enchanted ladies of distinction, because it was only a few days before that they had made their appearance in those meadows; but I was not surprised by that, because there were many other ladies there of the past and present, enchanted in various strange shapes, and among them I recognised Queen Guinevere and her lady Quintanona, she who poured the wine for Lancelot when he came from Britain."

When Sancho Panza heard his master say this he was ready die with laughter; because, as he knew the real truth about the fabricated enchantment of Dulcinea, in which he himself had been the enchanter and concocter of all the evidence, he made up his mind at last that, beyond all doubt, his master was out of his mind and raving mad, and so he said to him, "It was an evil hour, a worse season, and a sorrowful day, when you, dear master of mine, went down to the other world, and an unlucky moment when you met with Señor Montesinos, who has sent you back to us like this. You were well enough, here above ground, in your full senses, such as God had given you, delivering proverbs and giving advice at every turn, and not as you are now, talking the greatest nonsense that can be imagined."

"As I know you, Sancho," said Don Quixote, "I do not acknowledge your words."

"Neither do I yours sir," said Sancho, "whether you beat me or kill me because those I have spoken, I will say again if you don't correct and mend your own. But tell me, while there is still peace, how did you recognise lady Dulcinea; and if you spoke to her, what did you say, and what did she answer?"

"I recognised her," said Don Quixote, "by her wearing the same garments she wore when you pointed her out to me. I spoke to her, but she did not say a word in reply; on the contrary, she turned her back to me and ran, at such a pace that a crossbow shot could not have overtaken her. I wished to follow her, and would have done so if Montesinos had not told me not to take the trouble as it would be useless, particularly as the time was drawing near when it would be necessary for me to leave the cave. He told me, additionally, that in the course of time he would let me know how he and Belerma, and Durandarte, and all who were there, were to be disenchanted. But out of all I saw and observed down there, what gave me the most pain was, that while Montesinos was speaking to me, one of the two companions of the unfortunate

Dulcinea approached me without me noticing her coming, and with tears in her eyes said to me, in a low, agitated voice, 'My lady Dulcinea del Toboso kisses your hands, and asks you to do her the favour of letting her know how you are; and, being in great need, she also asks you as sincerely as she can to be so kind and lend her half a dozen gold coins, or as much as you may have on you; and she promises to repay them very promptly.' I was amazed and surprised by such a message, and turning to Señor Montesinos I asked him, 'Is it possible, Señor Montesinos, that people of distinction under enchantment can be in need?' To which he replied, 'Believe me, Señor Don Quixote, that which is called need is to be found everywhere, and penetrates all residences and reaches everyone, and does not spare even the enchanted; and as the lady Dulcinea del Toboso sent her lady to beg for those six gold coins, there is nothing else to do than to give them to her, because no doubt she must be in some trouble.' 'I will not take any begging from her,' I replied, 'neither can I give her what she asks for, because all I have is four gold coins; (those which you, Sancho, gave me the other day to give to the poor I met along the road), and I said, 'Tell your mistress, my dear, that I am saddened to the heart because of her distress, and wish I was a rich wealthy man to remedy it, and she should know that I cannot be in health while deprived of the happiness of seeing her and enjoying her discreet conversation, and that I ask her as sincerely as I can, to allow herself to be seen and spoken to by this man, her captive servant and lonely Knight. Tell her, too, that when she least expects it she will hear it announced that I have made an oath and vow to take no rest, and to roam the seven regions of the earth more thoroughly than the Prince Don Pedro of Portugal ever roamed them, until I have disenchanted her.' And the lady's answer to me was 'All that and more, you owe my lady,' and taking the four gold coins, instead giving a curtsey she leapt two full yards into the air."

"Good God!" exclaimed Sancho aloud, "is it possible that these things can exist in the world, and that enchanters and enchantments can have such a power to have changed my master's good senses into a craze so full of absurdity! O señor, for God's sake, consider yourself, have care for your honour, and give no credit to this silly stuff that has left you deprived and short of brain."

"You talk in this way because you love me, Sancho," said Don Quixote; "and not being experienced in the world, everything that has some difficulty seems to you to be an impossibility; but time will pass, as I said before, and I will tell you some of the things I saw down there which will make you believe what I have said now, the truth of which requires neither a reply or question."

CHAPTER 24

A THOUSAND INSIGNIFICANT MATTERS, AS TRIVIAL AS THEY ARE NECESSARY TO THE CORRECT UNDERSTANDING OF THIS GREAT HISTORY

He who translated this great history from the original written by its first author, Cide Hamete Benengeli, says that when coming to the chapter giving the adventures of the cave of Montesinos he found written on the margin of it, in Hamete's own hand writing, these exact words:

"I cannot convince or persuade myself that everything that is written in the preceding chapter could have precisely happened to the courageous Don Quixote; and for this reason, all the adventures that have occurred up to the present have been possible and probable; but in regards to this one of the cave, I see no way of accepting it as true, as it passes all reasonable boundaries. For me to believe that Don Quixote could lie, when he is the most truthful gentleman and the noblest Knight of his time, is impossible; he would not have told a lie even if he were shot to death with arrows. On the other hand, I reflect that he told the story with all the circumstances detailed, and that he could not have in such a short space of time fabricated such a vast array of absurdities; if, then, this adventure seems fictional, it is no fault of mine; and so, without affirming its fiction or its truth, I write it down. Decide for yourself with your wisdom, reader; because I am not bound, neither is it in my power, to do more; although they say that at the time of his death he retracted it, and said he had invented it, thinking it harmonised and corresponded with the adventures he had read of in his histories." And then he goes on to say:

The cousin was amazed as well at Sancho's boldness as at the patience of his master, and concluded that the good mood Don Quixote displayed arose from the happiness he felt after having seen his lady Dulcinea, even enchanted as she was; because otherwise the words and language Sancho has used deserved punishing; because he seemed to him to have been rather disrespectful to his master, and he said, "I, Señor Don Quixote of La Mancha, look at the time I have spent travelling with you as very well spent, because I have gained four things in its course; the first is that I have got to know you, which I consider great good fortune; the second, I have learned what the cave of Montesinos contains, together with the transformations of Guadiana and the lakes of Ruidera; which will be of use to me for the Spanish pride that I have; the third, I have discovered the antiquity of cards, that they were in use at least in the time of Charlemagne, as may be inferred from the words you say Durandarte spoke when, at the end of that long spell while Montesinos was talking to him, he woke up and said, 'Patience.' This phrase and expression he could not have learned while he was enchanted, but only before he had become so, in France, and in the time of the already mentioned emperor Charlemagne. And this demonstration is just the thing for the next book I am writing, the 'Supplement to Polydore Vergil on the Invention of Antiquities;' because I believe he never thought of inserting that about cards in his book, as I intend to do in mine, and it will be a matter of great importance, particularly when I can cite such a serious and genuine authority as Señor Durandarte. And the fourth thing is, that I have ascertained the source of the river Guadiana, up until now unknown to mankind."

"You are right," said Don Quixote; "but I would like to know, if by God's favour they grant you a licence to print those books of yours (which I doubt) who do you intend to dedicate them to?"

"There are lords and ladies in Spain to whom they can be dedicated to," said the cousin.

"Not many," said Don Quixote; "not that they are unworthy of it, but because they do not care to accept books and incur the obligation of giving something in return that seems due to the author's labour and thoughtfulness. One prince I know who makes up for all the rest, and more - how much more, I dare to say, because perhaps I might stir up envy in many; so let this wait for a more convenient time, and let us go and look for some place to shelter ourselves tonight."

"Not far from here," said the cousin, "there is a monastery, where a hermit lives, who they say was a soldier, and who has the reputation of being a good Christian and a very intelligent and charitable man. Close to the monastery he has a small house which he built at his own cost, but although it is small it is large enough to welcome guests."

"Has this hermit got any hens?" asked Sancho.

"Few hermits are without them," said Don Quixote; "because those we see these days are not like the hermits of the Egyptian deserts who were covered in palm-leaves, and lived on the roots of the earth. But do not think that by praising these I am disparaging the others; all I mean to say is that the sacrifices of those of the present day do not compare to the self-denial and seriousness of former times; but it does not follow from this that they are all unworthy; at best I think they are; and the worst I think is a hypocrite who pretends to be good does less harm than the open sinner."

At this point they saw approaching a man on foot, advancing at a rapid pace, and beating a donkey loaded with lances and axes. When he arrived, he greeted them and passed by without stopping. Don Quixote called him, "Stay, good fellow; you seem to be making more haste than suits that donkey."

"I cannot stop, señor," answered the man; "because the weapons you see here are to be used tomorrow, so I cannot not delay; God be with you. But if you want to know what I am carrying them for, I am going to stay tonight at the inn that is beyond the monastery, and if you are going the same way you will find me there, and I will tell you some interesting things; once more may God be with you;" and he continued on his donkey at such a pace that Don Quixote had no time to ask him what these interesting things were that he intended to tell them; and as he was somewhat inquisitive, and always tortured by his anxiety to learn something new, he decided to leave immediately, and go and spend the night at the inn instead of stopping at the monastery, where the cousin wanted them to go. Accordingly, they mounted and all three took the direct road to the inn, which they reached a little before nightfall. On the road the cousin proposed they should go to the hermitage to drink something. The instant Sancho heard this he steered his donkey toward it, and Don Quixote and the cousin did the same; but it seems Sancho's bad luck ordered it that the hermit was not home, because a student of the hermit in the monastery told them so.

They asked for some of the best drink available, to which she replied her master had none, but if they liked cheap water she would give it to them with great pleasure.

"If I wanted any in water," said Sancho, "there are wells along the road where I could have had enough of it. Ah, Camacho's wedding, and abundant house of Don Diego, how often I miss you!"

Leaving the monastery, they pushed on towards the inn, and a little further they came to a youth who was pacing along in front of them at no great speed, so they overtook him. He carried a sword over his shoulder, and a bundle of his clothes, probably his trousers, and a shirt or two; because he had on a short jacket of velvet with a gloss like satin on it in places, and had his shirt on with no trousers to tuck it into; his socks were made of silk, and his shoes square-toed as they wear them at court. His age might have been eighteen or nineteen; he had a cheerful expression, and an appearance to all of an active fellow, and he went along singing songs to charm the wearisomeness of the road. As they came to him he was just finishing one, which the cousin learnt by heart and they say it went like this:

I'm off to the wars,
For my lack of pence,
Oh, if I had money,
Maybe I'd show more sense.

The first to speak to him was Don Quixote, who said, "You travel very light-heartedly, sir suave; where are you heading, may we ask, if it is your pleasure to tell us?"

To which the youth replied, "The heat and my poverty are the reason of my travelling so light-heartedly, and I am heading to the wars."

"Poverty?" asked Don Quixote; "the heat I can understand."

"Señor," replied the youth, "in this bundle I carry velvet trousers to match this jacket; if I wear them out on the road, I will not be able to make a decent appearance in them in the city, and I do not have the money to buy others; and so for this reason, as well as to keep myself cool, I am making my way in this manner to catch up with some groups of soldiers that are about 12 miles away, in which I will enlist myself, and there will be no lack of trains to travel to the place of embarking, which they say will be Carthagena; I would rather have the King for a master, and serve him in the wars, than serve a poor man."

"Are you offered a payment for joining?" asked the cousin.

476

"If I had been in the service of some grand man of Spain or person of distinction," replied the youth, "I would have been safe to get it; because that is the advantage of serving good masters, and those that retire from the servants' hall get a good pension. But I, to my misfortune, always served hunters and adventurers, whose wages were so dismal and insufficient that half went on paying for the starching of my shirts; it would be a miracle indeed if an unknown volunteer like me ever got anything like a reasonable reward."

"And tell me, for heaven's sake," asked Don Quixote, "is it possible, my friend, that all the time you served you never got any uniform?"

"They gave me two," replied the boy; "but just as when one quits a religious community before becoming a priest, they strip him of the dress of the order and give him back his own clothes, like my masters did to me; because as soon as the business they came to court for was finished, they went home and took back the uniforms they had given merely for show."

"What meanness!" said Don Quixote; "but despite that, consider yourself happy in having left court with as worthy an objective as you have, because there is nothing on earth more honourable or profitable than serving, first of all God, and then one's King and natural lord, particularly in the profession of was, by which, if not more wealth, at least more honour is to be won than by men of letters, as I have said many times before; because although letters may have founded more great houses than war, still those founded by war have a superiority over those founded by letters, and a certain magnificence belonging to them that distinguishes them above all. And keep in mind what I am now about to say to you, because it will be of great use and comfort to you in time of trouble; it is, not to let your mind dwell on the adverse circumstances that may occur to you; because the worst of all is death, and if it is a good death, the best of all is to die. They asked Julius Caesar, the heroic Roman emperor, what was the best death. He answered, that which is unexpected, which comes suddenly and unforeseen; and although he answered like a pagan, and one without the knowledge of the true God, yet, as far as sparing our feelings is concerned, he was right; because suppose you are killed in the first engagement, whether by a cannon ball or blown up by a mine, what does it matter? It is only dying, and all is over; and according to Terence, a soldier is more honourable dead in battle, than alive and safe in flight; and the good soldier gains fame in proportion to how obedient he is to his captains and those in command over him. And remember, my son, that it is better for the soldier to smell of gunpowder than of a coward, and that if you make it to your old age in this honourable calling, although you may be covered with wounds and crippled, it will not come without honour, and no poverty cannot weaken that; especially now that provisions are being made for supporting and relieving old and disabled soldiers; because it is not right to deal with them in the same manner of those who set free and get rid of their slaves when they are old and useless, and, turning them out of their houses under the pretence of making them free, make them slaves to hunger, from which they cannot expect to be released from except by death. But for the present I won't say more than you travel behind me on my horse as far as the inn, and drink with me there, and tomorrow you will pursue your journey, and God give you the good speed your intentions deserve."

The boy politely declined the invitation to mount Rocinante but said he would drink with him at the inn; and here they say Sancho said to himself, "God; is it possible that a man who can say things as good as he has said just now, can say he saw all the impossible absurdities he reports about in the cave of Montesinos? Well, well, we shall see."

And now, just as night was falling, they reached the inn, and it was not without satisfaction as Sancho perceived his master took it for a real inn, and not for a castle as usual. The instant they entered Don Quixote asked the landlord about the man with the lances and axes, and was told that he was in the stable feeding his donkey; which was what Sancho and the cousin both proceeded to do for theirs, and gave the best place in the stable to Rocinante.

CHAPTER 25

THE HARSH ADVENTURE, AND THE AMUSING ONE OF THE PUPPET-MAN, TOGETHER WITH THE MEMORABLE DIVINATIONS OF THE APE

Don Quixote's bread would not bake, as the common saying is, until he had heard and learned the curious things promised by the man who carried the weapons. He went to seek him where the innkeeper said he was and having found him, asked him to now say what he had to say in answer to the question he had asked him on the road. "The tale of my wonders must be taken more leisurely and not standing," said the man; "let me finish feeding my donkey, good sir; and then I'll tell you things that will astonish you."

"Don't wait for that," said Don Quixote; "I'll help you with it," and so he did, sifting the barley for him and cleaning out his place in the stable; a degree of humility which made the other feel bound to tell him with good grace what he had asked; so seating himself on a bench, with Don Quixote beside him, and the cousin, the boy, Sancho Panza, and the landlord for an audience, he began his story in this way:

"You must know that in a village four and a half miles from this inn, it so happened that one of the members of the local council, by the trickery and dishonesty of a servant girl of his (which I will not go into now), lost a donkey; and although he did all he possibly could to find it, it was all to no avail. A fortnight might have gone by, as the story goes, since the donkey had been missing, when, as the council member who had lost it was standing in the plaza, another council member of the same town said to him:

'Pay me for good news; your donkey has turned up.'

'That I will, and well,' said the other; 'but tell us, where has he turned up?'

'In the forest,' said the finder; 'I saw him this morning without a saddle or harness of any sort, and so lean that it went to my heart to see him that way. I tried to encourage him and bring him to you, but he is already so wild and shy that when I went near him he ran into the thickest part of the forest. If you want to go back and look for him with me, let me take this donkey here back to my house and I'll be back soon.'

'You will be doing me a great favour,' said the owner of the donkey, 'and I'll try to pay it back in the correct currency.'

It is the way, with all these circumstances, and in the exact same way I am telling it now, that those who know all about the subject tell the story. Well then, the two council men set off on foot, arm in arm, to the forest, and coming to the place where they hoped to find the donkey they could not find him, neither was he to be seen anywhere they searched. Seeing, then, that there was no sign of him, the council man who had seen him said to the other:

'Look; a plan has occurred to me, by which, beyond a doubt, we will manage to discover the animal, even if he is somewhere in the belly of the earth, not to say the forest. Here it is. I can make a loud sound like a donkey, and if you can a little, it's as good as done.'

'A little did you say?' said the other; 'God, I can be so loud, I will not give in to anybody, not even to the donkeys themselves.'

'We'll soon see,' said the second council man, 'because my plan is that you go one side of the forest, and I the other; and every now and then you will make the sound and I will make the sound; and the donkey will have to hear us, and answer us if he is in the forest.'

To which the owner of the donkey replied, 'It's an excellent plan, I say, and worthy of your great genius;' and the two separating as agreed, it so happened that they made sounds almost at the same moment, and each, deceived by the sound of the other, ran to look, thinking the donkey had turned up at last. When they came in sight of one another, the one who lost the donkey said:

'Is it possible, that it was not my donkey then?'

'No, it was I,' said the other. 'Well then, I can tell you,' said the donkey's owner, 'that between you and a donkey there is not an atom of difference as far as the sound goes, because I never in all my life saw or heard anything more natural.'

'Those praises and compliments belong to you more than to me,' said the inventor of the plan; 'because, I swear to the God that made me, the tone you have got is deep, your voice is well kept in time and pitch, and your finishing notes come thick and fast; in fact, I declare myself beaten, and yield, and give in to you in this rare accomplishment.'

'Well then,' said the owner, 'I'll set a higher value on myself for the future, and consider that I know something, as I have an excellence of some sort; because although I always thought I could make a donkey call well, I never thought I matched the pitch of perfection as you say.'

'And I say as well,' said the second, 'that there are rare gifts being wasted in the world, and that are poorly given to those who don't know how to make good use of them.'

'Ours,' said the owner of the donkey, 'unless it is in cases like this we have now in hand, cannot be of any service to us, and even in this God allows them to be of some use.'

They separated, and started donkey calling again, but every moment they were deceiving one another, and coming to meet one another again, until they arranged by way of a sign, so as to know that it was themselves and not the donkey, to make two calls, one after the other. In this way, doubling the calls at every step, they made the complete circuit of the forest, but the lost donkey never gave them an answer or even the sign of one. How could the poor donkey have answered, when, in the thickest part of the forest, they found him devoured by wolves? As soon as he saw him his owner said:

'I was wondering why he did not answer, because if he wasn't dead he would have called when he heard us, or he would have been no donkey; but for the sake of having heard you donkey call to such perfection, I count the trouble I have taken to look for him well spent, even though I have found him dead.'

'he is in good hands,' said the other; 'if God calls, the follower is not far away.'

So they returned unhappy and rough to their village, where they told their friends, neighbours, and acquaintances what had happened to them in their search for the donkey, each praising the other's donkey calling. The whole story was spread abroad through the villages of the neighbourhood; and the devil, who never sleeps, with his love for introducing disagreement and spreading conflict everywhere, blowing disruption about and making arguments out of nothing, contrived to make the people of the other towns make donkey calls whenever they saw anyone from our village, as if to throw the donkey calling of our councilmen in our faces. Then everyone started to do it, and donkey calling spread from one town to another in such a way that the men of the donkey calling town are as easy to be known as blacks are to be known from whites, and the unlucky joke has gone so far that several times the mocked have come out with weapons to battle with the ridiculers, and no King or Queen, fear or shame, can remedy this. Tomorrow or the day after, I believe, the men of my town, that is, of the donkey calling town, are going to meet another village on the field two miles away from ours, one of those that persecute us most; and so we can go well prepared I have bought these lances and axes you have seen. These are the interesting things I told you I had to tell, and if you don't think they are interesting, I have got no others;" and with this the worthy fellow brought his story to a close.

Just at this moment there came through the gate of the inn a man entirely covered in leather, trousers, and jacket, who said in a loud voice, "Señor host, do you have a room? The divining ape and the show about the Release of Melisendra are coming."

"Great God!" said the landlord, "it's Master Pedro! We're in for a grand night!"

I forgot to mention that Master Pedro had his left eye and nearly half his cheek covered with a patch of green material, showing that something affected that side.

"You are welcome, Master Pedro," continued the landlord; "but where are the ape and the show, because I don't see them?"

"They are close by," said the man in the leather, "but I came first to know if there was any room."

"I'd make the Duke of Alva himself clear off to make room for Master Pedro," said the landlord; "bring in the ape and the show; there's company in the inn tonight that will pay to see the cleverness of the ape."

"Absolutely," said the man with the patch; "I'll lower the price, and be well satisfied if I only receive my expenses; and now I'll go back and hurry with the cart to bring the ape and the show;" and with these words he left the inn.

Don Quixote immediately asked the landlord who this Master Pedro was, and what the show and the ape he had with him were; to which the landlord replied, "This is a famous puppet-man, who for some time has been going around Mancha de Aragon, exhibiting a show about the release of Melisendra by the famous Don Gaiferos, one of the best-represented stories that have been seen in this part of the Kingdom for many years; he has also got with him an ape with the most extraordinary gift ever seen in an ape or imagined in a human being; because if you ask him anything, he listens attentively to the question, and then jumps on his master's shoulder, and getting close to his ear tells him the answer which Master Pedro then relays. He says a lot more about the past than about things to come; and although he does not always hit the exact truth in every case, most times he is not far wrong, so that he makes us think he has got the devil in him. He gets two coins for every question if the ape answers; I mean if his master answers for him after he has whispered into his ear; and so it is believed that this same Master Pedro is very rich. He is a 'polite man' as they say in Italy, and good company, and leads the finest life in the world; talks more than six people, drinks more than a dozen, and all through his tongue, his ape, and his show."

Master Pedro now came back, and in a cart followed the show and the ape - a big one, without a tail and with bare buttocks, but not vicious-looking. As soon as Don Quixote saw him, he asked him:

"Can you tell me, sir fortune-teller, what fish do we catch, and how will it go for us? See, here are my two coins," and he asked Sancho to give them to Master Pedro; but he answered for the ape and said, "Señor, this animal does not give any answer or information concerning things that are to come; but when it comes to the past he knows something, and more or less about things of the present."

"God," said Sancho, "I would not give a penny to be told what my past is about, because who knows that better than I do myself? And to pay for being told what I know would be mighty foolish. But as you know about the present, here are my two coins, and tell me, most excellent sir ape, what is my wife Teresa Panza doing now, and what is she amusing herself with?"

Master Pedro refused to take the money, saying, "I will not receive payment in advance or until the service has been first given;" and then with his right hand he gave a couple of slaps on his left shoulder, and with one jump the ape perched himself on it, and putting his mouth to his master's ear began chattering his teeth rapidly; and having kept this up as long as one could say philosophy, with another jump he landed on the ground, and the same instant Master Pedro ran in great haste and fell on his knees in front of Don Quixote, and holding his legs exclaimed, "These legs I embrace as I would embrace the two pillars of Hercules, O illustrious reviver of Knighthood, so long consigned to oblivion! O not praised enough, exalted Knight, Don Quixote of La Mancha, courage of the faint-hearted, prop of the weak, arm of the fallen, supervisor and adviser of all who are unfortunate!"

Don Quixote was amazed, Sancho astounded, the cousin shocked, the boy astonished, the man from the donkey calling town open-mouthed, the landlord in confusion, and, in short, everyone astounded by the words of the puppet-man, who went on to say, "And you, worthy Sancho Panza, the best aide and aide to the best Knight in the world! Have good cheer, because your good wife Teresa is well, and she is at this moment sifting a pound of flax; and on her left she has a jug with a broken spout that holds a good drop of wine, with which she comforts herself during her work."

"That I can well believe," said Sancho. "She is a lucky one, and if it was not for her jealousy I would not change her for Andandona, who by my master's account was a very clever and worthy woman; my Teresa is one of those that won't let themselves want anything."

"Now I declare," said Don Quixote, "he who reads much and travels much sees and knows a great deal. I say this because what amount of persuasion could have persuaded me that there are apes in the world that can divine as I have seen now with my own eyes? Because I am that very Don Quixote of La Mancha this worthy animal refers to, although he has gone too far in my praise; but whatever I may be, I thank heaven that it has awarded me with a tender and compassionate heart, always willing to do good to all and harm to none."

"If I had money," said the boy, "I would ask señor ape what will happen to me on the journey I am making."

To this Master Pedro, who had by this time risen from Don Quixote's feet, replied, "I have already said that this ape does not answer in regards to the future; but if he did, not having money would be no trouble, because to please Señor Don Quixote, here present, I would give up all the profit in the world. And now, because I have promised, and to offer him pleasure, I will set up my show and offer entertainment to all who are in the inn, without any charge whatsoever." As soon as he heard this, the landlord, delighted beyond measure, pointed to a place where the show could be set up, which was done immediately.

Don Quixote was not very satisfied with the divinations of the ape, as he did not think it was appropriate that an ape should divine anything, either past, present or future; so while Master Pedro was arranging the show, he went with Sancho into a corner of the stable, where, without being overheard by anyone, he said to him:

"Look here, Sancho, I have been seriously thinking about this ape's extraordinary gift, and have come to the conclusion that beyond a doubt this Master Pedro, his master, has a deal, implicit or explicit, with the devil."

"If the agreement is from the devil," said Sancho, "it must be a very dirty agreement no doubt; but what good can it do for Master Pedro to have such agreements?"

"You do not understand me, Sancho," said Don Quixote; "I only mean he must have made some agreement with the devil to infuse this power into the ape, so he could make his living, and after he has become rich he will give him his soul, which is what the enemy of mankind wants; this I am led to believe by observing that the ape only answers about things from the past or present, and the devil's knowledge extends no further; because the future he knows only by guesswork; because it is reserved for God alone to know the times and the seasons, and for him there is neither past or future; all is present. This being as it is, it is clear that this ape speaks by the spirit of the devil; and I am astonished they have not condemned him to the Holy Office, and put questions to him, and forced it out of him with whose power it is that he divines; because it is certain this ape is not an astrologer; neither his master nor does he set up, or knows how to set up the courts, which are now so common in Spain that there is not a man, or boy, that would not like to be part of it as eagerly as they would like to pick up a jack when playing cards, bringing however to nothing the marvellous truth of this science by their lies and ignorance. I know a lady who asked one of these schemers whether her little dog would breed, and how many and of what colour the little puppies would be. To which señor astrologer, answered that the bitch would give birth, and would drop three puppies, one green, another bright red, and the third multi-coloured, provided she conceived between eleven and twelve either in the day or night, and on a Monday or Saturday; but as things turned out, two days after this the bitch died, and señor planet-ruler had the credit everywhere of being the most profound astrologer, as most of these planet-rulers are considered."

"Still," said Sancho, "I would be glad if you would make Master Pedro ask his ape whether what happened to you in the cave of Montesinos is true; because, begging you pardon, I, for my part, believe it to have been all nonsense, or at any rate something you dreamt."

"That may be," replied Don Quixote; "I will do what you suggest; as I have my own doubts about it."

At this point Master Pedro came in search of Don Quixote, to tell him the show was now ready and to come and see it, because it was worth seeing. Don Quixote explained his wish, and begged him to ask his ape to tell him whether certain things which had happened to him in the cave of Montesinos were dreams or realities, because to him they appeared to be a bit of both. Master Pedro, without answering, went back to get the ape, and, having placed it in front of Don Quixote and Sancho, said:

"See here, señor ape, this gentleman wishes to know whether certain things which happened to him in the cave called Montesinos were false or true." Making the usual sign the ape climbed on his left shoulder and seemed to whisper in his ear, and Master Pedro said immediately, "The ape says that the things you saw or that happened to you in the cave are, are part true, part false; and that he only knows this and no more in regards the question; but if you would like to know more, next Friday he will answer everything you ask him, because at the moment his virtue is exhausted, and will not return to him until Friday, as he has said."

"Did I not say, señor," said Sancho, "that I could not bring myself to believe that all you said about the adventures in the cave were true, or even half of it?"

"The course of events will tell, Sancho," replied Don Quixote; "time, that discloses all things, leaves nothing that it does not drag into the light of day, even if it is buried in the belly of the earth. But enough of that for now; let us go and watch Master Pedro's show, because I am sure there must be something novel in it."

"Something!" said Master Pedro; "this show of mine has sixty thousand novel things in it; let me tell you, Señor Don Quixote, it is one of the best-worth-seeing things in the world to this day; but actions speak louder than words, so let's begin, because it is getting late, and we have a great deal to do, to say and to show."

Don Quixote and Sancho obeyed him and went to where the show was ready and uncovered, surrounded with lighted wax candles which made it look glorious and bright. When they came, Master Pedro concealed himself inside it, because he had to work the puppets, and a boy, a servant of his, stood outside to act as showman and explain the mysteries of the exhibition, having a wand in his hand to point to the figures as they came out. And so, all who were in the inn were arranged in front of the show, some of them standing, and Don Quixote, Sancho, the boy, and cousin given the best places, the interpreter began to say what can be heard or seen by whoever reads or hears the next chapter.

CHAPTER 26

THE AMUSING ADVENTURE OF THE PUPPET-SHOW

All who were watching the show were listening attentively to the interpreter expressing its surprises, when drums and trumpets were heard to sound inside it – making a cannon like sound. The noise was soon over, and then the boy raised his voice and said, "This true story which is here represented to you is taken word for word from the French archives and from the Spanish poems that are on everyone's lips. Its subject is the release by Señor Don Gaiferos of his wife Melisendra, when she was a captive in Spain in the hands of the Moors, in the city of Sansuena, as it was called then but is now called Saragossa; and there you can see how Don Gaiferos is playing at the tables, just as they sing:

Don Gaiferos playing at the tables sits,
Because Melisendra is forgotten now.

And that person that appears there with a crown on his head and a sceptre in his hand is the Emperor Charlemagne, the supposed father of Melisendra, who, angered to see his son-in-law's inaction and indifference, comes in to reprimand him. Observe the forcefulness and energy he reproaches him with, you would believe he was going to give him half a dozen strikes with his sceptre; and indeed there are authors who say that he did, and thorough ones too; and after having said a great deal to him about endangering his honour by not achieving the release of his wife, he said, so the story goes: I've said enough, do it now.

Observe how the emperor turns away, and leaves Don Gaiferos furious; and you see now, in a burst of anger, he throws the table and the board far from him and calls for his armour, and asks his cousin Don Roland to borrow his sword, Durindana, and how Don Roland refuses to lend it, offering him instead his company in the difficult adventure he is undertaking; but he, in his spirit and anger, will not accept it, and says that he alone will suffice to rescue his wife, even if she were imprisoned deep in the centre of the earth, and with this he leaves to arm himself and to go on his journey immediately. Now turn your eyes toward that tower over there, which is supposed to be one of the fortresses of the moors in Saragossa, now called the Aljaferia; that lady who appears on that balcony dressed in Moorish attire is the incomparable Melisendra, many times she used to gaze from there toward France, and seek comfort in her captivity by thinking of Paris and her husband. Observe, as well, a new incident which is now occurring, perhaps which has never been seen before. Do you not see that Moor, who silently and stealthily, with his finger on his lip, is approaching Melisendra from behind? Observe now how he prints a kiss on her lips, and what a hurry she is in to spit, and wipe them with her white sleeve, and how she cries, and pulls her fair hair as though it were to blame for the wrong. Observe, as well, that the noble Moor in that corridor is King Marsilio of Sansuena, who, having seen the Moor's disrespect, immediately orders him (although he's relative and a great favourite of his) to be detained and given two hundred whippings, while carried through the streets of the city according to the customs, with announcers going first in front of him and officers of justice behind; and here you see them come out to execute the sentence, although the offence has been barely committed; because among the Moors there are no prosecutions or imprisonments as with us."

Here Don Quixote called out, "Child, child, go straight on with your story, and don't run into curves and slants, because to establish a fact clearly there is great deal of proof and confirmation needed;" and Master Pedro said from within, "Boy, stick to your text and do as the gentleman asks you; it's the best plan; maintain your simple song, and don't attempt harmonies, because they are likely to break down from being over tuned."

"I will," said the boy, and he went on to say, "This figure that you see on horseback, covered with a cloak, is Don Gaiferos. His wife, now redressed for the insult of the amorous Moor, taking her stand on the balcony of the tower with a calmer and more tranquil expression, has perceived him without recognising him; and she calls out for her husband, supposing this Knight to be some traveller, and says aloud the poem that goes:

If you, sir Knight, are heading to France,
Ask for Gaiferos -

I will not repeat the rest here because wordiness causes disgust; suffice it to observe that by her joyful gestures Melisendra shows us she has recognised him; and what is more, we now see her lower herself from the balcony to place herself on the hips of her good husband's horse. But ah! unhappy lady, the edge of her coat has caught on one of the bars of the balcony and she is left hanging in the air, unable to reach the ground. But you see how compassionate heaven sends aid in our times of need; Don Gaiferos advances, and without caring if the coat is torn or not, he holds her and by force brings her to the ground, and then with one lift places her on the hips of his horse, straddling it like a man, and asks her to hold on tight and wrap her arms around his neck, crossing them on his chest so she does not fall, because the lady Melisendra was not used to that style of riding. You see, as well, how the sound of the horse shows his satisfaction with the gracious and beautiful burden he carries: his lord and lady. You see how they turn round and leave the city, and in joy and gladness take the road to Paris. Go in peace, incomparable pair of true lovers! May you reach your long-awaited homeland in safety, and may fortune interrupt with no impediment to your prosperous journey; may the eyes of your friends and family behold you enjoying in peace and tranquillity the remaining days of your life - and that there may be as many as those of the King!"

Here Master Pedro called out again and said, "Simplicity, boy! None of your excess; all exaggeration is bad."

The interpreter made no answer, but went on to say, "There were no lack of eyes, that see everything, to see Melisendra come down and mount the horse, and news of this was taken to King Marsilio, who immediately gave orders to sound the alarm; see what was happening, and how the city is drowned with the sound of bells ringing in the towers of all the mosques."

"No, actually" said Don Quixote; "on that point about the bells Master Pedro is very inaccurate, because bells are not in use among the Moors; only drums, and a kind of small trumpet somewhat like ours; to ring bells like this in Sansuena is unquestionably great absurdity."

Hearing this, Master Pedro stopped ringing, and said, "Don't be a pedant, Señor Don Quixote, or want to have things at a height of perfection that is out of reach. Almost every day are there not a thousand comedies represented everywhere full of thousands of inaccuracies and absurdities, and, despite that, they are successful, and are listened to not only with applause, but with admiration and all the rest that goes with it? Go on, boy; because as long as I fill my pocket, it does not matter if I show as many inaccuracies as there are particles in a sunbeam."

"Fair enough," said Don Quixote; and the boy went on: "See what the numerous and impressive crowd of horsemen issue from the city in pursuit of the two faithful lovers, the blowing of the trumpets, sounding of horns, beating of drums; I fear they will overtake them and bring them back tied to the tail of their own horse, which would be a terrible sight."

Don Quixote, however, seeing a pack of Moors and hearing such loud unpleasant noise, thought it would be right to aid the fugitives, and standing up he exclaimed in a loud voice, "Never, while I live, will I permit foul play to be practised in my presence again such a famous Knight and fearless lover as Don Gaiferos. Halt! ill-born rabble, do not follow or pursue him, or you will have to face me in battle!" and matching the action to the words, he raised his sword, and with one leap forward placed himself close to the show, and with unimaginable rapidity and fury began to shower down blows on the puppet group of Moors, knocking some over, decapitating others, damaging this one and demolishing that one; and among many more he sent one down stroke which, if Master Pedro had not ducked, made himself small, and got out of the way, would have sliced his head off as easily as if it had been made of almond-paste. Master Pedro kept shouting, "Halt! Señor Don Quixote! Can't you see they're not real Moors that you're knocking down, killing and destroying, they're only little pasteboard figures! Look how you're wrecking and ruining all that I'm worth!" But despite this, Don Quixote did stop discharging a continuous rain of cuts, slashes, downstrokes and backstrokes, finally, in no time at all, he brought the whole show to the ground, with all its fittings and figures shaken and knocked to pieces, King Marsilio badly wounded, and the Emperor Charlemagne with his crown and head split in two. The whole audience was thrown into confusion, the ape ran to the roof of the inn, the cousin was frightened, and even Sancho Panza himself was in great fear, because, as he swore after the storm was over, he had never seen his master in this much fury.

Therefore, the complete destruction of the show being accomplished, Don Quixote became a little calmer and said, "I wish I had here in front of me now all of those who do not or will not believe how useful Knights are in the world; just think, if I had not been present here, what would have become of the brave Don Gaiferos and the fair Melisendra! You can believe it, by this time those dogs would have overtaken them and inflicted some violence on them. So, then, long live Knighthood beyond everything living on earth this to date!"

"Let it live on" said Master Pedro in a feeble voice, "and let me die, because I am so unfortunate that I can say like King Don Rodrigo:

Yesterday I was lord of Spain,
Today I do not have a turret left,
That I may call my own.

Half an hour ago, actually, barely a minute ago, I saw myself the lord of Kings and emperors, and my stables filled with countless horses, my bags filled with numerous dresses; and now I find myself ruined, poor, impoverished and a tramp, and above all without my ape, because, I will have to sweat before I could catch him; and all through the reckless fury of sir Knight here, who, they say, protects the fatherless, rights wrongs, and does other charitable deeds; but whose generous intentions have been found missing in my case only. Truly, Knight of the Sorrowful Face he must be to have given me one."

Sancho was touched by Master Pedro's words, and said to him, "Don't cry, Master Pedro; you break my heart; let me tell you my master, Don Quixote, is so catholic and an honourable Christian that, if he can see that he has done you any wrong, he will acknowledge it, and be willing to pay for it and make it right, and add something extra over and above."

"Let Señor Don Quixote pay me for some part of the work he has destroyed," said Master Pedro, "and I would be content, and this would ease his conscience, because he who keeps what is another's against the owner's will and makes no restoration cannot be saved."

"That is true," said Don Quixote; "but at present I am not aware that I have got anything of yours, Master Pedro."

"What!" returned Master Pedro; "are these remains lying here on the bare hard ground - scattered and shattered by the invincible strength of your mighty arm? And who else did they belonged to but me? And how did I make my living, if not with them?"

"Now am I fully convinced," said Don Quixote, "of what I have always believed; that the enchanters who persecute me do nothing more than put figures like these in front of my eyes, and then change and turn them into whatever they like. In truth and all sincerity, I assure you gentlemen, that to me everything that has happened here seemed to take place literally, that Melisendra was Melisendra, Don Gaiferos Don Gaiferos, Marsilio Marsilio, and Charlemagne Charlemagne. That was why my anger was roused; and to be faithful to my calling as a Knight I sought to give aid and protection to those who ran, and with this good intention I did what you have seen. If the result has been the opposite of what I intended, it is no fault of mine, but of those wicked beings that persecute me; but, despite that, I am willing to convict and fine myself for this error of mine, although it did not proceed from malice; let Master Pedro determine what he wants for the damaged figures, because I agree to pay it immediately in good and current money of Castile."

Master Pedro said, "I expected no less from the rare Christianity of the noble Don Quixote of La Mancha, true helper and protector of all poor and needy beggars; master landlord here and the great Sancho Panza will be the mediators and appraisers between you and me of what these incapacitated figures are worth or may be worth."

The landlord and Sancho gave their consent, and then Master Pedro picked up from the ground King Marsilio of Saragossa with his head missing, and said, "Here you see how impossible it is to restore this King to his former state, so I think, unless you deem otherwise, that for his death and demise, four and a half gold coins should be given to me."

"Proceed," said Don Quixote.

"Well then, for this cut from top to bottom," continued Master Pedro, picking up the split Emperor Charlemagne, "it would not be much if I were to ask five and a quarter gold coins."

"It's not a lot," said Sancho.

"Neither is it much," said the landlord; "make it even, and say five coins."

"Let him have the whole five and a quarter," said Don Quixote; "because the total sum of this notable disaster does not stand on a quarter more or less; and finish this quickly, Master Pedro, because it's almost dinner-time, and I have a hint of hunger."

"For this figure," said Master Pedro, "without a nose, and missing an eye, is the fair Melisendra, I ask, and I am reasonable, two coins."

"The very devil must be involved," said Don Quixote, "if Melisendra and her husband are on the French border by now, because the horse they rode on seemed to me to fly rather than run; so you cannot try to sell me the cat for the rabbit, showing me a noseless Melisendra when she is now, maybe, enjoying herself with her husband in France. Master Pedro, let us proceed fairly and honestly; and now go on."

Master Pedro, perceiving that Don Quixote was beginning to wander, and return to his original madness, was not willing to let him escape, so he said to him, "This cannot be Melisendra, but must be one of the damsels that waited on her; so if I'm given one coin for her, I'll be content and sufficiently paid."

And so he went on, putting values on each and every smashed figure, which, after the two peacemakers had adjusted them to the satisfaction of both parties, came to forty and three-quarter gold coins; and in addition to this sum, which Sancho immediately paid, Master Pedro asked for two coins for his trouble in catching the ape.

"Let him have them, Sancho," said Don Quixote; "not to catch the ape, but to get drunk; and I would give two-hundred right now for the good news, and to anyone who could tell me positively, that lady Dona Melisandra and Señor Don Gaiferos were now in France and with their own people."

"No one could tell us that better than my ape," said Master Pedro; "but there's no devil that could catch him now; I suspect, however, that affection and hunger will drive him to come looking for me tonight; but tomorrow is approaching so we will soon see."

In short, the puppet-show storm passed, and they all had dinner in peace at Don Quixote's expense, because he was at the height of generosity. Before it was daylight the man with the lances and axes continued on his journey, and soon after daylight came the cousin and the boy came to say farewell to Don Quixote, the cousin returning home, the boy resuming his journey, and to help him, Don Quixote gave him twelve coins. Master Pedro did not want to engage in any more trouble with Don Quixote; so he woke up before sunrise, and having gathered together the remains of his show and caught his ape, he went on his way to seek further adventures. The landlord, who did not know Don Quixote, was as astonished at his madness as at his generosity. To conclude, Sancho, by his master's orders, paid him very liberally, and they left the inn at about eight in the morning and took the road, where we will leave them to pursue their journey, because this is necessary in order to allow certain other matters to be put forward, which are required to clear up this famous history.

CHAPTER 27

WHO MASTER PEDRO AND HIS APE WERE, TOGETHER WITH THE MISHAP DON QUIXOTE HAD IN THE DONKEY CALLING ADVENTURE, WHICH HE DID NOT CONCLUDE AS HE WOULD HAVE LIKED OR AS HE HAD EXPECTED

Cide Hamete, the reporter of this great history, begins this chapter with these words, "I swear as a Catholic Christian;" which the translator says that Cide Hamete swearing as a Catholic Christian, he being - as no doubt he was - a Moor, only meant that, just as a Catholic Christian taking an oath swears, or should swear, what is true, and tell the truth in what he asserts, he was telling the truth, as much as if he swore as a Catholic Christian, in all he chose to write about Don Quixote, especially in declaring who Master Pedro was and what the divining ape that astonished all the villages with his divinations was. He says, then, that he who has read the First Part of this history will remember well enough Gines de Pasamonte whom, with the other ship slaves, Don Quixote set free in the Sierra Morena: a kindness for which he afterwards got little thanks and even worse payment for from that evil-minded group. This Gines de Pasamonte - Don Ginesillo de Parapilla, Don Quixote called was the one who stole the donkey from Sancho Panza; which, because of the fault of the printers neither how or when was stated in the First Part, and has been a puzzle to many people, who attribute to the bad memory of the author that which was the error of the press. In fact, however, Gines stole the donkey while Sancho was asleep on his back; and, as has been told, Sancho afterwards recovered him.

This Gines, then, afraid of being caught by the officers of justice, who were looking for him to punish him for his innumerable crimes and offences (of which there were so many that he himself wrote a big book giving an account of them), determined to move his home into the Kingdom of Aragon, and cover his left eye, and begin the trade of a puppet-man; because this, as well as juggling, he knew how to practise to perfection. He bought the ape, from some Christians who were released from North Africa, and he it taught to climb on his shoulder and make signs and whisper, or seem to do so, in his ear. Therefore, prepared, before entering any village he was going to with his show and his ape, he used to inform himself at the nearest village, or from the most likely person he could find, what particular things had happened there, and to whom; and keeping these in mind, the first thing he did was to exhibit his show, sometimes one story, sometimes another, but all lively, amusing, and familiar. As soon as the exhibition was over he discussed the accomplishments of his ape, assuring the public that he could tell all the past and the present, but in regards to the future he had no skill. For each question answered he asked for two gold coins, and for some he made a reduction, and sometimes he went to houses where things he knew of had happened to the people living there, and even if they did not ask him a question, as they did not want to pay for it, he would make the sign to the ape and then declare that it had told him something, which was exactly the case. In this way he acquired extraordinary fame and everyone wanted to meet him and his ape; on other occasions, being very crafty, he would answer in such a way that the answers matched the questions; and as no one questioned him or asked him to tell how his ape was able to do this, he made fools of them all and filled his pockets. The instant he entered the inn he knew Don Quixote and Sancho, and with that knowledge it was easy for him to astonish them and all who were there; but it would have cost him if Don Quixote had aimed his hand a little lower when he cut off King Marsilio's head and destroyed all his horsemen.

And now to return to Don Quixote of La Mancha. After he had left the inn he decided to visit, first of all, the reservoirs of the river Ebro and that neighbourhood, before entering the city of Saragossa, because there was ample time to spare before the contests. With this objective in mind he followed the road and travelled along it for two days, without meeting any adventure worth writing until on the third day, as he was climbing a hill, he heard a great noise of drums, trumpets, and gun-shots. At first he imagined soldiers were passing that way, and to see them he dug his heels into Rocinante and quickly ascended the hill. On reaching the top he saw over two hundred men at the base of it, as it seemed to him, armed with all sorts of weapons, lances, crossbows, axes, spears, a few guns and many shields. He descended the slope and approached near enough to see distinctly the flags, make out the colours and distinguish the weapons they carried, especially one on a banner of white satin, on which there was painted in a very life-like donkey, with its head up, its mouth open and its tongue out, as if it were in the act of donkey calling; and around it inscribed in large characters were these two lines:

Without cause were their calls,
Our mayors are not fools.

From this Don Quixote concluded that these people must be from the opposition of the donkey calling town, and he said so to Sancho, explaining to him what was written on the banner. At the same time, he noticed that the man who had told them about the matter was wrong in saying that the two were councilmen, because according to the lines of the banner they were mayors. To which Sancho replied, "Señor, he may not have been incorrect, because maybe the councilmen then became mayors of their town afterwards, and so they may go by both titles; furthermore, it has nothing to do with the truth of the story whether they were council men or mayors, provided they did call; because a councilman is just as likely to donkey call as a mayor." They noticed, in short, clearly that the town which had been made fun of, had come to battle with some other town that mocked it more than was fair or neighbourly.

Don Quixote proceeded to join them, which made Sancho uneasy, as he never enjoyed mixing himself up in adventures of that kind. The members of the group welcomed him among of them, thinking he was someone who was on their side. Don Quixote, putting up his visor, advanced with an easy attitude and

493

character to the banner with the donkey, and all the men of the army gathered round him to look at him, staring at him with the usual amazement that everybody felt when seeing him for the first time. Don Quixote, seeing them examining him so attentively, and that none of them spoke to him or asked any question, determined to take advantage of their silence; so, breaking his own, raised his voice and said, "Worthy men, I have something to ask you sincerely - I wish to address to you, until you find it displeases you; and if that happened, at the slightest hint you give me I will seal my lips."

They all asked him say what he liked, because they would listen to him willingly.

With this permission Don Quixote went on to say, "I, am a Knight whose calling is arms, and whose profession is to protect those who require protection, and give help to those in need of it. Some days ago I became acquainted with your misfortune and the cause which impels you to take action again and again to seek revenge on your enemies; and having many times thought over your situation in my mind, I find that, according to the laws of combat, you are mistaken in believing yourselves to be insulted; because a private individual cannot insult on behalf of an entire community; unless it is by defying it collectively as a traitor, because he cannot tell who in particular is guilty of the treason for which he defies it. Of this we have an example: Don Diego Ordonez de Lara, who defied the whole town of Zamora, because he did not know that Vellido Dolfos had committed the betrayal and murder of his King; and therefore he confronted them all, and the revenge and the reply concerned all; although, Señor Don Diego went rather too far, indeed very much beyond the limits of defiance; because he had no reason to defy the dead, or the waters, or the fish, or the unborn, and all the rest mentioned in that story; let it pass, because when anger breaks out there's no father, governor, or rein to restrain the tongue. The case being, then, that no one can insult a Kingdom, province, city, state, or entire community, it is clear there is no reason for going out to retaliate against the defiance of such an insult. It would be a catastrophe if the people of the clock town were to be going to battle every moment with everyone who called them by that name - or the holders of all the other names and titles that are always in the mouths of the boys and common people! It would chaos if all these illustrious cities were to take revenge themselves and go about perpetually wielding their swords in every minor disagreement! No, no; God forbid! There are four things which sensible men and well-ordered States should battle, draw their swords, and risk their people, lives, and properties for. The first is to defend the Catholic faith; the second, to defend one's life, which is in accordance with natural and divine law; the third, in defence of one's honour, family, and property; the fourth, in the service of one's King in a justifiable war; and if to these we choose to add a fifth (which may be included in the second), in defence of one's country. To these five, as it were capital causes, some others may be added that are justifiable and reasonable, and make it a duty to battle; but to battle for minor things worth laughing about and being amused by rather than offended, would look as though he who did was lacking in common sense. Furthermore, to take unjustified revenge is directly opposed to the sacred law that we acknowledge, which commands us to do good to our enemies and to love those that hate us; a command which, although it seems somewhat difficult to obey, is only difficult in the case of those who have less God in them than the world, and yield more to the flesh than the spirit; because Jesus Christ, who never lied, could not and cannot lie, as our law-giver, said, that his burden was easy and light; he would not, therefore, have given any command to us that was impossible to obey. Therefore, sirs, you are bound to keep quiet by human and divine law."

"The devil take me," said Sancho - to himself, "this master of mine is a theologian; or, if not, believe, he is like one, as one egg is like another."

Don Quixote paused to take a breath, and, noticing that silence was still maintained, would have liked to continue his speech, and would have done so if Sancho had not interrupted with his smartness; because he, seeing his master pause, took the lead, saying, "My lord Don Quixote of La Mancha, who once was called the Knight of the Sorrowful Face, but is now called the Knight of the Lions, is a gentleman of great prudence who knows Latin and his mother tongue like a graduate, and in everything that he does or advises proceeds like a good soldier, and has all the laws and orders of what they call combat at his finger tips'; so you have nothing to do but let yourselves be directed by what he says, and let it fall on my head if it is wrong. Besides, you have been told that it is foolishness to take offence at merely hearing a donkey call. I remember when I was a boy I made this noise as often as I liked, without anyone deterring me, and I did it so elegantly and naturally that when I did, all the donkeys in the town would raise their call; but I was not ridiculed, the son of my parents who were greatly respected; and although I was envied because of that by more than one of the high and mighty people in the town, I did not care one bit about it; and so you can see I am telling the truth, wait a bit and listen, because this art, like swimming, once learnt is never forgotten;" and then, holding his nose, he began to make a sound so loud that all the valleys around echoed.

One of those, however, that stood nearby, believing he was mocking them, lifted up a long stick he had in his hand and struck him with such a blow that Sancho dropped helplessly to the ground. Don Quixote, seeing him treated so roughly, attacked the man who had struck him, but so many others immediately placed themselves between them that he could not retaliate. Far from it, finding a shower of stones raining on him, and an unnumbered amount of crossbows and guns aimed at him, he swung Rocinante around and, as fast as his best pace could take him, bolted from their sights, calling on God with all his heart to lead him out of this danger, in fear at every step of some ball penetrating his back and coming out through his chest, and every minute taking a deep breath to see whether or not it had been taken from him. The members of the group, however, were satisfied with seeing him retreat, and did not fire at him. They put Sancho, barely restored to his senses, on his donkey, and let him go after his master; not that he was sufficiently in his mind to, but his donkey followed the footsteps of Rocinante, from whom he could not for a moment be separated.

Don Quixote having found himself at a fair distance looked back, and seeing Sancho coming, waited for him, as he noticed that no one followed him. The men of the group stood their ground until the night, and as the enemy did not come out to battle, they returned to their town in glory; and had they been aware of the ancient custom of the Greeks, they would have built a monument on the spot.

CHAPTER 28

MATTERS THAT BENENGELI SAYS HE WHO READS THEM WILL KNOW, IF HE READS THEM WITH ATTENTION

When the brave man retreats, cowardice becomes visible and it is up to wise men to reserve this only for suitable occasions. This proved to be the case with Don Quixote, who, before the fury of the townspeople and the hostile intentions of the angry group, withdrew and, without a thought for Sancho or the danger in which he was leaving him, retreated to a distance that he thought made him safe. Sancho, lying across his donkey, followed him, as has been said, and finally caught up to him, having by this time recovered his senses, and on joining him let himself drop off the donkey at Rocinante's feet, sore, bruised, and beaten. Don Quixote dismounted to examine his wounds, but finding him complete from head to foot, he said to him, angrily enough, "at such an evil hour did you start donkey calling, Sancho! With the music of donkey calling what harmony could you expect to get than a beating? Give thanks to God, Sancho, that they signed the cross on you just now with a stick, and did not mark you with a sword."

"I'm not able to answer," said Sancho, "because I feel as if I am speaking through my shoulders; let us mount and get away from here; I'll stop myself from donkey calling, but not from saying that Knights retreat and leave their good aides to be grounded down like olives, or given as a meal to their enemies."

"To withdraw is not to retreat," returned Don Quixote; "you need to know, Sancho, that courage which is not based on a foundation of prudence is called rashness, and the deeds of the rash man are to be credited to good fortune rather than courage; and so I admit that I withdrew, but not that I retreated; and with this I have followed the example of many valiant men who have preserved themselves for better occasions; the histories are full of instances of this, but as it would not be any good to you or pleasure to me, I will not list them to you now."

By this time, Sancho had mounted his donkey with the help of Don Quixote, who then mounted Rocinante, and at a relaxed pace they proceeded to take shelter in the woods which was in sight about a quarter of a mile away.

Every now and then Sancho gave deep sighs and miserable cries, and when Don Quixote asked him what caused such acute suffering, he replied that, from the end of his back-bone up to the top of his neck, he was so sore that it nearly drove him out of his mind.

"The cause of that soreness," said Don Quixote, "will be, no doubt, the stick they beat you with being a very long one, which caught you all over the back, where all the parts that are sore are situated, and had they beat you any longer you would be sorer."

"Thank you God," said Sancho, "you have relieved me of a great doubt, and cleared up the point in such elegant style! Is the cause of my soreness such a mystery that you need to tell me I am sore everywhere the stick hit me? If it was, my ankles that caused pain might require your help to figure out why they did, but it is not much to determine that I'm sore where they beat me. Believe, master, the pain of others hangs by a hair; every day I am discovering more and more how little I have to hope for when accompanying you; because if this time you have allowed me to be beaten, the next time, or a hundred times more, we'll have the blanketing of the other day all over again, and all the other troubles which, if they have fallen on my shoulders now, will be thrown at my teeth eventually. I would do much better (if I was not an ignorant fool that will never do any good in my life with you), it's much better, I say, to go home to my wife and children and support them and bring them up with whatever God may please to give me, instead of following you along roads that lead nowhere, with little to drink and even less to eat. And then when it comes to sleeping! You might say, brother, measure yourself some earth and if that's not enough for you, take some more, because you may stretch yourself on the ground to your heart's content. Oh that I could see being burnt and turned into ashes by the first man that interfered with Knighthood or at any rate the first who choses to be an aide to such fools as all the Knights of past must have been! But those of the present day I say nothing about, because, as you are one of them, I respect them, and because I know you know a bit more than the devil in all you say and think."

"I would make a bet with you, Sancho," said Don Quixote, "that now you are talking without anyone to stop you, you don't feel a pain in your whole body. Talk away, my son, say whatever comes into your head or mouth, because as long as you feel no pain, the irritation your insolence gives me will be a pleasure to me; and if you are anxious to go home to your wife and children, God forbid that I would prevent you; you have money of mine; see how long it has been since we left our village this third time, and how much you can and should earn every month, and pay yourself out of your own hand."

"When I worked for Tom Carrasco, the father of the graduate Samson Carrasco that you know," replied Sancho, "I used to earn two gold coins a month and my food; I can't tell what I can earn with you, although I know Knight's aides have harder times than those who work for a farmer; because after all, those who work for farmers, however much they labour all day, at worst, at night, they have their dinner and sleep in a bed, which I have not slept in since I have been in your service, if it wasn't the short time we were in Don Diego de Miranda's house, and the feast I had with the servings I took out of Camacho's pots, and that I ate, drank, and slept in Basilio's house; the rest of the time I have been sleeping on the hard ground under the open sky, exposed to what they call the weather of heaven, keeping life in me with scraps of cheese and crusts of bread, and drinking water either from the lakes or from the streams we pass by on the paths we travel."

"I admit, Sancho," said Don Quixote, "that all you say is true; how much, do you think, I should give you over and above what Tom Carrasco gave you?"

"I think," said Sancho, "that if you were to add on two coins a month I'd consider myself well paid; that is, as far as the wages of my labour go; but to make up to me for your pledge and promise to me to give me the government of an island, it would be fair to add six coins or more."

"Very good," said Don Quixote; "it has been twenty-five days since we left our village, so, Sancho, according to the wages you have made for yourself, add it all up and see how much I owe you in proportion, and pay yourself, as I said before, out of your own hand."

"Let me recount the days!" said Sancho, "because when it comes to the promise of the island we must count that from the day you promised it to me to this present moment which we are at now."

"Well, how long is it, Sancho, since I promised it to you?" said Don Quixote.

"If I remember correctly," said Sancho, "it must be over twenty years, give or take three days."

Don Quixote gave himself a great slap on the forehead and began to laugh wholeheartedly, and said, "I have not been wandering, either in the Sierra Morena or in the whole course of our adventures for barely two months, and you say, Sancho, that it has been twenty years since I promised you the island. I believe you would want all the money I have go into your wages. If so, and if that were your will, I would give it to you now, once and for all, because as long as I see myself get rid of such a good-for-nothing aide I'll be glad to be left as a peasant without a penny. But tell me, perverter of the aides rules of Knighthood, where have you ever seen or read that any Knight's aides made these terms with his lord, 'you must give me so much a month for serving you'? Delve, you crook, rogue, and scoundrel such as I take you to be, I say, into their histories; and if you find that any aide ever said or thought what you have said now, I will let you nail it on my forehead, and give me, over and above this, four slaps in the face. Turn the rein, or the halter, of your donkey, and be gone, go home; because you will not go a single step further in my company. Bread thanklessly received! Promises poorly-given! Man more beast than human being! When I was just about to raise you to such a position, that, despite your wife, they would call you 'my lord,' you are leaving me? You are going now when I had a firm and fixed intention of making you a lord of the best island in the world? Well, as you yourself have said before, honey is not for the mouth of the donkey. Donkey you are, donkey you will be, and donkey you will end when the course of your life is finished; because I know it will come to its close before you perceive or discern that you are a beast."

Sancho observed Don Quixote quite seriously while he was giving him this rating, and was so touched with remorse that tears came to his eyes, and in a pathetic and broken voice he said to him, "Master of mine, I confess that, to be a complete donkey, all I need is a tail; if you will fix one on to me, I'll consider it well deserved, and I'll serve you as donkey for the remaining days of my life. Forgive me and have pity on my foolishness, and remember I do not know much, and, if I talk a lot, it's more from illness than malice; but he who sins and repents turns himself to God."

"I would have been surprised, Sancho," said Don Quixote, "if you had not introduced a proverb into your speech. Well, well, I forgive you, provided you repent and do not show yourself to only consider your own interest in the future, but try to be cheerful and have spirit, and encourage yourself to look forward to the fulfilment of my promises, which, by being delayed, does not make them impossible."

Sancho said he would do so, and keep up his spirit as best as he could. They then entered the woods, and Don Quixote settled himself at the feet of an elm tree, and Sancho at another, because trees of this kind and others like them always have feet but no hands. Sancho spent the night in pain, because with the cold of the evening the pain from the blows of the stick was intensified. Don Quixote spent it in his never-failing meditations; but, despite that, they had some moments of sleep, and with the appearance of daylight they pursued their journey in quest of the banks of the famous river Ebro, where what happened to them will be told in the following chapter.

CHAPTER 29

THE FAMOUS ADVENTURE OF THE ENCHANTED BOAT

As described or left undescribed, two days after leaving the woods Don Quixote and Sancho reached the river Ebro, and the sight of it was a great delight to Don Quixote as he contemplated and gazed at the charm of its banks, the clearness of its stream, the gentleness of its current and the abundance of its crystal water; and the pleasant view renewed a thousand thoughts in his mind. Above all, he recalled what he had seen in the cave of Montesinos; because although Master Pedro's ape had told him that out of these things part was true, part was false, he held them more as true than false, the very opposite of Sancho, who held them all to be absolute lies.

As they were proceeding, they discovered a small boat, without oars or any other gear, that was at the water's edge tied to the stem of a small tree growing on the bank. Don Quixote looked all around, and seeing nobody, immediately, without any discussion, dismounted from Rocinante and asked Sancho to get down from the donkey and tie both animals securely to the trunk of a tree. Sancho asked him the reason for this sudden dismounting. Don Quixote answered, "You must know Sancho, that this boat is plainly, and without the possibility of any alternative, calling and inviting me to enter it, and go to give aid to some Knight or other person of distinction in need, who is no doubt experiencing some trouble; because this is common in the books of chivalry and of the enchanters who speak in them. When a Knight is involved in some difficulty from which he cannot be rescued except by the hand of another Knight, although they may be at a distance of two or three thousand miles from each other, they either take him on a cloud, or they provide a boat for him to get into, and in less than the blink of an eye they carry him where his help is required; and so, Sancho, this boat is placed here for the same purpose; this is as true as it is now day, so, tie the donkey and Rocinante together, and let God's hand guide us; because I would not hold back from embarking, even if barefooted priests were to beg me."

"As that's the case," said Sancho, "and you choose to go along with these - I don't know if I may call them absurdities – all the time, there's nothing for me to do but obey and bow my head, bearing in mind the proverb, 'Do as your master asks you, and sit down at the table with him;' but despite that, for the sake of easing my conscience, I warn you that it is my opinion this boat is not an enchanted one, but belongs to some of the fishermen of the river, because they catch the best herring in the world here."

As Sancho said this, he tied the donkey and horse, leaving them in the care and protection of the enchanters with sorrow in his heart. Don Quixote asked him not to be worried about deserting the animals, "because the enchanter who would carry them over such longinquus roads and regions would take care to feed them."

501

"I don't understand longinquus," said Sancho, "neither have I ever heard the word in all the days of my life."

"Longinquus," replied Don Quixote, "means far off; but it is no wonder you do not understand it, because you are not required to know Latin, like some who pretend to know it and don't."

"Now they are tied," said Sancho; "what do we do next?"

"What?" said Don Quixote, "place a cross over our chests and raise anchor; I mean, embark and cut the fastenings which the boat is held by;" and so they did, and the boat began to drift away slowly from the bank. But when Sancho saw himself about two yards out in the river, he began to tremble and consider himself lost; but nothing distressed him more than hearing his donkey call and seeing Rocinante struggling to get loose, and he said to his master, "the donkey is calling out in grief at us leaving him, and Rocinante is trying to escape and jump in the water after us. Oh dear friends, may peace be with you, and this madness that is taking us away from you be turned into sober sense and bring us back to you." And with this he began crying so excessively, that Don Quixote said to him, sharply and angrily, "What are you afraid of, cowardly creature? What are you crying about, heart of butter? Who pursues or attacks you, soul of a tame mouse? What do you want, unsatisfied in the very heart of abundance? Are you, by chance, walking barefoot over the Riphaean mountains, instead of being sat on a bench like a duke on the tranquil stream of this pleasant river, from which in a short space we will emerge onto the open sea? We must have already emerged and gone seven or eight hundred miles; and if I had an astrolabe here to measure the altitude of the pole, I could tell you how many we have travelled, although either I know little, or we have already crossed or will shortly cross the equinox which parts the two opposite poles midway."

"And when we come to that line you speak of," said Sancho, "how far will we have gone?"

"Very far," said Don Quixote, "because of the three hundred and sixty degrees that this globe contains, as computed by Ptolemy, the greatest cosmographer known, we will have travelled one-half when we come to the line I spoke of."

"God," said Sancho, "you taught me something about this disputed anomaly and geographer."

Don Quixote laughed at the interpretation Sancho gave for "computed," the name "Ptolemy," and "cosmographer" he said, "You must know, Sancho, that for the Spaniards and those who embark at Cadiz for the East Indies, one of the signs they have to show when they have passed the equinoctial line I told you about, is, that any lice which were to be found on those on board the ship will die, and not a single one will remain, or be found on the whole vessel; so, Sancho, you might as well run you hand down you thigh, and if you come across anything alive we will no longer be in any doubt; if not, then we have not crossed."

"I don't believe a bit of it," said Sancho; "still, I'll do as you ask me; although I don't know what need there is for trying these experiments, because I can see with my own eyes that we have not moved two yards away from the bank, or five yards from where the animals are, because there are Rocinante and the donkey in the very same place where we left them; and, I swear on everything that's good, we are not moving faster than the pace of an ant."

"Try the test I told you about, Sancho," said Don Quixote, "and don't bother with any other, because you know nothing about colures, lines, parallels, zodiacs, ecliptics, poles, solstices, equinoxes, planets, signs, bearings, and the measurements of which the celestial and terrestrial spheres are composed of; if you were acquainted with all these things, or any portion of them, you would see clearly how many parallels we have cut, what signs we have seen, and what constellations we have left behind and are now leaving behind. But again I tell you, feel and hunt, because I am certain you are cleaner than a sheet of smooth white paper."

Sancho felt, and running his hand gently and carefully down his left knee, he looked up at his master and said, "Either the test is false, or we have not come to where you say, neither are we within many miles of it."

"Why, how?" asked Don Quixote; "have you come across something?"

"Indeed," replied Sancho; and shaking his fingers he dipped his whole hand in the river which the boat was quietly gliding along, not provoked by any mystical intelligence or invisible enchanter, but simply by the current, smoothly and gently.

At this moment they came in sight of some large water mills that stood in the middle of the river, and the instant Don Quixote saw them he cried out, "You see there, my friend? There stands the castle or fortress, where there is, no doubt, some Knight in confinement, or mistreated Queen, or the daughter of a monarch, or Princess, who requires the aid I am brought here for."

"What the devil city, fortress, or castle are you talking about, señor?" said Sancho; "don't you see that those are mills that are in the river to grind corn?"

"Hold your tongue, Sancho," said Don Quixote; "although they look like mills they are not; I have already told you that enchantments transform things and change their original shapes; I do not mean to say they really change them from one form into another, but that it seems as though they have, as experience proved with the transformation of Dulcinea, the sole sanctuary of my hopes."

By this time, the boat, having reached the middle of the stream, began to move less slowly than it had up until now. When the millers working the mills, saw the boat coming down the river, and being sucked in by the breeze toward the wheels, ran out in haste, several of them, with long poles to stop it, and having their faces and garments covered with flour, they presented an evil appearance and raised loud shouts, "Men of devils, where are you going? Are you mad? Do you want to drown yourselves, or turn yourselves into pieces among these wheels?"

"Did I not tell you, Sancho," said Don Quixote, "that we are approaching the place where I am required to show what the might of my arm can do? See what ruffians and villains are coming out against me; see what monsters oppose me; see what hideous faces have come to frighten us! You will soon see, scoundrels!" And then standing up in the boat he began in a loud voice to shout threats to the millers, exclaiming, "poor-conditioned and even worse-advised herd, restore the liberty and freedom of the person you hold in confinement in this fortress or prison of yours, high or low or of whatever rank or quality he or she may be, because I am Don Quixote of La Mancha, otherwise called the Knight of the Lions, for who, by the order of heaven above, it is reserved to conclude happily the issue of this adventure;" and so he raised his sword and began waving it in the air at the millers, who, hearing but not understanding all this nonsense, attempted to stop the boat, which was now approaching the rushing passage of the wheels. Sancho fell on his knees religiously appealing to heaven to save him from such imminent danger; which it did by the action and rapidity of the millers, who, pushing against the boat with their poles, stopped it, not, however, without upsetting and throwing Don Quixote and Sancho into the water; and lucky for Don Quixote as he could swim like a swan, although the weight of his armour pulled him to the bottom twice; and had it not been for the millers, who jumped in and pulled them both out, it would have been the end for them both. As soon as they were out, Sancho immediately went down on his knees and with clasped hands and eyes looking up to heaven, gave a long and impassioned prayer to God to rescue him from any further uncontrolled plans and attempts of his master. The fishermen, the owners of the boat, which the mill-wheels had knocked to pieces, now came, and seeing it smashed they proceeded to strip Sancho and to demand payment for it from Don Quixote; but with great calmness, he, just as if nothing had happened, told the millers and fishermen that he would pay for the boat most gladly, on the condition that they delivered to him, free and uninjured, to the person or people that were in confinement in the castle of theirs.

"What people or what castle are you talking about, madman? Are you here to take the people who come to grind corn in these mills?"

"That's enough," said Don Quixote to himself, "it would be like preaching in the desert to attempt with appeals to induce this herd to do any virtuous action. In this adventure two mighty enchanters must have encountered one another, and one frustrates what the other attempts; one provided the boat for me, and the other attempts to upset me; God help us, this world is all conspiracies and schemes with differing purposes which go against one another. I can do no more." And then turning towards the mills he said aloud, "Friends, whoever you are that are confined in that prison, forgive me that, to my misfortune and yours, I cannot free you from your misery; this adventure is doubtlessly reserved and destined for some other Knight."

Saying this he settled the damage with the fishermen, and paid fifty coins for the boat, which Sancho handed to them very much against his will, saying, "With a couple more boat adventures like this we will have exhausted our whole capital."

The fishermen and the millers stood staring in amazement at the two figures, so very different in appearance to ordinary men, and were totally unable to make out the questions Don Quixote addressed to them; and coming to the conclusion that they were madmen, they left them and went their way, the millers to their mills, and the fishermen to their huts. Don Quixote and Sancho returned to the horse and donkey, and concluded the adventure of the enchanted boat.

CHAPTER 30

DON QUIXOTE'S ADVENTURE WITH A FAIR HUNTRESS

Both the Knight and aide reached the donkey and Rocinante in a low spirit and bad humour, Sancho particularly, because with him whatever touched their stock of money touched his heart, and when any was taken from him he felt as if he was robbed. Without exchanging a word, they mounted and left the famous river, Don Quixote absorbed in thoughts of his love, Sancho thinking about his advancement, which just then, it seemed to him, he was very far from achieving; because, although a fool as he was, he saw quite clearly that his master's acts were all or mostly entirely senseless; and he began to think about an opportunity for retiring from his service and going home someday, without giving any explanation or saying farewell to him. Fortune, however, ordered that matters continue very much the opposite of what he contemplated.

It so happened that the next day towards sunset, when coming out of a wood, Don Quixote observed a green meadow, and at the far end of it noticed some people, and as he got closer saw that it was a hunting group. Coming closer, he distinguished among them a lady with a graceful appearance, on a pure white horse covered with a green harness and a silver saddle. The lady was also in green, and so richly and magnificently dressed that splendour itself seemed to be personified in her. On her left hand she held a hawk, proof to Don Quixote's mind that she must be some great lady and the mistress of the whole hunting group, which was the fact; so he said to Sancho, "Run Sancho, my son, and say to that lady on the horse with the hawk that I, the Knight of the Lions, kiss the hands of her exalted beauty, and if her excellency will grant me permission I will go and kiss them in person and offer myself at her service for anything at all that may be in my power and her highness may command; careful, Sancho, how you speak, and take care not to slip in any of your proverbs into the message."

"Am I one likely to slip them in?" said Sancho; "don't worry about that and trust me! This is not the first time in my life I have carried messages to high and exalted ladies."

"Except that which you carried to the lady Dulcinea," said Don Quixote, "I do not know that you have carried any other, at least in my service."

"That is true," replied Sancho; "but offers don't distress a good buyer, and in a house where there's plenty - dinner is soon cooked; I mean there's no need of telling or warning me about anything; because I'm ready for anything and know a little of everything."

"That I believe, Sancho," said Don Quixote; "go and good luck to you, and God give you speed."

Sancho went off at top speed, forcing his donkey out of his regular pace, and came to where the fair huntress was standing, and dismounting knelt before her and said, "Fair lady, that Knight that you see there, the Knight of the Lions by name, is my master, and I am the aide of his, and at home they call me Sancho

Panza. This same Knight of the Lions, who was not long ago called the Knight of the Sorrowful Face, sent me to say if it pleases your highness to give him permission, approval, and consent, so he may come and carry out his wishes, which are, as he says and I believe, to serve your exalted loftiness and beauty; and if you give it, you will do a thing which will contribute to your honour, and he will receive a highly distinguished favour and happiness."

"You have indeed, aide," said the lady, "delivered your message with all the formalities such messages require; rise, because it is not right that the aide of such a great Knight as he of the Sorrowful Face, of whom we have heard a great deal about here, should remain on his knees; rise, my friend, and tell your master that he is welcomed to the services of myself and the duke my husband, in a country house we have here."

Sancho got up, charmed as much by the beauty of the good lady as by her high-bred manner and her courtesy, but, above all, by what she had said about having heard of his master, the Knight of the Sorrowful Face; because if she did not call him Knight of the Lions it was no doubt because he had only taken the name recently. "Tell me, brother aide," asked the duchess (whose title, however, is not known), "this master of yours, is he not the one of whom there is a history present in print, called 'The Ingenious Gentleman, Don Quixote of La Mancha,' who has for the lady of his heart a definite Dulcinea del Toboso?"

"He is one and the same, señora," replied Sancho; "and that aide of his who appears, or should appear, in the history under the name of Sancho Panza, is myself, unless they have changed me at birth, I mean in the press."

"I am delighted by all this," said the duchess; "go, brother Panza, and tell your master that he is welcome to my estate, and that nothing could happen to me that could give me greater pleasure."

Sancho returned to his master tremendously pleased with this flattering answer, and told him everything the great lady had said to him, praising heaven, in his countryside style, her rare beauty, her graceful tone, and her courtesy. Don Quixote elevated himself in his saddle briskly, fixed himself in his stirrups, raised his visor, gave Rocinante the heels, and with a relaxed manner advanced to kiss the hands of the duchess, who, having gone to the duke her husband, told him while Don Quixote was approaching all about the message; and as both of them had read the First Part of this history, and were aware of Don Quixote's madness, they awaited him with great pleasure and nervousness, meaning to go along with his humour and agree with everything he said, and, as long as he stayed with them, to treat him as a Knight, with all the formalities usually found in the books of chivalry they had read, because they themselves were very fond of them.

Don Quixote came approaching with his visor raised, and as he seemed about to dismount Sancho rushed forward to hold his stirrup for him; but in getting down off his donkey he was so unlucky to catch his foot in one of the ropes of saddle in such a way that he was unable to free it, and was left hanging by it with his face and chest on the ground. Don Quixote, who was not used to dismounting without having the stirrup held, thinking that by this time Sancho had come to hold it for him, threw himself off with a wobble and brought Rocinante's saddle down with him, which was no doubt incorrectly fixed by Sancho, and so the saddle and he both came to the ground; not without embarrassment to him and abundant profanities mumbled between his teeth about the unlucky Sancho, who had his foot still in the shackles. The duke ordered his huntsmen to go and help the Knight and his aide, and they raised Don Quixote, badly shaken by his fall; and he, limping, advanced as best he could to kneel in front the noble pair. This, however, the duke would not permit; on the contrary, dismounting from his horse, he went and hugged Don Quixote, saying, "I am distressed, Sir Knight of the Sorrowful Face, that your first experience on my ground has been such an unfortunate one; but the carelessness of aides is often the cause of worse accidents."

"That which has happened while meeting you, mighty prince," replied Don Quixote, "cannot be unfortunate, even if my fall were into the depths of a bottomless pit, because the glory of meeting you would have lifted me up and freed me from it. My aide, God curse him, is better at releasing his tongue to talk profanity than tightening the ropes of a saddle to keep it steady; but however I may be, fallen or standing, on foot or on horseback, I will always be at your service and your lady's, the duchess, your worthy companion, admirable Queen of beauty and paramount Princess of courtesy."

"Gently, Señor Don Quixote of La Mancha," said the duke; "just because you do not see lady Dulcinea here, it is not right that other beauties should be praised."

Sancho, by this time had released himself from his entanglement, was standing nearby, and before his master could answer he said, "There is no denying, and it must be maintained, that lady Dulcinea del Toboso is very beautiful; and I have heard it said that what we call nature is like a potter that makes cups of clay, and he who makes one good cup can make two, or three, or a hundred; I say this because, the duchess is in no way behind the lady Dulcinea del Toboso in beauty."

Don Quixote turned to the duchess and said, "Your highness may perceive that no Knight in this world ever had a more talkative or amusing aide than I have, and he will prove the truth of what I say, if your highness is pleased to accept my services for a few days."

To which the duchess answered, "worthy Sancho being amusing I consider a very good thing, because it is a sign that he is sharp; because humour and agile thought, Señor Don Quixote, as you very well know, do not take their home in dull minds; and as good Sancho is humorous and agile I consider him sharp."

"And talkative," added Don Quixote.

"More the better," said the duke, "because many humorous things cannot be said in a few words; but not to spend too much time now in talking, come, great Knight of the Sorrowful Face"

"Of the Lions, you must say," said Sancho, "because there is no Sorrowful Face or any such character now."

"He of the Lions it will be," continued the duke; "I say, let Sir Knight of the Lions come to a castle of mine close by, where he will be given the welcome which is due to such an exalted Knight, and which the duchess and I do not give to all Knights that come there."

By this time Sancho had fixed and tightened Rocinante's saddle, and Don Quixote now on his back and the duke on a fine horse, with the duchess's horse placed in the middle they headed to the castle. The duchess wanted Sancho to come to her side, because she found endless enjoyment in listening to his sharp comments. Sancho required no insistence, but pushed himself in between her and the duke, who thought it was rare good fortune to welcome such a Knight and such a simple aide into their castle.

CHAPTER 31

MANY GREAT MATTERS

Sancho felt supreme satisfaction seeing himself summoned, as it seemed he was an established favourite of the duchess, and looked forward to finding in her castle what he had found in Don Diego's house and in Basilio's; he was always fond of living well, and always taken by any opportunity to feast whenever it presented itself. The history informs us, then, that before they reached the country house or castle, the duke went on in advance and instructed all his servants how they were to treat Don Quixote; and so the instant he came to the castle gates with the duchess, two servants or officers of the house, covered in gowns of fine crimson satin reaching to their feet, rushed out, and holding Don Quixote in their arms before he saw or heard them, said to him, "Your highness should go and take my lady the duchess off her horse."

Don Quixote obeyed, and a great exchanging of compliments followed between the two over the matter; but in the end the duchess's determination conquered, and she refused to get down or dismount from her horse except in the arms of the duke, saying she did not consider herself worthy to impose such an unnecessary burden on such a great Knight. Finally the duke came out to take her down, and as they entered a spacious court two fair ladies came forward and threw over Don Quixote's shoulders a large layer of the finest scarlet cloth, and at the same moment all the corridors of the court were lined with the male-servants and female-servants of the household, saying, "Welcome, elite and cream of Knight-hood!" while all or most of them threw capsules filled with scented water over Don Quixote and the duke and duchess; at all which Don Quixote was greatly surprised, as this was the first time that he thoroughly felt and believed himself to be a Knight in reality and not merely in his mind, now that he saw himself treated in the same way he had read about Knights being treated in days of the past.

Sancho, deserting his donkey, followed the duchess and entered the castle, but feeling some pain of conscience having left the donkey alone, he approached a respectable lady who had come out with the rest to welcome the duchess, and in a low voice he said to her, "Señora, or however your elegance may be called"

"I am called Dona Rodriguez de Grijalba," replied the lady; "what is your request, brother?" To which Sancho answered, "I would be glad if you would do me the favour of going out the castle gate, where you will find a grey donkey of mine, and make them put him in the stable, or put him there yourself, because the poor little donkey is easily frightened, and cannot bear being alone."

"If the master is as wise as the man," said the lady, "we have been given a fine bargain haven't we? Go along, brother, bad luck for you and to him who brought you here; go look after your donkey, because we, the ladies of this house, are not used to work of that sort."

"Well then, in truth," returned Sancho, "I have heard my master, who is the very treasure-finder of stories, telling the story of Lancelot when he came from Britain, say that ladies waited on him and governing ladies of the house waited on his horse; and, when it comes to my donkey, I wouldn't change him for Señor Lancelot's horse."

"If you are a joker, brother," said the lady, "keep your humour for some place where people gather and pay for it; because you'll get nothing from me but an olive."

"Hopefully, it will be a very ripe one," said Sancho, "because you will not be able to hide its years."

"Son of a bitch," said the lady, glowing with anger, "whether I'm old or not, is with God, not with you, you garlic-stuffed rat!" and she said it so loud, that the duchess heard it, and turning around and seeing the lady in such a state of excitement, and her eyes flaming, asked who she was arguing with.

"With this fellow here," said the lady, "who has requested me to go and put a donkey of his that is at the castle gate into the stable, holding up to me an example that they did the same I don't know where - that some ladies waited on Lancelot, and others on his horse; and what is more, to finish it off, he called me old."

"That," said the duchess, "I would have considered as the greatest insult that could be given to me;" and addressing Sancho, she said to him, "You must know, friend Sancho, that lady Rodriguez is very youthful, and that she wears that hood more for authority and custom's sake than because of her years."

"May all the rest of my years be unlucky," said Sancho, "if I meant it in that way; I only spoke because the affection I have for my donkey is so great, and I thought I could not offer him to a more kind-hearted person than lady Dona Rodriguez."

Don Quixote, who was listening, said to him, "Is this an appropriate place for this conversation, Sancho?"

"Señor," replied Sancho, "everyone must mention what he wants wherever he may be; I thought of the donkey, and I spoke of him here; if I had thought of him in the stable I would have spoken there."

The duke observed, "Sancho is quite right, and there is no reason at all to find fault with him; the donkey will be fed to his heart's content, and Sancho may relax, because he will be treated well."

While this conversation, amusing to all except Don Quixote and Lady Rodriquez, was proceeding, they ascended the staircase and escorted Don Quixote into a room draped with rich cloth of gold; six ladies removed his armour and waited on him like servants, all of them prepared and instructed by the duke and duchess with what they were to do, and how they were to treat Don Quixote, so that he could see and believe they were treating him like a Knight. When his armour was removed, there stood Don Quixote in his tight-fitting trousers and leather jacket, lean, lanky, and long; such a figure, that if the ladies serving him had not taken care to withhold their amusement (which was one of the particular orders their master and mistress had given them), they would have burst with laughter. They asked him to allow himself to be stripped so they could put a shirt on him, but he would not allow it at all, saying that Knights practised modesty just as much as courage. However, he said they could give the shirt to Sancho; and shutting the door to a room where there was a luxurious bed, he undressed and put on the shirt; and then, finding himself alone with Sancho, he said to him, "Tell me, new-born comedian and old tit, do you think it is right to offend and insult a lady deserving of reverence and respect as that one just now? Was that a time to think of your donkey, or are these noble people likely to let the animals be treated badly when they treat their owners in such elegant style? For God's sake, Sancho, restrain yourself, and don't show the thread allowing them see what a rough, impolite texture you are made of. Remember, sinner that you are, a master who is more esteemed, the more respectable and well-bred his servants are; and that one of the greatest advantages that princes have over other men is that they have servants as good as themselves to wait on them. Do you not see - short-sighted being that you are, and unlucky mortal that I am! that if they perceive you to be a clown or a dull fool, they will suspect me to be some impostor? Actually, friend Sancho, keep clear, oh, keep clear of these stumbling-blocks; because he who falls into the way of being a chatterbox and comedian, falls the first time he trips; hold your tongue, consider the weight of your words before they escape your mouth, and bear in mind we are now in a place – from where, by God's help, and the strength of my arm, we will leave greatly advanced in fame and fortune."

Sancho promised him with much sincerity to keep his mouth shut, and to bite off his tongue before he said a word that was not consistent to the purpose and well considered, and told him he could relax his mind on that point, because it would never be discovered through him what they were.

Don Quixote dressed himself, put on his belt with his sword, threw the scarlet cloak over his shoulders, placed on his head a green satin hat that the ladies had given him, and therefore, arrayed as such, walked out into the large room, where he found the ladies lined up along the walls, the same number on each side, all with the resources for washing hands, which they presented to him with abundant respect and formalities. Then twelve other servants came, along with the senior of the court, to lead him to the dining room, where his hosts were already waiting for him. They placed him in-between them, and with much splendour and magnificence they led him into another room, where there was an extravagant table laid with four covers. The duchess and the duke came out to the door of the room to welcome him, and with them a priest, one of those who run noblemen's houses; one of those who, not being born exalted themselves, never know how to teach those who are how to behave as such; one of those who would have the greatness of great people measured by their own narrowness of mind; one of those who, when they try to introduce economy into the household they lead it into stinginess. One of this type, I say, must have been the serious churchman who came out with the duke and duchess to welcome Don Quixote.

A vast number of polite speeches were exchanged, and at length, taking Don Quixote between them, they proceeded to sit down at the table. The duke encouraged Don Quixote to take the head of the table, and, although he refused, the appeals of the duke were so insistent that he had to accept it.

The priest took his seat opposite him, and the duke and duchess at his sides. All this time Sancho stood by with amazement at the honour he saw shown to his master by these illustrious people; and observing all the persuasion between the duke and Don Quixote to induce him to take his seat at the head of the table, he said, "If you will give me your permission I will tell you a story of what happened in my village in regards to a matter of seats."

The moment Sancho said this Don Quixote shivered, thinking that he was about to say something foolish. Sancho glanced at him, and guessing his thoughts, said, "Don't be afraid of me going astray, señor, or saying anything that won't match the purpose; I haven't forgotten the advice you gave me just now about talking too much or too little, well or poorly."

"I have no recollection of anything, Sancho," said Don Quixote; "say what you like, but say it quickly."

"Well then," said Sancho, "what I am going to say is so true that my master Don Quixote, who is here present, will keep me from lying."

"Lie as much as you like for all I care, Sancho," said Don Quixote, "because I am not going to stop you, but consider what you are going to say."

"I have considered and reconsidered," said Sancho, "that the alarm bells can be put away safely; as will be seen by what follows."

"It would be wise," said Don Quixote, "if your highnesses would order this idiot to be thrown out, because he will talk a heap of nonsense."

"On the life of the duke, Sancho will not be taken away from me for a moment," said the duchess; "I am very fond of him, because I know he is very discreet."

"Discreet are the days of your holiness," said Sancho, "because you have a good opinion about my wit, although there's none in me; but the story I want to tell is this. There was an invitation given by a gentleman of my town, a very rich one, and one of high quality, as he was one of the Alamos of Medina del Campo, and married to Dona Mencia de Quinones, the daughter of Don Alonso de Maranon, Knight of the Order of Santiago, that drowned at the Herradura - he was part of that argument years ago in our village, that my master Don Quixote was mixed up in, to the best of my belief, that Tomasillo the scoundrel, the son of Balbastro, was wounded in. Isn't all this true, master of mine? Please say, so these gentle people may not take me for some lying chatterbox."

"So far," said the priest, "I take you to be more of a chatterbox than a liar; but I don't know what I will take you as eventually."

"You cite many witnesses and proofs, Sancho," said Don Quixote, "that I have no choice but to say you must be telling the truth; go on, and cut the story short, because you are on the path not to make an end for another two days."

"He is not to cut it short," said the duchess; "on the contrary, for my gratification, he is to tell it as he knows it, even if he could not finish it in these six days; and if he took that many they would be to me the most pleasant I have ever spent."

"Well then, sirs, I say," continued Sancho, "that this same gentleman, who I know as well as I do my own hands, because it's not a bowshot from my house to his, invited a poor but respectable labourer to his home"

"Hurry up, brother," said the churchman; "at the rate you are going you will not stop with your story before the beginning of the next world."

"I'll stop less than half-way, if God wishes," said Sancho; "and so I say this labourer, coming to the house of the gentleman I spoke of that invited him - rest his soul, is now dead; and symbolically he died the death of an angel, so they say; because I was not there, because just at that time I had left home to earn an income"

"As you live, my son," said the churchman, "hurry up, and finish your story without burying the gentleman, unless you want to make more funerals."

"Well then, it so happened," said Sancho, "that as the pair of them were going to sit down at the table - and I think I can see them now clearer than ever"

The enjoyment of the duke and duchess was so great and was derived from the irritation the churchman showed at the long-winded, and the awkward way Sancho had of telling his story, while Don Quixote was scratching with rage and aggravation.

"So, as I was saying," continued Sancho, "as the pair of them were going to sit down at the table, as I said, the labourer insisted on the gentleman taking the head of the table, and the gentleman insisted on the labourer taking it, as his orders should be obeyed in his house; but the labourer, who prided himself on his politeness and good breeding, would not on any account, until the gentleman, out of impatience, putting his hands on his shoulders, compelled him by force to sit down, saying, 'Sit down, you stupid fool, because wherever I sit will be the head to you; and that's the story, and, in truth, I think it hasn't been given inaccurately here."

Don Quixote turned all colours, which, on his sunburnt face, speckled it until it looked like jasper. The duke and duchess suppressed their laughter so as not to embarrass Don Quixote further, because they saw through Sancho's cheek; and to change the conversation, and keep Sancho from saying any more absurdities, the duchess asked Don Quixote what news he had about his lady Dulcinea, and if he had sent her any presents of giants or troublemakers lately, because he must have defeated many.

To which Don Quixote replied, "Señora, my misfortunes, although they had a beginning, will never have an end. I have conquered giants and I have sent her cowards and troublemakers; but how can they find her if she is enchanted and turned into the most ill-looking peasant that can be imagined?"

I don't know," said Sancho Panza; "to me she seems the finest creature in the world; at any rate, in nimbleness and jumping she won't be beaten by a gymnast; believe, señora duchess, she can leap from the ground on to the back of a horse like a cat."

"Have you seen her enchanted, Sancho?" asked the duke.

"What, seen her!" said Sancho; "who the devil was it but myself that first thought up the enchantment? She is as enchanted as my father is."

When the priest heard them talking about giants, troublemakers and enchantment, he began to suspect that this must be Don Quixote of La Mancha, whose story the duke was always reading; and he had himself often criticised him for reading it, telling him it was foolish to read such nonsense; and becoming convinced that his suspicion was correct, addressing the duke, he said very angrily to him, "Señor, your excellency will have to give account to God for what this good man does. This Don Quixote, or Don Foolish, or whatever his name is, cannot be, I imagine, such a fool as you encourage him to be, to go on with his madness and stupidity." Then turning to address Don Quixote he said, "And you, idiot born boy, who put it into your head that you are a Knight, and conquer giants and capture troublemakers? Go on your way in an hour. Go home and bring up your children if you have any, and attend to your business, and give up wandering around the world making a fool of yourself to all who know you and all who don't. Where, in heaven's name, have you discovered that there are or ever were Knights? Where are there giants in Spain or troublemakers in La Mancha, or enchanted Dulcineas, or all the rest of the silly things they say about you?"

Don Quixote listened attentively to the gentleman's words, and as soon as he perceived he had done speaking, regardless of the presence of the duke and duchess, he jumped to his feet with angry looks and an agitated appearance, and said: (the reply deserves a chapter of its own).

CHAPTER 32

THE REPLY DON QUIXOTE GAVE THE PRIEST, WITH OTHER INCIDENTS, BOTH SERIOUS AND HUMOUROUS

Don Quixote, then, having risen to his feet, shaking from head to toe like a man dosed up on drugs, said in a hurried, agitated voice, "The place I am in, the presence in which I stand, and the respect I have and always have had for the profession to which you belong, halt and bind the hands of my justified fury; and as well for these reasons, because I know, as everyone knows, that a priest's weapon is the same as a woman's, the tongue, I will with mine engage in equal combat with you, from whom one might have expected good advice instead of vulgar abuse. Sincere, well-meant criticism requires a different manner and arguments of another type; at any rate, to have criticised me in public, and so roughly, exceeds the boundary of proper criticism, because that is done better with gentleness than with rudeness; and it is not appropriate to call the sinner a fool and tit, without knowing anything about the sin that is criticised. Tell me, which stupidity have you observed in me and condemn and abuse me for, and ask me go home to look after my house, wife and children, without knowing whether I have any? Is nothing more needed than to get a foot in, perhaps without merit, in other people's houses to rule over the masters (and then, perhaps, after having been brought up there, and without having ever seen more of the world than what lies within twenty or thirty miles), to lay down the law recklessly for chivalry, and give judgment on Knights? Is it, by chance, a useless occupation, or is time poorly-spent when it is spent roaming the world in quest, not out of enjoyment, but for those difficult adventures where the good rise upwards to the home of everlasting life? If gentlemen, great lords and noblemen, were to rate me as a fool I would take it as an irreparable insult; but I do not care one bit if men who have never entered or walked the paths of chivalry think of me as foolish. Knight I am, and Knight I will die. Some take the broad road of unrestrained ambition; others shameful grovelling and flattery; others take the path of deceitful hypocrisy, and some follow true religion; but I, led by my star, follow the narrow path of Knighthood, and in pursuit of that calling I despise wealth, but not honour. I have mended injuries, righted wrongs, punished insolence, defeated giants, and crushed monsters; I am in love, for no other reason than that it is compulsory for Knights to be; but although I am no animal-minded lover, but one of the moral, platonic sort. My intentions are always directed to worthy ends, to do good to all and evil to none; and if he who means this, does this, and makes this his practice deserves to be called a fool, it is for you to say?."

"God!" cried Sancho; "say no more in your own defence, master of mine, because there's nothing more in the world that could be said, thought, or insisted; and besides, when this gentleman denies, as he has, that there are or ever have been any Knights in the world, it is obvious he knows nothing about what he is saying?"

"Perhaps," said the priest, "you are the Sancho Panza that has been promised an island by your master?"

"That is I señor," said Sancho, "and what is more, I am one who deserves it as much as anyone; I am one of the kind that believe 'attach yourself to one who does good, and you will be good,' and, 'not who you meet with - but who you eat with,' and, 'he who leans against a good tree, is covered with good shade' I lean on a good master, and I have been leaning on him for months now, and God willing, I will many more months to come; long life to him and long life to me, because he will have no lack of empires to rule, and I no lack of islands to govern."

"No, Sancho my friend, certainly not," said the duke, "because in the name of Señor Don Quixote I will offer you the government of an island, one of no small importance that I have at my disposal."

"Go down on your knees, Sancho," said Don Quixote, "and kiss the feet of his excellence for the favour he has presented to you."

Sancho obeyed, and on seeing this the priest stood up from table in complete rage, exclaiming, "on the position I hold, I am almost inclined to say that you are as great a fool as these sinners. No wonder they are mad, when people who are in their senses support their madness! I leave you with them, because as long as they are in the house, I will remain in my own, and spare myself the trouble of condemning what I cannot resolve;" and without saying another word, or eating another bit, he left the room. The duke and duchess appealed for him to stay but this was entirely ineffective to stop him; not that the duke said much to him, he could not, because of the laughter his uncalled-for anger provoked.

When he had finished laughing, he said to Don Quixote, "You have replied on your own behalf so firmly, Sir Knight of the Lions, that there is no occasion to seek further satisfaction for this, which, although it may look like an offence, is not at all, because, as women can give no offence, neither can priests, as you very well know."

"That is true," said Don Quixote, "and the reason is, that he who is not liable to offence cannot give offence to anyone. Women, children, and priests, as they cannot defend themselves, although they may receive an offence cannot be insulted, because between the offence and the insult there is, as your excellence very well knows, this difference: the insult comes from one who is capable of offering it. As an example: a man is standing unsuspectingly in the street and ten others come and beat him; he raises his sword and defends himself like a man, but the number of his adversaries make it impossible for him to retaliate; this man suffers an offence but not an insult. Another example will make the same thing clearer: a man is standing with his back turned, another comes and strikes him from behind, and after striking him he runs away, without waiting. The man pursues him but does not catch him; he who received the blow received an offence, but not an insult, because an insult must be maintained. If he who struck him, although he did so in a sneaky manner, had raised his sword and stood to face him, then he who had been struck would have received an offence and insult at the same time; an offence because he was struck, an insult because he who struck him maintained what he had done, standing his ground without running. And so, according to the laws of fighting, I may have received an offence, but not an insult, because no women or child can maintain it, neither can they wound, or have any way of standing their ground, and it is just the same with those connected with religion; because these three types of people are without offensive or defensive capability, and so, although naturally they are bound to defend themselves, they have no right to offend anybody; and although I said just now I might have received an offence, I now am certain I did not, because he who cannot receive an insult cannot give one; for this reason I should not feel, or do I feel, hurt by what that good man said to me; I only wish he had stayed a little longer, so I might have shown him the mistake he makes in supposing and maintaining that there aren't and never have been any Knights in the world; had Amadis or any of his countless descendants heard him say this, I am sure it would not have gone well for him."

"I would make an oath for that," said Sancho; "they would have given him a slice that would have split him down the middle, head to toe, like a ripe melon; they were not the type of men to put up with jokes of that sort! Believe, I'm certain if Reinaldos of Montalvan had heard the little man's words he would have given him such a punch in the mouth that he wouldn't have spoken for the next three years!"

As the duchess listened to Sancho, she was ready to die with laughter, and in her own mind she considered him funnier and madder than his master; and there were many others just then who had the same opinion.

Don Quixote finally calmed down, and dinner came to an end, and as the cloth was removed four ladies came in, one of them with a silver basin, another with a jug of water made of silver, a third with two fine white towels on her shoulder, and the fourth, in her white hands, a round ball of soap from Naples. The one with the basin approached, and shoved it under Don Quixote's chin, who, wondering what this ceremony was, did not say a word, supposing it must be the custom there to wash beards instead of hands; he therefore stretched his out as far as he could, and at the same moment the jug began to pour and the lady with the soap rubbed his beard vigorously, raising little white flakes, because the soap lather was no less white, not only over the beard, but all over the face, and over the eyes of the humble Knight, so that they were unavoidably obliged to keep shut. The duke and duchess, who had not known anything about this, waited to see what was to come from this strange washing. When the lady barber had him covered in lather, pretended that there was no more water, and asked the one with the jug to go and get some more, while Señor Don Quixote waited. So she did, and Don Quixote was left looking like the strangest and most absurd figure that could be imagined. All those present, and there were many, were watching him, and as they saw him there with half a foot of lather, his eyes shut, and his beard full of soap, it was amazing that with great discretion they were able to restrain their laughter. The ladies, the creators of the joke, kept their eyes down, not daring to look at their master and mistress; and as for them, laughter and anger struggled within them, and they did not know what to do, whether to punish the girls for the unannounced joke, or to reward them for the amusement they had received from seeing Don Quixote in such a predicament.

Finally, the lady with the jug returned and they finished washing Don Quixote, and the one who carried the towels very deliberately wiped him and dried him; and all four of them together paid him their respects and gave him a curtsey.

They were about to go, when the duke, so Don Quixote could not perceive the joke, called out to the one with the basin and said, "Come and wash me, and make sure there is enough water." The girl, sharp-witted and prompt, came and placed the basin for the duke as she had done for Don Quixote, and they soon had him well soaped and washed, and having wiped him dry they paid their respect and left. It appeared afterwards that the duke had sworn that if they had not washed him as they had Don Quixote he would have punished them for their audacity, which they completely atoned for by washing him as well.

Sancho was watching the ceremony of washing very thoughtfully, and said to himself, "God bless, if it were only the custom in this country to wash aides' beards as well as Knights'. Because I swear to God and on my soul I want it badly; and if they gave me a scrape of the razor as well I'd take it as a greater kindness."

"What are you saying to yourself, Sancho?" asked the duchess.

"I was saying, señora," he replied, "that in the courts of other princes, when the cloth is taken away, I have always heard it said they give water for the hands, but not for the beard; and that shows it is good to live long so you can see a lot; for sure, they say as well that he who lives a long life must go through much suffering, although to undergo washing of that sort is pure pleasure rather than pain."

"Don't be uneasy, friend Sancho," said the duchess; "I will take care that my ladies wash you, and even put you in the tub if necessary."

"I'll be content with the beard," said Sancho, "at any rate for the present; and as for the future, God has ordered what will be."

"Attend to worthy Sancho's request," said the duchess, "and do exactly what he wishes." All agreed that Señor Sancho's request should be obeyed. And with this Sancho left the room.

The duke and duchess and Don Quixote remained at the table discussing a variety of things, but all about the calling of arms and Knighthood.

The duchess begged Don Quixote, as he seemed to have an absorbent memory, to describe and portray to her the beauty and features of the lady Dulcinea del Toboso, because, judging by the fame advertised abroad of her beauty, she felt sure she must be the most beautiful creature in the world, not only in all of La Mancha.

Don Quixote sighed on hearing the duchess's request, and said, "If I could pull out my heart, and place it on a plate on this table here in front of your highness's eyes, it would spare my tongue the pain of telling what can hardly be thought of, because in it your excellence would see her portrayed in full. But why should I attempt to depict and describe in detail, and feature by feature, the beauty of the peerless Dulcinea, the burden being worthy of other shoulders than mine, a task wherein the pencils of Parrhasius, Timantes, and Apelles, and the engravers of Lysippus should be employed, to paint it in pictures and carve it in marble and bronze, and the Demosthenian and Ciceronian eloquence to praise it?"

"What does Demosthenian and Ciceronian mean, Señor Don Quixote?" said the duchess; "these are words I never heard in all my life."

"Demosthenian and Ciceronian eloquence," said Don Quixote, "means the eloquence of Demosthenes, as Ciceronian means that of Cicero, who were the two most eloquent orators in the world."

"True," said the duke; "you must have lost your mind to ask such a question. Nevertheless, Señor Don Quixote would greatly gratify us if he would depict her to us; because with no doubt, even in an outline or sketch he will display her to be someone who could make the fairest envious."

"I would do so certainly," said Don Quixote, "had she not been blurred to my mind's eye by the misfortune that fell on her a short time ago, one of such a nature that I am more ready to cry over it than to describe. Because your highnesses must know that, going a few days back to kiss her hands and receive her approval, consent, and permission for this third departure, I found her a different being from the one I sought; I found her enchanted and changed from a Princess into a peasant, from fair to foul, from an angel into a devil, from fragrant to putrid, from refined to clownish, from a dignified lady into a tomboy, and, in a word, from Dulcinea del Toboso into a troll."

"God bless!" said the duke, "who could have done the world such injustice? Who could have robbed it of the beauty that delighted it, of the grace that charmed it, of the modesty that shed a smooth sheen on it?"

"Who?" replied Don Quixote; "who could it be but some malevolent enchanter out of the many that persecute me out of envy - that appalling race born into the world to obscure and bring to nothing the achievements of the good, and glorify and exalt the deeds of the evil? Enchanters have persecuted me, enchanters still persecute me, and enchanters will continue to persecute me until they have ruined me and thrown my grand chivalry in the deep abyss of oblivion; and they injure and wound me where they know I feel it most. Because to deprive a Knight of his lady is to deprive him of the eyes he sees with, of the sun that gives him light, of the food he lives by. Many times before I have said it, and I say it again, a Knight without a lady is like a tree without leaves, a building without a foundation, or a shadow without the body that causes it."

"There is no denying that," said the duchess; "but still, if we are to believe the history of Don Quixote that has been met with general applause, it is to be inferred from it, if I am not mistaken, that you never saw lady Dulcinea, and that the lady is nothing in the world but an imaginary lady, one that you yourself produced and gave birth to in your brain, and beautified with whatever charms and perfections you chose."

"There is a lot to be said on that point," said Don Quixote; "God knows whether there is any Dulcinea or not in the world, or whether she is imaginary or not; these are things the proof of which must not be pushed to extreme lengths. I have not created or given birth to my lady, although I hold her as she must be, a lady who contains in herself all the qualities to make her famous throughout the world, beautiful without a blemish, dignified without arrogance, tender and yet modest, gracious from courtesy and courteous from good breeding, and lastly, from an exalted lineage, because beauty shines and excels with a higher degree of perfection in those of good blood than those from low birth."

"That is true," said the duke; "but Señor Don Quixote must grant me permission to say what I am obliged to say due to the story of his adventures that I have read, from which it is to be inferred that, granting there is a Dulcinea in El Toboso, and she is in the highest degree as beautiful that has been described, that in regards to her lineage she is not on a par with the Orianas, Alastrajareas, Madasimas, or others of that sort, with whom, as you well know, the histories proliferate."

"To that I may reply," said Don Quixote, "that Dulcinea is the daughter of herself, and that virtues cure blood, and that low virtue should be more esteemed than exalted vice. Dulcinea, besides, has within her what is necessary to raise her to be a crowned Queen; because the merit of a fair and virtuous woman is capable of performing greater miracles; and virtually, although not formally, she has in herself higher fortunes."

"I object, Señor Don Quixote," said the duchess, "in all you say, be cautious, I will believe that there is a Dulcinea in El Toboso, and that she is living, and that she is beautiful and deserves to have a Knight such as Señor Don Quixote in her service, and that is the highest praise that it is in my power to give her. But I cannot help having a doubt, and holding a grudge against Sancho Panza; the doubt is this, that in the history it is declared that Sancho Panza, when he carried a letter on your behalf to lady Dulcinea, found her sifting a sack of wheat; and this makes me doubt the height of her lineage."

To this Don Quixote answered, "Señora, your highness must know that everything or almost everything that happens to me transcends the ordinary limits of what happens to other Knights; whether it is directed by the unpredictable will of destiny, or by the malice of some jealous enchanter. Now it is an established fact that all or most famous Knights have some special gift, one invincible against enchantment, another made of invulnerable flesh so he cannot be wounded, known to the famous Roland, one of the twelve peers of France, of whom it is said that he could not be wounded except in the sole of his left foot, and that it must be with the point of a strong pin and not with any other sort of weapon whatsoever; and so, when Bernardo del Carpio attacked him at Roncesvalles, finding that he could not wound him with steel, he lifted him from the ground in his arms and strangled him, bringing to mind the death which Hercules inflicted on Antaeus, the fierce giant that they say was the son of Terra. I would infer from what I have mentioned that perhaps I may have some gift, not being invulnerable, because experience has proven many times to me that I am made from tender flesh and not impenetrable; or that I am invincible against enchantment, because I have already seen myself captured in a cage, in which all the world would not have been able to confine me except with the force of enchantment. But as I freed myself from that, I am inclined to believe that there is no one that can hurt me; and so, these enchanters, seeing that they cannot apply their vile craft against me, take their revenge on what I love most, and seek to rob me of life by mistreating Dulcinea; and therefore I am convinced that when my aide carried my message to her, they changed her into a common peasant girl, engaged in such a low occupation as sifting wheat; but I have already said, however, that this was not wheat at all, but grains of orient pearl. And as a proof of all this, I must tell your highnesses that, going to El Toboso a short time ago, I was unable to discover the palace of Dulcinea; and that the next day, although Sancho, my aide, saw her in her proper form, which is the most beautiful in the world, to me she appeared to be a hard, poor farm-girl. And so, as I am not and, as far as one can judge, cannot be permanently enchanted, it is her that is enchanted, that is altered, changed, and transformed; my enemies have revenged themselves on me through her, and for this I will live with never-ending tears, until I see her in her pristine condition. Dulcinea is well-known and well-born, and from one of the gentle families in El Toboso, it is assured, through the peerless Dulcinea, her town will be famous and celebrated in ages to come, as Troy was through Helen, and Spain through La Cava, though with a better title and tradition. Another thing; I wish you to know and understand that Sancho Panza is one of the funniest aides that ever served a Knight; sometimes there is a simplicity about him so acute that it is an amusement to try and make out whether he is simple or sharp; he has mischievous tricks that make him a rogue, and careless ways that prove him to be a tit; he doubts everything and believes everything; when I think he is on the verge of going straight down into sheer stupidity, he comes out with something sharp that sends him to the sky. After all this, I would not exchange him for another aide, even if I were given a city, and therefore I am in doubt whether it would be wise to send him to govern the island your highness has offered him; although I perceive in him a certain aptitude for the work of governing, so that, with a little trimming of his understanding, he would manage any government as easily as the King does his taxes; and additionally, we already know with ample experience that it does not require much intelligence or much education to be a governor, because there are a hundred around that barely know how to read. The main point is that they should have good intentions and be eager to do right in all things, because they will never be without people to advise and direct them in what they have to do, like those Knight-governors who, not being lawyers, give sentences with the aid of a judge. My advice to him will be to take no bribes and surrender no rights, and I have some other matters reserved, that will be produced in due course for Sancho's benefit and the advantage of the island he is to govern."

The duke, duchess, and Don Quixote had reached this point in their conversation, when they heard voices and a great commotion in the palace, and Sancho burst abruptly into the room glowing with anger, with a cloth round his neck like a bib, and followed by several servants, or, more properly speaking, kitchen-boys, one of whom carried a small bowl full of water, that from its colour and impurity was clearly dishwater. The one with the bowl followed him everywhere he went, attempting with the utmost persistence to place it under his chin, while another kitchen-boy seemed eager to wash his beard.

"What is all this about?" asked the duchess. "What are you trying to do to this good man? Did you forget he is an elected governor?"

To which the barber kitchen-boy replied, "The gentleman will not allow me to wash him as is customary, and as the señor his master has been."

"Yes, I will," said Sancho, in a great rage; "but I'd like it to be with cleaner towels, clearer water, and not with such dirty hands; because there's not so much difference between me and my master that he should be washed with angels' water and I with devil's dirt. The customs of palaces are only good as long as they give no annoyance; but the style of washing they have here is worse than doing atonement. I have a clean beard, and I don't require to be refreshed in that way, and whoever comes to wash me or touch a hair on my head, I mean to say my beard, with all due respect, I'll give him a punch that will leave my fist in his skull; because washing of this kind is more like a joke than the polite attention of one's host."

The duchess was ready to die with laughter when she saw Sancho's rage and heard his words; but it was no pleasure to Don Quixote to see him in such a state, with the dingy towel round his neck, and the kitchen boys following him; so asking the permission of the duke and duchess to speak, he addressed them in a dignified tone: "Gentlemen! you leave my aide alone, and go back to where you came from, or anywhere else if you like; my aide is as clean; take my advice and leave him alone, because neither of us take kindly to jokes of this sort."

Sancho picked up where he had stopped, "Actually, let them come and try their jokes on this country boy, because it's as likely I'll stand them as it's now midnight! Let them bring me a comb, or whatever they like, and wash this beard of mine, and if they get anything from it that offends cleanliness, let them clip my skin."

The duchess, laughing the whole time, said, "Sancho Panza is right, and always will be in all he says; he is clean, and, as he says himself, he does not require to be washed; and if our ways do not please him, he is free to choose. Besides, you promoters of cleanliness have been excessively careless and thoughtless, I don't know if I should say daring, to bring bowls and wooden utensils and kitchen dish cloths, instead of basins and jugs of pure gold and towels of cotton, to such a person and such a beard; but, after all, you are poor-conditioned and low-bred, and spiteful as you are, you cannot help showing the grudge you have against the aides of esteemed Knights."

The bold kitchen boys, took the duchess to be speaking seriously, so they removed the cloth from Sancho's neck, and with something like shame and confusion on their faces left them and left him; and he, seeing himself safe and out of extreme danger, as it seemed to him, ran and fell on his knees in front of the duchess, saying, "From great ladies great favours are given; this which your grace has done for me today cannot be repaid even if I was made a Knight, to devote myself for the rest of my life to the service of such an exalted lady as you. I am a working man, my name is Sancho Panza, I am married, I have children, and I am serving as an aide; if in any one of these ways I can serve your highness, I will not delay in obeying your command."

"It is easy to see, Sancho," replied the duchess, "that you have learned to be polite in the school of politeness itself; I mean to say it is easy to see that you have been taken under the wing of Señor Don Quixote, who is, of course, the top of good breeding and flower of ceremony, as you would so say yourself. Good fortune favour such a master and such a servant, one the centre of Knighthood, the other the star of loyalty! Rise, Sancho, my friend; I will repay your courtesy by taking care that my lord the duke honours the promised gift of the government as soon as possible."

With this, the conversation came to an end, and Don Quixote withdrew to take his midday siesta; but the duchess begged Sancho, unless he really needed to go to sleep, to come and spend the afternoon with her and her ladies in one of the rooms of the palace. Sancho replied that, although he certainly had the habit of sleeping four or five hours during the day due to the heat of summer, to serve her, he would try with all his strength not to sleep even one hour that day, and that he would go in obedience to her command, and with that he left.

The duke gave new orders with respect to treating Don Quixote as a Knight, without deviating in the slightest degree from the style in which, as the stories tell us, that they used to treat the Knights of the past.

CHAPTER 33

THE CHARMING DISCOURSE WHICH THE DUCHESS AND HER LADIES HELD WITH SANCHO PANZA, WELL WORTH READING AND NOTING

The history records that Sancho did not sleep that afternoon, but in order to keep his word went, well before dinner, to visit the duchess, who, finding enjoyment in listening to him, made him sit down beside her, although Sancho, out of pure goodness, did not want sit down; the duchess, however, told him he was to sit down as governor and talk as an aide, as in both respects he was worthy of the chair which belonged to Cid Ruy Diaz the great leader. Sancho shrugged his shoulders, obeyed, and sat down, and all the duchess's ladies gathered round him, waiting in profound silence to hear what he would say. It was the duchess, however, who spoke first, saying:

"Now that we are alone, and that there is nobody to overhear us, I would be glad if the señor governor would relieve me of certain doubts I have, rising from the history of the great Don Quixote that is now in print. One is: as Sancho never saw Dulcinea, I mean the lady Dulcinea del Toboso, or took Don Quixote's letter to her, because it was left in the conversation that occurred in the Sierra Morena, how did he dare to invent the answer about finding her sifting wheat, the whole story being deception and false, and so much to the detriment of the peerless Dulcinea's good name, a thing that is not fitting with the character and loyalty of a good aide?"

At these words, Sancho, without saying one in reply, got up from his chair, and with silent steps, and with his finger on his lips, went all around the room lifting up objects and paintings on the wall; and with this done, he came back to his seat and said, "Now, señora, that I have seen that there is no one here except these spectators listening, I will answer what you have asked, and all you may ask me, without any fear. And the first thing I have got to say is, that in my opinion I believe my master Don Quixote to be totally mad, although sometimes he says things that, to my mind, and to everybody's that listens to him, are wise, and are so correct, that Satan himself could not argue with them; but despite that, really, and beyond all question, it's my firm belief he is crackers. Well, then, as this is clear to my mind, I can make him believe most things, like the answer to the letter, and what happened six or eight days ago, which is not yet in print, that is to say, the enchantment of my lady Dulcinea; because I made him believe she is enchanted, although there's no more truth in it than the reply to the letter."

The duchess begged him to tell her about the enchantment or deception, so Sancho told the whole story exactly as it had happened, and his listeners were highly amused by it; and then resuming, the duchess said, "In consequence of what Sancho has told me, a doubt arises in my mind, 'If Don Quixote is mad, crazy, and crackers, and Sancho Panza his aide knows it, and, despite this, serves and follows him, and trusts his empty promises, there can be no doubt that he must be madder than his master; and that being so, it would be even crazier to give Sancho an island to govern; because how will one who does not know how to govern himself know how to govern others?'"

"God, señora," said Sancho, "that doubt comes well-timed; but you have total right to say it; because I know what you say is true, and if I were wise I should have left my master a long time ago; but this was my fate, this was my bad luck; I can't help it, I must follow him; we're from the same village, I've eaten his bread, I'm fond of him, I'm grateful, he gave me his donkeys, and above all I'm faithful; so it's quite impossible for anything to separate us, except a sword and shovel. And if your highness does not wish to give me the government you promised, God made me without it, and maybe you not giving it to me will be better for my conscience, because fool that I am I still know the proverb 'through pain the ant got wings,' and it may be that Sancho the aide will get to heaven sooner than Sancho the governor. And 'at night all cats are grey,' and 'there's no stomach bigger than another,' and it can be filled 'with straw or hay,' and 'the little birds in the field have God for their supplier,' and 'when we leave this world and are placed underground, the prince travels the same road as the highwayman,' and 'the Pope's body does not take up more feet of earth than the common man's,' because although one is higher than the other; when we go to our graves we all make ourselves small, or rather others pack us up and make us small, and then – it's good night for us. And I say again, if you would not like to give me the island because I'm a fool, like a wise man I will not trouble myself about it; I have heard it said that 'behind the cross there's the devil,' and that 'all that glitters is not gold,' and that from the ox, and the plough, and the reins, Wamba the farmer was taken to be made the King of Spain, and from among golden fabric, pleasure, and riches, Roderick was taken to be devoured by snakes, if the verses of the old poems are true."

"They do not lie!" exclaimed Dona Rodriguez, the older lady, who was one of the listeners. "There's a poem that says they put King Rodrigo into a tomb while he was alive, full of frogs, snakes, and lizards, and that two days afterwards the King, in a sorrowful, feeble voice, cried out from within the tomb:

They bite me now, they bite me now,
Where I sinned most.

And according to that the gentleman has a good reason to say he would rather be a working man than a King, if vermin are to eat him."

The duchess could not help laughing at the simplicity of her lady, or wondering about the language and proverbs of Sancho, to whom she said, "Worthy Sancho knows very well that when a Knight has made a promise he strives to keep it, although it could cost him his life. My lord and husband the duke, although not one of the Knights, is not less honourable for that reason, and will keep his word about the promised island, despite the envy and malice of the world. Let Sancho be in good spirit; because when he least expects it he will find himself sat on the throne of his island in his seat of dignity, and will take possession of his government. I advise him to be careful how he governs his servants, bearing in mind that they are all loyal and well-born."

"As to governing them well," said Sancho, "there's no need to advise me to do that, because I'm kind-hearted by nature, and full of compassion for the poor; there's no stealing the loaf from those who knead and bake the bread;' and you have my word it won't work with me to misrepresent the truth; I am an old dog, and I know all about work in the community; I can be wide-awake, and I don't let clouds cover my eyes, because I know when the shoe is tight; I say this, because with me the good will have support and protection, and the bad will have no help or access. And it seems to me that, in governments, to make a beginning is everything; and maybe, after having been governor for a fortnight, I'll enjoy the work and know more about it than the field labour I have been brought up doing."

"You are right, Sancho," said the duchess, "because no one is born already taught, and the bishops are made out of men and not out of stones. But to return to the subject we were discussing just now, the enchantment of lady Dulcinea, I consider it as certain, and something more than apparent, that Sancho's idea of practising deception on his master, making him believe that the peasant girl was Dulcinea and that if he did not recognise her it must be because she was enchanted, was all a plot created by of one of the enchanters that persecute Don Quixote. Because in truth and sincerity, I know from a trustworthy source that the rough country girl who jumped up on the horse was and is Dulcinea del Toboso, and that worthy Sancho, although he believes himself to be the deceiver, is the one that has been deceived; and that there is no reason to doubt the truth of this than there is to doubt anything else we have ever seen. Señor Sancho Panza should know that we also have enchanters here that are available to us, and tell us exactly what is going on in the world, clearly and distinctly, without any tricks or deception; and believe me, Sancho, that agile country girl was and is Dulcinea del Toboso; and when we least expect it, we will see her in true form, and then Sancho will be enlightened about the illusion he is under at present."

"All that's very possible," said Sancho Panza; "and now I'm willing to believe what my master says about what he saw in the cave of Montesinos, where he says he saw lady Dulcinea del Toboso in the very same dress and apparel that I said I had seen her in when I made up the enchantment to help myself. All of it must be the other way round, as you say; because it is impossible to believe that out of my foolish mind such an astute trick could be concocted, and neither do I think my master is so mad that with my weak and feeble persuasion he could be made to believe something beyond reason. But, señora, your excellence must not therefore think I am untrustworthy, because a fool like me is not bound to see into the thoughts and plots of those vile enchanters. I invented all that to escape my master's reprimand, and not with any intention of hurting him; and if it has turned out differently, there is a God in heaven who judges our hearts."

"That is true," said the duchess; "but tell me, Sancho, what is this you say about the cave of Montesinos, because I would like to know."

Sancho relayed to her, word for word, what has been said already about that adventure, and having heard it the duchess said, "From this occurrence it may be inferred that, as the great Don Quixote says he saw the same country girl there that Sancho saw on the way from El Toboso, it is, no doubt, Dulcinea, and that there are some very active and exceedingly busy enchanters around."

"So I believe," said Sancho, "and if my lady Dulcinea is enchanted, that is terrible for her, and I'm not going to argue with my master's many and spiteful enemies. The truth is, the one I saw was a country girl, and I believed her to be a country girl; and if that was Dulcinea I cannot be blamed for what I saw, and neither should I be called to answer for it or take the consequences. They must attack me at every step - 'Sancho said it, Sancho did it, Sancho here, Sancho there,' as if Sancho was nobody at all, and not the same Sancho Panza that's now going all over the world in books, as Samson Carrasco told me, and he's a graduate of Salamanca; and people of that sort can't lie, except when the impulse takes them or they have a very good reason for it. So there's no reason for anybody to argue with me; and then I have a good character, and, as I have heard my master say, 'a good name is better than great riches;' place me into this government and you will see wonders, because one who has been a good aide will be a good governor."

"All worthy Sancho's observations," said the duchess, "are Catonian sentences, or out of the very heart of Michael Verino himself, who in his blossoming years was killed. In fact, to speak in his own style, 'under a bad coat there's often a good drinker.'"

"Indeed, señora," said Sancho, "I never yet drank out of evil; from thirst I have very likely, because I have nothing of the hypocrite in me; I drink when I'm inclined, or, if I'm not inclined, when they offer it to me; because when a friend drinks to one's health what heart can be so hard not to return it? But if I put on my shoes I don't dirty them; besides, aides to Knights mostly drink water, because they are always wandering among woods, forests and meadows, mountains and cliffs, without a drop of wine to drink even if they gave their eyes for it."

"So I believe," said the duchess; "and now let Sancho go and take his sleep, and we will talk later at greater length, and settle how he may soon go and start governing, as he says.

Sancho once more kissed the duchess's hand, and asked her for good care of Dapple, because he was the light of his eyes.

"What is Dapple?" said the duchess.

"My donkey," said Sancho, "which, not to call him by that name, I call him Dapple; I asked this lady here to take good care of him when I came into the castle, and she got as angry as if I had said she were old and ugly, although it should be more natural and appropriate for the ladies of the castle to feed donkeys than to decorate rooms. God! what spite a gentleman of my village had against these ladies!"

"He must have been a clown," said Dona Rodriguez; "because if he had been a gentleman and well-born he would have exalted them higher than the moon."

"That will do," said the duchess; "no more of this; quiet, Dona Rodriguez, and let Señor Panza rest and leave the treatment of Dapple to me, because as he is a treasure of Sancho's, I'll make him the apple of my eye."

"It would be enough for him to be in the stable," said Sancho, "because neither he or I are worthy to rest a moment in the apple of your highness's eye; because although my master says that in respect it is better to lose by too many cards than a card too short, when it comes to respect for donkeys we must keep within a suitable boundary."

"Take him to your government, Sancho," said the duchess, "and there you will be able to make as much of him as you like, and even release him from work and provide him a pension."

"Don't think, señora duchess, that you have said anything silly," said Sancho; "I have seen more than two donkeys go to governments, and for me to take mine with me would be nothing new."

Sancho's words made the duchess laugh again and gave her great delight, and dismissing him to sleep she went away to tell the duke the conversation she had had with him, and between them they plotted and arranged to play a rare and unique joke on Don Quixote entirely in Knighthood style, and in the very same style, they practised several on him, so suitable and so clever that they form the best adventures this great history contains.

CHAPTER 34

HOW THEY LEARNED THE WAY TO DISENCHANT DULCINEA DEL TOBOSO, WHICH IS ONE OF THE RAREST ADVENTURES IN THIS BOOK

The duke and duchess took great pleasure in the conversations of Don Quixote and Sancho Panza; and now, more inclined than ever to initiate the plan they had of practising some jokes on them that were to have the look and appearance of adventures, they formed as their basis for action what Don Quixote had already told them about the cave of Montesinos. But what the duchess was so amused about above all was that Sancho's simplicity was great enough to make him believe as absolute truth that Dulcinea had been enchanted, when it was he himself who had been the enchanter and trickster. Having, therefore, instructed their servants in everything they were to do, six days afterwards they took him out to hunt, with as many huntsmen as a crowned King.

They presented Don Quixote with a hunting suit, and Sancho with another of the finest green cloth; but Don Quixote declined to wear it, saying that he must shortly return to the hard pursuit of Knighthood, and could not carry clothes with him. Sancho, however, took what they gave him, intending to sell it when the first opportunity arose.

The day arrived, Don Quixote armed himself, and Sancho organised himself, and mounted his donkey (because he would not give him up even if they offered him a horse), he placed himself in the middle of the group of huntsmen. The duchess came out wonderfully attired, and Don Quixote, in pure courtesy and politeness, held the rein of her horse, although the duke did not want to allow him to; and finally they reached a wood that was between two high mountains, where, after taking various positions and paths, and distributing the group, the hunt began with great noise and shouting, so that, between the barking of the dogs and the blowing of the horns, they could not hear one another. The duchess dismounted, and with a sharp spear in her hand posted herself where she knew the wild boars usually passed. The duke and Don Quixote also dismounted and placed themselves at each side of her. Sancho took a position in the rear behind all without dismounting from his donkey, who he could not desert in case some great mischief might happen to him.

They had barely taken their place in a line with several of their servants, when they saw a huge boar, closely pursued by the dogs and followed by the huntsmen, coming towards them, with large tusks, grinding his teeth, and foaming from the mouth. As soon as Don Quixote saw it, raising his shield on his arm, and lifting his sword, advanced to meet it; the duke with a spear did the same; but the duchess would have gone in front of them all if the Duke had not prevented her. Sancho alone, at the sight of the mighty beast deserted his donkey, and ran as fast as he could and struggled to climb a tall oak. As he was clinging to a branch, however, half-way up in his struggle to reach the top, to his bad luck, it gave way, and he was caught in his fall by another branch of the oak, which he hung suspended in the air from unable to reach the ground. Finding himself in this position, and that the green coat was beginning to tear, and reflecting that if the fierce animal came that way he might be able to attack him, he began to make such cries and calls for help, that all who heard him and did not see him felt he must be in the teeth of some wild beast. In the end the boar fell pierced by the blades of the many spears they held in front of him; and Don Quixote, turning round at the cries of Sancho (because by them he knew it was him), and saw him hanging from the oak upside-down, with his donkey, who did not leave him in his distress, close beside him; and Cide Hamete notes that he rarely saw Sancho Panza without his donkey, or the donkey without Sancho Panza; as their attachment and loyalty one to the other was so great. Don Quixote went over and unhooked Sancho, who, as soon as he found himself on the ground, looked at the tear in his hunting coat and was saddened in his heart, because he thought he could have bought an estate for that suit.

Meanwhile they had placed the mighty boar across the back of a donkey, and having covered it with sprigs of rosemary, they took it away as the prize of victory to some large field with tents which had been pitched in the middle of the wood, where they found the tables laid and dinner served, in such grand and luxurious style that it was easy to see the rank and magnificence of those who had provided it.

Sancho, as he showed the tear in his suit to the duchess, said, "If we had been hunting rabbits, or small birds, my coat would have been safe; I don't know what pleasure is to be found in waiting for an animal that may take your life with his tusk if he gets you. I recall having heard an old poem that says:

Devoured by the bears, who was once the King.

"That," said Don Quixote, "was a King, who, going hunting, was devoured by a bear."

"Exactly," said Sancho; "and I would not have Kings and Princes expose themselves to such danger for the sake of a pleasure which, to my mind, should not be pleasurable to anyone, as it consists in killing an animal that has done no harm whatsoever."

"Quite the contrary, Sancho; you are wrong there," said the duke; "because hunting is more suitable and for Kings and Princes than for anybody else. The chase is the symbol of war; it has tactics and crafty tricks for overcoming the enemy in safety; extreme cold and intolerable heat have to be endured, laziness and sleep are despised, the bodily powers are invigorated, for those who engage in it, the limbs are made supple, and in short, it is a pursuit which can be followed without injury to anyone and with enjoyment to all; and the best of it is, it is not for everybody, as field-sports are, except hawking, which is also only for Kings and great Lords. Reconsider your opinion therefore, Sancho, and when you are governor start hunting, and you will find the good in it."

"Actually," said Sancho, "the good governor should be like one with a broken leg and stay at home;" it would not be a nice thing if, after people had taken the trouble of coming to look for him on business, the governor was away in the forest enjoying himself; the government would be handled badly in that fashion. Believe, señor, hunting and amusement are more fit for timewasters than for governors; I intend to amuse myself during Eastertime, and on Sundays and holidays; because hunting does not suit my condition or agree with my conscience."

"God grant it may turn out like that," said the duke; "because it's a long step from saying to doing."

"Be that as it may," said Sancho, "'promises do not distress a good payer,' and 'he who God helps does better than he who gets up early,' and 'it's the stomach that carries the feet and not the feet the stomach;' I mean to say that if God helps me and I do my duty honestly, no doubt I'll govern better than any other. Actually, let them put a finger in my mouth, and they'll see whether I can bite or not."

"The curse of God on you, you appalling Sancho!" exclaimed Don Quixote; "when will the day come - as I have often said to you - when I will hear you make one single coherent, rational remark without proverbs? Pray, your highnesses, and leave this fool alone, because he will grind your souls between, not two, but two thousand proverbs!"

"Sancho Panza's proverbs," said the duchess, "although more numerous than a Greek Commander's, are not to be less esteemed due to the conciseness of the truisms. I can say they give me more pleasure than others that may be better brought in and introduced more seasonably."

During this pleasant conversation they left the tent and went into the wood, and the day was spent in visiting some of the posts and hiding-places, and then the night closed in, not, however, as brilliantly or tranquilly as might have been expected for the season, because it was midsummer; but bringing with it a kind of fog that greatly aided the plan of the duke and duchess; and therefore, as night began to fall, and a little after sunset, suddenly the whole wood on all four sides seemed to be on fire, and shortly after, a vast number of trumpets and other military instruments were heard, as if several troops of cavalry were passing through the wood. The blaze of the fire and the noise of the warlike instruments almost blinded the eyes and deafened the ears of those that stood by, and indeed of all who were in the wood. Then repeated screams were heard in the Moorish style when they rush in to battle; trumpets sounded and drums beat, so unceasingly and so fast that the sound of many instruments served to confuse the senses of any who heard them. The duke was speechless, the duchess amazed, Don Quixote speculating, Sancho Panza shaking in fear, and even those who were aware of the purpose were frightened.

In their fear, a leading horseman, in the disguise of a demon, passed in front of them, blowing a huge hollow horn that gave a horrible note.

"You there! brother messenger," said the duke, "Who are you? Where are you going? What troops are these that seem to be passing through the wood?"

To which the messenger replied in a harsh, disagreeing voice, "I am the devil; I am in search of Don Quixote of La Mancha; those coming this way are six troops of enchanters, who are bringing with them on a victorious cart the incomparable Dulcinea del Toboso; she comes under enchantment, together with the courageous Frenchman Montesinos, to give instructions to Don Quixote as to how she may be disenchanted."

"If you were the devil, as you say and as your appearance indicates," said the duke, "you would have known who the Knight Don Quixote of La Mancha was, because you have him here in front of you."

"I swear to God and on my conscience," said the devil, "I never noticed, because my mind is occupied with so many different things that I was forgetting the main purpose I came for."

"This demon must be an honest fellow and a good Christian," said Sancho; "because if he wasn't he wouldn't swear to God and on his conscience; I feel sure now there must be good souls even in hell itself."

Without dismounting, the demon turned to Don Quixote and said, "The unfortunate but courageous Knight Montesinos sends me to you, the Knight of the Lions, asking me tell you to wait for him wherever I may find you, as he brings with him her who they call Dulcinea del Toboso, so he may show you what is needed in order to disenchant her; and as I came for nothing else I will stay no longer; may the demons of my sort be with you, and good angels with these gentle people;" and so, he blew his huge horn, turned around and left without waiting for a reply from anyone.

They all were astonished, but particularly Sancho and Don Quixote; Sancho to see how, in defiance of the truth, Dulcinea really was enchanted; Don Quixote because he could not feel sure whether what had happened to him in the cave of Montesinos was true or not; and as he was deep in these thoughts the duke said to him, "Are you going to wait, Señor Don Quixote?"

"Why not?" he replied; "I will wait here, because I am fearless and firm, even if all of hell came to attack me."

Night closed in more completely, and many lights, those that look like shooting-stars to our eyes, soared through the heavens; a frightful noise, was heard: harsh, ceaseless creaking, one like that made by the ox-carts, which, they say, the bears and wolves are carried in. In addition to all this commotion, there was another disturbance to increase the commotion, because it now seemed as if in truth, on all four sides of the wood, four battles were going on at the same time; in one quarter there was a dull noise of a terrible onslaught, in another numerous gunshots were being discharged, the shouting of the warriors sounded close by, and further away the Moorish screams were raised again and again. In short, the trumpets, horns, drums, cannons, gunshots, and above all the tremendous noise of the carts, made such a sound that Don Quixote needed to summon all his courage to endure it; but Sancho's gave way, and he fell fainting in front of the duchess, who let him lie there and promptly asked the servants to throw water on his face. This was done, and he came to himself by the time that one of the carts with the creaking wheels reached the spot. It was pulled by four ox all covered with black harnesses; on the top of the cart was a raised seat, on which sat an esteemed old man with a beard whiter than snow, and so long that it was below his waist; he was dressed in a long black robe made of rough linen; because as the cart was covered with a multitude of candles it was easy to make out everything that was on it. Leading in front of it were two hideous demons, also covered in rough linen, with faces so frightful that Sancho, having seen them once, shut his eyes not to see them again.

As soon as the cart came opposite them, the old man rose from his grand seat, and standing up said in a loud voice, "I am the sage Lirgandeo," and without another word the cart then passed by. Behind it came another of the same form, with another old man on top, who, stopping the cart, said in a voice no less serious than the first, "I am the sage Alquife, the great friend of Urganda the Unknown," and passed on. Then another cart came at the same pace, but the occupant of the throne was not old like the others, but a strong and healthy man, with a stern face, who as he came up said in a voice much hoarser and devilish, "I am the enchanter Archelaus, the living enemy of Amadis of France and all his lineage," and then passed on. Having gone a short distance, the three carts stopped and the repetitive noise of their wheels ceased, and soon after they heard another, not noise, but sound of sweet, harmonious music, which Sancho was very glad about, taking it to be a good sign; and he said to the duchess, who he did not move a step from for a single moment, "Señora, where there's music there can't be trouble."

"And neither where there are lights and it is bright," said the duchess; to which Sancho replied, "Fire gives light, and it's bright where there are bonfires, as we see by those that are all around us and perhaps may burn us; but music is a sign of joy and pleasure."

"Currently, that remains to be seen," said Don Quixote, who was listening to all that passed; and he was right, as is shown in the following chapter.

CHAPTER 35

CONTINUING THE INSTRUCTIONS GIVEN TO DON QUIXOTE FOR THE DISENCHANTMENT OF DULCINEA, TOGETHER WITH OTHER MARVELLOUS INCIDENTS

Coming toward them they saw, to the sound of this pleasing music, what they call a victorious car, pulled by six grey donkeys covered with white linen, on each of them a repentant man was mounted, robed also in white carrying a lit candle. The car was twice or, perhaps, three times as large as the former ones, and in front and on the sides stood twelve more repentant men, all as white as snow and all with lit candles, a spectacle to excite fear as well as wonder; and on a raised throne a fairy was sat draped in a multitude of silver veils with an embroidery of countless gold glittering all over them, that made her appear, if not richly, at least brilliantly, embellished. She had her face covered with thin transparent silk, the texture of which did not prevent the beautiful features of the lady being distinguished, while the numerous lights made it possible to judge her beauty and her age, which seemed to be no less than seventeen but not to have reached twenty yet. Beside her was a figure in a formal robe as they call it, reaching to the feet, while the head was covered with a black veil. But the instant the car was opposite the duke and duchess and Don Quixote the music ceased, the figure in the robe rose up, and removing the veil from its face, revealed to their eyes the shape of Death itself, fleshless and hideous, at this sight Don Quixote felt disturbed, Sancho frightened, and the duke and duchess displayed a certain nervousness. Having risen to its feet, this living death, in a sleepy voice, said:

I am Merlin who the legends say,
The devil had for a father, and the lie,
Gathered credibility over a space of time.
A magic prince of this day,
Monarch and treasurer, with a jealous eye,
I can see what you cannot find.
The courageous deeds of the Knights,
Who are, and have always been, dear to me,
Enchanters and magicians and their kind,
Are mostly hard hearted; but I am not,
Because mine is tender, compassionate and soft,
And doing good to all is its delight.
In the gloomy caves,
Tracing mystic lines and characters,
Soon there came,
The sorrow-filled complaint of her,
The incomparable Dulcinea del Toboso.

I knew of her enchantment and her fate,
From high-born lady to peasant girl,
And touched with pity, I turned the leaves,
Exercised my devilish craft.
And then, in this skeleton I have come in haste,
To show the appropriate remedy,
To give relief in such a worthy case.

You, the unbreakable steel! The shining light,
The beacon, guiding star, path and leader of all,
Who, despising sleep and the lazy,
Adopt the demanding life of bloodstained arms!
To you, great hero who all praise transcends,
La Mancha's polish and Iberia's star,
Don Quixote, as wise as brave, to you I say:
For the incomparable Dulcinea del Toboso,
Her pristine form and beauty to be regained,
It is necessary that your aide Sancho,
On his own sturdy ass facing heaven will,
Be given three thousand and three hundred whippings,
That must sting and cause him pain.
This is what the authors of her suffering have decided.
And this is why I came.

"Good God," exclaimed Sancho, "I might as well stab myself three times with a knife: three thousand, whippings! The devil has to have this way of disenchanting? I don't see what my ass has got to do with enchantment. God, if Señor Merlin has not found out some other way of disenchanting lady Dulcinea del Toboso, she may go to her grave enchanted."

"I'll take you, Clown stuffed with garlic," said Don Quixote, "and tie you to a tree as naked as the day you were born, and give you, not three thousand three hundred, but six thousand six hundred lashes, and so well placed on you that they won't disappear; don't answer back or I'll tear your soul out."

Hearing this Merlin said, "That will not work, because the whipping Sancho has to receive must be welcomed by his own free will and not by force, and at whatever time he chooses, and there is no fixed limit assigned to him; but it is permitted if he likes to half the pain of this whipping, if he agrees to let them be given by the hand of another."

"No hand, my own or anybody else's, will touch me," said Sancho. "Was it I that gave birth to lady Dulcinea del Toboso, so my backside has to pay for her sins? My master, he is a part of her - because, he's always calling her 'my life' and 'my soul,' he should whip himself for her and take all the pain required for her disenchantment. But to whip me! No day!"

As soon as Sancho had done speaking the fairy in silver that was next to Merlin stood up, and removing the thin veil from her face revealed one that seemed exceedingly beautiful to all; and with a masculine freedom from embarrassment and in a voice not very lady like, addressing Sancho directly, said, "You worthless aide, soul of a mug, heart of a cork tree, with bowels of stone and pebbles; if, you insolent thief, were asked to throw yourself down from a tall tower; if, the enemy of mankind asked you to swallow a dozen toads, two lizards, and three snakes; if they wanted you to murder your own wife and children with a sharp tool, it would be appropriate for you to be stubborn. But to argue against three thousand three hundred whippings, what every poor little farm-boy gets each month - it is enough to surprise, shock, and amaze the compassionate hearts of all who hear it, actually, all who come to hear it in the course of time. Look you miserable, hard-hearted animal, turn those fearful eyes to these of mine that are compared to radiant stars, and you will see in them trickling streams of tears, and outlining tracks and paths all over the fields of my cheeks. Let it move you, devious, ill-conditioned monster, to see my youth - still in its teens, because I am not twenty yet, wasting and withering away underneath the mask of a poor peasant lady; and if I do not appear like that now, it is due to a special favour Señor Merlin here has granted to me, only so my beauty may soften you; because the tears of beauty in distress turn rocks into cotton and tigers into sheep. Whip that ass of yours, you untamed beast, rouse your lusty drive that urges you only to eat and eat, and set free the softness of my flesh, the gentleness of my nature, and the fairness of my face. And if you will not concede for me, do it for the sake of that poor Knight you have beside you; your master, whose soul I can see right now, stuck in his throat not far from his lips, and only waiting for your inflexible or yielding reply to make it escape through his mouth or go back into his stomach again."

Hearing this Don Quixote felt his throat, and turning to the duke he said, "God, señor, what Dulcinea says is true, I have my soul stuck in my throat."

"What do you have to say, Sancho?" said the duchess.

"I say, señora," returned Sancho, "that I repeat what I said before; as for the whipping, no day!"

"No way, you should say, Sancho, and not no day," said the duke.

"Leave me alone, your highness," said Sancho. "I'm not in the mood to look into details of a letter more or less, because this whipping that is meant to be given to me, or I give to myself, has upset me, I don't know what I'm saying or doing. But I'd like to know from this lady, my lady Dulcinea del Toboso, where she learned this way of asking favours. She comes to ask me to mark my flesh with whippings, and she says I have the soul of a mug, an untamed beast, and other filthier names that the devil knows well. Is my flesh metal? Does it mean anything to me whether she is enchanted or not? Does she offer me a basket of good clothing, shirts, hats, socks – as an incentive? No, nothing but one piece of abuse after another, although she knows the proverb that 'a donkey loaded with gold goes easily up a mountain,' and that 'gifts break rocks,' and 'praying to God and working with the hammer,' and that 'one "take" is better than giving two"' Then there's my master, who should respect me; but he says if he gets hold of me he'll tie me to a tree naked and double the amount whips. These such kind hearted people should consider that it's not merely an aide, but a governor they are asking to whip; let them learn, the right way to ask, beg, and behave themselves; because now all times are equal, or appropriate. Now I'm ready to burst with tears seeing my green coat torn, and they come to ask me to whip myself with my own free will, I have as little inclination for it as I do swimming."

Well then, the fact is, Sancho," said the duke, "that unless you become softer than a ripe fig, you will not get hold of the government. It would not be a nice thing for me to send my islanders a cruel governor with a heart of stone, who will not yield to the tears of tormented ladies or to the prayers of wise, authoritative, ancient enchanters and sages. In short, Sancho, either you must be whipped by yourself, or they must whip you, or you will not be governor."

"Señor," said Sancho, "can't two days be given to me for me to consider what is best for me?"

"No, certainly not," said Merlin; "here, right now, immediately, the matter must be settled; either Dulcinea will return to the cave of Montesinos and to her former condition of a peasant girl, or else in her present form she will be taken to the Elysian fields, where she will remain waiting until the whipping is completed."

"Now then, Sancho!" said the duchess, "show some courage, and gratitude for your master Don Quixote; we are all bound to assist and please him for his generous character and grand chivalrousness. Consent to this whipping, my son; leave the devil with the devil, and fear to cowards, because 'a strong heart breaks bad luck,' as you very well know."

To this Sancho replied with an unrelated remark, "Will you tell me, Señor Merlin - when the devil came, he gave my master a message from Señor Montesinos, asking him to wait for him here, as he was coming to arrange how the lady Dona Dulcinea del Toboso was to be disenchanted; but up to the present we have not seen Montesinos, or anything like him."

To which Merlin answered, "The devil, Sancho, is a fool and a great villain; I sent him to look for your master, not with a message from Montesinos but from myself; because Montesinos is in his cave expecting, or more appropriately speaking, waiting for his disenchantment; because there's a story yet to be told about him; if he owes you anything, or you have any business to transact with him, I'll bring him to you and you put him where you choose; but for the present make up your mind and consent to this whipping, and believe me it will be very good for you, for your soul as well as your body - for your soul because of the compassion you perform it with, for your body because it will do you no harm and draw no blood."

"There are many doctors in the world; even the enchanters are doctors," said Sancho; "however, as everybody tells me the same thing - although I can't see it myself - I am willing to give myself the three thousand three hundred whippings, provided I am to give them whenever I like, without any fixed days or times; and I'll try and get out of this debt as quickly as I can, so the world can enjoy the beauty of the lady Dulcinea del Toboso; as it seems, contrary to what I thought, that she is beautiful after all. It must be a condition, as well, that I am not to be bound to draw any blood, and that if any of the whippings happen to be slightly weak they are to count. In case I make any mistake in the counting, Señor Merlin, as he knows everything, should keep count, and let me know how many left or how many extra I have done."

"There will be no need to let you know of any extra," said Merlin, "because, when you reach the full number, the lady Dulcinea will immediately, that very instant, be disenchanted, and will come with gratitude to seek the worthy Sancho and thank him, and even reward him for the good work. So you have no reason to be worry about too many or too few; heaven knows I would not cheat anyone out of a hair of their head."

"Well then, it is in God's hands then," said Sancho; "in this hard case, I give in; I accept the whippings on the conditions given."

The instant Sancho said this the music of the trumpets and drums started again, and gunshots were discharged, and Don Quixote hung on Sancho's neck kissing him again and again on the forehead and cheeks. The duchess and the duke expressed great satisfaction, the cart began to move on, and as it passed the fair Dulcinea bowed to the duke and duchess and made a curtsey to Sancho.

And now bright happy dawn came rapidly; the flowers of the field, raised their heads, revived, and the crystal water of the streams, flowing over the grey and white pebbles, raced to pay their respect to the expectant rivers; the cheerful earth, the unclouded sky, the fresh breeze, the clear light, each and all showed that the day approaching would be calm and bright. The duke and duchess, pleased with their hunt and having carried out their plans so cleverly and successfully, returned to their castle determined to continue their joke; because to them there was nothing else that could offer more amusement.

CHAPTER 36

THE STRANGE AND UNIMAGINABLE ADVENTURE OF THE DISTRESSED LADY, NAMED THE COUNTESS TRIFALDI, TOGETHER WITH A LETTER WHICH SANCHO PANZA WROTE TO HIS WIFE

The duke had a main servant with a very serious yet light hearted manner, and it was he that played the part of Merlin, made all the arrangements for the adventure, composed the verses, and got a lady to represent Dulcinea; and now, with the assistance of his master and mistress, he made up another of the funniest and strangest plans that can be imagined.

The next day the duchess asked Sancho if he had begun the task which he had to perform for the disenchantment of Dulcinea. He said he had, and had given himself five whips overnight.

The duchess asked him what he had given them with.

He said with his hand.

"That," said the duchess, "is more like giving oneself slaps than a whipping; I am sure the sage Merlin will not be satisfied with such gentleness; worthy Sancho must leave a mark, and make it felt; because the release of such a great a lady as Dulcinea will not be granted so cheaply, or at such a worthless price; and remember, Sancho, that works of generosity done in a lukewarm and half-hearted way have no merit or benefit."

To which Sancho replied, "If you will give me a proper whip, I will do it, provided it does not hurt too much; because you must know, fool as I am, my flesh is more cotton than leather, and it does no good for me or anybody else to destroy it."

"Certainly," said the duchess; "tomorrow I' will give you a whip that will be suitable for you, and it will accommodate itself to the sensitivity of your flesh."

Then said Sancho, "Your highness must know, dear lady of my soul, that I have a letter written to my wife, Teresa Panza, giving her an account of all that has happened to me since I left her; I have it here in my pocket, and there's nothing left to do but to put the address on it; I'd be glad if you would read it, because I think it is written in a governor's style; I mean the way governors should write."

"And who dictated it?" asked the duchess.

"Who else could have dictated it but myself, fool as I am?" said Sancho.

"And did you write it yourself?" said the duchess.

"That I didn't," said Sancho; "because I can neither read or write, although I can sign my name."

"Let me see it," said the duchess, "and have no fear I am sure in reflects the quality and quantity of your wit."

Sancho pulled out an open letter from his pocket, and the duchess, taking it, found it went like this:

SANCHO PANZA'S LETTER TO HIS WIFE, TERESA PANZA

If I was whipped well I took it like a gentleman; if I have become governor it was at the cost of a good whipping. You will not understand this at the moment, my Teresa; eventually you will know what it means. I will tell you, Teresa, I want you to travel in a coach, as a matter of importance, because every other way of travel is like going on all-fours. You are a governor's wife; take care that nobody speaks evil about you behind your back. I send to you a green hunting suit that my lady the duchess gave to me; alter it so as to make a coat for our daughter. Don Quixote, my master, if I am to believe what I hear in these parts, is a madman with some sense, and an absurd fool, and I am no way behind him. We have been to the cave of Montesinos, and the sage Merlin has charged me with the disenchantment of Dulcinea del Toboso, who is called Aldonza Lorenzo over there. With three thousand three hundred lashes, less five, that I am to give to myself, and then she will be entirely disenchanted as the mother that gave birth to her. Say nothing about this to anyone; because, make your affairs public, and some will say they are white and others will say they are black. I will leave in a few days for my government, to which I am going with a great desire to make money, because they tell me all new governors go with the same desire; I will feel the pulse of it and will let you know if you are to come and live with me or not. Dapple is well and sends many respects to you; I am not going to leave him behind even if they took me away believing I was a Grand Turk. My lady the duchess kisses your hands a thousand times; will you return this with two thousand, because as my master says, nothing costs less or is cheaper than civility. God has not been pleased to provide another bag for me with a hundred coins, like the one the other day; but never mind, my Teresa, I am safe here, and all will end with me securing my government; the only thing that troubles me greatly is what they tell me - that once I have tasted it I will eat my hands off to keep it; and if that is true, then it will not come cheap for me; although to be sure the injured benefit from the money they beg for; so one way or another you will be rich and in luck. God bring this letter to you as he can, and keep me alive to serve you. From this castle, the 20th of July, 1614.

Your husband, the governor,

SANCHO PANZA

When she had done reading the letter the duchess said to Sancho, "On two points the worthy governor goes astray; one is in saying or hinting that this government has been given to you for the whipping you are to give himself, when you know (and cannot deny) that when my lord the duke promised it to you nobody ever dreamt of such a thing as whipping; the other is that you show yourself here to be very greedy; and the governor should not be a money-seeker, because 'greed bursts the bag,' and the greedy governor does ungoverned justice."

"I don't mean it that way, señora," said Sancho; "and if you think the letter doesn't go as it should, the only thing to do is to tear it up and make another one; and maybe it will be worse if it is left up to me."

"No, no," said the duchess, "this one will do, and I would like the duke to see it."

With this they took themselves to a garden where they were to eat, and the duchess showed Sancho's letter to the duke, who was highly delighted with it. They ate, and after the cloth had been removed and they had amused themselves for a while with Sancho's rich conversation, the sad sound of a flute and harsh drum made itself heard.

All seemed somewhat disturbed by this dull, confused harmony, especially Don Quixote, who could not stay in his seat; and for Sancho, it is unnecessary to say that fear drove him to his usual refuge, the side of the duchess; and indeed, and in truth, the sound they heard was miserable and depressing. While they were still in uncertainty, they saw advancing towards them through the garden two men covered in robes representing them to be in mourning, so long and flowing that they trailed on the ground. As they marched they beat two large drums which were also covered in black, and beside them there was a flute player, wearing black and sad like the others. Following these came a person with a gigantic stature enveloped rather than covered in a black robe, the edge of which was of extraordinary dimensions. Over the robe, a belt crossed his figure, which was also black, and from which hung a huge sword with a black scabbard. He had his face covered with a transparent black veil, through which could be seen a very long beard as white as snow. He marched in step to the sound of the drums with great seriousness and dignity; and, in short, his stature, his walk, the seriousness of his appearance would have struck with wonder, as it did, all who observed him without knowing who he was. With this pace and with this appearance he advanced to kneel in front of the duke, who, with the others, awaited him. The duke, however, would not allow him to speak until he had risen. The extraordinary figure obeyed, and standing up, removed the veil from his face and revealed the most enormous, the longest, the whitest and the thickest beard that human eyes had ever seen until that moment, and then in a serious, loud voice from the depths of his broad chest, and fixing his eyes on the duke, he said:

"Most high and mighty señor, my name is Trifaldin the White Beard; I am the aide to the Countess Trifaldi, otherwise called the Distressed Lady, on whose behalf I come with a request for your highness, which is: will your magnificence be pleased to grant her permission to come and tell you her trouble, which is one of the strangest that any mind in the world most familiar with trouble could have imagined; but first she desires to know if the courageous and never defeated Knight, Don Quixote of La Mancha, is in your castle, because she has come in search of him and without breaking her fast from the Kingdom of Candy to your realm here; a thing which may and should be regarded as a miracle or enchantment; she is at the gate of this fortress or castle, and waits for your permission to enter. I have spoken." And with that he coughed, and stroked his beard with both his hands, and stood very tranquilly waiting for the response of the duke, which was this:

"Many days ago, worthy aide Trifaldin the White Beard, we heard about the misfortune of my lady the Countess Trifaldi, whom the enchanters have caused to be called the Distressed Lady. Tell her to enter, remarkable aide, and tell her that the courageous Knight Don Quixote of La Mancha is here, and from his generous character she may safely promise herself every protection and assistance available; and you can also tell her, that if my aid necessary it will not be withheld, because I am bound to give it as a man of good quality, which involves the protection of women of all kinds, especially widowed, wronged, and distressed ladies, such as she seems to be."

On hearing this Trifaldin bent his knee to the ground, and making a sign for the flute player and drummers to start, he turned and marched out of the garden to the same notes and at the same pace as when he entered, leaving them all amazed at his manner and seriousness.

Turning to Don Quixote, the duke said, "After all, renowned Knight, the darkness of malice and ignorance are unable to hide or obscure the light of valour and virtue. I say so, because your excellence has barely been in this castle for six days, and already the unhappy and the afflicted come in search of you from distant and remote lands, and not in coaches or on camels, but on foot while fasting, confident that in your mighty arm they will find a cure for their sorrows and troubles; thanks to your great achievements, which are in circulation all over the known earth."

"I wish, señor duke," replied Don Quixote, "that the blessed priest, who was at the table the other day and showed such bitter spite against Knights were here now to see with his own eyes whether Knights are needed in the world; he would at any rate learn by experience that those suffering any extraordinary affliction or sorrow, in extreme cases and unusual misfortunes do not go to look for a remedy in the courts or village churches, or from a Knight who has never attempted to leave the boundary of his own town, or from the slothful womaniser who only seeks for news to repeat and talk about, instead of striving to do deeds for his own benefit and for others. Relief in distress, help in need, protection for ladies, comfort for widows, are to be found in no sort of people other than in Knights; and I give unceasing thanks to heaven that I am one, and regard any misfortune or suffering that may happen to me in the pursuit of such an honourable calling as endured for a good purpose. Let this lady come and ask me what she would like, because I will relieve her with the might of my arm and the fearlessness of my strong heart."

CHAPTER 37

CONTINUING THE NOTABLE ADVENTURE OF THE DISTRESSED LADY

The duke and duchess were extremely glad to see how easily Don Quixote fell for their plan; but at this moment Sancho observed, "I hope this lady won't be putting a difficulty in the way of my promised government; because I have heard from a Toledoan that when a countess is involved nothing good can happen. God bless me, he hated them! And so what I'm thinking is, if all countesses, whatever sort or condition they may be, are like the plague and are gossipers, what must they be when they're distressed, like this Countess."

"Hush, friend Sancho," said Don Quixote; "since this countess comes in search of me from such a distant land she cannot be one of those the man meant; moreover, this is a countess, and when countesses serve as ladies it is in the service of Queens and Empresses, because in their own houses they are supreme and have other ladies to wait on them."

To this Dona Rodriguez, who was present, answered, "My lady the duchess has ladies in her service that could be countesses if it was the will of fortune; 'but laws go as Kings like;' nobody should speak poorly of countesses, especially ancient unmarried ones; because although I am not one myself, I know and am aware of the advantage an unmarried countess has over one that is a widow; because 'he who holds us keeps the scissors.'"

"Despite that," said Sancho, "there's not much to cut off as my barber says, 'it will be better not to stir the rice even if it sticks.'"

"These aides," returned Dona Rodriguez, "are always our enemies; and as they are the haunting spirits of the halls and watch our every step, whenever they are not saying their prayers (and that's often enough) they spend their time gossiping about us, digging up our bones and burying our good name. But we live in spite of them, and in great houses too, although we die of hunger and cover our flesh, delicate or not, with widow's weeds, as one covers or hides a dunghill on a church day. Believe, if it were permitted and we had enough time, I could prove, not only to those here present, but to the whole world, that there is no virtue which cannot be found in a countess."

"I have no doubt," said the duchess, "that my good Dona Rodriguez is right; but she should wait for the right time for fighting her own battle and on behalf of countesses, so as to crush the slanderer of that vile Toledoan, and root out the prejudice in the great Sancho Panza's mind."

To which Sancho replied, "Ever since I have sniffed the governorship I have got rid of the humours of an aide, and I don't give an olive for all the countesses in the world."

They would have carried on this dispute further if they had not heard the notes of the flute and drums again, from which they concluded that the Distressed countess was making an entrance. The duchess asked the duke if it would be appropriate to go out and welcome her, as she was a countess and a person of rank.

"In respect of her being a countess," said Sancho, before the duke could reply, "I think your highnesses should go out to welcome her; but in respect of her being a lady, it is my opinion you should not take a step."

"Who asked you to interfere in this, Sancho?" said Don Quixote.

"Who, señor?" said Sancho; "I interfere because I have a right to, as an aide who has learned the rules of courteousness in the school of you my lord, the most well-mannered and best-bred Knight in the whole world of chivalry; and in these things, as I have heard you say, much is lost by a word too many as well as one too few, and to one who has his ears open, listen."

"Sancho is right," said the duke; "we'll see what the countess is like, and then measure the courtesy that is due to her."

And now the drums and flute continued as before; and here the author brought this short chapter to an end and began the next, continuing the same adventure, which is one of the most notable in the history.

CHAPTER 38

THE DISTRESSED LADY'S TALE OF HER MISFORTUNES

Following the sad musicians as many as twelve ladies filled the garden, in two lines, all dressed in mourning robes of fine twill, with hoods of white luxurious silk so long that they allowed only the border of the robe to be seen. Behind them came the Countess Trifaldi, and the aide Trifaldin the White Beard leading her by the hand, covered in the finest black woollen material; the tail, or skirt, or whatever it might be called, ended in three points which were held by the hands of three boys, likewise dressed for mourning, forming an elegant geometrical figure with the three acute angles made by the three points, from which all who saw concluded that it must be because the countess was called Trifaldi, as though it were Countess of Three Points; and Benengeli says it was so, and that her real name was Countess Wolves, because wolves bred in great numbers in her country; and if, instead of wolves, they had been foxes, she would have been called the Countess Fox, as it was the custom in those parts for lords to take distinctive titles from the thing or things which were most abundant in their territories; this countess, however, in honour of the fashion of her skirt, dropped wolves and took Trifaldi. The twelve ladies and the countess one after the other at slow pace, their faces being covered with black veils, not transparent ones like Trifaldin's, but so opaque that they allowed nothing to be seen through them. As soon as the group of ladies was fully in sight, the duke, the duchess, and Don Quixote stood up, as well as all who were watching the slow-moving procession. The twelve ladies halted and formed a line, along which the Distressed One advanced, Trifaldin still holding her hand. On seeing this the duke, the duchess, and Don Quixote went forward to meet her. She then, kneeling on the ground, said in a croaky and rough voice, rather than fine and delicate:

"perhaps it will not please your highnesses to offer such courteously to me your servant, because I am in such distress that I will never be able to make a proper return, because my strange and unparalleled misfortune has taken my wits, and I do not know where; but it must be a long way away, because the more I look for them the less I find them."

"I would be lacking wits, señora countess," said the duke, "If I did not perceive your worth as a whole, because at first glance it can be seen you deserve the height of courtesy;" and raising her up by the hand he led her to a seat beside the duchess, who likewise welcomed her warmly. Don Quixote remained silent, while Sancho was dying to see the features of Trifaldi and one or two of her many ladies; but there was no possibility of it until they displayed them themselves and with their own free will.

All kept quiet, waiting to see who would break silence, which the Distressed Lady did in these words: "I am confident, mighty lord, and fair lady, and most discreet company, that my most miserable despair will be given a reaction no less dispassionate than generous and condoling, because it is one that is enough to crack marble, soften diamond, and melt the steel of the most hardened hearts in the world; but first let me say, I would be glad to know whether there is present in this circle, or company, that Knight, immaculate Don Quixote de la Mancha, and his fine aide Panza."

"The Panza is here," said Sancho, before anyone could reply, "and Don Quixote too; and so, most distressed lady, you may say what you want, because we are all ready to serve you."

On this Don Quixote rose, and addressing the Distressed lady, said, "If your sorrows, afflicted lady, can indulge any hope of relief from the valour or might of any Knight, here I am, which, as limited as they may be, I will be entirely devoted to your service. I am Don Quixote of La Mancha, whose calling it is to give aid to the needy; and that being so, it is not necessary for you, señora, to make any appeal to my kindness, or give explanations, only to tell your sorrow clearly and straightforwardly: because you have listeners that will know how to remedy them, and if not, to sympathise with them."

On hearing this, the Distressed lady acted as though she would throw herself at Don Quixote's feet, and actually did fall in front of them and said:

"In front of these feet and legs I throw myself, unconquered Knight, as they are the foundations and pillars of Knighthood; these feet I desire to kiss, because on their steps hangs and depends the sole remedy for my misfortune, noble Knight, whose genuine achievements eclipse the famous ones of the Amadises, Esplandians, and Belianises!" Then turning from Don Quixote to Sancho Panza, and grasping his hands, she said, "O you, the most loyal aide that ever served a Knight in this present time or times gone by, whose goodness is more extensive than the beard of Trifaldin my companion, you may boast that, in serving the great Don Quixote, you are serving, summed up in one, all of the Knights that have ever taken the path of Knighthood. I request that you, with your kind goodness, ask your master to assist this most humble and unfortunate countess."

To this Sancho answered, "In regards to my goodness, señora, being as long and as great as your aide's beard, it does not matter much to me; I hope to have my soul thick bearded and moustached when it comes for my time to leave this life, that's the point; about beards I do not care much for them; but without all this flattery, I will ask my master (because I know he loves me, and also he needs me at the moment for a particular reason) to help and aid you as much as he can; unpack your worries and lay them out us, and leave us to deal with them, because we will all have one mind."

The duke and duchess, as they were the ones who had made the experiment of this adventure, were ready to burst with laughter at all this, and between themselves they applauded the clever acting of Trifaldi, who, returning to her seat, said, "Queen Dona Maguncia reigned over the famous Kingdom of Candy, which lies between the great Trapobana and the Southern Sea, two miles beyond Cape Comorin. She was the widow of King Archipiela, her lord and husband, and during their marriage they had an issue with the Princess

Antonomasia, heiress of the Kingdom. Princess Antonomasia was raised and brought up under my care and direction, I being the oldest and highest in rank of her mother's ladies. Time passed, and the young Antonomasia reached fourteen, and in such perfect beauty, that nature could not raise it higher. But, it must not be supposed her intelligence was childish; she was as intelligent as she was gorgeous, and she was more stunning than any other in the world; and still is, unless envious fate and three hard-hearted sisters have cut short her thread of life. But if they have not, Heaven will not do such a great wrong to the Earth, as it would be to pluck an unripe grape from the greatest vineyard. This beauty, which my poor weak tongue has failed to do justice, countless princes, not only from that country, but from others, were captivated, and among them a private gentleman, who was from the court, dared to raise his thoughts to the heaven about such great beauty, trusting his youth, his courteous manner, his numerous accomplishments and grace, his quickness and wit; because I may tell your highnesses, if I am not exhausting you, that he played the guitar so as to make it speak, and he was, besides, a poet and a great dancer, and he could make bird cages so well, that he could have made a good living from making those alone if he had found himself reduced to poverty; but gifts and grace like this is enough to bring down a mountain, not to say a young girl. But all his chivalry, wit, and joyfulness, all his grace and accomplishments, would have had no effect toward gaining access to the fortress of my pupil, if the insolent thief had not taken the precaution of winning me over first. First, the criminal sought to win my good-will and buy my compliance, so as to get me, like a disloyal guardian, to deliver him the keys to the fortress I was in charge of. In a word, he gained an influence over my mind, and overcame my resolve, I do not exactly know how; but it was some verses I heard him singing one night from a window that opened facing the street where he lived, that, more than anything else, made me give way and led to my fall; and if I remember correctly they went like this:

From that sweet enemy of mine
My bleeding heart has had its wound;
And to increase the pain I'm bound,
To suffer and to make no sign.

The lines seemed like pearls to me and his voice was as sweet as syrup; and afterwards, ever since then, looking at the misfortune into which I have fallen, I have thought that poets, as Plato advised, should be banished from all well-ordered States; at least the romantic ones, because they write verses, not like those that delight and draw tears from women and children, but sharp-pointed lines that pierce the heart like thorns, and like lightning, strike it, leaving the poet uninjured. Another time he sang:

Death comes, so subtly veiled that I,
Do not know, how or when,

Or it would give me life again,
To find how sweet it is to die.

And other verses of the same sort, which enchant when sung and fascinate when written. And then, when they decide to compose a type of verse that was in vogue in Candy at the time, which they call seguidillas! Hearts jump and laughter breaks out, and the body grows restless and all the senses change rapidly. And so I say, sirs, that these poets seriously deserve to be banished to an island of lizards. Although it is not they that are at fault, but the simple fools that praise them, and the idiots that believe in them; and if I had been the faithful lady I should have been, his musty verses would have never moved me, neither should I have been taken in by such phrases as 'in death I live,' 'in ice I burn,' 'in flames I shiver,' 'in hopelessness I hope,' 'I go and stay,' and paradoxes of that sort which his writings are full of. And then when poets promise the Phoenix of Arabia, the crown of Ariadne, the horses of the Sun, the pearls of the South, the gold of Tibar, and the balsam of Panchaia! It costs them little to make promises they have no intention or power of fulfilling. But where am I going with this? Poor me, unfortunate being! What madness or foolishness leads me to speak of the faults of others, when there is so much to be said about my own? Again, poor me, unlucky I am! it was not the verses that conquered me, but my own simplicity; it was not music that made me yield, but my own imprudence; my own ignorance, and little caution opened the way and cleared the path for Don Clavijo's advances, because that was the name of the gentleman I have referred to; and so, with my help as the go-between, he found his way many times into the room of the deceived Antonomasia (deceived not by him but by me) under the title of being her lawful husband; because, sinner as I was, I would not have allowed him to approach the edge of her shoe without being her husband. No, no, not that; marriage must come first in any business of this sort. But there was one problem in this case, which was the inequality of rank, Don Clavijo being a private gentleman, and the Princess Antonomasia, as I said, heiress to the Kingdom. The engagement remained secret for some time, hidden by my astute precaution, until I perceived that a certain expansion of Antonomasia's waist would soon disclose it, the fear of this made us seek advice from each other, and it was agreed that before it came to light, Don Clavijo should demand Antonomasia as his wife in front of the Vicar, with a written agreement for the Princess to marry him, which was drafted by my wit in such binding terms that the might of Samson could not have broken it. The necessary steps were taken; the Vicar saw the agreement, and took the lady's confession; she confessed everything in full, and he ordered her into the custody of a very worthy officer of the court."

"Are there officers of the court in Candy, too," said Sancho at this, "and poets? I swear I think the world is the same everywhere! But continue, Señora Trifaldi; because it is late, and I am dying to know the end of this long story."

"I will," replied the countess.

CHAPTER 39

TRIFALDI CONTINUES HER MARVELLOUS AND MEMORABLE STORY

The duchess was as delighted by Sancho's words as Don Quixote was driven to desperation. He asked him to hold his tongue, and the distressed lady went on to say:

"Finally, after a lot of questioning and answering, as the Princess stuck to her story, without changing or deviating from her previous declaration, the Vicar gave his decision in favour of Don Clavijo, and she was given to him as his lawful wife; which the Queen Dona Maguncia, the Princess Antonomasia's mother, took so badly, that within the space of three days she was buried."

"She died, no doubt," said Sancho.

"Of course," said Trifaldin; "they don't bury living people in Candy, only the dead."

"Señora," said Sancho, "an unconscious man has been known to be buried, with the belief that he was dead; and Queen Maguncia should have fainted rather than died; because in life many things go well, and the Princess's foolishness was not so great that she needed to take it so badly. If the lady had married some boy of hers, or some other servant of the house, as many others have done, then the situation would be beyond repair But to marry such an elegant accomplished gentleman as described to us, although it was foolish, was not as bad as you think; because according to the rules of my master here - and he won't allow me to lie - out of men of letters bishops are made, and of Knights, and especially if they belong to the order of Knighthood, they could become Kings and emperors."

"You are right, Sancho," said Don Quixote, "because with Knights of the order, if he has even slight good fortune, it is on the cards to become the mightiest lord on earth. But let señora the Distressed One proceed; because I suspect she is yet to tell us the bitter part of this, so far, sweet story."

"The bitter is indeed to come," said the countess; "and so bitter that acid is sweet in comparison. The Queen, then, being dead, we buried; and we had hardly covered her with earth and hardly had time to say our last farewells, because who can express such misery without tears? Over the Queen's grave appeared, mounted on a wooden horse, the giant Malambruno, Maguncia's first cousin, who besides being cruel is an enchanter; came to seek revenge for the death of his cousin, punish the audacity of Don Clavijo, and was in wrath over the disobedience of Antonomasia, and so, he left them both enchanted by his art on the grave itself; she was changed into an ape made of brass, and he was turned into a horrible crocodile made of some unknown metal; while between the two there is a pillar, also of metal, with certain characters in the Syriac language inscribed on it, which, being translated into Candian, and now into Castilian, contain the following sentence:

'These two rash lovers will not recover their former shape until the valiant Manchegan comes to battle me in single combat; because Fate reserves this adventure for his mighty valour alone.'

This done, he drew from its sheath a huge broad sword, and grabbing me by the hair he acted as though he was going to cut my throat and take my head clean off. I was in terror, my voice stuck in my throat, and I was in the deepest distress; nevertheless, I summoned up my strength as well as I could, and in an unsteady and pitiful voice I said such words to him to induce him to stop the infliction of a punishment so severe. He then called for all the ladies of the palace, those that are here present, to be brought to him; and after having dwelt upon the outrage of our offence, he condemned the ladies, their characters, their evil ways and worse plans, charging them all of what I alone was guilty of, he said he would not give us capital punishment, but with others of a slow nature which would be in effect civil death for ever; and the very instant he stopped speaking we all felt the pores of our faces opening, and pricking us, as if with the points of needles. We immediately put our hands to our faces and found ourselves in the state you see now."

Here the Distressed One and the other ladies raised the veils with which they were covered, and disclosed faces all covered with beards, some red, some black, some white, and some greyish, which filled the duke and duchess with wonder. Don Quixote and Sancho were overwhelmed with amazement, and the bystanders lost in astonishment, while Trifaldi went on to say:

"Therefore that malevolent villain Malambruno did punish us, covering the tenderness and softness of our faces with these rough bristles! It would have been better if he cut our heads off with his enormous sword instead of obscuring the light of our faces with these hairs that cover us! because if we look into the matter, sirs (and what I am now going to say I would say with eyes flowing like fountains only at that the thought of our misfortune, but the oceans they have already wept keep them as dry as spears, and so I say it without tears), where can a lady with a beard go to? What father or mother will feel pity for her? Who will help her? Because, when she has smooth skin, and a face abused by thousands of washes and cosmetics, she can hardly get anybody to love her, what will she do when she shows a face turned into a bush? Oh ladies, friends of mine! it was an unlucky moment when we were born and a worse hour when our fathers produced us!" And as she said this she showed signs of being about to faint.

CHAPTER 40

MATTERS BELONGING TO THIS ADVENTURE AND TO THIS MEMORABLE HISTORY

Truly all those who find pleasure in histories like this should show their gratitude to Cide Hamete and its original author, because with the scrupulous care he has taken the time to give us all its minute details, not leaving anything, however trivial it may be, there is nothing he does not make plain and clear. He portrays the thoughts, he reveals the desires, he answers indirect questions, clears up doubts, resolves objections, and, in a word, makes clear the smallest points the most inquisitive person could desire to know. Renowned author! Happy Don Quixote! Amusing Sancho! May each and all live countless ages to delight and amuse the people of the earth!

The history goes on to say that when Sancho saw the Distressed lady faint he exclaimed: "I swear as an honest man and on all of my ancestors the Panzas, that I never saw or heard of, neither has my master perceived or conceived in his mind, such an adventure like this. Send a thousand devils - not to curse you – but to take you, Malambruno you enchanter and evil giant! Could you not find another sort of punishment for these sinners but bearding them? Would it not have been better to have taken half their noses off, even though they'd have snuffled when they spoke, than putting beards on them? I'll bet they do not even have the means to pay anybody to shave them."

"That is the truth, señor," said one of the twelve; "we do not have the money to get ourselves shaved, and so we have, some of us, started using sticky-plasters as an economical remedy, because by applying them to our faces and ripping them off quickly we are left with skin as bare and smooth as a baby's bottom. There are, to be sure, women in Candy that go from house to house to remove hair, and trim eyebrows, and make cosmetics for the use of women, but we, the ladies of my lady, would never let them in, because most of them are potential agents that are no longer active; so if we are not relieved by Señor Don Quixote we will be taken to our graves with beards."

"I will pluck my own hair out in the land of the Moors," said Don Quixote, "if I don't remove yours."

At this moment Trifaldi recovered from her faint and said, "That promise, valiant Knight, reached my ears during my faint, and has been the remedy to revive me and bring me back to my senses; and so once more I appeal to you, illustrious Knight, indomitable sir, to let your gracious promises be turned into deeds."

"There will be no delay on my part," said Don Quixote. "Think, señora, of what I must do, because my heart is most eager to serve you."

"The fact is," replied the Distressed lady, "it is five thousand miles, a couple more or less, from here to the Kingdom of Candy, if you go by land; but if you go through the air and in a straight line, it is three thousand two hundred and twenty-seven. You must know, as well, that Malambruno told me that, whenever fate produced the Knight our liberator, he himself would send him a horse far better and with less problems than the previous-horse; because it will be the same wooden horse on which the valiant Pierres carried the fair Magalona; which is guided by a peg he has in his forehead that serves to direct him, and flies through the air with such rapidity that you would think the devils were carrying him. This horse, according to ancient tradition, was made by Merlin. He lent him to Pierres, who was a friend of his, and who made long journeys with him, and, as has been said, carried the fair Magalona, taking her through the air and making all who observed them from the earth stare with amazement; and he never lent him to anyone except to those he loved or those who paid him well; and since the great Pierres we know of no one having mounted him until now. From Pierres, Malambruno stole him using his magic art, and he has him now in his possession, and makes use of him in his journeys which he constantly makes through different parts of the world; he is here today, and in France tomorrow, and the next day in Bolivia; and the best of it is the horse does not eat, sleep or wear out shoes, and goes at an incredible pace through the air without wings, so that whoever has mounted him can carry a cup full of water in his hand without spilling a drop. He goes so smoothly and easily, which is the reason the fair Magalona enjoyed riding him so much."

"For going smoothly and easily," said Sancho, "give me my Dapple, although he can't go through the air; but on the ground he's better than all the slow donkeys of the earth."

They all laughed, and the Distressed lady continued: "And this same horse, if Malambruno is willing to put an end to our sufferings, will be here before night; because he told me that the sign he would give me when I had found the Knight I was in search of, would be to send me the horse wherever he might be, speedily and promptly."

"And how many is there room for on this horse?" asked Sancho.

"Two," said the Distressed lady, "one in the saddle, and the other on the back; and generally these two are the Knight and aide, when there is no lady that's being carried somewhere."

"I'd like to know, Señora," said Sancho, "what is the name of this horse?"

"His name," said the Distressed lady, "is not the same as Bellerophon's horse that was called Pegasus, or Alexander the Great's, called Bucephalus, or Orlando Furioso's, or Frontino like Ruggiero's, or Bootes or Peritoa, as they say the horses of the sun were called, neither is he called Orelia, like the horse on which the unfortunate Rodrigo, the last King of the Goths, rode to the battle where he lost his life and his Kingdom."

"I'll bet," said Sancho, "that as they have given him none of these famous well-known horse's names, they have not called him the name of my master's Rocinante, which surpasses all that have been mentioned."

"That is true," said the bearded countess, "still it suits him very well, because he is called Clavileno the Swift, which is in accordance with being made of wood, with the peg he has in his forehead, and with the swift pace at which he travels; and so, as far as the name goes, he can compare with the famous Rocinante."

"I have nothing to say against his name," said Sancho; "but without reins how is he managed?"

"I have said already," said Trifaldi, "that it is with a peg, by turning it to one side or the other the Knight who rides him makes him go as he pleases, either through the upper air, or skimming and almost sweeping the earth, or in the very middle which is sought and followed in all well-regulated flights."

"I'd like to see him," said Sancho; "but to think I'm going to mount him, either in the saddle or on the back, is to ask pears to grow on a banana tree. A good joke indeed! I can barely keep my seat on Dapple, and on a saddle softer than silk itself, and you want me to hold onto the legs of plank without a pad or cushion of any sort! God, I have no notion of bruising myself to get rid of anyone's beard; let each one shave himself the best he can; I'm not going to accompany my master on any such long journey; besides, I can't give any help to the shaving of these beards as I have to attend to the disenchantment of lady Dulcinea."

"Yes, you can, my friend," replied Trifaldi; "and so much, that without you, as I understand, we will not be able to do anything."

"In the King's name!" exclaimed Sancho, "what have aides got to do with the adventures of their masters? Do historians say, 'Such and such a Knight finished such and such adventure, but with the help of so and so, his aide, without which it would have been impossible for him to accomplish;' no, this is not the case, they write, "Don Paralipomenon of the Three Stars accomplished the adventure of the six monsters;' without mentioning any aide, who was there the whole time, just as if there was no such person. I repeat, my master may go alone; and I'll stay here in the company of my lady the duchess; and maybe when he comes back, he will find the resolution of lady Dulcinea's situation to be advanced; because I am to give myself a whipping."

"Despite that you must go if it is necessary, my good Sancho," said the duchess, "because they are worthy people who ask for you; and the faces of these ladies must not remain overgrown in this way because of your fears; that would not be right."

"In the King's name, again!" said Sancho; "If this charitable work were to be done for the sake of ladies in imprisonment, a man might expose himself to some hardship; but to bear it for the sake of removing beards! Let the devil do it! I'd rather see them all bearded, from the highest to the lowest."

"You are very hard on the ladies, Sancho my friend," said the duchess; "and you are wrong sometimes; there are ladies in my house that may serve as a pattern for ladies; and here is my lady Dona Rodriguez, who will not allow me to say otherwise

"Your excellence may say it if you like," said Dona Rodriguez; "because God knows the truth of everything; and whether we ladies are good or bad, bearded or smooth, we are mothers' and daughters like other women; and as

God sent us into the world, he knows why he did, and on his mercy I rely, and not on anybody's beard."

"Well, Señora Rodriguez, Señora Trifaldi, and those present," said Don Quixote, "I trust in Heaven that it will look with kind eyes on your troubles, because Sancho will do as I ask him. Let Clavileno come and let me find myself face to face with Malambruno, and I am certain no razor will shave you more easily than my sword will shave Malambruno's head off his shoulders; because 'God bears with the evil, but not forever.'"

"Ah!" exclaimed the Distressed lady, "may all the stars of the celestial regions look down on your greatness with compassionate eyes, valiant Knight, and shed prosperity and valour on your heart, so it may be the shield and safeguard of the abused ladies you see here, detested by men, mocked by aides, and made fun of by all. Unfortunate beings that we are, us ladies! Although we descended in the direct male line from Hector of Troy himself, our mistresses never fail to address us as 'you' if they think it makes Queens of them. Giant Malambruno, although you are an enchanter, you are true to your promises. Send us the peerless Clavileno, so our misfortune may be brought to an end; because if the hot weather arrives and these beards of ours are still there, pity for us!"

Trifaldi said this in such a pathetic way that she drew tears from the eyes of all and even Sancho's filled up; and he committed in his heart to accompany his master to the end of the earth, if this would assist the removal of the wool from those faces that depended on it.

CHAPTER 41

THE ARRIVAL OF CLAVILENO AND THE END OF THIS PROLONGED ADVENTURE

And now night came, and with it the appointed time for the arrival of the famous horse Clavileno, the non-appearance of which was already beginning to make Don Quixote uneasy, because it struck him that, as Malambruno was taking so long to send it, either he himself was not the Knight the adventure was reserved for, or Malambruno did not dare to meet him in single combat. But, suddenly into the garden came four wild-men covered in green ivy carrying on their shoulders a large wooden horse. They placed it on its feet on the ground, and one of the wild-men said, "Let the Knight who has the heart for it mount this machine."

Here Sancho exclaimed, "I don't mount, because I do not have the heart and am not a Knight."

"And let the aide, if he has one," continued the wild-man, "take his seat on the back, and let him trust the valiant Malambruno; because by no sword except his, or by the malice of any other, will he be attacked. All that is required is to turn this peg the horse has on his neck, and he will carry them through the air to where Malambruno awaits them; but in case the elevation of their course should make them dizzy, their eyes must be covered until the horse neighs, which will be the sign of completing their journey."

With these words, leaving Clavileno behind them, they left with dignity the same way they came. As soon as the Distressed lady saw the horse, almost in tears she exclaimed to Don Quixote, "Valiant Knight, the promise of Malambruno has proved to be trustworthy; the horse has come, our beards are growing, and all of us beg you to shave and shear us, as mounting him with your aide and making a happy beginning with your new journey is all that is needed."

"That I will, Señora Countess Trifaldi," said Don Quixote, "most gladly and with goodwill, without stopping to take a rest, so as not to lose time, such is my desire to see you and all these ladies shaved clean."

"That I won't," said Sancho, "with good-will or bad-will, or any way at all; and if this shaving can't be done without my mounting on the back, my master had better look for another aide to go with him, and these ladies for some other way of making their faces smooth; I'm no witch to have a taste for travelling through the air. What would my islanders say when they heard about their governor going, wandering about on the winds? And another thing, as it is three thousand or so miles from here to Candy, if the horse tires, or the giant blows, it will take half a dozen years to return, and there won't be an island in the world that will know me: and so, as it is a common saying 'in delay there's danger,' and 'when they offer you a cow run with the reins,' these ladies' beards must excuse me; 'Saint Peter is very well in Rome;' I mean I am very well in this house where so much is offered to me, and I hope for good things from the master who promised to make me a governor."

"Friend Sancho," said the duke, "the island that I have promised you is not a moving one, or one that will run away; it has roots so deeply buried in the belly of the earth that it will be no easy matter to pick it up or shift it from where it is; you know as well as I do, that there is no sort of office of any importance that is not obtained by a bribe of some kind, great or small; well then, that which I look to receive for this government is that you go with your master Don Quixote, and bring this memorable adventure to a conclusion; and whether you return on Clavileno as quickly as his speed seems to promise, or adverse fortune brings you back on foot travelling as a pilgrim from inn to inn, you will always find your island on your return where you left it, and your islanders will with the same eagerness they have always had welcome you as their governor, and my good-will will remain the same; do not doubt the truth of this, Señor Sancho, because that would be seriously insulting to my character."

"Say no more, señor," said Sancho; "I am a poor aide and not equal to having as much courtesy; let my master mount; cover my eyes and hand me to God's care, and tell me if I may call on our Lord or call on the angels to protect me when we go up there."

To this Trifaldi answered, "Sancho, you may freely call on God or whoever you like; because Malambruno although an enchanter is a Christian, and carries out his enchantments with great caution, taking very good care not to fall out with anyone."

"Well then," said Sancho, "God give me help!"

"Since the memorable adventure of the mills," said Don Quixote, "I have never seen Sancho as afraid as now; if I were as superstitious as others his severe fear would cause my spirit some anxiety. Come with me Sancho, because without these present I want to say a word or two to you in private;" and drawing Sancho aside among the trees of the garden and holding both his hands he said, "You see, brother Sancho, the long journey we have ahead of us, God knows when we will return, or what rest or opportunities this business will allow us; therefore I want you to go to your room now, as though you were going to get something required for the road, and instantly give yourself five hundred whippings out of the three thousand three hundred which you are bound to do; it will be for the good, and to make a start toward it and have it half finished."

"God," said Sancho, "you must be out of your mind! This is like the common saying, 'You see me with a child, and you want me to be a virgin.' Just as I'm about to sit on wooden horse, you want me to mark my backside! I am not stupid. Let's leave now, to shave these ladies; and on our return I give my word that I will hurry to wipe off all the debt that's due from me to satisfy you; I can't say more."

"Well, I will comfort myself with that promise, my good Sancho," replied Don Quixote, "and I believe you will keep it; because as stupid as you are, you are truthful."

"I'm not truthful," said Sancho, "only hungry; but even if I was a little, I would still keep my word."

With this they went back to mount Clavileno, and as they were about to do so Don Quixote said, "Mount and cover your eyes, Sancho; because one who sends for us from lands so far distant cannot intend to deceive us for the sake of the worthless glory to be derived from deceiving people who trust in him; even if all turns out to be the opposite of my hopes, no malice will be able to dim the glory of having undertaken this adventure."

"Let us leave, señor," said Sancho, "because I have taken the beards and tears of these ladies so deeply to my heart, I will not eat a bit until I have seen them restored to their former smoothness. Mount, my lord, and blindfold yourself, because if I am to go on the rear, it is clear the rider in the saddle must mount first."

"That is true," said Don Quixote, and, taking a handkerchief out of his pocket, he asked the Distressed Lady to cover his eyes very carefully; but after having them covered he uncovered them again, saying, "If my memory does not deceive me, I have read in Virgil, the Palladium of Troy, a wooden horse the Greeks offered to the goddess Pallas, afterwards led to the destruction of Troy; so it would be wise to see, first of all, what Clavileno has in his stomach."

There is no need for that," said the Distressed Lady; "I will vouch for him, and I know that Malambruno will play no tricks, you may mount without any fear, Señor Don Quixote; if any harm comes your way let it fall on my head."

Don Quixote thought that to say anything further in regards to his safety would be putting his courage in an unfavourable light; and so, without any more words, he mounted Clavileno, and tried the peg, which turned easily; and as he had no stirrups and his legs hung down, he looked like a Roman figure in triumph painted or embroidered on a tapestry.

Really against his will, and very slowly, Sancho proceeded to mount, and, after settling himself as well as he could on the rear, found it rather hard, and not soft at all, and asked the duke if it would be possible to provide him with a pad of some kind, or a cushion; even if it were from the couch of his lady the duchess, or from the bed of one of the servants; as the rear of that horse was more like marble than wood. Trifaldi observed that Clavileno would not carry any kind of harness or accessories, and that his best plan would be to sit sideways woman fashion, as in that way he would not feel the hardness so much.

Sancho did so, and, saying farewell, allowed his eyes to be covered, but immediately afterwards uncovered them again, and looking sad and tearfully on those in the garden, asked them to help him in his current situation with plenty of prayers, so God might provide someone to say as many for them, whenever they found themselves in a similar emergency.

At this Don Quixote exclaimed, "Are you about to be hung like a thief, or at your last moment, to make such pathetic requests like that? Cowardly, spiritless creature, are you not in the very place the fair Magalona occupied, and from which she descended, not into the grave, but to become the Queen of France; unless the histories lie? And I am I not the one beside you, on par with or surpassing the valiant Pierres? Cover your eyes, cover your eyes, miserable animal, and do not let your fear escape your lips, at least in my presence."

"Blindfold me," said Sancho; "as you won't let myself or anyone else on my behalf call for God's help, is it surprising that I am afraid there is a region of devils about to take us away?"

They were both blindfolded, and Don Quixote, finding himself settled, felt for the peg, and the instant he placed his fingers on it, all the ladies and all who stood by raised their voices exclaiming, "God guide you, valiant Knight! God be with you fearless aide! Now you go slicing through the air more swiftly than an arrow! Now you begin to amaze and astonish all who watch you from the earth! Take care not to wobble, valiant Sancho! Careful not to fall, because your fall will be worse than that impulsive youth who tried to steer the chariot of his father the Sun!"

As Sancho heard the voices, holding on tightly to his master and wrapping his arms round him, he said, "Señor, how do they perceive us to be going so high, if their voices can reach us here and they seem to be speaking quite close to us?"

"Don't mind that, Sancho," said Don Quixote; "because as adventures of this sort, and flights like this are out of the common course of things, you can see and hear as much as you like a thousand miles away; but don't squeeze me so tight or you will upset me; and really I do not know what you have to be uneasy or frightened about, because I can safely swear I never mounted a smoother-going horse in all the days of my life; one would believe we were not even moving. Get rid of your fear, my friend, because indeed everything is going as it should, and we have the wind behind us."

"That's true," said Sancho, "because such a strong wind comes against me on this side, that it seems as if people were blowing on me with a thousand fans;" which was the case; they were all fanning him; because the whole adventure was so well planned by the duke and the duchess, that nothing was omitted to make it perfectly successful.

Don Quixote now, feeling the air, said, "Without a doubt, Sancho, we must have already reached the second region of the air, where the hail and snow are generated; the thunder, the lightning, and the thunderbolts are created in the third region, and if we go on ascending at this rate, we will shortly plunge into the region of fire, and I do not know how to control this peg, so as not to go where we will be burned." And now they began to warm their faces, from a distance, with candles that could be easily set on fire and extinguished again, fixed on the end of a stick. Feeling the heat Sancho said, "May I die if we are not already in that place of fire, or very near it, because a good part of my beard has been singed, and am inclined señor, to uncover my face to see whereabouts we are."

"Do nothing of the kind," said Don Quixote; "remember the true story of the vicar Torralva that the devils carried flying through the air riding on a stick with his eyes shut; who in twelve hours reached Rome and dismounted at Torre di Nona, which is a street in the city, and saw the whole attack and the death of

Bourbon, and was back in Madrid the next morning, where he gave an account of all he had seen; and he said that as he was going through the air, the devil asked him to open his eyes, and he did so, and saw himself so near the surface of the moon, so it seemed to him, that he could have touched it with his hand, and that he did not dare to look at the earth or else he would be nauseous. So Sancho, it will not be right for us to uncover ourselves, because he who is in charge will be responsible for us; and perhaps we are gaining an altitude to enable us to descend in one plunge into the Kingdom of Candy, as the Eagle does on its prey, so as to catch it however high it may soar; and although it seems to us not even half an hour since we left the garden, believe me we must have travelled a great distance."

"I don't know how that could be," said Sancho; "all I know is that if Señora Magallanes or Magalona was satisfied with this rear, she could not have had very sensitive flesh."

The duke, the duchess, and all in the garden were listening to the conversation of the two heroes, and were beyond amused by it; and now, eager to put a finishing touch on this rare and well-contrived adventure, they lit the end of Clavileno's tail with a candle, and the horse, being full of fireworks and crackers, immediately blew up with an extraordinary noise, and brought Don Quixote and Sancho Panza to the ground half singed. By this time the bearded group of ladies, Trifaldi and all, had vanished from the garden, and those that remained lay stretched on the ground as if they had fainted. Don Quixote and Sancho got up rather shaken, and, looking around, were amazed to find themselves in the same garden from which they had started, and seeing such a number of people stretched on the ground; and their astonishment was increased when at one side of the garden they noticed a tall lance planted in the ground, and hanging from it by two cords of green silk a smooth white notice on which there was the following inscription in large gold letters: "The illustrious Knight Don Quixote of La Mancha has, by merely attempting it, finished and concluded the adventure of the Countess Trifaldi, otherwise called the Distressed Lady; Malambruno is now satisfied on every point, the chins of the ladies are now smooth and clean, and King Don Clavijo and Queen Antonomasia in their original form; and when the aide completes the whipping, the white dove will find herself freed from the evil enchanters that persecute her, and in the arms of her beloved mate; because this is the ruling of the sage Merlin, enchanter of enchanters."

As soon as Don Quixote had read the inscription on the notice he perceived clearly that it referred to the disenchantment of Dulcinea, and giving many thanks to heaven that he had with such little danger achieved such a grand adventure to restore to their former complexion the faces of those esteemed ladies, he advanced towards the duke and duchess, who had not yet come to themselves, and taking the duke by the hand he said, "Be happy, worthy sir, be happy; it's nothing at all; the adventure is now over and without any harm done, as the inscription fixed on this post clearly says."

The duke came to himself slowly and like one recovering consciousness after a heavy sleep, and the duchess and all who had fallen in the garden did the same, with such demonstration of wonder and amazement that they would have almost persuaded one that what they pretended so skilfully had happened to them in reality. The duke read the notice with his eyes half shut, and then ran to embrace Don Quixote with open arms, declaring him to be the best Knight that had ever lived. Sancho kept looking for the Distressed Lady, to see what her face was like without the beard, and if she was as fair as her elegant manner indicated; but they told him that, the instant Clavileno descended flaming through the air and came to the ground, the whole group of ladies vanished along with Trifaldi, and that they were already shaved without a hair left.

The duchess asked Sancho how he had felt on that long journey, to which Sancho replied, "I felt, señora, that we were flying through the region of fire, as my master told me, and I wanted to uncover my eyes for a bit; but my master, when I asked to uncover myself, would not let me; but as I have a little bit of curiosity, and a desire to know what is forbidden and hidden from me, quietly and without anyone seeing me I uncovered my eyes a little, and looked towards the earth, and it seemed to me that it was no bigger than a mustard seed, and that the men walking on it were a little bigger than hazel nuts; so you can tell how high we must have been."

To this the duchess said, "Sancho, my friend, careful what you are saying; it seems you could not have seen the earth, but only the men walking on it; because if the earth looked to you like a mustard seed, and each man like a hazel nut, one man would have covered the whole earth."

"That is true," said Sancho, "but despite that I got a glimpse of one side of it, and saw it all."

"Take care, Sancho," said the duchess, "with a bit of one side one does not see the whole of what one looks at."

"I don't understand that way of looking at things," said Sancho; "I only know that you should bear in mind that as we were flying by enchantment I might have seen the whole earth and all the men in whatever direction I looked; and if you won't believe this, no more will you believe that, uncovering myself, I saw myself so close to the sky that there was not a hand's length between me and heaven; and I can swear to you, señora, it is great! And it so happened that we came to where the seven goats are, and by God and on my soul, as in my youth I was a goatherder in my own country, as soon as I saw them I felt a longing to be among them for a little while, and if I had not given in to it I think I would have burst. So what did I do? Without saying anything to anybody, not even to my master, softly and quietly I got down from Clavileno and amused myself with the goats - which are like roses, like flowers - because for not even three-quarters of an hour Clavileno never moved from one spot."

"And while the good Sancho was amusing himself with the goats," said the duke, "how did Señor Don Quixote amuse himself?"

To which Don Quixote replied, "As all these things and similar occurrences are out of the ordinary course of nature, it is no wonder that Sancho says what he does; for my part I can only say that I did not uncover my eyes, neither did I see the sky, earth, sea or shore. It is true I felt that I was passing through different regions of air, and even that I touched the region of fire; but I cannot believe we passed any further than that; because the region of fire being between heaven and the last region of air, we could not have reached heaven where the seven goats Sancho speaks of are without being burned; and as we were not burned, either Sancho is lying or Sancho is dreaming."

"I am neither lying or dreaming," said Sancho; "ask me to prove they were the same goats, and you'll see whether I'm telling the truth or not."

"Tell us then, Sancho," said the duchess.

"Two of them," said Sancho, "are green, two red, two blue, and one a mixture of all colours."

"An odd sort of goat, that," said the duke; "in this earthly region of ours we have no such colours; I mean goats of such colours."

"That's obvious," said Sancho; "of course there must be a difference between the goats of heaven and the goats of the earth."

"Tell me, Sancho," said the duke, "did you see any male goat among those goats?"

"No, señor," said Sancho; "but I have heard that none ever passed the moon."

They did not care to ask him anything else about his journey, because they knew he was rambling about going all over heaven giving an account of everything that went on there, without having ever moved from the garden. So, in short, this was the end of the adventure of the Distressed Lady, which gave the duke and duchess great laughter not only for the present, but for their whole lives, and Sancho something to talk about for ages, if he lived long; but Don Quixote, coming close to his ear, said to him, "Sancho, if you want me to believe what you saw in heaven, I require you to believe me in regards to what I saw in the cave of Montesinos; I say no more."

CHAPTER 42

THE ADVICE WHICH DON QUIXOTE GAVE SANCHO PANZA BEFORE HE BEGAN TO GOVERN THE ISLAND, TOGETHER WITH OTHER WELL-CONSIDERED MATTERS

The duke and duchess were so pleased with the successful and humorous result of the adventure of the Distressed Lady, that they decided to carry on the joke, seeing what else they could do to make it pass for reality. So having made their plans and given instructions to their servants on how to behave toward Sancho in his government of the promised island, the next day, following Clavileno's flight, the duke told Sancho to prepare and get ready to go and be a governor, because his islanders were already anticipating him like the showers of May.

Sancho paid him respect, and said, "Ever since I came down from heaven, and from the top of it observed the earth, and saw how little it is, the great desire I had to be a governor has been cooled in me; because what grandeur is there in being a ruler on a mustard seed, or what dignity or authority in governing half a dozen men as big as hazel nuts; because, so far as I could see, there were no more on the whole earth? If you would be so kind to give me even a small bit of heaven, even if it were no more than half a meter, I'd rather have it than the best island in the world."

"Remember, Sancho," said the duke, "I cannot give a bit of heaven, not even as much as the width of my nail, to anyone; rewards and favours of that sort are reserved for God alone. What I can give, I give you, and that is a real, genuine island, compact, well proportioned, and unusually fertile and fruitful, where, if you know how to use your opportunities, you may, with the help of the world's riches, gain those of heaven."

"Well then," said Sancho, "let the island come; and I'll try and be such a governor, that in spite of crooks I'll go to heaven; and it's not from any craving to quit my own humble condition or better myself, but from the desire I have to try what it tastes like to be a governor."

"If you try it, Sancho," said the duke, "you'll eat your fingers off after you leave the government, such a sweet thing is it to command and be obeyed. Believe it when your master comes to be an emperor (as he will be beyond a doubt from the course his affairs are taking him), it will be no easy matter to take the dignity from him, because he will be sore from having taken so long to become one."

"Señor," said Sancho, "it is my belief it's a good thing to be in command, even if it's only over a herd of cattle."

"May I be buried with you, Sancho," said the duke, "you know everything; I hope you will make as good a governor as your wisdom promises; and that is all I have to say; and now remember tomorrow is the day you leave for the government of the island, and this evening they will provide you with the proper attire for you to wear, and all the things requisite for your departure."

"Let them dress me as they like," said Sancho; "however I'm dressed I'll be Sancho Panza."

"That's true," said the duke; "but one's dress must be suited to the office or rank one holds; because it would not do for a judge to dress like a soldier, or a soldier like a priest. You, Sancho, will go partly as a lawyer, partly as a captain, because, in the island I am giving you, arms are needed as much as letters, and letters as much as arms."

"Letters I know little about," said Sancho, "because I don't even know the A B Cs; but it is good enough for me to have Christ in my memory to be a good governor. As for weapons, I'll handle whatever they give me until I drop, and then, God help me!"

"With such a good memory," said the duke, "Sancho cannot go wrong in anything."

Here Don Quixote joined them; and learning what was discussed, and how soon Sancho was to go to his government, he with the duke's permission took him by the hand, and went into a room with him for the purpose of giving him advice as to how he was to humble himself in his office. As soon as they had entered the room he closed the door behind him, and almost by force made Sancho sit down beside him, and in a quiet tone addressed him:

"I give infinite thanks to heaven, friend Sancho, that, before I have met with any good luck, fortune has come forward to meet you. I who counted on my good fortune to discharge you for the payment of your services, find myself still lacking in my advancement, while you, before the time, and contrary to all reasonable expectation, see yourself blessed in the fulfilment of your desires. Some will bribe, beg, petition, rise early, plead and persist, without attaining the object of their desire; while another comes, and without knowing why or from where, finds himself provided with the place or office so many have pursued; and here the common saying, 'There is good luck as well as bad luck in pursuits,' applies. You, who, to my thinking, are beyond all doubt a fool, without early rising or staying up late nights or taking any trouble, with the mere breath of Knighthood that has blown on you, see yourself without more to do and become governor of an island, as though it were a mere matter of course. This I say, Sancho, you attribute not the favour you have received for your own merit, but give thanks to heaven that arranged these matters beneficially, and secondly give thanks to the great power the profession of Knighthood contains in itself. With a heart, then, inclined to believe what I have said to you, join yourself, my son, with Cato who would counsel you and be your guide to direct you to a safe haven out of this stormy sea where you are about to immerse yourself; because offices and positions of great responsibility are nothing else but a sea of troubles. First of all, my son, you must fear God, because in the fear of him is wisdom, and being wise you cannot make an error. Secondly, you must keep in view what you are, striving to know yourself, the most difficult thing to know that the mind can imagine. If you know yourself, it will follow that you will not inflate yourself like the frog that tried to make himself as large as an ox; if you do, the recollection of having kept pigs in your own country will serve as the ugly feet for the wheel of your foolishness."

"That's the truth," said Sancho; "but that was when I was a boy; afterwards when I was more of a man it was geese that I kept, not pigs. But to my thinking that has nothing to do with it; because all who are governors don't come from a Kingly lineage."

"True," said Don Quixote, "and for that reason those who are not from a noble origin should take care that the dignity of the office they hold should be accompanied with a gentle smoothness, which wisely managed will save them from the malice that no fame escapes from. Glory in your humble birth, Sancho, and do not be ashamed of saying you are peasant-born; because when it is seen that you are not ashamed, no one can make you blush; and pride yourself on being one of lower virtue rather than a grand sinner. There are countless who, born of poor parentage, have risen to the highest distinctions, grandiose and Lordly, and for the truth of this I could give enough instances to weary you."

"Remember, Sancho, if you make virtue your aim, and take a pride in doing virtuous actions, you will have no cause to envy those who are Princely or Lordly, because blood is an inheritance, but virtue is an acquisition, and virtue has in itself alone a worth that blood does not possess."

"This being so, if by chance anyone of your family should come to see you when you are on your island, you are not to repel them, but on the contrary to welcome them, entertain them; because in so doing you will be approved of in heaven (which is not pleased that any should despise what it has made), and will comply with the laws of well-ordered nature. If you take your wife with you (it is not well for those that administer governments to be long without their wives), teach and instruct her, and strive to smooth down her natural roughness; because all that may be gained by a wise governor may be lost and wasted by a rough stupid wife."

"If by chance you are left a widower - a thing which may happen - and in virtue of your office seek a partner of higher degree, do not choose one purely to serve your fishing-rod, because I tell you, you will be held accountable at the general calling at the end of life; where those have to repay in death four times the items that in life they regarded as nothing. Never go by subjective law, which is favoured by ignorant men who pride themselves on cleverness. Let the tears of the poor man find you with more compassion, but not more justice, than the pleadings of the rich. Strive to speak the bare truth, as well among the promises and presents of the rich man, as among the crying and pleading of the poor."

"When fairness may and should be brought into play, do not impose the utmost rigour of the law against the guilty; because the reputation of the stern judge does not stand higher than that of the compassionate."

"If by chance you permit the staff of justice to veer, do not let it be by the weight of a gift, but by that of mercy."

"If it happens that you are required to give judgment on one who is your enemy, turn your thoughts away from your injury and fix them on the justice of the case."

"Do not let your own passion blind you in another man's cause; because the errors you will commit like this will be most frequently irremediable; or if not, only to be remedied at the expense of your good name and even your fortune."

"If any beautiful woman comes to seek justice from you, turn away your eyes from her tears and your ears from her cries, and consider deliberately the merit of her demand, if you do not want to have your reason swept away by her weeping, and your righteousness by her sighs."

"Do not abuse with words those who you have punished with deeds, because the pain of punishment is enough for the unfortunate without the addition of your words."

"Bear in mind that the offender who comes under your jurisdiction is a miserable man subject to all the tendencies of our depraved nature, and so far as it may be in your power show yourself lenient and merciful; because although the attributes of God are all equal, to our eyes, mercy is brighter and grander than justice."

"If you follow these precepts and rules, Sancho, your days in office will be long, your fame eternal, your rewards abundant, your happiness unimaginable; you will marry your children to whoever you like; they and your grandchildren will hold titles; you will live in peace and harmony with all men; and, when life draws to a close, death will come to you in calm and ripe old age, and the light and loving hands of your great-grandchildren will close your eyes."

"These instructions are for the adornment of your mind; now listen to those which attend to that of the body."

CHAPTER 43

THE SECOND SET OF ADVICE DON QUIXOTE GAVE TO SANCHO PANZA

Who, hearing the previous discourse of Don Quixote, would not have considered him to be a person of great sense and even greater morality of purpose? But, as has been frequently been observed in the course of this great history, he only talked nonsense when he touched on chivalry, and in discussing all other subjects showed that he had a clear and unbiased understanding; so in the case of this second set of advice that he gave to Sancho, he showed himself to have a sense of humour, and evidently displayed his wisdom, and also his foolishness.

Sancho listened to him with the deepest attention, and endeavoured to fix his advice in his memory, like one who intended to follow it and with it bring the full promise of his government to a happy conclusion. Don Quixote, then, went on to say:

"With regard to the mode in which you should govern yourself and your house, Sancho, the first advice I have to give you is to be clean, and to cut your nails, not letting them grow as some do, whose ignorance makes them believe that long nails are an enhancement to their hands, as if those outgrowths they neglect to cut were nails, and not the claws of a lizard catching falcon - a filthy and unnatural abuse to the self."

"Do not go about undisciplined and loose, Sancho; because disordered attire is a sign of an unstable mind, unless indeed the untidiness and slackness is due to a craft, as the common opinion was in the case of Julius Caesar."

"Ascertain cautiously what your office may be worth; and if it will allow you to give uniforms to your servants, give them respectable and serviceable ones, rather than tasteless and flashy ones, and divide them between your servants and the poor; that is to say, if you can clothe six servants, clothe poor men, and therefore you will have servants for heaven and servants for earth; the conceited never think of this way of giving uniforms."

"Do not eat garlic or onions, or they might believe you to have a disrespectful origin by the smell; walk slowly and speak deliberately, but not in such a way as to make it seem you are listening only to yourself, because all pretention is bad."

"Eat lightly and drink even more sparingly still; because the health of the whole body is produced in the workshop of the stomach."

"Be moderate in drinking, keeping in mind that wine in excess does not keep secrets or promises."

"Take care, Sancho, not to burp in anybody's presence."

"Burp!" said Sancho; "I don't know what that means."

"To burp, Sancho," said Don Quixote, "means to belch, and that is one of the filthiest words in language."

"In truth, señor," said Sancho, "one of the cautions I will bear in mind most will be this, not to belch, because I'm constantly doing it."

"Burp, Sancho, not belch," said Don Quixote."

"Ok burp, I swear not to forget it," said Sancho."

"Likewise, Sancho," said Don Quixote, "you must not mix so many of your proverbs into your conversation as you do; because although proverbs are short sayings of wisdom, you drag them in so often that they appear more like nonsense than wise words."

"God alone can cure that," said Sancho; "because I have more proverbs in me than the bible, and when I speak they come so thick together into my mouth that they fight amongst themselves to get out; that's why my tongue lets the first one that comes fly out, although it may not be suitable for the purpose. But I'll be careful from now on to use those that suit the dignity of my office; because 'in a house where there's plenty, dinner is soon cooked,' and 'giving and keeping require brains.'"

"That's it, Sancho!" said Don Quixote; "keep string proverbs together; nobody is stopping you! 'The mother beats the child, and the child continues the tricks.' I am asking you to avoid proverbs, and here in a second you have shot more of them, which have as much to do with what we are talking about as 'nothing.' Careful, Sancho, I do not say that a proverb suitably brought in is objectionable; but to pile up and string together proverbs at random makes conversation uninteresting and discourteous."

"When you ride on horseback, do not go slouching with your body on the back of the saddle, or carry your legs stiff, or sticking out from the horse's belly, or sit so loosely that one would suppose you were on Dapple; because the seat on a horse makes gentlemen of some and animals of others."

"Be moderate in your sleep; because he who does not rise early does not get the benefit of the day; and remember, Sancho, diligence is the mother of good fortune, and indolence, sloth and laziness are its opposite, which had never yet attained the object of an honest ambition."

"The last one I will give to you now, although it does not lead to bodily improvement, I want you to carry carefully in your memory, because I believe it will be no less useful to you than those I have already given you, and it is this - never engage in a dispute about family, at least in the way of comparing them one with another; because one of those compared will be better than the other, and you will be hated by the one you have disparaged, and get nothing in any shape or form from the one you have exalted."

"Your clothing should be full length, a long jacket, and a cloak a little longer; no loose trousers, because they are not appropriate for a gentlemen or for governors."

"For the present, Sancho, this is all the advice I can think of to give to you; as time goes by and occasions arise my instructions will follow, if you take care to let me know how you are doing."

"Señor," said Sancho, "I see well enough that all these things you have said to me are good, holy, and profitable; but what use will they be to me if I don't remember one of them? Not letting my nails grow, and marrying again if I have the chance, will not slip out of my head; but all that other jumble, I don't and can't recollect any more of it than last year's clouds; so it must be given to me in writing; because although I can't read or write, I'll give it to my vicar, to drive it into me and remind me of it whenever it's necessary."

"Ah, sinner that I am!" said Don Quixote, "how bad it looks for governors not to know how to read or write; because let me tell you, Sancho, when a man does not know how to read, or is poor-handed, it argues one of two things; either that he was the son of exceedingly lowly parents, or that he himself was so hopeless and ill-conditioned that neither good company or good teaching could make any impression on him. That is a great defect that you will need to work on, and therefore I advise at least learn to sign your name."

"I can sign my name well enough," said Sancho, "because when I was the overseer of the brotherhood in my village I learned to make certain letters, like the marks on the side of goods, which they told me made out my name. Besides I can pretend my hands are disabled and make someone else sign for me, because 'there's a remedy for everything except death;' and as I will be in command of the staff, I can do as I like; moreover, 'like he who has a magistrate for a father,' and I'll be governor, and that's higher than a magistrate. You will see! Let them make fun and abuse me; 'they'll come for wool and go back shaved;' 'whoever God loves, his house is known to Him;' 'the silly sayings of the rich pass for proverbs in the world;' and as I'll be rich, being a governor, and at the same time generous, as I intend to be, no fault will be seen in me. 'But make yourself honey and the flies will stick to you;' 'as much as you have as much you're worth,' as my grandmother used to say; and 'you can have no revenge on a man of affluence.'"

"Oh, God curse you, Sancho!" exclaimed Don Quixote; "sixty thousand devils take you away and your proverbs! For the last hour you have been stringing them together and inflicting torture on me with every one of them. Those proverbs will bring you to the gallows one day, I promise; your people will take the government from you, or there will be revolts among them. Tell me, where do you pick them up, you tit? How do you apply them, fool? Because with me, to say one and make it apply properly, I have to sweat and work as if I were digging."

"God, master of mine," said Sancho, "you are making a fuss about very little. Why the devil should you be angry if I make use of what is my own? And I have got nothing else, or any other stock to trade with except proverbs and more proverbs; and I have three that just came into my head, suitable for the purpose like pears in a basket; but I won't repeat them, because 'Sancho will be called sage silence.'"

"That, Sancho, you are not," said Don Quixote; "because not only are you not sage silence, but you are virulent and perversity; still I would like to know what three proverbs have just come into your mind, because I have been going over my own - and none occur to me."

"What can be better," said Sancho, "than 'never put your thumbs between your two back teeth;' and that there is no answer to "get out of my house" and "what do you want with my wife?" and 'whether the jug hits the stove, or the stove the jug, it's a bad for the jug;' all of these fit, because no one should argue with his governor, or one in authority over him, because he will come out worse, as one who puts his finger between two back teeth and if they are not back teeth it makes no difference, as long as they are teeth; and to whatever the governor may say there's no answer, for it any more than there is to 'get out of my house' and 'what do you want with my wife?' and then, as for that about the stove and the jug, a blind man could see that, and you know well that 'the fool knows more in his own house than the wise man in another's.'"

"Actually, Sancho," said Don Quixote, "the fool knows nothing, either in his own house or in anybody else's, because no wise structure of any sort can stand on a foundation of foolishness; but let us say no more about it, Sancho, because if you govern badly, the fault will be yours and the shame will be mine; but I comfort myself with having done my duty in advising you as sincerely and as wisely as I can; and therefore I am released from my obligations and my promise. God guide you, Sancho, and govern you in your government, and free me from the worry I have that you will turn the whole island upside down, a thing I might easily prevent by explaining to the duke what you are and telling him that the fat little person you are is nothing but a sack full of proverbs and impudence."

"Señor," said Sancho, "if you think I'm not fit for this government, I give it up; because the mere black of my nail is dearer to me than my whole body; and I can live just as well, simple Sancho, on bread and onions, as governor, on chicken and hens; and what's more, while we're asleep we're all equal, great and small, rich and poor. But if you look into it, you will see it was you alone that gave me this idea of governing; because I know no more about the government of islands than an eagle; and if there's any reason to think that because of me being a governor the devil will get hold of me, I'd rather take Sancho to heaven than take a governor to hell."

"God, Sancho," said Don Quixote, "for those last words you have said, I consider you deserve to be governor of a thousand islands. You have good natural instincts, without which no knowledge is worth anything; call on God, and try not to swerve in the pursuit of your main objective; I mean, always make it your aim and fixed purpose to do right in all matters that come to you, because heaven always helps good intentions; and now let us go to dinner, because I think my lord and lady are waiting for us."

CHAPTER 44

HOW SANCHO PANZA WAS LED TO HIS GOVERNMENT, AND THE STRANGE ADVENTURE THAT HAPPENED TO DON QUIXOTE IN THE CASTLE

It is stated, they say, when Cide Hamete came to write this book, that the true original of this history was not translated correctly – as a kind of complaint the Moor made against himself for having taken in hand a story so boring and of so little variety as this of Don Quixote, because he found himself forced to speak perpetually about him and Sancho, without attempting to indulge in detours and episodes more serious and more interesting. He said, too, that to go on, with his mind, hand, pen always restricted to writing on one single subject, and speaking through the mouths of a few characters, was unbearable work, the result of which was never equal to the author's ability, and that to avoid this he had in the First Part liberated himself from this with novels like, like "The Ill-advised Curiosity," and "The Captive Captain," which stand, as it were, apart from the main story. He also thought, he says, that many, engrossed by the interest attached to the adventures of Don Quixote, would take no interest in the novels, and pass over them hastily or impatiently without noticing the elegance and art of their composition, which would be very evident if theory were published by themselves and not as mere additions to the madness of Don Quixote or the simplicities of Sancho. Therefore in this Second Part he thought it best not to insert novels, either separate or interwoven, but only episodes, or something like them, arising out of the circumstances the facts present; and even these sparingly, and with no more words than that which suffice to make them clear; and as he confines and restricts himself to the narrow limits of the narrative, although he has ability; capacity, and enough brains to deal with the whole universe, he requests that his work is not detested, and that credit be given to him, not only for what he writes, but for what he has refrained from writing.

And so he goes on with the story, saying that the day Don Quixote gave the advice to Sancho, the same afternoon after dinner he handed them to him in writing so that he might get someone to read them to him if needed. They had barely, however, been given to him when he let them drop, and they fell into the hands of the duke, who showed them to the duchess and they were both given fresh amazement at the madness and wit of Don Quixote. To carry on the joke, then, the same evening they sent Sancho with a large following to the village that was to serve as his island. It happened that the person who was in charge was a chief of the duke's, a man of great discretion and humour (there can be no humour without discretion) and the same man who played the part of the Countess Trifaldi in the comical way that has been already described; and therefore qualified, and instructed by his master and mistress how to deal with Sancho, he carried out their scheme admirably. Now it came to pass that as soon as Sancho saw this chief he seemed to recognise in him the features of Trifaldi, and turning to his master, he said to him, "Señor, either the devil will take me away, here on this spot, righteous and believing, or you will admit to me that the face of this chief of the duke's is the very face of the Distressed Lady."

Don Quixote stared at the Chief attentively, and having done so, said to Sancho, "There is no reason why the devil should take you away, Sancho, either righteous or believing - and what you mean by that I do not know; the face of the Distressed Lady is that of the Chief, but despite that the Chief is not the Distressed Lady; because him being so would involve a mighty contradiction; but this is not the time for going into questions of the sort, which would be involving ourselves in a complex labyrinth. Believe me, my friend, we must pray sincerely to our Lord that he frees us both from evil wizards and enchanters."

"It is no joke, señor," said Sancho, "because before this I heard him speak, and it seemed exactly as if the voice of Trifaldi was hitting my ears. Well, I'll hold my peace; but I'll take care to be on the look-out from now for anything that may confirm or rid me of this suspicion."

"That would be wise, Sancho," said Don Quixote, "and you will let me know anything you discover, and all that happens during your government."

Sancho finally left attended by a large number of people. He was dressed in the clothing of a lawyer, with a robe of tweed and a cap of the same material, and mounted on a donkey. Behind him, in accordance with the duke's orders, followed Dapple with a brand new saddle and harness covered in silk, and from time to time Sancho turned around to look at his donkey, so well pleased to have him with him that he would not have changed places with the emperor of Germany. On leaving he kissed the hands of the duke and duchess and got his master's blessing, which Don Quixote gave to him with tears.

Let worthy Sancho go in peace, and good luck to him, Gentle Reader; and look out for two heaps of laughter, which the account of how he behaved himself in office will give you. In the meantime, turn your attention to what happened to his master the same night, and if you do not laugh, you will at least stretch your mouth with a grin; because Don Quixote's adventures must be admired either with wonder or with laughter.

It is recorded, then, that as soon as Sancho had gone, Don Quixote felt his loneliness, and had it been possible for him to revoke the mandate and take away the government from him he would have done so. The duchess observed his dejection and asked him why he was so down; because, she said, if it was for the loss of Sancho, there were aides, servants, and ladies in her house who would wait on him to his full satisfaction.

"The truth is, señora," replied Don Quixote, "that I do feel the loss of Sancho; but that is not the main cause of my sadness; and out of all the offers you make me, I only accept the good-will with which they are made, and as to the remainder I ask you to permit and allow me to wait on myself in my room."

"Señor Don Quixote," said the duchess, "that cannot be; because four of my ladies, as beautiful as flowers, will wait on you."

"To me," said Don Quixote, "they will not be flowers, but thorns to pierce my heart. They, or anything like them, as soon enter my room like flies. If your highness wishes to gratify me, although I do not deserve it, allow me to please be by myself, and wait on myself in my own room; because I place a barrier between my inclinations and my virtue, and I do not wish to break this rule through the generosity your highness is disposed to display towards me; and, in short, I will sleep in my clothes, sooner than allow anyone to undress me."

"Say no more, Señor Don Quixote, say no more," said the duchess; "I assure you I will give orders that not even a fly will enter your room. I am not the one to undermine the decency of Señor Don Quixote, because it strikes me that among his many virtues, one that is pre-eminent, is that of modesty. You may undress and dress in private and in your own way, as you please and when you please, because there will be no one to hinder you; and in your room you will find all the utensils requisite to supply the wants of one who sleeps with his door locked, so there would be no need to compel you to open it. May the great Dulcinea del Toboso live a thousand years, and may her fame extend all over the world, because she deserves to be loved by a Knight so courageous and so virtuous as you; and may kind heaven infuse zeal into the heart of our governor Sancho Panza to finish off his task promptly, so that the world may once more enjoy the beauty of such a grand lady."

To which Don Quixote replied, "Your highness has spoken like what you are; from the mouth of a noble lady nothing bad can come; and Dulcinea will be more fortunate, and better known to the world by the praise of your highness than by all the tributes the greatest orators on earth could give to her."

"Well, well, Señor Don Quixote," said the duchess, it is nearly diner-time, and the duke is probably waiting; come let us go to eat, and retire to rest early, because the journey you made yesterday from Candy was so long that it must have caused you some fatigue."

"I feel none señora," said Don Quixote, "because I would go as far to say that in my whole life I never mounted a quieter horse, or travelled on a better paced one, than Clavileno; and I don't know what could have induced Malambruno to discard a horse so swift and so gentle, and burn it so recklessly as he did."

"Probably," said the duchess, "repenting for all the evil he had done to Trifaldi and the bearded ladies, and others, and the crimes he must have committed as a wizard and enchanter, and so he decided to set fire to all the instruments of his craft; and burned Clavileno as the main one, and that which primarily made him restless, wandering from land to land; and with its ashes, the bravery of the great Don Quixote of La Mancha is established for ever."

Don Quixote renewed his thanks to the duchess; and after dinner went to his room alone, refusing to allow anyone to enter with him, due to his fear of encountering temptations that might lead or drive him to forget his loyalty to his lady Dulcinea; because he had always present in his mind the virtue of Amadis, that flower and mirror of Knights. He locked the door behind him, and by the light of two wax candles undressed himself, but as he was taking off his socks - a disaster unworthy of such a person! - there was a burst, not of tears, but of two dozen stitches in one of his socks, that made it look like a lattice. The gentleman was extremely distressed, and at that moment he would have given an ounce of silver to have had some green silk there; I say green silk, because the socks were green.

Here Cide Hamete exclaimed as he was writing, "Poverty, poverty! I do not know what could have possessed the great Cordovan poet to call you 'a holy gift ungratefully received.' Although a Moor, I know well enough from the discussions I have had with Christians that holiness consists in charity, humility, faith, obedience, and poverty; but despite that, I say he must have a great deal of godliness who can find any satisfaction in being poor; unless, indeed, it be the kind of poverty one of their greatest saints refers to, saying, 'possess all things as though you did not possess them;' which is what they call poverty in spirit. But that other poverty – because that is what I am speaking of now - why do you love to fall out with gentlemen and men of good birth more than with other people? Why do you compel them to have cracks in their shoes, and to have the buttons of their coats stitched up, one with silk and another with wool? Then he goes on: "Poor gentleman from good families! Always ruining their honour, eating miserably and in secret, making a hypocrite of the toothpick with which he goes out into the street after having nothing to encourage him to use it! Poor fellow, I say, with his nervous honour, thinking they notice a mile away the patch on his shoe, the sweat-stains on his hat, the shabbiness of his coat, and the hunger of his stomach!"

Similar feelings came to Don Quixote by the bursting of his stitches; however, he comforted himself on noticing that Sancho had left behind a pair of travelling boots, which he decided to wear the next day. Finally, he went to bed, unhappy and depressed, not only because he missed Sancho but because of the irreparable disaster to his socks, so much so, he would have even stitched them up with silk of another colour, which is one of the greatest signs of poverty a gentleman can show in the course of his never-failing embarrassments. He put out the candles; but the night was warm and he could not sleep; he rose from his bed and opened a grated window slightly, that looked out onto a beautiful garden, and as he did he noticed and heard people walking and talking in the garden. He began to listen attentively, and those speaking had their voices raised enough so he could hear these words:

"Emerencia if you try to encourage me to sing, I could not, because you know that ever since this stranger entered the castle and I saw him, I cannot sing, I only cry; besides my lady is such a light sleeper, I would not sing for all the wealth in the world in case she found us here; and even if she were asleep and did not wake up, my singing would be in to no avail, if this strange leader, who has come into my neighbourhood to disobey me, sleeps and does not wake to hear it."

"Do not worry about that, dear Altisidora," replied a voice; "no doubt the duchess is asleep, and everybody in the house except the lord of your heart and disturber of your soul; because just now I noticed him open the grated window of his room, so he must be awake; sing, my poor sufferer, in a low sweet tone to the accompaniment of your harp; and even if the duchess hears us we can blame it on the heat of the night."

"That is not the point, Emerencia," replied Altisidora, "it is that my singing may clearly open my heart, and that I would be thought of as a light and unrestrained lady by those who do not know the mighty power of love; but whatever happens; it is better to have blush on the cheeks than a pain in the heart;" and here a harp softly made itself heard.

As he listened to all of this Don Quixote was in a state of breathless amazement, because immediately the countless adventures like this, with windows, gardens, serenades, love making, and desires, that he had read about in his books of chivalry, came to his mind. He immediately concluded that some lady of the duchess's was in love with him, and that her modesty forced her to keep her passion a secret. He was shaking and worried he may fall, and so he made an inward resolution not to yield; and calling with all his might and soul on his lady Dulcinea he made up his mind to listen to the music; and to let them know he was there he gave a pretend sneeze, at which the ladies were more than delighted, because all they wanted was Don Quixote to hear them. So having tuned the harp, Altisidora, running her hand across the strings, began this poem:

O you who are above in bed,
Between the silky sheets,
Lying there from the night till morn,
With outstretched legs asleep;

O you, most valiant Knight of all
The famous Manchegan Knight,
Height of purity and virtues tall,
Greater than any diamond however bright;

Lend your ears for a suffering maid,
Not knowing where to start,
You are the sun and have lit,
A fire within her heart.

Adventure seeking on the road,
Helping others with alarm;
Healing wounds, as you have the balm,
Which in your hands you do hold!

Valiant Knight, and so may God
Give you speed,
You are the light of crystal sands,
Helping those who are in need.

576

Did the little snakes let you suck?
Who nursed you as a babe?
Were you cradled in the forest?
Or in gloomy mountain cave?

O Dulcinea must be proud,
That plump and lusty maid;
Because she alone had the power,
To make a fierce tiger tame.

And for this famous she will be,
From Spain worldwide,
From no corner her name will hide,
On Earth, water, and every mountain side,

To change her for me - my attempt,
May be viewed as contempt,
But I offer the best I have to hold,
All laced and trimmed with gold.

To be happy,
I, in your mighty arms enrol,
Or even sit beside your bed
And scratch your dusty pole!

I seek to give favours such as these,
Unworthy to aspire high;
To tickle your feet would be enough,
For someone so poor as I.

What cap, what slippers silver-laced,
And the finest coats!
What trousers I would make for you;
And fine long tweed cloaks!

And I would give you pearls that should
Make themselves as big as oaks be shown;
So matchless that each might as well
Be called the greatest one alone.

Manchegan hero, do not look down,
From your high perch,
On this burning heart, or add,

The fuel of your fury to make it worse.

A virgin young and soft am I,
Not yet seventeen years old;
(I'm only three months past sixteen,
I swear on my soul).

I do not hobble and neither do I limp,
Blemishes I am without,
And as I walk my lovely locks,
Are trailing on the ground.

And although my nose is rather flat,
And although my mouth is wide,
My teeth like precious stones exalt,
My beauty to the sky.

You know that my voice is sweet,
That is if you hear;
And I am moulded in a form
Somewhat below the mean.

These charms, and many more are,
Yours, to accompany you, your lance and all; A,
Lady of this house am I,
By the name Altisidora.

At this point the heart stricken Altisidora concluded her poem, while the pursued Don Quixote began to feel worried; and with a deep sigh he said to himself, "O am such an unlucky Knight, no lady can set their eyes on me and not fall in love! The peerless Dulcinea should be so unfortunate that they cannot let her enjoy my incomparable constancy in peace! What you do to her, you Queens? Why do you persecute her, you Empresses? Why do you pursue her, you virgins? Leave the lady to triumph in glory with the love I have been pleased to give her in surrendering my heart and yielding my soul to her. You love-struck lady, know that to Dulcinea only I am soft and sweet as sugar, stone to all others; for her I am honey, for you nettles. For me Dulcinea alone is beautiful, wise, virtuous, graceful, and high-bred, and all others are unpleasant, foolish, light, and low-born. Nature sent me into the world to be hers and no other's; Altisidora may cry or sing, and may give way to misery, but I must be Dulcinea's, pure, courteous, and faithful, in spite of all the magic-working powers on earth."

And with that he shut the window with a bang, and with such temper that it would appear that some great misfortune had happened to him. He proceeded to stretch himself on his bed, where we will leave him for the present, as the great Sancho Panza, who is about to set up his famous government, now demands our attention.

CHAPTER 45

HOW THE GREAT SANCHO PANZA TOOK POSSESSION OF HIS ISLAND, AND HOW HE MADE HIS BEGINNING

Light of the world, eye of heaven, sweet stimulator of the water! An archer, now physician, father of poetry, inventor of music; you that always rise and, apart from appearance, never set! To you, Sun, by whose aid man brought into existence man, to you I appeal to help me and lighten the darkness of my mind so I may be able to proceed with honourable thoroughness in giving an account of the great Sancho Panza's government; because without you I feel myself as frail, weak, and unsure.

To come to the point, then - Sancho with all his attendants arrived at a village of about a thousand inhabitants, and one of the largest the duke possessed. They informed him that it was called the island of Barataria, because the name of the village was Baratario. On reaching the gates of the town, which was a walled, the vicar came forward to meet him, the bells, and the inhabitants showed every sign of general satisfaction; and with great ceremony they led him to the principal church to give thanks to God, and then with more ceremony and dance they presented him with the keys to the town, and acknowledged him as governor of the island of Barataria. The costume, the beard, and the fat figure of the new governor astonished all those who were not aware of the secret, and for those who were, (which was not a few).

Finally, leading him out of the church they carried him to the judgment seat and sat him on it, and the duke's chief of the home said to him, "It is an ancient custom in this island, señor governor, that he who comes to take possession of this famous island is bound to answer a question which will be put to him, and which is a somewhat difficult one; and from his answer the people will measure their new governor's wit, and welcome him with joy or criticise his arrival accordingly."

While the chief was making this speech Sancho was gazing at several large letters inscribed on the wall opposite his seat, and as he could not read he asked what was painted on the wall. The answer was:

"Señor, there it is written and recorded the day on which you took possession of this island, and the inscription says, 'This day, of this month and year, Señor Don Sancho Panza took possession of this island; and for many years may he enjoy it.'"

"And who do they call Don Sancho Panza?" asked Sancho.

"You, my lord," replied the chief; "because no other Panza except the one who is now sat in that chair has ever entered this island."

"Well then, let me tell you, brother," said Sancho, "I haven't got the 'Don,' and no one in my family ever had it; my name is plain Sancho Panza, and Sancho was my father's name, and Sancho was my grandfather's and they were all Panzas, without any Dons added; I suspect that in this island there are more

Dons than stones; but never mind; God knows what I mean, and maybe if my government lasts four days I'll weed out these Dons that no doubt are as great a nuisance as the mice, as there are so many. Let the chief go on with his question, and I'll give the best answer I can, whether the people criticise or not."

At this moment two old men came into the court, one carrying a cane as a walking-stick, and the one who had no stick said, "Señor, some time ago I lent this good man ten gold-coins on the condition that he was to return them to me whenever I would ask for them. A long time passed before I asked for them, because I would not ask at any moment which could put him in a worse situation than when I lent them to him; but thinking he was becoming careless about payment I asked for them several times; and not only will he not give them back, but he denies that he owes them to me, and says I never lent him anything at all; or if I did, that he repaid them; and I have no witnesses either of the loan, or the payment; I want you to put him under oath, and if he swears he returned them to me I will consider the debt repaid right now before God."

"What do you say about this, good old man, you with the stick?" said Sancho. To which the old man replied:

"I admit, señor, that he lent them to me; but I swear to God."

The old man who had the stick handed it to the other old man to hold for him while he swore; and then laid his hand on the cross, saying that it was true the ten coins had been lent to him; but that he had with his own hand given them back into the hand of the other, and that he, not recalling it, was always asking for them.

Seeing this the great governor asked the creditor what he had to say in answer to what his opponent had said. He said that no doubt his debtor had told the truth, because he believed him to be an honest man and a good Christian, and he himself must have forgotten when and how he had given the coins back; and from that time forward he would make no further demand for payment.

The debtor took his stick again, and bowing his head left the court. Observing this, and how, without another word, he left, and observing too the resignation of the other, Sancho buried his head in his chest and remained in deep thought for a short space of time, with his hand on his chin; then he raised his head and asked them to call back the old man with the stick. They brought him back, and as soon as Sancho saw him he said, "Honest man, give me that stick, because I want to see it for a moment."

"Sure," said the old man; "here it is señor," and he place it in Sancho's hand.

Sancho then passed it to the other old man and said to him, "Go, and God be with you; because now you are paid."

"Paid señor?" returned the old man; "is this cane worth ten gold-coins?"

"Yes," said the governor, "or if not I am the greatest fool in the world; now you will see whether I have got the head to govern a whole Kingdom;" and he ordered the cane to be broken in two, there, in the presence of all. It was done, and in the middle of it they found ten gold-coins. All were filled with amazement, and looked at their governor as another King Solomon. They asked him how he had come to the conclusion that the ten coins were inside the cane; he replied, that observing how the old man who swore gave the stick to his opponent while he was taking the oath, and swore that he had really given him back the coins, and how as soon as he had done swearing he took the stick back, it came into his head that the sum demanded must be inside it; and from this he said it might be seen that God sometimes guides those who govern in their judgment, even though they may be fools; besides this he had himself heard the vicar of his village mention another similar case, and he had such a good memory, that it would not allow him to forget even that which he did not wish to remember, and that there would not be a memory like his on the whole island. To conclude, the old men went off, one deflated, and the other highly contented, all who were present were astonished, and he who was recording the words, deeds, and movements of Sancho could not make up his mind whether he was to look at him and put him down as a fool or as a man of sense.

As soon as this case was concluded, a woman came into the court holding on with a tight grip to a man dressed like a wealthy cattle dealer, and she came forward making a great outcry and exclaiming, "Justice, señor governor, justice! And if I don't get it on earth I'll go look for it in heaven. Señor governor of my soul, this evil man caught me in the middle of the fields and used my body as if it was a wash rag, and took from me what I had kept for twenty-three years, defending it against Moors and Christians, natives and strangers; did I stay hard as an oak tree, and keeping myself as pure as flowers compared to the weeds, for this man to come with his hands to handle me!"

"It remains to be proven whether this man's hands are clean or not," said Sancho; and turning to the man he asked him what he had to say in response to the woman's accusation.

He in confusion answered, "Sir, I am a poor pig dealer, and this morning I left the village to buy four pigs, and between fees and payment I got less than I paid for. As I was returning to my village I encountered this good lady, and the devil who makes a mess out of everything, pulled us together. I paid her fairly, but she not being content grabbed me and never let go until she brought me here; she says I forced her, but she is lying under oath I swear or am ready to swear; and this is the whole truth and every bit of it."

The governor asked him if he had any silver on him; he said he had about twenty coins in a leather wallet in his pocket. The governor asked him take it and place it in the hand of the lady; he obeyed while shaking; the woman took it, and gave a thousand thanks and made a prayer to God to give long life and health to the governor who had such a high regard for distressed ladies. She then hurried out of court with the wallet grasped in both her hands, first looking, however, to see if the money it contained was silver.

As soon as she was gone Sancho said to the pig dealer, whose tears were already starting to show, and whose eyes and heart were following his wallet, "Good man, go after that woman and take the wallet from her, by force if

582

necessary, and come back here with it;" and he did not say it to someone who was deaf, because the man was gone like a flash of lightning, and ran to do as he was told.

All the spectators waited anxiously to see the end of the case, and then both the man and woman came back with a tighter grip of each other than before, she with her coat done up and the wallet inside it, and he struggling hard to take it from her, but all to no avail, so strong was the woman's defence all the while crying out, "Justice from God and the world! see here, señor governor, the shamelessness of this thief, who in the middle of the town, in the middle of the street, wanted to take the wallet which you made him give to me."

"And did he take it?" asked the governor.

"Take it!" said the woman; "I'd let my life be taken from me sooner than the wallet. Hammers, mallets and chisels would not get it out of my grip; no, or lions' claws; the soul has to come out of my body first!"

"She is right," said the man; "I am beaten and powerless; I confess I haven't got the strength to take it from her;" and he let go of her.

The governor said to the woman, "Let me see that wallet, my worthy and strong friend." She handed it to him immediately, and the governor returned it to the man, and said to the unforced lady of force, "Sister, if you had shown as much, or only half as much spirit and vigour in defending your body as you have shown in defending the wallet, the strength of Hercules could not have forced you. Go away, and God give you speed, and bad luck to you, and don't show your face in this island again, or within six miles of it on any side, under pain of two hundred lashes; leave immediately, now, you shameless cheating mouse."

The woman was shamed and went off miserably, hanging her head; and the governor said to the man, "Honest man, go home with your money, and God give you speed; and for the future, if you don't want to lose it, see that you don't take it into your head to get too close to this type of woman."

The man thanked him as much as he could and went on his way, and the witnesses were again filled with admiration at their new governor's judgments and sentences.

Next, two men, one apparently a farm worker, and the other a tailor, because he had a pair of scissors in his hand, presented themselves before him, and the tailor said, "Señor governor, this labourer and I come to you because this man came to my shop yesterday, and putting a piece of cloth into my hands and asking me, 'Señor, will there be enough in this cloth to make me a cap?' Measuring the cloth, I said that there would. He probably suspected - as I thought, and I was right - that I wanted to steal some of the cloth, and was led to think so by his own mischief and the bad opinion people have about tailors; and he told me to see if there would be enough for two. I guessed what he was trying to do, and I said 'yes.' He, following up his original unworthy notion, went on adding cap after cap, and I 'yes' after 'yes,' until we got as far as five. He has just come for them; I gave them to him, but he won't pay me for making them; actually, he asks me to pay him, or return his cloth."

"Is all of this true, brother?" said Sancho.

"Yes," replied the man; "but will you ask him to show the five caps he has made?"

"Sure," said the tailor; and drawing his hand from under his coat he revealed five tiny caps stuck to each of his fingers, and said, "these are the caps this good man asked for; and by God and upon my conscience I haven't got a scrap of cloth left, and I'll let the work be examined by the inspectors of the trade."

All present who witnessed laughed at the number of caps and the uniqueness of the case; Sancho gave himself a moment to think, and then said, "It seems to me that in this case it is not necessary to deliver long-winded arguments, but only to give the judgment of an honest man; and so my decision is that the tailor loses the payment and the labourer loses the cloth, and that the caps go to the prisoners in the jail, and let that be it."

If the previous decision about the cattle dealer's wallet excited the admiration of the bystanders, this provoked their laughter; however, the governor's orders were executed after all. All of this, having been writen down by his chronicler, was immediately sent to the duke, who was looking forward to it with great eagerness; and here let us leave good Sancho; because his master, deeply troubled in his mind by Altisidora's music, has pressing issues for us to attend to now.

CHAPTER 46

THE TERRIBLE BELL AND CATS THAT FRIGHTENED DON QUIXOTE IN THE COURSE OF ALTISIDORA'S COURTING

We left Don Quixote deep in thought due to the music of the infatuated maid Altisidora. He went to bed with these thoughts, and just like bedbugs they would not let him sleep or get a moment's rest, and the broken stitches of his socks assisted them. But as time is slippery and no obstacle can stop its course, he came gliding through the hours, and morning very soon arrived. Seeing which Don Quixote left the soft bed, with no appearance of sloth, dressed himself in his suit and put on his travelling boots to hide the disaster of his socks. He threw on his scarlet coat trimmed with green velvet and a silver edging, put across his shoulder the belt which carried his good sharp sword, picked up a large rosary that he always carried with him, and with great seriousness and precision of style proceeded to the main room where the duke and duchess were already dressed and waiting for him. But as he passed through the hallway, Altisidora and the other lady, her friend, were waiting for him, and the instant Altisidora saw him she pretended to faint, while her friend caught her in her arms, and began quickly loosening the lace of her dress.

Don Quixote observed this, and approaching them said, "I know very well what this faint arises from."

"I do not know why," replied the friend, "because Altisidora is the healthiest lady in this house, and I have never heard her complain the whole time I have known her. A plague should pursue all the Knights in the world, if they are all ungrateful! Go away, Señor Don Quixote; because this poor child will not come to herself again as long as you are here."

To which Don Quixote replied, "Do me the favour, señora, have a guitar placed in my room tonight; and I will comfort this poor lady to the best of my ability; because in the early stages of love a prompt disappointment is the best remedy;" and with this he left, not to be observed by any who might see him there.

He had barely walked away when Altisidora, recovering from her faint, said to her companion, "The guitar must be left, because no doubt Don Quixote intends to play us some music; and coming from him it will surely be worth it."

They went to inform the duchess of what was going on, and about the guitar Don Quixote had asked for, and she, delighted beyond measure, plotted with the duke and her two ladies to play a trick on him that would be amusing but harmless; and in joy they waited for the night, which came as quickly as the day had come; and as for the day, the duke and duchess spent it in charming conversation with Don Quixote.

When eleven o'clock came, Don Quixote found a guitar in his room; he tried it, opened the window, and noticed that some people were walking in the garden; and having passed his fingers over the frets of the guitar and tuned it as well as he could, he spat and cleared his chest, and then with a voice a little rough but full, he sang the following, which he had composed himself that day:

Mighty Love the hearts of ladies,
Does unsettle and perplex,
And the instrument it uses,
Most of all is idleness.

Sewing, stitching, any labour,
Having always work to do,
For the poison Love instils,
Is the antidote for you.

And to proper-minded ladies,
Who desire a respectable name,
Caution is respect's potion,
Modesty their highest fame.

Men of prudence and discretion,
All men and courteous Knights,
Who the lustful ladies seek,
But the modest take one wife.

There are passions, passing, brief,
Loves in Inns for the day,
Sunrise loves, which sunset ended,
When the guest has gone his way.

Love that comes so swift,
Here today, gone tomorrow,
Plants no trace of it,
And leaves no image on the soul.

Painting that is laid on painting,
Makes no display or show;
Where one beauty's in possession,
There no other can take hold.

Dulcinea del Toboso,
On my heart engraved;
Never from this place, never,
Can her image be erased.

The quality of all in lovers,

Most esteemed is constancy;
It is by this that love works wonders,
It allows the boat to sail, peacefully on the sea.

Don Quixote had got so far with his song, to which the duke, the duchess, Altisidora, and nearly the whole household of the castle were listening to, when all of a sudden from a room which was exactly above his window they let down a rope with more than a hundred bells attached to it, and immediately after that dropped a large sack full of cats, which also had bells of smaller size tied to their tails. The sound of the bells and those of the cats was so loud, that although the duke and duchess were the contrivers of the joke even they were shocked by it, while Don Quixote stood paralysed with fear; and as luck would have it, two or three of the cats made their way in through the window of his room, and flying from one side to the other, made it seem as if there was a legion of devils in it. They extinguished the candles that were burning in the room, and jumped around seeking some way of escape; the cord with the large bells never ceased rising; and most of the people in the castle, not knowing what was happening, were in complete astonishment. Don Quixote jumped to his feet, and drawing his sword, began waving it at the window, shouting out:

"Go away, wicked enchanters! Go away witchcraft-working rabble! I am Don Quixote of La Mancha, against whom your evil manoeuvres will not work and have no power." And turning to the cats that were running around the room, he made several slices at them. They ran to the window and escaped through it, except one that, finding itself cornered, flew at his face and held on to his nose with no intention of letting go, the pain of this induced him to shout his loudest. The duke and duchess hearing this, and guessing what it was, ran with all haste to his room, and as the poor gentleman was striving with all his might to detach the cat from his face, they opened the door with a master-key and went in to witness the unequal combat. The duke ran to part the combatants, but Don Quixote cried aloud:

"Let no one take him from me; leave me, hand to hand with this demon, this wizard, this enchanter; I will teach him who, I myself, who Don Quixote of La Mancha is." The cat, however, not heeding these threats, growled and held on; but finally the duke pulled it off and threw it out the window. Don Quixote was left with a face full of holes, like a sieve, and a nose in poor condition, and angry that they did not let him finish the battle he had been winning with that evil enchanter. They requested some oil, and Altisidora bandaged all the wounded parts with her own hands; and as she did she said to him in a low voice:

"All these mishaps that have happened to you, hard-hearted Knight, due to the sin of your insensibility and stubbornness; God grant your aide Sancho might forget to whip himself, so that your dearly beloved Dulcinea may never be released from her enchantment, so you may never go to her bed, at least while I who adore you am alive."

To this Don Quixote gave no reply except to produce deep sighs, and then stretched himself on his bed, thanking the duke and duchess for their kindness, not because he was in any fear of that bell-ringing bunch of enchanters in cat form, but because he recognised their good intentions in coming to his rescue. The duke and duchess left him to recover and left him deeply saddened by the unfortunate result of the joke; as they never thought the adventure would have been so bad for Don Quixote, because it cost him five days of confinement in his room, during which he had another adventure, better than the most recent, which his chronicler will not relay yet in order that he may turn his attention to Sancho Panza, who was proceeding with great diligence and humour with his government.

CHAPTER 47

CONTINUING THE ACCOUNT OF HOW SANCHO PANZA CONDUCTED HIMSELF IN HIS GOVERNMENT

The history says that from the court they carried Sancho to a sumptuous palace, where in a spacious room there was a table laid out with royal magnificence. The trumpets sounded as Sancho entered the room, and four servants came forward to present him with water for his hands, which Sancho received with great dignity. The music halted, and Sancho sat himself at the head of the table. Someone, who it appeared afterwards was a physician, stood by his side with a wand in his hand. They then lifted up a fine white cloth covering fruit and a great variety of dishes of different sorts; one who looked like a student said grace, and a servant put a bib on Sancho, while another who played the part of head carver placed a dish of fruit in front of him. But he hardly had tasted it when the man with the wand touched the plate with it, and they took it away from him with the greatest speed. The carver, however, brought him another dish, and Sancho proceeded to try it; but before he could touch it, not even to say taste it, already the wand had touched it and a servant had carried it away with the same speed as the fruit. Seeing this Sancho was puzzled, and looking from one to another asked if this dinner was to be eaten or was some kind of trick.

The man with the wand replied, "It is not to be eaten, señor governor, perhaps in other islands, but I, señor, am a physician, and I am paid a salary in this island to serve its governors, and I have a great regard for their health, studying day and night and making myself acquainted with the governor's composition, in order to be able to cure him when he falls sick. The main thing I have to do is to attend his dinners and allow him to eat what appears to me to be fit for him, and keep from him what I think will do him harm and be detrimental to his stomach; and therefore I ordered that plate of fruit to be removed as being too moist, and that other dish I ordered to be removed as being too hot and containing many spices that stimulate thirst; because he who drinks too much kills and consumes the radical moisture of which life consists."

"Well then," said Sancho, "that dish of roasted hens over there seems so savoury it will not do me any harm."

To this the physician replied, "those my lord, the governor will not eat as long as I live."

"Why?" said Sancho.

"Because," replied the doctor, "our master Hippocrates, the beacon of medicine, says in one of his precepts to be full is bad, and to fill up with hens is the worst of all."

"In that case," said Sancho, "let señor doctor see among the dishes that are on the table what will be best and what will cause the least harm, and let me eat it, without tapping it with his stick; for the life of the governor, let God allow me to enjoy it, because I'm dying of hunger; and despite the doctor and all he may say, to deny me food is the way to take my life instead of prolonging it."

"You are right, señor governor," said the physician; "and therefore you, I consider, should not eat those stewed rabbits there, because it is a furry kind of food; if that beef was not roasted and served with pickles, you could have it; but it is out of the question."

"That big dish that is cooking over there," said Sancho, "seems to me to be a stew, and out of the diversity of things in stews, I can't fail to find something tasty and good for me."

"Abstain from that," said the doctor; "there is nothing in the world less nourishing than stew; vicars, heads of colleges, or peasants' weddings have stews, but let us have none of them on the tables of governors, where everything that is present should be delicate and refined; and the reason is, that everywhere and by everybody, simple medicines are more esteemed than compound ones, because we cannot go wrong with those that are simple, while with the compounds we can, by merely altering the quantity of the things in them. But my opinion as to what the governor should eat now in order to preserve and fortify his health is a hundred or so waffle cakes and a few thin slices of pome fruits, which will settle his stomach and help his digestion."

On hearing this Sancho threw himself back in his chair and observed the doctor firmly, and in a sincere tone asked him what his name was and where he had studied.

He replied, "My name, señor governor, is Doctor Pedro Recio de Aguero, I am a native of a place called Tirteafuera which lies between Caracuel and Almodovar del Campo, on the right-hand side, and I have the degree of doctor from the university of Osuna."

To which Sancho, glowing all over with rage, returned, "Then let Doctor Pedro Recio de Malaguero, native of Tirteafuera, a place that's on the right-hand side, graduate of Osuna, get out of my presence immediately; or I swear I'll take a bat, and by way of beatings I will make a beginning with him, I'll not leave a doctor in the whole island; at least of those I know to be ignorant; but for wise, sensible physicians, I will give them reverence and honour as divine people. Once more I say: Pedro Recio get out of here or I'll take this chair I am sitting on and break it on your head. And if they call me to account for it, I'll clear myself by saying I served God in killing a bad doctor. And now give me something to eat, or else take your government; because a trade that does not feed its master is not worth two beans." The doctor was distressed when he saw the governor in such fury, and he would have left but that same instant a horn sounded in the street; and the carver putting his head out of the window turned round and said:

"It's a courier from my lord the duke, no doubt with some news of importance."

The courier came in sweating and flustered, and taking a paper from his pocket, placed it in the governor's hands. Sancho handed it to the chief and asked him to read the message, which went as follows:

To Don Sancho Panza, Governor of the Island of Barataria, for his own hands or those of his secretary. When Sancho heard this said, "Which of you is my secretary?"

"I am, señor," said one of those present, "because I can read and write, and am a Biscayan."

"With that addition," Sancho said, "you could be secretary to the emperor himself; open this paper and see what it says." The new secretary obeyed, and having read the contents said the matter was one to be discussed in private. Sancho ordered the room to be cleared, with only the chief and the carver remaining; so the doctor and the others left, and then the secretary read the letter, which was as follows:

It has come to my knowledge, Señor Don Sancho Panza, that certain enemies of mine and of the island are about to make a furious attack on it soon, but I do not know when. It is a duty for you to be alert and keep watch, so they will not surprise you. I also know through trustworthy spies that four people have entered the town in disguise in order to take your life, because they fear your great capability; keep your eyes open and observe carefully those that approach you, do not eat anything that is offered to you. I will send assistance if you find yourself in difficulty, but in all things you will act as may be expected from your judgment. From here, the Sixteenth of August, at four in the morning.

Your friend,

THE DUKE

Sancho was astonished, and those who stood by appeared to be as well, and turning to the chief he said to him, "What we have to do first, and it must be done at once, is to put Doctor Recio in the prison; because if anyone wants to kill me it is him, with a slow death, the worst of all, from hunger."

"Likewise," said the carver, "it is my opinion you should not eat anything that is on this table, because all of it was a present from some nuns; and as they say, 'behind the cross there's the devil.'"

"I don't deny it," said Sancho; "so for the present give me a piece of bread and four pounds or so of grapes; no poison can come in them; because the fact is I can't continue without eating; and if we are to be prepared for these battles that are threatening us, we must be well provisioned; because it is the stomach that carries the heart and not the heart the stomach. And you, secretary, answer my lord the duke and tell him that all his commands will be obeyed, exactly as he directs; and say from me to my lady the duchess that I kiss her hands, and that I beg her not to forget to send my letter and bundle to my wife Teresa Panza; and I will consider it as a great favour and will not fail to serve her with all that is in my power; and you may enclose a kiss for the hand to my master Don Quixote so he may see I am grateful man; and as a good secretary and a good Biscayan you may add whatever you like and whatever is best; and now take this cloth away and give me something to eat, and I'll be ready to meet all the spies, assassins and enchanters that may come against me or my island."

At this moment a servant entered saying, "Here is a farmer on business, who wants to speak to you my lord, about a matter of great importance, he says."

"It's very odd," said Sancho, "the way of these men on business; is it possible they can be such fools not to see that an hour like this is no hour for coming on business? We who govern and we who are judges - are we not men of flesh and blood, and are we not to be allowed the time required for taking rest, it seems they want us to be made of marble. On my conscience, if the government remains in my hands (which I have a belief it won't), I'll bring more than one man on business to court. However, tell this good man to come in; but take care first of all that he is not some spy or one of my assassins."

"No, my lord," said the servant, "he looks like a simple man, and either I know very little or he is as good as bread. "

"There is nothing to be afraid of," said the chief, "we are all here."

"Would it be possible, carver," said Sancho, "now that Doctor Pedro Recio is not here, to let me eat something solid and substantial, even if it were a piece of bread and an onion?"

"Tonight," said the carver, "the shortcomings of the dinner will be made up for, and you will be fully content."

"God grant it," said Sancho.

The farmer came in, a privileged man that one could see a thousand miles away was honest with a good soul. The first thing he said was, "who is the lord governor here?"

"Who else could it be," said the secretary, "but he who is sat in the chair?"

"Then I humble myself before him," said the farmer; and going on his knees he asked for his hand to kiss it. Sancho refused, and asked him to stand up and say what he wanted. The farmer obeyed, and then said, "I am a farmer, señor, a native of Miguelturra, a village two miles from the city of Real."

"Another from Tirteafuera!" said Sancho; "continue, brother; I know Miguelturra very well, because it's not very far from my own town."

"The case is this, señor," continued the farmer, "through God's mercy I am married with the permission and licence of the holy Roman Catholic Church; I have two sons, students, and the younger is studying to become a graduate, and the elder to be vicar; I am a widower, as my wife died, or more properly speaking, a bad doctor killed her, giving her a purge when she was pregnant; and if it had pleased God that the child had been born, and was a boy, I would have made him study to be a doctor, so he would not envy his brothers the graduate and the vicar."

"And if your wife had not died, or had not been killed, you would not now be a widower," said Sancho.

"No, señor, certainly not," said the farmer.

"We've got that much settled," said Sancho; "continue, brother, because it's more bed-time than business-time."

"Well then," said the farmer, "this son of mine who is going to be a graduate, fell in love with a lady called Clara Perlerina from our town, daughter of Andres Perlerino, a very rich farmer; and this name of Perlerines does not come to them by ancestry or descent, but because all the family are paralytics, and for a better name they call them Perlerines; although to tell the truth the lady is as fair as an Oriental pearl, and like a flower of the field, if you look at her on the right side; and not so much on the left, because on that side she is missing an eye that she lost through small-pox; and although her face is deeply pitted, those who love her say those are not pits, but graves where the hearts of her lovers are buried. Her face carries her nose turned upward, as they say, so that one would think it was running away from her mouth; and with all this she looks extremely good, because she has a wide mouth; and except for missing ten or so teeth she could compare and compete with the most attractive. As for her lips I say nothing, because they are so fine and thin that, if lips could be taken, one would make good skin from them; but being of a different colour from ordinary lips they are wonderful, because they are mottled, blue, green, and purple - let my lord the governor pardon me for painting so intricately the charms of the lady who some time or other will be my daughter; because I love her, and I don't find her unsuitable."

"Paint what you like," said Sancho; "I enjoy your painting, and if I had eaten already there could be no dessert more to my taste than your portrait."

"That I still have to complete," said the farmer; "but a time will come when we may be able to if we are not now; and I can tell you, señor, if I could paint her gracefulness and her tall figure, it would astonish you; but that is impossible because she is bent with her knees touching her chest; but despite that it is easy to see that if she could stand up she'd knock her head against the ceiling; and she would have given her hand to my graduate, except she can't stretch it out, because it is restricted; but still one can see its elegance and fine long nails."

"That will do, brother," said Sancho; "consider you have painted her from head to toe; what is it you want? Come to the point without all this beating about the bush."

"I want you, señor," said the farmer, "to do me the favour of giving me a letter of recommendation to the girl's father, begging him to be so good as to let this marriage take place, as we are not poorly-matched either in the gifts of fortune or of nature; because to tell the truth, señor governor, my son is disturbed by the devil, and there is not a day that passes that the evil spirits do not torment him three or four times; and from having once fallen into the fire, he has his face screwed up like a piece of paper, and his eyes watery and always running; but he has the character of an angel, and if it was not for overstressing and beating himself up all the time he'd be a saint."

"Is there anything else you want, good man?" said Sancho.

"There's another thing I'd like," said the farmer, "but I'm afraid to mention it; however; despite that, I can't let it rot inside me forever. I mean, señor, that I'd like you to give me three hundred or six hundred coins as a to help my son, to help him set up his house; because they must live by themselves, without being subject to the interference of their fathers-in-law."

"Just see if there's anything else you'd like," said Sancho, "and don't hold back from mentioning it out of modesty."

"No, indeed there is no more," said the farmer.

The moment he said this the governor got to his feet, and taking the chair he had been sitting on exclaimed, "By all that's good, you fool, rude peasant, if you don't get out of here immediately and hide yourself from my sight, I'll break your head open with this chair. Mischievous devil's painter, at this hour you come to ask me for six hundred coins! How would I have them? And if I did, why should I give them to you, you stinking clown? Fool. What do I have to do with the whole family of the Perlerines? Get out I say, or on the life of my lord the duke I'll do as I said. You're not from Miguelturra, but some joker sent from hell to tempt me. Why, villain, I have not yet had the government half a day, and you want me to have six hundred coins already!"

The carver made signs to the farmer to leave the room, which he did with his head down, and to all in the appearance of terror as the governor may put his threats into effect, because the rogue knew very well how to play his part.

But let us leave Sancho in his fury; and let us return to Don Quixote, who we left with his face bandaged and doctored after the cat wounds, of which he was not cured for eight days; and the adventure that happened on one of those days Cide Hamete promises to relay soon, with the precision and truth he relays everything connected with this great history, however intricate it may be.

CHAPTER 48

WHAT HAPPENED TO DON QUIXOTE WITH DONA RODRIGUEZ, THE DUCHESS'S LADY, TOGETHER WITH OTHER OCCURRENCES WORTHY OF RECORD AND ETERNAL REMEMBRANCE

Don Quixote was very unhappy, with his face bandaged and marked, not by the hand of God, but by the claws of a cat, an unusual way for a Knight to be hurt.

Many days passed without him appearing in public, and one night as he was awake thinking of his misfortunes and about Altisidora's pursuit of him, he noticed that someone was opening the door to his room with a key, and he immediately believed that the infatuated lady was coming in to make an assault on his chastity and put him in danger of failing the faithfulness he owed to his lady Dulcinea del Toboso.

"No," he said, firmly convinced of the truth of his idea (and he said it loud enough to be heard), "the greatest beauty on earth cannot make me renounce my love for her who is stamped and engraved in the core of my heart and the secret depths of my mind; you, lady of mine, whether transformed into a clumsy country girl, or into a golden woman weaving a web of silk, let Merlin or Montesinos hold you captive wherever they like; because wherever you are, you are mine, and wherever I am, I must be yours."

The very moment he had said these words, the door opened. He stood up on the bed wrapped from head to toe in a yellow satin cover, with a cap on his head, and his face bandaged up, which made him look like the most extraordinary scarecrow that could be imagined. He kept his eyes fixed on the door, and just as he was expecting to see the love-sick Altisidora make her appearance, he saw coming in, a respectable looking lady, in a long white gown that covered and enveloped her from head to toe. Between the fingers of her left hand she held a candle, while with her right she shaded it to keep the light from her eyes, which were covered by large spectacles, and she walked forward with noiseless steps, treading very softly.

Don Quixote kept an eye on her from his bed, and observing her appearance and noting her silence, he concluded that it must be some witch or sorceress that was coming in disguise to bring some trouble, and so he began making a cross across his chest quickly. The lady continued advancing, and on reaching the middle of the room, looked up and saw the energy with which Don Quixote was crossing himself; and if he was scared by seeing such a figure as hers, she was terrified at the sight of his; because the moment she saw his tall yellow form with the cover and the bandages that disfigured him, she gave a loud scream, and exclaiming, "Jesus! What is this I see?" she dropped the candle in her fright, and then finding herself in the dark, turned to run away, but tripping over her long gon in her panic, she came down with an all mighty fall.

Don Quixote in his fear began saying, "I ask you, ghost, or whatever you are, tell me what you are and what you intend to do with me. If you are a tormented soul, say so, and I will do what I can for you with all my power; because I am a Catholic Christian and love to do good for the world, and to this end I have joined the order of Knighthood to which I belong, the jurisdiction of which extends to doing good, even to souls in torment."

The unfortunate lady hearing herself addressed in this way, by her own fear guessed it was Don Quixote and in a quiet voice answered, "Señor Don Quixote - if indeed you are Don Quixote - I am no ghost or tormented soul, as you seem to think, but Dona Rodriguez, lady of the duchess, and I come to you with one of those injustices for you to rectify."

"Tell me, Señora Dona Rodriguez," said Don Quixote, "do you by chance come to conduct any go-between business? Because I must tell you I am not available for that, thanks to the peerless beauty of my lady Dulcinea del Toboso. In short, Señora Dona Rodriguez, if you will put aside all love messages, you may light your candle and we will discuss all the commands you have for me and whatever you wish, except, as I said, any seductive communication."

"I carry nobody's messages, señor," said the lady; "you know me very little. Actually, I'm far enough advanced in years not to take to any such childish acts. Praise God I still have a soul in my body, and all my teeth in my mouth, except one or two that the cold weather, so common in this Aragon country, have robbed me of. But wait a little, while I go and light my candle, and I will return immediately and tell you my sorrows as you are one who aims to relieve those;" and without staying for an answer she left the room and left Don Quixote tranquilly meditating while he waited for her. A thousand thoughts suggested themselves to him on the subject of this new adventure, and it struck him as being unsafe to expose himself to the danger of breaking his faith to his lady; and said he to himself, "Who knows, the devil being cunning, may be trying now to catch me with this lady, having failed with empresses, Queens, duchesses and countesses? I have heard it said many times and by many men of sense that he will always offer you a flat-nosed lady rather than a roman-nosed one; and this privacy, this opportunity, this silence, may awaken my sleeping desires, and lead me in these my older years to fall where I have never fell before? In cases of this sort it is better to run than to await the battle. But I must be out of my senses to think and say such nonsense; because it is impossible that a long, white-hooded lady could stir up or excite any disgraceful actions. Is there a lady in the world that escapes being bad-tempered, wrinkled, and prudish? Go away, you ladies, un-delightful to all mankind"

He jumped off the bed, intending to close the door and not allow Señora Rodriguez to re-enter; but as he went to shut it Señora Rodriguez returned with another wax candle, and having a closer view of Don Quixote, with the yellow cover round him, and his bandages and night-cap, she was alarmed again, and taking a couple of steps back, exclaimed, "Am I safe, sir Knight? because I don't see it as a sign of good virtue that you got up out of bed."

"I ask the same, señora," said Don Quixote; "Am I safe from being attacked and forced?"

"Who do you demand that security from, sir Knight?" said the lady.

"I ask it from you," said Don Quixote; "because I am not marble, and you are not brass, and it is not ten o'clock in the morning, but midnight, or a little past it I believe, and we are in a secluded room like a cave. Give me your hand, señora; I require no better protection than my own continence, and my own sense of modesty;" and saying this, he kissed her right hand and took it in his own, she yielding it to him with equal ceremoniousness.

Don Quixote finally got into bed, and Dona Rodriguez took her seat on a chair at a little distance from there, without taking off her spectacles or putting aside the candle. Don Quixote wrapped the covers round him and covered himself completely, leaving nothing but his face visible, and as soon as they had both regained their composure he broke the silence, saying, "Now, Señora Dona Rodriguez, you may unload yourself and relieve everything you have in your sorrowful heart; and you will be heard with attentive ears, and aided by compassionate action."

"I believe it," replied the lady; "from your gentle presence only a Christian answer could be expected. The fact is, then, Señor Don Quixote, that though you see me sat in this chair, here in the middle of the Kingdom of Aragon, and in the attire of a despised outcast, I am from the Asturias of Oviedo, and from a family with which many of the best of the province are connected by blood; but my poor fate and the carelessness of my parents, who, I do not know how, were unexpectedly reduced to poverty, brought me to the court of Madrid, where as a provision and to avoid greater misfortune, my parents placed me as a seamstress in service to a lady of quality, and I want you to know that in regards to sewing I have never been surpassed by anyone my whole life. My parents left me in service and returned to their own country, and a few years later went, no doubt, to heaven, because they were good Catholic Christians. I was left an orphan with nothing but the low wage and trivial presents that are given to servants of my sort in palaces; but around this time, without any encouragement on my part, one of the men of the household fell in love with me, a man somewhat advanced in years, full-bearded and friendly, and above all as good a gentleman as the King himself. We did not carry on our love with much secrecy so it came to the knowledge of my lady, and she, had us married with the full sanction of the holy Roman Catholic Church, from this marriage our daughter was born which put an end to my good fortune, if I had any; not that she died at birth, because she passed through it safely and in due season, but because shortly afterwards my husband died of a certain shock he received, and if I had time to tell you about it I know you would be surprised;" and here she began to cry bitterly and said, "Pardon me, Señor Don Quixote, if I am unable to control myself, because every time I think about my unfortunate husband my eyes fill up with tears. God bless me, with such dignity he used to carry my lady behind him on a such a strong donkey! because in those days they did not use coaches or chairs, as they do now, ladies always rode behind their aides. This I cannot help telling you, so you may observe the good breeding of my worthy husband. As he was turning into the road called Santiago in Madrid, which is rather narrow, one of the magistrates of the Court, with two ministers in front of him, was coming out of it, and as soon as my good husband saw him he turned his donkey and went toward him as if he would accompany him. My lady, who was riding behind him, said to him in a quiet voice, 'What are you doing, informant, don't you see that I am here?'

Still my husband, persisted in trying to accompany the magistrate, and seeing this my lady, filled with rage and anger, pulled out a big pin, or, rather I think, a thick long needle, out of her needle-case and pushed it into his back with such force that my husband gave a loud yell, twisted and fell to the ground with his lady. Her two servants ran to pick him up, and the magistrate and the ministers did the same; those by the gate were all in commotion - I mean the sloths congregated there; my mistress came back on foot, and my husband was rushed to a doctor protesting that he was pierced right through the guts. The courtesy of my husband was spoken about abroad to such an extent, that the boys in the street gave him no peace; and because of this, my lady dismissed him; and this humiliation I am convinced beyond a doubt brought on his death. I was left a helpless widow, with a daughter growing up in beauty like the sea; finally, however, as I had the character to be an excellent seamstress, my lady the duchess, then married to my lord the duke, offered to take me with her to this Kingdom of Aragon, along with my daughter, and here as time went by my daughter grew up and she was filled all the graces of the world; she sings and dances, quick in thought, reads and writes like a schoolmaster, and does mathematics like a miser; I say nothing about her organisation, because the running water is not purer, and her age now is, if my memory serves me correctly, sixteen years five months and three days, one more or less. To come to the point, the son of a very rich farmer, living in a village of my lord the duke's not very far from here, fell in love with this girl of mine; and in short, I do not know how, they came together, and with the promise of marrying her he made a fool of my daughter, and will not keep his word. And although my lord the duke is aware of it (because I have complained to him, not once but many times, and asked him to order the boy to marry my daughter), he turns a deaf ear and will barely listen to me; the reason being that as the deceiver's father is so rich, and lends him money, and offers security for his debts, he does not like to offend or annoy him in any way. Now, señor, I want you to take it upon yourself to rectify this wrong either by your appeal or with weapons; because the whole world says you came into it to recompense injustices and right wrongs and help the unfortunate. Please keep in mind the unprotected condition of my daughter, her youth, and all the perfections I have said she possesses; and before God and on my conscience, out of all the ladies my lady has, there is not one that compares to the sole of my daughter's shoe, and the one they call Altisidora, who they say is the best of them all, when in comparison with my daughter, does not come within two miles of her. I would like you to know, señor, all that glitters is not gold, and that same little Altisidora has more forwardness than good looks, and more audacity than modesty; besides not being very sound, because she has such a disagreeable manner about her, that one cannot bear to be near her for a moment; and even my lady the duchess - but I'll hold my tongue on that, because they say that walls have ears."

"For heaven's sake, Dona Rodriguez, what bothers my lady the duchess?" asked Don Quixote.

"Asked in that way," replied the lady, "I cannot help but answering your question and telling you the whole truth. Señor Don Quixote, have you observed the charm of my lady the duchess, that smooth complexion of hers like a polished sword, those two cheeks of milk and crimson, that happy lively step with which she treads or rather seems to bounce on the earth, so that one would think she was radiating health wherever she passed? Well then, let me tell you she may thank, first of all God, for this, and another reason."

"Blessed Virgin!" exclaimed Don Quixote.

Dona Rodriquez was about to continue when the door flew open with a loud bang, the noise it gave made Dona Rodriguez drop the candle from her hand, and the room was left in darkness. Suddenly the poor lady felt two hands grab her by the throat, so tightly that she could not speak, while someone else, without saying a word, with what seemed to be a slipper began to beat her so firmly that anyone would have felt sorry for her; but although Don Quixote knew something was happening he never moved from his bed, but lay quiet and silent, actually apprehensive that his turn for a beating might be coming. And the apprehension was not for no reason; because leaving the lady (who did not dare to make a noise), the silent executioners attacked Don Quixote, and taking the sheet off him, they pinched him so fast and so hard that he was driven to defend himself with his fists, and all of this happened in marvellous silence. The battle lasted nearly half an hour, and then the invisible attackers ran away; Dona Rodriguez gathered her things, and cursing her fate left without saying a word to Don Quixote, and he, sorely pinched, confused, and miserable, remained alone, and there we will leave him, wondering who could have been the perverse enchanter who had reduced him to such a state; but that will be told in due course, because now Sancho claims our attention, and the methodical arrangement of the story demands it.

CHAPTER 49

WHAT HAPPENED TO SANCHO WHEN GOVERNING HIS ISLAND

We left the great governor angered and irritated by that portrait-painting rogue of a farmer, who then said "Now I see plainly enough that judges and governors must be made of brass not to feel the requests of the applicants that at all times and all seasons insist on being heard, and having their business posted, and their own affairs and no others attended to; and if the poor judge does not hear them and settle the matter - either because he cannot or because it is not the time for hearing them - they abuse him, and run him down, and try to open holes in his honour. You silly, stupid applicants, don't be in a hurry; wait for the proper time and season for this business; don't come at dinner-hour, or at bed-time; because judges are only flesh and blood, and must give Nature what it naturally demands from them; all except myself, because in my case I give it nothing to eat, thanks to Señor Doctor Pedro Recio here, who would have me die of hunger, and declares that death is life; so hopefully the same sort of life God may give him and all his kind - I mean the bad doctors of the earth; because the good ones deserve awards and praise."

All those who knew Sancho Panza were astonished to hear him speak so elegantly, and did not know what to attribute it to unless it were that the office and serious responsibility either sharpen or overwhelm a man's mind. At last Doctor Pedro Recio promised to let him have dinner that night although it might be in breach of all the sayings of Hippocrates. With this the governor was satisfied and looked forward to the approach of dinner-time with great anxiety; and although time, to his mind, stood still and made no progress, nevertheless the hour he longed for finally came, and they gave him a beef salad with onions and some boiled cows' feet. This he ate with greater relish than if they had given him birds from Milan, pheasants from Rome, veal from Sorrento, partridges from Moron, or geese from Lavajos, and turning to the doctor at dinner he said to him, "Look here, señor doctor, for the future don't trouble yourself about giving me delicate things or optimal dishes to eat, because it will only take my stomach off its hinges; it is accustomed to goat, cow, bacon, beef, turnips and onions; and if by any chance it is given these palace dishes, it receives them squeamishly, and sometimes with disgust. What the head-carver had best do is to serve me with what they call pork bean stew (and the rottener they are the better they smell); and he can put whatever he likes in the stew, as long as it is good to eat, and I'll be thankful to him, and will repay him some day. Nobody play jokes on me; let us live and eat in peace, because when God sends the dawn, he sends it for all. I mean to govern an island without giving up a right or taking a bribe; let everyone keep his eyes open, and look out for the arrows; because I can see them' and if they aim at me they'll see something that will astonish them. Make yourself honey and the flies will come."

"Truth, señor governor," said the carver, "you are right in everything you have said; and I promise you in the name of all the inhabitants of this island that they will serve you with enthusiasm, affection, and good-will, because the kind of government you have given a sample of to begin with, leaves them no ground for doing or thinking anything to your disadvantage."

"That I believe," said Sancho; "and they would be great fools if they did or thought otherwise; once more I say, someone feed my Dapple because that is most appropriate right now; and when the hour comes let us begin the work, because it is my intention to purge this island of all uncleanness and of all lazy good-for-nothing drifters; because you should know that lazy sloths are the same thing in a State as the bees in a hive, that eat up the honey the industrious bees make. I mean to protect the gardener, to preserve for the gentleman his privileges, to reward the virtuous, and above all to respect religion, and honour its ministers. What do you say to that, my friends? Is there anything in what I say, or am I talking non-sense?"

"There is so much in what you say, señor governor," said the head, "that I am filled with wonder when I see a man like you, entirely without education (because I believe you have none at all), say such things, and so full of sound truisms and sage remarks, very different from what was expected of your intelligence. Every day we see something new in this world; jokes become reality, and the jokers find the tables turned on them."

Night came, and with the permission of Doctor Pedro Recio, the governor had a snack. Then they got ready to begin the work, and he left with the head, the secretary, the head-carver, the chronicler charged with recording his deeds, and enough ministers and notaries to form a fair-sized army. Sancho marched with his staff, as fine a sight as one could wish to see, but only a few streets of the town had been navigated when they heard a noise which sounded like the clashing of swords. They rushed to the spot, and found two combatants, who seeing the authorities approaching stood still, and one of them exclaimed, "Help, in the name of God and the King! Are men allowed to rob in the middle of this town, and rush out to attack people in the streets?"

"Be calm, my good man," said Sancho, "and tell me what the cause of this disagreement is; because I am the governor."

The other combatant said, "Señor governor, I will tell you in a very few words. You must know that this gentleman has just won more than a thousand coins in the gambling house opposite, and God knows how. I was there, and I favoured him slightly very much against my conscience. He made off with his winnings, and when I made sure he was going to give me a coin or so at least by way of a gift, as it is usual and customary to give men of my sort who stand by to see fair or foul play, and uncover scams, and prevent arguments, he pocketed his money and left the house. Annoyed at this I followed him, and speaking to him fairly and civilly asked him to give me only eight coins, because he knows I am an honest man and that I have no property, because my parents never brought me up to gain any or leave me anything; but the rogue, who is a great thief, would not give me more than four coins; so you may see how little shame and conscience he has. I swear to God if you had not come I would have made him hand over his entire winnings, and he'd have learned the hard way."

"What do you say about this?" asked Sancho. The other replied that all his antagonist said was true, and that he did not choose to give him more than four coins because he gave him money quite often; and that those who expected gifts should be civil and take what is given to them with a cheerful attitude, and not make any accusations against winners unless they know for certain that their winnings were unfairly won; but there is no better proof of an honest man than one who refuses to give anything; because thieves always offer gifts to those who observe them.

"That is true," said the head; "Señor Sancho consider what should be done with these men."

"What should be done," said Sancho, "is this; you, the winner, good or bad, or indifferent, give this attacker of yours a hundred coins at once, and you, who have no profession or property who hang about the island in idleness, take these hundred coins now, and sometime during the day tomorrow leave the island - sentenced to banishment for ten years, and you will complete this sentence in another life if you disobey, because I'll hang you, or at least the hangman will by my orders; not a word from either of you, or I'll make you feel my hand."

One paid the money and the other took it, and the latter left the island, while the other went home; and then the governor said, "Either I am not good for much, or I'll get rid of these gambling houses, because it strikes me they are very mischievous."

"This one at least," said one of the notaries, "you will not be able to get rid of, because a great man owns it, and what he makes every year is beyond all comparison more than what he loses. On the minor gambling houses, you may exercise your power, as it is they that do most harm and shelter the most shameless practices; because in the houses of lords and gentlemen of quality the notorious thieves do not dare to play their tricks; and as the vice of gambling has become common, it is better men play in the houses with good reputation than in some tradesman's, where they catch an unlucky man in the early hours of the morning and take all he has."

"I already know, notary, that there is a good deal to be said on that point," said Sancho.

And now an officer came holding a young man, and said, "Señor governor, this youth was coming towards us, and as soon as he saw the officers of justice he turned around and ran like a deer, proof that he must be some evil-doer; I ran after him, and had it not been that he stumbled and fell, I would never have caught him."

"What did you run for, fellow?" said Sancho.

To which the young man replied, "Señor, it was to avoid answering all the questions officers of justice ask."

"What is your trade?"

"A craftsman."

"And what do you make?"

"Lance heads."

"Don't try to fool me! Do you pride yourself on being a joker? Where were you going just now?" said Sancho.

"To get some fresh air, señor."

"And where does one take in fresh air on this island?"

"Wherever it blows."

"Good! your answers are very much to the point; you are a smart youth; but take notice that I am the air, and that I will blow you away to jail. Hold him and take him away; I'll make him sleep tonight without air."

"God," said the young man, "you will make me sleep just as soon as they make me King. "

"Why should I not make you sleep?" said Sancho. "Do I not have the power to arrest you and release you whenever I like?"

"You have all the power," said the young man, "but you won't be able to make me sleep."

"How? not able to!" said Sancho; "take him away immediately where he will see his mistake with his own eyes; and see that the jailer does not release him, because I'll give put penalty on the head of anyone who allows him to take a step outside of the prison."

"That's ridiculous," said the young man; "the fact is, all the men on earth will not make me sleep in prison."

"Tell me, you devil," said Sancho, "have you got any angel that will free you, and take the iron off that I am going to order them to put on you?"

"Now, señor governor," said the young man in an active manner, "let us be reasonable and come to the point. Granted you may order me to be taken to prison, and to have iron and chains put on me, and to shut me in a cell, and may put heavy penalties on the jailer if he lets me out; if I don't choose to sleep, and choose to remain awake all night without closing an eye, will you with all your power be able to make me sleep if I choose not to?"

"Not, truly," said the secretary, "and the fellow has made his point."

"So then," said Sancho, "it would be entirely your own choice if you would stay awake; in opposition to my will?"

"No, señor," said the youth, "certainly not."

"Well then, go, and God be with you," said Sancho; "Go home to sleep, and God give you good sleep, because I don't want to rob you of it; but for the future, let me advise you don't joke with the authorities, because you may come across someone who will turn the joke around on you."

The young man went his way, and the governor continued his journey around the town, and shortly afterwards two officers came with a man in custody, and said, "Señor governor, this person, who seems to be a man, is actually a woman." They raised two or three lanterns to her face, and distinguished the features of a woman to all with an appearance aged sixteen or a little more, with her hair gathered into a gold and green silk net, and fair as a thousand pearls. They scanned her from head to toe, and noticed that she wore red silk socks with white tights bordered with gold and pearl; her trousers were green and gold, and under an open jacket she wore another made of the finest white and gold cloth; her shoes were white; she carried no sword on her belt, but only a richly decorated dagger, and on her fingers she had several stunning rings. In short, the girl seemed beautiful to look at, and none of those who saw her knew her, the people of the town said they could not imagine who she was, and those who were in on the secret of the jokes that were being practised on Sancho were the ones who were most surprised, because this incident or discovery had not been arranged by them; and they watched anxiously to see how the matter would end.

Sancho was fascinated by the girl's beauty, and he asked her who she was, where she was going, and what had induced her to dress herself as a man. She with her eyes fixed on the ground answered in modest confusion, "I cannot tell you, señor, in front of so many people; however, one thing I wish to be known is, that I am no thief or sinner, but only an unhappy lady whom the power of jealousy has led to break through the respect that is due to modesty."

Hearing this the head said to Sancho, "Make the people stand back, señor governor, so this lady can say what she wants to with less embarrassment."

Sancho gave the order, and all except the head, the head-carver, and the secretary fell back. Finding herself then in the presence of no more, the lady continued to say, "I am the daughter, of Pedro Perez Mazorca, the wool-farmer of this town, who is in the habit of going to my father's house."

"That won't do, señora," said the head; "because I know Pedro Perez very well, and I know he has no child at all, son or daughter; and besides, although you say he is your father, you add that he goes very often to your father's house."

"I had already noticed that," said Sancho.

"I am confused, sirs," said the lady, "and I don't know what I am saying; but the truth is that I am the daughter of Diego de la Llana, who you all must know."

"That will do," said the head; "because I know Diego de la Llana, and know that he is a gentleman of high rank and a rich man, and that he has a son and a daughter, and that since he was left a widower nobody in this town has seen his daughter's face; because he keeps her so closely shut away that he does not even give the sun a chance to see her; but there are reports that she is extremely beautiful.

"It is true," said the lady, "and I am that daughter; whether the report lies or not as to my beauty, you, sirs, can decide, as you have seen me;" and with this she began to cry bitterly.

On seeing this the secretary leant over to the head-carver's ear, and said to him in a quiet voice, "Something serious has no doubt happened this poor lady, that makes her wander from her home in such an outfit and at such an hour, and one of her rank too."

"There can be no doubt about it," returned the carver, "and moreover her tears confirm your suspicion."

Sancho gave her the best comfort he could, and asked her to tell them without any fear what had happened to her, as they would all sincerely and by every means in their power endeavour to relieve her.

"The fact is, sirs," she said, "that my father has kept me shut away for the last ten years, as it has been this long since the earth received my mother. Prayers are said at home in a magnificent chapel, and all this time I have only seen the sun during the day, and the moon and the stars at night; but I do not know what the streets are like, or plazas, or churches, or even men, except my father and a brother I have, and because Pedro Perez the wool-farmer; came frequently to our house, I took it into my head to call him my father, to avoid naming my own. This seclusion and the restrictions on me going out, even if it were only to church, have been keeping me unhappy for a very long time; I longed to see the world, or at least the town where I was born, and it did not seem to me that this wish was inconsistent with the respect ladies of good quality should have for themselves. When I heard them talking about bull-fights taking place, and about javelin games, and plays, I asked my brother, who is a year younger than myself, to tell me what sort of things these were, and about many other things I had never seen; he explained them to me as well as he could, but the only effect was to ignite in me a stronger desire to see them. At last, to cut short the story, I begged and pleaded with my brother – I wish I had never made such a request" And again she began to cry.

"Proceed, señora," said the head, "and finish your story about what has happened to you, because your words and tears are keeping us all in suspense."

"I have little more to say, but many tears to shed," said the lady; "because desires can only be paid for in some way."

The lady's beauty had made a deep impression on the head-carver's heart, and he again raised his lantern for another look at her, and although they were not tears she was shedding, but pearls or dew, actually, he exalted them higher, and believed them to be Oriental pearls, and passionately hoped her misfortune would not be as great as her tears and cries seemed to indicate. The governor was losing patience at the length of time the girl was taking to tell her story, and told her not to keep them waiting any longer; because it was late, and there was still a large part of the town left to go through.

She, with cries and half-suppressed sighs, went on to say, "My misfortune, is simply this, that I asked my brother to dress me up as a man in his clothes, and take me some night, when our father was asleep, to see the whole town; he, overcome by my pleading, consented, and dressing me in this suit and himself in clothes of mine that fitted him as if made for him (because he does not have a hair on his chin, and might pass for a very beautiful young girl), and about an hour ago, more or less, we left the house, and guided by our youthful and foolish impulse made a circuit of the whole town, and then, as we were about to return home, we saw a large group of people coming, and my brother said to me, 'Sister, put wings on your feet, and follow me as fast as you can, in case they recognise us, because it would be bad news if they did;' and so saying he turned around and began, I cannot say to run but to fly; in less than six feet I fell from fright, and then the officer of justice came up and carried me to you, where I find myself put to shame along with all the people who are impulsive and vicious."

"So then, señora," said Sancho, "no other mishap has happened to you, and it was not jealousy that made you leave home, as you said at the beginning of your story?"

"Nothing has happened me," she said, "no it was not jealousy that brought me out, but merely a longing to see the world, which did not go beyond seeing the streets of this town."

The appearance of the officers with her brother in custody, whom one of them had overtaken as he ran away from his sister, now fully confirmed the truth of what the girl said. He had nothing on but a rich coat and a short blue cloak with fine gold lace, and his head was uncovered and adorned only with its own hair, which looked like rings of gold, as they were so bright and curly. The governor, the head, and the carver went to one side with him, and, unheard by his sister, asked him how he came to be in that dress, and he with no less shame and embarrassment told exactly the same story as his sister, to the great delight of the infatuated carver; the governor, however, said to them, "In truth, young lady and gentleman, this has been a very childish affair, and to explain your foolishness and impulsiveness there was no necessity for all this delay and all these tears and sighs; because if you had said we are so-and-so, and we escaped from our father's house in this way in order to roam about, out of mere curiosity and with no other objective, that would have been the end of the matter, and none of these little cries and tears and all the rest of it."

"That is true," said the girl, "but you see the confusion I was in was so great it did not let me behave as I should."

"No harm has been done," said Sancho; "come, we will leave you at your father's house; perhaps he will not have missed you; and another time don't be so childish or eager to see the world; because a respectable lady should behave like one with broken legs and stay at home; because she who is eager to see is also eager to be seen; I say no more."

The youth thanked the governor for his kind offer to take them home, and they directed their steps towards the house, which was not far away. On reaching it the youth threw a pebble at the window, and immediately a female servant who was waiting for them came down and opened the door, and they went in, leaving the group admiring their grace and beauty in wishing to see the world at night and without leaving the village; which, however, they put down to their youth.

The head-carver was left with a broken heart, and he made up his mind on the spot to demand for her hand in marriage from her father the following day, making sure she would not be refused to him as he was a servant of the duke's; and even Sancho had ideas and schemes of marrying the boy to his daughter Sanchica, and he decided to open the negotiation up at the proper time, persuading himself that no husband could be refused to a governor's daughter. And so the night's work came to an end, and a couple of days later so did the government, where all his plans were overthrown and swept away, as will be seen shortly.

CHAPTER 50

WHO THE ENCHANTERS WERE THAT FLOGGED THE LADY AND PINCHED DON QUIXOTE, AND ALSO WHAT HAPPENED TO THE SERVANT WHO TOOK THE LETTER TO TERESA PANZA, SANCHO'S WIFE

Cide Hamete, the painstaking investigator of the intricate points of this veracious history, says that when Dona Rodriguez left her room to go to Don Quixote's, another lady who slept with her, saw her, and as all ladies are fond of prying, listening, and gossiping followed her so silently that lady Rodriguez never noticed it; and as soon as the lady saw her enter Don Quixote's room, not to fail a lady's invariable practice of gossiping, she went that moment to report to the duchess how Dona Rodriguez was alone with Don Quixote. The duchess told the duke, and asked him to let her and Altisidora go and see what the lady wanted with Don Quixote. The duke gave permission, and the pair cautiously and quietly opened the door of the room and posted themselves so close that they could hear everything that was said inside. But when the duchess heard how Rodriguez had made public her issues she could not restrain herself, and neither could Altisidora; and so, filled with rage, they burst into the room and tormented Don Quixote and flogged the lady in the manner already described; because shame aimed toward the charm and self-esteem of women provoke their anger and make them eager for revenge. The duchess told the duke what had happened, and he was quite amused by it; and she, in pursuit of her plan and playing tricks on Don Quixote, despatched the servant who had played the part of Dulcinea in the negotiations for her disenchantment (which Sancho Panza, while governing, had completely forgotten about) to Teresa Panza his wife with her husband's letter and another from herself, and also a large number of flowers as a present.

Now the history says this servant was very sharp and quick-witted; and eager to serve his lord and lady she set off very willingly to Sancho's village. Before she entered it she observed a number of women washing clothes in a lake, and asked them if they could tell her whether a woman named Teresa Panza lived there, wife of one Sancho Panza, aide to a Knight called Don Quixote of La Mancha. At the question a young girl who was washing stood up and said, "Teresa Panza is my mother, and Sancho is my father, and that Knight is our master."

"Well then, miss," said the servant, "come and show me where your mother is, because I have a letter and a present for her, from your father."

"That I will do with all my heart, Señorita," said the girl, who seemed to be about fourteen, more or less; and leaving the clothes she was washing to one of her companions, and without putting anything on her head or feet, as she was bare-legged and had her hair hanging down, she went in front of the servant's horse, saying, "Follow me Señorita, our house is at the entrance of the town, and my mother is there, with such sorrow for not having had any news of my father for so long."

"Well," said the servant, "I am bringing her such good news that she will have good reason to thank God."

And then, running, and prancing, the girl reached the town, but before going into the house she called at the door, "Come out, mother Teresa, come out, come out; here's a lady with letters and other things from my good father." At these words her mother Teresa Panza came out in a grey coat (so short one would have thought it had been cut it short), a grey dress of the same material. She was not very old, but clearly past forty, strong, healthy, vigorous, and sun-dried; and seeing her daughter and the servant on horseback, she exclaimed, "What is this, child? What lady is this?"

"A servant of my lady, Teresa Panza," replied the servant; and matching her actions to her words she jumped off her horse, and with great humility advanced to kneel in front of lady Teresa, saying, "Let me kiss your hand, Señora Teresa, as the lawful and only wife of Señor Don Sancho Panza, rightful governor of the island of Barataria."

"Ah, Señorita, get up, do not do that," said Teresa; "I am not a lady of the court, but a poor country woman, the daughter of a farmer, and the wife of an aide, not of a governor."

"You are," said the servant, "the worthiest wife of the worthy governor; and as proof of what I say accept this letter and this present;" and at the same time she handed her a bunch of flowers with gold string, and said, "This letter is from my lord the governor, and the other as well as these flowers from my lady the duchess, who sends me to you."

Teresa stood lost in amazement, and her daughter just as much, and the girl said, "I bet our master Don Quixote's has something to do with this; he must have given our father the government or county he often promised him."

"That is the truth," said the servant; "because it is through Señor Don Quixote that Señor Sancho is now governor of the island of Barataria, as will be seen by this letter."

"Will you read it to me, noble lady?" said Teresa; "because although I can sew I can't read, not a word."

"Neither can I," said Sanchica; "but wait a bit, and I'll go and get someone who can read it, either the vicar or the graduate Samson Carrasco, and they'll come gladly to hear any news about my father."

"There is no need to summon anybody," said the servant; "because although I cannot sew, I can read, and I'll read it;" and so she read it, but as it has been already mentioned, it is not inserted here; and then she took out the other one from the duchess, which went as follows:

Friend Teresa, your husband Sancho's good qualities, of heart as well as of head, induced and compelled me to request my husband the duke to give him the government of one of his many islands. I am told he governs like a hawk, of which I am very glad, and my lord the duke, of course, is also; and I am very thankful to heaven that I have not made a mistake in choosing him for government; because I would like Señora Teresa to know that a good governor is hard to find in this world and may God make me as good as Sancho's way of governing. I send to you, my dear, flowers with gold string; I wish they were Oriental pearls; but a time will come when we will become acquainted and meet one another, but God knows the future. Mention me to your daughter Sanchica, and tell her from me to hold herself ready, because I intend to make a high match for her when she least expects it. They tell me there are big chestnuts in your village; send me a couple dozen or so, and I will value them greatly coming from your hand; and write to me to assure me of your health and well-being; and if there is anything you are in need of, all you need to do is say, and it will be prescribed. God keep you well.

From this place.
Your loving friend,
THE DUCHESS.

"Ah, what a good lady!" said Teresa when she heard the letter; "may I be buried with ladies of that sort, and not the women we have in this town, that think because they are women the wind must not touch them, and go to church with as much arrogance as if they were Queens, no less, and seem to think they are disgraced if they look at a farmer's wife! And see how this good lady, is a duchess, and she calls me 'friend,' and treats me as if I was her equal - I see her equal to the tallest church-tower in the whole of La Mancha! And as for the chestnuts, Señorita, I'll send her a bunch and such big ones that one would be in amazement. And now, Sanchica, see that the lady is comfortable; take her horse to the stable, and take some eggs from there, cut plenty of bacon, and let's give her dinner like a princess; for the good news she has brought, and as her beautiful face deserves; and meanwhile I'll run out and give the neighbours the news of our good luck, and the vicar, and Master Nicholas the barber, who are and always have been such good friends of your father's."

"That I will, mother," said Sanchica; "but you must give me half of that string; because I don't think my lady the duchess could have been so stupid as to send it all to you."

"It is all for you, my child," said Teresa; "but let me wear it round my neck for a few days; because it seems to make my heart happy."

"You will be happy too," said the servant, "when you see what is in this bag, because it is a suit of the finest cloth, that the governor only wore one-day hunting and now sends, all for Señora Sanchica."

"May he live a thousand years," said Sanchica, "and the bearer as many, actually two thousand."

With this Teresa hurried out of the house with the letters, and with the golden string around her neck, and went along tapping the letters as if they were a tambourine, and by chance coming across the vicar and Samson Carrasco she began dancing and saying, "None of us are poor now! We've got a little government! Let the finest lady try to tackle me, and I'll put her in her place!"

"What is all of this, Teresa," they said; "what madness is this, and what papers are those?"

"The madness is only this," said she, "that these are the letters from duchesses and governors, and this gold thread I have on my neck signify that I am a governess."

"God help us," said the vicar, "we don't understand you, Teresa, or know what you are talking about.

"Here, you may see it for yourselves," said Teresa, and she handed them the letters.

The vicar read them out for Samson Carrasco to hear, and Samson and he regarded one another with looks of astonishment at what they had read, and the graduate asked who had brought the letters. Teresa in reply asked them to come with her to her house and they would see the messenger, a most elegant youth, who had brought another present which was worth much more. The vicar took the gold thread from her neck and examined it again and again, and having satisfied himself with its fineness he began wondering even more, and said, "By the gown I wear I don't know what to say or think about these letters and presents; on one hand I can see and feel the fineness of the thread, and on the other I read how a duchess begs for a dozen chestnuts."

"Reconcile that if you can," said Carrasco; "and let's go and see the messenger, and we'll learn something about this mystery that has turned up."

They did so, and Teresa returned with them. They found the servant sifting a little barley for her horse, and Sanchica cutting the bacon to be made with eggs for her dinner. Her looks and her elegant attire greatly pleased them both; and after they had greeted her, and her to them, Samson begged her to give them the news, of Don Quixote as well as Sancho Panza, because, he said, although they had read the letters from Sancho and the duchess, they were still puzzled and could not make out what was meant by Sancho's government, and above all of an island, when all or most of those in the Mediterranean belonged to his Majesty the King.

To this the servant replied, "In regards to Señor Sancho Panza being a governor there is no doubt whatsoever; but whether it is an island or not, that I cannot say; but it is a town of more than a thousand inhabitants; with regard to the chestnuts I may tell you that my lady the duchess is so unpretentious and modest that, not only would she ask for chestnuts from a peasant, she has been known to ask to borrow a comb from one of her neighbours; because ladies of Aragon, although they are just as illustrious, are not so pretentious and conceited as the Castilian ladies; and they treat people with greater familiarity."

In the middle of this conversation Sanchica came in with her skirt full of eggs, and she said to the servant, "Tell me, Señorita, does my father wear trousers since he has been governor?"

"I have not noticed," said the servant; "but no doubt he wears them."

"Ah! my God!" said Sanchica, "what a sight it must be to see my father in those! Isn't it odd that ever since I was born I have had a longing to see my father in trousers?"

"As things go you will soon see that," said the servant; "he is on the way to take the road into the shade of prosperity if the government lasts him only two more months."

The vicar and the graduate could see clearly enough that the servant spoke in a humorous manner; but the fineness of the thread, and the hunting suit that Sancho sent (as Teresa had already shown it to them) removed the impression; and they could not help laughing at Sanchica's wish, and even more when Teresa said, "Señor vicar, look around to see if there's anybody here going to Madrid or Toledo, to buy me a coat, a proper fashionable one of the best quality; because I must do honour to my husband's government as well as I can; actually, if I am put into it and have to, I'll go to Court in a coach; because she who has a governor for her husband may very well have one and keep one.

"And why not, mother!" said Sanchica; "if only it were today instead of tomorrow, even if they were to say when they saw me sat in the coach with my mother, 'See that rubbish, that garlic-stuffed governor's daughter, how she goes stretched at ease in a coach as if she was the pope!' But let them walk through the mud, and let me go in my coach with my feet off the ground. Bad luck to the malicious all over the world; 'I will be sincere and the people may laugh.' Isn't that right, mother?"

"It sure is, my child," said Teresa; "and all this good luck, and even more, my good Sancho told me would come; and you will see, my daughter, he won't stop until he has made me a countess; because to make a beginning in anything brings luck; and as I have heard your good father say many times (because besides being your father he's the father of proverbs too), 'When they offer you a cow, run with the reins; when they offer you a government, take it; when they give you a county, seize it; when they say, "Here, here!" and give you something good, swallow it.' Or else! Go to sleep, and don't answer the calls of good fortune and the lucky chances that are knocking at the door of your house!"

"What do I care," added Sanchica, "whether anybody says when they see me holding my head up, 'The dog found herself in hemp trousers'?"

Hearing this the vicar said, "I believe that the family of Panzas are born with sacksful of proverbs in their heads, every one of them; I never saw one of them that does not pour them out at all times and on all occasions."

"That is true," said the servant, "because Señor Governor Sancho utters them all the time; and although many of them are not to the purpose, still they amuse me, and my lady the duchess and the duke praise them highly."

"Then you still maintain that all this about Sancho's government is true, Señorita," said the graduate, "and that there actually is a duchess who sends him presents and writes to him? Because we, although we have seen the presents and read the letters, don't believe it and suspect it to be something in the line of our fellow-townsman Don Quixote, who believes that everything is done by enchantment; and for this reason I am almost ready to say that I'd like to touch and feel you to see whether you are an ambassador of the imagination or a woman of flesh and blood."

"All I know, sirs," replied the servant, "is that I am a real ambassador, and that Señor Sancho Panza is governor as a matter of fact, and that my lord and lady the duke and duchess can give, and have given him this government, and that I have heard it said Sancho Panza carries himself very solidly; whether there be any enchantment in all this or not, it is for you to settle between you; because that's all I know, I swear, and that is on the life of my parents who are still alive, and who I love dearly."

"It may be so," said the graduate; "but I doubt it."

"Doubt if you like," said the servant; "but what I have told you is the truth, and that will always rise above falsehood like oil above water; if not let the deeds prove the words. Let one of you come with me, and he will see with his own eyes what he does not believe with his ears."

"It's for me to make that trip," said Sanchica; "take me with you, Señorita, behind you on your horse; because I'll go with all my heart to see my father."

"Governors' daughters," said the servant, "must not travel along the roads alone, but accompanied by coaches and large number of attendants."

"By God," said Sanchica, "I can go just as well mounted on a donkey as in a coach; what a weak lady you must take me for!"

"Hush, girl," said Teresa; "you don't know what you're talking about; the lady is quite right, because 'the behaviour matches the time."

"Señora Teresa says more than she is aware of," said the servant; "and now give me something to eat and let me go, because I intend to return this evening."

"Come with me," said the vicar; "because Señora Teresa has more will than means to serve such a worthy guest."

The servant refused, but had to agree at last for her own sake; and the vicar took her home with him very gladly, in order to have an opportunity of questioning her further about Don Quixote. The graduate offered to write the letters in reply for Teresa; but she did not want to let him mix himself up in her affairs, because she thought he was someone who was inclined to make jokes; and so she gave a cake and a couple of eggs to a young man who was good with the pen, and he wrote two letters for her, one for her husband and the other for the duchess, dictated out of her own head, which are not the worst inserted in this great history, as will be seen shortly.

CHAPTER 51

THE PROGRESS OF SANCHO'S GOVERNMENT, AND OTHER ENTERTAINING MATTERS

The following day after the night of the governor's round; a night which the head-carver passed without sleeping, absorbed in his thoughts of the face and beauty of the disguised lady, while the head spent what was left of it writing an account to his lord and lady of everything Sancho said and did, being as much amazed at his sayings as at his actions, because there was a mixture of wisdom and simplicity in all his words and deeds. The governor got up, and with Doctor Pedro Recio's directions they made him breakfast which was jam and four cups of cold water, which Sancho would have readily exchanged for a piece of bread and a bunch of grapes; but seeing there was no help for it, he submitted with great sorrow in his heart and discomfort in his stomach; Pedro Recio having persuaded him that a light and delicate diet invigorated the mind, and that was what was most essential for people placed in command and in responsible situations, where they have to employ not only the bodily powers but those of the mind as well.

Due to this Sancho was made to endure hunger, and hunger so strong that in his heart he cursed the government, and even those who had given it to him; however, with his hunger and his jam he undertook to deliver judgments that day, and the first thing that came to him was a question that was submitted by a stranger, in the presence of the head and the other attendants, and it was in these words: "Señor, a large river separated two regions - will you please pay attention, because the case is an important and a rather complex one? On this river there was a bridge, and at one end of it some sort of court, where four judges commonly sat to administer the law which the lord of river, bridge and the land was legislated, and which was to this effect, 'If anyone crosses this bridge from one side to the other he will declare under oath where he is going and with what objective; and if he is truthful, he will be allowed to pass, but if he is not honest, he will be sentenced to death, being hung from the beams erected there.' Although the law and its severe penalty were known, many people crossed, but in their declarations it was easy to see they were telling the truth, and the judges let them pass. It happened, however, that one man, when they came to take his declaration, swore and said "I am going to die, being hung from the beams that stand there, and nothing else". The judges held a consultation over the oath, and they said, 'If we let this man pass then his oath is false, and by the law he should die; but if we hang him, as he swore he was going to die in that manner, and therefore swore the truth, by the same law he should go free.' It is asked of you, señor governor, what are the judges to do with this man? Because they are still in doubt and perplexity; and having heard of your acute and exalted intellect, they have sent me to ask you on their behalf to give your opinion on this very intricate and puzzling case."

To this Sancho answered, "Indeed those gentlemen the judges that send you to me might have spared themselves the trouble, because I have more of a simple mind than an acute one in me; but repeat the case again, so that I may understand it better, and then perhaps I may be able to come to the conclusion."

He repeated again and again what he had said before, and then Sancho said, "It seems to me I can set the matter right in a moment, and in this way; the man swears that he is going to die being hung from the beams; but if he dies he has sworn the truth, and by the law enacted deserves to go free and pass over the bridge; but if they don't hang him, then he has passes on a false oath, and by the same law deserves to be hanged."

"It is as señor governor says," said the messenger; "and as you have a complete comprehension of the case, there is nothing left to understand or hesitate about."

"Well then I say," said Sancho, "they should let pass the part of this man that has sworn truly, and hang the part that has lied; and in this way the conditions of the law will be fully complied with."

"But then, señor governor," replied the enquirer, "the man will have to be divided into two parts; and if he is divided of course he will die; and so none of the requirements of the law will be carried out, and it is absolutely necessary to comply with it."

"Look here, my good sir," said Sancho; "either I'm a fool or else the reasons are the same for this man to die or live and pass over the bridge; because if the truth saves him the falsehood equally condemns him; and that being the case it is my opinion you should say to the gentlemen who sent you to me that as the arguments for condemning him and for absolving him are exactly balanced, they should let him pass freely, as it is always more praiseworthy to do good than to do evil; this I would give signed with my name if I knew how to write; and what I have said in this case is not out of my own head, but one of the many teachings my master Don Quixote gave me the night before I left to become governor of this island, that came into my mind, and it was this, that when there was any doubt about the justice of a case I should lean toward mercy; and it is God's will that I recalled it now, because it fits this case as if it was made for it."

"That is true," said the head; "and I maintain that Lycurgus himself, who gave laws to the Lacedemonians, could not have pronounced a better decision than the great Panza has given; let the morning's audience close with this, and I will see that the governor has a dinner entirely to his liking."

"That is all I ask for - fair play," said Sancho; "give me my dinner, and then let it rain cases and questions on me, and I'll resolve them in an instant."

The head kept his word, because it went against his conscience to kill such wise a governor through hunger; particularly as he intended to finish playing the last joke he was commissioned to practise on him that evening.

It came to pass, then, that after he had dinner that day, in opposition to the rules and sayings of the Doctor, as they were taking away the cloth there came a courier with a letter from Don Quixote for the governor. Sancho ordered the secretary to read it to himself, and if there was nothing in it that demanded secrecy to read it aloud. The secretary did so, and after he had skimmed the contents he said, "It can be read aloud, because what Señor Don Quixote writes to you deserves to be printed or written in letters of gold, and it is as follows:"

DON QUIXOTE OF LA MANCHA'S LETTER TO SANCHO PANZA, GOVERNOR OF THE ISLAND OF BARATARIA.

When I was expecting to hear of your stupidities and blunders, friend Sancho, I have received intelligence of your display of good sense, which I give a special thanks to heaven for, as it can raise the poor from the dunghill and turn fools into wise men. They tell me you govern as if you were a man, and are a man as if you were an animal, as you conduct yourself with great humility. But I want you to bear in mind, Sancho, that very often it is suitable and necessary for the authority of office to resist the humility of the heart; because the display of one who is accountable with serious duties should be such as they require and not measured by what his own humble tastes may lead him to prefer. Dress well; a stick dressed up does not look like a stick; I do not say you should wear jewels or fine clothing, or that being a judge you should dress like a soldier, but that you should array yourself in the apparel your office requires, and that at the same time it should be neat and handsome. To win the good-will of the people you govern there are two things, among others, that you must do; one is to be civil to all (this, however, I told you before), and the other to take care that food is abundant, because there is nothing that angers the heart of the poor more than hunger and high prices. Do not make many declarations; but those you do make take care that they are good ones, and above all that they are observed and carried out; because declarations that are not observed are the same as if they did not exist; actually, they encourage the idea that the Prince who had the wisdom and authority to make them did not have the power to enforce them; and laws that threaten and are not enforced come to be like the King of the frogs, that frightened them at first, but in time they despised and attacked him. Be a father of virtue and a stepfather of vice. Do not always be strict, or always lenient, but observe a balance between these two extremes, because in that is the aim of wisdom. Visit the prisons, the slaughter-houses, and the market-places; because the presence of the governor is of great importance in such places; it comforts the prisoners who are hoping for a speedy release, it calms the worry of the butchers who have to provide, and it is comforts the terror of the market-women for the same reason. Do not let it be seen that you are (even if by chance you are, which I do not believe) desirous, a follower of women, or a glutton; because when the people and those that have connections with you become aware of your special weakness they will bring their attacks to you in that region, until they have brought you down to the depths of hell. Consider and reconsider, the advice and the instructions I gave you before your departure in regards to your government, and you will see that in them, if you follow them, you have a helping hand that will lighten the troubles and difficulties for you that surround governors at every step. Write to your lord and lady and show yourself grateful to them, because ingratitude is the daughter of pride, and one of the greatest sins we know of; and he who is grateful to those who have been good to him shows that he will be grateful to God also who has granted and still grants so many blessings to him. My lady the duchess sent a messenger with your suit and another present to your wife Teresa Panza; we expect the reply soon. I have been scratching a bit recently, not very much to the benefit of my nose; but it is nothing; because if there are enchanters who mistreat me, there are also some who defend me. Let me know if the head who is with you had any share in the Trifaldi performance, as you suspected; and keep me informed of everything that happens to you, as the distance is so short. While I was thinking of giving up this idle life I am leading, as I was not born for it, something has occurred to me which I am inclined to think will put me out of favour with the duke and duchess; but although I am sorry for it I do not care, because after all I must obey my calling rather than their pleasure, in accordance with the common saying, Plato is my friend but truth is a better friend. I quote this to you because I am sure that since you have been a governor you will have learned it. Bye for now; let God keep you from being an object of pity to anyone.

Your friend,
DON QUIXOTE OF LA MANCHA.

Sancho listened to the letter with great attention, and it was praised and considered wise by all who heard it; he then got up from the table, and calling his secretary shut himself in his own room with him, and without waiting he intended to reply to his master Don Quixote immediately; and he asked the secretary to write down what he told him without adding or suppressing anything, which he did, and the answer was to the following effect:

SANCHO PANZA'S LETTER TO DON QUIXOTE OF LA MANCHA.

The pressure of business is so great on me that I have no time to scratch my head or to even cut my nails; and I have them so long - God please send a remedy for it. I say this, master of my soul, so you may not be surprised if I have not until now sent you a word of how I am doing, well or poorly, in this government, in which I am suffering more hunger than when we were wandering through the woods. My lord the duke wrote to me the other day to warn me that certain spies had got into this island to kill me; but up to the present I have not found any except a certain doctor who receives a salary in this town for killing all the governors that come here; he is called Doctor Pedro Recio. This doctor says that he does not cure diseases, but prevents them coming, and the medicines he uses are diet and more diet until he makes one skin and bones; as if leanness was not worse than fever. In short he is killing me with hunger, and I am dying of anger; because when I thought I was coming into this government to get my hot food and cool drinks, and rest between my cotton sheets on feather beds, I find I have come for atonement as if I was a hermit; and as if I do it willingly I suspect that in the end the devil will take me away. So far I have not taken any bribes, and I don't know what to think of it; because here they tell me that the governors that come to this island, before entering it have plenty of money either given to them or lent to them by the people of the town, and that this is the usual custom not only here but with all who become governors. Last night doing the rounds I came across a fair lady in men's clothing, and a brother of hers dressed as a woman; my head-carver has fallen in love with the girl, and has in his mind chosen her as a wife, so he says, and I have chosen the boy as a son-in-law; today we are going to explain our intentions to the father of the pair, who is one Diego de la Llana, a gentleman and an old Christian. I have visited the market-places, as you advised me, and yesterday I found a stall-keeper selling new hazel nuts but proved that she had mixed a heap of old rotten nuts with the new; I confiscated all of them for the children of the local charity, who will know how to distinguish them well enough, and I sentenced her not to sell in the market-place for a fortnight; they told me I did well. I can tell you it is commonly said in this town that there are no people worse than the market-women, because they are all shameless, immoral, and ill-mannered, and I can believe it from what I have seen of them so far. I am very glad my lady the duchess has written to my wife Teresa Panza and sent her the present you speak about; and I will strive to show my gratitude when the time comes; kiss her hands for me, and tell her she has not thrown her generosity into a sack with a hole in it, as she will see in the end. I would like you not to have any differences with my lord and lady; because if you fall out with them clearly it will do me harm; and as you give me the advice to be grateful it would wise for you to do the same to those who have shown you such kindness, as you have been treated so hospitably in their castle. About the scratching, I don't understand; but I suppose it must be one of those wicked enchanters always pursuing you; when we meet I am sure I will hear more about it. I wish I could send something; but I don't know what to send, but if the office remains with me I'll find something to send, one way or another. If my wife Teresa Panza writes to me, pay the postage and send me the letter, because I have a great desire to hear how my house, wife and children are doing. And so, I hope God frees you from evil-minded enchanters, and carries me well and peacefully out of this government, which I doubt, because I expect to leave it and my life together, from the way Doctor Pedro Recio treats me.

Your servant,

SANCHO PANZA THE GOVERNOR.

The secretary sealed the letter, and immediately sent the courier; and those who were carrying out the joke against Sancho putting their heads together arranged how he was to be dismissed from the government. Sancho spent the afternoon drawing up certain regulations relating to good governing of what he believed to be an island; and he ordered that there were to be no hustlers in the State, and that men could import wine into it from any place they liked, provided they declared where it came from, so a price may be put upon it according to its quality, reputation, and the esteem it was held in; and any one that watered down his wine, or changed the name, was to give his life for it. He reduced the prices of all types of shoes, boots, and socks, but shoes in particular, as they seemed to him to be priced extravagantly high. He established a fixed rate for servants' wages, which were becoming unreasonably low. He placed extremely heavy penalties on those who sang disrespectful songs either during the day or night. He declared that no blind man should sing of any miracle, unless he could produce authentic evidence that it was true, because it was his opinion that most that they sing were false, to the detriment of the ones which are true. He established and created officials of the poor, not to harass them, but to examine them and see whether they really were; because many thieves or drunks go around pretending to be crippled. In a word, he made so many good rules that to this day they are preserved there, and are called The constitutions of the great governor Sancho Panza.

CHAPTER 52

THE ADVENTURE OF THE SECOND DISTRESSED LADY, CALLED DONA RODRIGUEZ

Cide Hamete says that Don Quixote being now cured of his scratches felt that the life he was leading in the castle was entirely inconsistent with the order of chivalry he followed, so he determined to ask the duke and duchess to allow him to leave for Saragossa, as the time of the festival was approaching, and he hoped to win a suit of armour which is the prize at festivals of this type. But one day at the table with the duke and duchess, just as he was about to carry his plan into effect and ask for their permission, suddenly there came in through the door of the great hall two women, as they afterwards proved to be, draped in mourning attire from head to toe, one approaching Don Quixote threw herself at his feet, pressing her lips to them, and giving moans so sad, so deep, and so miserable that all who heard and saw her where put into a state of confusion; and although the duke and duchess thought it must be some joke their servants were playing on Don Quixote, still the way the woman sighed and moaned and wept puzzled them and made them feel unsure, until Don Quixote, touched with compassion, raised her up and made her unveil herself and remove the cover from her tearful face. She complied and disclosed what no one could have ever anticipated, because she revealed the face of Dona Rodriguez, the lady of the house; the other female in mourning being her daughter, who had been made a fool of by the rich farmer's son. All who knew her were filled with astonishment, the duke and duchess more than any; because although they thought she was a simple weak creature, they did not think she was capable of crazy pranks. Dona Rodriguez, finally, turning to her master and mistress said to them, "Will you please permit me to speak to this gentleman for a moment, because it is necessary for me to successfully get out of the business in which the boldness of an evil-minded clown has involved me?"

The duke gave his permission, and said that she could speak with Señor Don Quixote as much as she liked.

She then, turning to Don Quixote said, "Some days ago, brave Knight, I gave you an account of the injustice and treachery of a wicked farmer against my dearly beloved daughter, I bring the unhappy lady here in front of you, and you promised me you would right the wrong that has been done to her; but now I have heard that you are about to leave this castle to enter the games at a fair, before you take the road, I ask that you challenge this fool, and compel him to marry my daughter in fulfilment of the promise he gave her to become her husband before he seduced her; because to expect that my lord the duke will do this justice is to ask for pears from the oak tree; may God grant you good health and that you do not desert me now."

Don Quixote replied very seriously and sincerely, "Worthy lady, hold your tears, or rather dry them, and spare your sighs, because I take it on myself to obtain redress for your daughter, for whom it would have been better not to have been so ready to believe lovers' promises, which are for the most part quickly made and very slowly performed; and so, with my lord the duke's permission, I will go immediately in search of this cowardly youth, and I will find him, challenge him and slay him, if he refuses to keep his promise; because the main objective of my profession is to forgive the humble and punish the proud; I mean, to help the distressed and destroy the bullies."

"There is no necessity," said the duke, "for you to take the trouble of seeking this youth who this worthy lady complains about, neither is there any necessity, either, for asking for my permission to challenge him; because I will take care that he is informed of the challenge, and accepts it, and comes to this castle of mine in person to answer, where I will offer you both a fair field, observing all the conditions which are usually and properly observed in such battles, and observing justice to both sides, as all Princes who offer a free field to combatants are bound to do."

"Then with that assurance and your highness's blessing," said Don Quixote, "I renounce my privilege of gentle blood, and will put myself on a level equal to the low born wrong-doer, making myself equal with him and enabling him to enter into combat with me; and so, I challenge him, although absent, for breaking the faith of this poor lady; and say that he should fulfil the promise he gave her to become her lawful husband, or else he will sacrifice his life."

And then pulling a glove off his hand he threw it down in the middle of the hall, and the duke picked it up, saying, as he had said before, that he accepted the challenge on behalf of his servant, and fixed the date six days from then, the courtyard of the castle as the place, and for weapons the customary ones of Knights, lance, shield and full armour, with all the other accessories, without tricks, craftiness, or charms of any sort, and will be examined and approved by the judges of the field. "But first of all," he said, "it is requisite that this worthy lady and worthy young lady should place their claim for justice in the hands of Don Quixote; because otherwise nothing can be done, neither can the challenge be issued lawfully."

"I place it," replied the lady.

"And I do too," added her daughter, in tears and covered with shame and confusion.

This declaration having been made, and the duke having settled in his own mind what he would do in the matter, the ladies left, and the duchess gave orders that for the future they were not to be treated as servants of hers, but as ladies who came to her house to demand justice; so they gave them a room to themselves and waited on them as they would on strangers, to the dismay of the other female-servants, who did not know where the foolishness and carelessness of Dona Rodriguez and her unlucky daughter would stop.

And now, to complete the enjoyment of the food and bring the dinner to a satisfactory end, the servant who had carried the letters and presents to Teresa Panza, the wife of the governor Sancho, entered the hall; and the duke and duchess were very pleased to see her, being anxious to know the result of her journey; but when they asked her the servant said in reply that she could not reply in front of so many people or in a few words, and begged them to wait for a private opportunity; and taking out the letters she placed them in the duchess's hand. One addressed: To my lady the Duchess; and the other: To my husband Sancho Panza, governor of the island of Barataria. The duchess's bread would not bake, as the saying is, until she had read her letter; and having looked over it herself and seen that it could be read aloud for the duke and all those present to hear, she read it out as follows:

TERESA PANZA'S LETTER TO THE DUCHESS.

The letter your highness wrote to me, my lady, gave me great pleasure, because I found it very welcoming indeed. The string is very fine, and my husband's hunting suit is equal to it. All in this village are very pleased that you have made a governor of my good man Sancho; although nobody will believe it, particularly the vicar, and Master Nicholas the barber, and the graduate Samson Carrasco; but I don't care about that, because as long as it is true, as it is, they may say whatever they like; although, to tell the truth, if the string and the suit had not come I would not have believed it either; because in this village everybody thinks my husband is a fool, and except for governing a herd of goats, they cannot understand what sort of government he could be fit for. I am determined with your permission, lady of my soul, to make the most of this day, and go to Court to stretch myself at ease in a coach, and make all those I have envying me already cry their eyes out; so I beg you to order my husband to send me a small amount of money, enough to cover everything, because one's expenses are quite heavy at the Court; a loaf of bread costs a coin, and meat is expensive; and if he does not want me to go, ask him to tell me, because my feet are anxious to go; and my friends and neighbours tell me that if my daughter and I make a good show at the Court, my husband will come to be known far more by me than I by him, because of course plenty of people will ask, "Who are those ladies in that coach?" and some servant of mine will answer, "The wife and daughter of Sancho Panza, governor of the island of Barataria;" and in this way Sancho will become well known, and I'll be thought well of. I am as angry as angry can be that they have gathered no chestnuts this year in our village; because all I can send your highness is half a dozen that I went to the woods to gather and pick out one by one by myself, and I could find no bigger ones; I wish they were as big as ostrich eggs. Please do not forget to write to me; and I will take care to answer, and let you know how I am, and whatever news there may be in this place, where I remain, praying to our Lord to keep your highness under his protection and not to forget me.

I, Sancha my daughter, and my son, kiss your hands.

She who would rather see you than write to you,

Your servant,

TERESA PANZA.

All were amused by Teresa Panza's letter, but particularly the duke and duchess; and the duchess asked Don Quixote's opinion whether they could open the letter that had come for the governor, which she suspected must be very good. Don Quixote said that to gratify them he would open it, and did so, and found that it went as follows:

TERESA PANZA'S LETTER TO HER HUSBAND SANCHO PANZA.

I got your letter Sancho, man of my soul, and I promise you and swear as a Catholic Christian that I was within days of going mad before receiving it. I am so happy. I can tell you, brother, when I came to hear that you were a governor I thought I would drop dead with joy; and you know they say sudden joy kills as well as great sorrow; and as for Sanchica your daughter, she cried out of sheer happiness. I had in front of me the suit you sent me, the thread my lady the duchess sent to me around my neck, and the letters in my hands, and there was the carrier of them standing by, and in spite of all this I truly believed and thought that what I saw and handled was a dream; because who could have thought that a goat herder would come to be a governor of islands? You know, my friend, what my mother used to say, that one must live long to see much; I say it because I expect to see more if I live longer; because I don't expect to stop until I see you a farmer of taxes or a collector of revenue although the devil takes those who make bad use of them, still they make and handle money. My lady the duchess will tell you the desire I have to go to the Court; consider the matter and let me know what you think; I will honour you by going in a coach. Neither the vicar, the barber, or the graduate can believe you are a governor, and they say the whole thing is a delusion or enchantment, like everything belonging to your master Don Quixote; and Samson says he must go in search of you and drive the government out of your head and the madness out of Don Quixote's skull; I laugh, and look at my thread, and plan the dress I am going to make for our daughter out of your suit. I sent some chestnuts to my lady the duchess; I wish they had been gold. Send me a string of pearls if they are in fashion in that island. Here is the latest news of the village; La Berrueca has married her daughter to a good-for-nothing painter, who came here to paint anything he could. The council gave him an order to paint his Majesty's weapons over the door of the town-hall; he asked for two gold coins, which they paid him in advance; he worked for eight days, and at the end of them he had painted nothing, and then he said he had no desire to paint such things; he returned the money, and despite that has married on the pretence of being a good workman; to be sure he has now put aside his paint-brush and taken a spade instead, and goes to the field like a gardener. Pedro

Lobo's son has received the first orders and shaved his head, with the intention of becoming a priest. Minguilla, Mingo Silvato's grand-daughter, found out, and has disputed this as he had given her promise of marriage. Many say she is expecting a child by him, but he denies it firmly. There are no olives this year, and there is not a drop of vinegar in the whole village. Sanchica is making pillow cases; she earns eight coins a day clear, which she puts into a moneybox as help towards furnishing the house; but now that she is a governor's daughter you will give her an allowance without working for it. The fountain in the plaza has run dry. A flash of lightning struck the wooden beams where criminals are hung, and I wish it set fire to it. I look forward to your reply, and to know your wishes about me going to the Court; and so, God keep you well, longer than me, because I would not leave you in this world without me.

Your wife,

TERESA PANZA.

The letters were applauded, laughed over, enjoyed, and admired; and then, as if to put the seal on everything, the courier arrived, bringing the one Sancho sent to Don Quixote, and this, too, was read aloud, and it raised some doubts in regards to the governor's simplicity. The duchess left to hear from the servant about her adventures in Sancho's village, which she discussed fully without leaving anything unmentioned. She gave her the chestnuts, and also some cheese which Teresa had given her, which she said was very good and superior to that from Tronchon. The duchess received it with great delight, in which we will leave her, to describe the end of the government of the great Sancho Panza, the cream of all governors of islands.

CHAPTER 53

THE TROUBLE AND TERMINATION OF SANCHO PANZA'S GOVERNMENT

To think that in this life anything belonging to it will remain for ever in the same state is an illusion; on the contrary, everything seems to go in a circle, I mean round and round. The spring is replaced by the summer, the summer by the autumn, the autumn by the winter, and the winter by the spring, and so time rolls in a never-ceasing wheel. Man's life alone, swifter than time, speeds onward to its end without any hope of renewal, except in that other life which is endless and boundless. Therefore, Cide Hamete the philosopher says; because there are many that by the light of nature, without the light of faith, have a notion of the transitory nature and instability of this present life and the endless duration of that eternal life we hope for; but our author is speaking about the rapidity with which Sancho's government came to an end, melted away, disappeared, vanished as it were into the abyss. Because as he lay in bed on the night of the seventh day of his government, full, not with bread and wine, but with providing judgments and giving opinions and making laws and declarations, just as sleep, despite his hunger, was beginning to close his eyelids, he heard the noise of bell-ringing and shouting that one would have believed the whole island was going to sink. He sat up in bed and listened intently to try and make out what could be the cause of such great commotion; not only, however, was he unable to discover what it was, but as countless drums and trumpets now accompanied the sound of the bells and shouting, he was more confused than ever, and filled with fear and terror; and getting up he put on a pair of slippers because the floor was damp, and without putting on a dressing gown or anything over him he rushed out of the door, just in time to see, along a corridor, a group of more than twenty people with torches and swords in their hands, all shouting out, "War, señor governor, war! The enemy is on the island in countless numbers, and we are lost unless your skill and bravery come to our support."

Continuing this noise and chaos, they came to where Sancho stood confused and disoriented by what he saw and heard, and as they approached one of them said to him, "Arm yourself, my lordship, if you do not want yourself and the whole island destroyed."

"What have I got to do with war?" said Sancho. "What do I know about weapons or supporting? Better to leave this to my master Don Quixote, who will settle it all and make everything safe; because God help me, I don't understand these things."

"Ah, señor governor," said another, "what laziness is this! Arm yourself; here are weapons for you, offensive and defensive; come out and be our leader and captain; it falls on you, because you are our governor."

"Arm me then, in God's name," said Sancho, and they covered him with two large shields, and placed them over his shirt, without letting him put on anything else, one shield in front and the other behind, and passing him more weapons through the openings they had made, they bound him tight with ropes, so that there he was enclosed and unable to bend his knees or take a single step. In his hand they placed a lance, which he leant on to keep himself from falling, and as soon as they had him fixed they asked him to march forward and lead them and give them courage; because with him as their guide, light and star, they were sure to bring the battle to a successful conclusion.

"How am I going to march, unlucky being that I am?" said Sancho, "when I can't move my knee-caps, and these boards that are bound so tight to my body won't let me. What you must do is carry me, and put me at some entrance, and I'll defend it either with this lance or with my body."

"On, señor governor!" cried another, "it is fear more than the boards that stop you from moving; quickly, move yourself, because there is no time to lose; the enemy is increasing in numbers, the shouts grow louder, and the danger is rising."

Urged by these appeals the poor governor made an attempt to advance, but fell to the ground with such a crash that he thought he had broken himself into pieces. He lay there like a tortoise enclosed in its shell. The group of jokers did not feel any compassion for him when they saw him on the floor; far from it, extinguishing their torches they began to shout louder and renew the calls for war with such energy, trampling on poor Sancho, and hitting his shield with their swords in such a way that, if he had not made himself into a little ball between the shields, things would have gone badly for the poor governor. Squeezed into that narrow enclosure, he lay, sweating and sweating, and calling with his whole heart for God to free him from his present danger. Some stumbled over him, others fell on him, and one took his position on top of him for some time, and from there as if from a watchtower gave orders to the men, shouting, "There, on that side! There the enemy is fullest! Hold the opening there! Shut that gate! Barricade the doors! Block the streets!" In short, in his passion he mentioned every little thing, every method and instrument of war which an assault on a city is to be warded off with, while the bruised and battered Sancho, who heard all and suffered, was saying to himself, "If it would only please the Lord to let the island be lost right now, and I could see myself either dead or out of this torture!"

Heaven heard his prayer, and when he least expected it he heard voices exclaiming, "Victory, victory! The enemy retreats - beaten! Come, señor governor, get up, and come and enjoy the victory, and divide what has been won from the enemy by the might of our invincible arms."

"Lift me up," said poor Sancho in a distressed voice. They helped him to his feet, and as soon as he was up he said, "I don't want to divide what has been won from the enemy, I only beg that some friend, if I have one, give me a sip of wine, because I'm parched with thirst, and wipe me dry, because I'm turning into water."

They wiped him down, got some wine and removed the shields, and he sat himself on his bed, and with fear, agitation, and fatigue he fainted. Those who had orchestrated the joke were now sorry they had pushed it so far; however, the anxiety his fainting had caused them was relieved when he returned to himself. He asked what time it was; they told him it was sunrise. He said no more, and in silence began to dress himself, while they all watched him, waiting to see what putting on his clothes in such a rush meant.

He got himself dressed, and then, slowly, because he was very bruised and could not go fast, he walked to the stable, followed by all those who were present, and going up to Dapple embraced him and gave him a loving kiss on the forehead, and said to him, with tears in his eyes, "My companion, friend and partner of my sorrow; when I was with you and had no care except mending your harness and feeding you, my hours were happy, my days, and my years; but since I left you, and climbed the towers of ambition and pride, a thousand miseries, a thousand troubles, and a thousand anxieties have entered my soul;" and while he was speaking in this manner he was fixing the saddle to the donkey, without a word from anyone. Then having Dapple saddled, he, with great pain and difficulty, got on him, and addressing the head, the secretary, the head-carver, and Pedro Recio the doctor and several others who stood by, he said, "Make way, gentlemen, and let me go back to my old freedom; let me go look to my past life, and raise myself up from this present death. I was not born to be a governor or protect islands or cities from the enemies that choose to attack them. Cultivating, digging and pruning, are more suitable than defending provinces or kingdoms. 'Saint Peter is very well in Rome;' I mean each of us is best following the trade he was born to do. A shovel fits my hand better than a governor's stick; I'd rather fill myself with soup' than be subject to the misery of a meddling doctor who tortures me with hunger, and I'd rather lie in summer under the shade of an oak, and in winter wrap myself in a double sheepskin jacket in freedom, than go to bed between cotton sheets and dress in a suit under the restraint of a government. God be with you all, and tell my lord the duke that 'I was born naked, and now I find myself naked, I neither lose or gain;' I mean that I came into this government without anything, and I leave it without anything, very different from the way governors usually leave islands. Stand aside and let me go; I have to bandage myself, because I believe every one of my ribs is broken, thanks to the enemies that have been trampling on me."

"That is unnecessary, señor governor," said Doctor Recio, "because I will give you a dose which will soon make you as strong as ever; and in regards to your diet I promise to behave better, and let you eat abundantly and whatever you like."

"Too late," said Sancho. "I'd prefer to be a Turk than stay any longer. Those jokes won't happen a second time. I am as likely to remain in this government, or take another, even if it was offered to me on a plate, as I am to fly to heaven without wings. I am one of the Panzas, and every one of them is unmoved, and if they say 'no,' no it must be, even if it is yes, despite what the whole world says. Here in this stable I leave the wings that lifted me up into the air for the birds to eat me, and I will stand on the level ground and on my feet again; and if they're not enclosed in cordovan shoes, they won't desire sandals of hemp; no one should stretch his legs beyond the length of the sheets; and now let me pass, because it's getting late."

To this the head said, "Señor governor, we would let you go with all our hearts, although it truly grieves us to lose you, because your wit and Christian conduct naturally make us regret your departure; but it is well known that every governor, before he leaves the place where he has been governing, is bound first of all to give an account. Please do so for the ten days you have held the government, and then you may go and the peace of God will go with you."

"No one can demand it from me," said Sancho, "but whoever my lord the duke appoints; I am going to meet him, and to him I will give an exact account; besides, when I leave naked as I do, there is no other proof needed to show that I have governed like an angel."

"God, the great Sancho is right," said Doctor Recio, "and we should let him go, because the duke will be surely glad to see him."

They all agreed to this, and allowed him to go, first offering to accompany him and provide him with all he needed for his own comfort or for the journey. Sancho said he did not want anything other than a little barley for Dapple, cheese and half a loaf of bread for himself; because as the distance was so short there was no cause for any larger supplies. They all embraced him, and he with tears embraced them all, and left them filled with admiration not only with his remarks but with his firm and sensible disposition.

CHAPTER 54

OTHER MATTERS RELATING TO THIS HISTORY

The duke and duchess decided that the challenge Don Quixote had, for the reason already mentioned, given by their servant, should be carried out; and as the young man was in Flanders, where he had fled to escape having Dona Rodriguez as a mother-in-law, they arranged to substitute him for a servant, named Tosilos, first of all carefully instructing him in all he had to do. Two days later the duke told Don Quixote that in four days from that time his opponent would present himself on the battle field armed as a Knight, and would argue that the lady lied, if she maintained that he had given her the promise of marriage. Don Quixote was very pleased with the news, and promised to perform wonders in the battle, and considered it rare good fortune that an opportunity had presented itself for letting his noble hosts see what the might of his arm was capable of; and so in high spirits and satisfaction he awaited the end of four days, which measured by his impatience seemed to be four hundred years. Let us leave them to pass as we turn our attention to other things, and give Sancho some company.

As he mounted Dapple, half glad, half sad, he travelled along the road to join his master, under whose guidance he was happier than being governor of any island in the world. It so happened that before he had gone very far from the island of his government (and whether it was island, city, town, or village that he governed he never bothered to inquire) he saw coming along the road six pilgrims with bags, foreigners that beg for donations while singing; who as they drew near arranged themselves in a line and lifting their voices began to sing in their own language, one that Sancho could not understand with the exception of a word which sounded like "donations," from which he gathered that it was a donation they asked for in their song; and being, as Cide Hamete says, remarkably charitable, he took from his saddle bag the half loaf and cheese he had been provided with, and gave both to them, explaining to them with hand gestures that he had nothing else to give them. They received them gladly, but exclaimed, "Geld! Geld!"

"I don't understand what you want from me, good people," said Sancho.

One of them took a wallet out and showed it to Sancho, by which he comprehended they were asking for money, and shaking his head he gave them the understanding that he had no coins on him, and urging Dapple forward he broke through them. But as he was passing, one of them who had been asking for money rushed towards him, and throwing his arms around him exclaimed in a loud voice, "God bless me! What is this I see? Is it possible that I hold in my arms my dear friend, my good neighbour Sancho Panza? There can be no doubt about it, because I'm not asleep, or drunk."

Sancho was surprised to hear himself called by his name and to find himself embraced by a foreign pilgrim, and after observing him carefully without speaking he was still unable to recognise him; but the pilgrim noticing his confusion cried, "What! Is it possible, Sancho Panza, that you do not know your neighbour Ricote, the Morisco shopkeeper of your village?"

Sancho looked at him again more carefully and began to recall his features, and finally recognised him perfectly, and without getting off the donkey threw his arms around his neck saying, "Who the devil could have recognised you, Ricote, in the attire you are in? Tell me, who has turned you French, and how do you dare return to Spain, where if they catch you and recognise you it will not go well for you?"

"If you do not betray me, Sancho," said the pilgrim, "I am safe; because in this attire no one will recognise me; but let us turn off of this road into the woods over there where my companions are going to eat and rest, and you will eat with them there, because they are all very good men; I'll have enough time to tell you all that has happened to me since I left our village in obedience to his Majesty who threatened such cruelty against the unfortunate people of my nation, as you have already heard."

Sancho complied, and after Ricote instructed the other pilgrims they withdrew to the woods, proceeding a considerable distance out of the road. They put down their bags, took off their pilgrim's coats and remained in their under-clothing; they were all good-looking young men, except Ricote, who was quite advanced in years. They all carried saddle-bags, and all appeared to be well filled, at least with things that provoke the thirst, enough to summon it from two miles away. They stretched themselves on the ground, and making a tablecloth of the grass they spread on it bread, salt, knives, walnuts, bits of cheese, and pork ribs which if they were past chewing on were not past sucking. They also put down a delicacy called, they say, caviar, made from fish eggs, a great thirst-arouser. But what made the best show in the field of the banquet was half a dozen bottles of wine, as each of them produced his own from his saddle-bags; even the good Ricote, who from a Morisco had transformed himself into a Frenchman, took out his, which in its size might have contended with five others. They then began to eat with very great relish and leisure, making the most of each bite; and then all at the same moment raised their bottles, and all eyes fixed on heaven just as if they were taking aim at it; and in this attitude they remained for a long time, waving their heads from side to side as if in acknowledgment of the pleasure they were enjoying while they emptied the contents of the bottles into their stomachs.

Sancho observed all, "and nothing gave him pain;" far from it, acting on the proverb he knew so well, "when you are in Rome do as you see," he asked Ricote for his bottle and took aim like the rest of them, and with no less enjoyment. Four times the bottles were raised, but the fifth time was ineffective, because they were drier than hot sand by that time, which made the cheerfulness that had been ongoing begin to fade.

Every now and then one of them would hold Sancho's right hand and say, "Spanish and French make good peasants;" and Sancho would answer,

"Good peasants pray to God!" and then he gave a burst of laughter that lasted an hour, without a thought for the moment of anything that had happened to him during his government; because troubles have very little effect on us while we are eating and drinking. Finally, as the wine had come to an end, drowsiness began to affect them, and they fell asleep on their table and tablecloth. Ricote and Sancho were the only ones to remain awake, because they had eaten more and drunk less, and Ricote took Sancho aside, and they sat themselves at the base of an oak tree, leaving the pilgrims deep in sweet sleep; and without using his own language Ricote spoke as follows:

"You very know well, neighbour and friend Sancho, how the declaration of his Majesty commanded to be issued against those of my nation filled us all with terror; at least it did to me, to the extent that before the time given to us for leaving Spain was complete, the full force of the penalty had already been given to me and my children. I decided, then, and I think wisely (just like one who knows that at a certain date the house he lives in will be taken from him, and looks for another one beforehand), I decided, to leave the town myself, alone and without my family, and go to seek some place to take them to comfortably and not in the hurried manner in which the others made their departure; because I saw very clearly, and so did all the older men among us, that the proclamations were not mere threats, as some said, but declarations which would be enforced at the appointed time; and what made me believe this, was what I knew of the vile and excessive plans which our people harboured, plans of such a nature that I think it was a divine inspiration that moved his Majesty to carry out a resolution so forcefully; not that we were all guilty, because some were true and loyal Christians; but there were so few that they could not stop this plan against those who were not; and it was not prudent to value snakes in the land by having enemies in the house. In short, it was appropriate that we were met with the penalty of banishment, a mild and lenient one in the eyes of some, but to us the most terrible that could be inflicted on us. Wherever we are we cry for Spain; because after all we were born there and it is our natural homeland. Nowhere else do we find the welcome our unhappy condition needs; and in all the parts of Africa where we counted on being supported and welcomed, it is there they insult and mistreat us most. We did not know our good fortune until we lost it; and this creates the yearning almost all of us have to return to Spain, and most of those who like myself know the language, and there are many who do, return to it and leave their wives and children abandoned somewhere else, as their love for Spain is so great; and now I know by experience the meaning of the saying, sweet is the love of one's country.

"I left our village, as I said, and went to France, but although they gave us a kind welcome there I was anxious to see as much as I could. I crossed into Italy, and reached Germany, and there it seemed to me we could live with more freedom, as the inhabitants do not pay any attention to insignificant matters; everyone lives as he wants to, because in most parts they enjoy freedom of conscience. I took a house in a town near Augsburg, and then joined these pilgrims, who are in the habit of going to Spain in great numbers every year to visit the shrines, which they look on as their idols and a sure and certain source of gain. They travel nearly all over it, and there is no town which they do not leave with a belly full of meat and drink, as the saying is, and with a coin, at least, in money, and they end their travels with more than a hundred coins saved, which, when changed into gold, they smuggle out of the Kingdom in the patches of their pilgrim's coats, and carry it to their own country despite the guards at the posts where they are searched. Now my purpose is, Sancho, to take the treasure that I left buried, which, as it is outside the town, I will be able to do without any risk, and to write, or cross over from Valencia, to my daughter and wife, who I know are in Algeria, and find some method of bringing them to a French port and from there into Germany, to await what God's will - will be for us; because, after all, Sancho, I know well that Ricota my daughter and Francisca Ricota my wife are Catholic Christians, and although I am not as much, I am still more of a Christian than a Moor, and it is always my prayer to God that he will open the eyes of my understanding and show me how I am to serve him; but what amazes me and what I cannot understand is why my wife and daughter would have gone to Africa rather than to France, where they could live as Christians."

To this Sancho replied, "Remember, Ricote, that may not have been open to them, because Juan Tiopieyo your wife's brother took them, and being a true Moor he went where he could go easily; and another thing I can tell you, it is my belief you are going to look for what you have left buried for no reason, because we heard they took from your brother-in-law and your wife a great quantity of pearls and money in gold."

"That may be," said Ricote; "but I know they did not touch what I buried, because I did not tell them where it was, in fear of this type of accident; and so, if you will come with me, Sancho, and help me to take it and conceal it, I will give you two hundred coins with which you can relieve your necessities, and, as you know, I know there are many."

"I would do it," said Sancho; "but I am not at all greedy, because I gave up an office this morning in which, if I was, I might have made the walls of my house golden and ate off silver plates within six months; and so for this reason, and because I feel I would be guilty of treason to my King if I helped his enemies, I would not go with you even if instead of promising me two hundred coins you were to give me four hundred in my hand right now."

"And what office is this you have given up, Sancho?" asked Ricote.

"I have given up being governor of an island," said Sancho, "and one, believe me, the type you won't find easily."

"And where is this island?" said Ricote.

"Where?" said Sancho; "two miles from here, and it is called the island of Barataria."

"Nonsense! Sancho," said Ricote; "islands are away out in the sea; there are no islands on the mainland."

"What? No islands!" said Sancho; "I am telling you, friend Ricote, I left it this morning, and yesterday I was governing it however I chose; but despite that I gave it up, because it seemed to me the governor's office is a dangerous one."

"And what have you gained from your government?" asked Ricote.

"I have gained," said Sancho, "the knowledge that I am not good for governing, unless it is a herd of sheep, and that the riches that are to be gained by these governments are gained at the cost of one's rest and sleep, in fact, even one's food; because in islands the governors must eat little, especially if they have doctors to look after their health."

"I don't understand you, Sancho," said Ricote; "but it seems to me you are talking nonsense. Who would give you an island to govern? Is there a lack in the world of cleverer men than you are for governors? Hold your tongue, Sancho, and come back to your senses, and consider whether you will come with me as I said to help me take the treasure I left buried (because indeed it may be called treasure, as it is so large), and I will give you enough to keep yourself well, as I have told you."

"And as I have told you already, Ricote, I will not," said Sancho; "let it relieve you to know that by me you will not be betrayed, and go your way in God's name and let me go mine; because I know that which is gained fairly may be lost, but that which is gained unfairly is lost, itself and its owner also."

"I will not insist, Sancho," said Ricote; "but tell me, were you in our village when my wife, daughter and brother-in-law left it?"

"I was indeed," said Sancho; "and I can tell you your daughter left it looking so lovely that all the village came out to see her, and everybody said she was the finest creature in the world. She cried as she went, and embraced all her friends and acquaintances and those who were there, and she begged them all to ask for Jesus's and Our Lady his mother's assistance for her, and in such a touching way that it made me cry as well, although I do not commonly shed tears; and, believe me, many people would have liked to hide her, or take her on her journey; but the fear of going against the King's command kept them back. The one who showed himself most moved was Don Pedro Gregorio, the rich young heir you know of, and they say he was deep in love with her; and since she left he has not been seen in our village again, and we all suspect he has gone after her to take her away, but so far nothing has been heard about it."

"I always had a suspicion that gentleman had a passion for my daughter," said Ricote; "but as I felt sure of my Ricota's virtues it gave me no anxiety to know that he loved her; because you must have heard it said, Sancho, that the Morisco women rarely or never engage in lovemaking with the Christians; and my daughter, who I believe thought more of being a Christian than of lovemaking, would not trouble herself about the attention of this heir."

"God grant it," said Sancho, "because it would be bad business for both of them; but now let's go, friend Ricote, because I want to reach my master Don Quixote is by this evening."

"God be with you, brother Sancho," said Ricote; "my companions are beginning to wake, and it is time, too, for us to continue our journey;" and then they both embraced, Sancho mounted Dapple, Ricote went back to his companions, and so they parted.

CHAPTER 55

WHAT HAPPENED TO SANCHO ON THE ROAD, AND OTHER THINGS THAT CANNOT BE WITHHELD

The time taken with Ricote prevented Sancho from reaching the duke's castle that day, although he was only half a mile away from it when night came, somewhat dark and cloudy. This, however, as it was summer time, did not give him much worry, and he turned off of the road intending to wait for the morning; but his bad luck decided that as he was searching for a place to make himself as comfortable as possible, he and Dapple fell into a deep dark hole. As he fell he called for God's assistance with his whole heart, thinking he was not going to stop until he reached the depths of the bottomless pit; but it did not turn out so, because at a little more than three times a man's height Dapple touched bottom, and he found himself sitting on him without receiving any injury or damage whatsoever. He felt himself all over to see if he was unhurt, and finding himself all right and whole and in perfect health he gave generous thanks to God our Lord for the mercy that had been shown to him, because he made sure he had not been broken into a thousand pieces. He also felt along the sides of the pit with his hands to see if it were possible to get out of it without help, but he found that they were very smooth and he was unable to get a grip anywhere, which greatly distressed him, especially when he heard how pathetically and unhappily Dapple was moaning, and no wonder he complained, because in truth he was not in a very good state. "Unfortunately," said Sancho, "unexpected accidents happen at every step to those who live in this miserable world! Who would have said that one who saw himself yesterday sitting on a throne, governor of an island, giving orders to his servants, would see himself buried in a pit today without a soul to help him, or servant to come to his relief? Here we must die with hunger, my donkey and myself, if indeed we don't die first, he from his bruises and injuries, and I from grief and sorrow. At any rate I won't be as lucky as my master Don Quixote of La Mancha, when he went down into the cave of that enchanted Montesinos, where he found people to look after him, more than if he had been in his own house; because it seems he went in for a laid out table and a readymade bed. There he saw pleasant visions, but here I'll see, I imagine, snakes and frogs. Unlucky fool that I am, what an end my foolish desires have come to! They'll dig up my bones out of here, when it is heaven's will that I'm found, and my good Dapple's with them, and by that, perhaps, it will be found out who we are, at least by hearing that Sancho Panza never separated from his donkey, and neither the donkey from Sancho Panza. Unlucky fools, I say again, that our unlucky fate should not let us die in our own country and among our own people, where if there was no help for our misfortune, at any rate there would be someone to grieve over it and to close our eyes as we passed away! O friend, how poorly I have repaid your faithful services! Forgive me, and ask Fortune, as well as you can, to free us from of this miserable situation we are both in; and I promise to put a crown on your head, and make you look like a monarch, and give you double portions of feed."

Sancho continued to moan in this manner, and his donkey listened to him, but did not reply with a word, due to the distress and anguish the poor creature found himself in. Finally, after spending a night in bitter moaning and crying, day came, and by its light Sancho observed that it was totally impossible to escape from the pit without help, and he began to moan about his fate and making loud shouts to find out if there was anyone who might hear him; but all his shouting was only crying in the wilderness, because there was not a soul anywhere in the region to hear him, and then, finally, he considered himself dead. Dapple was lying on his back, and Sancho helped him onto his feet, which he was barely able to keep; and then taking a piece of bread out of his saddle-bags which had shared their misfortune of the fall, he gave it to the donkey, who welcomed it, saying to him as if he understood him, "With bread all sorrows are improved."

And now he noticed on one side of the pit a hole large enough to allow a person through if he squeezed himself into a small shape. Sancho attempted it, and entered, and found it wide and spacious on the inside, which he was able to see as a ray of sunlight penetrated through what might be called the roof. He observed that it opened and widened out into another spacious cavity; upon seeing this he made his way back to where the donkey was, and with a stone began to break down the clay from the hole until in a short time he had made room for the donkey to pass through easily, and with this accomplished, taking him by the reins, he proceeded to navigate the hollow to see if there was any opening at the other end. He advanced, sometimes in the dark, sometimes without light, but never without fear; "God Almighty help me!" he said to himself; "this that seems like a misadventure to me would make a good adventure for my master Don Quixote. He would have taken these depths and dungeons to be flowery gardens or palaces, and would have believed he would leave this darkness and imprisonment and enter into some blooming meadow; but I, unlucky as I am, hopeless and spiritless, expect at every step another pit deeper than the first to open under my feet and swallow me up for good; 'welcome evil, do you come alone?'"

In this manner and with these reflections he believed he had travelled more than half a mile, when at last he noticed a dim light that looked like daylight and found its way in on one side, showing that this road, which appeared to him to be the road to the other world, led to some opening.

Here Cide Hamete leaves him, and returns to Don Quixote, who in high spirit and satisfaction was looking forward to the day fixed for the battle where he was to fight with the one who had robbed Dona Rodriguez's daughter of her honour, for whom he hoped to obtain contentment for the insult shamefully inflicted on her. It so happened, then, that going out one morning to practise and exercise himself in what he would have to do in the encounter he expected to find himself engaged in the next day, as he was exerting Rocinante practising his charge, he brought his feet so close to a pit that if he had not reined him in tightly it would have been impossible for him to avoid falling into it. He managed to bring him to a stop, however, without a fall, and coming a little closer examined the hole without dismounting; but as he was looking at it he heard loud cries coming from it, and by listening attentively was able to make out that he who pronounced them was saying, "Hello, above there! Is there any Christian that hears me, or any charitable gentleman that will take pity on a sinner buried alive, or on an unfortunate disgoverned governor?"

It struck Don Quixote that it was the voice of Sancho Panza, at which he was shocked and amazed, and raising his own voice as much as he could, he cried out, "Who is down there? Who is that complaining?"

"Who else could be here, or who should complain," was the answer, "but the lost Sancho Panza, for his sins and for his bad-luck, ex-governor of the island of Barataria, and once aide to the famous Knight Don Quixote of La Mancha?"

When Don Quixote heard this his amazement was doubled and his agitation grew greater than ever, because it suggested itself to his mind that Sancho must be dead, and that his soul was in torment down there; and carried away by this idea he exclaimed, "I summon you by everything that I as a Catholic Christian can summon you with, tell me who you are; and if you are a tortured soul, tell me what you would like me do for you; because as my profession is to give aid and assistance to those that need it in this world, it will also extend to aiding and assisting the distressed in the other world, who cannot help themselves."

"In that case," answered the voice, "you who speak to me must be my master Don Quixote of La Mancha; actually, from the tone of the voice it is clear it cannot be anybody else."

"Don Quixote I am, whose profession it is to aid and assist the living and the dead in need; therefore tell me who you are, because you are keeping me in suspense; because, if you are my aide Sancho Panza, and are dead, since the devil has not carried you away, and you are by God's mercy in limbo, our holy mother the Roman Catholic Church has methods sufficient enough to release you from the pain you are in; and I for my part will plead with her for that purpose, as much as I am able to; without further delay, therefore, declare yourself, and tell me who you are."

"On all that's good," was the answer, "and on the life of whoever you choose, I swear, Señor Don Quixote of La Mancha, that I am your aide Sancho Panza, and that I have never died in my whole life; but that, having given up my government for reasons that would require more time to explain, I fell last night into this pit where I am now, and Dapple is my witness and won't let me lie, because he is also here with me."

One would have believed the donkey understood what Sancho said, because at that moment he began to make noises so loudly that the whole cave echoed.

"Legendary testament!" exclaimed Don Quixote; "I know that noise as well as if I was its mother, and your voice as well, my Sancho. Wait while I go to the duke's castle, which is close by, and I will bring someone to take you out of this pit into which you have been placed no doubt for your sins."

"Go, my lord," said Sancho, "and come back quickly for God's sake; because I cannot bear being buried alive any longer, and I'm dying of fear."

Don Quixote left him, and rushed to the castle to tell the duke and duchess what had happened to Sancho, and although they were astonished by it; they could easily understand a fall into the pit, as the cave had been in existence for centuries; but they could not imagine how he had left the government without them receiving any hint of him leaving. To be brief, they got the ropes, and with the help of many hands and much labour they hoisted Dapple and Sancho Panza out of the darkness into the light of day. A student who saw him remarked, "That's the way all bad governors should come out of their governments, as this sinner comes out of the depths of the pit, dead with hunger, pale, and I suppose without a penny to his name."

Sancho overheard him and said, "It has been eight or ten days, since I entered the government of the island they gave me, critic, and all that time I never had a bellyful of food, not even for an hour; doctors persecuted me and enemies crushed my bones; I had no opportunity for taking bribes or levying taxes; I don't deserve, I think, to leave in this manner; but 'man proposes and God disposes;' and God knows what is best, and what suits each man; God knows what I mean and that's enough, and although I could; I say no more."

"Do not be angry or annoyed by what you hear, Sancho," said Don Quixote, "or it will never end; keep a clear conscience and let them say whatever they like; because trying to stop attackers' tongues is like trying to put gates on the open field. If a governor comes out of his government rich, they say he must have been a thief; and if he comes out poor, that he has been a fool."

"They'll surely, this time," said Sancho, "put me down as a fool rather than a thief."

While talking, and surrounded by boys and a crowd of people, they reached the castle, where in one of the corridors the duke and duchess stood waiting for them; but Sancho would not go to see the duke until he had first put Dapple in the stable, because he said he had spent a very bad night in his last accommodation; then he went upstairs to see his lord and lady, and kneeling in front of them he said, "Because it was your wish, I went to govern your island of Barataria, which 'I entered naked, and naked I find myself; I neither lose or gain.' Whether I have governed well or poorly, I have had witnesses who will say what they think about it. I have answered questions, I have resolved cases, and all while dying of hunger, because Doctor Pedro Recio of Tirteafuera, the island and governor's doctor, gave this prescription. Enemies attacked us during the night and put us in a great dilemma, but the people of the island say they came out safe and victorious by the might of my arm; and may God give them as much health as there's truth in what they say. In short, during that time I have weighed the care and responsibly governing brings with it, and by my calculation I find my shoulders can't bear it; and so, before the government kicked me out, I preferred to leave the government; and yesterday morning I left the island as I found it, with the same streets, houses, and roofs it had when I entered it. I asked for no loan from anybody, neither did I try to fill my pockets; and although I intended to make some useful laws, I hardly made any, as I was afraid they would not be kept; because in that case, it would be the same to make them or not to make them. I left the island, as I said, without any escort except my donkey; I fell into a pit, I pushed on through it, until this morning by the light of the sun I saw an outlet, but not an easy one, but had heaven not sent me my master Don Quixote, I'd have stayed there till the end of the world. So now my lord and lady, duke and duchess, here is your governor Sancho Panza, who in the ten days he has held the government has come to the conclusion that he would not give anything to be a governor again, not even of an island, but of the whole world; and that point being settled, kissing your hands, I leave the government and pass back into the service of my master Don Quixote; because after all, although during my service I ate my bread in fear, I was full; and as long as I'm full, it's all the same to me whether it's full with carrots or with chicken."

Here Sancho brought his long speech to an end, while the whole time Don Quixote was in fear of him expressing a bunch of absurdities; and when he observed him finish with so few, he thanked heaven from the bottom of his heart. The duke embraced Sancho and told him he was very sorry he had given up the government so soon, but that he would see that he was provided with some other post on his estate less burdensome and more profitable. The duchess also embraced him, and gave orders that he should be taken good care of, as it was clear to see he had been badly treated and thoroughly bruised.

CHAPTER 56

THE EXTRAORDINARY AND UNPARALLELED BATTLE THAT TOOK PLACE BETWEEN DON QUIXOTE OF LA MANCHA AND THE SERVANT TOSILOS IN DEFENCE OF THE DAUGHTER OF DONA RODRIGUEZ

The duke and duchess had no reason to regret the joke that had been played on Sancho Panza in giving him the government; especially as their head returned the same day, and gave them a detailed account of almost every word and deed that Sancho said and did during the time; and to finish, he articulately described to them the attack on the island and Sancho's fear and departure, with which they were thoroughly amused. After this the history goes on to say that the day fixed for the battle had arrived, and that the duke, after having repeatedly instructed his servant Tosilos how to deal with Don Quixote so as to defeat him without killing or wounding him, gave orders to have the tips removed from the lances, telling Don Quixote that Christian charity, on which he prided himself, could not allow the battle to be fought with so much risk and danger to life; and that he must be content with the offer of a battlefield on his territory (although that was against the orders of the holy Council, which prohibits all challenges of the sort) and not to push such a difficult adventure to its extreme limits. Don Quixote asked his excellence to arrange all the matters connected with the affair as he pleased, as on his part he would obey him in everything he requested. The day then, having arrived, and the duke having ordered a spacious stand to be erected facing the court of the castle for the judges of the field and the ladies, mother and daughter - encouraged massive crowds to come from all the villages of the neighbourhood to see the unusual spectacle of the battle; nobody, dead or alive, in those areas having ever seen or heard of such a thing.

The first person to enter the field was the master of the ceremony, who surveyed and patrolled the whole ground to see that there was nothing unfair and nothing concealed to make the competitors stumble or fall; then the ladies entered and sat themselves, enveloped in veils covering their eyes. Shortly afterwards, accompanied by several trumpets and mounted on a powerful horse that threatened to crush the whole earth, the great servant Tosilos made his appearance on one side of the field with his visor down and enclosed in a suit of strong shining armour. The courageous combatant came well prepared by his master the duke as to how he was carry himself against the valiant Don Quixote of La Mancha; being warned that he must on no account kill him, but strive to evade the first encounter to avoid the risk of killing him, as he was sure to do if he struck him with full power. He crossed the courtyard slowly, and coming to where the ladies were, he stopped to look at her who demanded him for a husband; the officer of the field then summoned Don Quixote, who had already presented himself in the courtyard, and standing by the side of Tosilos he spoke to the ladies, and asked them if they consented that Don Quixote of La Mancha should battle on their behalf. They said they did, and that whatever he does on their behalf they declared rightly done, final and valid. By this time the duke and duchess had taken their places on a balcony overlooking the field, which was filled with a mass of people eager to see this dangerous and unparalleled encounter. The conditions of the combat were that if Don Quixote was the victor his antagonist was to marry the daughter of Dona Rodriguez; but if he was defeated his opponent was released from the promise that was claimed against him and from all other obligations to give satisfaction. The master of the ceremony positioned them, each on the spot where he was to stand. The drums beat, the sound of the trumpets filled the air, the earth trembled under their feet, the hearts of the gazing crowd were full of anxiety, some hoping for a happy result, some apprehensive of an unfortunate ending to the affair, and lastly, Don Quixote, calling with all his heart to God our Lord and to lady Dulcinea del Toboso, stood waiting for them to give the necessary signal for the commencement. The servant, however, was thinking of something very different; he only thought of what I am now going to mention.

It seems that as Tosilos stood contemplating his enemy (the daughter of Dona Rodriquez) she struck him as the most beautiful woman he had ever seen in his whole life; and the little blind boy who they commonly call Love had no desire to let the chance of triumphing over a servants heart slip, and adding it to the list of his conquests; and so, subtly approaching him unseen, he drove a dart two foot long into the poor servant's left side and pierced his heart thoroughly; which he was able to do quite easily, because Love is invisible, and comes in and goes out as he likes, without anyone calling him to account for what he does. Well then, when they gave the signal for the commencement the servant was in ecstasy, absorbed in the beauty of her whom he had already made mistress of his freedom, and so he paid no attention to the sound of the trumpet, unlike Don Quixote, who was off the instant he heard it, and, at the highest speed Rocinante was capable of, determined to meet his enemy.

His good aide Sancho was shouting loudly as he saw him start, "God guide you, cream and flower of Knighthood! God give you the victory, because you have righteousness on your side!"

But although Tosilos saw Don Quixote coming toward him he never moved from the spot where he was posted; and instead called loudly to the officer of the field and said, "Señor, is this not a battle to decide whether I marry or do not marry that lady?"

"Indeed," was the answer.

"Well then," the servant said, "I feel the pain of conscience, and I would put a-heavy burden on it if I were to proceed any further with the combat; I therefore declare that I am defeated, and that I am willing to marry the lady immediately."

The officer of the field was lost in amazement by the words of Tosilos; and as he was one of those who were privy to the arrangement of the affair he did not know what to say in reply. Don Quixote pulled up in mid-charge when he saw that his enemy was not coming forward to attack. The duke could not determine the reason why the battle did not continue; but the officer of the field ran to him to let him know what Tosilos had said, and he was amazed and extremely angry by it. In the meantime, Tosilos advanced to where Dona Rodriguez sat and said in a loud voice, "Señora, I am willing to marry your daughter, and I have no wish to obtain by fighting what I can obtain in peace and without any risk to my life."

The fearless Don Quixote heard him, and said, "As that is the case I am released and absolved from my obligation; let them marry, and as 'God our Lord has given her, may Saint Peter add his blessing.'"

The duke had now appeared in the courtyard of the castle, and going up to Tosilos he said to him, "Is it true, that you surrender, and that moved by conscience you wish to marry this lady?"

"It is, señor," replied Tosilos.

"And he does well to do so," said Sancho.

Meanwhile Tosilos was trying to remove his helmet, and he begged them to help him, as his power of breathing was failing him, and his head could not remain for so long shut in that confined space. They removed it as quickly as possible, and his features were revealed to the public's eye.

At this sight Dona Rodriguez and her daughter raised a mighty outcry, exclaiming, "This is a trick! This is a trick! They have put Tosilos, the duke's servant, in place of the real husband. Administer the justice of God and the King against such trickery and deceit!"

"Do not distress yourselves, ladies," said Don Quixote; "because this is not trickery or deceit; or if it is, it is not the duke who has done it, but those wicked enchanters who persecute me, and are jealous of me earning the glory of this victory, and so they have turned your husband's features into those of this person, who you say is a servant of the duke's; take my advice, and despite the malice of my enemies marry him, because no doubt he is the one you wish for as a husband."

When the duke heard this, all of his anger was beginning to morph into a burst of laughter, and he said, "The things that happen to Señor Don Quixote are so extraordinary that I am ready to believe this servant of mine is not one; but let us follow this plan; let us pause the marriage for, say, a fortnight, and let us keep this person who we are uncertain about in close confinement, and perhaps in the course of that time he might return to his original shape; because the malice which the enchanters do against Señor Don Quixote cannot last long, especially as it is of little advantage to them to practise these deceptions and transformations."

"Oh, señor," said Sancho, "those villains are very used to changing whatever concerns my master from one thing into another. A Knight that he conquered some time ago, called the Knight of the Mirrors, they turned into the shape of the graduate Samson Carrasco from our town and a great friend of ours; and they have turned my lady Dulcinea del Toboso into a common country girl; so I suspect this servant will have to live and die a servant."

Here Dona Rodriguez's daughter exclaimed, "Let him be whoever he is, this man that claims me for a wife; I am thankful to him, because I would rather be the lawful wife of a servant than the cheated mistress of a gentleman; although he who lied to me is nothing of the kind."

To be brief, all the talk and all that had happened ended in Tosilos being shut in confinement until it was seen how his transformation turned out. All praised Don Quixote as the victor, but a greater number of people were angry and disappointed as the combatants they had been anxiously waiting for had not smashed one another to pieces. The people dispersed, the duke and Don Quixote returned to the castle, they locked Tosilos away, Dona Rodriguez and her daughter remained perfectly contented when they saw that the affair will end in marriage, and Tosilos wanted nothing else.

CHAPTER 57

HOW DON QUIXOTE LEFT THE DUKE, AND WHAT FOLLOWED WITH THE WITTY AND SASSY ALTISIDORA, ONE OF THE DUCHESS'S LADIES

Don Quixote now felt it right to leave a life of such inactivity; because he believed that the world was missing his service by being shut up and inactive among the countless luxuries and enjoyments his hosts bestowed on him as a Knight, and he felt that he would have to give an account to heaven about the inactivity and seclusion; and so one day he asked the duke and duchess to grant him permission to make his departure. They gave it, showing at the same time that they were very sad he was leaving them.

The duchess gave his wife's letters to Sancho Panza, who shed tears over them, saying, "Who would have thought that the grand hopes of my wife Teresa Panza inspired by the news of my government would end in me going back to the wandering adventures of my master Don Quixote of La Mancha? Still I'm glad to see my Teresa behaving as she should when sending the chestnuts, because if she had not sent them I'd have been upset, and she'd have shown herself ungrateful. It is a comfort to me that they can't say that present was a bribe; because I was given the government before she sent them, and it's reasonable that those who have had good done for them should show their gratitude, even if it's only with something simple. After all I went into the government naked, and I come out of it naked; so I can say with a safe conscience - and it's no small matter 'I was born naked, naked I find myself, I neither lose, or gain.'"

Sancho expressed these thoughts aloud on the day of their departure, as Don Quixote, who made his appearance at an early hour in full armour in the courtyard of the castle. The whole household of the castle were watching him from the corridors, and the duke and duchess came out to see him. Sancho was mounted on his donkey, with his saddle bags full, and was extremely happy because the duke's head, the same that had acted the part of Trifaldi, had given him a little purse with two hundred gold coins to meet the necessary expenses of the journey, but Don Quixote knew nothing about this yet. While all were, as has been said, observing him, suddenly from among the ladies the bold and witty Altisidora raised her voice and said in a pathetic tone:

Give me your ear, cruel Knight,
Stop your course,
There is no need to leave tonight,
On that broken horse.

From what do you leap?
No dragon I am,
Not even a sheep,
But a soft young lamb.

You have rejected a lady,
What could have been between us,
Instead of a maybe,
I should be worshipped like Venus.

What worse can I call you?
Let the devil go with you! All evil befall you!

In your claws, ruthless thief,
You stole away,
The heart of a meek,
Loving maid of your prey,

Three handkerchiefs you stole,
Knickers a pair,
Tears from my eyes and the whole,
Situation unfair.

And the sighs all around,
Would burn to the ground,
Two thousand large Towns,
If that many were found.

What worse can I call you?
Let the devil go with you! All evil befall you!

May no mercy,
To Sancho be granted,
And your Dulcinea,
Be left forever enchanted.

May your falsehood to me
Find its punishment in her,
Because in my land the good,
Often pays for the sinner.

May your grandest adventures,
Bring you embarrassment,
May your joy be all dreams,
And your love fail, from its mismanagement.

What worse can I call you?
Let the devil go with you! All evil befall you!

May your name be banished,
For your conduct to ladies,
From Bilbao to Malaga,
From Murcia to Cadiz;

May all your cards be unlucky,
No King, Queen, jack, ace or joker,
Your hands contain nothing,
When you play poker.

When your calluses be cut,
May it be painful and quick,
When your teeth are falling out,
May the roots of them stick.

What worse can I call you?
Let the devil go with you! All evil befall you!

While the unhappy Altisidora was moaning in the above manner, Don Quixote stood staring at her; and without saying a word in reply to her he turned round to Sancho and said, "Sancho my friend, I ask you to swear on the life of your forefathers tell me the truth; have you by any chance taken the three handkerchiefs and a pair of knickers that this love-sick lady speaks of?"

To this Sancho answered, "I did take the handkerchiefs señor, but as for the knickers I did not.'"

The duchess was amazed at Altisidora's declaration; she knew that she was bold, lively, and brazen, but not as much to behave in this fashion; and not being prepared for the joke, her astonishment was all the greater. The duke had a mind to keep up the joke, so he said, "It does not seem right to me, sir Knight, that after having received the hospitality that has been offered you in this castle, you should have attempted to take three kerchiefs, not to say my maid's knickers. It shows a bad heart and does not match your reputation. Restore her knickers, or else I challenge you to combat, because I am not afraid of mischievous enchanters changing or altering my features as they changed those of who you encountered into those of my servant, Tosilos."

"God forbid," said Don Quixote, "that I should raise my sword against such a noble person from whom I have received such great favours. The handkerchiefs will be restored, as Sancho says he has them; but as for the knickers that is impossible, because I have not got them, neither has he; and if your maid will look in her hiding-places, I am sure she will find them. I have never been a thief, my lord duke, neither do I intend to be as long as I live, even if God decides not to have me in his custody. This lady by her own confession speaks as someone in love, for which I am not to blame, and therefore do not need to ask for a pardon, either from her or from you, who I ask to hold a better opinion of me, and once more to give me permission to continue my journey."

"And may God grant you a wonderful journey, Señor Don Quixote," said the duchess, "and that we may always hear good news about your deeds; God give you speed; because clearly, the longer you stay, the more you ignite the hearts of the ladies who observe you; and as for this one of mine, I will discipline her so she will not misbehave again, either with her eyes or with her words."

"One word and no more, valiant Don Quixote, that I ask you to hear," said Altisidora, "I beg your forgiveness about the theft of the knickers; because I have them on, and I have fallen into the same foolish error as he who went looking for his donkey while the whole time he was mounted on it."

"Didn't I say so?" said Sancho. "I am not one to hide thefts! If I wanted to deal in them, enough opportunities came to me during my government."

Don Quixote bowed his head, and saluted the duke and duchess and all the bystanders, and turning Rocinante around, Sancho following him on Dapple, he rode out of the castle, making his course for Saragossa.

CHAPTER 58

HOW ADVENTURES CAME TO DON QUIXOTE IN SUCH NUMBERS THAT THEY GAVE HIM NO TIME TO BREATHE

When Don Quixote saw himself in the open country, free, and relieved from the attention of Altisidora, he felt at ease, and in a renewed spirit to continue the pursuit of chivalry again; and turning to Sancho he said, "Freedom, Sancho, is one of the most precious gifts that heaven has given men; no treasure that the earth holds buried or the sea conceals can compare with it; because freedom, like honour, life should consist of; and on the other hand, captivity is the greatest evil that can happen to a man. I say this, Sancho, because you have seen the exuberance, the abundance we have enjoyed in the castle we have left; and among those banquets and cold beverages I felt as though I were dying of hunger, because I did not enjoy them with the same freedom as if they had been my own; because the sense of being under an obligation to return benefits and favours received is a restraint that captures the independence of the spirit. A man is happy when heaven has given him a piece of bread for which he is not bound to give thanks to anyone but heaven itself!"

"All you say," said Sancho, "does not consider the thanks we should give on our part for two hundred gold coins that the duke's head has given to me in a little purse which I carry next to my heart, like a warming plaster or comforter, to meet any circumstance which may arise; because we won't always find castles where they'll entertain us; now and then we'll drift from the roadside into inns where they'll beat us instead."

During this the Knight and aide were pursuing their journey, when, after they had gone a little more than half a mile, they noticed a dozen men dressed like labourers sitting on their coats on the grass of a green meadow eating their dinner. They had beside them what seemed to be white sheets concealing some objects under them. Don Quixote approached and greeting them courteously at first, but then he asked what it was the cloths covered.

"Señor," answered one of the party, "under these cloths are some carved images intended for a frame we are putting up in our village; we carry them covered up so they will not get dirty, and so they will not be broken by our shoulders when we carry them."

"With your permission," said Don Quixote, "I would like to see them; because images that are carried so carefully no doubt, must be fine ones."

"I would hope they are!" said the other; "let the money they cost speak for that; because as a matter of fact none of them have cost us less than fifty coins; and you may judge; wait a moment, and you will see with your own eyes;" and getting up from his dinner he went and uncovered the first image, which was one of Saint George on horseback with a snake twisting at his feet and the lance thrust down its throat with all the fierceness that is usually depicted. On seeing it Don Quixote said, "That Knight was one of the best Knights the army of heaven ever owned; he was called Don Saint George, and he was a strong defender of ladies. Let us see the next one."

The man uncovered it, and it was that of Saint Martin on his horse, sharing his coat with a beggar. The instant Don Quixote saw it he said, "This Knight was one of the Christian adventurers, but I believe he was generous rather than valiant, as you can perceive Sancho, by him sharing his coat with the beggar and giving him half of it; no doubt it was winter at the time, because otherwise he would have given him all of it, as he was so charitable."

"It was most likely," said Sancho, "that he knew the proverb that says, 'Giving and keeping require brains.'"

Don Quixote laughed, and asked them to take off the next cloth, which concealed the image of the patron saint of Spain sat on horseback, his sword stained with blood, trampling on Moors and treading on heads under his feet; and on seeing it Don Quixote exclaimed, "This is a Knight, from the group of Christ! This one is called Don Saint James the Moor slayer, one of the bravest saints and Knights the world ever had or heaven has now."

They then raised another cloth which covered Saint Paul falling from his horse, with all the details that are usually given in representations of him. When Don Quixote saw it rendered in such lifelike style that one would have said Christ was speaking and Paul answering, "This," he said, "during his time was the greatest enemy that the Church of God, our Lord had, and the greatest champion it will ever have; a Knight in life, a committed saint in death, a tireless labourer in the Lord's vineyard, a teacher of the irreverent, whose school was heaven, and whose instructor and master was Jesus Christ himself."

There were no more images, so Don Quixote asked them cover them up again, and said to those who had brought them, "I take it as a god sign, brothers, to have seen what I have today; because these saints and Knights were from the same profession as myself, which is the calling of arms; only there is this difference between them and me, that they were saints and fought with divine weapons, and I am a sinner and fight with human ones. They won heaven by force of arms, because heaven suffered violence; and I, so far, do not know what I have won for all my suffering; but if my lady Dulcinea del Toboso were to be released from hers, perhaps with better fortune and a mind restored to itself my steps might be directed in a path better than I am following at present."

"May God hear you and sin be deaf," said Sancho.

The men were filled with surprise, at both the figure and the words of Don Quixote, although they did not understand half of what he meant by them. They finished their dinner, put their images on their backs, and saying farewell to Don Quixote resumed their journey.

Sancho was amazed at the extent of his master's knowledge, as much as if he had never known him, because it seemed to him that there was no story or event in the world that he did not know about and had fixed in his memory, and he said to him, "In truth, master of mine, if this that has happened to us today is to be called an adventure, it has been one of the sweetest and most pleasant that has occurred during the whole course of our travels; we have come out of it without being beaten or troubled, we have not drawn a sword or hit the ground with our bodies, and we have not been left starving; bless God that he has let me see such a thing with my own eyes!"

"All you say is right, Sancho," said Don Quixote, "but remember all times are not the same and neither do they end equally; and these things the ill-mannered commonly call omens, which are not based on any normal reason, will be esteemed as happy accidents by the wise man. One of these believers in omens will get up in the morning, leave his house, and meet a priest, and, as if he had met a mythic creature, he will turn around and go home. Another spills the salt on his table, and believes evil has been spilt on his heart, as if nature was obliged to give us warnings of coming misfortunes with such trivial methods as these. The wise man and the Christian should not bother with what heaven decides to do. Scipio when going to Africa stumbled as he reached the shore; his soldiers took it as a bad omen; but he, touching the soil with his hands, exclaimed, 'You cannot escape me, Africa, because I hold you tight between my arms.' Therefore, Sancho, observing those images has been a happy occurrence to me."

"I can believe it," said Sancho; "but I would like you to tell me what the reason is that Spaniards, when they are about to battle, call on Saint James the Moorslayer, and say 'Santiago and close Spain!' Is Spain then, open, so that it is needed to be closed; what is the meaning of this?"

"You are very simple, Sancho," said Don Quixote; "God gave that great Knight of the Red Cross to Spain as its patron saint and protector, especially in those hard struggles the Spaniards had with the Moors; and therefore they call on him as their defender in all their battles; and in these he has been seen many times beating down, trampling, destroying and slaughtering the Moors in clear sight of all; and I could give you many examples of this fact recorded in truthful Spanish histories."

Sancho changed the subject, and said to his master, "I am amazed, señor, by the boldness of Altisidora, the duchess's lady; he who they call Love must have cruelly pierced and wounded her; they say he is a little blind rogue who, though blurry-eyes, or more properly speaking sightlessness, aims at a heart, however small it is, hits it and pierces it with his arrows. I have heard as well that the arrows of Love are blunt and their points are removed by modesty; but with this Altisidora, it seems they have been sharpened rather than made blunt."

"Bear in mind, Sancho," said Don Quixote, "that love is influenced by no reflection, recognises no restraint of reason, and consists of the same nature as death, it attacks the grand palaces of Kings and the humble cabins of shepherds alike; and when it takes entire possession of a heart, the first thing it does is to remove fear and shame from it; and so without shame Altisidora declared her passion, which provoked embarrassment in my mind rather than commiseration."

"What cruelty!" exclaimed Sancho; "unheard-of ingratitude! I can only say for myself that the very smallest loving word of hers would have subdued me and made me a slave. The devil! What a heart of marble, what a soul of cement! But I can't imagine what it is that this lady saw in you that could have conquered and captivated her so much. What brave figure was it, what bold manner, what grace, what attractiveness, which of these things by itself, or all together, could have made her fall in love with you? Because in truth many times I stop to look at you from the sole of your foot to the hair of your head, and I see something more to frighten than to make someone fall in love; actually I have heard that beauty is the first and main thing that excites love, and as you have none at all, I don't know what the poor lady fell in love with."

"Remember, Sancho," replied Don Quixote, "there are two sorts of beauty, one of the mind, the other of the body; that of the mind displays and exhibits itself in intelligence, modesty, honourable conduct, and generosity; and all of these qualities are possible and may exist in an ugly man; and when it is this sort of beauty and not that of the body that is the attraction, love is likely to occur suddenly and violently. I, Sancho, perceive clearly enough that I am not beautiful, but at the same time I know I am not repulsive; and it is enough for an honest man not to be a monster to be an object of love, if he possesses the endowments of mind I have mentioned."

While engaged in this conversation they were making their way through a wood, when suddenly, without expecting it, Don Quixote found himself caught in some green nets stretched from one tree to another; and unable to understand what it could be, he said to Sancho:

"Sancho, it strikes me this matter of nets will prove to be one of the strangest adventures imaginable. May I die if the enchanters that persecute me are not trying to entangle me in them and delay my journey, by way of revenge for my inflexibility towards Altisidora. Well then let me tell them that if these nets, instead of being green cord, were made of the hardest diamonds, or stronger than that which the jealous god entangled Venus and Mars, I would break them as easily as if they were made of cotton threads."

But just as he was about to move forward and break through, suddenly from among some trees two shepherdesses of superior beauty presented themselves to his sight. Their jackets were made of richly woven silver with gold embroidery. Their hair, in its golden brightness contending with the beams of the sun itself, fell loose upon their shoulders and was crowned with flowers twisted with green leaves; and their appearance was between fifteen to eighteen.

Sancho was filled with amazement, Don Quixote was fascinated, and stopped in his course to observe them, while all four were in a strange silence. Finally, one of the shepherdesses, first to speak, said to Don Quixote, "Stop, sir Knight, and do not break these nets; because they are not spread here to do you any harm, but only for our amusement; and as I know you will ask why they have been put there, and who we are, I will tell you in a few words. In a village about two miles from here, where there are many people of quality, it was agreed by a number of them to come with their wives, sons, daughters, neighbours and friends, and have a holiday here, which is one of the most pleasant places in the whole neighbourhood, and us ladies dressed ourselves as shepherdesses and the youths as shepherds. We have prepared two plays, one by the famous poet Garcilasso, the other by the most excellent Camoens, but we have not yet acted them. Yesterday was the first day of our arrival here; we have a few tents pitched among the trees on the bank of an ample stream that fertilises these meadows; last night we spread these nets in the trees here to catch the silly little birds that, frightened by the noise we make, may fly into them. If you would like to be our guest, señor, you will be welcomed politely, because here neither a care or a sorrow can enter."

She said no more, and Don Quixote answered, "In truth, fair lady, when Actaeon unexpectedly observed Diana bathing in the stream he could not have been more fascinated and in awe than I am at the sight of your beauty. I applaud your mode of entertainment, and thank you for the kindness of your invitation; and if I can serve you, you may command me with the full confidence of being obeyed, because my profession is none other than to show myself grateful, and ready to serve people of all conditions, but especially people of quality such as your appearance indicates; and if, instead of taking up, as they probably do, a small space, these nets took the whole surface of the globe, I would seek new worlds of which to pass through, so as not to break them; and so you may give some acceptance to this exaggerated language of mine, know that it is no other than Don Quixote of La Mancha that makes this declaration to you, if indeed such a name has reached your ears."

"Ah! friend of my soul," instantly exclaimed the other shepherdess, "what great good fortune has been granted to us! You see this gentleman we have in front of us? Well then let me tell you he is the most valiant, the most devoted and the most courteous gentleman in the whole world, unless a history of his achievements that has been printed and I have read is telling lies and deceiving us. I will bet that this good fellow who is with him is one Sancho Panza his aide, whose humour no one can equal."

"That's true," said Sancho; "I am that same aide you speak of, and this gentleman is my master Don Quixote of La Mancha, the same that's in the history that they talk about."

"Oh, my friend," said the other, "let us beg him to stay; because it will give our fathers and brothers infinite pleasure; I have also heard what you mentioned about the valour of one and the humour of the other; and what is more, they say he is the most consistent and loyal lover that was ever heard of, and that his lady is Dulcinea del Toboso, who all over Spain is awarded the height of beauty."

"And justly awarded," said Don Quixote, "unless, indeed, your unequalled beauty makes it a matter of doubt. But do not trouble yourselves, ladies, of begging me to stay, because the urgent calls of my profession do not allow me to take rest under any circumstances."

At this moment the brother of one of the two shepherdesses came, also in a shepherd's attire, and as richly dressed as they were. They told him that their companion was the valiant Don Quixote of La Mancha, and the other Sancho Panza his aide, of whom he already knew about from having read their history. The shepherd offered his services and begged them to accompany him to their tents, and Don Quixote finally gave way and complied.

Now the game had started, and the nets were filled with a variety of birds that deceived by the colour fell into the danger they were flying from. Over thirty people, all dressed as shepherds and shepherdesses gathered on the spot, and were informed who Don Quixote and his aide were, which delighted them, as they knew of him already through his history. They withdrew to the tents, where they found tables laid out, abundant and carefully furnished. They treated Don Quixote as a person of distinction, giving him the seat of honour, and all observed him, and were full of astonishment at the spectacle. Finally, the cloth was removed and Don Quixote with great composure raised his voice and said:

"One of the greatest sins that men are guilty of is: some will say pride, but I say it is ingratitude, going by the common saying that hell is full of ingrates. This sin, as far as it is in my power, I have endeavoured to avoid ever since I have enjoyed the faculty of reason; and if I am unable to repay good deeds that have been done for me by other deeds, I substitute the desire to do so; and if that is not enough I make them known publicly; because he who declares and makes known the good deeds done to him clearly would repay them by others if it were in his power to do so, and for the most part those who receive are inferiors of those who give. Therefore, God is superior to all because he is the supreme giver, and the offerings of men fall short by an infinite distance of being a full return for the gifts of God; but gratitude in some degree makes up for this deficiency and shortcoming. I therefore, am grateful for the favour that has been extended to me here, and unable to make a return in the same measure, restricted as I am by the narrow limits of my power, offer what I can and what I have to offer in my own way; so I declare that for two full days I will stay in the middle of this road leading to Saragossa, and maintain that these ladies disguised as shepherdesses, who are here present, are the fairest and most well-mannered ladies in the whole world, excluding the incomparable Dulcinea del Toboso, sole mistress of my thoughts."

On hearing this Sancho, who had been listening with great attention, cried out in a loud voice, "Is it possible there is anyone in the world who will dare to say and swear that this master of mine is a madman? Say it, gentle shepherds, is there a village priest, so wise or educated, who could say what my master has said is wrong; or is there a Knight, whatever status he may have as a man of valour, that could offer what my master has offered now?"

Don Quixote turned to Sancho, and with a face glowing with anger said to him, "Is it possible, Sancho, there is anyone in the whole world who will say you are not a fool, and without the embellishments of impudence and mischief? Who asked you to meddle in my affairs, or to inquire whether I am a wise man or a fool? Hold your tongue; do not say a word; saddle Rocinante if he is unsaddled; and let us go and put my offer into execution; because with what I am maintaining you may consider vanquished all who dare to question it;" and in a great rage, and showing his anger, he got up from his seat, leaving the company lost in amazement, and making them feel unsure whether they should regard him as a madman or a rational being. In the end, although they attempted to dissuade him from involving himself in such a challenge, assuring him they acknowledged his gratitude as fully established, and needing no other deed to be convinced of his valiant spirit, as those told in the history of his adventures were sufficient, still Don Quixote persisted; and mounted Rocinante, and bracing his shield on his arm and holding his lance, he posted himself in the middle of the road that was not far from the green meadow. Sancho followed on Dapple, together with all the members of the gathering, eager to see what would be the outcome of his proud and extraordinary proposal.

Don Quixote, then, placed himself in the middle of the road, and shouted words to this effect: "You travellers, Knights, aides, people on foot or on horseback, who pass this way or will pass in the course of the next two days! Know that Don Quixote, Knight of La Mancha, is posted here to maintain by arms that the beauty and courtesy preserved in the ladies that inhabit these meadows and woods surpass all on earth, putting aside the lady of my heart, Dulcinea del Toboso. Upon this, let him who is of the opposite opinion prepare for battle, because here I await him."

He repeated the same words twice, and twice they were unheard by any adventurer; but fate, that was guiding affairs for him, ordered it that shortly afterwards a crowd of men on horseback, leading a herd of bulls, appeared there on the road, many of them with lances in their hands, all riding in formation and in a great rush. As soon as those who were with Don Quixote had seen them they turned around and withdrew to some distance from the road, because they knew that if they stayed some harm might come to them; but Don Quixote with a fearless heart stood his ground, and Sancho Panza shielded himself behind Rocinante's back legs. The group came, and one of them who was at the front began shouting to Don Quixote, "Get out of the way, son of the devil, or these bulls will knock you to pieces!"

"Vile Herd!" returned Don Quixote, "Confess immediately villains, that what I have declared is true; or else you have to deal with me in combat."

The herdsman had no time to reply, and Don Quixote no time to get out of the way even if he wished; and so the fierce bulls, together with the crowd of herdsmen and others who were taking them to a village where they were to run the next day, passed over Don Quixote and over Sancho, Rocinante and Dapple, throwing them all to the earth and rolling them over on the ground. Sancho was left crushed, Don Quixote scared, Dapple beaten and Rocinante in a poor condition.

They all got up, however, finally, and Don Quixote in great rush, stumbling here and falling there, started running after the herd, shouting out,

"Hold! you wicked rabble, a single Knight awaits you, and he is not of the opinion of those who say, 'Flying from the enemy makes a bridge of silver.'" The retreating party in their haste, however, did not stop, or heed his threats. Finally, weariness brought Don Quixote to a stop, and more enraged than avenged he sat down on the road to wait until Sancho, Rocinante and Dapple came. When they reached him, the master and man mounted again, and without going back to say goodbye to those who had hosted them, and more in humiliation than contentment, they continued their journey.

CHAPTER 59

THE STRANGE THING, WHICH MAY BE REGARDED AS AN ADVENTURE, THAT HAPPENED DON QUIXOTE

Don Quixote and Sancho discovered a spring to relieve them of their thirst and fatigue due to the impolite behaviour of the bulls, and by the side of this, having let Dapple and Rocinante loose, the lonely pair, master and man, sat themselves. Sancho searched through the store of his saddle-bags; Don Quixote rinsed his mouth and bathed his face, and through this cooling process his flagging energies were revived. Out of pure anger he remained without eating, and out of pure politeness Sancho did not attempt to touch any of the food in front of him, but instead waited for his master to act as the taster. Seeing, however, that, absorbed in thought, he was forgetting to carry the bread to his mouth, and never said a word, he began to put away the bread and cheese.

"Eat, Sancho my friend," said Don Quixote; "support life, which is more appropriate for you than for me, and leave me to die by the pain of my thoughts and pressure of my misfortune. I was born, Sancho, to live dying, and you to die eating; and to prove the truth of what I say, look at me, printed in histories, famous for arms, courteous in behaviour, honoured by Princes, pursued by ladies; and after all, when I looked forward to honours, triumphs, and crowns, won and earned by my valiant deeds, I have this morning seen myself trampled on, kicked, and crushed by the feet of unclean filthy animals. This thought robs me of all appetite for food; so much so that I may let myself die of hunger, the cruellest death of all deaths."

"So then," said Sancho, chewing the whole time, "you do not agree with the proverb that says, 'Let a man die, but let him die with a full belly.' I, at any rate, have no intention to kill myself; far from that, I intend to do as the shoemaker does, who stretches the leather with his teeth until he makes it reach as far as he wants. I'll stretch out my life by eating until it reaches the end heaven has determined for it; and let me tell you, señor, there's no greater foolishness than to think of dying of misery as you do; take my advice, and after eating lie down and sleep a bit on this green grass, and you will see that when you wake up you'll feel better."

Don Quixote did as recommended, because it struck him that Sancho's reasoning was more like a philosopher's than a fool's, and he said, "Sancho, if you will do for me what I am going to tell you, my mind would be more relaxed and my heaviness of heart not so great; and it is this: to go away little while I am sleeping in accordance with your advice, and, bare your buttocks in the air, and give yourself three or four hundred whips with Rocinante's reins, on account of the three thousand or so you are to give yourself for the disenchantment of Dulcinea; because it is a great pity that the poor lady should be left enchanted through your carelessness and negligence."

"There is a good deal to be said on that point," said Sancho; "let us both go to sleep now, and after that, God has already declared what will happen. Let me tell you that for a man to whip himself is a hard thing, especially if its falls on an under-nourished and poorly-fed body. Let my lady Dulcinea be patient, and when she is least expecting it, she will see me make a start with the whipping, and 'until death it's all life;' I mean that I have life left in me, and the desire to do what I have promised."

Don Quixote thanked him, and ate a little, and Sancho ate a lot, and then they both laid down to sleep, leaving those two inseparable friends, Rocinante and Dapple, to their own free will and to feed themselves unrestrained on the abundant grass with which the meadow was covered. They woke up rather late, mounted again and resumed their journey, pushing on to reach an inn which was in sight, apparently a mile away. I say an inn, because Don Quixote called it so, contrary to his usual practice of calling all inns castles. They reached it, and asked the landlord if they could stay there. He said yes, with as much comfort and as good welcoming as they could find in Saragossa. They dismounted, and Sancho stored away his saddle-bags in a room of which the landlord gave him the key to. He took the animals to the stable, fed them, and came back to see what orders Don Quixote, who was sat on a bench at the door, had for him, giving special thanks to heaven that this inn had not been taken for a castle by his master.

Dinner-time came, and they went to the dining room, and Sancho asked the landlord what he had to give them to eat. To this the landlord replied whatever he desired; he only had to ask what he wanted; because the inn was always stocked with birds of the air, fowl of the earth and fish of the sea.

"There's no need for all that," said Sancho; "if they'll roast us a couple of chickens we'll be satisfied, because my master is delicate and eats little, and I'm not over and above insatiable."

The landlord replied he had no chickens, because they had been stolen.

"Well then," said Sancho, "let señor landlord tell them to roast any bird, make it a tender one."

"A bird!" said the landlord; "impossible and in truth only yesterday I sent over fifty to the city to sell; but apart from birds ask for something else."

"In that case," said Sancho, "you will not be without veal."

"Right now," said the landlord, "there's none in the house, it's all finished; but next week there will be enough and more to spare."

"What good that does us," said Sancho; "I'll lay a bet that all these short-comings are going to end up in plenty of bacon and eggs."

"By God," said the landlord, "my guest's wits must be dull; I tell him I have no birds or veal, and he wants me to have eggs! Ask for something else, if you like, and don't ask for birds again."

"God!" said Sancho, "let's settle the matter; tell me what you have, and let us have no more words about it."

"In truth, señor guest," said the landlord, "all I have is a couple of cow-heels like calves' feet, or a couple of calves' feet like cow-heels; they are boiled with chick-peas, onions, and bacon, and at this moment they are saying 'Come eat me, come eat me."

"I mark them as mine right now," said Sancho; "let nobody touch them; I'll pay more for them than anyone else, because I could not wish for anything more; and I don't care a bit whether they are feet or heels."

"Nobody will touch them," said the landlord; "because the other guests I have, being people of high quality, brought their own cook, caterer and food with them."

"If you speak about people of quality," said Sancho, "there's nobody more so than my master; but the calling he follows does not allow for much food to store; we lay ourselves down in the middle of a meadow, and fill ourselves with acorns or apples."

Sancho ended his conversation with the landlord, not caring to carry it any further by answering him; because he had already asked him what calling or what profession it was his master followed. And so, the landlord brought in the stew, and Sancho sat himself down very eagerly to eat it.

It seemed that coming from another room, which was next theirs, with nothing but a thin partition to separate it, the following words could be overheard:

"Señor Don Jeronimo, while they are having dinner, let us read another chapter of the Second Part of 'Don Quixote of La Mancha.'"

The instant Don Quixote heard his own name, he jumped to his feet and listened with open ears to catch what they said about him, and Don Jeronimo who had been addressed said in reply, "Why do you want us to read that absurd stuff, Don Juan, when it is impossible for anyone who has read the First Part of the history of 'Don Quixote of La Mancha' to take any pleasure in reading this Second Part?"

"Despite that," said Don Juan, "we will do well to read it, because there is no book so bad that doesn't have something good in it. What displeases me most about it is, that it represents Don Quixote as now cured of his love for Dulcinea del Toboso."

On hearing this Don Quixote, full of anger and outrage, raised his voice and said, "Whoever you may be who says that Don Quixote of La Mancha has forgotten or can forget Dulcinea del Toboso, I will teach you with arms that what you say is very far from the truth; because the incomparable Dulcinea del Toboso cannot be forgotten, and neither can forgetfulness have a place in Don Quixote; his motto is constancy, and his profession to maintain the same with his life and never deviate."

"Who is this that answers us?" said those in the next room.

"Who else could it be," said Sancho, "but Don Quixote of La Mancha himself, who will prove all he has said and all he will say; because pledges don't trouble a good payer."

Sancho had hardly said these words when two gentlemen, entered the room, and one of them, throwing his arms round Don Quixote's neck, said to him,

"Your appearance cannot leave any question as to your name, neither can your name fail to identify your appearance; unquestionably, señor, you are the real Don Quixote of La Mancha, pinnacle and star of Knighthood, despite and in defiance of he who has sought to shame your name and bring to nothing your achievements, as the author of this book which I here present to you has done;" and with this he placed a book which his companion carried, into the hands of Don Quixote, who took it, and without replying began to run his eyes over it; but he returned it saying: "In the little I have seen, I have discovered three things in this author that deserve to be censured. The first is some words that I have read in the preface; the next that the language is incorrect, because sometimes he writes without articles; and the third, which above all proves him to be ignorant, is that he departs from the truth in the most important part of the history, because here he says that my aide Sancho Panza's wife is called Mari Gutierrez, when she is called Teresa Panza; and when a man makes an error on such an important point as this there is good reason to fear that he makes errors on every other point in the history."

"A nice sort of historian, indeed!" exclaimed Sancho; "he must know a lot about our affairs when he calls my wife Teresa Panza, Mari Gutierrez; take the book again, señor, and see if I am in it and if he has changed my name."

"From your talk, friend," said Don Jeronimo, "no doubt you are Sancho Panza, Señor Don Quixote's aide."

"Sancho, I am," said Sancho; "and I'm proud of it."

"Believe, then," said the gentleman, "this new author does not handle you with the decency that you display in person; he makes you out to be an overeater and a fool, and extremely stupid, a very different being from the Sancho described in the First Part of your master's history."

"God forgive him," said Sancho; "he might have put me to one side without researching my history to focus on my master Don Quixote'"

The two gentlemen asked Don Quixote to come into their room and have dinner with them, as they knew very well there was nothing in that inn fit for someone of his kind. Don Quixote, who was always polite, yielded to their request and ate with them. Sancho stayed behind with the stew. and with full delegated authority sat himself at the head of the table, and the landlord sat down with him, because he was no less fond of cow-heels and calves' feet than Sancho was.

While at dinner Don Juan asked Don Quixote what news he had about lady Dulcinea del Toboso, was she married, did she have children, or was she still in her modesty preserving her delicacy, and cherishing the memory of the tender passion of Señor Don Quixote?

To this he replied, "Dulcinea is still modest, and my passion more firmly rooted than ever, however her beauty has been transformed into that of a foul country girl;" and then he proceeded to give them a full and particular account of the enchantment of Dulcinea, and of what had happened to him in the cave of

Montesinos, together with what the sage Merlin had prescribed for her disenchantment, namely the whipping of Sancho.

The amusement the two gentlemen derived from hearing Don Quixote recount the strange incidents of his history was exceedingly great; and if they were amazed by his absurdities they were equally amazed by the elegant style in which he delivered them. On one hand they regarded him as a man of intelligence and sense, and on the other he seemed to them a madman and fool, and they could not make up their minds whereabouts between wisdom and foolishness they should place him.

Sancho having finished his dinner, left the landlord and went to the room where his master was, and as he came in he said, "May I die, sirs, if the author of this book you have does not encourage the wrong view of me; as he calls me glutton (according to what you say) he might as well call me drunkard too."

"But he does," said Don Jeronimo; "I cannot remember, however, in what way, although I know his words are offensive, and what is more, false, as I can see plainly by the appearance of the worthy Sancho in front of me."

"Believe me," said Sancho, "the Sancho and the Don Quixote of this history are different people from those that appear in the one Cide Hamete Benengeli wrote; my master courageous, wise, and true in love, and I simple, but neither a glutton or a drunkard."

"I believe it," said Don Juan; "and if it were possible, an order should be issued that no one should deal with anything relating to Don Quixote, except his original author; just as Alexander commanded that no one should paint his portrait except Apelles."

"Let whoever paint me," said Don Quixote; "but as long as he does not abuse me; because my patience will often break down when I find myself insulted."

"No offence can be offered to you Señor Don Quixote," said Don Juan, "that you will not be able to avenge, if you do not ward it off with the shield of your patience, which, I take it, is great and strong."

A considerable portion of the night passed in conversation of this sort, and although Don Juan wished Don Quixote to read more of the book to see what it was all about, he was not to be persuaded, saying that he treated it as read already and declared it completely silly; and, if by any chance its author's ears should find out that he had it in his hand, he did not want to flatter him with the idea that he had read it; and also because our thoughts, and furthermore our eyes, should keep themselves detached from what is obscene and filthy.

They asked him where he was going to direct his steps. He replied, to Saragossa, to take part in the contests which were held in the city each year. Don Juan told him that the new history described how Don Quixote, took part there in the ring, completely lacking inventiveness, dressed poorly, although rich in foolishness.

"For that very reason," said Don Quixote, "I will not go to Saragossa; and that means I will expose to the world the lie of this new history writer, and people will see that I am not the Don Quixote he speaks of."

"That's quite right," said Don Jeronimo; "and there are other contests in Barcelona in which Señor Don Quixote may display his expertise."

"That's what I intend to do," said Don Quixote; "and now it is time, I ask your permission to allow me to leave and go to bed, and to count me as one of your greatest friends."

"And me too," said Sancho; "maybe I'll be good for something."

With this they said goodbye to each other, and Don Quixote and Sancho went to their room, leaving Don Juan and Don Jeronimo amazed to see the mix of his good sense and his craziness; and they felt thoroughly convinced that this pair, and not those their Aragonese author described, were the genuine Don Quixote and Sancho.

Don Quixote said goodnight to his hosts by knocking on the partition of the other room. The following day Sancho paid the landlord well, and recommended that he either say less about the food in his inn or to keep it better stocked.

CHAPTER 60

WHAT HAPPENED TO DON QUIXOTE ON HIS WAY TO BARCELONA

A new morning gave the promise of a cool day as Don Quixote left the inn, first of all taking care to determine the most direct road to Barcelona without going anywhere near Saragossa; he was so eager to make out this new historian, who they said abused him, to be a liar. Nothing worthy of being recorded happened to him for six days, at the end of which, having turned off the road, he was taken over by night in a wood of oak or cork trees; because on this point Cide Hamete is not as precise as he usually is on other matters.

Master and man dismounted from their animals, and as soon as they had settled themselves at the base of the trees, Sancho, who had eaten a good afternoon meal that day, let himself pass through the gates of sleep. But Don Quixote, was kept awake by his thoughts far more than hunger, and could not close his eyes, and was lost in thought going back and forth through all sorts of places. At one moment it seemed to him that he was in the cave of Montesinos and saw Dulcinea, transformed into a country girl, jumping on her donkey; and then the words of the sage Merlin were in his ears, giving the conditions to be observed and the exertions to be made for her disenchantment. He lost all patience when he considered the laziness and lack of compassion from his aide Sancho; because to the best of his belief he had only given himself five lashes, a worthless number and disproportioned to the number required. At this thought he felt such anger that he reasoned the matter as this: "If Alexander the Great cut the Gordian knot, saying, 'To cut is the same thing as to untie,' and yet did not fail to become a lord paramount of all Asia, nothing more or less could happen now with Dulcinea's disenchantment if I hit Sancho against his will; because, if it is a condition of the remedy that Sancho receives three thousand or so lashes, what does it matter to me whether he inflicts them himself, or someone else does, when the essential point is that he receives them?"

With this idea he went over to Sancho, having first taken Rocinante's reins and held them in a way to be able to flog him with them, but as soon as he approached him Sancho woke up in his full senses and shouted, "What is this?

"It is I," said Don Quixote, "and I come to repay the debt of your shortcomings and relieve my own distresses; I come to whip you, Sancho, and wipe off a portion of the debt you have left. Dulcinea is suffering, and you are living on regardless, and I am dying of deferred hope; therefore, accept this with good will, because here in this remote location, I will give you at least two thousand lashes."

"Not at all," said Sancho; "you must keep quiet, or else God and the deaf will hear us; the lashes I agreed to must be voluntary and not forced on me, and right now I have no desire to whip myself; it is enough if I give you my word to flog myself when I am in the right mood."

"It will not do to leave it to your mood, Sancho," said Don Quixote, "because you lack heart and, although you are a clown, soft of flesh;" and at the same time he struggled to tie him.

Seeing this Sancho got up, and grappling with his master he held him with all his might, tripping him with his heel, and putting him on the ground on his back, and pressing his right knee on his chest held his hands so that he could not move and barely breathe.

"Traitor!" exclaimed Don Quixote. "You dare to rebel against your master and natural lord? You rise against one who gives you his bread?"

"I would not put down a King," said Sancho; "I only stand up for myself as my own lord; if you promise to be quiet, and not to try whip me, I'll let you go free and unrestricted; if not...

Before Sancho had finished speaking Don Quixote gave his promise, and swore on the life of his thoughts not to touch so much as a hair on his head, and leave him entirely free and to his own discretion to whip himself whenever he pleased. Sancho got up and went some distance from the spot, but as he was about to place himself leaning against another tree he felt something touch his head, and raising his hands he encountered somebody's feet with shoes on them. He shivered with fear and ran to another tree, where the very same thing happened to him, and he began shouting, calling for Don Quixote to come and protect him. Don Quixote came, and asked him what had happened to him, and what he was afraid of. Sancho replied that all the trees were full of men's feet and legs. Don Quixote felt them, and guessed what it was, and said to Sancho, "You have nothing to be afraid of, because these feet and legs that you feel no doubt belong to some criminals that have been hanged from these trees; because the authorities here hang twenty or thirty of them at a time when they catch them; therefore, in my estimation we must be near Barcelona;" and it was, in fact, as he suggested; they looked up and saw that the fruit hanging on those trees were criminals' bodies.

And now day came; and if the dead criminals had scared them, their hearts were no less troubled by forty living ones, who all of a sudden surrounded them, and in the Catalan tongue asked them stand and wait until their captain came. Don Quixote was on foot with his horse untied and his lance leaning against a tree, and in short completely defenceless; therefore, he thought it was best to fold his arms and bow his head and reserve himself for a more favourable occasion and opportunity. The robbers rushed to search Dapple, and did not leave a single thing out of all he carried in the saddle-bags; and lucky for Sancho that the duke's coins and those he brought from home were in belt he wore underneath around his chest; despite that these criminals would have stripped him, and even looked to see what he had hidden between his skin and flesh. At that moment their captain arrived, who was about thirty-four years old, strongly built, above the average height, with a strict manner and an olive complexion. He was mounted on a powerful horse, and had four guns on his waist. He saw that his aides were about to shoot at Sancho Panza, but he ordered them not to and was immediately obeyed. He went over to see the lance leaning against the tree, the shield on the ground, and the unhappy Don Quixote, with the saddest face that sadness itself could produce; and going up to him he said, "Do not be so down, good man, because you have not fallen into the path of any inhuman hands, but into Roque's, those which are more merciful than cruel."

"The cause of my sadness," returned Don Quixote, "is not that I have fallen into your hands, valiant Roque, whose fame on earth is no doubt renowned, but that my carelessness has been so great that your soldiers caught me unarmed, when it is my duty, according to the rules of Knighthood which I follow, to always be alert and at all times on the lookout; because let me tell you, great Roque, had they found me on my horse, with my lance and shield, it would not have been so easy for them to subdue me, because I am Don Quixote of La Mancha, who has filled the whole world with his achievements."

Roque perceived that Don Quixote's weakness was more similar to madness than boasting; and although he had sometimes heard him spoken about, he never regarded the things attributed to him as true, and he could not persuade himself that such eccentricity could become dominant in the heart of man; he was extremely glad, therefore, to meet him and test in close range what he had heard of him at a distance; so he said to him, "Do not despair, valiant Knight, or regard the position you are in as bad; it may be that your crooked fortune will make itself straight; because by strange indirect ways, heaven which is mysterious and incomprehensible to man, raises the fallen and makes the rich poor."

Don Quixote was about to thank him, when they heard a noise from behind them which sounded like horses; there was, however, only one, coming at a furious pace with a youth mounted, about twenty years of age, covered in green edged with gold and loose trousers, with a slanted hat, tight-fitting polished boots, a dagger and sword, and in his hand a musket, and a pair of guns on his waist. Roque turned round at the noise and observed this figure, which coming closer addressed him, "I came in search of you, valiant Roque, to find in you a remedy, if not, at least relief for my misfortune; and not to keep you in suspense, because I see you do not recognise me, I will tell you who I am; I am Claudia Jeronima, the daughter of Simon Forte, your good friend, and special enemy of Clauquel Torrellas, who is yours as well from the group opposed to you. You know that Torrellas has a son who is called, Don Vicente Torrellas. Well, to cut the story short, I will tell you in a few words what this youth has done to me. He saw me, he wanted me, I listened to him, and, unknown to my father, I loved him; because there is no woman, however secluded or guarded she may be, who will not have opportunities to follow her impulses. In a word, he pledged himself to be mine, and I promised to be his, without taking matters any further. Yesterday I learned that, forgetful of his pledge to me, he was about to marry another, and that this morning he was going to pledge his loyalty to her, intelligence which overwhelmed and infuriated me. As my father was not at home I was able to wear this costume you see, and urging my horse to rush I overtook Don Vicente about a mile from here, and without waiting to hear excuses I fired this musket at him, and these two pistols, and to the best of my belief I must have stuck more than two bullets in his body, opening doors to let my honour flow free, enveloped in his blood. I left him there in the hands of his servants, who did not dare and were not able to interfere in his defence, and I come to seek from you a safe escort into France, where I have relatives with whom I can live; and also to beg you to protect my father, so that Don Vicente's numerous relatives will not attempt to seek vengeance on him."

Roque, filled with admiration by the bravery, spirit, figure, and adventure of the fair Claudia, said to her, "Come, Señorita, let us go and see if your enemy is dead; and then we will consider what will be best." Don Quixote, who had been listening to what Claudia and Roque said, replied to her, "Nobody trouble himself with the defence of this lady, because I take it upon myself. Give me my horse and weapons, and wait for me here; I will go in search of this Knight, and dead or alive I will make him keep his word to such a great beauty."

"Nobody need have any doubt about that," said Sancho, "because my master has a flair for matchmaking; it's not been many days since he forced another man to marry, who in the same way backed out of his promise to another lady; and if it had not been for his persecutors the enchanters changing the man's proper shape into a servant's, the lady would not be one right now."

Roque, who was paying more attention to Claudia's adventure than to the words of master or man, did not hear them; and ordering his aides to restore to Sancho everything they had taken from Dapple, he directed them to return to the place where they had slept during the night, and then he left with Claudia at full speed in search of the wounded or dead Don Vicente. They reached the spot where Claudia shot him, but found nothing there, except freshly spilt blood; looking all round, however, they observed some people on the slope of a hill above them, and concluded, as indeed it proved to be, that it was Don Vicente, whom either dead or alive, his servants were carrying to attend to his wounds or to bury him. They rushed to overtake them, which, as the group moved slowly, they were able to do with ease. They found Don Vicente in the arms of his servants, who he was asking in a broken feeble voice to leave him there to die, as the pain of his wounds would not allow him to go any further. Claudia and Roque jumped off their horses and advanced towards him; the servants were restrained by the appearance of Roque, and Claudia was moved by the sight of Don Vicente, and going up to him half caringly, half seriously, she held his hand and said to him, "Had you given me this hand according to our promise, this would have never happened."

The wounded gentleman opened his closed eyes, and recognising Claudia said, "I see clearly, mistaken lady, that it is you that has killed me, a punishment not deserved by my feelings towards you, because I never meant to, and neither could I, wrong you in thought or deed."

"It is not true, then," said Claudia, "that you were going this morning to marry Leonora the daughter of the rich Balvastro?"

"Certainly not," replied Don Vicente; "sad fortune must have carried that information to you to drive you in jealousy to take my life; and to assure you of this, hold my hands and take me for your husband if you will; I have no better satisfaction to offer you for the wrong you thought you had received from me."

Claudia squeezed his hands, as her own heart was squeezed so tight that she lay fainting on the bleeding chest of Don Vicente, whom a spasm of death seized at the same instant. Roque was in confusion and did not know what to do; the servants ran to get water, and returning with some, sprinkle their faces with it. Claudia recovered from her faint, but Don Vicente did not recover from the spasm that had overtaken him, because his life had come to an end. On perceiving this, Claudia, when she had convinced herself that her beloved husband was no more, filled the air with her sighs and made the heavens hear her cries; she tore her hair out and scattered it in the wind, she beat her face with her hands and showed all the signs of grief and sorrow that could be observed to come from a distressed heart. "Cruel, reckless woman!" she cried, "how easily you moved to carry out such a wicked thought! Furious force of jealousy, to what desperate lengths you lead those that give you room to live in their chests! My husband, whose unhappy fate has taken you from the bed of marriage to the grave!"

The cries of Claudia were so intense and so sad that they drew tears from Roque's eyes, never before used in this way, as no occasion had ever drawn tears from them. The servants cried, Claudia fainted again and again, and the whole place seemed like a field of sorrow and a home of misfortune. In the end Roque directed Don Vicente's servants to carry his body to his father's village, which was close by, for the burial. Claudia told him she intended to go to a monastery, of which her aunty was the head of, where she would spend the rest of her life with a better and everlasting husband - God. He applauded her religious disposition, and offered to accompany her to wherever she wished, and to protect her father against the relatives of Don Vicente and the whole world, if they sought to injure him. Claudia would not on any account allow him to accompany her; and thanking him for his offers as well as she could, left him with tears in her eyes. The servants of Don Vicente carried his body, and Roque returned to his companions, and here ended the love of Claudia Jeronima; but is it any wonder, when it was the unbeatable and cruel might of jealousy that wove the web of her sad story?

Roque found his aides in the place which he had sent them to, and Don Quixote on Rocinante among them delivering a lecture to them in which he urged them to give up a mode of life so full of danger to their souls as well as their bodies; but as most of them were criminals, rough lawless men, his speech did not make much of an impression on them. Roque came and asked Sancho if his men had returned and restored to him the treasure and jewels they had taken from Dapple. Sancho said they had, but that three handkerchiefs that were worth three cities were missing.

"What are you talking about?" said one of the bystanders; "I have got them, and they are not worth three pence."

"That is true," said Don Quixote; "but my aide values them at the rate he says, as he was given them by me."

Roque ordered them to be returned immediately; and making his men form a line he directed all the clothing, jewellery, and money that they had stolen recently to be produced; and making a rough valuation, he divided all of it among the whole group so equally and carefully, that in no case did he exceed or fall short of strict distributive justice.

When this had been done, and all were left satisfied, Roque said to Don Quixote, "If this accuracy were not followed, there would be no living with these men."

Sancho remarked, "From what I have seen here, justice is such a good thing that there is no point to be without it, even among thieves."

One of the aides heard this, and raising the butt-end of his gun would have no doubt broken Sancho's head with it had Roque not called out to him to put his hand down. Sancho was frightened out of his mind, and vowed not to open his mouth as long as he was in the company of these people.

At this moment one or two of those aides who were posted as lookouts on the roads, to watch who came along and report to their chief, came and said, "Señor, there is a large group of people not far away coming along the road to Barcelona."

To which Roque replied, "Have you determined whether they are the sort that are after us, or the sort we are after?"

"The sort we are after," said the aide.

"Well then, go," said Roque, "and bring them to me immediately without letting any of them escape."

They obeyed, and Don Quixote, Sancho, and Roque, left by themselves, waited to see who the aides brought back, and while they were waiting Roque said to Don Quixote, "Our type of life must seem strange to Señor Don Quixote, strange adventures, strange incidents, and all full of danger; because in truth I must admit there is no mode of life more restless or anxious than this. What led me into it was a certain thirst for vengeance, which is strong enough to disturb the quietest of hearts. I am by nature soft-hearted and kind, but, as I said, the desire to seek revenge for a wrong that was done to me overturned all my better impulses and keeps me living this way of life despite what my conscience tells me; and as one depth calls on another, and one sin another sin, revenge links together with the next, and I have now taken it upon myself not only my own but those of others: it pleases God, however, that, although I see myself in this maze of entanglements, I do not lose the hope of escaping from it and reaching a safe port."

Don Quixote was amazed to hear Roque say such excellent and fair thoughts, because he did not think that among those who followed this trade, robbing and murdering, there could be anyone capable of a virtuous thought, and he said in reply, "Señor Roque, the beginning of health lies in knowing the disease and in the sick man's willingness to take the medicines which the physician prescribes; you are sick, you know what afflicts you, and heaven, or more properly speaking God, who is our physician, will administer medicines that will cure you, and cure gradually, and not all of a sudden or by a miracle; besides, sinners of discernment are nearer correction than those who are fools; and as you have shown good sense in your remarks, all you have to do is to keep a good heart and trust that the weakness of your conscience will be strengthened. And if you have any desire to shorten the journey and put yourself easily on the path of redemption, come with me, and I will show you how to become a Knight, a calling where so many hardships and mishaps are encountered that if they are considered as atonement they will place you in heaven in an instant."

Roque laughed at Don Quixote's appeal, and changing the conversation he relayed the tragic affair of Claudia Jeronima, at which Sancho was extremely saddened; because he had not found the young lady's beauty, self-assurance, and spirit at all bad.

And now the aides returned, bringing with them two gentlemen on horseback, two pilgrims on foot, and a coach full of women with six servants on foot and on horseback, and a couple of men on donkeys whom the gentlemen had with them. The aides made a ring round them, both the victors and vanquished maintaining a profound silence, waiting for the great Roque to speak. He asked the gentlemen who they were, where they were going, and what money they carried with them; "Señor," replied one of them, "we are two captains of Spanish infantry; our comrades are in Naples, and we are on our way to embark on four ships which they say are at Barcelona heading for Sicily; and we have about two or three hundred coins, with which we are, according to us, rich and contented, because a soldier's poverty does not allow a more extensive supply."

Roque asked the pilgrims the same questions he had put to the captains, and was answered that they were going to take ship heading for Rome, and that between them they have about sixty coins. He asked also who was in the coach, where they were going and what money they had, and one of the men on horseback replied, "Those in the coach are my lady Dona Guiomar de Quinones, wife to the adviser of the Vicar in Naples, her little daughter, a maid and six servants are in attendance for her, and the money we have amounts to six hundred coins."

"So then," said Roque, "we have got here nine hundred and sixty coins; my soldiers require sixty; how much there goes to each, because I am a bad mathematician." As soon as the robbers heard this they shouted "Long life to Roque, despite those that seek his ruin!"

The captains showed the concern they felt, the advisor's lady was sad, and the pilgrims did not enjoy seeing their property confiscated. Roque kept them in suspense in this way for a while; but he had no desire to prolong their distress, which could be seen a mile away, and turning to the captains he said,

"Sirs, will you kindly lend me sixty coins, and you, the advisor's wife eighty, to satisfy this group that follows me, and then you may proceed on your journey, free and unhindered, with a safe-passage which I will give you, so that if you come across any other groups of mine that I have scattered around, they will do you no harm; because I have no intention of injuring soldiers, or to any woman, especially one of quality."

The captains gave expressions of gratitude and thanked Roque for his courtesy and generosity. Señora Dona Guiomar de Quinones wanted to throw herself out of the coach to kiss the feet and hands of the great Roque, but he would not allow it; far from it, he begged her to forgive him for the wrong he had done to her under the pressure of the inevitable requirements of his unfortunate calling. The advisor's lady ordered one of her servants to give the eighty coins that had been asked from her, because the captains had already paid their sixty. The pilgrims were about to give the whole of their money, but Roque asked them to keep quiet, and turning to his men he said, "Out of these coins which go to each man, twenty extra remain; let ten be given to these pilgrims, and the other ten to this worthy aide so he may be able to speak favourably about this adventure;" and then having writing materials, with which he always had with him, he gave them in writing a letter of safe-passage to the leaders of the group; and saying farewell let them go free and filled with admiration at his nobility, his generous disposition, and his unusual conduct, and were persuaded to regard him as an Alexander the Great rather than a notorious robber.

One of the aides observed the mixture of generousness and Catalan, "This captain of ours would make a better priest than highwayman; if he wants to be so generous again, let it be with his own property and not ours."

The unlucky aide was overheard by Roque, and drawing his sword almost split his head in two, saying, "That is the way I punish disrespectful impertinent men." They were all shocked, and none of them dared to say a word, such was the respect they paid him. Roque then withdrew to one side and wrote a letter to a friend of his in Barcelona, telling him that the famous Don Quixote of La Mancha, the Knight of whom there was so much talk, was with him, and was, he assured him, the funniest and wisest man in the whole world; and that in four days from that date, that is to say, on Saint John the Baptist's Day, he was going to send him in full armour mounted on his horse Rocinante, together with his aide Sancho on a donkey, to the middle of the city; and asking him to give notice of this to his friends the Niarros, so they could amuse themselves with him. He also said, that he wishes his enemies the Cadells could be deprived of this pleasure; but that was impossible, because the craziness and sharp sayings of Don Quixote and the humour of his aide Sancho Panza could not help giving general pleasure to all. He sent the letter by one of his aides, who, exchanging the costume of a highwayman for that of a peasant, made his way into Barcelona and gave it to the person to whom it was addressed.

CHAPTER 61

WHAT HAPPENED TO DON QUIXOTE WHEN ENTERING BARCELONA, ALONG WITH OTHER MATTERS

Don Quixote spent three days and three nights with Roque, and if he had spent three hundred years he would have found enough to satisfy his wonder about in his mode of life. During the morning they were in one spot, at dinner-time another; sometimes they ran without knowing from who, at other times they lay waiting, not knowing for what. They slept standing, breaking their sleep to shift from place to place. There was nothing but sending out spies, posting lookouts and firing guns. Roque spent his nights in some place separate from his men, so they would not know where he was, because the ruler of Barcelona had issued so many announcements against his life he was in constant fear and uneasiness, and he did not trust anyone, afraid that even his own men would kill him or take him to the authorities for a reward; in truth, a weary miserable life!

Finally, through neglected roads, short cuts, and secret paths, Roque, Don Quixote, and Sancho, together with six aides, set out for Barcelona. They reached Barcelona on Saint John's Eve during the night; and Roque, after embracing Don Quixote and Sancho (to whom he gave the ten coins he had promised but had not given until then), left them with many expressions of good-will on both sides.

Roque went back, while Don Quixote remained on horseback, just as he was, waiting for the day, and it was not long before the sun began to show itself at the balconies of the east, charming the grass and flowers, and at that moment to delight the ear, the sound of trumpets drums, bells, and cries of "Clear the way!" seemed to come from the city.

The morning made way for the sun, that with a face broader than a shield, began to rise slowly above the low line of the horizon; Don Quixote and Sancho looked around, they observed the sea, a sight until then unseen by them; it struck them as exceedingly spacious and wide, much more so than the lakes of Ruidera which they had seen in La Mancha. They saw the ships along the beach, which, lowering their anchors, displayed themselves decked with flags and banners that shook in the breeze and kissed the water, while on board, the trumpets were filling the air with warlike notes. Then they began to move and execute a kind of battle on the calm water, while a vast number of men on fine horses and in flashy attire, coming from the city, engaged on their side in a somewhat similar movement. The soldiers on board the ships kept up a ceaseless fire, which those on the walls and forts of the city returned, and the heavy cannons filled the air with the tremendous noise they made, to which the guns of the ships replied. The bright sea, the smiling earth, the clear air - although at times darkened by the smoke of the guns - seemed to fill all with unexpected delight. Sancho could not make out how it was that all of those that moved over the sea had so many feet.

And now the horsemen came galloping with shouts, cries and cheers to where Don Quixote stood in amazement; and one of them, who Roque had sent word to, addressed him as follows: "Welcome to our city, beacon and star of all Knighthood! Welcome, I say, valiant Don Quixote of La Mancha; not the false, the fabricated, the fictional, that these recent days have offered us in lying histories, but the true, the legitimate, the real one that Cide Hamete Benengeli, top of all historians, has described to us!"

Don Quixote gave no reply, and neither did the horseman wait for one, but turning around again with all his followers, they began circling around Don Quixote, who, turning to Sancho, said, "These gentlemen have clearly recognised us; I will bet they have read our history, and even that newly printed one by the Aragonese."

The Knight who had addressed Don Quixote approached him again and said, "Come with us, Señor Don Quixote, because all of us are your servants and great friends of Roque's;" to which Don Quixote returned, "If courtesy breeds courtesy, yours, sir Knight, is the daughter or very nearly similar to the great Roque's; take me wherever you please; I will have no will but yours, especially if you deem it worthy to use it in your service."

The Knight replied with words no less polite, and then, all closing in around him, they led him to the city, to the music of the trumpets and the drums. As they were entering it, the evil one, who is the author of all trouble, and the boys who are worse than the evil one, arranged that a couple of these impudent irrepressible mischievous children could force their way through the crowd, and lifting up the tails of Dapple and Rocinante, inserted a bunch of yellow shrubs under each. The poor animals felt a strange feeling, so much so that, making a number of jumps, they threw their masters to the ground. Don Quixote, covered with shame, ran to pluck the shrubs from his poor horse, while Sancho did the same for Dapple. Those leading them tried to punish the disrespect of the boys, but there was no possibility of doing so, because they hid themselves among the hundreds of others that were following them. Don Quixote and Sancho mounted again, and with the same music and cheers reached their host's house, which was large and imperial, that of a rich gentleman; and there we will leave them for the present, as this is Cide Hamete's desire.

CHAPTER 62

THE ADVENTURE OF THE ENCHANTED HEAD, TOGETHER WITH OTHER MATTERS WHICH CANNOT BE LEFT UNTOLD

Don Quixote's host was one Don Antonio Moreno, a gentleman of wealth and intelligence, and very fond of amusing himself in any good-natured way; and having Don Quixote in his house he commenced devising methods of making him reveal his madness in a harmless style; because jokes that give pain are not jokes, and not worth anything if it hurts another. The first thing he did was to make Don Quixote put on his full armour, and led him, in that tight suit we have already described and depicted more than once, out on to a balcony overlooking one of the main streets of the city, in full view of the crowd and of the boys, who stared at him as they would at a monkey. The Knights in uniform galloped toward him again as if it was purely for him, and not to invigorate the festival of the day; and Sancho was highly delighted, because it seemed to him that, without knowing how, he was attending another Camacho's wedding, another house like Don Diego de Miranda's, another castle like the duke's. Some of Don Antonio's friends dined with him that day, and all showed honour to Don Quixote and treated him as a Knight, and as a consequence he could not help himself becoming puffed up and inflated with high satisfaction. The humour of Sancho was so impressive that all the servants of the house, and all who heard him, were kept hanging upon his words. While at the table Don Antonio said to him, "We hear, worthy Sancho, that you are so fond of custard and meat balls, that if you have any left, you keep them for the next day."

"No, señor, that's not true," said Sancho, "because I am more clean than greedy, and my master Don Quixote here knows well that us two are used to living for a week on a handful of acorns or nuts. To be sure, if it so happens that they offer me a donkey, I run with the reins; I mean, I eat what I'm given, and make use of the opportunities as I find them; but whoever says that I'm an overeater or not clean, let me tell him that he is wrong; and I'd put it in another way if I did not respect the honourable beards that are at this table."

"Indeed," said Don Quixote, "Sancho's moderation and cleanliness in eating might be inscribed and engraved on plates of brass, to be kept in eternal remembrance for all ages to come. It is true that when he is hungry there is a certain appearance of greediness about him, because he eats at a great pace and chews with both jaws; but cleanliness he is always mindful of; and when he was governor he learned how to eat lightly, so much so that he eats grapes, and even pips, with a fork."

"What!" said Don Antonio, "Sancho has been a governor?"

"Ay," said Sancho, "of an island called Barataria. I governed it for ten days perfectly; and lost all my time for rest; and learned to look down on all the other governments in the world; I got out of it due to a war, and fell into a pit where I considered myself dead, and out of this pit I escaped alive by a miracle."

Don Quixote then gave them an account of Sancho's government, with which he greatly amused the listeners.

The cloth was removed and Don Antonio, taking Don Quixote by the hand, passed with him into a distant room in which there was nothing except a table, apparently of jasper, and a bronze head on top of it which was set up in the fashion of the Roman emperors. Don Antonio searched the whole apartment with Don Quixote and walked around the table several times, and then said, "Now, Señor Don Quixote, that I am satisfied that no one is listening to us, and that the door is shut, I will tell you of one of the rarest adventures, or more properly speaking strange things, that can be imagined, on the condition that you will keep what I say to you in the furthest recesses of your mind."

"I swear it," said Don Quixote, "and for greater security I will put a stone over it; because I want you to know, Señor Don Antonio, that you are addressing one who, although he has ears to hear, has no tongue to speak; so you may safely transfer whatever you have on your chest into mine, and rely on it that you have committed it to the depths of silence."

"In reliance on that promise," said Don Antonio, "I will astonish you with what you will hear, and relieve myself of some of the anger it gives me to have no one to whom I can confide my secrets, because they are not the type to be entrusted to everybody."

Don Quixote was confused, wondering what the cause of such precautions were; Don Antonio took his hand, passing it over the bronze head and the whole table of jasper on which it stood, and then said, "This head, Señor Don Quixote, has been made by one of the greatest magicians and wizards the world ever saw, Polish, I believe, by birth, and a pupil of the famous Escotillo of whom such marvellous stories are told. He was here in my house, and for the thousand coins that I gave him he constructed this head, which has the property and virtue of answering whatever questions one may ask. He knew the points of the compass, he studied the stars, he foretold favourable moments, and finally created what we will see tomorrow, because on Fridays it is mute, and this being Friday we must wait until the next day. In the interval you may consider what you would like to ask it; and I know by experience that in all its answers it always tells the truth."

Don Quixote was amazed by the virtue of the head, and was leaning to disbelieve Don Antonio; but seeing what a short time he had to wait to test the matter, he did not choose to say anything except that he thanked him for having entrusted him with such a great secret. They then left the room, Don Antonio locked the door, and they returned to where the rest of the gentlemen were gathered. In the meantime, Sancho had told them about several of the adventures and mishaps that had happened to his master.

That afternoon they took Don Quixote out for a walk, not in his armour but in casual attire, with a coat of yellowish-brown cloth, that during that season would have made ice itself sweat. Orders were left with the servants to entertain Sancho and not to let him leave the house. Don Quixote was mounted, not on

Rocinante, but on a tall donkey of a slow easy pace and handsomely accessorised. They put the coat on him, and without him noticing it, they stitched on the back of it a parchment on which they wrote in large letters, "This is Don Quixote of La Mancha." As they went on their excursion the words attracted the eyes of all who saw him, and as they read out, "This is Don Quixote of La Mancha," Don Quixote was amazed to see how many people stared at him, called him by his name, and recognised him, and turning to Don Antonio, who rode by his side, he said to him, "The privileges of Knighthood are great, because it makes him who follows it known and famous in every region of the earth; see, Don Antonio, even the boys of this city know me without having ever seen me."

"True, Señor Don Quixote," returned Don Antonio; "because as fire cannot be hidden or kept secret, virtue cannot escape being recognised; and that which is attained by the profession of arms shines distinguished above all others."

It so happened, however, that as Don Quixote was proceeding among the praise that has been described, a Castilian, reading the inscription on his back, shouted out in a loud voice, "The devil take you, Don Quixote of La Mancha! How are you here, and not dead from the countless beatings that your ribs have taken? You are mad; and if you were by yourself, and kept yourself within your madness, it would not be so bad; but you have the gift of making fools out of all who have anything to do with you. Look at these gentlemen giving you their company! Go home, idiot, and see to your affairs, your wife and children, and give up this foolishness which is draining your brains and skimming away your mind."

"Go your own way, brother," said Don Antonio, "and don't offer advice to those who don't ask you for it. Señor Don Quixote has his full senses, and we who give him company are not fools; virtue is to be honoured wherever it may be found; go, and bad luck to you, and don't involve yourself where you are not wanted."

"God, you are right," replied the Castilian; "because to advise this good man is to pee against the wind; despite that it fills me with pity that the intelligence they say this fool has wastes away through the channel of his Knighthood; but may the bad luck you talk of follow me and all my descendants, if, from this day onward, although I may live a long life, I ever give advice to anybody even if he asks me for it."

The advice-giver went away, and they continued their walk; but the boys and people were so eager to read the writing on the jacket, that Don Antonio was forced to remove it.

Night came and they went home, and there was a ladies' dancing party, because Don Antonio's wife, a lady of distinction, beauty and intelligence, had invited some friends of hers to come and honour her guest and amuse themselves with his strange delusions. Several of them came, they ate extravagantly, and the dance began at about ten o'clock. Among the ladies were two with a mischievous and lively manner, and, although perfectly modest, somewhat free in playing tricks for harmless fun. These two were so remorseless in taking Don Quixote to dance that they tired him, not only in body but in spirit. It was such a sight to see the figure Don Quixote made, long, lanky, lean, and yellow, his garments clinging tightly to him, awkwardly, and above all - anything but loose.

The happy ladies acted as though they were secretly attracted to him, and on his part he secretly repelled them, but finding himself showered by their flattery he raised his voice and exclaimed, "Be gone all evil powers! Leave me in peace, unwelcome advances; halt with your desires, ladies, because she who is my Queen, the incomparable Dulcinea del Toboso, is the only one to make me captive and subdue me;" and he sat down on the floor in the middle of the room, tired out and worn down by all the exertion of dancing.

Don Antonio ordered that he be carried to bed, and the first to lift him was Sancho, saying as he did so, "In an evil hour you took to dancing, master of mine; do you think all mighty men of valour are dancers? If you do, I can tell you, you are mistaken; there's many men that would rather undertake to kill a giant than dance."

With these and other observations Sancho had everyone laughing, and then put his master to bed, covering him up well so that he might sweat out any chill caught after his dancing.

The next day Don Antonio thought he might as well test the enchanted head, and with Don Quixote, Sancho, and two others, friends of his; and the two ladies that had worn out Don Quixote the night before (as they had stayed the night with Don Antonio's wife). He locked them all in the room where the head was. He explained to them the qualities it possessed and entrusted them with the secret, telling them that now for the first time he was going to test the virtue of the enchanted head; but apart from Don Antonio's two friends, no one else was aware of the mystery of the enchantment, and if Don Antonio had not revealed it to them they would have been certainly in the same state of amazement as the rest.

The first to approach the ear of the head was Don Antonio himself, and in a low voice but not so low not to be heard by all, he said to it, "Head, tell me by your virtue what am I thinking of at this moment?"

The head, without any movement of the lips, answered in a clear and distinct voice, so as to be heard by all, "I cannot judge thoughts."

All were amazed by this, and even more so because they saw that there was nobody anywhere near the table or in the whole room that could have answered. "How many of us are here?" asked Don Antonio; and it was answered him in the same way, "You and your wife, with two friends of yours and two of hers, and a famous Knight called Don Quixote of La Mancha, and an aide of his, Sancho Panza."

Now there was even further astonishment; everyone's hair was standing on end with awe; and Don Antonio stepping away from the head exclaimed, "This proves to me that I have not been deceived by him who sold you to me, O sage head, talking head, answering head, wonderful head! Let someone else go and put whatever question he likes to you."

And as women are commonly impulsive and inquisitive, the first to come forward was one of the two friends of Don Antonio's wife, and her question was, "Tell me, Head, what can I do to be very beautiful?" and the answer she got was, "Be very modest."

"I have no further questions," said the fair lady.

Her companion then came and said, "I would like to know, Head, whether my husband loves me or not;" the answer given to her was, "Think of if he uses you or not, and you may guess;" and the married lady went on saying, "For that answer no question was needed; because of course the treatment one receives shows the character of whom it is received from."

Then one of Don Antonio's two friends advanced and asked it, "Who am I?" "You know," was the answer. "That is not what I asked you," said the gentleman, "but to tell me if you know me who I am." "Yes, I know you, you are Don Pedro Noriz," was the reply.

"I do not seek to know more," said the gentleman, "because this is enough to convince me, O Head, that knows everything;" and as he stepped away the other friend came forward and asked it, "Tell me, Head, what are the wishes of my eldest son?"

"I have already said," was the answer, "that I cannot judge thoughts; however, I can tell you the wish of your son is to bury you."

"What I see with my own eyes I point out with my finger,'" said the gentleman, "so I ask no more."

Don Antonio's wife came forward and said, "I do not know what to ask you, Head; I only seek to know from you, if I will have many years of enjoyment with my good husband;" and the answer she received was, "you will, as his vigour and his temperate habits promise many years of life, which by overindulgence others so often cut short."

Then Don Quixote came forward and said, "Tell me, you that answers, was that which I describe as having happened to me in the cave of Montesinos the truth or a dream? Will Sancho's whipping be accomplished? Will the disenchantment of Dulcinea be manifested?"

"As to the question of the cave," was the reply, "there is much to be said; there is a bit of both in it. Sancho's whipping will continue leisurely. The disenchantment of Dulcinea will attain its due completion."

"I seek to know no more," said Don Quixote; "let me see Dulcinea disenchanted, and I will consider that all the good fortune I could wish for has come to me all at once."

The last questioner was Sancho, and his questions were, "Head, will I by any chance have another government? Will I ever escape from the hard life of an aide? Will I get back to see my wife and children?" To which the answer came, "You will govern in your house; and if you return to it you will see your wife and children; and on ceasing to serve you will cease to be an aide."

"Good God!" said Sancho Panza; "I could have said myself that."

"What answer would you have wanted, beast?" said Don Quixote; "is it not enough that the replies this head has given suit the questions put to it?"

"Yes, it is enough," said Sancho; "but I would have liked it to have made itself clear and told me more."

The questions and answers came to an end here, but not the wonder which all were filled with, except Don Antonio's two friends who were in on the secret, which Cide Hamete Benengeli thought fit to reveal, not to keep the world in suspense, thinking that the head had some strange magical mystery in it.

He says, therefore, that based on the model of another head, which he had seen in Madrid, Don Antonio made this one at home for his own amusement and to astonish ignorant people; and its method was as follows:

The table was made of wood painted and varnished to imitate jasper. The head, which resembled a Roman emperor, and was coloured like bronze, was hollow throughout, as was the table, onto which it was fitted so precisely that no trace of the joining was visible. The legs of the table were also hollow and joined the throat and neck of the head, which was in communication with another room underneath the room in which the head stood. Through the entire cavity in the table legs, throat and neck of the head, there passed a tube carefully adjusted and concealed from sight. In the room below corresponding to the one above a person was placed to answer, with his mouth to the tube, and the voice, when whispered in the ear of the head passed from above downwards, and was returned from below upwards. The words passed so clearly and distinctly it was virtually impossible to detect the trick. A nephew of Don Antonio's, a smart sharp-witted student, was the voice of the head, and as he had been told beforehand by his uncle who the people were that would come with him that day into the room where the head was, it was an easy for him to answer the first question immediately and correctly; the others he answered by guess-work, and, being clever, cleverly. Cide Hamete adds that this marvellous head stood for ten or twelve days; but that, as it became known through the city that he had in his house an enchanted head that answered all questions put to it, Don Antonio, fearing it might come to the ears of the watchful priests of our faith, explained the matter to the questioners, who ordered him to break it up. Don Quixote and Sancho however were to remain believing the head was still enchanted, and capable of answering questions, although this was more to Don Quixote's satisfaction than Sancho's.

The gentlemen of the city, to gratify Don Antonio and also to honour Don Quixote, and give him an opportunity of displaying his foolishness, made arrangements for a battle in the ring six days from that time, which, however, for reasons that will be mentioned shortly, did not take place.

Don Quixote wanted to walk around the city quietly and on foot, because he feared that if he went on horseback the boys would follow him; so he, Sancho and two servants of Don Antonio left for a walk. It so happened, that going along one of the streets Don Quixote raised his eyes and saw written in very large letters over a door, "Books printed here," at which he was very pleased, because until then he had never seen a printing office, and he was curious to know what it was like. He entered it with those following, and saw them printing sheets in one place, editing in another, agreeing the font here, and revising the text there; in short, all the work that is to be seen in great printing offices. He went up to one man and asked what he was doing there; the workmen told him, he watched with wonder what went on. He approached another man, among others, and asked him what he was doing. The workman replied, "Señor, this gentleman here" (pointing to a man of attractive appearance and a certain seriousness of look) "has translated an Italian book into our Spanish language, and I am setting it up for printing."

"What is the title of the book?" asked Don Quixote; to which the author replied, "Señor, in Italian the book is called Le Bagatelle."

"And what does Le Bagatelle mean in Spanish?" asked Don Quixote.

"Le Bagatelle," said the author, "is as we would say in Spanish 'The Toys'; but although the book has a humble name it has good solid matter in it."

"I," said Don Quixote, "know a little bit of Italian, and I pride myself on singing some of Ariosto's poems; but tell me, señor - I do not say this to test your ability, but merely out of curiosity - have you ever discovered the word pentola in your book?"

"Yes, often," said the author.

"And how would you say that in Spanish?"

"How else would I say it," returned the author, "but olla?"

"My God," exclaimed Don Quixote, "how proficient you are in the Italian language! I would bet that the word in Italian 'piace' you say in Spanish 'gusta', and where they say 'piu' you say 'mas', and you translate 'scalata' and 'escalada'."

"Of course," said the author, "because those are their proper equivalents."

"I would dare to say," said Don Quixote, "that you are not known in the world, which always withholds the rewards from rare intellects and praiseworthy work. What talents are wasted! What genius put in the corner! What work left neglected! Still it seems to me that translation from one language into another, if it is not from the Queens of languages, the Greek and the Latin, is like looking at interwoven tapestries; because letters are visible, they are full of threads that make them indistinct; and translation from easy languages demands neither ingenuity or command of words, any more than transcribing or copying out one document from another. But by this I do not mean to draw the conclusion that no credit is to be awarded to the work of translating, because a man may employ himself in worse and less profitable ways. This estimate does not include two famous translators, Doctor Cristobal de Figueroa and Don Juan de Jauregui, who by their competence leave it in doubt which is the translation and which is the original. But tell me, are you printing this book at your own risk, or have you sold the copyright to some bookseller?"

"I print at my own risk," said the author, "and I expect to make a thousand coins profit at least from this first edition, which will be from one hundred and sixty-six copies sold at six coins each."

"A fine calculation there!" said Don Quixote; "it is clear you don't know anything about the printers. I promise you when you find yourself loaded with one hundred and sixty-six copies you will feel so sore that it will astonish you, particularly if the book is a little out of the ordinary and not in any way highly seasoned."

"What!" said the author, "you advise me to give it to a bookseller who will give three hundred coins for the copyright and think he is doing me a favour? I do not print my books to win fame in the world, because I am known in it already by my work; I want to make money, which without a reputation is not worth anything."

"God send you good luck," said Don Quixote; and he moved on to another case, where he saw them correcting a page of a book with the title "Light of the Soul;" noticing it he said, "Books like this, although there are many of them, are the ones that deserve to be printed, because there are many sinners these days, and when the lights are outnumbered all are in darkness."

He passed on, and saw some correcting another book, and when he asked what its title was, they told him it was called, "The Second Part of the Ingenious Gentleman Don Quixote of La Mancha," by a Toledoan.

"I have heard of this book already," said Don Quixote, "by now, truly and on my conscience I thought it had been burned to ashes as an intruder; but its Saint Martin's Day will come to it as it does to every pig; because fiction has more merit and charm the closer they approach the truth or what looks like it; and true stories, the truer they are the better they are;" and he walked out of the printing office with a certain amount of displeasure on his face.

That same day Don Antonio arranged to take him to see the ships that were on the beach, which highly delighted Sancho, as he had never been on any his whole life.

Don Antonio sent word to the commander of the ships that he intended to bring his guest, the famous Don Quixote of La Mancha, of whom the commander and all the citizens had already heard of, that afternoon to see them; and what happened on board will be told in the next chapter.

CHAPTER 63

THE MISHAP THAT HAPPENED TO SANCHO PANZA DURING THE VISIT TO THE SHIPS, AND THE STRANGE ADVENTURE OF THE FAIR MOOR

Don Quixote's reflections about the enchanted head were profound, not however, discovering the secret of the trick, he concentrated on the promise, which he regarded as a certainty, of Dulcinea's disenchantment. This he went over in his mind again and again with great satisfaction, fully persuaded that he would shortly see its fulfilment; and as for Sancho, although, as it has been said, he hated being a governor, he still had a longing to give orders and find himself obeyed again; this is the misfortune that being in authority, even as a joke, brings with it.

To continue; that afternoon their host Don Antonio Moreno and his two friends, with Don Quixote and Sancho, went to the ships. The commander had been already made aware of his good fortune when seeing two famous people such as Don Quixote and Sancho, and the moment they came to the shore all the ships sounded their trumpets and the drums beat. A small rowing boat covered with rich carpet and cushions of crimson velvet was immediately lowered into the water, and as Don Quixote stepped on board of it, the leading ship fired its gun, and the other ships did the same; and as he climbed the ladder on the right side of the ship the whole crew saluted him (as this is the custom when a person of great distinction comes on board) by shouting "Hu, hu, hu," three times. The general, which we will call, a Valencian gentleman of high rank, gave him his hand and embraced him, saying, "I will mark this day with a white stone as one of the happiest I can expect to enjoy in my lifetime, since I have seen Señor Don Quixote of La Mancha, the pattern and image of which we see condensed and contained all that is worthy in Knighthood."

Don Quixote was elated beyond measure by such a grand welcoming, and replied to him in words no less courteous. All then proceeded to the highest deck of the ship, which was generously decorated, and sat themselves on the benches; the ships officer in charge of equipment and crew passed along the walkway and whistled for them all to remove their shirts, which they did in an instant. Sancho, seeing such a number of men stripped to their skin, was shocked, and even more when he saw them spread the canopy so quickly that it seemed to him as if the devil was at work; but all of this was butter to the bread of what I am going to tell now. Sancho was sat in the captain's seat, close to the rower on the right-hand side. He, previously being instructed in what he was to do, held Sancho, picking him up in his arms, and the whole crew, who were standing ready, beginning on the right, proceeded to pass him along from hand to hand and from bench to bench with such speed that it took the sight out of poor Sancho's eyes, and he was now sure that the devil himself was taking him; and they did not leave him alone until they had sent him back along the left side and placed him on upper deck; and poor Sancho was left bruised and breathless, in a sweat, and unable to comprehend what had happened to him.

When Don Quixote saw Sancho's flight without wings asked the general if this was a usual ceremony with those who came on board ships for the first time; because, if so, as he had no intention of partaking in this, he said if anyone offered to pick him up and pass him about, he swore to God he would kick the soul out of him; and as he said this he stood up and slapped his hand on his sword.

At this moment they dropped the beam which the sail hung from, which crashed down with a remarkable rattle. Sancho thought heaven was falling and going to land on his head, and full of terror he ducked and buried his head between his knees; and neither were Don Quixote's knees altogether under control, because he also shook a little, squeezed his shoulders together and lost colour. The crew then hoisted the beam back up with the same rapidity and as when they let it drop, all the while remaining in silence as though they neither had a voice or breath. The officer in charge of the crew gave the signal to raise the anchor, and standing in the middle of the walkway began to whip the shoulders of the crew.

When Sancho saw so many red feet (as he took the oars to be feet) moving all together, he said to himself, "It is these that are the real enchanted things, and not the ones my master talks about. What can those victims have done to be whipped; and how does that man who goes along there whistling dare to whip so many? I say this must be hell, or at least limbo!"

Don Quixote, observing how attentively Sancho considered what was going on, said to him, "Ah, Sancho my friend, how quickly you could finish off the disenchantment of Dulcinea, if you would strip to the waist and take your place among those gentlemen! Among the pain and suffering of so many you would not feel your own so much; and perhaps the sage Merlin would allow each of these lashes, being given with a good hand, to count for ten of those which you must give yourself."

The general was about to ask what these lashes were for, and what was Dulcinea's disenchantment, when a sailor exclaimed, "Signals that there is an oared vessel off the coast to the west."

On hearing this the general jumped to the upper deck shouting, "Now then, my sons, don't let her get away! It must be some Algerian pirate ship that the watchtower signals to us." Three other ships immediately came alongside to receive their orders. The general ordered two to go out to sea while the main ship stayed with his on the shore, so that in this way the vessel could not escape them. The crews worked the oars driving the ships so furiously that they seemed to fly. The two that had gone out to sea, after a couple of miles saw the vessel which, as soon as it had realised it had been discovered went off in the hope of making an escape with its speed; but the attempt failed, because the main ship was the fastest vessel, and overtook her so rapidly that those on board the pirate ship saw clearly there was no possibility of escaping, and therefore it would have been best to drop their oars and give themselves up so as not to provoke the captain in command of our ships to anger. But chance, directing things otherwise, so ordered it that just as the main ship came close enough for those on board the vessel to hear the calling of them to surrender, two Turks, both drunken, with a dozen more that were on board the pirate ship, fired their guns, killing two of the soldiers that lined the sides of our ship. Seeing this the general swore he would not leave any of those he found on board the pirate ship alive, but as he pursued furiously she slipped away from him. The ship shot a good distance ahead; those on board saw their case was desperate, and with the ship approaching they set the sail, and by sailing and rowing once again tried to get away; but their activity did not do them as much good as their impulsiveness did them harm, because the ship coming up to them in a little more than half a mile threw her oars over them and took the whole of them alive. The other two ships now joined company and all four returned with the prize to the beach, where a vast crowd stood waiting for them, eager to see what they brought back. The general anchored close to the shore, and noticed that the mayor of the city was on the shore. He ordered the small rowing boat to go and retrieve him, and the beam to be lowered for the purpose of hanging the sail and the men of the pirate ship to be taken on board, about thirty-six in total, all smart and most of them Turkish gunners. He asked who was the captain of the pirate ship, and was answered in Spanish by one of the prisoners (who afterwards proved to be a Spanish traitor):

"This young man, señor that you see here is our captain," and he pointed to one of the most handsome suave-looking youths that could be imagined. He did not seem to be more than twenty years of age.

"Tell me, dog," said the general, "what led you to kill my soldiers, when you saw it was impossible for you to escape? Is that the way to behave? Do you know that impulsiveness is not courage? Faint prospects of success should make men brave, but not careless."

The captain was about to reply, but the general could not at that moment listen to him, as he had to rush to welcome the mayor of the city, who was now coming on board the ship, and with him came a few of his attendants.

"You have had a good chase, señor general," said the mayor.

"Your excellency will soon see how good, by what will be fastened to this beam," replied the general.

"How so?" returned the mayor.

"Because," said the general, "against all law, reason, and purpose of war they have killed two of the best soldiers on board these ships, and I have sworn to hang every man that I have taken, but above all, this is the youth who is the captain of the pirate ship," and he pointed to him as he stood with his hands already tied and the rope round his neck, ready for death.

The mayor looked at him, and seeing such a handsome man, so graceful, and so submissive, he felt a desire to let him live, the attractiveness of the youth gave him a letter of recommendation. He therefore questioned him, saying, "Tell me, captain, are you a Turk, Moor, or traitor?"

To which the youth replied, also in Spanish, "I am not a Turk, Moor, or traitor."

"What are you, then?" said the mayor.

"A Christian woman," replied the youth.

"A woman and a Christian, in this attire and in such circumstances! It is more amazing than credible," said the mayor.

"Suspend the execution of the sentence," said the youth; "your punishment will not lose much by waiting while I tell you the story of my life."

What heart could be so hard as not to be softened by these words, at any rate so far as to listen to what the unhappy youth had to say? The general asked her to say what she liked, but not to expect a pardon for her offence. With this permission the youth began in these words.

"Born of Morisco parents, I am from that nation, unhappier than wise, which lately a sea of troubles has rained on. In the course of our misfortune I was taken to Africa by two uncles of mine, because it was not believed that I was a Christian, as I am in fact, and not one who pretends, but a true Catholic Christian. It was of no use to protest this to those overseeing our extradition, and neither would my uncles believe it; on the contrary, they treated it as a lie and a trick set up to enable me to remain behind on the land of my birth; and so, more by force than my own will, they took me with them. I had a Christian mother, and a father who was a man of good sense and a Christian too; I absorbed the Catholic faith with my mother's milk, I was brought up well, and neither in word or in deed did I, I think, show any sign of being a Morisco. To accompany these virtues, because that's what I believe them to be, my beauty, if I possess any, grew as I grew; and although the seclusion in which I lived was great, it was not so great to stop a young gentleman, Don Gaspar Gregorio, the eldest son of a gentleman who is lord of a village near ours, finding opportunities to see me. How he saw me, how we met, how his heart was lost to me, and mine not kept from him, would take too long to tell, especially at a moment when I am in fear of the cruel rope that threatens to be between my tongue and throat; I will only say, therefore, that Don Gregorio chose to accompany me when we were banished. He joined the Moriscos who were leaving the other villages, because he knew their language very well, and on the voyage he made a friendship with my two uncles who were taking me with them; because my father, like a wise and far-sighted man, as soon as he heard the first order for our expulsion, left the village and departed in search of some refuge for us abroad. He left hidden and buried, somewhere which only I alone have the knowledge, a large quantity of pearls and precious stones of great value, together with a sum of money in gold. He ordered that on no account I should touch the treasure, if by any chance they expelled us before his return. I obeyed him, and with my uncles, as I have said, and others of my kind, went to Africa, and the place where we set up our home was Algeria, which is basically the same as if we had set it up in hell itself. The King heard about my beauty, and of my wealth, which was in some degree fortunate for me. He summoned me, and asked me what part of Spain I came from, and what money and jewels I had. I mentioned the place, and told him the jewels and money were buried there; and they could easily be recovered if I myself went back for them. All this I told him, in fear that my beauty and not his own greed would influence him. While he was engaged in conversation with me, they told him that along with me was one of the most handsome and graceful youths that could be imagined. I knew immediately that they were speaking about Don Gaspar Gregorio, whose attractiveness surpasses the most highly praised beauty. I was troubled when I thought of the danger he was in, because among those cruel Moors a fair youth is more esteemed than a woman, even if she is ever so beautiful. The King immediately ordered him to be brought to him so he could see him, and asked me if what they said about the youth was true. I then, almost as if inspired by heaven, told him it was, but that he should know it was not a man, but a woman like myself, and I asked him to allow me to go and dress her in the attire of a woman, so that her beauty might be seen to perfection, and that she might present herself in front of him with less embarrassment. He told me go by all means, and said that the next day we should discuss the plan to be adopted for my return to Spain to retrieve the hidden treasure. I saw Don Gaspar, I told him the danger he was in if he let it be seen he was a man, I dressed him as a Moorish woman, and that same afternoon I brought him to the King, who was charmed when he saw him as her, and decided to keep the lady and give her as a present to a grand nobleman; and to avoid the risk that she might be among the women of his house, and distrustful of himself, he commanded her to be placed in the house of some Moorish ladies of high rank who would protect and attend to her; and to there she was taken immediately. What we both suffered (because I cannot deny that I love him) may be left to the imagination of those who are separated if they love one another dearly. The King then arranged that I should return to Spain in this ship, and that two Turks, those who killed your soldiers, should accompany me. And this Spanish rebel also came with me" - and here she pointed to him - "whom I know to secretly be a Christian, and desires more to be left in Spain than return to Africa. The rest of the crew of the ship are Moors and Turks, who merely serve as rowers. The two Turks, greedy and insolent, instead of obeying the orders they had to take me and this rebel in Christian attire to the first Spanish ground we came to, chose to run along the coast and win some prize if they could, fearing that if they put us ashore first, we might, in case of some accident happening to us, make it known that the ship was at sea, and therefore, if there happened to be any ships on the coast, they might be taken. We saw this shore last night, and knowing nothing about these ships, we were discovered, and the result was what you have seen. To sum it up, there is Don Gregorio in a woman's dress, among women, in imminent danger of his life; and here am I, with my hands tied, in expectation, or rather in fear, of losing my life, of which I am already tired. Here, sirs, ends my sad story, as true as it is unhappy; all I ask from you is to allow me to die like a Christian, because, as I have already said, I am not to be charged with the offence of which those from my nation are guilty of;" and she stood silent, her eyes filled with moving tears, accompanied by plenty from the bystanders.

The mayor, touched with compassion, went up to her without speaking untied the rope that held the hands of the Moorish girl.

But all the while the Morisco Christian was telling her strange story, an elderly pilgrim, who had come on board the ship at the same time as the mayor, kept his eyes fixed on her; and the instant she stopped speaking he threw himself at her feet, and embracing them said in a voice broken by cries and sighs, "O Ana Felix, my unhappy daughter, I am your father Ricote, who came back to look for you, unable to live without you, my soul!"

At these words of his, Sancho opened his eyes and raised his head, which he had been holding down between his knees, thinking over his unlucky excursion; and looking at the pilgrim he recognised in him as the same Ricote he met the day he left his government, and felt satisfied that this was his daughter. She being now unbound embraced her father, mingling her tears with his, while he addressing the general and the mayor said, "This, sirs, is my daughter, unhappier in her adventures than in her name. She is Ana Felix, surnamed Ricote, celebrated as much for her own beauty as for my wealth. I left my native land in search of some shelter or refuge for us abroad, and having found one in Germany I returned in this pilgrim's dress, in the company of some other German pilgrims, to seek my daughter and retrieve a large quantity of treasure I had left buried. I did not find my daughter, but the treasure I found and have with me; and now, in this strange way you have seen, I find the treasure that more than anything else makes me rich, my beloved daughter. If our innocence, her tears and mine can with justice open the door to mercy, grant it to us, because we never had any intention of injuring you, and neither do we agree with the aims of our people, who have been rightly banished."

"I know Ricote well," said Sancho, "and I know what he says about Ana Felix being his daughter is true; but as for those other details about coming and going, good or bad intentions, I say nothing."

While all those present stood in amazement by this strange occurrence the general said, "Your tears will not allow me to keep my oath; live, fair Ana Felix, all the years that heaven has apportioned to you; but these foolish insolent men must pay the penalty of the crime they have committed;" and with that he gave orders to have the two Turks who had killed his two soldiers hung immediately. The mayor, however, begged him sincerely not to hang them, as their behaviour seem to be madness rather than audacity. The general yielded to the mayor's request, because revenge is not always easily taken. They then tried to devise a scheme to rescue Don Gaspar Gregorio from the danger which he had been left in. Ricote offered more than two thousand coins that he had in pearls and gems for his safe return; they proposed several plans, but none as good as that suggested by the rebel already mentioned, who offered to return to Algeria in a small boat, manned by Christian rowers, as he knew where, how, and when he could and should land, and he knew the house in which Don Gaspar was staying. The general and the mayor had some hesitation about placing confidence in the rebel and entrusting him with the Christians who were to row, but Ana Felix said she could vouch for him, and her father offered to go and pay the ransom for the Christians if by any chance they were captured. This, then, being agreed upon, the mayor left the ship, and Don Antonio Moreno took the fair Morisco and her father home with him, the mayor ordering him to give them the best treatment and welcome in his power, while he also offered all that his house contained for their entertainment; as the beauty of Ana Felix had infused into his heart such good-will and compassion.

CHAPTER 64

THE ADVENTURE WHICH GAVE DON QUIXOTE MORE UNHAPPINESS THAN ALL THAT HAD HAPPNED TO HIM

The wife of Don Antonio Moreno, so the history says, was extremely happy to see Ana Felix in her house. She welcomed her with great kindness, charmed by her beauty as well as by her intelligence; because in both respects the fair Morisco was richly endowed, and all the people of the city gathered to see her as though they had been summoned by the ringing of bells.

Don Quixote told Don Antonio that the plan approved for releasing Don Gregorio was not a good one, because its risks were greater than its advantages, and that it would be better for him to land with his weapons and horse in Africa; because he would carry him away despite the Moorish hosts, as Don Gaiferos carried off his wife Melisendra.

"Remember, my lord," said Sancho, "Señor Don Gaiferos carried his wife from the mainland, and took her to France by land; but in this case, if by chance we carry Don Gregorio, we have no way of bringing him to Spain, because there's a sea in-between."

"There's a remedy for everything except death," said Don Quixote; "if they bring the ship close to the shore we will be able to get on board even if the whole world strove to prevent us."

"You could be right," said Sancho; "but 'it's a long step from saying to doing;' and I trust in the rebel, because he seems to me an honest good-hearted fellow."

Don Antonio then said that if the rebel was not successful, the plan of the great Don Quixote's expedition to Africa should be adopted.

Two days afterwards the rebel was put to sea in a light boat of six oars on each side manned by a strong crew, and two days later the ships sailed eastward, the general having begged the mayor to let him know all about the release of Don Gregorio and about Ana Felix, and the mayor promised to do as he requested.

One morning as Don Quixote went out for a stroll along the beach, arrayed in full armour (because, as he often said, that "his only rest was the fight," and he never was without his armour for a moment), he saw coming towards him a Knight, also in full armour, with a shining moon painted on his shield, who, on approaching sufficiently near enough to be heard, said in a loud voice: "Illustrious Knight, and never sufficiently exalted Don Quixote of La Mancha, I am the Knight of the White Moon, whose unheard-of achievements would have perhaps recalled me to you memory. I come to battle you and prove the might of my arm, to make you acknowledge and confess that my lady, is supremely fairer than your Dulcinea del Toboso. If you do acknowledge this fairly and openly, you will escape death and save me the trouble of inflicting it on you; if you fight and I vanquish you, I demand no other satisfaction than, putting aside your weapons and abstaining from going in search of adventures, you withdraw and take yourself to your own village for a year, and live there without putting your hands on your sword, in peace and quiet and beneficial rest, which will be needed for your recovery and the salvation of your soul; and if you vanquish me, my head will be at your disposal, my weapons and horse, yours, and the renown of my deeds transferred and added to yours. Consider which will be your best course, and give me your answer promptly, because this day is all the time I have for this business."

Don Quixote was amazed and astonished, at the Knight of the White Moon's arrogance, as well as at his reason for distributing the defiance, and with calm dignity he answered him, "Knight of the White Moon, of whose achievements I have never heard of until now, I will dare to swear you have never seen the renowned Dulcinea; because if you had seen her I know you would have taken care not to undertake this issue, because the sight would have removed all doubt from your mind that there ever has been or can be a beauty compared with hers; and so, not saying you lie, but merely that you are not correct in what you state, I accept your challenge, with the conditions you have proposed, and immediately, so the day you have fixed will not expire; and from your conditions I do not agree that of the fame of your achievements will be transferred to me, because I do not know what they are or what they amount to; I am satisfied with my own. Take whatever side of the field you choose, and I will do the same; and to whoever God will give it may Saint Peter add his blessing."

The Knight of the White Moon had been seen from the city, and the mayor was told how he was in conversation with Don Quixote. The mayor, thinking it must be a new adventure planned by some gentleman from the city, hurried to the beach accompanied by Don Antonio and several other gentlemen, just as Don Quixote was wheeling Rocinante round in order to create the necessary distance. Seeing that the pair were preparing to charge, the mayor put himself between them, asking them what it was that led them to engage in combat all of a sudden in this way. The Knight of the White Moon replied that it was a question of superiority of beauty; and briefly told him what he had said to Don Quixote, and how the conditions of the defiance agreed upon on both sides had been accepted. The mayor went over to Don Antonio, and asked in a low voice did he know who the Knight of the White Moon was, or was it some joke they were playing on Don Quixote. Don Antonio replied that he did not know who he was or whether the defiance was a joke or serious. This answer left the mayor in a state of confusion, not knowing whether he should let the combat go ahead or not; but unable to persuade himself that it was anything but a joke he stepped back, saying, "If there is no other way out of it, brave Knights, except to confess or die, and Don Quixote is unyielding, and you Knight of the White Moon are as well, in God's hands it will be."

The Knight of the White Moon thanked the mayor in courteous and well-mannered words for the permission he gave them, and so did Don Quixote, who then, calling with his whole heart to heaven and to his Dulcinea, as was his custom before any combat that awaited him, proceeded to take a little more distance, as he saw his antagonist was doing the same; then, without the blast of a trumpet or other warlike instrument to give them the signal to charge, both at the same instant turned their horses; and the Knight of the White Moon, being faster, met Don Quixote after having travelled two-thirds of the course, and there encountered him with such violence that, without touching him with his lance (because he held it high), he hurled Don Quixote and Rocinante to the ground, a dangerous fall. He jumped on him, and placing the lance over his visor said to him, "You are vanquished, sir Knight, actually dead unless you admit the conditions of our combat."

Don Quixote, bruised and dazed, without raising his visor said in a weak feeble voice, "Dulcinea del Toboso is the fairest woman in the world, and I am the most unfortunate Knight on earth; it is not fitting that this truth should be affected by my feebleness; drive your lance in me, sir Knight, and take my life, since you have taken away my honour."

"That I will not do," said the Knight of the White Moon; "the fame of lady Dulcinea's beauty may live undimmed as ever; as long as the great Don Quixote returns to his own home for a year, which is what we agreed before engaging in this combat."

The mayor, Don Antonio, and several others who were present heard all of this, and heard how Don Quixote replied that as long as nothing against Dulcinea was demanded from him, he would follow all the rest like a true and loyal Knight. The Knight of the White Moon turned around, and showing respect to the mayor with a movement of the head, rode away into the city. The mayor asked Don Antonio to go after him, and find out who he was. They raised Don Quixote up and uncovered his face, and found him pale and covered in sweat.

Rocinante lay unable to move for the present. Sancho, totally sad and sorrowful, did not know what to say or do. He thought it was all a dream, or the whole business was a piece of enchantment. Here his master was defeated, and bound not to seek any further adventures for a year. He saw the light of the glory of his achievements obscured; the hopes of the promises made to him swept away like smoke in the wind; Rocinante, he feared, was crippled for life, and his master's bones out of their sockets; because if he were only shaken out of his madness it would be pure luck. In the end they carried him to the city which the mayor had requested them to do, and to there the mayor returned as well, eager to ascertain who this Knight of the White Moon was who had left Don Quixote in such a sad state.

CHAPTER 65

WHO THE KNIGHT OF THE WHITE MOON WAS; AND GREGORIO'S RELEASE

Don Antonia Moreno followed the Knight of the White Moon, and a number of boys followed him as well, actually pursued him, until they surrounded him in a house in the heart of the city. Don Antonio, eager to find out who he was, entered; an aide was seen accompanying him, and he shut himself into a room, but was still followed by Don Antonio, whose bread would not bake until he had found out who he was. The Knight of the White Moon, seeing then that the gentleman was following him, said, "I know very well, señor, what you have come for; it is to find out who I am; and as there is no reason why I should conceal it from you, while my servant here is taking off my armour I will tell you the true state of the case, without leaving anything out. You must know, señor, that I am called the graduate Samson Carrasco. I am from the same village as Don Quixote of La Mancha, whose madness and foolishness make all of us who know him feel sorry for him, and I am one of those who have felt it the most; and persuaded that his chance of recovery lay in keeping him at home and in his own house, I came up with this plan for keeping him there. Three months ago, therefore, I went out to meet him as a Knight, under the name: the Knight of the Mirrors, intending to engage him in combat and overcome him without hurting him, making it the condition of our combat that the vanquished should follow the wishes of the victor. What I meant to demand from him (as I regarded him as vanquished already) was that he should return to his own village, and not leave it for a whole year, by which time he might be cured. But fate ordered it otherwise, because he vanquished me and knocked me off my horse, and so my plan failed. He went his way, and I returned conquered, covered with shame, and sorely bruised from my fall, which was a particularly dangerous one. But this did not quench my desire to meet him again and overcome him, as you have seen today. And as he is so dependable in his observance of the laws of Knighthood, he will, no doubt, in order to keep his word, obey the order I have given him. This, señor, is how the matter stands, and I have nothing more to tell you. I ask you not to betray me, or tell Don Quixote who I am; so that my honest undertaking may be successful, he is a man of excellent wits if only he got rid of his foolish chivalry – and so, he may get them back again."

"O señor," said Don Antonio, "may God forgive you for the injustice you have done to the whole world in trying to bring the most amusing madman in it back to his senses. Do you not see, señor, that the gain by Don Quixote's sanity can never equal the enjoyment his madness gives? My belief is that all of your pain to execute this plan will be of no avail to bring a man so hopelessly cracked, back to his senses again; and if it were not heartless, I would say may Don Quixote never be cured, because from his recovery we lose not only his own humour, but his aide's, Sancho's as well, any one of them is enough to turn sadness itself into laughter. However, I'll say nothing to him, and we'll see whether I am right in my suspicion that Señor Carrasco's effort will be fruitless."

The graduate replied that the results of the affair gave promise of the recovery, and he hoped for a happy result from it; and here he left Don Antonio; and having had his armour packed and placed on a donkey, he rode away from the city the same day he rode to battle, and returned to his own country without meeting any adventure worth recording in this genuine history.

Don Antonio reported to the mayor what Carrasco had told him, and the mayor was not pleased to hear it, because Don Quixote's retirement brought to an end the amusement of all who knew about his madness.

Don Quixote stayed in his bed for six days, sad and depressed, moping over the unhappy event of his defeat. Sancho strove to comfort him, and among other things he said to him, "Hold your head up señor, and be happy if you can, and give thanks to heaven that if you have had a tumble to the ground you have not broken a rib; and you know that 'where they give they take.' Let us go home, and give up searching for adventures in strange lands and places; I am the greater loser here, with the government I gave up I would never wish to be a governor again, but I did not give up the desire to be a count; and that will never happen if you give up becoming a King by renouncing the calling of chivalry; and so my hopes are going to turn into smoke.

"Peace, Sancho," said Don Quixote; "you see my suspension is not going to exceed a year; I will return to my honoured calling soon, and there will always be a Kingdom to win and a county to give to you."

"May God hear it and the Devil be deaf," said Sancho; "I have always heard it said that 'a good hope is better than a bad doubt.'"

As they were talking Don Antonio came in looking extremely pleased and exclaiming, "Reward me for my good news, Señor Don Quixote! Don Gregorio and the rebel who went to save him have come ashore. They are already in the mayor's house, and will be here soon."

Don Quixote cheered up a little bit and said, "In truth I am almost ready to say I would have been glad if had it turned out the other way, because it would have obliged me to cross over into Africa, where by the might of my arm I would have restored to liberty, not only Don Gregorio, but all the Christians that are there in captivity. But what am I saying, miserable fool that I am? Am I not the one who has been conquered? Am I not the one who has been overthrown? Am I not the one who must not seek adventures for a year? Then what am I saying; what am I bragging about; when it is more appropriate for me to handle the sowing machine than the sword?"

"No more of that, señor," said Sancho; "'today for you and tomorrow for me;' in these encounters and whacks one must not mind them, because he that falls today may get up tomorrow; unless indeed he chooses to lie in bed, I mean gives way to weakness and does not pluck up fresh spirit for fresh battles; get up now to welcome Don Gregorio; because the household seems to be in commotion, and no doubt he has come now;" and it proved to be the case, because as soon as Don Gregorio and the rebel had given the mayor an account of the voyage, Don Gregorio, eager to see Ana Felix, came with the rebel to Don Antonio's house. When they carried him away from Algeria he was in woman's clothing; on board the ship, however, he exchanged it for that of a captive who escaped with him; but in whatever dress he might be he looked like one to be loved, served and esteemed, because he was exceedingly well-favoured, and to judge by appearances about seventeen or eighteen years of age. Ricote and his daughter came out to welcome him, the father with tears, the daughter with nervousness. They did not embrace each other, because where there is deep love there will never be extreme boldness. Seen side by side, the attractiveness of Don Gregorio and the beauty of Ana Felix were the admiration of all who were present. It was silence that spoke for the lovers in that moment, and their eyes were the tongues that declared their pure and happy feelings. The rebel explained the actions and methods he had taken to rescue Don Gregorio, and Don Gregorio finally, but in a few words, in which he showed that his intelligence was advanced for his years, described the danger and embarrassment he found himself in among the women with whom he had lived. To conclude, Ricote generously paid and rewarded the rebel as well as the men who had rowed; and the rebel achieved his admission into the body of the Church and was reconciled with it, and from a rotten limb became by atonement and repentance a clean one.

Two days later the mayor discussed with Don Antonio the steps they should take to enable Ana Felix and her father to stay in Spain, because it seemed to them there could be no objection to a daughter who was such a good Christian and a father who appeared to all so well disposed remaining there. Don Antonio offered to arrange the matter in the city, where he was compelled to go on some other business, hinting that many difficult affairs were settled there with the help of favour and bribes.

"Actually," said Ricote, who was present during the conversation, "it will not do to rely on favours or bribes, because with the great Don Bernardino de Velasco, to whom his Majesty has entrusted our expulsion, no begging or promises, bribes or appeals to compassion, are of any use; because although it is true he combines mercy with justice, still, seeing that the whole body of our nation is tainted and corrupt, he applies it more to that which burns rather than that which soothes; and there, by prudence, wisdom, care and the fear he inspires, he has carried on his mighty shoulders the weight of this great policy and carried it into effect, all our schemes and plots, appeals and tricks, being ineffective to blind his eyes, which are always on the watch in case one of us remained behind in concealment like a hidden root which sprouts and bears poisonous fruit in Spain, which is now cleansed, and relieved of the fear in which our vast numbers kept it."

"At any rate," said Don Antonio, "when I am there I will make all possible effort, and let heaven do as it wishes; Don Gregorio will come with me to relieve the anxiety which his parents must be suffering due to his absence; Ana Felix will remain in my house with my wife; and I know the mayor will be glad that the worthy Ricote should stay with him until we see what terms I can make."

The mayor agreed to all that was proposed; but Don Gregorio who heard all that had passed, declared he could not and would not on any account leave Ana Felix; however, as it was his purpose to go and see his parents and devise some way of returning for her, he complied with the proposed arrangement. Ana Felix remained with Don Antonio's wife, and Ricote in the mayor's house.

The day for Don Antonio's departure came; and two days later, that for Don Quixote's and Sancho's as well, because Don Quixote's fall did not allow him to take the road any sooner. There were tears and sighs, at the parting between Don Gregorio and Ana Felix. Ricote offered Don Gregorio a thousand coins if he needed them, but he did not want any except five which Don Antonio lent him and he promised to repay. So the two of them made their departure, and Don Quixote and Sancho did afterwards, as has already been said, Don Quixote without his armour and in travelling attire, and Sancho on foot, Dapple being loaded with the armour.

CHAPTER 66

WHAT HE WHO READS WILL SEE, OR WHAT HE WHO HAS IT READ TO HIM WILL HEAR

As he left Barcelona, Don Quixote turned to the spot where he had fallen. "Here Troy was," he said; "here my bad-luck, not my cowardice, robbed me of all the glory I had won; here Fortune made me the victim of its impulses; here the sparkle of my achievements was dimmed; here, in a word, my happiness fell never to rise again."

"Señor," said Sancho, "brave hearts must be patient in adversity just as much as being glad in prosperity; I judge by myself, because, if when I was a governor I was glad, now that I am an aide and on foot I am not sad; and I have heard it said that she who they call Fortune is a drunken impulsive lady, and, what is more, blind, and therefore does not know what she does, who she puts down or who she lifts up."

"You are a great philosopher, Sancho," said Don Quixote; "you speak very sensibly; I do not know who taught you. But I can tell you there is no such thing as Fortune in the world, and nothing which takes place there, good or bad, comes about by chance, but by the preordained plan of heaven; and hence the common saying that 'each of us is the maker of his own Fortune.' I have been the maker of mine; but not with the proper amount of prudence, and my self-confidence has therefore made me pay; because I should have known that Rocinante's lack of strength could not resist the mighty weight of the Knight of the White Moon's horse. In a word, I attempted it, I did my best, I was overthrown, but although I lost my honour I did not lose and cannot lose the virtue of keeping my word. When I was a Knight, brave and valiant, I supported my achievements with my hands and actions, and now that I am a humble man I will support my words by keeping the promise I have given. Let us go then Sancho my friend, to spend the year of probation in our own town, and in that seclusion we will gain fresh strength to return to the calling of Knighthood."

"Señor," returned Sancho, "travelling on foot is not such a pleasant thing that it makes me feel willing or tempted to make long journeys. Let us leave this armour hung on some tree, in place of some one that has been hanged; and then with me on Dapple's back and my feet off the ground we will arrange the journey as you plan; but to think that I am going to travel on foot, so far, is to think nonsense."

"You speak well, Sancho," said Don Quixote; "let my armour be hung up as a trophy, and under it or round it we will carve on the trees what was inscribed on the trophy of Roland's armour: No one moves this, whoever dares faces the might of Roland."

"That's it," said Sancho; "and if we did not need Rocinante on the road, we could leave him hung up too."

"I would rather not have him or the armour hung up," said Don Quixote, "because that which renders good service should not be given a bad return."

"You're right," said Sancho; "because, as sensible people say, 'the fault of the donkey must not be laid on the saddle-bag;' and, as in this affair the fault is yours, punish yourself and don't let your anger go against the already battered and bloody armour, or the poor Rocinante, or on my feet by trying to make them travel more than is reasonable."

During conversation of this type the whole went by, along with the following four, without anything occurring to interrupt their journey, but on the fifth day as they entered a village they found a large number of people at the door of an inn enjoying themselves as if it was a holiday. As Don Quixote approached, a peasant called out, "One of these two gentlemen who come here, and who don't know any of us, will tell us what we should do about our bet."

"Certainly," said Don Quixote, "and according to the rights of the case, if I can manage to understand it."

"Well, here it is sir," said the peasant; "a man of this village who is so fat that he weighs twenty stone challenged another, a neighbour of his, who does not weigh more than nine, to run a race. The agreement was that they were to run a distance of a hundred meters with equal weights; and when the challenger was asked how the weights were to be equalised he said that the other, as he weighed nine stone, should put eleven stone of iron on his back, and that in this way the twenty stone of the thin man would equal the twenty stone of the fat one."

"Not at all," exclaimed Sancho, before Don Quixote could answer; " only a few days ago I stopped being a governor and a judge, as the world knows, so it is up to me to settle these doubtful questions and give an opinion in disputes of this sort."

"Answer, Sancho my friend," said Don Quixote, "because I am not fit to give meat to a dog, my mind is so confused and upset."

With this permission Sancho said to the peasants who stood around him, waiting for his decision to come, "Brothers, what the fat man asks for does not have a shadow of justice in it; because, if it is true, as they say, that the challenged may choose the weapons, the other has no right to choose anything that will prevent and keep him from winning. My decision, therefore, is that the fat challenger trim, remove, peel off and correct himself, and take eleven stone of fat off his body, here or there, however he likes, and as suits him best; and being in this way reduced to nine stone in weight, he will make himself equal and even with the nine stone of his opponent, and they will be able to run on equal terms."

"That's good," said one of the peasants as he heard Sancho's decision, "the gentleman has spoken like a saint, and given judgment like a lord! But I'll bet the fat man won't remove an ounce of his flesh, not to say eleven stone."

"The best plan will be for them not to run," said another, "so the thin man will not break down under the weight, and the fat does not have to rid himself of his flesh; let half the betting money be spent on wine, and let's take these gentlemen to the tavern where it has the best."

"I thank you, sirs," said Don Quixote; "but I cannot stop for a moment, because sad thoughts and unhappy circumstances force me to seem impolite and to travel quickly;" and urging Rocinante he went on, leaving them wondering about what they had seen and heard, at his strange figure and the shrewdness of his servant, because that's what they believed Sancho to be; and another of them observed, "If the servant is so clever, what must the master be? I'll bet, if they are going to Salamanca to study, they'll become magistrates of the Court in an instant."

The master and man spent the night in the fields and open air, and the next day as they were continuing their journey they saw coming towards them a man on foot with saddle-bags on the neck and a javelin or spiked stick in his hand, who, as soon as he came close to Don Quixote, increased his pace and half running came up to him, and embracing his right thigh, because he could reach no higher, exclaimed with evident pleasure, "O Señor Don Quixote of La Mancha, what happiness it will be to the heart of my lord the duke when he knows you are coming back to his castle, because he is still there with my lady the duchess!"

"I do not recognise you, friend," said Don Quixote, "and I do not know who you are, unless you tell me."

"I am Tosilos, my lord the duke's servant, Señor Don Quixote," replied the courier; "he who refused to fight you over marrying the daughter of Dona Rodriguez."

"God bless me!" exclaimed Don Quixote; "is it possible that you are the one who my enemies the enchanters changed into the servant you speak of in order to rob me of the honour of that battle?"

"Nonsense, good sir!" said the messenger; "there was no enchantment or transformation at all; I entered as the servant Tosilos just as I came out of it as the servant Tosilos. I thought to marry without fighting, because the girl had caught my interest; but my scheme had a very different result, because as soon as you left the castle my lord the duke gave me one hundred strokes of the stick for opposing to the orders he gave me before engaging in the combat; and the end of the whole matter is that the girl has become a nun, and Dona Rodriguez has gone back to Castile, and I am now on my way to Barcelona with a packet of letters for the mayor which my master is sending to him. If you would like, I offer you a drop of the best wine I have here, and some scraps of cheese that will serve to awaken your thirst if it is asleep."

"I accept the offer," said Sancho; "pour it out, good Tosilos."

"You are indeed the greatest glutton in the world, Sancho," said Don Quixote, "and the greatest fool on earth, not to be able to see that this courier is enchanted and this Tosilos is not the real one; stay with him and fill yourself; I will go on slowly and wait for you to catch up with me."

The servant laughed, poured his wine, unpacked his cheese, and taking out a small loaf of bread he and Sancho sat themselves on the green grass, and in peace and good fellowship finished off the contents of the saddle-bags, so resolutely that they licked the wrapper of the letters, merely because it smelt of cheese.

Tosilos said to Sancho, "Beyond a doubt Sancho my friend, this master of yours should be a madman."

"Should!" said Sancho; "he owes no man anything; he pays for everything, especially when the payment is madness. I see it clear enough, and I tell him clearly; but what's the use? Especially now that it is over for him, because he was beaten by the Knight of the White Moon."

Tosilos begged him to explain what had happened to him, but Sancho replied that it would not be good manners to leave his master waiting for him; and that some other day if they met again there would be time for that; and then getting up, after shaking his jacket and brushing the crumbs out of his beard, he mounted Dapple, and saying goodbye to Tosilos, he left him and re-joined his master, who was waiting for him under the shade of a tree.

CHAPTER 67

THE DECISION DON QUIXOTE FORMED TO BECOME A SHEPHERD AND LIVE A LIFE IN THE FIELDS WHILE THE YEAR RAN ITS COURSE

If a great number of reflections used to harass Don Quixote before his fall, now a great number more had been added. He was under the shade of a tree, as has been said, and there, like flies on honey, thoughts came swarming and stinging him. Some of them turned to the disenchantment of Dulcinea, others on the life he was about to lead in his compulsory retirement.

Sancho approached and spoke in high praise of the generous disposition of the servant Tosilos.

"Is it possible, Sancho," said Don Quixote, "that you still think that he is a real servant? Apparently it has escaped your memory that you have seen Dulcinea turned and transformed into a peasant, and the Knight of the Mirrors into the graduate Carrasco; all the work of the enchanters that persecute me. But tell me now, did you ask this Tosilos, as you call him, what has happened to Altisidora, did she cry over my absence, or has she already committed to extinction the thoughts of love that used to distress her when I was present?"

"The thoughts that I had," said Sancho, "did not leave time for asking fool's questions señor! are you now in a condition to inquire into other people's thoughts, above all love thoughts?"

"Look, Sancho," said Don Quixote, "there is a great difference between what is done out of love and what is done out of gratitude. A Knight may very well be against someone's love for him; but it is impossible, strictly speaking, for him to be ungrateful. Altisidora, loved me truly; she gave me the three handkerchiefs you know about; she cried during my departure, she abused me, putting her shame aside as she done this in public; all signs that she adored me; because the wrath of lovers always ends in abuse. I had no hope to give her, or treasures to offer her, because mine are given to Dulcinea, and the treasures of Knights are like those of the fairies,' illusory and deceptive; all I can give her is a place in my memory that I keep for her, without prejudice, however, to that which I hold devoted to Dulcinea, who you are wronging with your hesitation to whip yourself and marking that flesh – it is like I will see that eaten by wolves or worms, before I see the relief of that poor lady."

"Señor," replied Sancho, "if the truth is told, I cannot persuade myself that whipping my backside has anything to do with the disenchantment of the enchanted; it is like saying, 'If your head aches rub ointment on your knees;' I'll dare to swear that in all the histories dealing with Knighthood that you have read you have never come across anybody disenchanted by whipping; but whether you have or not, I'll whip myself when I feel to, and when the opportunity serves to do it comfortably."

"God grant it," said Don Quixote; "and heaven give you the grace to take it to heart and own the obligation you are under to help my lady, who is yours also, inasmuch as you are mine."

As they continued their journey talking in this way they came to the same spot where they had been trampled on by the bulls. Don Quixote recognised it, and said to Sancho, "This is the meadow where we came across those shepherdesses and shepherds, who were trying to revive the good calling, which gives me a novel idea, Sancho, I believe we should become shepherds, for the time I have to live in retirement. I will buy some sheep and everything else required; and, I under the name of the shepherd Quixotize and you as the shepherd Panzino, we will roam the woods and meadows singing songs here, weeping in poems there, drinking from the crystal waters of the springs, streams or flowing rivers. The oaks will give us their sweet fruit abundantly, the trunks of the hard cork trees a seat to sit on, the willows shade, the roses perfume, the meadows carpets tinted with a thousand dyes; the clear pure air will give us breath, the moon and stars will light the darkness of the night, songs will be our delight, weeping our joy, the sun will supply us with verses, and love with the skill which will make ourselves famous forever, not only in the present but in all time to come."

"Shepherds," said Sancho, "that sort of life matches my ideas; and what is more the graduate Samson Carrasco and Master Nicholas the barber might want to follow and turn into shepherds along with us; and God grant it may come into the vicar's head to join us as well, he's so cheerful and fond of enjoying himself."

"You are right, Sancho," said Don Quixote; "and if the graduate Samson Carrasco enters upon the shepherd's life, as no doubt he may call himself the shepherd Samsonino, or perhaps the shepherd Carrascon; Nicholas the barber may call himself Nicoloso, and as for the vicar I don't know what name we can call him unless it is something derived from his title, the shepherd Vicarioso. For the shepherdesses whose lovers we shall be, we can pick names as we would pears; and as my lady's name does just as well for a shepherdess as for a Princess, I do not need to trouble myself to look for one that will suit her better; to yours, Sancho, you can give her whatever name you like."

"I have no other name to give her but Teresona," said Sancho, "which will go well with her strength and with her own name, as she is called Teresa; and then when I sing about her in my verses I'll show how chaste my passion is, because I'm not going to look for better bread in other men's houses. The vicar can't have a shepherdess, for the sake of setting a good example; and if the graduate chooses to have one, that is up to him."

"God bless me, Sancho my friend!" said Don Quixote, "what a life we will lead! We will hear oboes and bagpipes, drums and tambourines! And then among all the different sorts of instruments we will hear the cymbals."

"What are cymbals?" asked Sancho, "because I have never in my whole life heard of them or seen them."

"Cymbals," said Don Quixote, "are brass plates that when struck against one another, the hollow inside makes a noise which, if not very pleasing or harmonious, is not disagreeable and harmonises very well with the strong notes of the bagpipe and tambourine. I mention this as it will be of great assistance to us when practicing this calling that includes being a poet, and as you know, the graduate Samson Carrasco is an accomplished one. I say nothing about the vicar; but I will bet he has some spice of a poet in him, and no doubt Master Nicholas has as well, because all barbers, or most of them, are guitar players and verse creators. I will cry about my separation; you will glorify yourself as a constant lover; the shepherd Carrasco will act as a rejected one, and the vicar Vicarioso as whatever pleases him best; and so, all of us will go along as happily as our hearts could wish."

To this Sancho answered, "I am so unlucky, señor, that I'm afraid the day will never come when I'll see myself good at such a calling. O what spoons I will make, what cream and cheese! And if they don't give me a name for my wisdom, they'll not fail to give me one for ingenuity. My daughter Sanchica will bring us our dinner to the field. But as she's good-looking, and shepherds are more mischievous than simple; I would not have her 'come to sheer the sheep and go back trimmed;' love-making and lawless desires are just as common in the fields as in the cities, and in shepherds' dwellings as in royal palaces; 'remove the cause, and you remove the sin;' 'if eyes don't see, hearts don't break' and 'better a clear escape than good man's prayers.'"

"A cease-fire for your proverbs, Sancho," exclaimed Don Quixote; "any one of those you have said would suffice to explain your meaning; many times I have recommended that you not to be so extravagant with proverbs and to exercise some moderation when delivering them; but it seems to me it is only 'preaching in the desert;' 'the mother beat the son and he continue the mischief."

"It seems to me," said Sancho, "that you are like the common saying, 'The pot calling the kettle black.' You scold me for saying proverbs, and then you string them together yourself."

"Observe, Sancho," replied Don Quixote, "I bring in proverbs appropriately, and when I quote them they fit like a ring on the finger; you drag them in by their heads and shoulders, rather than introduce them; and if I am not mistaken, I have told you already that proverbs are short maxims drawn from the experience and observation of historic wise men; but a proverb that is out of context is a piece of nonsense and not a maxim. But enough of this; as night is coming, let us retire some distance from the road to pass the night; what is in store for us tomorrow only God knows."

They turned aside, and ate late and poorly, very much against Sancho's will, who turned over in his mind the hardships of Knighthood in woods and forests, even though at times abundance presented itself in castles and houses, as at Don Diego de Miranda's, the wedding of Camacho the Rich, and at Don Antonio Moreno's; he reflected, however, that it could not always be day, or always night; and so that night he spent sleeping, while his master was awake.

CHAPTER 68

THE ROUGH ADVENTURE THAT HAPPENED TO DON QUIXOTE

The night was somewhat dark, because although there was a moon in the sky it was not in a position to be seen; because sometimes the moon likes to hide behind clouds, and leaves the mountains black and the valleys in darkness. Don Quixote obeyed nature and slept his first sleep, but did not give way to the second, very different from Sancho, who never had a second, because with him sleep lasted from night until morning, which showed how few cares he had. Don Quixote's cares kept him restless, so much so that he woke Sancho and said to him, "I am amazed, Sancho, by the unconcern of your temperament. I believe you are made of marble or hard brass, incapable of any emotion or feeling whatsoever. I stay awake while you sleep, I cry while you sing, I am faint with fasting while you are sluggish from pure repletion. It is the duty of good servants to share the sufferings and feel the sorrows of their masters. See the calmness of the night, the solitude of the spot, inviting us to break our sleep. Rise and live, and retire a little distance, and with a good heart and cheerful courage give yourself three or four hundred lashes on account of Dulcinea's disenchantment; and this I ask from you, making it a request, because I have no desire to ask a second time, as I know you have a heavy hand. As soon as you have laid them on yourself we will spend the rest of the night, I singing about my separation, you about your constancy, and both of us thinking about making a start with the shepherd's life we are to follow in our village."

"Señor," replied Sancho, "I'm no monk to get up in the middle of my sleep and whip myself, neither does it seem to me that one can pass from one extreme of the pain to the other of music. Will you let me sleep, and not bother me about whipping myself? Or you'll make me swear never to touch a hair on my head, not to say my flesh."

"What a hard heart!" said Don Quixote, "merciless aide! O bread poorly given, O favours unacknowledged, both of those done for you and more I intend to do for you! Through me you have seen yourself a governor, and through me you see yourself in immediate expectation of being a count, or obtaining some other equivalent title, because after darkness I hope for light."

"I don't know what that means," said Sancho; "all I know is that as long as I am asleep I have no fear or hope, trouble or glory; good luck for he that invented sleep, the coat that covers all men's thoughts, the food that removes hunger, the drink that drives away thirst, the fire that warms the cold, the cold that lowers the heat, and, to wind up with, the universal coin with which everything is bought, the weight and balance that makes the shepherd equal with the King and the fool with the wise man. Sleep, I have heard it said, has only one fault, that it is like death; because between a sleeping man and a dead man there is very little difference."

"I have never heard you speak so elegantly as now, Sancho," said Don Quixote; "and here I begin to see the truth of the proverb you sometimes quote, 'Not with whom you are bred, but with whom you are fed.'"

"Ha, master of mine," said Sancho, "it's not I that am stringing proverbs together now, they drop in pairs from your mouth faster than from mine; only there is this difference between mine and yours, that yours are well-timed and mine are untimely; but anyhow, they are all proverbs."

At this point they became aware of a harsh faint noise that seemed to spread through all the valleys around. Don Quixote stood up and placed his hand on his sword, and Sancho hid himself under Dapple and put the bundle of armour on one side of him and the donkey's saddle-bags on the other, in fear and trembling as great as Don Quixote's disturbance. Each instant the noise increased and came nearer to the two terrified men, or at least to one, because as to the other, his courage is well known to all. The fact of the matter was that some men were taking over six hundred pigs to sell at a fair, and were on their way with them at that hour, and the noise was so loud, their grunting and blowing, that they deafened the ears of Don Quixote and Sancho Panza, and they could not make out what it was. The wide-spread grunting herd came in a mass, and without showing any respect for Don Quixote's or Sancho's dignity, went right over the pair of them, demolishing Sancho's shields, and not only upsetting Don Quixote but sweeping Rocinante off his feet; and with the trampling and the grunting, and the pace at which the unclean beasts went, saddle-bags, armour, Dapple and Rocinante were left scattered on the ground and Sancho and Don Quixote in distress.

Sancho got up as well as he could and begged his master to give him his sword, saying he wanted to kill a dozen of those dirty unmannerly pigs, because by this time he had found out that was what they were.

"Let them be, my friend," said Don Quixote; "this insult is the penalty of my sin; and it is the righteous chastisement of heaven that dogs should devour a vanquished Knight, wasps sting him and pigs trample him under their feet."

"I suppose it is the chastisement of heaven, as well," said Sancho, "that flies should prick the aides of vanquished Knights, and lice eat them, and hunger attack them. If us aides were the sons of the Knights we serve, or their very near relations, it would be no wonder if the penalty of their misdeeds fell on us as well, even to the fourth generation. But what have the Panzas got to do with the Quixotes? Let's lie down again and sleep for what little of the night there is left, and God will send us dawn and we will be all right."

"You sleep, Sancho," returned Don Quixote, "because you were born to sleep as I was born to watch; and during the time from now until dawn I will give a loose rein to my thoughts, and seek a vent for them in a little song which, unknown to you, I composed in my head last night."

"I should think," said Sancho, "that the thoughts that allow one to make verses cannot be of much bother to me; let you string verses together as much as you like and I'll sleep as much as I can;" and taking the space of ground he required, he curled himself up and fell into a deep sleep, undisturbed by anything.

Don Quixote, sat up against the trunk tree, and sang this, to the accompaniment of his sighs:

In my mind,
I recollect, Love, oh your cruelty,
To death I flee,
The end from all to find.

But drawing near,
Heaven will welcome my sea of woe,
Joy I no longer know,
That world revives, yet still I linger here.

Therefore, life does kill,
And death restores life,
Strange destiny,
That deals with life and death, a mess to me!

He accompanied each verse with many sighs and tears, just like one whose heart was pierced with grief by his defeat and his separation from Dulcinea.

And now daylight came, and the sun hit Sancho on the eyes with its beams. He woke up, shook himself and stretched his lazy limbs, and seeing the havoc the pigs had made with his saddle-bags he swore aloud. Then the pair resumed their journey, and as evening closed in they saw coming towards them about ten men on horseback and four or five on foot. Don Quixote's heart began to beat quickly and Sancho's shook with fear, because the people approaching them carried lances and shields, and were moving in a very warlike manner. Don Quixote turned to Sancho and said:

"If I could make use of my weapons, and my promise had not tied my hands, I would count this group that comes against us nothing but cakes and fancy bread; but perhaps it will be something different from what we apprehend."

The men on horseback now came, and raising their lances surrounded Don Quixote in silence, and pointed them at his back and chest, threatening him with death. One of those on foot, putting his finger to his lips as a sign to him to be silent, grabbed Rocinante's reigns and took him out of the road, and the others driving Sancho and Dapple in front of them, and all maintaining a strange silence, followed the steps of the one who led Don Quixote. Don Quixote made two or three attempts to ask where they were taking him and what they wanted, but the moment he began to open his lips they threatened to close them with the points of their lances; and the same was the case with Sancho, because the moment he seemed as if he were to speak one of those on foot hit him with a stick, and Dapple as well, as if he also wanted to talk. Night set in, they increased their pace, and the fear of the two prisoners grew greater, especially as they heard themselves attacked with these words: "Come on, you cave men;" "Silence, you barbarians;" "March, you animals;" "No speaking, you Illiterates;" "Don't open your eyes, you murderous Giants, you blood-thirsty lions," and other names of this sort with which their abductors agitated the ears of the poor master and man. Sancho went along saying to himself, "barbarians, animals! I don't like those names at all; 'misfortune comes to us all at once like dogs that return with sticks,' and I hope God does not make it worse for us than he has for them."

Don Quixote rode completely dazed, unable to make out the meaning of these abusive names that they called him, and the only conclusion he could come to was that there was no good to be hoped for and much evil to be feared. And now, about an hour after midnight, they reached a castle which Don Quixote immediately recognised as the duke's, where they had been not too long ago. "God bless me!" he said, "what does this mean? There is civility and respect in this house; but with the vanquished good turns into evil, and evil into worse."

They entered the main gate of the castle and found the courtyard prepared in a style that added to their amazement and doubled their fears, as will be seen in the following chapter.

CHAPTER 69

THE STRANGEST AND MOST EXTRAORDINARY ADVENTURE THAT HAPPENED TO DON QUIXOTE IN THE WHOLE COURSE OF THIS GREAT HISTORY

The horsemen dismounted, and, together with the men on foot, without a moment's delay seized Sancho and Don Quixote, and carried them into the court, which had a hundred burning candles placed in holders all around, and more than five hundred lamps in the corridors, so that despite being night, which was somewhat dark, the lack of daylight could not be perceived. In the middle of the court was a wooden frame, raised about six feet above the ground and covered completely by an immense covering of black velvet, and on the steps surrounding it white wax candles burned in more than a hundred silver candlesticks. On the wooden frame was the dead body of a lady so lovely that her beauty made death itself look beautiful. She lay with her head resting on a cushion of rich woven fabric and crowned with sweet-smelling flowers, her hands crossed on her chest. On one side of the court was a stage, with two chairs were two people sat, who from having crowns on their heads and sceptres in their hands appeared to be Kings of some sort, whether real or fake ones. By the side of this stage, which was reached by steps, were two other chairs on which the men carrying the prisoners sat Don Quixote and Sancho, all in silence, and with signs indicated to them that they were to remain silent; which, however, they would have been anyway, without any signs, because their amazement of what they had seen made them tongue-tied. And now two people of distinction, who were immediately recognised by Don Quixote as his hosts the duke and duchess, ascended the stage and sat themselves on two gorgeous chairs close to the two Kings, as they seemed to be. Who would not have been amazed by this? This wasn't all, because Don Quixote had perceived that the dead body on the frame was that of the fair Altisidora.

As the duke and duchess mounted the stage Don Quixote and Sancho stood up and gave them deep respect, which they returned by bowing their heads slightly. At this moment an officer came, and approaching Sancho threw over him a robe of black painted all over with flames of fire, and taking off his cap put on his head, in the style of those undergoing the sentence of the Holy Office; and whispered in his ear that he must not open his lips, or they would put a gag on him, or take his life. Sancho observed himself from head to toe and saw himself covered with flames; but as they did not burn him, he did not care about it. He took off the cap, and seeing it painted with devils he put it on again, saying to himself, "Well, so far they don't burn me or take me away." Don Quixote observed him too, and although fear had got the better of his faculties, he could not help smiling to see the figure Sancho presented.

And now from underneath the frame, so it seemed, there was a low sweet sound of flutes, which, coming unbroken by a human voice (because even silence kept its silence), had a soft sentimental effect. Then, next to the pillow of what seemed to be the dead body, suddenly a youth of a Roman appearance appeared, who, to the accompaniment of a harp which he played himself, sang in a sweet and clear voice these two poems:

Fair Altisidora, the sport,
Of the cold Don Quixote's cruelty had been,
Returns to life, and in this magic court,
The ladies in fur come to grace the scene,
And while her ladies all of a good sort,
Dressed her in the robes to be seen,
Her beauty and her sorrows to report,
Of her pain and that of the mean.

But not in life, it seems to me,
This Lady deserved such a wrong,
Cold death, I believe, clear to see,
My voice gives this consoling song.
A soul, from this prison-house set free,
On the lake it floats along,
Your praise I am singing and it holds its way,
And makes the waters of silence stay.

At this point one of the two that looked like Kings exclaimed, "Enough, enough, divine singer! It would be an endless task to tell us about the death and the charms of the incomparable Altisidora, not dead as the ignorant world would believe, but living in fame and in the self-punishment which Sancho Panza, here present, has to undergo to restore her to the long-lost light. Do you, therefore, Rhadamanthus, who sit as a judge with me, as you know that mysterious fate has directed the resuscitation of this lady, announce and declare, that the happiness we look forward to from her restoration should no longer be deferred."

As soon as Minos the associate judge of Rhadamanthus said this, Rhadamanthus got up and said:

"Officials of this house, high and low, great and small, hurry immediately, and print on Sancho's face twenty-four slaps, and give him twelve pinches; because the ceremony of the restoration of Altisidora depends on this."

On hearing this Sancho broke his silence and cried out, "For all that is good, I'll turn into a Moor before I allow my face to be slapped. Poor me! What has handling my face got to do with the resurrection of this lady? They enchant Dulcinea, and whip me in order to disenchant her; Altisidora dies from the ailments God sent her, and to bring her to life again they must give me twenty-four slaps, and pinch my body! Try these jokes on someone else; 'I'm an old dog, and this will not work on me.'"

"You will die," said Rhadamanthus in a loud voice; "concede, you tiger; humble yourself, proud hunter; suffer and be silent, because nothing impossible is asked of you; it is not for you to inquire into the difficulties of this matter; you must be slapped, and made to cry with pinches. I say, officials, obey my orders; or by the word of an honest man, you will dislike your punishment."

Six ladies, advanced across the court, making their appearance in procession, one after the other, and all with their right hands raised. As soon as Sancho caught sight of them, roaring like a bull, he exclaimed, "I might let myself be handled by the whole world; but to allow these ladies to touch me - not a bit! Scratch my face, pierce me with daggers; pinch my arms with red-hot metal; I'll take all patiently to serve these noble people; but I won't let these ladies touch me, even if the devil would take me away!"

Here Don Quixote, broke his silence, saying to Sancho, "Have patience, my son, and gratify these noble people, and give thanks to heaven that it has infused such virtue into you, that by your suffering you can disenchant the enchanted and restore the dead to life."

The ladies were now close to Sancho, and he, having become more obedient and reasonable, sat himself well in his chair presented his face and beard to the first, who delivered to him a very strong slap, and then gave him a bow.

"Less politeness señora, it doesn't make this any less bad," said Sancho; "and God your hands smell like vinegar."

All the ladies slapped him and several others of the household pinched him; but he could not stand it; and so, apparently losing patience, he stood up, and grabbing a lit torch that was near attacked the ladies and the rest of his tormentors, exclaiming, "Be gone, administers of hell; I'm not made of brass not to feel this torture."

At this moment Altisidora, who probably was tired of lying on her back for so long, turned onto her side; and seeing this the bystanders cried out almost with one voice, "Altisidora is alive! Altisidora lives!"

Rhadamanthus asked Sancho to control his wrath, as the objective they had was now attained. When Don Quixote saw Altisidora move, he went on his knees to Sancho saying to him, "Now is the time, my son, for you to give yourself some of those lashes you are bound to give for the disenchantment of Dulcinea. Now, I say, is the time when the virtue that is in you is ripe, and presented with the value to work the good that is looked for from you."

To which Sancho answered, "This is a trick on a trick, I think, and not honey on pancakes; what a nice thing it would be for a whipping to come now, on top of the pinches and slaps! You might as well take a big stone and tie it round my neck, and throw me down a well; I would not mind it much, if I'm always going to be made the cure of other people's ailments. Leave me alone; or else I swear to God I'll feed myself to the dogs, if they come my way."

Altisidora had by this time sat up on the wooden frame, and as she did the trumpets sounded, accompanied by the flutes, and the voices of all those present exclaiming, "Long life to Altisidora! long life to Altisidora!" The duke and duchess and the Kings Minos and Rhadamanthus stood up, and all, together with

Don Quixote and Sancho, advanced to welcome her and take her down from the frame; and she, acting as though she were recovering from a faint, bowed her head to the duke and duchess and to the Kings, and looking sideways at Don Quixote, said to him, "God forgive you, insensitive Knight, because through your cruelty I have been, to me it seems, in the other world for more than a thousand years; and to you, the most compassionate man on earth, I give thanks for the life I am now in possession of. From this day onward, friend Sancho, you may count as your own, six dresses of mine which I give to you, to make as many shirts for yourself as you can, and if they are not all quite whole, at least they will be clean."

Sancho, kneeling with the cap in his hand, kissed her hands in gratitude. The duke asked them to take it from him, and give him back his jacket and remove the flaming robe. Sancho begged the duke to let him keep the robe and cap; as he wanted to take them home as a souvenir of that unique adventure. The duchess said they must leave them with him; as he was a great friend of hers. The duke then gave orders that the court should be cleared, and that all should return to their rooms, and that Don Quixote and Sancho should be guided to theirs.

CHAPTER 70

DEALING WITH MATTERS CRUCIAL FOR THE CLEAR COMPREHENSION OF THIS HISTORY

That night, Sancho slept in a small bed in the same room as Don Quixote, a thing he would have rather avoided, as he knew that the questions his master would ask would not allow him to sleep, and he was not in the mood for talking, as he still felt the pain of his recent torture, which interfered with his freedom of speech; and it would have been more to his taste to sleep in a field alone, than in that luxurious room accompanied. And his apprehension proved to be the case, and his anticipation so correct, that barely had his master got into bed when he said, "What do you think about tonight's adventure, Sancho? The power of cold-hearted scorn can be great, as you with your own eyes have seen Altisidora dead, not by arrows, by the sword, or by any warlike weapon, or by deadly poison, but by the thought of the severity and scorn with which I have always treated her."

"She might have died," said Sancho, "when she pleased and how she pleased; and she might have left me alone, because I never made her fall in love with me or scorned her. I don't know and cannot imagine how the recovery of Altisidora, a lady more whimsical than wise, can have, as I have said before, anything to do with the suffering of Sancho Panza. Now I begin to see plainly and clearly that there are enchanters and enchanted people in the world; and may God free me from them, since I can't free myself; and so I beg you to let me sleep and not ask me any more questions, unless you want me to throw myself out of the window."

"Sleep, Sancho my friend," said Don Quixote, "if the pinches and the slaps you have received will let you."

"No pain can match the insult of the slaps," said Sancho, "for the simple reason that it was ladies, that gave them to me; but once more I ask you to let me sleep, because sleep is the relief from misery to those who are miserable when awake."

"So be it, and God be with you," said Don Quixote.

Both of them fell asleep, and Cide Hamete, the author of this great history, took this opportunity to record what it was that induced the duke and duchess to create the elaborate plot that has been described.

The graduate Samson Carrasco, he says, not forgetting how he as the Knight of the Mirrors had been vanquished and overthrown by Don Quixote, decided to try again, hoping for better luck than he had before; and so, having learned where Don Quixote was from the servant who brought the letter and present to Sancho's wife, Teresa Panza, he decided to get himself some new armour and another horse, and put a white moon on his shield, and to carry his weapons he had a donkey led by a peasant, not by Tom Cecial his former aide as he feared he would be recognised by Sancho or Don Quixote. He came to the duke's castle, and the duke informed him of the road and route Don Quixote had taken with the intention of being present at the contests in Saragossa. He told him, as well, about the jokes they had practised on him, and the plan for the disenchantment of Dulcinea at the expense of Sancho's backside; and finally he gave him an account of the trick Sancho had played on his master, making him believe that Dulcinea was enchanted and turned into a country girl; and about how the duchess, his wife, had persuaded Sancho that it was he himself who was deceived, inasmuch as Dulcinea was really enchanted; at which the graduate could not stop laughing, and marvelled at both the sharpness and simplicity of Sancho and at the extent to which Don Quixote's madness went. The duke begged him if he found him, to return that way and let him know the result; this the graduate agreed to.

He left in search of Don Quixote, and not finding him in Saragossa, he continued to search, and what happened has already been told. He returned to the duke's castle and told him everything, what the conditions of the combat were, and how Don Quixote was now, like a loyal Knight, returning, to keep his promise of retiring, to his village for a year; by which time, the graduate said, he might perhaps be cured of his madness, because that was the objective that had led him to adopt these disguises, as it was a sad thing for a gentleman of such good sense as Don Quixote to be a madman.

And so he left the duke, and went home to his village to wait there for Don Quixote, who was coming behind him. Here the duke seized the opportunity of performing this joke on him, as he enjoyed everything connected with Sancho and Don Quixote. He had the roads around his castle, everywhere he thought Don Quixote was likely to pass on his return, occupied by large numbers of his servants on foot and on horseback, who were to bring him to the castle, however necessary, if they met him. They did meet him, and sent the word to the duke, who, having already plotted what was to be done, as soon as he heard of his arrival, ordered the candles and lamps in the court to be lit and Altisidora to be placed on the frame with all the spectacle and ceremony that has already been described, the whole affair being so well arranged and acted that it contrasted very little from reality. And Cide Hamete says, moreover, that for his part he considers the concocters of the joke as crazy as the victims of it, and that the duke and duchess were not too far from being something like fools themselves when they took such actions to play such a trick on a pair of fools.

As for the two fools, one was sleeping soundly and the other awake occupied with his erratic thoughts, when daylight came to them bringing with it the desire to rise; because being lazy was never a delight to Don Quixote, whether he was a victor or vanquished.

Altisidora, came back from death as Don Quixote believed, and following her lord and lady, entered the room, crowned with the flowers she had worn on the frame and in a robe of white embroidered with gold silk, her hair flowing loose over her shoulders, and leaning on a fine stick. Don Quixote, unsettled and in confusion by her appearance, curled himself up and covered himself with the sheets and cover of the bed, tongue-tied, and unable to offer her any courtesy.

Altisidora sat herself on a chair at the end of the bed, and after a deep sigh, said to him in a soft voice, "When women of rank and modest ladies trample their honour under their feet, and let the tongue loose that breaks through every barrier, publishing the inner most secrets of their hearts, they are open and vulnerable. I am one of those ladies, Señor Don Quixote of La Mancha, crushed, conquered, love-sick, but yet patient through suffering and virtuous, and so much so that my heart broke with grief and I lost my life. For the last two days I have been dead, murdered by the thought of the cruelty with which you have treated me, stubborn Knight, harder than marble to my appeal; or at least believed to be dead by all who saw me; and had it not been that Love, taking pity on me, let my recovery rest on the suffering of this good aide, I would have remained in the other world."

"Love might as well have let it rest on the suffering of ass." Said Sancho, "But tell me, señora - and may heaven send you a better lover than my master - what did you see in the other world? What goes on in hell? Because of course that's where one who dies in despair goes."

"To tell the truth," said Altisidora, "I cannot have died completely, because I did not go into hell; had I gone in, it is very certain I would have never come out again. The truth is, I came to the gate, where about a dozen or so devils were playing tennis, all in trousers and jackets, with falling collars and ruffled shirts; in their hands they held rackets of fire; but what amazed me more was that books, apparently full of nonsense and rubbish, were their tennis balls, a strange and marvellous thing; this, however, did not astonish me so much as to observe that, although with players it is usual for the winners to be glad and the losers upset, in that game all of them were growling, all were angry, and all were cursing one another."

"That's no wonder," said Sancho; "because devils, whether playing or not, can never be content, win or lose."

"Very likely," said Altisidora; "but there is another thing that surprises me as well, I mean surprised me then, and that was that no ball was of any use a second time; and the constant succession of books was beyond belief, new and old. To one of them, a brand-new, well-bound one, they gave such a stroke that they knocked the insides out of it and scattered the pages everywhere. 'What book that is,' said one devil to another, and the other replied, 'It is the "Second Part of the History of Don Quixote of La Mancha," not by Cide Hamete, the original author, but by a Toledoan.' 'Into the depths of hell with it out of my sight,' said the first. 'Is it so bad?' said the other. 'So bad,' said the first, 'that if I had set myself deliberately to make it worse, I could not have done it.' They then went on with their game, knocking other books around; and I, having heard them mention the name of Don Quixote whom I love and adore so much, took care to retain this vision in my memory."

"A vision it must have been, no doubt," said Don Quixote, "because there is no other I in the world; this history has been going around here for some time from hand to hand, but it does not stay long in any, because everybody passes it on. I am not disturbed by hearing that I am also heard of in the darkness of hell or in the daylight above, because I am not the one that history speaks of. If it were good, faithful, and true, it will live forever; but if it is bad, from its birth to its burial will not be a very long journey."

Altisidora was about to proceed with her complaint against Don Quixote, when he said to her, "I have several times told you, señora that it upsets me that you have set your affections on me, as they can never be gratified by mine. I was born to belong to Dulcinea del Toboso, and fate, if there is such thing, dedicated me to her; and to believe that any other beauty can take the place she occupies in my heart is to believe an impossibility. This clear declaration should suffice to make you retire within the boundary of your modesty, because no one can bind himself to do impossibilities."

Hearing this, Altisidora, with a show of anger and agitation, exclaimed, "God's life! Don soul of mortar, stone, stubborner than stubborn, if I attack you I'll tear your eyes out! Do you think, Don Vanquished, Don beaten, that I died for your sake? All that you have seen tonight has been made up; I'm not the woman to suffer for such a camel, and even less to die!"

"That I can well believe," said Sancho; "because all that about lovers pining to death is absurd; they may talk about it, but doing it only the fools would believe that!"

While they were talking, the musician, singer, and poet, who had sung the two poems given above came in, and giving deep respect to Don Quixote said, "Will you, sir Knight, retain me as one of your most faithful servants, because I have always been a great admirer of yours, because of your fame as well as your achievements?"

"Will you tell me who you are," replied Don Quixote, "so that my courtesy may be able to answer your question?"

The young man replied that he was the musician from the night before.

"In truth," said Don Quixote, "you have an excellent voice; but what you sang did not seem to me very suitable; because what have Garcilasso's poems got to do with the death of this lady?"

"Don't be surprised by that," returned the musician; "because for poets of our time, it is the way for everyone to write as he pleases and steal parts where he chooses, whether it be suitable for the matter or not, and these days there is no piece of music they can sing that has not already been written in some way or other."

Don Quixote was about to reply, but was prevented by the duke and duchess, who came in to see him, and following was a long and delightful conversation, in the course of which Sancho said so many funny things that he left the duke and duchess amazed not only by his simplicity but by his sharpness. Don Quixote begged their permission to make his departure, as for a vanquished Knight like himself it was more appropriate for him to live in a pig-sty than in a royal palace. They gave their permission, and the duchess asked him if Altisidora treated him better now.

He replied, "Señora, let me tell you that this lady's ailment comes entirely from idleness, and the cure for it is honest and constant employment. She has told me that jackets are worn in hell; and as she must know how to make them, let her be occupied in shifting the needle to and fro, because the image or images of what she loves will not remain in her thoughts while she is busy; this is the truth, this is my opinion, and this is my advice."

"And mine," added Sancho; "because I never in my whole life saw a jacket maker that died from love; when ladies are working their minds are more set on finishing their tasks than on thinking about their loves. I speak from my own experience; because when I'm digging I never think of my wife; I mean my Teresa Panza, whom I love more than my own eyelids."

"You speak well, Sancho," said the duchess, "and I will take care that my Altisidora employs herself from now on in needlework of some sort; because she is an expert at it."

"There is no reason to resort to that remedy, señora," said Altisidora; "because the mere thought of the cruelty with which this villain has treated me will suffice to delete him from my memory without any other method needed; with your highness's permission I will leave now, not to have in front of my eyes, I won't say his beautiful face, but his repulsive ugly looks."

"That reminds me of the common saying, that 'he who protests is ready to forgive,'" said the duke.

Altisidora then, pretending to wipe away her tears with a handkerchief, gave respect to her master and mistress and left the room.

"Bad luck to you, poor lady," said Sancho, "bad luck to you! You have gained a soul as dry as wind and a heart as hard as an oak; had it been me, 'believe 'another rooster would have crowed at you.'"

So the conversation came to an end, Don Quixote dressed himself and had dinner with the duke and duchess, and then left the same evening.

CHAPTER 71

WHAT PASSED BETWEEN DON QUIXOTE AND SANCHO ON THE WAY TO THEIR VILLAGE

The vanquished and afflicted Don Quixote went along very sad in one respect and very happy in another. His sadness arose from his defeat, and his satisfaction from the thought that the virtue in Sancho had been proven by the resurrection of Altisidora; although it was difficult to persuade himself that the love-sick lady had really been dead. Sancho went along far from cheerful, because it upset him that Altisidora had not kept her promise of giving him the dresses; and thinking about this in his mind he said to his master, "Surely, señor, I'm the most unlucky doctor in the world; there's many physicians that, after killing the sick man he had to cure, are still paid for their work, although all they do is prescribe the list of medicines that are to be given, and this is already decided, and there his labour comes to an end; but with me although to cure somebody else costs me drops of my blood, slaps and pinches, and even whippings, nobody gives me anything. Well, I swear on all that's good if they put another patient in my hands, they'll have to pay me first before I cure him; because, as they say, 'by his preaching the priest gets his dinner,' and I'm not going to believe that heaven has given me the virtue I have, so that I should be giving it to others all for nothing."

"You are right, Sancho my friend," said Don Quixote, "and Altisidora has behaved very badly in not giving you the dresses she promised; and although that virtue of yours is complimentary grace - as it has cost you nothing, still you deserved your payment. I can say for myself that if payment was required for the lashes on account of the disenchant of Dulcinea, I would have given it to you freely. However, I am not sure, whether payment will agree with the cure, and I do not want the reward to interfere with the medicine. I think there will be nothing lost by trying it; consider how much you would like Sancho, and whip yourself immediately, and pay yourself out of your own hand, as you have money of mine."

This proposal opened the eyes and ears of Sancho, and in his heart very readily accepted the whipping of himself, and he said to his master, "Very well then, señor, I'll hold myself ready to gratify your wishes if I'm to profit from it; because the love of my wife and children forces me to seem greedy for money. Tell me how much you will pay me for each lash I give myself."

"If Sancho," replied Don Quixote, "I was to repay you for the cure you can provide, the treasures of Venice and the mines of Bolivia, would be insufficient. See what you have of mine, and put a price on each lash."

"There are three thousand three hundred or so lashes to be given," said Sancho, "and out of those I have given myself five, the rest remain; let the five go for free, and let us take the three thousand three hundred, which at a quarter coin each (because I will not take less even if the whole world asked me) make three thousand three hundred quarter coins; the three thousand are one thousand five hundred half coins, which make seven hundred and fifty full coins; and the three hundred make a hundred and fifty half coins, which come to seventy-five full coins, which added to the seven hundred and fifty make eight hundred and twenty-five coins in total. These I will take out of what I have belonging to you, and I'll return home rich and content, although well whipped, because 'there's no receiving without giving' but I say no more."

"O blessed Sancho! O dear Sancho!" said Don Quixote; "we will be bound to serve you, Dulcinea and I, for the rest of our lives, as long as heaven grants to us! If she returns to her former shape, her misfortune will have been good fortune, and my defeat a real triumph. But, Sancho; when will you begin the whipping? Because if you get it done quickly, I will give you a hundred coins extra."

"When?" said Sancho; "tonight without fail. Let us go into the open air, and I'll whip myself."

The night, longed for by Don Quixote with the greatest anxiety in the world, finally came, although it seemed to him that the revolution of the sun had broken down, and that the day was drawing itself out longer than usual, which is the case with lovers, who desires never seem to reconcile with time. Finally, they made their way among some pleasant trees that stood a little distance from the road, and dismounting from Rocinante's and Dapple's saddle, they stretched themselves on the green grass and made their dinner out of Sancho's supplies, and he making a powerful and flexible whip out of Dapple's reins walked about twenty paces from his master among some oak trees. Don Quixote observed him walk away with such determination and spirit, and said to him, "Take care, my friend, not to cut yourself into pieces; allow the lashes to wait for one another, and do not hurry as to run yourself out of breath midway; I mean, do not whip so vigorously as to make your life end before you have reached the desired number; and to make sure you do not give too much or too little, I will stay here and count on my rosary the lashes you give yourself. May heaven help you as your good intention deserves."

"'Promises don't distress a good payer,'" said Sancho; "I intend to whip myself in such a way, without killing myself, because in that, no doubt, lies the essence of this miracle."

He then stripped himself from the waist upwards, and snatching the rope he began to whip himself and Don Quixote started to count the lashes. He had given himself about six or eight when he began to think this was no little matter, and its price very low; and stopping his hand for a moment, he told his master that he had made a blind bargain, because each of those lashes should have been paid for at the rate of half a coin instead of a quarter.

"Go on, Sancho my friend, and do not be disheartened," said Don Quixote; "because I will double the price."

"In that case," said Sancho, "in God's hand it is, and let it rain lashes." However, he no longer whipped his shoulders, but instead started to whip the trees, with such shouts every now and then, that one would have thought his soul was being plucked out by the roots. Don Quixote was so touched, and fearing he might kill himself, and that through Sancho's carelessness he might not gain his objective, and so said to him, "Let the matter rest where it is for now my friend, because the remedy seems to me to be a very rough one, and it is best to have patience; 'Rome was not built in day.' If I am not wrong you have given yourself over a thousand lashes; that is enough for the present; 'because the donkey,' to put it in simple way, 'bears the load, but not an overload.'"

"No, no, señor," replied Sancho; "that could not be said of me, 'The money paid, the arms broken;' stand back a little and let me give myself another thousand lashes; because in a couple of rounds like this we will have finished off the lot."

"As you are in such a willing mood," said Don Quixote, "may heaven aid you; continue and I'll step back."

Sancho returned to his task with so much spirit that he soon had the bark stripped off several trees, such was the severity with which he whipped them; and one time, raising his voice, and giving an oak a tremendous lash, he cried out, "Here dies the devil, and all with him!"

At the sound of his cry and of the stroke of the cruel lash, Don Quixote ran to him, and grabbing the twisted reins that served him for a whip, said to him, "Heaven forbid, Sancho my friend, that to please me you should lose your life, which is needed for the support of your wife and children; let Dulcinea wait for a better opportunity, and I will content myself with hope soon to be realised, and have patience until you have recovered fresh strength to be able to finish off this business to the satisfaction of everybody."

"As you will have it, señor," said Sancho, "so be it; but throw your coat over my shoulders, because I'm sweating and I don't want to catch a cold; it's a risk that rookie disciplinarians run."

Don Quixote obeyed, and removing his coat covered Sancho with it, who slept until the sun woke him; they then resumed their journey, which for the time being they brought to an end at a village that was about three miles away. They dismounted at a inn which Don Quixote recognised as such and did not take to be a castle with a moat, towers, a gate, and a drawbridge; because ever since he had been beaten he talked more rationally about everything. They gave him a room on the ground floor, which had hanging canvass paintings. On one of them was, painted very poorly, the Abduction of Helen, when she was carried away from the King of Sparta, and on the other was the story of Dido and Aeneas, where it could be seen that he was abandoning her, and she was making signals to the fugitive who was out at sea on a ship. He noticed in the two stories that Helen did not go very reluctantly, because she was laughing slyly and wickedly; but the fair Dido was shown dropping tears the size of chestnuts from her eyes. As Don Quixote looked at them he said to himself, "These two ladies were very unfortunate not to have been born in this age, and I unfortunate above all men not to have been born in theirs. Had I been alongside those gentlemen, Troy would not have been burned, because all I would have done is defeated Paris, and all these misfortunes would have been avoided."

"I'll bet," said Sancho, "that soon there won't be a tavern, inn, or barber's shop that won't have paintings of our adventures; but I'd like it painted by a better painter than whoever painted these."

"You are right, Sancho," said Don Quixote, "because this painter is like the one who was in Andalusia, who when they asked him what he was painting, used to say, 'Whatever it may turn out to be; and if he decided to paint a hen he would write under it, 'This is a hen,' in fear they might think it was a fox. The painter or writer, because it's all the same, who published the history of this new Don Quixote that has come out, must have been one of this kind I think, Sancho, because he painted or wrote 'whatever it might turn out to be;' or perhaps he is like a poet called Mauleon that was in the Court some years ago, who used to answer carelessly whatever he was asked, and when someone asked him what from God meant, he replied 'from to give'. But, putting this aside, tell me, Sancho, are you able to give yourself some more tonight, and would you rather do it indoors or in the open air?"

"Señor," said Sancho, "what I'm going to give myself, is the same to me whether it is in a house or in the fields; but I guess I'd like it to be among some trees; because I think they are good company for me and help me to bear my pain gracefully."

"And yet it is not so graceful, Sancho my friend," said Don Quixote; "but, to enable you to recover strength, we could keep it for our own village; because the latest we will get there will be the day after tomorrow."

Sancho said he would do as he pleased; but he would prefer to finish off the business quickly before his blood cooled and while he had the desire, because "in delay there is danger" very often people "pray to God and neglect the work," and "one take was better than two later," and "a bird in the hand is worth two in the bush."

"For God's sake, Sancho, no more proverbs!" exclaimed Don Quixote; "it seems to me you are becoming whatever you want to be again; speak in a plain, simple, straight-forward way, as I have often told you, and you will find the good in it."

"I don't know what bad luck it is of mine," said Sancho, "but I can't say a word without a proverb; however, I intend to mend if I can;" and so for the present the conversation ended.

CHAPTER 72

HOW DON QUIXOTE AND SANCHO REACHED THEIR VILLAGE

That day Don Quixote and Sancho remained in the village inn waiting for night, one to finish off his task of whipping himself in the field, and the other to see it accomplished, because within that lay the triumph of his wishes. Meanwhile a traveller arrived at the inn on horseback with three or four servants, one of whom said to him who appeared to be the master, "Here, Señor Don Alvaro Tarfe, you may take your siesta today; the rooms seem to be clean and cool."

When he heard this Don Quixote said to Sancho, "Look, Sancho; when turning over the pages of that book, the Second Part of my history I think I came across this name: Don Alvaro Tarfe."

"If that is so," said Sancho; "let him dismount, and then we can ask about it."

The gentleman dismounted, and the landlady gave him a room on the ground floor opposite Don Quixote's, adorned with paintings of the same sort. The newly arrived gentleman put on a summer coat, and coming out to the gateway of the inn, which was wide and cool, addressing Don Quixote, who was pacing up and down there, he asked, "In what direction are you heading, sir?"

"To a village near here, which is my own village," replied Don Quixote; "and you, where are you heading for?"

"I am going to Granada, señor," said the gentleman, "to my own town."

"And a good town," said Don Quixote; "but will you do me the favour of telling me your name, because it is of more importance for to me to know it than I can tell you."

"My name is Don Alvaro Tarfe," replied the traveller.

To which Don Quixote returned, "I have no doubt that you are Don Alvaro Tarfe who appears in print, in the Second Part of the history of Don Quixote of La Mancha, lately published by a new author."

"I am one and the same," replied the gentleman; "and that same Don Quixote, the principal person in the history, was a very great friend of mine, and it was I who took him from his home, or at least induced him to go to some contests that were to be held in Saragossa, where I was going myself; indeed, I showed him much kindness, and saved him from having his shoulders touched by the executioner because of his extreme rashness."

"Tell me, Señor Don Alvaro," said Don Quixote, "am I at all like that Don Quixote you know of?"

"No," replied the traveller, "not a bit."

"And that Don Quixote" he said, "did he have with him an aide called Sancho Panza?"

"He did," said Don Alvaro; "but although everyone said he was very funny, I never heard him say anything humorous."

"That I can well believe," said Sancho, "because to come out with jokes is not in everyone's nature; and that Sancho you speaks of, gentle sir, must be some great crook, fool, and thief, all in one; because I am the real Sancho Panza, and I have more jokes in me than if it rained them; you will see; come along with me for a year or so, and you will find they fall from me like leaves from trees, and so rich and abundantly that although I don't always know what I am saying I make everybody that hears me laugh. And the real Don Quixote of La Mancha, the famous, the valiant, the wise, the lover, the righter of wrongs, the guardian of orphans, the protector of widows, the saviour of ladies, he who has for his sole mistress the incomparable Dulcinea del Toboso, is this gentleman in front of you, my master; all other Don Quixotes and all other Sancho Panzas are fakes."

"God I believe it," said Don Alvaro; "because you have said more jokes, my friend, in the few words you have spoken than the other Sancho Panza in all I ever heard from him. He was greedier than well-spoken, and duller than funny; and I am convinced that the enchanters who persecute Don Quixote the Good have been trying to persecute me with Don Quixote the Bad. But I don't know what to say, because I am ready to swear I left him trapped in Saragossa, and here another Don Quixote turns up, though a very different one from the one I knew."

"I don't know whether I am good," said Don Quixote, "but I can safely say I am not 'Bad;' and to prove it, let me tell you, Señor Don Alvaro Tarfe, I have never in my life been to Saragossa; so far from that, when it was told that this imaginary Don Quixote had been present at the contests in that city, I declined to enter it, in order to expose this falsehood to the whole world; and so I went straight to Barcelona, the treasure-house of courtesy, haven of strangers, asylum of the poor, home of the valiant, champion of the wronged, pleasant exchange of firm friendships, and a city unrivalled in beauty. And although the adventures that happened to me there are not by any means matters of enjoyment, but rather of regret, I do not regret them, simply because I have had the pleasure to see it. In a word, Señor Don Alvaro Tarfe, I am Don Quixote of La Mancha, the one that fame speaks of, and not the unlucky one that has attempted to use my name and pretended to be me. I ask you, as a duty of a gentleman to make a declaration to the magistrate of this village that you have never seen me in your whole life until this moment, and that am I not the Don Quixote in print in the Second Part, and neither is this Sancho Panza, my aide, the one you knew."

"That I will do most willingly Señor," replied Don Alvaro; "although it amazes me to find two Don Quixotes and two Sancho Panzas, so alike in name but so different in manner; and again I say and declare that what I saw, I cannot have seen, and that what happened to me cannot have happened."

"No doubt you are enchanted, like my lady Dulcinea del Toboso," said Sancho; "and if your disenchantment rested on me giving myself another three thousand or so lashes like what I'm giving myself for her, I'd do it without looking for anything."

"I don't understand that about the lashes," said Don Alvaro.

Sancho replied that it was a long story to tell, but he would tell him if they happened to be going the same way.

Dinnertime arrived, and Don Quixote and Don Alvaro ate together. The magistrate of the village came into the inn along with a notary, and Don Quixote petitioned, stating that it was requisite for his rights that Don Alvaro Tarfe, the gentleman present, should make a declaration to him that he did not know Don Quixote of La Mancha, who was also present, and that he was not the one that was in print in a history entitled: "The Second Part of Don Quixote of La Mancha, by Avellaneda of Tordesillas."

The magistrate finally put it into legal form, and the declaration was made with all the formalities required in such cases, at which Don Quixote and Sancho were in high delight, as if this declaration was of great importance to them, and as if their words and deeds did not clearly show the difference between the two Don Quixotes and the two Sanchos. Much courtesy was exchanged between Don Alvaro and Don Quixote, in the course of which the great Manchegan forgave Don Alvaro for the error he was under; and he, on his part, felt convinced he must have been enchanted, now that he had been brought in contact with two completely opposite Don Quixotes.

The evening came, and they left the village, and after about half a mile two roads branched off, one leading to Don Quixote's village, the other, the road in the direction Don Alvaro was going. In this short interval Don Quixote told him about his unfortunate defeat, and about Dulcinea's enchantment and the remedy, which gave Don Alvaro fresh amazement, and after embracing Don Quixote and Sancho he went his way, and Don Quixote went his.

He spent that night among trees again in order to give Sancho an opportunity of whipping himself, which he did in the same manner as the night before, at the expense of the bark on the trees, much more than his back, of which he took great care that the lashes would not have even knocked off a fly if there had been one. Don Quixote being fooled did not miss a single lash while counting, and he found that together with those from the night before they made up three thousand and twenty-nine.

The sun apparently had got up early to witness the sacrifice, and with its light they resumed their journey, discussing the deception of Don Alvaro, and saying how well they did to have taken his declaration in front of a magistrate in such impeccable form.

That day and night they continued their travels, with nothing happening to them worth mentioning, apart from that during the course of the night Sancho finished off his task, which made Don Quixote joyful beyond measure.

He waited for daylight, to see if he would find his disenchanted lady Dulcinea along the road; and as he pursued his journey there was no woman that he did not go up to, to see if she was Dulcinea del Toboso, as he held it absolutely certain that Merlin's promises could not lie. Full of these thoughts and anxiety, they ascended a hill from where they observed their own village, at the sight of which Sancho fell on his knees exclaiming, "Open your eyes, my home, and see how your son Sancho Panza comes back to you, if not very rich, very well whipped! Open your arms and welcome, as well, your son Don Quixote, who, if he comes defeated by another, comes victorious over himself, which, as he himself has told me, is the greatest victory anyone can desire. I'm bringing back money, because if I was well whipped, I conducted myself as a gentleman."

"Are you done with this foolishness," said Don Quixote; "let us go home first, before we give free range to our thoughts, so we can settle our plans for our future life as shepherds."

With this they descended the slope and directed their footsteps to their village.

CHAPTER 73

THE SIGNS DON QUIXOTE HAD AS HE ENTERED HIS OWN VILLAGE, AND OTHER INCIDENTS THAT ENHANCE AND GIVE COLOUR TO THIS GREAT HISTORY

At the entrance of the village, as Cide Hamete says, Don Quixote saw two boys arguing, one said to the other, "Take it easy, Periquillo; you will never see it again as long as you live."

Don Quixote heard this, and said to Sancho, "Did you hear, friend, what that boy said, 'You will never see it again as long as you live'?"

"Well," said Sancho, "what does it matter if the boy said that?"

"What!" said Don Quixote, "do you not see that, applied to the objective of my desires, the words mean that I am never to see Dulcinea again?"

Sancho was about to answer, when his attention was diverted by seeing a rabbit running across the field pursued by several greyhounds and huntsmen. In its terror it ran to take shelter and hide itself under Dapple. Sancho caught it alive and presented it to Don Quixote, who was saying, "A bad sign, a bad sign! A rabbit runs, greyhounds chase it, Dulcinea does not appear."

"You are a strange man," said Sancho; "let's suppose that this rabbit is Dulcinea, and these greyhounds chasing it are the evil enchanters who turned her into a country girl; she runs, and I catch her and put her into your hands, and you hold her in your arms and cherish her; what bad sign is that, or what bad sign can be seen here?"

The two boys who had been arguing came over to look at the rabbit, and Sancho asked one of them what their argument was about. He was answered by the one who had said, "You will never see it again as long as you live," that he had taken a cage full of crickets from the other boy, and did not intend to give it back to him as long as he lived. Sancho took out four coins from his pocket and gave them to the boy for the cage, which he placed back into the hands of the other boy, saying, "There, señor! The bad signs are broken and destroyed, and they have no more to do with our affairs, to my thinking, fool as I am; if I remember correctly, I have heard the vicar of our village say that it was not suited to Christians or sensible people to give any notice to these silly things; and even you yourself said the same to me some time ago, telling me that all Christians who considered signs were fools; but there's no need to talk more about it; let us continue to our village."

The huntsmen came and asked for their rabbit, which Don Quixote gave to them. They then went on, and on the green at the entrance of the town they saw the vicar and the graduate Samson Carrasco giving a service. It should be mentioned that Sancho had thrown over Dapple the bundle of armour, and the robe painted with flames which they had put on him at the duke's castle the night Altisidora came back to life. He had also placed the cap on Dapple's head, the weirdest transformation that any donkey in the world underwent.

They were immediately recognised by both the vicar and the graduate, who came towards them with open arms. Don Quixote dismounted and embraced them; and the boys, who were like tigers that nothing escapes, observed the donkey's cap and came running to see it, one shouting, "Come on boys, come and see Sancho Panza's donkey dressed up, and Don Quixote's horse leaner than ever."

Finally, with the boys around them, and accompanied by the vicar and the graduate, they made their entrance into the town, and proceeded to Don Quixote's house, where they found his housekeeper and niece at the door, who had already heard the news of his arrival. It had been brought to Teresa Panza, Sancho's wife, as well, and with her hair loose and half dressed, she dragged Sanchica her daughter by the hand and ran out to meet her husband; but seeing him coming in no appearance of a governor, she said to him, "How is it you come in this way, husband? It seems to me like you come walking with sore feet, and looking more like a messy drifter than a governor."

"Hold your tongue, Teresa," said Sancho; "not all, is always as it seems;' let's go into the house and I'll tell you some strange things. I bring money, and that's the main thing, earned by my own industry without wronging anyone."

"You bring money, my good husband," said Teresa, "and no matter whether it was earned this way or that way; you would not have brought any new practice into the world."

Sanchica hugged her father and said she had been looking out for him just like the showers of May. She took hold of him by the belt on one side, and he took his wife by the hand, while the daughter led Dapple, they walked toward their house, leaving Don Quixote in his, with his niece and housekeeper, and in the company of the vicar and the graduate.

Don Quixote immediately, without any regard for the time or season, went to another room in private with the gradate and the vicar, and in a few words told them about his defeat, and that the penalty meant he was not able to leave his village for a year, which he intended to respect, as a Knight bound by honourable good faith and the laws of Knighthood should; and about how he thought of becoming a shepherd for that year, and diverting himself in the solitude of the fields, where he could with perfect freedom give range to his thoughts of love while he followed the virtuous calling; and he requested, if they did not have a lot to do and were not prevented by more important tasks, to consent to be his companions, because he would buy enough sheep to qualify them all as shepherds; and the most important point of the whole matter he told them was settled, because he had given them names that would suit them. The vicar asked what they were. Don Quixote replied that he himself was to be called shepherd Quixotize, the graduate shepherd Carrascon, the vicar shepherd Vicarioso, and Sancho Panza shepherd Panzino.

Both were amazed at Don Quixote's new craze; however, to ensure he did not leave the village in pursuit of his chivalry again, and thinking that in the course of the year he might be cured, they agreed to his new project and approved his wild idea, and offered to share the life with him.

"And what's more," said the graduate Carrasco, "I am, as all the world knows, a very famous poet, and I'll be always making verses to pass our time in those secluded regions where we will be roaming. But what is most useful, sirs, is that each of us should choose the name of the shepherdess he intends to worship in his verses, and that we should not pass a tree, however hard it is, without carving her name on it, as this is the habit and custom of lovesick shepherds."

"That's the thing," said Don Quixote; "I do not need to create the name of an imaginary shepherdess, because there's the incomparable Dulcinea del Toboso, the glory of these streams, the decoration of the meadows, the backbone of beauty, the elite of all the grace, and, the lady to whom all praise is appropriate, however extravagant it may be."

"Very true," said the vicar; "but we the others must look for willing shepherdesses that will satisfy our purpose one way or another."

"And," added Samson Carrasco, "if we fail to find them, we can call them by the names of the ones in print that the world is filled with; because as they sell them in the market-places we may fairly buy them and make them our own. If my lady, or I should say my shepherdess, happens to be called Ana, I'll call her Anarda, and if Francesca, I'll call her Francenia, and if Lucia, Lucinda, because it is all the same thing; and Sancho Panza, if he joins, may glorify his wife Teresa Panza as Teresiana."

Don Quixote laughed at the name, and the vicar praised the worthy and honourable plan he had made, and again offered to give him company during the time he could spare from his essential duties. And so they left him, recommending and asking him to take care of his health and giving himself a suitable diet.

It so happened that his niece and the housekeeper overheard the three of them; and as soon as they were gone they both came in to Don Quixote, and the niece said, "What is this uncle? Now that we were thinking you had come back to stay at home and lead a quiet respectable life, you are getting yourself into new entanglements, and turning yourself into a shepherd"

"And," added the housekeeper, "will you be able to bear, out in the fields, the heat of summer, the cold of winter, and the howling of the wolves? Not you; because that's a life for hard men, bred and seasoned to work like this almost from the time they were children. Why, make this evil choice? It's better to be a Knight than a shepherd! Señor; take my advice - stay at home, look after your affairs, go often to confession, be good to the poor, and if any evil comes to you let it be on my soul."

"Hold your peace, my daughters," said Don Quixote; "I know very well what my duty is; help me into bed, because I don't feel very well; and rest assured that, Knight now or wandering shepherd to be, I will never fail to care for your interests, as you will see in the end."

725

And the good ladies (as they undoubtedly were), the housekeeper and niece, helped him into bed, where they gave him something to eat and made him as comfortable as possible.

CHAPTER 74

HOW DON QUIXOTE FELL SICK, THE WILL HE MADE, AND HOW HE DIED

As nothing that is a man's can last for ever, all descends downwards from its beginning to its end, and above all a man's life, and as Don Quixote's had no special exemption from heaven to have a different course, its end and close came when he least expected it. Because whether it was the misery the thought of his defeat produced, or heaven's will had ordered it – he developed a fever which kept him in his bed for six days, during which he was often visited by his friends the vicar, the graduate, and the barber, while his good aide Sancho Panza never left his bedside. All of them believed that it was grief at finding himself defeated, and the objective of his heart, the freedom and disenchantment of Dulcinea, unattained, that kept him in this state, and they strove with everything in their power to cheer him up; the graduate asking him to have a good spirit for his upcoming new life as a Shephard, for which he himself, he said, had already composed a poem that would take the shine out of all of the others ever written, and had bought with his own money two famous dogs to guard the herd, one called Barcino and the other Butron, which a herdsman had sold him. But despite this Don Quixote could not shake off his sadness.

His friends called in the doctor, who felt his pulse and was not very satisfied with it, and said that it would be wise for him to attend to the health of his soul, as his body was in a bad condition. Don Quixote heard this and was calm; but his housekeeper, his niece, and his aide, cried inconsolably, as if he were already dead in front of them. The doctor's opinion was that sadness and depression were bringing him to his end. Don Quixote begged them to leave him by himself, as he wanted to sleep a little. They obeyed, and he slept more than six hours, which made the housekeeper and niece think he was going to sleep for ever. But at the end of that time he woke up, and in a loud voice exclaimed, "Bless Almighty God, who has shown me such goodness. In truth his compassions are unlimited, and the sins of men can neither limit them or keep them away!"

The niece listened with attention to her uncle's words, and they struck her as more coherent than what usually came from him, at least during his illness, so she asked, "What are you saying, señor? Has anything strange happened? What compassions or what sins of men are you talking about?"

"The compassions, niece," said Don Quixote, "are those that God has this moment shown me, and with him, as I said, my sins are no obstruction to them. My reason is now free and clear, rid of the dark shadows of ignorance that my unhappy constant study of those vile books of chivalry cast over it. Now I see through their absurdity and deception, and it only saddens me that this destruction of my illusions has come so late that it leaves me no time to compensate by reading other books that might be a light to my soul. Niece, I feel myself at the point of death, and I would not be please to meet it in such a way that I should leave behind me the name of a madman; because although I have been one, I would not like that the fact would be made clearer at my death. Call for me, my dear, my good friends the vicar, the graduate Samson Carrasco, and Master Nicholas the barber, because I wish to confess and make my will."

But his niece was saved the trouble by the entrance of the three. The instant Don Quixote saw them he exclaimed, "Good news for you, good sirs, that I am no longer Don Quixote of La Mancha, but Alonso Quixano, whose way of life gave him the name of Good. Now I am the enemy of Amadis of France and of the whole group of his descendants; all the irreligious stories of Knighthood are now detestable to me; now I realise my foolishness, and the danger into which reading them brought me; now, by God's mercy guided into my senses, I detest them."

When the three heard him speak in this way, they had no doubt that some new craze had taken hold of him; and Samson said:

"What? Señor Don Quixote! Now we have intelligence that lady Dulcinea has been disenchanted, you are taking this line; now, just as we are on the point of becoming shepherds, to spend our lives singing, like Princes, you are thinking of turning into a recluse? Be quiet, for heaven's sake, be rational and let's have no more nonsense."

"All that nonsense," said Don Quixote, "that up until now has been the cause of my pain, my death will, with heaven's help, turn into good. I feel, sirs, that I am rapidly drawing near death; no more jokes; let me have someone to confess to, and a notary to make my will; because in matters like this, a man must not play with his soul; and while the vicar hears my confession, someone, I beg, go and get the notary."

They looked at one another, amazed by Don Quixote's words; but, although uncertain, they were inclined to believe him, and one of the signs which gave them the conclusion he was dying was this sudden and complete return to his senses after having been mad; because along with the words already quoted he added many more, so well expressed, so sincere, and so rational, that they banished all doubt and convinced everyone that he was in his senses. The vicar asked them all to leave, and left alone with him he heard his confession. The graduate went to retrieve the notary and returned shortly afterwards with him and with Sancho, who, having already hearing from the graduate the condition his master was in, and finding the housekeeper and niece crying, began to cry and shed tears.

With the confession over, the vicar came out saying, "Alonso Quixano the Good is dying, and is indeed in his senses; we may now go in to him while he makes his will."

This news gave a tremendous impulse to the eyes of the housekeeper, niece, and Sancho Panza his good aide, making the tears burst from their eyes and a mass of sighs leave their hearts; because in truth, as has been said more than once, whether as Alonso Quixano the Good, or as Don Quixote of La Mancha, he was always of a gentle character and kind in all his behaviour, and therefore he was loved, not only by those in his own house, but by all who knew him.

The notary came in with the rest, and as soon as the preface of the will had been set out and Don Quixote had called out to God with all the sincere formalities that are usual, coming to the inheritance, he said, "it is my will that in regards to certain money in the hands of Sancho Panza (whom in my madness I made my aide), between him and me there have been certain debits and credits, no claim can be made against him, or any account demanded from him in respect of that money; but that if anything remains over and above, after he has paid himself what I owe him, the balance, which will be a little, will also be his; and if, as when I was mad I had a share in giving him the government of an island, so, now that I am in my senses, if I could give him a Kingdom, it would be his, because the simplicity of his character and the faithfulness of his conduct deserve it." And then, turning to Sancho, he said, "Forgive me, my friend, that I led you to seem as mad as myself, making you fall into the same error I myself fell into, that there were and still are Knights in the world."

"Ah!" said Sancho crying, "don't die, master, but take my advice and live for many years; because the worst thing a man can do in this life is to let himself die without a reason, without anybody killing him, or by anything except sadness making an end of him. Come on, don't be lazy, get up from your bed and let us go to the fields as shepherds as we agreed. Perhaps behind some bush we will find lady Dulcinea disenchanted, as fine as fine can be. If you are dying of anger at having been defeated, place the blame on me, and say you were overthrown because I prepared Rocinante badly; besides you must have seen in your books of chivalry that it is common for Knights to upset one another, and the one who is conquered today to be the conqueror tomorrow."

"Very true," said Samson, "and good Sancho Panza's view of these cases is quite right."

"Not so fast, sirs," said Don Quixote, "'in last year's nests there are no birds this year.' I was mad, now I am in my senses; I was Don Quixote of La Mancha, I am now, as I said, Alonso Quixano the Good; and may my repentance and sincerity restore me to the esteem you used to have for me; and now let the Notary proceed.

"I leave all my property to Antonia Quixana my niece, present with us, after all has been deducted from the most available portion of it that may be required to satisfy the obligations I have made. And the first disbursement I desire to be made is the payment of the wages I owe for the time my housekeeper has served me, with two hundred coins, over and above. The vicar and the graduate Samson Carrasco, now present, I appoint as my executors.

"It is my wish that if Antonia Quixana, my niece, desires to marry, she marries a man who first of all, ascertained by any information noted, does not know what books of chivalry are; and if it is be proved that he does, and if, despite this, my niece insists on marrying him, and does marry him, then she will forfeit all of what I have left her, which my executors will donate to charity as they please.

"I ask the gentlemen my executors, that, if any chance leads them to discover the author who is said to have written a history now going about under the title of: 'The Second Part of Don Quixote of La Mancha,' they ask him on my behalf as sincerely as they can to forgive me for having been, without intending it, the cause in his writing of so many absurdities; because I am leaving the world with a feeling of regret at having provoked him to write about it."

With this, he closed his will, and with a faintness coming over him he stretched himself out at full length on the bed. All were in a state of agitation and rushed to relieve him, and during the three days after he made his will he fainted very often. The house was in a state of confusion; but still the niece ate and the housekeeper drank and Sancho Panza enjoyed himself; because inheriting property wipes out or softens the feeling of grief the dead man might be expected to leave behind him.

Finally, Don Quixote's end came, after he had received all the rituals, and had fully expressed his hatred for books of chivalry. The notary was there at the time, and he said that in no book of chivalry had he ever read of any Knight dying in his bed so calmly and so like a Christian as Don Quixote, who among the tears of all who were present, gave his spirit to heaven, that is to say died. On observing this the vicar begged the notary to be a witness that Alonso Quixano the Good, commonly called Don Quixote of La Mancha, had passed away from this present life, and died naturally; and said he desired this testimony in order to remove the possibility of any other author except Cide Hamete Benengeli bringing him to life again falsely and making new stories out of his achievements.

This was the end of the Ingenious Gentleman of La Mancha, whose village Cide Hamete would not indicate precisely, in order to leave all the towns and villages of La Mancha to contend among themselves for the right to adopt him and claim him as a son, as the seven cities of Greece contended for Homer. The cries of Sancho, the niece and housekeeper are omitted here, as well as the new inscription on his tomb; Samson Carrasco, however, created the following lines:

A brave gentleman lies here;
A stranger his whole life to fear;
Not even in his death could Death dare,
In his last hour, to give him a scare.
The world may have cared little for him,
But his amazing deeds they could not dim,
A crazy man in his life he passed,
But in his senses he died at last.

And the sage Cide Hamete said to his pen, "Rest here, I place you on this shelf, O my pen, whether skilfully crafted or poorly cut I do not know; here you will remain for ages to come, unless arrogant or evil story-tellers take you down

730

to disrespect you. But if they touch you, here you warn them, and, as best you can, say to them:

Stop! Weakling;
Remove your hands! And do not roam,
Because this, my lord the King,
Was meant for alone.

Don Quixote was born for me alone, and I for him; it was for him to act, and me to write; us two together make one, nevertheless and despite that, that Toledoan writer ventured and might venture again with his dirty pen to write the achievements of my valiant Knight; if by any chance you come across him, you should warn him to leave to rest where the weary decaying bones of Don Quixote lie, and not to dig him up, in opposition to all the privileges of death, and take him to Castile, making him rise from the grave where in reality and truth he lies, powerless to make any third expedition or new adventures; because the two that he has already made, much to the enjoyment and approval of everybody, in this as well as in foreign countries, are quite sufficient for the purpose of turning into ridicule the whole set of those made by all Knights; and doing so, completes my Christian calling, giving good advice against the one who offers evil to you. And I will remain satisfied, and proud to have been the first who has ever enjoyed the fruit of his writings as fully as he could desire; because my desire has been no other than to deliver to the detestation of mankind the false and foolish stories of the books of chivalry, which, thanks to my true Don Quixote, are now wobbling, and no doubt doomed to fall forever. Farewell."

END

For more adapted classics by James Harris please visit:

Http://ViewAuthor.at/JamesHarris

Made in United States
Troutdale, OR
08/30/2023

12495166R20407